JENNA RHODES

THE ELVEN WAYS:
THE FOUR FORGES
THE DARK FERRYMAN
KING OF ASSASSINS
THE COURT OF GODS*

Coming soon from DAW Books

KING OF ASSASSINS

The Elven Ways: Book Three

JENNA RHODES

DAW BOOKS, INC.

DONALD A. WOLLHEIM, FOUNDER

375 Hudson Street, New York, NY 10014

ELIZABETH R. WOLLHEIM
SHEILA E. GILBERT
PUBLISHERS
www.dawbooks.com

First Paperback Printing, November 2015

1 2 3 4 5 6 7 8 9

DAW TRADEMARK REGISTERED
U.S. PAT. AND TM. OFF. AND FOREIGN COUNTRIES
—MARCA REGISTRADA
HECHO EN U.S.A.

PRINTED IN THE U.S.A.

Chapter One

*I*T IS SAID in the lands of Kerith, "It is better to have Death knock on your door than a Vaelinar." I may well be the proof of that old Dweller proverb. I am Vaelinar, after all, or half of their blessed and cursed blood, and we are the invaders of these lands, blasted here by some magical or immortal meddling that we have not been able to decipher. Yet here we are on Kerith and many regret our coming. It is no wonder, for we arrived clad in battle gear and ready to ride into a fight and, from the feuds which exist among our various bloodlines to this day, I have no doubt we were prepared to wage war upon each other rather than some arcane enemy. Welcome or not, we carved out our places here, particularly in the western provinces known as the First Home of the continent. We found Kerith malleable to our will, for we can see the very threads of its physical being and cast, tangle, and weave those threads to our wishes in varying degrees. We have forced Ways upon the land which betray its natural laws but have given us both wealth and convenience. We remembered our old dominance and arrogance which cloaks us still, while we have forgotten the name of our mother world, and even yet plan to replace the very Gods which all mortals should respect. Then there are those like myself, born in between, who hope only to know the truth and live to see its justice.

My name is Sevryn Dardanon and I am the bastard son of the Vaelinar traitor Daravan and Mista, the Kernan witch woman he abandoned. She soon abandoned me as well, trusting that the streets would be kinder than her maternal bond to me. I looked for them both until I realized that neither of them searched for me and I was alone. The two of them left me with only anger to fire my survival. Thus was I forged.

I took to thieving like any boy hiding in the back streets until Gilgarran found me and brought me up to be his apprentice, to make a spying and killing tool of me. A spymaster himself, an occupation that is redundant for a Vaelinar, he nonetheless fostered me well in the years we had together. He told me there would be more to come in my schooling, but then he was murdered by Quendius while taking me on a quest to uncover secrets which were not ready to be revealed. His failure brought me down with him and left me enslaved. The hammer of this fate left me tempered.

For twenty-some years I worked the foundries of the smuggler and weaponmaster Quendius, living through degradation that the Gods have been kind enough to let time blur for me. I brought out of that pit, buried and sharpened inside my core, the fierce will to do what was right by the world, as sharp as any edged blade.

I was found again by the Warrior Queen Lariel and her brother Jeredon, taken in and valued. Rulers of the valley kingdom Larandaril used my Talents and gave me a home in return. But none of this compares to meeting the love of my life who restored not only my faith but my soul. What can I say of Rivergrace who rode the tide of the Silverwing River into the lives of the Dweller family called Farbranch? I met her when she was still a girl, poised on the threshold of becoming an incredible woman, and she captured my heart and holds it still in her slender hands. For Rivergrace and any of

*the Farbranches—Nutmeg, Tolby, Lily, and the three brothers—
I would die a thousand more deaths. Rivergrace and I have
died once, and it was her light that brought me back. I no
longer fear death, just the separation and the pain. Her love
anchors me as steady as a sheath, as the time for my wielding
draws close.*

*I am but a weapon. I have no illusions beyond that I only
question who will wield me. Will it be the queen to whom I
vowed my service, or the woman to whom I gave my heart,
or a shadowy, unknown figure I have yet to meet?*

*May the Gods treat me with the respect a good weapon
deserves, show me my destination, and aim me truly. Being
Vaelinar, however, I should know that the Gods never grant
us anything but what we rip from Their hands . . .*

There is a quarter of Calcort where city walls do not hold
back the wilderness, and the city streets thin to nothing
more than dirt lanes, and those in turn fade to stony hills
landscaped with vineyards as far as the eye can see. One
might presume it would be the weakest point of the city, but
none have ever succeeded in invading over those hills and
across those vineyards. It might be because of wards set
long ago by the Mageborn before that class destroyed itself,
or it might be attributed to the catacomb of caves scattered
underneath the hillsides, a brittle rock strata waiting to collapse under the weight of an approaching army with its
many men, its cavalry, and wagons. No one knew for certain.
He didn't know and it made him nervous. Sevryn had never
trusted Calcort; his senses, his Vaelinarran nerves, told him
not to. The city gates had been assailed again and again
through the history of the First Home, with occasional success, yet the vineyards had stood fast. But he could not trust
them to do so again. The need to stand and protect pricked
at his nerves.

Sevryn walked past an aged yet well-loved farmhouse,
the last true house on the lane and one which ruled the

biggest of the vineyards. A beamed cider house stood to the left, with wine-making barns to the far rear of the property, sided by the barn and pastures.

"Kisses or coins?"

Against the lowering of the sun, two young women stepped out of the weathered building and smiled as they drew close. The taller of the two, by far, slipped her hand to the back of his neck and massaged him gently, repeating, "Kisses or coins for your thoughts?"

He made a noncommittal grunt. "You wouldn't like them." He reached back to cover her hand with his for a moment. "But I'll take payment in kisses. Always." Her skin was slightly cooler than his and he tried to warm her. "I'm on watch."

Rivergrace laughed teasingly. "You are the most suspicious presence in this quarter, right now."

"And you the most luminous."

His gaze swept the two, her slender Vaelinar self with gleaming auburn hair that reached almost to her waist and her sister, Nutmeg, who looked not a bit like her: a Dweller who stood as tall as Grace's elbow, with bouncing brunette hair in curls, and almost too pregnant for any one woman to bear. Nutmeg grinned up at him, Rivergrace's sister of her heart, bonded as close as any kin could be. She did not look like she carried the heir to the throne of the Warrior Queen of Larandaril, wrapped in the hardy body of the Dweller folk, but she did. Not that she did not look pregnant, because she most certainly did, but Dwellers usually did not carry royalty. And because she did, a tension thick enough to be cut with a knife ran through this end of Calcort and through Sevryn as well. No one connected with any of the ruling Houses of Vaelinar was ever safe. He had not been able to save his friend Jeredon from blood feuds and conspiracies of the ild Fallyn, but he would lay down his life to protect Rivergrace and Nutmeg.

As for his love—she was as pure a Vaelinar as he was not: willowy, ears curving to a graceful point, hair of auburn tumbling down nearly to her waist, and eyes . . . oh, those eyes.

Eyes of aquamarine, and cobalt, and sky blue, eyes that shouted of magic. Sevryn felt he could fall into those eyes forever and know that he was loved. His own plain gray eyes disguised his inheritance of Talents and abilities. For the Vaelinar it was simple: multihued eyes could see the very threads of the world and meddle with them, and uncomplicated eyes could not. He'd spent a lifetime making good use of the arrogance of being overlooked and underrated.

Rivergrace's gaze swept over darkening shadows and she frowned before she sat, undoubtedly noting the three Vaelinar guards across the street who melted back into the dimming light as watchers took notice of their appearance. She looked back to Sevryn. "And you are watching them guard us?"

"No. I seem to be watching the intangible. There is that which they can't—nor can I—quite see. I'm a half blood, but if I can feel, they ought to be able to as well. Yet I see no sign that they do. Something is not right. How can they be missing it, and what the cold hells is it I'm missing?" He longed for the touch of her withdrawn hand even as he scowled at the trio on the lane's other side. Their watch post was next to the shop and home of the herbalist, her own yards blending into the edges of the vineyard grapes. Next to the herbalist across the way stood the cobbler's abode, his back fence hanging with tanned leathers getting an airing before storage. Beside him, sat the pottery shed and kiln, and the small, gabled house which made up the home of the ceramics maker. Beyond those businesses, a crude sidewalk and gutter began, curving slightly and leading back into the city proper.

Her words warmed him. "If you worry, then I will worry. I trust your instincts."

"Mmmm." Sevryn ran his hand through his hair. "I'm walking," he said. "I can't stand here and do nothing."

She watched him stride off, shedding energy like tiny sparks as he did, like a firebrand being carried through twilight. Nutmeg put her hand on Rivergrace's arm to steady herself a bit as she sat down with a muffled sigh.

"What was that all about?"

"Just a feeling. A shiver down the back of the neck. A pinch in the gut. Nothing definite and yet ... something awry."

"I thought you weren't superstitious." Nutmeg leaned upon Rivergrace slightly.

"Of course I am, I was raised Dweller!" She pinched her sister. "But neither am I flinching at shadows. You?"

"No idea what I am at th' moment, except one big stomach." Nutmeg folded her hands about her abdomen. She looked down at it solemnly, her curls bouncing about to settle in a gentle cascade upon her shoulders.

There was nothing palpable upon the air that Rivergrace sighted, except a very slight darkness flowing where darkness should not be despite the coming evening, and moving against the wind. How could shadows move against the wind? Perhaps a trick of the light as it changed how it fell upon the street, or the way the buildings shifted in its reflection, or did she even see such a thing? Sevryn had gone in a different direction, but had he doubled back and could that be his elusive form she almost saw? She didn't think so. She knew the way he moved, even when he could only be seen in the corner of the eye or the sigh of the twilight. Every fiber of her being was attuned to him, as it should be, for all that they shared including death.

Rivergrace didn't discount what she thought she saw, any more than she would Sevryn's restlessness, for Vaelinars viewed the world in a different way. If she concentrated, she could perceive the tiny strands of light that made up the falling dusk. She could see the edges of every tiny grain of dirt that went into the brickwork, the fibers of the wood cut into planks and shingles. She could sense the water in the air, nearly gossamer drops of dew waiting to coalesce into something heavier, more substantial as nighttime fell. She could feel the pull of water in the bodies across the way, coursing in their blood, collecting in their tissues. More, she could sense the potency and the wiles of the River Goddess of the Silverwing, the Goddess whose being had become inexplicably and inexorably intertwined within her own essence. Life was water and it called to her, drop by drop, stream by stream. Grace blinked, shedding her inner sensing of the world, before she felt compelled to pluck at its strands and . . . do what? Create havoc? Call the water to her when she had no right to do so? How would that help anything? With a sigh of her own, she tried to shake off the mood Sevryn had handed to her. Her attention dropped to Nutmeg and the commanding size of her stomach as her sister contemplated herself. The sight halted her and led to another thought entirely.

Without preamble, Rivergrace said, "What *were* you thinking?"

"Only that I was in love." Nutmeg rubbed the palm of her hand over her ample tummy and sat back wryly. "It seemed enough at th' time. But it was never a kind of lusty, must scratch that itch kind of love. It was a gentle, nurturing love. He needed me." She shrugged and cast a sideways glance. "I was wonderin' when you'd ask."

Rivergrace leaned against her Dweller sister. In every way but blood she counted, she was more than adopted into the Farbranch family, she was bonded, woven into the very fabric of their lives as skillfully as Lily and Nutmeg Farbranch's hands upon a loom could weave true. Nutmeg hadn't known whom she rescued that day from a small raft on the raging River Silverwing and, if she had, Rivergrace did not think her sister would have acted any differently. Nutmeg had pulled her sister into her family and woven her firmly into its fabric. Such impetuousness had always ruled her bold sister's life. "I wasn't going to ask."

"But you did, and rightly so. Mom and Dad have not. I rushed into it, did I not? Sometimes I wonder what it would have been like after the wars. Would he have come back all full of confidence and then we would have had sparks? I canna decide what I think about that. I want to love someone the way Mom and Dad love. A deep, abiding trust."

"With lust and sparks."

"Aye! With lots of sparks. I cannot even think about that

now. Now I'm to be a mum, and I have doubts about a fu-
turc beyond that."

"There's time enough later, but I'm pretty sure there is
always a possibility for sparks."

"There had better be! I don't want to be missing out."
Nutmeg sat with one arm upon her burgeoning stomach
and her brow faintly twisted as she looked across the dirt
lane at the guards who stood just behind the shadow of the
eaves, waiting and watching. "I want to throw rotten apples
at them."

"Meg!"

"I know, I know. But they are here and Jeredon . . . Jeredon
is gone. Where's th' fairness in that, I ask you? Where?" The
brace of guards across the lane sprawled on a bench, looking
at ease even as their very heritage spoke of quickness in reaction unlikely to be matched by the average city folk. They
could afford to be indolent—and arrogant. Both Rivergrace
and Nutmeg sighed and looked away from the ever-present
guards.

Grace straightened again, something tickling at the edge
of her senses. She had thought Sevryn overkeen. Now she
wondered. She shook it off as her sister looked up and into
her face.

"If we're askin' questions never asked before . . ."

Oh, no. But she smiled faintly. "What?"

"Nothing I would ask, for myself, but because of Jeredon." Nutmeg pushed back a heavy lock of hair from her
temple. "Did you feel anything when you died? I wonder
because, well, I wonder if Jeredon feels anything?"

Grace held her features perfectly still. Her thoughts
darted about until she reached out to grab and steady them,
wondering what she could say. She had died, and so had
Sevryn, on that quest they all took to cleanse the sacred
River Andredia. Two had died and Lariel had maimed herself, given a part of her flesh, to mend the river and her
family's pact with it to protect the valley of Larandaril. And
Jeredon had been paralyzed. But she'd come back and so
had Sevryn; Jeredon recovered, eventually, with Nutmeg's

love and nursing. Finally, she answered, "I can't say what Sevryn felt, but my experience was all interwoven with the Goddess of the Silverwing, and she couldn't die. A peace surrounded me, peace with healing, and I felt my mother's presence, and I—I felt whole. I knew a kind of sorrow for leaving you all behind, but I knew the way ahead waited and I was eager to go. Then I got reknit and returned, but I had no sense of the timing of all of it. I was hardly there, Nutmeg, and there was something tugging at me, but I never got to it, never touched the awe of it before I was back."

"Was it . . . dark?"

Her sister held her gaze, although Rivergrace wanted very much to look away. Slowly, she said, "Dying is not something I want to remember. It was cold and hurtful and frightfully lonely. But Death itself is entirely different."

"There is something beyond."

"I think so."

"Does Sevryn think so?"

She tilted her head. "We don't really talk about it. There's too much to do here." Rivergrace looked at Nutmeg's hand, thinking of Lariel's maimed hand and the sacrifice of flesh. "I'm sorry I can't give you the comfort you want about Jeredon."

"If you don't fear death, what do you fear?"

Rivergrace could feel the color leaving her face, the warmth draining away, and her head jerked imperceptibly. "Quendius," she said, her voice barely loud enough to be heard. "And Tressandre ild Fallyn."

Taken aback for a moment at the name of the weapon-maker outlaw as well as the rival Vaelinar, Nutmeg found the breath to make a rude noise. "Two blights on th' face of the earth! Rotten apples they are, trying to spoil the barrel. At least they never allied."

"No. Not yet. Even Tressandre knows better than to partner with the venom that one is." She shook herself. "At least we have that for luck. How much gloomier can you be, Meg?"

"Just thoughtful. Some days the babe is so heavy, it seems all I can do is sit and think."

"Then think about life and baby names!"

"It's no matter—it's—" Nutmeg's hand on her belly moved, almost imperceptibly. She beamed and her expression showed the change of her thoughts.

"Oh, there he kicks again. Want to feel it? You're never here, and soon it'll be too late."

"Too late?"

"He'll be born before you get back here again."

"You don't know that."

"I know it's been forever since I've seen you." Nutmeg's face twisted wryly. "I think if Master Trader Bregan hadn't had a caravan comin' this way, you would never have visited."

"The caravan made for good cover. As much as I want to see you, I can't. It could be taken as a sign that the queen has made a decision about the child, and that could be dangerous for the two of you. Lariel has not declared an heir yet, because of that. If Bregan hadn't been coming this way, I might not have been able to come." Machinations. Motives within motives, webs within webs. She knew that Nutmeg knew, even if both of them did not embrace the politics they'd fallen into.

"But he kicks so strongly. Just feel it."

"No," refused Grace gently, as she had every time the offer had been made on this visit. The thought of some being living inside her sister and kicking as though in protest made her faintly queasy. "And you don't know it's a he. You kicked a lot, according to Mother." She pushed her hair back from her forehead, trying to hide her unease. That shadow amongst shadows had moved again, like a river of dark water across the side of the herbalist's house. Or had it?

"She does say that." Nutmeg rubbed the end of her nose. She circled back to Rivergrace's question. "What did I think beyond Jeredon?" She waved her hand to indicate the guards. "Not of that, to be certain. Not that Lariel would have guards set upon me and others there," she twitched her thumb to indicate an even more shadowy corner a little down the street, not far from a small but raucous tavern. "Diort has three Galdarkans who come and go, but mostly stay." She made a huff. "Did I ever think I would attract th' attention of the Galdarkans and the east? Never."

Rivergrace tried not to show her surprise that Meg was aware of the Galdarkans, for she'd been in Calcort three days on this visit and Sevryn had only informed her that eve of the watch he had been keeping, not only on Lariel's guards but the others he tabbed as being from the warlord Diort. The Vaelinars had been assigned for protection but there was no knowing why Diort's men stood watch. She dragged her concern back to the ox in the middle of the room, as it were. "You must have had some inkling of complications. Jeredon was the Warrior Queen's brother. His death doesn't diminish that. You can't tell me you didn't think of it. You've never climbed a tree where you did not know exactly where you'd land, if you fell."

Nutmeg rolled her eyes. "Listen to you. If we ever get home, no one will know a thing you say. You sound just like one of the elven with words of honey and spidersilk to trap the listener."

By home, Nutmeg meant the orchards and fields of the groves by the Silverwing, a place of hard work sunup to sundown and faraway neighbors, a home overrun by Ravers and abandoned because of that. The folk they'd left behind were not city folk, far from it, and their ways held a directness of their own. The diplomacy and tact she'd learned in the courts of the Warrior Queen would not go far there. Grace bumped her shoulder. "Forget what I was saying. What are you saying?"

Nutmeg fussed with her hair, pulling it off her shoulders and away from her face, fastening her heavy tresses into a ponytail which, the moment she took her nimble fingers away, sprang out of its knot and came tumbling back down. "I was thinking," she said quietly, "that I was foolish t'expect that he might ever stay with me, but while I had him, when he was wounded and healing, I was good for him. He needed Dweller common sense and care in heaping spoonfuls, and he got it. When he began to walk again, a step at a time, the beauty of his happiness took my breath away. An' I did that. Part of it. I think he loved me then. When he left me for the war, and he went to Tressandre, I told myself he was decoying the ild Fallyn away from me. Keeping me safe so that they would not harm me or use me t' twist him in their ways. I told myself that—over and over."

"And I think you were right. But . . ." Grace hesitated to ask. "Did he know you were with child? Did you ever get a chance to tell him?"

Nutmeg shook her head. "No. I barely knew it myself, and he . . ." She stopped as memory flooded her eyes and an unshed tear sparkled on her eyelashes. "I think somehow he sensed it at the end. War and blood all around us. Yet he touched me, and said my name, and a wonder seemed to fill him, just for a moment, before his life winked out. Did I imagine that? I hope not. I hope it was real." She put her hand on Grace's arm. "I knew how t' dance. Kiss. Laugh an' flirt. But I had never been with a man before. I took what precautions I knew about, but Vaelinars have such a power runnin' within them." She looked into Rivergrace's eyes. "If you're asking questions for Lariel, I don't plot against her rule. If you're asking for yourself, it happened, Grace, because I loved him so blessed much. And now look where we are. I have a babe the size of a tree growing inside me, and a pack of guard hounds on my heels. And you wearin' a sword on your belt. Who'd have thought?"

Rivergrace reached out and took Nutmeg's hand, found it chilled despite the lingering warmth of the day, and she squeezed gently. "I wear this sword as much because of Sevryn as I do for any other. I wish I could say the others don't matter, but we know they do. Still," and she did not resist this time when Nutmeg took their laced hands and placed them over her stomach and she could feel the tiny but insistent bumps under her palm, "it would be nice if you could raise him as a Farbranch like you did me."

"Would it not? Just think, a Vaelinar with th' roots and

sense of a Dweller! Look at you. Lariel could do worse for an heir."

Rivergrace freed her hand to place her finger across Nutmeg's lips. "Words like that could cause a wagon load of trouble."

Nutmeg flashed a look. "I may be small, but I am not simple."

Lily Farbranch emerged from the doorway of the farmhouse, wiping her hands on the hem of her apron, a half-smile curving her lips. "Grace has not been gone from us long enough to think such things, Meg." She smoothed her apron down as both her daughters adjusted on the bench to make room for her, but she stayed in the doorway, leaning a shoulder against it. The dusk softened the lines in her face and laugh creases about her eyes, but added to the shimmer of gray strands among her dark hair. Nutmeg echoed some of her looks, but not all, for she carried her father Tolby's looks as well. Their mother watched them for a long moment before adding, "I know it's getting late, but the two of you need t'be thinking of letters to draft in thanks to Lord Bistane and Lord Tranta for their birthing gifts."

"Think of," Nutmeg responded. "An aryn wood cradle. D' you wonder if Lord Bistane carved it himself?"

"I think he might have planned the crafting of it. He's been at Ashenbrook so much cleaning the battlefield and preparing for another, it's hard to tell if he's had time while bolstering the lines there. The wood, though, came from his forests, no doubt of that."

Aryn wood was a wonder, a bane against wild magic and corruption still lingering in the lands from the wars among the Mageborn centuries ago. It was considered such a beneficial wood that baby toys were made from it, when it could be gotten, to carry good fortune and guardianship for the young. To have an entire cradle made of it—well, that was a gift beyond compare. Bistane took after his father Bistel, stepping into his position as a warlord whose strategy and execution were incomparable, but who also held a deep love for his land and for the aryn trees which had come from the unknown lands of their Vaelinar past, a handsome, straight-backed man who carried his legacy well. Rivergrace smiled in fond remembrance.

"I had not expected anything from th' Lords, what with all that." Meg fell silent, her gaze dropping to the dirt lane. When she looked up, it was to say, "Lord Bistel protected me, you know. At Ashenbrook. From the Raymy and all. I heard his last words."

Lily dropped her hand onto her daughter's shoulder. "We know. You told us the tale."

Nutmeg opened her mouth as if to add more, but tightened her lips instead, her hand working on her lap, twisting a knot and then letting it go.

"What about the baby cart?" Rivergrace prompted, to ease Meg's sudden mood. "Not aryn wood, but a fine mahogany ship, with those ocean waves carved into it."

"It is a fine carriage, with a ride as soft as wool."

"Tranta said the making of it was one of the things that eased the loss of his brother."

Lily murmured, "Every war has its losses, but this last is almost too much to bear." She dropped one hand to caress the top of Nutmeg's head.

In the memory of dark times, a flicker of movement caught Rivergrace's eye.

"He still works on the Jewel of Tomarq, does he not?" Lily asked softly. "Putting the Jewel to rights after it was shattered?"

"Aye, he does. Obsessed with it. He says he can see the Way pulsing still within those bits of gem and Jewel, and swears he will find a way to put the Jewel back together. I don't know if he can, but Lariel says if anyone can, it will be Tranta Istlanthir. I say it cannot come quickly enough, for I miss his light and quick wit." The lord of the coast, with his sea-blue hair, was one of her favorites. Even as she rued the loss of his humor, something sharp stabbed at her senses like a knife in the dark. She turned her head about.

Nutmeg stood abruptly. "I'd better get t' those letters. They have to be grand ones. I'll be glad for your help, Rivergrace."

Grace surged to her feet as well, but not because her sister stood. She saw a movement in the shadows, a thrusting lunge that caught her attention, and she cried out, throwing the bench over and Meg behind it, as men and steel launched at them. Even as Nutmeg rolled in the dirt, she reached out and grabbed the heavy three legged stool next to the bench and grasped it firmly in her hands.

Rivergrace pulled her weapon and unlatched the chain belt worn about her waist, snapping it into the air, thick and sturdy, into the face of the first Vaelinar coming at them, sending his sword arm awry. She slashed him across the throat, and took a second out with the back swing of her blade. Nutmeg got the third in the knees with a smashing blow of her stool, and then a second to the head. He moaned but once. Grace cried out, "Attack!" worried, as she saw no sight of Sevryn. Lily made a smothered sound in the doorway before getting out, "I'll find Hosmer," and disappearing into the depths of the farmhouse, no doubt to go out the back way in search of Nutmeg's brother who had joined the city's Guards.

Grace moved cautiously behind the small barricade of the wooden bench, searching the deepening shadows across the way. No movement, not of Sevryn or Vaelinar or Galdarkan. She glanced down at the one attacker who remained alive at their feet, the second she'd caught with her backhand. Crimson spilled over his chest and bubbled from the corner of his mouth, but he lived. His eyelids fluttered as she knelt over him.

"Who sent you?"

His mouth pulled. His breath bubbled as he answered, "No survivors." With a hand too quick to stay, he grabbed her sword to slit his own throat.

"*Velk,*" muttered Nutmeg.

Rivergrace stood carefully. "To be expected, I suppose." Though the assailant was undoubtedly a Vaelinar, she did not recognize him and he did not wear the colors of any affiliation.

A sound across the way caught her attention, and a body toppled from the depths of the dusk. One of the queen's

Vaelinar guards. Just beyond, she could see shadows grappling, one being shrugged off with a grunt and a cry that stopped abruptly. That body, too, fell out into the street, and Sevryn jumped into the open, clear of it. So Lariel's guards had been at work defending Nutmeg, although not successfully. She wondered how big a force had been sent against them and tightened her grip on both the sword and chain.

"Get her inside," Sevryn ordered. He turned to set himself in the street.

Grace hesitated but a moment, before seeing what he turned to meet.

Kobrir, the assassins all assassins hoped to be one day, spilled out into the lane. Sevryn stepped into a stance to face them.

Chapter Two

THEY ATTACKED WITHOUT WARNING. What assassin worth his salt would do otherwise?

He pivoted and countered by letting fly with daggers readily at hand: one, two, and three. They dropped and lay unmoving in the afternoon shadows, but from the quiet, he knew there were more and he was also fairly certain his downed opponents were not dead or dying but injured enough to stay out of the fray. Sevryn drew back quickly to find a defensible spot among the shanties footing the dirt lane and when he turned around; the three bodies were gone, melted into the late afternoon shadow, retreated. The Kobrir did not leave their dead or wounded behind.

He could tell the Kobrir by the deadly stealth with which they moved and how quickly and soundlessly they closed on him out of the sidelines even as they blurred in and out of the narrow buildings and ditches. He recognized the odd smell of their skin and the stain of *kedant* venom on the weapons they grasped. And he knew that as soon as they regrouped, they would attack again.

He felt strangely alone in the middle of the street, not

liking it. He made his way down it, toward the city itself until he reached a tavern. The Kobrir did not kill just for the sake of it. They had their targets and kept their collateral damage as low as possible. So if they were after him and him alone, it behooved him to add numbers to the fight, milling about in the street, engulfing both forces. He backed up and kicked the door twice, hard, yelling "Fight! Fight!"

The tavern doors flung open with a crash, spilling out spectators both drunk and sober. A few took to their heels, shouting for the Guard. Master Trader Bregan emerged into the last of the sunlight and threw his head back, taking in the Kobrir just out of range.

"Ho, Sevryn. What are you up to here?"

"I appear to be having a bit of contract problems."

"Let me help you with the negotiations." Pulling at his leather sheaths, Bregan ended up next to Sevryn, his own vicious swords in his hands. "Trouble always did shadow a Vaelinar's heels," he said, kicking away a drunk who staggered off, muttering. His own breath held a faint haze of liquor.

"Good timing."

"Too early for dinner and too late for lunch. Truth be told, I should be down at the stables, packing for the road." Sevryn knew Bregan had been a sword master in his youth before his accident, and despite a weakness in his right side, he was still formidable. And game. He had not always been thus; he had fallen into drunken ways in self-sorrow after his maiming, but judging from his current form, those self-destructive times were far behind him. A master trader with a powerful guild and an even more powerful father behind him, Bregan still fought most of his own battles. Sevryn felt him move instinctively to his flank as the two of them backed into an alley. "What're we facing?"

"A few traitorous Vaelinar besides the handful or two of Kobrir."

Bregan swallowed a curse and raised his blades as shadows heaved and the attack came at them.

Sevryn swung away from the first knife with a hiss, stepping away with a vicious parry, and found himself with precious little time to do anything more than react. He shouldered away the lunge of a second assailant, blades whining as they slid off one another. The alley gave them close quarters and shadows in the late afternoon sun, and the experienced Kobrir knew how to work the scene to their advantage. Assassination was all they had been trained to do, its dark art swam in their veins instead of blood. They maneuvered him about as Sevryn found himself blinded by a shard of unexpected light one second and then doused in inky darkness the next. He let his ears and his hands do the work then, sensing what his eyes could not. Another step into the fray, letting Bregan guard his back, the Kernan trader prince nearly as good with his weapons as those the two of them faced.

An assassin took his measure with a slow blink of his eyes, the only part of his face visible under his veil. He raised both hands in a salute to Sevryn before stepping into his assault. Sevryn met him hand to hand before sweeping his boot out and catching the other in the kneecap, crumpling him to the ground. A dagger to the throat and Sevryn leaped over the body, carrying Bregan with him. He held two in a frontal assault, now in cautious movement, assessing him further. Still at his back, Bregan grunted harshly as he took a blow, and his sword sang a steel-driven note as he met blade with blade.

He looked to make certain Grace had not come after them, braver than she should be but, to his relief, saw no sign of her. He could fight his best if he knew they were clear, and he knew that she knew that.

Then Sevryn lost all thought except for the need to meet attack and mount attack, to give as good as he got as the tide of Kobrir descended upon them.

He didn't intend to die that day. So when Death granted a respite, Sevryn grabbed at it and Bregan and hauled his comrade up, clambering above the fray like a creature going tree-born, as the Kobrir fell back in disarray and confusion and lost them momentarily. Sevryn crouched on the edge of the roof, eyes intent upon the alley below. A cold moist wind off the river bathed his heated face, hiding his scent, barely rippling the edge of his cloak, and curling off the edge of the daggers he held. Unsure of the exact moment it had happened, Sevryn had gone from prey to hunter. That quickly the tide had turned.

Without doubt, living remained imperative. He put his hand out, stilling the companion who moved restlessly beside him. He could appreciate the other's stiffness, the leg brace that helped more than it hindered although the limb the brace contained remained unwieldy. Bregan quieted with a slow inward hiss of breath. Sevryn winced, but none of the shadows below—the shadows which moved in spite of the torchlight and the moonlight—seemed to take notice. They were searching, quietly and effectively, save that none of them looked up. When the Kobrir did, the pitched battle would begin again. They would swarm up walls to the roof-top as handily as they had swarmed the alleys. He could almost swear that the laws of flat and incline did not hold for them. He had once seen a Kobrir creep across a ceiling, although with some effort that made him think later that they might have been using climbing gear of some sort to achieve that. As assassins, they had no peers.

Except perhaps a man like himself who had been trained by both the street and by Gilgarran, which did not give him an edge, just an opportunity. He could hold his own against one. Two. Even three. But more than that boiled down below him, shadows merging and dividing until he lost count of the twilight shapes. He remained convinced they had come for him although the Master Trader would be a far richer prey if hostage taking were their intent. Yet in the skirmish below they had—had he imagined it?—acted as if Bregan were an inconvenient obstacle to be put aside with as little harm as possible, so that their target might be achieved.

He let his mind wander down twisted ways as dark as the shadowed and misty alleys below him. If Sevryn were taken out, how vulnerable would Nutmeg be? Lariel? With her brother only two seasons dead, who could stand for Lariel if he were gone? Not that the Warrior Queen needed anyone to raise a blade for her; she was nearly as swift and sure as he was with a weapon, but who would have her back? Only Bistane after him. Sevryn told himself it should be too dangerous to so openly assassinate him.

Shouldn't it?

Who could be so bold?

He felt that the tyrant Quendius did not hire the Kobrir. Likely they would no longer work for him, if they had ever worked for him in the past. The rogue Vaelinar weaponmaker did not keep bargains, knew no boundaries, and had little respect for anyone but himself. If he wished Sevryn dead, he and his bound servant Narskap would come do the deed themselves and relish the doing.

Perhaps the ild Fallyn had hired these blades. That would fall naturally to their bloodline. Tressandre ild Fallyn, known for ambition without measure, would not hesitate to cut him away from Lariel if she could. Yet Tressandre's actions would not be blunt but sharp and hidden, unaccountable, untraceable. The Kobrir attack would be too obvious for her, unless she were desperate. Of all things the sultry woman could be at this moment, he did not think desperate was among them. She had converts now who would be less subtle than she, but they would hesitate to act independently for fear of her retaliation. It was well that they should be afraid of her. He was. But not here, and not now.

His thoughts spun a dark web about him, weighing whether he might live or die. Yet none of them could explain or shake from him the sense that he indeed stood at a crossroads. He would make decisions in the next few moments which would inalterably change his course. They would impact his world and the few he would either stand with or leave behind, and nothing would be the same. He'd felt this fate upon him only a few times in his life, and he had never thought to feel it again. Mentally he flipped a silver coin and sent it spinning through the air, waiting for it to fall . . .

He leaped from the rooftop, killing two as he landed, dancing backward in a slight retreat. They grouped to follow. Another step backward as they closed. And another as he drew the fray down the street. Away from the Farbranch farmhouse and cider mill. Back toward the wards of town and city. Back to the alleyways and gutters and streets like those where he'd lived his early life. Like a mother bird would fake a broken wing to draw the tree foxes and other predators away from her nestlings, he drew them away from his loved one. Bregan, at his flank, moved with him without question as he took to the rooftops a second time. The cloud of Kobrir circled about him below, ravens after the kill, intent on their mission. He decided to strike while he still had some advantage. Sevryn extended his senses, felt his mind identifying the pattern of the reality about him, inhaling long and deep and silently as he learned it intimately. Then he spoke, loosing his Voice Talent that began deep in his diaphragm and pushed out of his throat, vibrating the very air, and the Kobrir reacted. They could not help but respond as he compelled them to submit. Even Bregan started at his side.

He heard his taunt echo from the alley juxtaposed to their current position. He lifted a finger to Bregan and leaped the span, landing softly behind them.

They struck in the darkened maze of alleys behind the Trader and the Yoke pub. He heard them coming, at least five, his hands open and stance wary. Shards of black splintered apart and reformed. He had no fear of street cutthroats and bullies, but as they rushed him, he could hear the hiss of their breaths as they sucked inward, preparing.

"Blades high," he said. He slashed backhanded across his right flank, catching the first who had hoped to come in under his guard. Swathed in black, the assailant crumpled at his boots but it was Bregan who kicked the body aside. He parried a blow and struck under it, only to have it firmly parried back to him. Bregan let out a grunt which might have been in sympathy, but Sevryn knew was more likely to have come from shielding.

He would have to trust Bregan to take care of himself. He had his own concerns. The trader had grown up with a sword in his hand, and even if he had been forced to change from one lead to the other because of a grievous injury, he had come back nearly as strong and twice as clever, no longer being able to count entirely on his strength. The trader could fight.

Sevryn twisted a knife blade off his sword and countered with a punch of his left fist, his own dagger buried deeply in his hold save for four inches of the point. The Kobrir fell back. Under his veiled face, Sevryn thought he could see pain in the eyes, but the moment fled so quickly, he couldn't be certain. He hadn't time. Three Kobrir rushed him, and thoughts fled to reflex, movements honed into him by years of hard training and sparring with some of the best fighters in the world. The trade of killing by body and blade took him over, possessed him, and when he blinked to wipe sweat off his brow with the bloodied back of one hand, he saw two more bodies fallen before him, while three fresh Kobrir glided quietly from the back alley to replace the dead.

They barely gave him time to register that before they were on him again.

He fought with the awareness that they held back. Perhaps it was Bregan shielding part of his vulnerability, but they could have worked that. The Kobrir took every advantage they could. He had faced them before, and barely lived to tell about it. But they had to know, even as he and Bregan protected each other, the two men also hampered each other's full movement. The assassins had to know that, and waited to use it. But why did they wait?

Sword and daggers bit and clashed. Hisses of pain were sucked in and muttered warnings grunted out. He sheathed his sword in favor of another dagger. He'd never used a shield, he wore scarred and supple leather vambraces to

protect his forearms, and dagger work, wet work, seemed to
be the only way to beat the attackers back. They would take
him down. No two of them fought the same, and he no
sooner mastered the rhythm and attack of one when he
would drop back and another step into his place. They were
growing canny. His thoughts scattered before their strikes
and blows. He took another Kobrir down before he found
time for a second, deep breath. If he had been hurt, he did
not feel it, would not until later. His pulse pounded in his
ears, loud but steady, and he could feel the warmth of kedant coursing through his veins. *That* told him he had been
hit, at least once, but he no longer had the sensitivity that
many Vaelinar had. He'd been shown his vulnerability and
he'd fought it, building up a slow but definite immunity to
the venom which had been particularly virulent once. If
the Kobrir had thought to lay him low, they missed their
bet. The veiled and shrouded being in front of him dropped
back on his heels, retreating, as if reading his thoughts, and
he took the precious moments offered to recover his stamina.

The inside of his right arm quivered a bit with the strain.
He shook it to loosen his muscles. Blood splattered off him
as he did. It ran into a black-crimson runnel in the hard-
packed dirt. He could feel Bregan at his back, trembling
from boot to shoulder. Was it weariness or fear? Either way,
Sevryn couldn't blame him. He'd never had such a number
of assassins come after him so relentlessly. He'd fought
them before, though never in such numbers, and they would
retreat rather than assault a target futilely. This time was
different. It would not halt until he was either dead or he
had killed all those mustered against him.

Bregan jostled him roughly, with an inhaled hiss, and
Sevryn broke their stances to whirl about. Three Kobrir
snarled and ranged against his sword mate, like war hounds
worrying at a breach, seeking to bring him down and leave
Sevryn standing alone. Bregan dropped to one knee, his
braced one, shielding the good leg and letting the golden
metal brace of the bad one act as a shin guard and more. He,
like Sevryn, had gone to hand daggers in place of his sword,

for the Kobrir pressed him close and desperately. To kill him was one thing, but to kill those he loved and that Lariel had put under her protection, as she had all the citizens of the western lands, was another. Anger filled Sevryn, a hot anger that fed new blood to tired muscles and nerves, surging inside him like an irresistible tide. He would ride that anger as long and far as he could.

Sevryn filled his left hand with both of his fighting daggers to reach inside his vest for his throwing knives. One, two, three, they left his fingers with growing accuracy until the last thunked home, centered in one of the revealed eyes of the Kobrir on Bregan's left. The veil fluttered as he hissed out in pain, and fell with a truncated wail. A man down with the Kobrir did not always mean death, but he knew this one would not rise again.

Fighting stopped a moment. He had assassins at his flank who froze as if listening to silent instructions. The heated beat of his own heart filled his mind.

Then Bregan pivoted on his heel, bringing around his braced leg, the leg covered from mid-thigh to calf within a golden, enruned cage designed and crafted by Vaelinar hand. He swept his leg out, catching Sevryn behind the knee, sweeping him to the ground.

Kobrir swooped over Sevryn, covering him, pinning him down as the trader began to back away. He paused. Bent. Whispered in his ear. "I'm sorry, Sevryn Dardanon. Very sorry. The Gods spoke to me and I had to listen. They've awakened, finally! Awake! They told me to bring you here."

Then Bregan's voice was gone, shouldered away, the trader dragged off by Kobrir hands, his heels digging a groove into the alleyway dirt before he twisted free and took to a run; then all Sevryn knew was many, many hands upon his body, hands like steel claws.

Another dry breath upon his ear, grazing his cheek, carrying the scent with it of a drug that tickled at his memory, a drug he should have known, but which he could not place, and why in God's name did he think now of drugs and Gilgarran's teachings about drugs and spying when he was about to die and he should be thinking of his Rivergrace and the sorrow he would be bringing her? His heart ticked once, twice, and the killing blow did not fall.

Instead, the Kobrir at his neck said, "We were betrayed." Breath sprayed hot on his face. The low husky whisper continued. "We know the secret of the death of life. We were brought here to kill you, but we now break our contract. We honor your mother, and we have been shown you must live. As you love your soul and those of others, come find the king of assassins. Find him and find answers. Or your Rivergrace is lost. Her sister is lost. The queen to whom you are sworn is lost. And more." He dropped a pair of handcuffs into the grime of the alleyway where they smoldered as if newly forged. A second item, a thin shiv of unique make with a D stamped on its slender hilt followed.

And then they all disappeared like the black smoke of which they seemed to be made, black smoke with hands as hard as obsidian. He tried to look for them, and his vision blurred. Sevryn groaned as he tried to rise to give chase and could not.

He knew nothing more until someone kicked him in the shoulder.

Chapter Three

"**STAY IN THE GUTTER** this close to the tavern and they'll be pissin' on you, lad." Tolby Farbranch reached down to Sevryn whose ears rang as he looked upward uncertainly. Stunned, he hadn't moved for . . . how long? Sevryn blinked as the rough and callused hand reached down and pulled him to his feet. He fought for his balance, and the grip shifted to his shoulder where it stayed, fingers biting into the flesh beneath his light armor. Tolby had come from the fields, it seemed, for he smelled of grape leaves and late sun, and he wore his short sword and a wickedly sharp pruning hook tucked into his belt, a man as solid and welcome as a good rock wall at his back.

Sevryn patted his old friend's hand. "I think I already have been. You should have been here earlier." He stomped one foot and then another, steadying himself. He'd been unable to do anything but lie still while the Kobrir retreated, and then his thoughts had addled on him. Who would think to mention his mother to him, a woman gone and long thought dead? She had to have gone to dust long ago, born of Kernan blood that lived a tenth of the lifespan of the Vaelinar. She had to be long gone . . . but not forgotten, and why remembered by the Kobrir?

Sevryn couldn't understand why they had refused their Kill. The knowledge that the assassins had turned on their contractor . . . impossible! He'd still be lying in the alley effluvium if Tolby hadn't rousted him, his thoughts spinning a cocoon about him. A glint caught his eye.

He bent, scooping up the handcuffs and dagger before Tolby's sharp gaze could spot them and palming them inside his shirt. "Nutmeg? Grace?"

"A little shaken and their mettle is up, but they be fine. Hosmer is standing guard." Tolby's mouth curled. "Sorry I missed th' action." A caravan guard in his youth, Tolby Farbranch could more than hold his own. He dusted Sevryn off. "Grace said there were two of you?"

"One fell back." Sevryn wiped his nose and mouth with the back of his hand. "Let's see how he fared."

"You did for the others?"

"As well as I could."

Tolby nodded and said gruffly, "That's as well, then. I won't have killers after my daughters."

"Hosmer can hold them?"

"With his brothers." Tolby shifted his belt on his hips. "I will feel a bit better after we send word to th' queen."

"Soon as I check on Trader Bregan."

"He stood with you?"

"For most of it." Sevryn did not part with more detail than that as he surveyed the alley. Tavern first, but if the trader had well and truly fled, he'd not catch up to him for a few days, not until things were settled here. Tolby fell in step with him as he strong-armed the tavern door open, a structure of solid wood, smelling of beer and raw hard liquor, and smoke. Few enough faces outlined by sooty lamplight turned to squint warily at them in the doorway. He saw no sign of Bregan. A low growl of disappointment escaped his throat. He shouldered the door shut before muttering, "Bregan turned tail on me."

"There will be a season for that one," Tolby said.

"Without doubt." His temples throbbing, Sevryn attempted the street, Tolby in step with him. His head cleared more with every step. "Rivergrace will be wanting to know where we are."

"Oh, she knows where we are. She'll be wantin' to know what trouble we're in."

Sevryn smiled in spite of himself. He would be held accountable for his actions, and he did not mind it. Despite his shortness of stature, common to all Dwellers, Tolby nearly matched him stride for stride. At the farmhouse, Keldan, the youngest Farbranch, met them at the front door with a wry grin, saying only, "Things are quietin' a bit." He brushed his dark hair from his eyes, his longish wavy cut reminding Sevryn of the hot-blooded elven horses the Dweller so admired.

Nutmeg was the center of attention. She sat, her feet up, her face scrunched in consternation over the display of concern as Lily moved back and forth between her and the kitchen. Rivergrace perched on a stool nearby, a cleaning rag in one hand and her sword in the other, taking slow, deliberate wipes along the blade, her head bent in thought. The moment the two men stepped in the room, her face came up and her gaze fixed on Sevryn, searching, and then she relaxed into a smile.

Nutmeg put her hand up at Tolby. "Now, Dad, don't be yelling at Grace for putting me on the ground. I was a prize target before that."

"Mmmmm," her father said, leaning over to kiss one, then the other on the cheek. He turned to Hosmer. "Two different groups of assassins, or am I wrong in my thinking?"

"No, you're right. The Vaelinars swept in first and they would have taken Nutmeg if you had not been here, Sevryn."

"Ild Fallyn?"

Hosmer, a shorter and stockier version of his father, shrugged. "Not wearing th' black and silver, but that would be a fair guess, we're all thinking. What we cannot guess is who the Kobrir came after." Not a question outright, but Hosmer locked his gaze on Sevryn.

He did not answer, thinking that the Kobrir might not have been in Calcort at all, save for his drawing them there. But he could not be sure. Their targets had been many and their contract broken. Had he just proved too costly and they changed their minds? Or was finding the king of assassins a deeper trap? The handcuffs tucked away inside his shirt smoldered, and he thought of Rivergrace and the faint scars about her forearms from just such a binding when she was a child, cuffs commissioned and used by Quendius to enslave her and her family. His jaw tightened. Grace blinked up at him as if she'd caught that in his face, and he reminded himself how sensitive she was to him now. It was the way they were meant to be. He dropped a hand to her shoulder and squeezed it lightly.

She put her weapon and cleaning cloth away briskly. "We have to get word to Lariel."

"Pigeon master is at the nor'eastern quarter, near the curve of the river, edge of the lanes. Night is falling, but he can still set them on their way. I'll come with you," Hosmer offered, tugging at his City Guard's tunic, the rest of his uniform consisting of cuffed horse boots over plain trousers. His light brown hair curled down to his collar, and his expressive hazel eyes darted a look between his father and Sevryn.

"Good, then."

Keldan bounded to his feet and out the door before anyone could suggest he go saddle the horses. He held all three mounts by their reins when Sevryn drew Rivergrace out to the courtyard, Hosmer on their heels. Keldan's face warmed at Sevryn's raised eyebrow. "I had 'em ready."

"Indeed. That, or the tack appeared out of thin air."

Keldan gave both the tashya-bred horses a muzzle rub before giving Sevryn his reins and lending Rivergrace a leg up to her saddle. The hot-blooded creatures arched their necks and snuffled the palm of his hand eagerly as if still searching for the sweet-grain he must have fed them earlier.

They tossed their heads in disappointment at finding his hand empty. Grace took up her reins gently.

Keldan lit a hand torch and passed it to his brother, for the other side of the city, like this quarter, would be dark on the fringes, night having fallen well and truly. He opened the courtyard gate to wave the mounts through.

The City Guard had already gathered the bodies that they could find and were carting them through the streets to the city surgery as they rode past. Rivergrace looked down to the carts, where cloaks and tarps covered the dead.

"No Kobrir."

"No. They always take their own."

Her mouth tightened slightly. "The one Vaelinar who lived but briefly made sure he could not tell me who sent them."

"But it must be obvious," Hosmer remarked. "Vaelinars opposed to Queen Lariel. It has to be the Stronghold of ild Fallyn."

"And you'd likely not be wrong, but proving it would be nigh impossible. The ild Fallyn are as shrewd as they are treacherous."

"So nothing will come of this."

"For the moment. They have tipped their hand, so Lara is forewarned, and that has some worth."

"Surely you can mark them as ild Fallyn, somehow, some way. Would not their bloodline give them away? Ears? Eyes?"

"While it's known that the ild Fallyn breed true, it's also known that they take in many half-breeds. Those are most likely the ones trained and sent, for if they had sent true of their line, we might not have stood so easily against them."

"Why?"

"The ild Fallyn can levitate," Grace told him. "That's how they build their Ways, and how they built their Stronghold. Tressandre or Alton could have crossed lanes in a single bound and been on us before we scarce knew they were there."

The torch he held wavered slightly in his hand. Then he

shook his head slowly. "It's a wonder any of you are still alive."

Her mouth quirked. "I am only by the grace of your family."

He dropped his reins to grip her skirted knee. "That's not what I meant!"

"No, but it's true." She clasped the back of his hand before moving it aside gently as their horses bumped shoulders in the lane. "Which brings to mind . . ." She turned to look at Sevryn. "It might not be ild Fallyn. It could be Quendius."

Did she sense the cuffs he had hidden away? "It could."

Her brows knotted a moment. "He would have sent Narskap to oversee it."

"Narskap died at Ashenbrook."

"So it was said, but no one has found the body." She stroked the neck of her horse. "No one has seen Quendius either, although signs of his movement have been found. He would have taken Narskap back, if he could have gotten his hands on his old hound."

She did not call Narskap father, nor would she, although he had been, in another lifetime. Now the being burning inside out with his Vaelinar magic could hardly be called human, or alive, he thought. The man she'd known as her father, Fyrvae, had not existed in decades, not since he had failed in his escape from the mines of the weaponmaker, and the loss of his wife and child had broken him. He watched Rivergrace's face as she absently tucked a strand of hair back behind her ear. So young, still, her journey from the underground caverns of her escape having been put in suspension, held in the arms of a Kerith River Goddess until released tens of years after onto the flood-swollen waters of the River Silverwing which had carried her and her tiny raft past the apple orchards of the Farbranch family. Because of her, the Farbranches had eventually had to flee their ranch and take up residence in Calcort, but their hard work and shrewdness and family bonds ensured they would succeed.

Hosmer held their horses as they reached the pigeon master's coops and home. The smell of bird dung drifted on the damp night air, Rivergrace wrinkling her nose as she stepped into the front lobby of the home with Sevryn.

A Kernan, smoking his pipe in the corner, as he set the wing of a bird, put both his charge and pipe down carefully. He moved to the counter fronting his lobby. "Business, is it?"

"Yes, and we'll need nightfliers. Word must go out now."

The Kernan nodded. "Distance?"

"We'll need three teams. To the Istlanthir hold on the coast, to Larandaril, and to the Vantane House in the north."

The pigeon master sucked on his lower lip for a moment. "That'll be pricey."

"Coin does not matter. Speed and sure arrival does."

He nodded in understanding. "I have but seven birds who can manage those routes."

"And we'll need six. They will be sent back when rested."

The Kernan flushed briefly. "Oh, I have no doubt your lords will see right by my birds. No doubt." He drew out six containers, with fine slips of paper for the messages to be written upon, and quills and ink. He turned his back on them, saying, "I'll get my fliers."

Sevryn inked the warnings to Tranta and Bistane and Lara quickly, passing them to Grace to be blotted and rolled into the copper tubes. Spare messages, but he wrote more to Lariel using the shorthand he and the queen had developed over the years for the work he'd done for her. Rivergrace filled her slender hands with the tubes, and let out a small cry when the pigeon master came back from his coops. One of the birds on his arm was a silverwing. It cooed when it saw her, putting its head out for her finger to stroke. He did not know the affinity of such creatures toward Grace, but it existed and he could not explain it. Some Vaelinar had the Talent for animals, but her Talents were Water and Fire. No. This perhaps was born from her association with the Kerith Goddess, or her years with the Far-branches at the edge of the wilderness, or perhaps merely from the goodness of her heart.

"She goes to Larandaril?"

"Aye. That's her range."

Rivergrace stroked the bird's head one last time. She handed him the tube Sevryn had marked for Lariel, and its twin for the next bird.

The other five fliers were skyhawks, nightfliers who also ranged in the day, and whose wider wingspread and deeper chests marked them as longer-distance birds. Each had a paint smear upon its head: blue for the coastal regions and green crossed with white for the Vantane hold. Sevryn would ordinarily marvel that a pigeon master in Calcort had such messenger birds for those routes, but with the Raymy invasion and battle at Ashenbrook, and the subsequent military maneuvers throughout the Vaelinar and Galdarkan forces, it only made sense that communication would be necessary. He and the pigeon master fastened the tubes to the birds' legs quickly, and then the Kernan sent them winging into the night.

He paid the pigeon master, who thanked him and said, "Good news?"

That was the only thing out of character. Why would the man ask what sort of news he sent? Sevryn stared at him for a moment before answering, "Who asks?"

The man had the grace to flush and stammer back, "N-no one, good sir. No one at all."

"There had better not be." He took Grace by the elbow and steered her back outside.

Now he had to wonder if his messages would be delivered to whom he had intended. Message agents were sworn to be discreet and this one had been . . . almost. Hosmer looked down from his mount. "Done?"

"No. Is there another messenger in town?"

Hosmer sat back in his saddle, thinking. "One," he answered slowly. "A dodgy fellow, though."

"Nonetheless, we'll stop there as well."

Hosmer looked to his sister. "Not safe for her there."

Rivergrace put her chin up. "I can hold my own."

"No time to waste, Hosmer, arguing with her." Sevryn

made sure Rivergrace was seated before swinging up himself. "Take us there."

And so Hosmer did. The dodgy fellow smelled of beer, and his birds were field owls, their big yellow eyes blinking as they entered the birder's hut and aviary.

"How much?"

The bird man gave a twisted grin, only half his face obeying the attempt. Half-brained, Sevryn thought, as he watched the man limp across the dirt floor of his cottage, one arm hanging slightly, one leg dragging a bit behind. But the floor of the cottage was well-raked and clear of bird debris, a difficult task with as many bird perches as were set into the dirt. He revised his opinion of the fellow. Perhaps a stroke had rendered him but half a man.

"A gold bit each."

Sevryn winced, thinking of old days when he might have killed to have a gold bit pass his palm. Still, a bit was less than a half and far less than a full coin. Reminding himself that most of the coins in his purse had come from Queen Lariel, he nodded. "Done." He watched the shrewd intelligence gleaming in the man's eyes. "Another bit if you can tell me if Master Trader Bregan has left town."

"Oh, that one! Aye. Lit off like his tail was on fire. Took his caravan back to the coast empty. No profit in that. Someone put the fear of the Gods into that one."

Rivergrace turned her back slightly to hide her expression as he dropped the promised bits into the man's good hand. He tucked his fee into his own coin purse and made a sweeping bow only slightly affected by his condition. "Ink 'n paper on the counter. Write what you will. I'll attach them."

"We can do that," Grace murmured.

The birder shot her a look as if assessing her ability. The field owl at her elbow clacked his beak, and she put her hand out to gently stroke his throat feathers. The man gave his grimaced smile again. "As you wish. Loose them, too?"

"I will."

The bird perches were marked with the flags of the cities

and holds to which they'd been trained to fly as destinations. He chose his birds swiftly as Grace penned the notes, her handwriting even smaller and clearer than his. Sevryn and Grace braved their clacking beaks to fasten the letter tubes to their legs before they were set free. As Sevryn watched them take flight as only an owl does, swift and silent, he felt more certain that the word he sent would be carried to its destination, one way or another. He watched them take wing, the birder silent at their backs, letting them do as they would, but ensuring that his birds were being handled safely.

They were. Sevryn had chosen his messengers carefully before setting them to the sky.

He could not afford to be silenced.

Chapter
Four

"**WHAT IS THAT?**" Rivergrace asked quietly, her words muffled as she did not wish them to carry, to disturb the quiet which had finally fallen in the Dweller farmhouse. She sat behind him, her body cushioned in quilts and linens, her hair tickling his face as she leaned toward him. She watched what he held.

"A present from the Kobrir," Sevryn told her, as he turned the shiv over and over in his hands, carefully, for it was as keenly sharp as any stabbing/slicing weapon he'd ever come across, and it reeked faintly of kedant as well.

"They know us well enough to leave presents now?" She smiled faintly as she sat on the small bed behind him with the point of her chin on his shoulder so that she could look down at his hands as he examined his gift.

"So it seems." He did not wish to let her know about the cuffs, so he kept them close, burning his skin even as he did so, from the malignant, binding magic which was twisted into the fiber of the steel. He paused, letting the engraved, ornate letter D shine in the candlelight.

She sucked in her breath. "Daravan?"

"My thoughts exactly, yet how can it be?"

"The Ferryman."

He thought of how they had last seen Daravan and his brother who resided neither in the flesh nor entirely in the phantasmic, a Way in and of himself, linked inextricably with Daravan who, as the named brother, held the only life the two of them shared. It was Daravan who told them that the Vaelinars were not the *Suldarran*, the Lost, as they believed themselves but the *Suldarrat*, the Exiled, traitors against Trevilara their world and queen. It had struck them deeply, and hard. Yet, even as Daravan had exhorted them, railed against them for their trespasses in Trevilara's war, he took the tide of Raymy, lizard men who had no heart and souls as any man would reckon them, and sent them on a journey where only a Way could take them. Perhaps it had been to a when rather than a where, for such was the twisted nature of the Way known as the Ferryman, but the invading force had been swept from the field of Ashenbrook. It was but a temporary diversion, but without it, the battle, and all, would have been lost.

That troubled him. He did not hold Daravan as the sacrificial type. Why had he swept up the Raymy? When would they come back, a massive tide of war and destruction? What had been Daravan's true intentions? At Ashenbrook, the massed armies of the Vaelinars and the Galdarkans had stood to do what damage they could. If the Raymy, turned aside from the battlefield of Ashenbrook, returned elsewhere and could not be met by an army, what destruction could they truly wreak upon Kerith? He knew that Lariel, as Warrior Queen, kept forces marshaled at Ashenbrook. But what if she were wrong?

The Raymy would return. Perhaps any day. Perhaps in a decade. They did not know. So an army camped. Waiting.

Sevryn turned the shiv in his hands yet again.

"If he's found his way back . . ." Rivergrace began and then halted.

"We know the Way he created to take them is not perfect. We have handfuls of Raymy who drop here and there, as whimsical as frogs dropping from a raincloud and as lethal as the deadliest viper."

"But the bulk of the army stays . . . wherever it is he took them."

"As far as we know." Sevryn traced the D. "I know Daravan had dealings with the Kobrir. He admitted as much. He meddled. He assassinated. He did whatever it took to keep us from regaining our heritage and our truth. Whatever. I would not put it past him to have returned and be doing it again."

"I saw—" Rivergrace hesitated.

"What?"

"A shadow that did not fall as other shadows did. A river of darkness moving past and against the flow of dimming light."

"Even the Kobrir don't move like that, although they would like to."

"I'm thinking of a story Lily told us once of a man who brought her a cloth, a weave unlike any other. Nightweave, she called it. He left her a number of coins to tailor a hooded cloak for him—"

"I remember. She kept the remnants."

"Aye." Rivergrace moved from her position behind his shoulder to sit next to him. "She thinks it was Daravan who commissioned the cloak. She never knew for certain. And if it was, and if he had such a garment with such powers, then a river of darkness could indeed flow against the pattern of falling light."

"Well, then." Carefully, Sevryn put the shiv away in his wrist sheath. "We have two votes for Daravan."

"The Raymy cannot be far behind."

"If he can control it, he will use their return to destroy us. He endeavored to do it in the past, and I doubt he's given up his goals."

"For Trevilara."

The corner of Sevryn's mouth twitched. "She must," he said, in slow deliberation, "be a hell of a woman, like you."

Rivergrace slapped the back of his hand lightly. "I don't know if I've been complimented or reviled!"

"Come close, and I'll tell you." He turned his head to blow the candle out, reaching for her as he fell back onto the bed. His hands traced messages of love and longing over her skin.

Chapter Five

ON THE COAST OF THE COUNTRY, Tranta Istlanthir paused, hanging halfway between the sky and the ocean, the wind tugging at his gear as it strained to pull him free. Rough waves far below him futilely sent fingers of spray after him, thinning to a salty damp mist before they fell back into the sea in a foam of white and green. He set his hands to his ropes again, balanced on his feet to check the setting of his spikes, and looked up to the cliff's edge which loomed perhaps three body lengths above him. Nearly there.

The ild Fallyn had sent one of their best levitators to assist in building a footbridge across the chasm on the land side of the cliff, from the rough hills which held the now deserted Istlanthir and Drebukar guard barracks. Work on the bridge progressed rapidly, but he did not wish to wait. He climbed, as he had always climbed, and his father before him had, to the cradle which held the Jewel of Tomarq. It was a kind of sacrifice to the gem which had caught the fire of sun and magic to aim her wrath upon trespassers of the bay and coast. Did she know of the sacrifice? Had she sensed his brother's death leap to protect her before she herself was shattered? She was only a stone, but he had always thought of her as more, for she had been made a Way and that, in itself, made her unique. The wind twisted him upon his gear and he took a deep, stabbing breath. He had fallen from her heights once. He had caught himself upon the same capricious wind and broken the fall, saving his life but laming himself and losing the memory of it for days. If he had but remembered in time, he would have known that a spy had been observing her weaknesses up close, and he had met with her potential attacker who had driven him off the cliff. He would have deduced that that enemy would return until he had accomplished his goal in destroying her entirely. Instead, it was his brother who had met the return and failed. But it was not his brother's fault. No. Tranta owned that himself, even if it would not bring his brother back.

Tranta wiped his face dry with the back of his hand and set to finishing the climb. It proved farther than three lengths, but it mattered little, for when he topped the edge and pulled himself onto the summit, it was done.

No one else had ever stood in the shattered remains of the Jewel. He'd set a barrier for the bridge workers which no one could cross. He did not wish the ruins to be disturbed or picked over by those who thought her relics might make a pretty ring or bauble. True to her majesty, the Jewel of Tomarq had not broken into dust, but into shards as big as his fist and bigger, into splinters that would rival a throwing dagger, into rocks the size of a man's head. He dropped his gear on the ground and sat to remove the harness of spikes from his boots. The sun had risen while he climbed, and it was still bitter cold on the cliff as he squatted in the ruins and looked at the failure of his House.

It was said that when the Drebukar miners unearthed the gem, she came free willingly from the dark under the mountain's vein, already near polished and whole although she would be faceted later and when the mine's patron, the head of the House of Istlanthir laid his hands on her, she asked to be set forever in the sun. It was also said that the heads of both Houses dreamed of her destiny and that they worked together to forge the Way that would make her the Jewel, the Shield, of Tomarq. It was the first and only time two Houses made a Way between them.

Tranta did not doubt it. The gem had always held a majesty and an affinity for the sun's fire, her judgment and justice an apocalyptic spear which burned to ashes whatever it struck. Lariel had told him to give up. To gather the remnants together and bring them to Larandaril until they could decide how best to dispose of them, while House Drebukar reopened the mines of Tomarq to search for her likeness. He did not think the mines would hold a twin to her might, and even if it did, the Way that was made into her depths could never be unmade and laid upon another. Ways did not survive their unmaking and, often, an insufficiently skilled Vaelinar did not survive the attempt to create a Way. It was, for a bloodline, a once-in-a-lifetime happening.

He touched the gem nearest him. He could see from its shape that it belonged melded to the crooked splinter lying next to it. He mated them to one another upon the ground, moving through the bits and pieces, putting the puzzle back together as he had attempted once, twice, a dozen times before. She bit at his fingers and palms, some of her edges sharper than the finest made sword. His hands went raw and bloody before the sun had even begun to climb on the eastern horizon and workers began to arrive on the other side of the barrier. This here, which must go . . . no, not there, but *there* . . . And yet, it would not be enough. It had never been enough. He paused at the edge of the fire pit, its charcoal interior now cold and dead. He could not create enough heat to meld her edges back together. If he could bring the mouth of a volcano to her, perhaps . . . even then, it would only be a perhaps. Who knew what fires and pressures had created her in the first place? He was not a God.

He ground his teeth in frustration, kneeling among the hundreds of other pieces he had not yet fit together, and looked at the travesty of his attempts. Blood from his torn hands dripped slowly and thinly upon the glittering bits. Sweat from his brow trickled down his face and jaw to fall upon the splinters. If it were enough to give his soul to make the Jewel whole, he would have given it. But it was not. Yet, even as he squatted and his blood dripped down, a heat reflected from his shattered puzzle and light dazzled over his hands with a faint sizzling sound, and the thousand tiny, jagged cuts healed. He sat down in shock.

Tranta rubbed his hands. Usually she did not cut him. The fragments would turn in his fingers and hands so as not to harm him, but today he had been frustrated and she had responded in kind, twisted at his maddened touch upon her. Yet—and yet—she knew his touch on her and rose to protect him. Tranta examined his hands minutely. Not a scar. No pinkness or so much as tenderness. He twisted his hands back and forth in examination. The Jewel of Tomarq had healed him, but she was never a healer. Always a guardian. Had he discovered a new power within her depths? He needed to test it. Perhaps he was not meant to return her to her former glory because a new destiny awaited them both. Fatigue swept over him, and he put the heels of his hands to his eyes. With his brother gone, he was the only guardian the Jewel had left, and he feared he was failing her. Seeing things he did not really see. Hoping for a restoration that he could not possibly affect. He sighed.

Spring clouds filled the sky, dimming the day. Someone shouted at him over the barrier, and Tranta went to answer the call, parting the ward with his body to see what the problem might be. The Kernan foreman with more than a few hints of Vaelinar in his blood, leaned on his stone-working pick, a knife-like smile parting his lips. "His lordship says we are nearly done. The anchor is set and set deep on this side. We've got nets below, three of 'em," and he paused long enough to spit to one side, although Tranta could not be sure if it was an opinion of safety nets for the rope bridge or not. "When we hitch it up, it should hold. Even if typhoon winds hit. Though," and he squinted through one plain brown eye, "I wouldn't want to be on it then."

"Nor I. Sounds like good work from you and all your lads."

"Thanks for that. His Lordship might walk on air, but it's we who bite the rock, and bite it deep." He hefted his pick. Before joining his crew, who sat on break waiting for the ild Fallyn engineer, he surveyed his side of the cliff. His jaw worked a bit as if chewing the words up first. "I be sorry for the Jewel," he offered, finally. "My brother is a fisherman, my father a short voyage trader. She guarded the harbor well for all of our lives. Our words of sorrow for the loss of your lordship."

Tranta dropped his chin. "I thank you for that."

The foreman nodded back and sauntered over to his crew. On the far side, Tranta could see the rest of the workers busy, and no sign of the ild Fallyn yet.

Tranta traced the barrier with his sigil and passed through again. It parted reluctantly, with a shiver, and he knew that its force was weakening. He would have to decide, and soon, what to do with the remains of the fiery mistress who had dictated all of his life before she could be carted off and sullied by hands that would hold her only for wealth and greed.

A ray dazzled his eye. Clouds thinned overhead and the rubble lit up, and he could hear a hum in his ears. The empty cradle turned in its stead at his elbow, but the noise did not come from the machine's near silent workings. Tranta bent cautiously. He put his hand out. Warmth flooded his senses and vibration his hearing, and his nerves fired into vigilance. The hairs at his temples and back of his neck prickled. The gem nearest his palm nearly leaped into his grasp, burning, twisting in his hold.

There, there, there.

The stone fired in his hand, burning, glowing, and sending a beam striking outward. Not enough to destroy, no, but undeniably it pulsed in frantic warning.

Tranta fumbled at his belt for his telescope as he strode to the seaward edge and knelt there, one hand full of the fiery eye and looked upon the waters. He swept the stretch once and then caught it, where the beam fell upon glittering waters, its red eye bobbing on the ocean's tide.

Intruder.

He could see the helm of the boat cutting through the waters swiftly, and the lens brought into detail not the exact shape of the rowers, but enough of them to know they did not move like men.

Tranta shot to his feet and bellowed, "Send a bird down to the port. On the leeward side of the cliff, near the cove of Keniel, intruders."

Excited shouts and cries followed his orders and in another breath, a bird took wing, followed by a second a long moment after as the work crew fumbled to send word. The first bird, undoubtedly, had escaped when they'd opened the cage to get the second. Someone had the presence of mind to yell, "Message away!" to confirm the obvious.

Raymy. Scouts from the remnants of the original force, perhaps, lying off the coast and out of sight, venturing timidly into their waters to look for their army. Or perhaps not. Whoever or whatever sailed that boat did not bear a badge which gave them clearance to ply their trade upon these waters, the badge which allowed the Jewel of Tomarq to overlook them.

Tranta's hand trembled. He looked down at it, as the stone remained hot and heavy in his hand, pulsing with its wispy voice. Dare he call it that? Its voice thinned and then tailed off, as if knowing the alarm had been called and heard. Or had he heard anything but the wail of the wind over the cliff and across the cradle and through his hair? How could he have heard anything? It was his mind, only his mind, and the alarm he had called, had he condemned innocent men? He retrained his scope on the waters below, to the leeward side of the cliff where the boat cut the water closer and closer and he could no longer say with any surety if its occupants moved as men did or not. They had tarps up to cut off the sea spray and wore oil skin cloaks and floppy hats as further protection against the water, hunched over their oars as they rowed with quick and steady strokes. He dropped the orb, pain throbbing through his hand as if it had burned to his very core.

It fell among its mates and rolled to a stop on the bruised and tender green grasses of the cliff top, shaded by the workings of the cradle. He folded one hand over the other gingerly in protection, but the heat fled as quickly as it had come, and his flesh seemed none the worse for it. How could he have felt such heat and not been seared by it?

Tranta stared down. Shaded, no longer refracting the light of the sun, he expected to see the dazzle dim and then bleed out altogether, but the orb glowed steadily. Then, one by one, other orbs caught fire in the rubble. His head felt muzzy as the vibration picked up strength to thrum louder and stronger in warning. He stood among them as belief forced its way into his body and mind. The Jewel of Tomarq lived still. She served, even broken and shattered and unable to strike as she had been faceted to strike, but she sounded the alarm. He squatted again, to be closer to the glowing stones. Their color grew even more brilliant as he knelt over them, as his belief in them grew. The Way had been changed, malformed by the attack, but she had not been broken.

Triumph surged through him. She had been made to be used, freed to face the sun in all its glory, and she wanted to be used still. He had only to find a new Way for her. He filled his pouch with a handful of the larger pieces, gems the size of his fist, experiments flooding his mind.

The Kernan foreman cut short the moment he was savoring. "Istlanthir! Lord. A bird has come to the field post."

Warmth still flooded his mind. He blinked it away. "Back to roost?"

"Nay, lordship, a new bird. Field owl, it looks like. Has th' other birds all in a fright. No one dares go near it, so the master sent me for you."

That cleared his mind like a dash of cold seawater. "Field owl, you say?"

"So the coop lad marked it. He's a bit dim, that lad, but he knows his fowl."

"He should." Tranta opened his barrier and stepped through again, the afternoon sun on the back of his neck. He tightened his hair in its brace, the ponytail snagging a few blue strands on his rough hands as he did so. He shook them off and watched them drift away like spiderwebs on the wind off the sea cliffs. The ild Fallyn engineer sat on a stump, charts and diagrams held down by rocks on a table in front of him, but lifted his gaze long enough to give Tranta a jerk of a nod as he passed.

Tranta did not trust the man any further than he could throw him, but it was not politic to slight him any more than it would have been to refuse his help. Was that a bird feather drifting off the hem of the man's short cloak as Tranta passed? And if it was . . . why?

Before Tranta could think much more on it, the coop lad came pelting up the crest of the hill. He carried the field owl in both hands, unaware of the creature's ability to rip him open with either beak or talon. He thrust the carrier at Tranta. "Sir! Sir!" Then he stood panting, too winded to say anything else.

Tranta put his forearm out and spoke a soothing word, and the owl turned harvest moon eyes on him, blinking. "Fed him yet?"

"Just a scrap, sir. Just a shred."

"See to it, then, soon as I get the tube off." Tranta felt the owl settle on his arm and close its claws tight about him. Owls felt even lighter than most birds. It swiveled its head about to fix its gaze on his face. Tranta spoke a few more words, nonsense really, part of a sea chantey that had been in his head all day, and the owl settled, eyes half-closed. He rubbed the knuckle of his finger down its chest. It radiated heat just as the Jewel of Tomarq rubble had. He found the tube and untied it quickly. The owl dipped its beak down to rub the back of his hand as he did so, and found itself transferred briskly back to the coop lad's arm. "Go and feed him. Settle him in, but keep him isolated."

"No fear, sir! Lordship." The lad took a deep breath. "The other birds are scared spitless of this one."

No doubt. The owl was probably a predator of their kind. He kept no vantane in his roost, but if he had, that proud war bird would have scared this field owl even as it terrified the others. Pecking order.

Tranta found himself grinning at his thought, as he twisted the tube open and popped the tiny scroll out. His smile disappeared immediately.

"What is it, Lord?"

"Word from afar. I may be gone for several days. No one crosses that barricade, not even the Stronghold of ild Fallyn. To do so will mean death. Understand me?"

The Kernan squinted his brown eyes as he looked back to Tranta's warding, and he nodded, tightly. "No one, Lord."

Tranta thrust the note in his pocket and took the easy way down from the cliffs, whistling for a groom to bring up a horse.

Chapter Six

IN THE NORTHERN HILLS and forests of the lands known as First Home, a manor house sprawled at the edge of mighty aryn groves, with far-flung fields beyond them. They did not look like the holdings of a warlord, but they were, and now, the inheritance of a man who had lived long and well among the Vaelinar. Bistane Vantane felt the welcome weight of his family's estate fold about him like a cloak as he rode in, dismounted from his weary horse, and turned his reins over to one of the waiting stable lads. "Rub him down well, Cathen. He deserves it, he brought me all the way from Ashenbrook."

He watched them move toward the open stalls in the back, the horse dampened with sweat and blowing lightly, but walking soundly. Then he turned away.

"Welcome home, Lordship."

Bistane paused in the stable doorway. His leathers creaked faintly as he looked to see who called his name, and spotted his brother Verdayne standing half-shadowed.

"Brother, will you never learn not to stand unrevealed unless you intend not to be revealed?"

"Someday, I'll learn. I just keep forgetting what a jumpy lot you elven-blooded are." The corner of Verdayne's mouth twisted wryly. He shoved his hands into his jacket, and a glint came into his eyes that, for the briefest of moments, echoed that of the father they shared, though his height and diffident posture came from the mother they did not.

"Bastard," said Bistane fondly and grabbed for his brother, bringing him close in a rough hug. He ruffled Dayne's hair. "You'd be jumpy, too, waiting for the Raymy to rain down on you."

"I'd gladly go in your place, but I think the women fighters would throw me back." Verdayne twisted out of his hold and stepped back, grinning.

"Perhaps." Bistane considered. "No, undoubtedly they would. No one attracts the fair sex like I do."

"Bah. Sounds and smells like the mulch and fertilizer I spent most of the last three days spreading down on the sapling orchard."

Bistane laughed as they exited the barn. "How do they look?"

"Excellent, if I do say so myself. I have that much of our father in me, I can grow aryns."

"Indeed you can, but don't doubt yourself. There is much, much more of him in you than that."

Verdayne tossed him a look. "I'd rather have heard it from him."

"I know. I would have, too. A spare man with praise, he was." Bistane stripped off his riding gloves.

"I can fight."

"And well I know it." Bistane rubbed his rib cage ruefully. "I have the scar to prove it."

Verdayne flushed. His dark blue eyes, blue upon indigo, Vaelinar eyes with their multiple shades of color, darkened even more. "I never meant to—"

"Of course you did! But not to hurt." Bistane threw an elbow at him, Dayne dodging easily, with a Dweller's grace. Dayne's dark curls bounced as he did. His hair was not black like Bistane's, but a rich, dark brown, with a curl that kept it close to his head until it needed cropping so badly that his brow could hardly be seen. In his youngest days, catching Dayne for a haircut was like rounding up wild cattle or sheep. It seemed like only yesterday. It wasn't, quite, for all that he was half-Dweller, his brother had already outlived much of his family, including his mother. He would probably live two to three hundred years, near three times the age of most of his race, unless war or assassination took him first, or some dire plague that even stout Dweller constitution couldn't withstand. But Dayne was like Bistane in that he would age slower and that thick, dark hair would someday go snow white, like that of their Vaelinar father.

Something stirred on the wind. Bistane lifted his chin, and his attention, from his brother who went stock-still.

"What is it?"

"Don't know. Something." Bistane rubbed his bare hand across the back of his neck. He'd gone with his hair shorn close to his head lately, to keep his battle helm better fitting and to . . . well, he supposed, to emulate his warlord predecessor and father.

"I can tell that much." Verdayne put his shoulders back.

Bistane shook his head apologetically. "I don't know more than that. There are times when . . ." he paused. He would not say it aloud, but there were times when the presence of his father walked these lands as strongly as he did when he was alive. He'd never told Dayne he'd seen him or asked if the other had, as well. He was a warlord now. Questions of his sanity would not be wise. This, though. He lifted his index finger. "It doesn't feel like . . ."

"Father," finished Dayne.

They traded a long look. Did Verdayne feel his father's presence as he did? Dayne did not blink.

"Oh," Bistane breathed. "And you never said anything. You will pay for that."

"What would I say? Ghosts don't exist." The corner of Verdayne's mouth quirked up. "And you think you're man enough to take the toll from me?"

"I know I am."

Dayne set his feet. They both knew that stance, the readying for a quick, fleet start. Dayne's first offense was usually a quick and lithe retreat. Then he would circle back when he thought he had the advantage. It was a strategy which worked for him, playing off the height disadvantage.

Bistane curled his hand. "Come here, *little* brother."

"You have far more years than I do, but not the wisdom that goes with them!" taunted Dayne.

Bistane readied to chase after him as Dayne moved, but it was not to take to his feet and run this time. The other put his head down and charged, with a snort just like a recalcitrant wild bull. He hit Bistane low, knocking him clean off his feet and gasping in surprise in the stable yard grit and grasses. They rolled around, both of them whooping for breath for even as Bistane had lost his, so had his brother when they had collided.

Dayne finally ended up on top, pinning him. "You, Brother, are built like a stone wall." He inhaled gustily.

"I am just biding my time," he warned.

"Well, and I know that." Dayne hopped off and put his hand down. "But I got you."

"That you did." Bistane got up, shaking himself off. "And I will wager you never learned that from Father or any of the teachers he lined up for us."

"No, I learned that from old gardener Magdan." Verdayne's eyes went a little moist, for he had been as close to the Dweller gardener as he had to his warlord Vaelinar father, his booted feet planted firmly in both worlds. Both of his fathers, real and foster, had died in the last year.

Bistane moved as if to pass him, put his foot out and swept Verdayne's feet out from under him before his brother could blink away the tears. Verdayne went down with a whoop. Bistane looked at him. "I learned from old Magdan as well." He grinned and headed to the main house with a swagger to his steps.

Then he heard a whistling. He looked up. A silverwing raggedly rode the wind in from the south dipping up and down on the uneasy currents, a bird rarely seen in this northern land, but he'd had a few trained to messenger for him. This one looked exhausted, its wings flapping erratically. Behind it, as if stalking the bird, glided a field owl.

"Get the owl," Bistane ordered.

Verdayne dashed back in the barn to retrieve a bow and arrow, a utilitarian set, and nocked the arrow before Bistane could purse his lips to whistle the silverwing down as it neared them. The arrow flew past it, and caught the owl in the wing, bringing it down with a screech. As if relieved, the silverwing circled slowly and then plunged in a ragged dive to Bistane's outstretched hand.

"Did you kill it?" He focused his attention on the messenger, for a tube did indeed glitter upon its leg.

"No, and good thing, too. It's carrying a scroll." Verdayne bent over his quarry and stretched his hands out. "The birder will be furious I shot it."

"Both carry messages?" Frowning, Bistane whistled for Habbane, the head stables lad, as he worked at the thong to get his tube freed from the silverwing as it gasped and quivered in his hold. The poor thing's journey had nearly done it in. He tried to think who could have sent it, and how far.

"I can set the wing, I think." Dayne clucked soothingly to the owl, and it settled in the crook of his arm. "They're both played out, Brother. They've come a long way."

Habbane came running with the limp he'd had since he'd been kicked by one of Bistel's warhorses a decade back, and he bowed. "Lordship, Lord, forgive me. I was in the mares' barn. Your Ilytha is about to drop her foal."

"No explanations. Take this silverwing and put it to roost. See it's fed, but slowly. It may be famished, but I don't want it to choke."

"And the owl?"

Verdayne said, "Broken wing from the arrow."

"Can be set, or I can wrench its neck."

"Set it," both Bistane and Verdayne said as one.

"Hold it, then. No sense having it scare the wits out of this little one. I'll be back soon as this one's settled." Habbane staggered off, whistling through his half-toothed mouth for the lads who helped him run his stable yards and coops.

Bistane opened his scroll. He read it, frowning, then looked to Dayne. "Give me yours."

The scroll flashed through the air. It startled the owl who flung both wings out, then gave a screech of pain as it did so. Verdayne settled it back down, folding it back into quiet.

"Same message."

"Someone wanted to be certain."

"Indeed, he did. This is from Sevryn. They tried to assassinate Nutmeg."

Dayne had been worrying at the owl's injury, snapping the shaft in two and working it through the creature's wing as gently as he could. He looked up sharply. "At Calcort?"

"None other."

"You'll be heading there, then."

"No. I've been at Ferstanthe, on the way back from Ashenbrook, and what I find there sends me to Larandaril. Faster now, for I can wager that we'll get a bird from Lara sometime tomorrow."

"Why were you at Ferstanthe?"

"Because Azel sent for me. What I have to tell you, though, is best not discussed out here in the open, but it must be said before I leave." Dayne nodded solemnly. Neither spoke another word when Habbane returned for the injured owl, and they walked to the manor house that had been Warlord Bistel's domain.

Chapter
Seven

BISTANE TAPPED OUT A BOTTLE and decanted it into two handblown glasses meant to be gripped in the palm of a man's hand, barrel-shaped glasses, and the caramel liquor filled each glass halfway. He left the lid off the bottle before taking up his glass and settling back into his chair. The messenger birds had been cared for and safely tucked away in the croft built for such creatures. Dayne took his drink up as well, speculatively, and both of them eyed the massive chair on the other side of the study desk: their father's chair. Empty. Likely never to be filled and equally as likely never to be taken out of the study and put away. Bistane took a deep sip of his drink and stayed quiet for such a long time that Dayne, despite his inner promise to himself to be quiet and content and certainly not impatient as Dwellers could be (after all, they did not have the time, let alone the lifespan, of the average Vaelinar) and finally blurted, "Why Ferstanthe?"

Bistane's eyes came back into focus and he looked over as though realizing he wasn't alone and had forgotten that.

He took a very short sip of his drink before answering, "I was looking for something."

"And you didn't find it."

"No. But I did find something else." Bistane sat back even further, swung his boot heels up on the edge of the desk, and began a tale. "I was riding home from Ashenbrook, to see how you were doing, and the farmlands, and to swing by the Library because of something gone missing that bothered me, and because Azel had sent me a note that I decided I should answer. Despite the fact worry carried me there, I enjoyed the journey. I like the northern lands with their evergreens and free-flowing brooks and . . ."

Dayne sat back and listened to his brother launch into his story.

There was a wind in the high forests, and the evergreens shook and moaned against one another, sounding like both the sea and a ship sailing upon it, its timbers creaking and echoing the force of nature which carried it. Azel d'Stanthe of Ferstanthe came to the gate of the library grounds when summoned, one hand wrapped firmly at the collar of his cloak, his towering body hunched as though the winds could lift and carry even his substantial figure away with it.

"Bistane! My lad. Good of you to come. I hope I did not thwart any battle plans by asking you to detour here."

"You would never ask lightly, Azel. Whatever your concerns, I'll do what I can."

The wind whistled as if it would cut through both of them, and Azel hurried them through the gate and gardens and into the library's front rooms, closing the massive wooden doors with a resounding thud at their heels. The foyer and corridors smelled of aromatic woods and faint incense and the metallic odors of various inks. He could hear students rustling in the background, but no one came to take his coat or Azel's cloak, and he had the feeling that the master of these great woods and its library had ordered complete and total solitude. He draped his cloak coat over his arm as he followed after d'Stanthe to a study deep within the library complex.

"My father intended to visit you before Ashenbrook."

"And so he did, Lord Vantane, so he did. His journal rests with the other *Books of All Truth*."

A tension left Bistane. It was a duty he knew his father had taken most seriously and he had made his intent known that he would visit Ferstanthe. But Bistane had never been certain that Bistel had actually relinquished the book even though his visit had been well known and, since the journal had not been found with what little remains his Returned body left behind, he had worried that it might have been lost in battle. Like his father, Bistane had seen that worn leather journal nearly every day of his life. He would have liked to see it again. Just for old times' sake, and perhaps a bit more.

Azel set his hands on his knees and said, as if reading Bistane's mind, "It is beyond sharing now. It is in the trust with the other books, until that time prophesied when they will be needed and unleashed."

Bistane sat with a faint misgiving. "Unleashed? So strong a word?"

"Repeated as it was given and lessoned to me. It is strong, isn't it? It makes me worry about my charges even more." Azel leaned forward, removing a quilted cover over an ornate tray on the table between them. He poured drinks and sliced from a loaf and piled cold meats and cheese on it, and gave a share balanced on a clean linen napkin to Bistane. "Eat and listen."

So he did.

Azel looked gray about the face, his eyes lined more than Bistane remembered, and there was a gauntness about his hands that seemed new as well. He leaned forward and fell into a long pause, as if drawing his thoughts from a great well. The mulled wine had stayed mostly warm, if not piping hot, and imparted a good feeling against the knifing effect of the wind. Bistane kept his silence as promised, even when the quiet between them stretched for a very long time. Finally, Azel stirred, lifting up an ink-stained great mitt of a hand.

"I have sifted through it and there's no easy way to say it. No way to tell the tale that won't have you wondering if I have lost my mind. So here it is. There is a ... thing ... skulking about the immediate grounds. And somewhat in the forest, too, although my lumbermen aren't talking about it. I've had a scholar lad or two, scarcely babes, blurt something out, but these others, their fathers and brothers, are hard men, few jobs more risky than cutting and processing timber, and they don't like being taken for cowards. The saw mills and paper mills still run, but the workers are scared." Azel paused, leveling his eyes upon Bistane. Bistane nodded to show he understood.

"There is a dead man haunting." Azel let his breath out in a great puff and sat back. "I've said it, there. Incomprehensible as it is. Perhaps not dead, but Undead. Walking. Hiding. He has a smell not unlike the books from centuries ago: dry, musty, faintly decaying."

"Hurt anyone?" Bistane couldn't keep silent a moment longer.

"I'm not certain. There's nothing like this in our tales, and I hadn't run across it much in the stories of Kerith, but it does crop up from time to time. A soulless, unloving thing that exists only to bring disaster upon the living." Azel's gaze bored into his. "Even so, I wouldn't have believed it until I saw it myself."

"Where?"

"In these Halls. Attempting, so it seemed, to gain entrance into the inner sanctum."

Where his father's journal lay, among countless others, rumored to hold the truth and nothing but the truth as written by the Vaelinars themselves. If rumors were true.

"And did it?"

"No. Although that brings me to another part of my tale. The black mold which corrupted many of my texts is gone, thanks to the preservative invented by Tolby Farbranch and the tireless efforts of my students, but it left something insidious in its wake. The books are simply disintegrating."

"What? No fungus and yet we're losing them? How can that be?"

Azel nodded sadly, his great face drooping in folds of defeat. "Little more than crumbles. So far it hasn't hit the *Books of All Truth*, but it might. It could." He turned away, unable to look at Bistane any longer. "*It will*."

"What then?"

"We don't copy those books because the magic that lies within them comes from the hands that have penned the pages. When they are gone, there is nothing. We lost a few to the black mold, but very few in the inner sanctum, by Tree's blood, and none of the All Truth yet. This new contagion has different . . ." Azel stopped. He lifted both hands in entreaty, searching for a word and then giving up. "Rules, for lack of a better word."

"And you surmise this dead man might have something to do with it."

"I couldn't say. It can't get into that part of the collection, but who's to say . . . who's to say what it is and what it can do."

"And you are scholars, not swordsmen."

Azel's eyebrows lowered ponderously. "Yes."

Bistane rocked back in his chair, now empty napkin over one thigh, his cup in his hand. "Two things."

"Yes?"

"I want a book in the early stages of this disintegration wrapped and packaged, to be taken to Tolby Farbranch, with all due caution. Can such a thing be done?"

"All right. I don't know if we can do it, but we can certainly try."

"And I want the *Books of All Truth* separated. Each to its own private chamber or drawer or whatever you can manage. Handle them as meticulously as you would a victim of plague."

"That goes without saying; however, there are a few hundred of them . . ."

"And each is as valuable as the next, as far as we know. Separate them or have each contaminate the other until none is left."

Azel scratched at his chin. "Nothing fancy as the sanctum now, but . . . yes, there are possibilities. I will have to set wards."

"One of your many Talents, as I recall, Master Librarian."

That garnered a small smile. "Yes. Not widely known but true. It will take me some time, however. And I will have to set a guard upon myself because one day those wards will have to be taken down and only I will know the undoing of them." He pushed himself to his feet. "Such is power. It both makes and imprisons a man."

Bistane tilted his head to one side. "And a third thing, nearly forgotten."

"What?"

"Have I time to nap a bit and sharpen my sword before I go after that skulker?"

"I think you might. These deeds always seem best done after the sundown."

Bistane could see signs aplenty that the scholars were wary and some downright frightened. Doors had heavy bolts newly added to them. The main entry door now had a massive board that could be lowered across it, and as Bistane examined it, he could feel the tingle of a ward on it as well. They'd done everything they knew how to do but have a cleric come bless the place with sacred flame and cleansing water, but as the students were, for the most part, Vaelinars, they didn't believe in the Gods of Kerith.

He made the rounds outside, twice, knowing that night might draw it out, and not just the curtain of nightfall, but the depths of it when most souls were hidden deep in dreams. As it came to pass, the skulker was never found or dispatched. It, perhaps, with an uncanny intelligence, found out it was being hunted and fled. Or perhaps it was never quite what Azel and his students and timber men had made it out to be. There were some small signs of a presence. A scratched lock. A shutter hinge bent and easily loosened on a back window. Beds of twigs and leaves and grass in the woods that stank of something that made the dogs paw at their noses and growl. But nothing Bistane could face and skewer on the point of his sword. He left after a few days with two parcels in his saddlebags and Azel distracted with his current feat of re-housing his important library collection and coming up with the energy and will to ward each book separately. He looked even grayer when Bistane rode out.

Verdayne took a deep breath as though just realizing he'd been holding it. He sat back and rolled his empty glass between his palms as his brother finished.

"And so that brought me here."

"Did you run across sign of that thing, whatever it was?"

"I'm not sure. In the wilderness, you can find subtle signs of death wherever you look. Animals prey upon each other and not always neatly. Whatever it was, it appeared to flee south. I didn't follow. I'd been gone too long from home, and I had this —" He withdrew a small parcel, wrapped solidly in oilcloth, tied and sealed with wax. He dropped his heels from the desk so that he could lean forward and place the bundle on the top between himself and Dayne. "For you." He topped off both glasses before settling back.

"Me? Do I look like a Tolby Farbranch to you?"

"No, but you look like the only one I can trust to deliver it to him."

Silence followed. Bistane put his glass down next to the book. "Father hired and trained a good many men to help him with his holdings, but he only had two sons. The lands will prosper for a time without us when there are things only one of us can do."

"You want me to go to Calcort."

"Now, more than ever. Not just to take the book to Far-branch but now also to see to Nutmeg."

"I'm not a swordsman! I won't be much use as a body-guard."

"Of course you are. You just don't like to admit it because seeming not to be gives you an advantage." Bistane eyed his brother shrewdly. "Admit it. You like being under-estimated."

"I like not being a bloodthirsty warlord."

"Dayne."

Dayne felt a slight smile creep over his mouth, almost unbidden. "All right. I do like having a leg up. A fellow like me sometimes needs the odds on his side." He swirled his drink before setting it down. "Why send me to Calcort?"

"Because you're my brother."

"That is not always a good thing among the Vaelinar."

Bistane leveled a look at him, smoldering, his lips thin-ning. Dayne shrugged. "You know what I mean, Bis."

"This is as much about Nutmeg as it is the decaying books."

"The books are Ways, or part of one. The library is para-mount among our memories, and you want me to go be-cause of a girl? An unwed Dweller girl flush with child?"

"Not just any girl. Father thought a lot of her."

"Yes, as I recall, he called meeting her a 'feisty breath of fresh air.' She wasn't so impressed by him that she forgot how to speak. He thought that her friendship with Lariel ensured that our Warrior Queen would stay in touch with the more common peoples. Not that I think she needs to be reminded. She keeps her pact with the sacred river well and honestly, and with the people who depend upon that river all the way to the sea. I've always wondered why she is called a Warrior Queen when she's more of a mother on guard."

Bistane raised an eyebrow, and Verdayne flushed slightly in response. He turned away for a moment. "Not that she gives off a maternal air in any way. To me. Or you."

He cleared his throat with a noise that indicated it had suddenly become rather tight.

Bistane took a deep breath, then another. He looked away, across the study, at the artifacts of his father's life. "The books are, of course, paramount." He leaned forward on his elbows. "Ways are changing. Snapping back into that from which they originally came or warping into something unknowable. We twisted the threads of creation and now those threads are being knotted or slashed undone altogether. I need you at Calcort with Tolby Farbranch and his daughter. Will you do as I ask?"

"Never a doubt."

"Accordingly, I also ask you to watch out for Nutmeg. Tell her a bit of your life. What you've been through. It can only help the child later."

"I've not had such a rough life here."

Bistane met his brother's eyes evenly. "Nor has it been as welcoming as it could have been, from myself and others."

That brought a flush to Verdayne's cheeks, bringing the Dweller looks out in him even more. "You've been a good enough brother!"

"I could have been better."

"You were insulted at first."

Bistane nodded. "I was. That our father should have needed another son! I realized later that it was family and love he needed, and you and yours provided."

"I thought you told him he should have gotten another dog."

"No, I told him that I was going to treat you like a puppy." Bistane grinned suddenly. "And I did, rather! You were a round, rollicking child."

"And sturdy. Don't forget sturdy."

"You needed to be."

"Anyone who touched me had to fear being beat down by you. Or old Magdan." Verdayne leaned back in his chair, a thoughtful expression on his face. "You taught me what it was to be Vaelinar. He taught me what it meant to be Dweller."

"And Dad?"

"He taught me everything. But you don't always believe

your parent, do you? It took the two of you to convince me. You can depend upon me."

"Good. I leave for Larandaril tomorrow morning."

"Then you can bid me good-bye at first light."

"Done."

"And, hopefully," Verdayne added, picking up his glass again, "Done well."

Chapter Eight

Abayan Diort

TO THE EAST, and to the south, were the lands that the Wars of the Mageborn ruined and left to pool with magic gone corrupt, a fractured boundary between the provinces of the First Home and the far-flung nomadic holdings of the Galdarkans. An encampment lay there, pitched in the desert.

A soft wind rose off the oasis, shivering the many tents grouped about it, and moving particularly the one great canopy. It lifted the words being spoken softly, as a wave might crest under a ship or a sporting dolphin, and carried them to a listener.

"A Vaelinar comes to your house."

Abayan Diort shifted in his leather-slung chair at the words, the beginning of night breezes rippling the canopy of his tent overhead, the noise like the sails of a ship upon a great and restless sea. He responded. "Like Death, a Vaelinar is as inevitable and unwanted in my house." He pushed his boot out and toed a line of colored sand at his feet, not moving a grain. He studied the Galdarkan woman, one of his own, as she knelt among the colored sands. "One doesn't have to be a prophet to utter that."

She flinched, her cupped hand scattering sand haphazardly over her design. She looked down at it in dismay. "I can't—I cannot—"

"I know," he acknowledged, not unkindly. "You cannot tell me how to rule, and what kind of man would I be if I asked you to, and if I took your readings as such? I would no longer deserve the regard I've earned. As for you. Tell me truly, can you read?"

The oracle rocked back to settle on her heels. After a very long moment, and a sigh, she shook her head. "Not this. Not now."

"Will you be able to read again?" He had heard many things from her before and knew that, as sometimes they all did, her well had gone dry. It happened. She feared him for it, but she shouldn't. He couldn't blame her.

She lifted her face up to meet his gaze, before dropping to look down at the colored sands. "I don't know. I hope so."

He stood, and bent to take her hands in his. They were trembling. "Don't worry. You will be honored for your service. And your honesty." He walked out of his tent then, to go stand in the wind, leaving her to clean up and cry in solitude.

A Vaelinar comes to your house. Would that one would, one particular Vaelinar, a proud and beautiful woman, a Warrior Queen as he was a warlord. He favored her, with her cascade of gold-and-silver hair and her eyes of bright blue studded with gold stars and streaks in the remarkable way of the elven, the Vaelinarran eyes. Abayan put his head back and gazed at the bright multitude of stars overhead. As above, so below. A field of races walked under them. The beastlike Bolgers, the invader Vaelinars, the majority of Kernans, the short and sturdy Dwellers, and his own, the golden-skinned Galdarkans. Each had their strengths and shortcomings. There were Kernan who claimed they could read the future in the fields of lights which shone down upon their lands of Kerith, but he laid little stock in them. If you could not read the future in your own self, how could you perceive it in the firmament of something as distant and untouchable as a star? He knew, as his own prophet did, that the spreading and reading of colored sands was only a focus for that which she brought forth from within herself. And he did not judge her harshly for not being able to prophesy at the drop of a grain of dirt. No one could, nor be expected to. No matter how he wished his indecisions and worries could be prophesied away.

He could not rely on battles to gain the destiny he wanted, but . . . Abayan tightened his jaw. The destiny he had begun upon, solid in his choices, had started to twist in his mind. He could not place the blame on any one circumstance, nor even upon a solid event. He had set out to unite his nomadic people, to give them union with one another and present a front to those of the First Home, the Kernan and Vaelinar who ruled the western lands. The years of a Galdarkan empire lying fallow had been long enough. They had atoned for the brutal indifference of the Mageborn and Mage Kings who had ruled in the east before destroying themselves, leaving only their servant guardians the Galdarkan behind in their dust and ruins. Centuries after, he had been born, and he had looked into their past and present and decided on what kind of future he wished his people to gain. Had they agreed with him? Not all. Most but not all. And it was his bringing those who disagreed with him to their knees before they would join him that had angered Queen Lariel of the Vaelinars. She alone held the true power to withstand him.

And had.

Yet he thought she understood him.

Dare he still hope that she might come to want to ally with him, to wed their ambitions and their peoples? After meeting her in battle and then standing with her in war, he had thought perhaps there still lay a chance . . . but she had not asked to speak with him in weeks, other than to discuss the logistics of keeping a standing force in place against that time when their mutual enemy would return. For what did she wait? Did she wish him to speak first?

Abayan's throat dried as it never did when contemplating a maneuver. It was not that courting Lariel Anderieon was not formidable, it was. But what stayed him now was that she had not become his obsession. Her alliance and love his goal. Her being with him the only right answer among all the other answers in his world.

That stayed his hand.

He did not know what he wanted. He did not know the best way to go forward or retreat. He had lost his bearing.

Why?

He knew that he was desirable. A scroll from Tressandre ild Fallyn lay upon the small side table in his tent. Her words had prompted his call for his oracle and yet, the failure of his servant did not perturb him overly. The ild Fallyns were a hard, ambitious people even among the hard and ambitious Vaelinars. He'd seen them glory in the blood of the battle-field and he knew from the glittering of their eyes and the flash of their weapons that it did not truly matter whose blood showered them from head to foot. Any blood would do. Any blood would give an ild Fallyn both the power and pleasure desired. He had no doubt that Tressandre walked in beauty . . . and cruelty. Did he wish to take a woman of that ilk to his people and his bed?

His oracle left the tent and began to move past him, and then she hesitated. Abayan took his attention and thoughts from the stars to look to her. "Yes?"

She swallowed tightly. Afraid, he knew. Afraid of him and her failure.

"It's all right."

She shifted her slight weight. "As . . . not as an oracle, but as a woman of your clan and a . . . a friend . . ." Her voice thinned away entirely.

"Go on."

She gathered her nerve. A familiar sight, he'd seen it in his soldiers again and again. He did not speak, but he watched her and let his mouth soften in encouragement. "I'm listening."

"I feel you've lost your way. You don't falter, but you've many thoughts." She tried to clear a rasp from her throat and failed. "You've made yourself a king of us, but . . . but you were made to be a guardian. Is it one and the same, or do you fight yourself? Warlord. Diort." And she bowed her head, unable to say more.

He waited a long moment to allow her to continue if she could, but she did not try. He put his hand on her shoulder briefly. "Thank you. I shall consider that."

The oracle spun away from him, and disappeared into the night among the tents, her slim figure there one moment and gone the next as Abayan watched.

A wisdom, then, which he had sought; the barest of crumbs, and yet there it was.

He was Galdarkan. By their very nature, they were guardians. The right hands of the rightful rulers of the eastern lands, yet . . . there were no more kings to vouchsafe. The Mageborn rulers had killed one another, and the Gods themselves had killed off their remaining bloodlines, however faint they might be. That very same past had scattered his people, made them nomads with little more than clan allegiances until, for their own survival, he decided to knit them back together. Now that he had done so, he felt . . . Abayan clenched his fist. He had denied the feeling but now it flooded him, unwelcome, dark, and terrible. Now that he had stitched a nation together, he wanted to hand it over to . . . someone.

Someone the Gods decreed could no longer exist.

His bloodline had been created to hand his people to a Mageborn, and then stand at his right hand, protecting as he had been created to do. He could not do it. He should not. But if he did. If he did, would it be Queen Lariel Anderieon or Tressandre ild Fallyn in the place of the impossible since no Mageborn existed?

Abayan stood, his teeth clenched until the sinews of his neck ached, overwhelmed by his failure.

Chapter
Nine

AWAY FROM THE FOREST and field lands of the north, standing near the cove which held the bridged city of Hawthorne, Bregan staggered into the front yards of his home, his legs weary and his mind fogged. The horse which had brought him home trailed along listlessly after he slipped off its bridle and saddle and dropped them on the ground carelessly. He was a dead man. A dead man. He rubbed the back of his hand across his mouth. He could barely remember what possessed him, what drove him to treachery except that the Gods of Kerith had leaned low from the heavens to speak to him, and he'd had no choice.

None.

Be that as it may, he highly doubted that they would give him much more of a bargain than that. There would be no heavenly intervention when Sevryn caught up with him. And Sevryn would, for he had survived Bregan's treachery. It was only a matter of time.

He made it into the villa and yelled for a bottle. He did not intend to be sober when Sevryn kicked down his door. And the man would. Bregan had turned him over to the enemy, but he had survived, and he would come hunting.

Chapter
Ten

SEVRYN LEANED THROUGH the doorway. "It's time to say your farewells."

"I know." Rivergrace tossed her head, a mannerism she seldom used unless she'd been around Nutmeg. It was her sister's familiar gesture, like that of a mountain pony, a showing of reluctance and sometimes, downright mulish, defiance. "I wish I could stay until after the baby is born. She needs me. Mother does, too. I need to be here."

"As if we'd have any way of knowing when that might be."

Grace sighed and looked down at her hands as she twisted her fingers. "Being of both races, the midwives can't tell us. Later than a Dweller birth might be, but earlier than a Vaelinar. It depends, I guess, on Nutmeg."

"I don't think she can get much bigger."

She turned on him. "Then let me stay!"

"I can't." He caught her hands. "You increase the danger to her, you must know that."

"Me? How?"

"Because anyone wanting to unseat Lariel will chip away at her support. Me. Houses Istlanthir and Drebukar

and Vantane. Her allies. Her friends. All are at risk now, not
just her possible heir."

She tugged away from his hold but not enough to free
herself entirely as his hands closed tighter about hers.
"Tree's blood, Sevryn. What a world I've entered."

He leaned over to kiss her brow. "I never would have
found you otherwise. Would you turn that back on us?"

"My soul not find yours? Who knows?" She stepped
close to him, then. "We leave tomorrow?"

"Tomorrow."

"Aderro," she said, and hugged him, before going to find
Nutmeg.

Nutmeg sat in the tiny courtyard where the old well flourished
and flowers grew at random as if birds had scattered their
seeds, and she waited for her sister to find her because Grace
would be coming, and soon, to tell her good-bye. It would happen, whether she hid or not, because Queen Lariel had sent
birds out, they'd been received, and Sevryn had been ordered
home, with new guards on their way, and so forth.

So forth.

Nutmeg sighed. She had overheard her sister talking.
They could have been killed despite their defense. Grace
surmised that they survived because whomever had sent
the assassins wanted Nutmeg alive. Not for long, undoubtedly, but initially. And what then? Where would she be
taken, how long would her lifeblood flow before they cut it
off, and why?

She twisted one thumb about the other. It wouldn't be
because they wanted the baby alive. No. They wanted her
alive because they wanted information. What did they think
she knew? Something Jeredon had told her? Or details from
the awful battle at the Ashenbrook and Revela Rivers?

She closed her eyes in memory.

As if it were yesterday, Nutmeg was there again, trying to warn Bistel of the arrows aimed at them. He moved, to protect Bistane and her, and took the shaft to his chest. He sent Bistane away to do what could be done to stem the tide of the battle, and she had been left alone with him. She wrenched her hands together as the remembrance swept her up, and she could not break away as it all happened again. She still had Jeredon's blood on her and now watched another dying.

Bistel turned back. He stumbled. His chest gurgled. He broke the arrow shaft. He looked down at Nutmeg and seemed to really see her for the first time. He touched her wet face.

She could see the copse he led her to, and put her small weight under his shoulder, and helped him to the shelter. Behind them, the Raymy and Ravers quarreled amongst themselves among the carcasses of their own, and the two of them were forgotten. He sank gratefully to the ground. He took off his helmet and let it drop and he lay down beside it, his snow-white hair glistening with sweat.

"Did you . . . find what you needed . . . at the library?"

"Not what I hoped."

"And . . ." He paused to take a long, sucking breath. She could only wonder why the arrow had not eaten him inside out, but it mattered little. It had killed him anyway. "And what had you hoped for?"

"I wanted to find out if I could love a Vaelinar, and if he could love me back."

"Ahhhh." He touched her wet cheek again. "That is not . . . the sort of thing . . . we Vaelinar write in our books. We feel it, but we do not write it." His chest bubbled and she could see his pulse throb in his neck, and his skin pale.

"I have something . . . I want you to take. It is a burden, a trust." He licked his lips. "You can say no."

"There is no one else here."

He smiled thinly. "Bistane will come back for . . . me. But it is not something . . . I wish him to have . . . yet. You are honest. By the very stock of your blood, you are honest."

He gathered another breath, in great pain from the creases across his face. "Take the book from inside my mail, tucked in my shirt. Keep it. Give it to your sons to keep . . . until the day you feel it should be given."

His eyes of brilliant blues locked onto hers. She did not quite know what to answer.

"I will," vowed Nutmeg. She unlaced his chain and found the book inside as he told her, wrapped in cloth that had become drenched with blood. She pushed the cloth aside and then put the book inside her bodice. "Until the day comes when I think it should be given."

"Thank you." Bistel managed a half breath and then shuddered. His body gave a terrible wrench as if it fought to hold on, and failed.

With a shudder of her own, Nutmeg broke free of that past and its remembrances. If only she had said no, as he'd offered her, but how could she have? He'd just saved her life and there was more than that to his request, an importance she couldn't have denied.

She could be fairly certain someone might think she knew something. She was the only one at Warlord Bistel's side when he died.

Did they know about the book he'd entrusted to her and made her swear on?

Did they? Her fingers laced together as she wrung her hands.

It was known, though quietly, that Bistel had placed his journal at the library of Ferstanthe. That's when they'd met and talked, tall, impressive warlord and her impulsive Dweller self. Whoever hunted her down for information had to know that, even though it hadn't been widely talked about. The *Books of All Truth* weren't discussed among the Vaelinars, at least not with other ears to hear. But this book was not his journal. She wasn't sure of its contents, but she knew that much. She'd seen the worn journal when they'd met at the library. She knew that wasn't what she had hidden. The hidden book was thinner, newer looking though nearly as worn, the edges of its pages gilt in gold. One could never mistake one book for another. She wondered who had originally been meant to inherit her burden. Bistel? His other son, the half-blooded one? Perhaps another Vaelinar like Lariel Anderieon? Whom had she robbed of their legacy?

Twist. Her fingers curled as she wrung them.

Rivergrace couldn't tell her much because she was more of a Dweller, her sister, and the machinations of Vaelinar plots were often as obscure to her as they were to Nutmeg. Or they had been. Grace had changed since she'd met Sevryn and would continue to change. Maybe the day would come when Nutmeg couldn't recognize her sister at all, when the labyrinth of Vaelinar planning would come as naturally to her as her own breath.

Turn.

If Jeredon had lived, perhaps they would have stayed together, and she close to Grace at Larandaril, and privy to the lives of the high elven. Certainly she would not have been shut out, shut away, here at Calcort, like a favorite broodmare turned out to pasture to wait until foaling. She could possibly even have turned the burden over to another wiser person, more able to carry it.

Twist.

Nutmeg winced as she gave herself a burn and forced her hands apart. She flapped them in the air to chase the sting away.

"Feeling a'right, Nutmeg?" Lily Farbranch drifted out of the back doorway, dusting biscuit flour off her hands as she moved to stand by her daughter. A comforting smell of baking bread followed in her wake from the kitchen snuggled behind the weathered timbers of the farmhouse.

Nutmeg leaned against a stout post as she hid her reddening hands from sight. She sighed and retrieved a thought that would not be an untruth. "I'm going to miss Rivergrace."

"So will I." Lily ruffled Nutmeg's hair the way she used to do when both were younger. She put her hand familiarly on Nutmeg's swollen belly. Her face stretched in a smile. "Feel that baby kick!"

"Oh, I am. It tumbles about like a street acrobat." She stumbled a bit on the unfamiliar word before letting out a pony-like huff. "Hasn't it been long enough?"

"Vaelinars age far slower than we do. Stands to reason even their babes would take their time."

"I could be pregnant for years!" Nutmeg's hand flew up to smother a wail.

Her mother patted her belly. "Doubtful."

"Don't tease."

"Never, I would never. Now your father and your brothers . . ." Her voice trailed off. Nutmeg did not answer. Both knew that Tolby and her brothers doted on her even as they ragged her with teasing. Perhaps a little too much. Sometimes she felt smothered.

Nutmeg peered across the way. It was a far cry from their home and orchards on the banks of the Silverwing, where one might ride the better part of a morning to greet a neighbor. Far from the gnarled and fragrant apple trees. Those days were gone, their neighbors the Barrels mostly dead, killed by Ravers, the farms and orchards gone fallow or — worse — feral. Other neighbors had moved closer to villages and farther away from the mountains and the ridgelines where wild things prowled. Life here was good in its way just as their life there had been good until danger forced them off their lands. She wondered how their fate might have been had she not pulled a girl child from the river and claimed her as her own sister. The Silverwing gave life and, like any river in its occasional rages, could take it away. The Ravers had come for Rivergrace because of her Vaelinar blood as if they had scented her on the wind.

She braced herself in her chair, a rocking chair, and glared at the hitching rail. Her father and Keldan had built it for Hosmer, now a captain in the City Guard, with a proud horse of his own to tie to it. Not a mountain pony which suited the shorter stature of the Dwellers more, nor a hot-blooded tashya from the Vaelinar herds, but a long-limbed Kernan horse, as befit the city patrol. Hosmer patrolled the city street in front of the farmhouse now to replace Lariel's guards until new ones arrived, his horse inside the stable.

Nutmeg shifted one hip and felt the baby roll slightly inside her. She thought that the child would be like its father, tall and rangy. It was hard to think that any of her blood might show in the child's heritage. She thought of it as Jeredon's child, hardly ever just . . . hers. "Do you think Tressandre ild Fallyn sent the killers?"

"That bitch."

Nutmeg's jaw dropped as she whipped her head around to stare at Lily Farbranch. "Mother!"

Her mother's mouth tightened momentarily. "I can think that. Say it, too."

"City ways are rubbing off on you."

"Is that not the truth?" Lily sat on the hitching post railing with a little bit of a hop. Her feet did not touch the ground once she perched her body on the precarious seat. "I weave fine fabrics for them and sew gracious tailoring and I hear what they say, some of it to my face but most of it behind my back. There are many who carry the venom of envy in their words. There are many who are as deceitful as any of our old tales would have them. Yet my daughters have befriended the Warrior Queen. What should I think, then? And what should I think when they send assassins?"

Nutmeg cradled her stomach for a moment.

Lily took a deep breath, as if to shake off her mood. She leaned down. "Do you wonder who it is you carry?"

"Boy or girl? Aye, of course, Mom! It's strong and feisty, that I know."

Lily laughed softly. "Shall I swing a ring for you?"

"Like we used to do when we were just villagers? Before we moved to this great city?"

Nutmeg sombered a bit. "I would, very much. I thought of asking you, but it seemed . . ."

"Meg. Never doubt that we love this baby as much as we

love you. And we are not disappointed. Do you hear me?"
Lily hid the glimmer of a tear in the corner of her eye as she
roughly tugged off her wedding ring. "Let me get a bit of
string." She felt about in the pockets of her apron to come
up with a long piece of embroidery thread. "This will do."
She affixed her ring to it and held the ring in the air over
Nutmeg's swollen belly. "Now. Both of us need to be quiet
for this to work."

"Tell the baby that," Nutmeg muttered before pressing
her lips together tightly.

They watched the ring hanging still from its thread. It did
not stir, not even in the growing breeze that always came as
the day moved toward evening. Nutmeg fidgeted one foot,
and bit the corner of her lip. Long moments passed. Then . . .
did it move? Just a tad? Before she could open her mouth
to exclaim that it had, the ring began to swing back and
forth in an undeniable arc. A circle would have foretold a
girl, but this—most emphatically—heralded a boy.

"A boy!"

"So it seems."

"Jeredon would have loved either."

"And you?" Lily looked down at her with a gentle expression on her face.

"I fancied a boy. I wanted to see him, somehow, I guess."
She closed her eyes, briefly, seeing Jeredon and wondering
how she'd see him in their child. And a lingering echo of
Bistel's "Pass it on to your sons." He'd known then, somehow. She took a deep breath to watch Lily unfasten her ring
and slip it back on her finger.

Nutmeg added, "I know I would see his blood in a girl,
too. But a boy. This time I wanted a boy."

"The ring isn't always right."

"It has been every time I've seen it swung," Nutmeg said
confidently. She rubbed one eye vigorously.

"You're lonely. I know you miss him . . . but are you
empty?"

Nutmeg looked up. Her face wrinkled a bit in thought.
The two of them had never discussed all that her love for

Jeredon had portended. Her parents had never questioned her, just as Rivergrace hadn't till a day or so ago. She tilted her head slightly. "I never expected," she began, "that I would have a long future with him. I never thought that far ahead. It was like a call to me, Mother, that I couldn't ignore. I wanted to answer it. I gave him all that I could in hopes he would heal. And he did. Then the war took him, war and treachery." Nutmeg inhaled sharply. "It hurt when he left me behind for Tressandre, but I knew what he was doing. I just wanted him for whatever moments we could have. I never thought it would be so short. Or that I would have this memory of him."

Nutmeg inhaled again, this time deeper and slower. "This babe will need grounding and roots, as deep and solid as anything before the machinations of a Vaelinar can be grafted on it."

Lily slipped her arm about Nutmeg's shoulders. "Who would have thought orchard growers could have such wisdom, eh?"

Nutmeg rubbed her cheek on her mother's arm, getting flour, no doubt, on her face. "I miss our orchards. I never thought there wouldn't be a tall enough tree that I could climb so that I could see for leagues around, to get a clear view on things. But this." She shook her head lightly. "There are no trees that reach to the heavens to give me a view now, are there?"

Lily kissed the top of her daughter's head. "Not yet, dear. Not yet."

They stayed like that for a very long time until Grace found them, and they told her of the ring's findings, and they talked of many things, but avoided saying good-bye.

As Sevryn brought her horse out of the stables, Rivergrace turned the collar of her cloak against the brisk morning. The corner of it seemed damp. Tears, she thought. Hers or Nutmeg's. Spring had failed that day, it seemed, and winter whispered down at them again. Her breath sent white gusts against the chilled air. Uneasiness tugged against her, far sharper than that of winter's touch. She turned on one heel, scouting the landscape about her, trying to understand the strangeness that tugged at her. Threads seemed to fall through the air, multicolored, writhing aimlessly before fading abruptly away as if to tell her that somewhere, a weaving had gone awry. It left a foreboding coiled just under the edge of her rib cage. She couldn't see anything amiss, but the sense of wrongness pricked and jabbed at her. She threw a hand up in warding.

He pressed her reins into the palm of her free hand before turning to go get his own mount and their pack animal. She caught his arm.

"What is it?"

She looked over her shoulder. "Can't you feel it?"

"The cold? Do you want a coat under your cloak?"

"It's not that." She searched the courtyard and street beyond it, looking for threads among the threads again, meaning to catch them if she could. "There's a gap, Sevryn. Something is wrong." Her hands winged through the air. "A river of darkness moving against the natural rivers of shadows. Like I felt before."

"Afraid?"

Her nose wrinkled a little as she frowned up at him. "No. I sense it. Can't you? There is a tangle among the threads."

Sevryn stood still for a moment, opening his mind. She could see his eyes harden and knew that it wasn't as easy for him as others, his half-bloodedness blocking him sometimes, but Gilgarran had drilled him relentlessly when he was young, and he could use his Voice at will. Other perceptions were harder. He lifted a hand, as she had, to give a brusque nod as if he felt it. "Not a tangle, no. A rip." The expression on his face chilled. "Grace—something is very wrong."

"Nutmeg?"

"Not sure." He took to his heels, horses behind him, running down the dirt lane, back toward the city, back to where she thought she felt the contradiction of universes twisting violently, beginning to rend . . .

"Sevryn!" Hosmer called behind them and began to run after. "What is it?"

"Trouble!" Sevryn pulled his sword. Rivergrace drew hers at the same time and knew that behind them, her brother, Hosmer Farbranch of the Calcort City Guard, did as well.

Hosmer passed them on the street, his Dweller feet fleet and without the burden of pulling horses behind. Dust flew from his boot heels. Grace felt the sky shiver overhead. Sevryn pulled to a stop. "Rivergrace, stay behind me!" She did. He dropped the horses' reins and shooed them away.

The ground rumbled. She fell to one knee as buildings swayed, shutters flew open, and bricks tumbled down from a nearby structure. Sevryn's gaze stayed fixed upward, where a brilliantly blue sky turned dark with storm clouds, swirling over and downward. Funnels surged to the earth before the clouds sucked them back up. He narrowed his vision, trying to pick through the chaos to see the threads of instability behind the unnatural storm. The force of the vision set him back on his heels, shocked for a heartbeat or two as his eyes locked with another's.

Daravan.

Locked in the storm's center, or perhaps he was its epicenter, power flaring about him, from the darkest of grays to silvery white, blinding and yet compelling. Looking into that sharp-paned face was like looking into a still water reflection of himself, but he had never felt that kind of power flowing through his own frame. Daravan's strength rolled off him like tongues of flame that he could feel radiating hotly. He put a hand up to shade his eyes, uncertain of just what it was he was seeing.

"Sevryn . . . what are you seeing?"

"A vision. Perhaps."

He was no more certain when Daravan's eyes widened slightly and fixed upon him.

His father. Not a man he remembered in that position,

because his mother had raised him alone until she left to follow, without telling him just who she went after. If Gilgarran had known whose son he adopted off the streets, he never mentioned it, nor had he stored the information away within his spymaster diaries. Gilgarran had either never known it or known it so well he had no need to write the truth down to remember it. Sevryn chose to believe that his own ignorance had been Gilgarran's as well.

"Father." Barely audible, yet filled with the power of his Voice, in case it might be heard.

Daravan's focus stayed locked upon him, and then the figure stretched out his arm, hand extended. Instinctively, he reached back. Vision touched flesh, and Sevryn staggered as a force slammed into him and reached deep inside, grabbing his essence and shaking him like a dog shakes a seized prey. He fought for release, but the thing that was and was not Daravan towered over him. Time slowed to a near stop. He thought he heard a soft murmur of surprise at his back which would have come from Rivergrace, but he couldn't be certain. An ice so cold it felt like fire encased his hand.

"Give me all that you are. Give me back the life I gave you." An intense need accompanied Daravan's demand, a need that shivered inside of Sevryn, icy and determined, splintering him from the inside out.

Sevryn could not speak his denial, but Daravan felt it and shook him harder. He clenched his teeth. "Don't do this. You saved us at Ashenbrook."

The scalding ice encasing his hand moved up his arm, burning through his clothes as though they weren't there and perhaps in Daravan's existence, they weren't. Stormy gray eyes with all the shadows of darkness falling bored into him.

"You know nothing of what I did or why and the only good you can do me now is to surrender. All or nothing," Daravan replied. "The aid I want is what I can take from your thin blood. I hold an army at bay. What is that worth to you and your precious Kerith?" He spat to one side as if the word befouled his mouth.

Sevryn realized coldly that the actions taken at Ashenbrook that he'd thought heroic had begun to unravel. Whatever Daravan intended, whatever he plotted, lay still in front of them and he meant no good. He could feel it in the bond that stretched unwillingly between them now. Daravan had done what he'd done to save his army of Raymy, to retreat and attack when he had the advantage, not when three armies joined to meet them. Sevryn struggled to free himself, his heartbeat thrumming in his ears, fire and ice devouring him, Daravan taking what he could. He could feel himself losing bit by bit.

And then Grace touched his shoulder. He heard her voice although he couldn't discern her words. It didn't matter. Her warmth flooded him. With a gut-wrenching twist, he tore his hand free from Daravan and dropped to his knees. Time caught up with a rush and a roar, punctuated by a voice laced with fury. It battered his hearing to numbness and then bled away to nothing.

Faintly, he heard Rivergrace say, "What is happening?"

"Daravan. He is either losing control, or he has far more control than we know and should fear." He pulled himself to his feet. "Catastrophe lies in either instance." He watched as rolling clouds closed in about them.

Lightning struck from boiling black to glistening darkness. And then ... the sky opened and the enemy broke through.

Chapter
Eleven

RAYMY RAINED FROM ABOVE. Twisted and tumbling to right themselves, hissing and stinking of saltwater and lizard slime, they hit the dirt mostly on their feet, still clad in battle gear. Gore splattered their green-and-gray bodies and weapon-filled hands as if no time had passed for them between the battle of Ashenbrook and now. Ravers fell with them, their carapaced bodies wrapped in sodden rags of dark cloth, once disguising them but now their likeness poking through with sticklike projections. Bred to ravage the pathway in front of the Raymy, they were also fodder. They rose on their oddly stilted legs, buffeted aside by their betters. The reptilian warriors stood like men, legs bent oddly, shoulders humped and spined, mouths sneering open to reveal nothing but sharp, shining teeth. An army which eats its dead. A bitterness rose in the back of Sevryn's throat.

He threw an arm across Rivergrace to shield her; the only thing Sevryn could be thankful for was that it wasn't the entire army. Maybe two to three dozen dropped down, but with only him and Hosmer on the ground to face them, and Rivergrace there as well, he didn't like the odds. Raymy didn't have central hearts where they might be expected, but the enemy certainly knew where *his* vulnerable spots were. "Grace, stay as far back as you can."

She replied calmly, "I'll be at your back."

He heard her move into a guard position. She moved with him like his shadow as he stepped into his own defensive stance.

Hosmer did not hesitate, although his face had gone white with astonishment. He blew three sharp blasts on the whistle around his neck, the piercing noise bouncing down the lane and off the buildings. In the far distance, Sevryn could hear a two-blast answer. Backup, on the way. They could not arrive soon enough.

He remembered the days when it took himself, Jeredon, and Lariel combined to take down a charging Raymy warrior. Now he had a better idea of how to bring one down. Take them off at the legs, both Raymy and Raver, before they could leap. Then go for the head. Cripple them, if nothing else, step into the next and leave the wounded until you could return for the kill. A brutal way of fighting, but he wasn't in it for honor. He had only to last until reinforcements arrived.

To Hosmer, he shouted, "Take their legs out first. Then their heads if you can."

Not that the City Guard would be prepared to meet such as these, he thought as he stepped in, cutting low, ducking the blade swung at his face. He fought dirty. No legs, no warrior. At least, not a standing one. He could feel Grace moving at his flank, with the sense to imitate his actions. He could hear her faint grunts as she connected, her following gasp of dismay that she had, thinking that this was his Grace who ought never to have to swing a weapon. And yet, he knew that she had carried the Souldrinker, that immense broadsword Cerat, when no one else could have survived the burden. She had taken the weapon to destroy it when no one else could bear to take it up. He reminded himself, as a Raymy grinned fangs in his face and Sevryn stabbed him in the torso to double him over, then swept his ankles out from under the beast, that Rivergrace stood alone. The Raymy toppled. He had no time for satisfaction as two jumped him, one at his flank and the other at his back. He surged in the opposite direction, letting their momentum swing them off balance before kicking the weaker-looking one away, and burying his sword to the hilt in the guts of the remaining reptile. Warmish blood spilled over his hand. The color disconcerted him for a moment. Red yet with a green-and-black cast to it that reflected in the sun, like an oily sheen. He kneed the second one back, took off a leg, and left it to bleed out. He found it mildly disconcerting and distracting that the fallen appendage flopped and kicked a pace away from the body.

He heard a flurry behind him, followed by a triumphant noise from Rivergrace. Across from them, Hosmer also followed his lead and, to Sevryn's relief, three more guards galloped up, jumping from their horses to join the fray. They drew weapons and shields and fell into formation, leaving no flank open as they attacked. Shrewdly assessing the handiwork, the guards flew on the Raymy with the same determination to cut them out from below and leave them fallen.

Overhead, the sky rumbled darkly and shuddered, and a drum of thunder rolled through him, shaking his very bones. With it, the sky split open a second time, and Raymy fell through as if poured from a bucket. The street and alley filled with their hissing forms.

Rivergrace uttered a small sound. Sevryn backed up and caught her by her free wrist.

"Run," he told her. "I'll hold them."

"No one holds that many. I can't leave you." She tossed her head futilely to clear her hair from her brow, frowning. "And, look, there's something . . . wrong . . . with them." She pivoted him to his right.

One of the Raymy she had cut down lay curled in the dust, bleeding and panting, but his wound did not keep him down so much as the bubbling pustules that covered his already warty form, pustules that leaked a foul yellowish-green fluid to join his blood in the dirt. "They're revolting, but I don't remember this from Ashenbrook."

The Raymy snarled at him, forked tongue slicking in and out of his jaw, swollen and blackening at the edges. He recoiled. Sevryn split his lungs open and stepped back a pace as foulness spilled out.

Recognition jolted him. "He's sick." Sevryn jerked her back, uselessly; they were both doused with the gore of battle, but he could not help himself. "Plague." He looked at the others downed, writhing nearby. Disgusting blisters blanketed them, and the Raymy wheezed as if they could barely breathe, yet struggled to get to their feet, ready to fight and kill if they could. Wherever they had been, they had been contaminated, and now they carried it like a blanket wrapped tightly about them like a second skin. A deadly blanket. His hand closed tightly on her shoulder. "Stay away from them."

"Have you ever seen anything like it?" Rivergrace shook under his touch.

"No. Never. Whatever it is, it's bad." He stepped back and swung her around with him. A Raymy surged at them. Rivergrace jabbed to impale him, and Sevryn swept his head off as the beast stumbled to a stop. It bounced away from him, still spitting in hatred and battle fervor.

Hosmer looked at them from across the wide ring of enemies, readying to join them, as the force weakened down the center.

"Don't touch the bodies!" Rivergrace cried to him. "Plague!" She threw Sevryn a wild look. "We have to stop this."

"How?"

She dropped her sword and straightened, taking as deep a breath as she could, and with a short cry of defiance, she set the world on fire.

Flame shivered out of her, drawn from her slender form like a thread which expanded and burst into conflagration as it gained the air, and she aimed it to the blood-coated earth where it anchored itself into a river, a spiraling river, of fire. Sevryn reached to grasp her hand, but the heat shimmering off her drove him back.

Beyond Hosmer and his brace of guards, the sky still rained down Raymy, though the quantity had slowed to a mere handful or two at a time, filling the entire quarter of the city. Yet these fighters did not rise to battle. They lay in miserable heaps, sisssssing and gnashing their teeth in agony.

"Quarantine," muttered Sevryn. He raised his voice and sent his Talent thundering toward Hosmer, as he repeated, "Quarantine!"

Hosmer raised his blade in knowledge.

Sevryn turned to Rivergrace. "How long will the fire hold here?" he asked as the thread snapped off and she stumbled back in weariness.

"Till dark, I think. I don't . . . know."

He caught her just before she fell.

Chapter
Twelve

"YOU LEFT HOSMER THERE? In the circle of fire? In the middle of plague?" Nutmeg's face looked at her, shock-white, her eyes stricken.

"Yes." Grace hung her head down, unable to look at her sister's face any longer.

"How could you?" Nutmeg swung from one to the other.

"There was no choice. You have to understand that."

Tolby clasped Sevryn's shoulder in response. "I know that, lad, no need t'explain further. We have to accept what's been done. Hosmer is a smart man. I've raised him to know how to deal with contamination, be it an orchard or a sick animal. He'll make do."

"He shouldn't have to make do," Lily said tightly. She would not look at either Rivergrace or Sevryn as she spoke, one of her hands twisting in her apron.

"It will be fine," Tolby reassured her.

"You're his sister," Lily added, unrelenting, to Grace. "How could you leave him?"

Rivergrace's mouth worked, but no words came out. She

cleared her throat and tried again. "To protect Nutmeg. I have to keep her safe if I can. He was on the other side."

Meg looked at her wildly. "Did I ask for protecting?"

Tolby stepped forward, his voice dropping. "That will be enough. From everyone. What's done is done, and Hosmer is a man full grown. He's a son of mine, and he will do the job he took on when he took th' uniform of the City Guard. Settle that within yerselves, for I won't hear another word on it. Understand?"

Lily turned sharply on her heel and left for the kitchen where the pans and crockery could be heard clashing upon the tables and shelves. Tolby grunted as the noise reached them.

Keldan tilted his head at his father. "They still have to leave." He beckoned at Sevryn and Rivergrace. "But the streets to the gates are cut off."

"Aye. Through the fields, I'm thinking."

"Can we get out that way?"

Tolby's eyes narrowed a bit in thought, and the corner of his mouth quirked as though he bit down on the stem of a pipe in rumination. "Mayhap," he answered, finally. "Mayhap."

Even that answer was a bit more certain than the actual probability, Sevryn thought, as he sat his horse and watched Keldan and Nutmeg at the edge of the vineyards, where the rock rose to meet the ground and the bases of the vines were old, gray, and gnarled, until they sprouted fresh green sprouts to join the framework meant to hold them as they grew. The perimeter of the vineyards, however, stood as a wild tangle of old, never trimmed or cropped vines, unproductive yet singularly determined to weave together, as high as one man standing upon another's shoulders. Still, the barrier didn't look insurmountable.

"You'll not be getting through this way," Nutmeg threw over her shoulder. She rode their stout little mountain pony stallion who had mellowed in his years in Calcort, it seemed, and only snorted in mild annoyance at being held to bridle and saddle at Nutmeg's hands.

"And why not?"

"No one ever has. It's been warded since even before th' time of the Mageborns, is all we were told. Cannot your own eyes see?"

"I'm not that trained," Rivergrace murmured. "I can see a kind of weaving, but that just may be the vines. I don't think I could manipulate it. If it were water or fire . . ." She shrugged.

Sevryn ran a fingernail along the edge of his jaw in thought. He'd been trained by Gilgarran, but it didn't come easily to him. Daravan's taunt about thin blood echoed through him for a moment. He narrowed his eyes, glowering at the edge of the vineyard, and then he caught it. An immense, golden wire weaving that reached high enough to stave off even a catapult hit. Little things could get through: mice, bees, songbirds, but nothing of substance. The barrier stood as nothing a Vaelinar would make; he would tweak and bind together the natural threads of the earth, but this stood like an alien edifice, something smelted out of will and metal. He let out a whistle. "I can see why no one's breached it yet." His horse did a lazy turnabout, and Sevryn put the side of his boot flat into his side to halt him. "What makes you think we can get out this way?"

Keldan grinned, as he shadowed Nutmeg, and came around the end row of vines. "Because there's a backdoor, a-course."

"Naturally," said Grace dryly as she pushed her horse past Sevryn.

He did not like backdoors. Traitors could make use of them. Keldan saluted his frown as if reading his mind, saying, "Not this one. You'll be lucky to get your horses through it, and the only reason you'll make it through is because you've magic of your own."

"And you know this because?"

"We've been through the gate. Or Garner has, mostly.

There's an archway, more like a short cave, and it leads out to a wash above the river. He said it made his skin crawl, told us not to try it. Made it sound like we'd be skinned alive if we did."

"Keldan," warned Nutmeg.

"He did!" Keldan leaped onto his horse, which he rode without bridle or saddle, and wrapped one hand in the mane. Both tossed their heads at the same time. "Thisaway."

Scowling, Nutmeg fell in behind him, and just shook her head at Grace when they traded looks. Sevryn brought up the rear, warily, making sure they had not been followed. He did not fear the Raymy breaking quarantine, but assassins were another matter. Having failed, they would be back. Not the Kobrir, but the others, he had little doubt. He'd had private words with Tolby. They could, and would, use the quarantine to mask Nutmeg's comings and goings as much as they could, but there would be those who would come, by rooftop if they had to, past the City Guard. The only question in their minds was when. It would be best in any plan to do the deed before the child was born, because once there was a baby and its sex was known, its death had to be suspect. Someone would always try to put forth a half-Dweller, half-Vaelinar heir, valid or not. That's how fortunes were made in the shadows. No, it would be better by far for Tressandre's plans to have mother and unborn child indisputably dead. Tolby had told him as much, and Sevryn uncomfortably agreed with him. Impetuous Nutmeg had not thought of those consequences, of any of them, really, except the immutable condition of love.

The line of horses and ponies came to a halt again, downslope, where the vines were a bit sheltered from the wind, and tangled a little less as they put forth their greenery, spindly and yet lusciously colored, to reach the fork-like frames which would hold them and guide the runners. Sevryn stretched in his stirrups, looking back yet again. Tendrils of the vineyard curled verdantly from their posts, masking trespassers.

Keldan slipped to the ground, twisted the ear of his

mount, and spoke a hushed word or two. When he stepped away, the horse relaxed into a stand, disinclined to wander off despite there being no hold upon him.

"The man's a witch," he said aside to Grace.

"There are a few among the Kernan. He's always had a way with animals, especially horses. Didn't you tell me your mother had a touch of witchery in her?"

"Supposedly she was a weather woman, but that was long enough ago that I find it difficult to remember. I don't have any of it in me."

She reached out, her hand brushing his knee in apology, but she said nothing as if knowing that her words might sting even more. They were opposites, he and Grace. Her mother had sacrificed herself to save her child. His mother had sacrificed her child to save herself. Or, with as little information as he had about what had actually happened in his past, so it seemed.

Nutmeg dismounted from her pony carefully, taking a moment to steady herself. She saw Grace watching her and flashed a grin. "Mom and I rigged a sling this morning. Holds the baby's weight a bit for me, but I won't be runnin' anywhere today."

"You shouldn't even be here."

Meg winked at Rivergrace's scolding tone. "And miss my last chance to say good-bye for a while? What kind of a sister do you think I am?"

"Right now, I'd say it was obvious."

"That would be the truth!" Laughing, she held her hand up for Grace's as Grace swung down and, leaning on each other, they followed Keldan over the rocky slope to a bowl-shaped depression. Sevryn kicked pebbles aside as he trailed behind.

"Too rocky here even for vines."

"Dad always says that it's good to force the vines, to parch them a bit. Gives them flavor. Says a born-to-it vine-man would curse an over-wet spring, brings fungus to the grapes."

"So last year wouldn't hurt the crop."

"Supposedly not." Meg paused a moment, to tweak her

hair back in place, her curls as recalcitrant as always. She wrinkled her nose at Rivergrace. "Do you suppose—?"

"Probably just as bad. Jeredon had wavy hair himself, you remember."

Sevryn stopped behind them. "What?"

Grinning, both women looked to him. "We were wondering if the baby would have curly hair. Both at the same time, it seems."

"Ah." He hadn't wondered that, although he had wondered if he would recognize his friend's tall and slender grace in the child, broad shoulders if a boy and wide eyes if a girl. What of Jeredon would remain? Wavy hair seemed as likely as not. He looked ahead, realizing that Keldan had disappeared. "And where would our horse witch be?"

"Right here." Keldan stepped sideways out of a boulder, or so it appeared. Sevryn craned his neck a bit as he walked around to see a natural wall of rock jutting out and switching back, a zigzag of an entrance to what appeared to be a cave. A rock-blocked cave. Behind him, he could feel a twitch as Rivergrace shuddered. She did not like closed-in places, for all that the two of them had had their adventures in them. He didn't worry about her; she'd soldier through. She would be fearless for him, but he could not be for her. The handcuffs he kept secreted in his waistband, now wrapped in a cloth to stop them from burning his skin, the cuffs meant for her, he would fear a thousand years and more until he could find a way to permanently keep them from her. For the moment, it meant getting away from Calcort and then getting his true bearings. He put his hand up to the fallen rocks, seeing if he could put his fingers into the small crevices, worry at them, tumble one or two out of place, breaking the wall down. His touch met a different reality than his vision did: one of solid masonry, not a rockfall. He tried to look at it, at the way of it, but his gaze slid off it unfailingly, again and again.

"Grace. Come have a look at this."

"Nutmeg says it's a door, of sorts."

"Mayhap. Difficult to tell. Look at it with your eyes and tell me what you see."

He stepped back a pace to make room for her, could hear Nutmeg's lusty breathing at his elbow. Her body heat radiated about her, warming his arm as well. "Are you all right, Meg?"

"A-course. Just feeling it, a bit." She gulped down a breath or two. "Be fine in a twitch. Don't fret at me, it's bad enough having strangers on the street gawk at me like I should have my belly in a wheelbarrow."

"That," said Keldan slowly, "might be an idea."

Out of breath as she was, her hand flew out fast enough to clip her brother in the ear, bringing a sharp "Ow!" out of him. "My body might be dragging a bit but not my reach or my hearing!"

Grace smothered a laugh as she positioned herself beside the shaded rock. Here, behind the wall of a true rock, and heavily shaded from the afternoon sun, rested the blockage. She put her hand up, palm out, not quite touching. "A door, indeed. Hard to see, but I can. It keeps trying to slip away, as though it's been greased, but I can catch sight of it well enough."

"Well enough to what?"

She glanced over her shoulder to Sevryn. "To see it. To see the lock on it. It's been etched by fire."

"Can you tell the making of the door? Is it one of ours, or Mageborn, or hedge witch?"

Rivergrace shifted her weight from one foot to another as she considered the object. "That, I couldn't say."

Meg ducked her head under her sister's elbow. "That's a blacksmith lock on it, and it ought to have tumblers in it, three in all. I'd say any street thief could pop it off, wouldn't you?"

Keldan, Grace, and Sevryn all looked at her.

"Well, it's obvious, is it not?"

"That's just the point. It isn't obvious, not to any of us. It's not even *visible*."

Meg tilted her head. "I've had just about enough making fun of the fat lady." Pulling a hairpin from her obstinate curls, she muscled past Grace to the rock wall. "It does slip a bit, but like Keldan, you just stare at it hard and it settles down." She put her hands out and when her fingers met the heavy padlock she'd described, it became evident, oddly set in a jumble of rock, but easily seen. Her fingers nimbly applied the hairpin while Keldan made a sputtering noise as if he'd just discovered his sister picking pockets on the streets outside a tavern.

"Where'd you learn—never mind, I don't think I want to be knowing. That way I won't have to be telling Dad."

"Who d' you think taught me?" Meg laughed at her brother, as the lock fell open in her hands, and suddenly, a door entire came to view.

She bowed to Keldan and said, "Open if you dare" before shoving her hairpin back into her hair, catching what stray curls she could with it.

The air that tumbled out of the doorway smelled of limestone and old rock, with a hint of mosses to it, stale but not deadly, quiet but not totally undisturbed. Sevryn bowed his head a bit as he inhaled. "The other end of the passage is open."

"But a far bit off, I'd say."

Sevryn nodded to Keldan.

Meg dusted her hands. "Then it's here we say farewell. For a bit." She caught her sister's chin. "Will you be coming back in time?"

"I don't know. I will try, if you have enough notice. I want to be here. I do." She put her hand about Nutmeg's and squeezed gently.

"I know that well. We'll send a bird on all the winds to reach you, if we can."

"Good."

Sevryn stepped through the massive doorway. "We can lead the horses through, single file."

"You're sure?"

"I'm sure of this far."

Rivergrace frowned before adding, "I don't want to be backing my horse out of here."

"Nor do I. I can't make promises about what I don't know, and I haven't got time to go ahead to scout it. We need to make time, aderro."

Rivergrace inhaled deeply. She hugged Nutmeg as tightly as she could, then she embraced her youngest brother. Abruptly, she turned, hiding her face as she went to get their horses, leaving Sevryn standing awkwardly on the threshold. Both Keldan and Nutmeg stared at him with narrowed eyes. He held his hands up in surrender. "I know. Take care of her."

"Indeed." Meg closed her full lips tightly.

"Use the quarantine as a barricade. It'll help keep you safe. When Lariel's guards get here, get them word to come over the rooftops, and then to fortify that way as well."

Keldan nodded. "Got it."

"Hosmer should be all right." He put his hand on Nutmeg's shoulder. "I cannot certify it for you, Meg, but I think he will. And there is a good chance that, before Rivergrace set the place on fire, she warded him. She has those kinds of powers at times."

Meg nodded wordlessly. The clop of hooves on stone stopped her from saying anything in answer, and she moved aside for suddenly there was no room for Dwellers if the horses pushed in behind the rock wall.

She stared at Rivergrace with her eyes brimming, forced a smile, and then ran out into the sunlight and the vineyard. Keldan ducked after her. Grace stood for a moment in the doorway, looking past the horses, her lips parted as though she could throw her love after them, but did not. Her shoulders dropped as she pressed reins into his hand and nudged him into the tunnel.

They walked for a while, getting used to the dankness, which reminded Sevryn of many a river's wayside ditch in the bad streets of towns he'd grown up in, some carved by water and some by tool.

"She would not have seen that door before."

"Before this." Her hand cut the air about her own stomach.

Sevryn stopped in his tracks. He considered her words, her voice faint behind him.

"What do you mean?"

"She's my sister, and something more."

"Do you think so?"

"I know so. Those were not her senses she drew upon, couldn't have been. She's not got Kernan witch-blood or Mageborn, or even Dweller tree and animal sense, not more than a smidge. She's many things but filled with power like that, no."

"How, then?"

A long pause followed, broken only by the click of horses' shoes upon the hard ground and occasional stone, and the closed-in noise of their breathing.

"She tapped into a power within I don't think she knew she could do."

"The child?"

"It has to have been. Jeredon's child, of Vaelinar blood."

"She saw because the child within her had the power to see."

"Yes."

"But you and I—"

"Your Talents don't use sight much and I—I have a Goddess that shields my sight from time to time, just as she shields my body."

"The babe is half-blooded."

"Yes, and yet it seems the Vaelinar blood is very strong in it. Him, I think."

"Can you tell? That Nutmeg bears a son?"

"It's only a feeling. No more than I can tell the future." Rivergrace sighed softly. "If I could, things would be very different."

He didn't quite know how to take that, until she added, "Aderro." With a slight smile, he went back to leading the way.

Chapter Thirteen

A LOUD AND VIOLENT DRUM pounded its cadence through the otherwise silent villa and sank its rhythm into Bregan's bones. The only part of his body that did not throb was his leg encased in his Vaelinarran splint. He wiped at grimed eyes and rolled to one elbow. He hadn't gone to bed drunk, had he? Of course he had, awash in drink, but it hadn't lasted. He'd sweated it out somehow and now he was not as drunk as he was miserable. He hadn't done that in years. He scrubbed his hand over his eyes again. He'd been days in this state, his foggy memory told him. His servants had all slunk out, by ones and twos, leaving one last disgruntled old retainer to throw blasphemy in his face. And what had he done, really? Told them the truth about their miserable lives.

He needed new staff. Unfortunately, there was no one left to assign for hiring one. He'd have to ride over to his father's and commandeer old Grigenhilda, she of the one immense eyebrow you could hang socks on for drying, to take care of things. As formidable as she seemed, she was brisk, organized, and incredibly uncanny at knowing one's

strengths and faults and assigning household jobs accordingly. His father's estate ran like an elven-made clockwork
piece to everyone's envy, and the praise could justifiably be
laid at Grigenhilda's feet. Or hung from her eyebrow. She
had always been old from his perspective, but it seemed she
hadn't aged beyond the initial ravage of years, for she hadn't
changed a bit since he'd become a grown man and a trader
in his own right. He ought, surely, to be able to look her in
the face now. He hadn't much choice.

Bregan kicked off his last remaining blanket and staggered to his feet. The room swung around alarmingly before
the drum trapped inside his skull settled down to a reason-
able hammering and his ears buzzed along to keep time
with it. He realized as he walked down the hallway, at a lean
with his right shoulder brushing the wall, seemingly unable
to stand up straight just yet, that his stable was no doubt as
near empty as his household. Damned, superstitious staff.
Willing and able to take whatever coin he'd stuffed in their
pockets and unwilling to stay when their view of the world
and its Gods turned just a bit risky. That was like a Kernan,
his own people though he grudging allowed it was so. If
only he'd been born tough and practical like a Dweller. His
friend Garner Farbranch, now there was a man worth his
salt, and a fair gambler, too. They had met at cards more
than once, but it was the war in the tunnels and on the fields
of Ashenbrook that took their real measure. Garner took a
shrewd measure on whatever life dealt him, and handled it
accordingly. Mayhap Bregan could suggest to Grigenhilda
to contact Garner and see if he knew any likely candidates
for household and stable staff. But he'd have to warn Garner off Sevryn Dardanon first. Yes, or he was a dead man.
Bregan sighed. Must everything be so complicated?

In the meantime, though, there was this pesky problem
with a hallway and subsequent staircase which would not
stand up squared and impeded his progress more so by every foot. Bregan came to a last slide at the bottom of the
stairs, his legs going out from under him, his brace no help
at all since both limbs had gone the way of limp noodles.

Bregan gave a frustrated snort and managed to sit straight up. At least he thought it was up. Without a light in the house or any shutter or door thrown open, he could barely see his boots on the end of his feet. "Is there nobody about?"

Silence answered the cadence inside his skull. It made an odd combination, one muffling the other, only to be overcome by the noise eventually. He ground his teeth before bellowing, "Come on, there must be one of you left, cowering in the pantry or thereabouts if only to rob me! Throw open a window, a door. Light a candle! I'll pay for it." *Help me back on my feet.*

His voice echoed dimly back at him. Something scurried at the far end of the house, noise so faint that he imagined it to be a wee rodent of some sort, frightened out of its whiskers, nothing bigger or of any use to him.

Bregan dragged in a deep breath. He clicked his teeth shut on it. He wasn't drunk, and he had no damn excuse for lying on the floor near helpless in a darkened house. Aye, he'd preyed on his fellows, and that had come back to kick him in the ass, good and hard, and he'd no one to blame but himself. If the Gods were paying attention, they would be laughing. There was a justice to it that he could not deny. He'd lined his pockets on the deliberate spread of rumors and the ready supply of goods to fulfill those rumors. It had seemed harmless if highly profitable at the time, and he'd never had regrets until he had been taken in by his own scam.

Bregan scrubbed his chin. The pounding in his skull settled to a steady beating that no longer felt as if it might shatter his excuse for a head, and feeling had returned to his legs. He got up and stood, as shaky as a newborn colt on legs that felt as if they did not quite belong to him. In truth, one did not. He smiled ruefully as he straightened the brace on his right, workmanship that had no equal in all the lands of the First Home or even in the wide stretches to the east. Even as he cursed the Vaelinars, he needed them.

He slapped his hand on the wall as vertigo threatened to

undo him all over again. If he had light, he might convince his body which way was up. Bregan hastily searched his pockets, but not a strike met his touch. The toback that the Dwellers prized so much was not his vice, he reflected, although he might take it up if it kept him from being left in the dark. He slapped his hand on the wall again in frustration.

"Kitchen, you fool," he muttered. "Get yourself to the kitchen and quit yammering like an orphaned babe."

His eyes adjusted to the lack of light as he made his way, tripping once over a fallen object ... a coat tree was it? ... that lay hidden at shin height. Bregan roared in his anger and self-disgust. "Light! I need light by Tree's blood!"

The room flared, white flame, about him. It stunned him as neatly as a backhand across the face and knocked him on his ass.

Bregan flung his hands in front of his face, gasping for breath. Heated air roared around him, and then all became still. Light bled through his protective fingers, brilliant and blinding, and he sat up, slowly, and squinted as he lowered his hands. Illumination swam before his vision as moisture dripped unbidden from his eyes. He scrubbed them dry and shook his head. Every lamp, sconce, and candle as far as he could see across the room and into the next room was lit, flames burning blue-white hot. He could feel their blazing heat. He turned his face from the sight and saw, where he had slapped his hand on the wall, an imprint. Rectangular in shape, it held a sigil across its face, a lilting symbol. Mouth and throat like cotton, Bregan attempted a swallow, but his tongue stayed glued to the roof of his mouth. He knew that sign. Knew it almost as well as he knew the gold stamp and seal of his trading house. Knew it better than the lines across the palms of his hands. Knew it to be a twin to the signs emblazoned on tiles placed on cavern walls on the Pathways of the Guardians. He held a fingertip over the imprint, hesitating. Some workman or craftsman had placed this here, right under his nose, and he had never noticed it.

He'd built this house from the ground up when he knew

that he could no longer live under his father's roof and boot, just as his father had one day learned that he could not live under the rule of Bregan's grandfather. That dispute had not turned out well, although the dynasty had passed successfully from one grand trader to another. Bregan had never held patricide as an option. He had simply had his bags packed and gotten out. He had made his own fortune by then, nothing as it was now, but his coffers had paid for the raising of this manor and the buying of his own string of caravans and more. Guards not only to secure his goods and businesses but his person. His father, after all, had already stained his hands once with familial blood. Bregan had never doubted that he could do it again.

He traced the tile upon his wall. This, however, he would swear had not manifested from his father's greed. This had come from who knew where and must surely have been here all along, and he'd simply never seen it.

But the hairs rose on the back of his neck and told him differently. He had never noticed it because it hadn't been there before. He placed his finger onto the imprint. A blue spark flew from his skin to the tile with a sizzle of heat, jumping as his heartbeat jumped, before the shock shivered away. And as the sensation and sound faded, he heard an echo at the back of his thoughts.

Listen, O Mageborn.

White heat curled at his back. That settled it. The drink had poisoned him, curdled his brain, tainted his blood, and corrupted his very soul. He could not afford to listen!

Bregan took to his heels. He flew through the rooms and corridors, a shriek stuck in his throat and desperation in his shaking hands. He squelched out every candle and sconce he could reach before their heat set the timbers and walls on fire as if they were only so much dry kindling. Every room stood ablaze in light, light he'd been cursing for and, it seemed, his need had been answered. Now, in fear for his life and property, he fumbled to put it all out. In the last room, little more than a storage closet, he stood, trembling and out of breath, and put his shoulder to the wall. Lest he doubt it had been real, his fingers throbbed, singed and stained with the soot from wicks and his cuffs stained from the oil splashed from lamp basins and sconces as he'd snuffed them out. He stood in darkness again and closed his eyes.

He had an enemy. An enemy that would use him and set him against Sevryn, and through Sevryn, against the Warrior Queen herself. And there was no way he could protect himself against this unknown enemy who could conjure up such power. Deceit and manipulation, he had used before and would again. He thought he had heard the voices of the Gods before. What made him think now was any different?

What made him think it wasn't?

Because there were no more Mageborn. Had not been for centuries untold. The Gods themselves had put a plague upon them, scourging them from the face of Kerith for their transgressions, and the people had died, leaving no root or seed behind them. The death toll had been devastating and final. No one with even a jot, a token drop, of Mageborn blood lived. Not one. If he thought he listened to Mageborn and they taunted him, he would be a dead man. The Gods themselves would put him down, like a diseased and broken animal.

Someone had set a trap for him. Someone who coveted his position and his assets and, likely, his life. There could be no other explanation. Except there was one . . . Bregan scrubbed his hand over his chin, found both trembling, and stopped.

The Gods, if he did hear Gods, had a most twisted sense of humor if they thought to label him one of the destroyed people. Did they now tell him that he, too, was marked? Not likely. The Gods would not bend to talk to the likes of him. He returned to the scenario of his ruin being plotted. A great possibility was that one of the Vaelinar tormented him, although he had never heard of talents among the elven people to be like those of the Mageborn. Still, it was the invaders who held powers over earth, air, fire, and water alike. He would need the skills of a trader guild apprentice to count all his enemies among the Vaelinar. He would have no allies if the Vaelinars had declared him anathema. No one, not even his father, would stand by his side. The invaders had proven themselves too strong, century after century, and he knew his own actions lay suspect because of the Raymy. He was doomed. No one would stand by his side, no one would come to tell him if what happened was real or imagined, magic or insanity. Bregan dabbed at his eyes, now watering from the smoke, and moved out of the storage area. Two lone lamps burned downstairs and he went to them, drawn like a moth to dancing flames. He stood there without a coherent thought in his head for so long that the only thing holding him still on his feet was the clever golden brace of elven make. His hand dropped to the top of it, mid-thigh, and he drummed it for a moment mindlessly before the touch of it woke him to his actions. He turned and slapped the imprint again. At his action, and his thought of darkness, the two remaining lamps sputtered out.

Light blossomed when he placed his palm upon the wall again. Not blindingly, but the room he stood in illuminated itself as if he himself had put a spark to every wick. White heat invaded his thoughts, blindingly, and he closed his eyes against the onslaught, shuttering it away. It went, reluctantly. His hand began to shake uncontrollably, and he snatched it from the imprint and hugged his arms to himself. Strength bled away from him as surely as darkness had bled from the room. Back to the wall, he slowly slid down it until he crouched upon the floor, enveloped in a power for which he had no word and no control and which, he could feel in his bones, would be the death of him. He had nowhere he could go and no one he could trust with whatever shreds of a mind he had left.

Alcohol had pickled his brain. He'd gone insane and, like most crazed people, he did not even know it. Did he hallucinate as old, drunken wicks of men did lying in the black gutters of the worst hellholes in town? Was he even in his own home, still? Bregan thought and thought but couldn't find any reassurance in himself. Despite all he'd drunk, he felt as dried out as a salt creek wash in a desert. His body cried out for water, his lips cracked and sore, but he couldn't bring himself to stand up and fetch a cup. He didn't trust himself to draw water and not more alcohol. He couldn't trust himself at all.

He hugged himself tighter as the lamps and candles put forth enough light to create mocking and dancing shadows of a cage about him. Bregan swallowed down a breath. He began to make a list of his options and found it distressingly short.

Chapter Fourteen

SPRING WHISTLED THROUGH THE TREES of Hold Vantane when he led his horse out of the stable and checked the carriage as well, all the equines stomping their hooves and snorting white breaths into the early morning as they signaled him their readiness to be off and on the road. He saw no sign of Bistane about, but the stable lads were all up and awake, so his brother might have left even earlier. He swung up on the wagon, and turned upon the road south, his saddle horse following on a lead.

The Hold had been his home for most of his life, ever since that day Bistel had come to claim him, and he glanced back as he left. He squared his shoulders. He had only one suspicion which he had not told his older brother. Dayne smiled to himself as he thought that, for Bistane was much older than he, and it was not likely he'd ever again be related to anyone older since the death of their mutual father. His suspicion nudged its way back to the fore of his thoughts. The books resisting the virulent corruption of the libraries were those which had been printed on paper made from aryn pulp, a rarity in itself for the trees were not so populous that they could afford to harvest them for ordinary things like lumber and paper. Yet, even those trees could not totally withstand the black mold and the devastation it left behind even when treated and thought eradicated. He was a gardener and a steader, not a warrior and not a librarian, and he was not at all sure what Bistane had in mind for him by carrying these parcels, except for the trust imparted upon him to do so. And perhaps that was all it was. His brother trusted him more than anyone to do this task and placed the burden of the histories of their people upon him. The books of Ferstanthe contained irreplaceable writings.

If he were a suspicious man, he might wonder if his brother had ulterior motives for sending him to the Dweller family who would be raising a crossed child like himself, and perhaps could use a bit of wisdom personally gained. If he were suspicious. If Bistane were anything like the strategist their father had been. Perhaps he was. He'd hailed one of the stead's artists and had a small painting made of the Farbranch girl from Bistane's memory of her, and when it had dried, his brother had pressed it into his hand.

"This is the lass you look for."

"I thought I was searching out the Farbranch vineyards on the river."

"That, too." Bistane's head had tilted as he considered the canvas. "It's a good likeness, for having not seen her, but he didn't quite catch the . . ." Bistane's hand had danced over the canvas a moment as if rearranging in his mind what he saw. "The liveliness. The spark of humor and intelligence in her eyes. Hard to explain."

Verdayne had looked down on the canvas. He saw eyes of cinnamon and brown, a generous mouth, a tumble of light brown hair that no doubt would catch the sunlight, brows arched gracefully, and a dainty nose. The chin held a stubborn jutting. He could understand why Jeredon had fallen for the girl who'd pushed and pulled him out of self-pity and marched him into healing. He folded the canvas over to protect the likeness. "I'll take care to see she's as protected as the Ferstanthe books," he'd promised.

Verdayne turned back and settled onto his cart seat. When the time came, and he reached Calcort, he was not certain how he could advise the Farbranches. How could he look Tolby and his wife in their faces, and into the eyes of young Nutmeg, and tell them that their lifespan in comparison to the child would be as that of the family dog to their own lives? Could he explain the acute loneliness of seeing your family age and die before you without hope of saving them or yourself that pain? Should he? Could he advise them how to avoid the prejudices against half-breeds? He hadn't dodged those unpleasantries, even as sheltered as Bistel had kept him, although in the last ten decades it had gotten better. And what about siblings if Nutmeg should go on with her life, and marry, and bear other children, Dweller children? He and his brother had had words and deeds between them that, now, he realized any brothers had. Then, he had taken it to heart as bullying rather than the head butting any siblings did. He had finally learned to tell the difference. Had he any hope at all in instructing Nutmeg Farbranch how to deal with it?

If Bistane had thought to send Verdayne only as a teacher, the least he could have done was ask him if it was a task he would accept.

Perhaps it was wiser Bistane had not. Verdayne had no idea what his answer would be and likely would not even when he reached Calcort even though he had days and days to think upon it. Open his past up to strangers, peeling away walls he'd taken decades to build to shield himself? He did not think he could. He knew he didn't wish to. Better for them to head into their tomorrows without knowing the inevitable sorrow and bitterness that could await them. Foreknowledge wouldn't avert their future and it might be better for them simply to face it one bleak day at a time. He had faced little at home, but away from home, he had not always been sheltered. Better to concentrate upon the books. As perplexing and despairing as that problem was, it was far better than trying to understand the hearts and minds of others. Gods knew, he did not understand his own. He clucked to his ponies and let them think about the road ahead, as he held the reins lightly between his hands.

Two days out, the road had become little more than a rough lane where wheels and hooves might have passed—or might not. The early spring day had begun with drizzles, but the sun forced its way through before midday, and by the time he reached his destination, the cart ponies were tossing their heads and stepping out sprightly, their nostrils flared wide to catch the intoxicating scent of the aryns on the wind.

The trees had leafed out nicely, after a two-year drought and much worry on his part. It did not look, Verdayne thought, as if the lack of rain had affected this part of the forest greatly. He stood in the cart for a bit, letting his legs take the jostle and bounce over what could barely be called a road, reins firmly wrapped in his hands to telegraph his needs to the two ponies who shook their manes and pranced their hooves in a bit of wildness. He brought the cart to a halt and set the brake with a kick of his boot. His ponies snorted as if to say they had come to a standstill because it had been their will, not his, and the caramel-patched one rolled a white-ringed eye at him as he passed by. Verdayne slapped it lightly on the neck, both rewarding and reminding the pony who was boss here. His saddle horse, tied to the back rail of the cart, snorted as if in scorn at pony antics. He would leave the cart at a homestead along the way, but he saw no reason he should not work a bit as he made his way to Calcort. There was urgency, he supposed, but nothing a few days would harm. He had work to do, work that Bistel had raised him in, and he loved to do.

Although, as Verdayne stepped clear of his cart, putting his head back and resting fists on his hips, to take a good look at the aryns, anyone could see they were the kings here. Their palm-sized leaves rippled in the breeze, their varying spring colors of dark green and light green and even golden green moving in a sea current from branch to branch, tree to tree. More than their majesty, he could sense their magic. Where the aryns stood, the tides of burned-out sorcery from the Mageborn Wars and their spillover of chaotic magic stopped. Were repulsed by wood and leaf, turned back from lands never meant to be touched. Were cleansed in roots that thrust deep into the earth and the earth's underground rivers. Were unmade and dispersed as though never called up and woven by power-mad Magi. That was not to say peace ruled here in the aryn groves. No. But the happenings here sprang from natural elements, just as fearsome and devastating as the unnatural but, once expended, they did not twist back upon themselves in vengeance and hatred as though a living beast. Verdayne looked upon the trees and not for the first time wondered what these lands would have suffered if the aryns had not taken root here and turned back the remnants of a long ago yet still smoldering war. The aryns were not native to the lands of Kerith, but the Mageborn had been.

"Vaelinars came to our country in a blast of lightning and thunder, but the Mageborn," his long-passed mother would whisper to him, "the Mageborn created fire and wind to carry death across our country. They tried to raise themselves to be Gods upon the backs of our dead. And they failed, but their deeds live after them, foul and smoldering, pools of arrogance and ill-will and poison. Never forget them, my Verdayne. Not the Vaelinars who fathered you or the Mageborn who would have killed you rather than look at you twice. Never." And she would kiss him on his forehead as if sealing her words into his memory.

She had, or he would not think of them now. Verdayne let out a small sigh. Her talents had been passed to him, the knowledge of earth and growing things, of the cycles of life which vibrated through all things Kerithian. She had never questioned the dual nature of his Vaelinar father, a man who waged war as no other had or could and yet spent most of his years farming and cultivating the groves of aryns. "There is light and there is shadow," she would say. "Your father is both, but to me he is love." That, then, had embarrassed him, but he had been young. Young in only the way a native born of Kerith can be when held accountable against the long-lived Vaelinar. His mother's lifespan had been a tenth or even less than that of Bistel's.

He had lost her, and his half brothers and sisters, before he could scarcely know what it meant to have Vaelinar blood intertwining with his own. He would not live a stretch of life such as the elven did, but still would see three or more generations of his Dweller blood flourish, wither, and die in his own lifetime. It came as a harsh realization. He felt guilt for his lifespan and for his inability to hold onto the short-lived members of his family. After his mother passed, the others seemed to have slipped through his fingers like water.

He rode a wagon because he carried aryn saplings to be planted where needed and the farm where he intended to leave his cart was the holding of a great-niece although Verdayne didn't think she knew she was related by blood to him. Her children certainly did not. There was no meaning to it, he thought, having an uncle and then a great-uncle and then a great great-uncle who stayed in his prime while they fell to dust. He resented it on his end, and Gods knew, he had the better part of the bargain. No. It was a burden he felt best unmentioned. Also, and he hated to think it, there was that small part of him that thought they might seek to take advantage of him, of his relationship to them, rather than his love for them and theirs for him. It was a tricky business being part of the Vaelinar culture.

He frowned and walked around, stretching his legs and letting the horses rest a bit, the afternoon upon the road and wild grove.

He took an aryn branch in hand, lightly, spreading its leaves out, looking upon its stem and branches, checking for any sign of the awful blight which had begun to take root even among the near indestructible aryn. None here in this grove. He released the branch which sprang back into place, releasing its aromatic scent as it did, and he inhaled deeply. It lifted his spirits even as it filled his lungs. There were many who cursed where Vaelinars set foot on First Home and the rest of Kerith, but there was no one who cursed the aryn trees. Except for the bastard who'd spread the black fungus among them, but they had a handle on that, finally, thanks to Tolby Farbranch.

He walked the grove, the cart ponies following behind him, used to doing this work with him, stopping when he did to crop at the various grasses and flowers which grew outside the shaded grove. Every step reassured him.

And that was when he found the fire circle. Small, almost insignificant, hidden by the deep shaded interior of the grove—which made it all the more insidious. What if the grove had caught fire? Unlikely, true, in this wet spring, and the aryns rarely burned all the way through. They had a tough skin and a resiliency to fire, but the idea that a camper had dared to start a fire here, in the depths of the grove, rather than out in the meadow or down by the nearby stream—what madness was this? But he could tell from the ring that it was not laid out with the intentions of harming the grove, but rather to cook a simple meal and warm a body throughout the still chill night.

Verdayne stirred the ashes with a finger. More than cold, now dewy, the fire had been out for days. He could smell it but without any great intensity. The wood used had been kindling gathered from nearby trees, none of it aryn. The few bones were of fish, and ground into the ashes so they would meld into a fertilizer of sorts, given time. A transgressor with sensibility then, if twisted. He sat back on his heels, thinking.

His jaw tightened. What if he'd come across the very bastard whose work sent him here? He'd skewer the man alive for poisoning the aryns. But he'd have to find him, first, wouldn't he? Dayne could feel his nostrils flare, almost like a hound on the hunt. Fortune had led him to this site, along

with his task of scouting the groves to see which needed
spraying and which did not, and if he had the chance to
catch the bastard, book delivery or no book delivery, by
Gods he'd do it!

When he stood, it was to see if he could find a trail, however faint, hidden in the grove. The ponies nickered nervously as he moved in and out of their sight, so he whistled
to them and they trotted to catch up, the cart bouncing at
their heels, and his tashya steed jogging along behind with
a bored set to his arched neck and head. He found what he
was looking for: signs of a horseman moving deliberately
through the grove, weaving through the trees. There was no
sign on the aryns of the fungus or the salve that contained
it. No damage. Havoc did not seem to be the goal here; sub-
terfuge had been paramount on the intruder's mind. Who
would do such a thing and for what reason?

The horseman had moved swiftly, and Verdayne wasn't
about to catch up to his next camp without getting back in
the cart and hustling. A second campsite caught the corner
of his eye, so well hidden that even searching for it, he
barely saw it. Dayne moved to it, and the smell of ash and
woodsmoke filled his senses, meager but much sharper than
at the other site and hence more recent.

He went to one knee beside it, hands out, palms down,
and let his Vaelinar blood sense what it could. A faint stirring tingled along his skin, as if from a breeze no one else
could sense as he moved through the grass, through the
growing things, and among the living things in the immediate area. The fire was cold, but he could feel the muted intensity with which it had burned when it had been lit. Smell
the charred flesh of a small coney on a stick across the rocks
which banked and kept the flames in check. Felt the bruised
grasses where the intruder had sat to cook and then eat. A
wider spot which bore an imprint of resting. Not sleep.
Dayne's head tilted a bit as he contemplated this realization, and the smell of old, musty, mummified death. Not
decomposition for living flesh, but as if a body had been
stored for years and no longer existed as flesh but as some-

thing else. He did not like the sensation and, dropping his hands, stood quickly.

He'd still no idea of what had disturbed the forest or why, but if the intent had been to spread the black fungus, it had never been made. Therefore, the camper had another purpose in mind. What? As he moved out of the canopy and looked skyward, spotting the sun's movement, he realized the direction the horseman headed. The trail had been circuitous, but his instincts pinged. He sighted what he'd followed so far, and where he was headed, and where that other's trail led.

His mysterious camper moved toward Larandaril. Verdayne could follow further, but he'd been given his task to reach Calcort, another road forking away. He couldn't be in both places at once. He had no excuse for mere curiosity. Bistane would skin him alive for delaying as long as he had, even if it was to track an intruder. A chill danced down the back of his neck like an angry insect, and he swung his hand to smack at it.

He could almost smell the essence of Vaelinar on the branches floating about him, and in the bent grasses, and against the leaves brushing him in turn.

A Vaelinar. Through here. In hiding.

A Vaelinar who did not smell like a living thing.

A being using the aura of the aryns to obscure his presence. Trespassing where nothing could scent or see him, something which wanted to be undiscoverable. Something skulked through his groves, and Dayne didn't like that at all.

He thought of his brother's tale at the library, and his skin went cold. Something similar had been haunting Ferstanthe. Infecting the books? Done there and moving on to Larandaril with a new purpose? Yet without a sighting, he didn't have enough evidence to change his quest.

He took a great gulping breath, and tasted death upon it, at the back of his throat, like rusty iron. Not good at all. When he got to Calcort, he'd send to Bistane to tell him what he'd discovered, but he couldn't do anything until then, unless the crofters he would meet in the next day had messenger birds of their own. Not likely. No need to. Dwellers had their own means of communication, and rarely was anything urgent enough to be sent on wing. Life was shorter there, but moved slower, an oxymoron if ever he'd found one.

He whistled and his ponies heard him, came trotting through the glade reluctantly, sweet spring shoots still hanging from their whiskery lips, a meal interrupted. He patted both of them and murmured words of praise for their intelligence and their work, and they both whickered into his hands, proud of themselves and somewhat mollified. Lastly, he moved to his tashya mount, small for one of the Vaelinarran hot bloods but good-sized for his own stature. The horse put his head down and blew over his hands, but it was an uneasy gesture, for the horse flung his head back up, high, looking over the grasses and through the trees as if sensing what Dayne had been following.

Verdayne reached his hand up to scratch behind the gelding's ear. "You feel it, too. I'll find some sugar grass to thank you for that—don't like feeling as if I have gone wobbly in the brain."

The gelding snorted and ducked his head down to butt him in the chest, knocking the wind out of him. Laughing, even as he struggled to catch a deep breath, Dayne staggered back a step and hung an elbow over the cart's bed. The gelding had a cantankerous nature and was known for his head butts, and still he'd been suckered into standing close enough and long enough with his guard down to receive one.

He rubbed his chest and gave a last coughing whoop as the breath came back to him.

Dayne showed the horse his fist. "See that? All the sugar grass you get will fit in there!"

The gelding curled his lip in disdain before swinging about and leaning on him, pressing him against the side of the cart. Dayne took it for a few moments, the warmth and ordinariness of the horse comforting, before he shoved the animal away and then slapped his rump. "Don't go thinking you and I are friends now," he growled.

He returned to the front of the cart and pulled himself up, chirping as he did. His ponies swung into an easy trot even before he had the reins settled into his hands. He had places to be.

Chapter
Fifteen

MEG TRIED TO FIND a comfortable position in which to recline, a seemingly impossible task because the child within was all angles and strong, pushing at her in determined nudges. Night had fallen, Rivergrace and Sevryn were several days into their journey, the family meal had been shared, and her father had gone off to an early bed as he had early work. Garner had come and gone, drifting off without much explanation, but Lily had frowned after him, muttering something about "tempting the luck of the Gods," meaning she thought he'd gone off to gamble somewhere. Keldan kept nearly the same hours as their father, for he worked shoulder to shoulder with him, although there were occasional nights when he spent some time with a local girl or two. And Hosmer. She tried not to think of Hosmer behind the lines of quarantine. She'd been reassured, but she would not believe it until he returned, safe. That left Lily who sat by a lantern in the kitchen, her hands working on something for the baby that she kept hidden from Nutmeg if not entirely successfully.

She rubbed her stomach and the fragrance of the herbal

oils she'd been using to soothe her skin drifted up. "If you could smell this," she told the baby, "you'd like it. Maybe you'd think your Mom always smells like this." That made the corner of her mouth quirk. The floral fragrance also held an underlying essence of qynch oil, a pressed oil with many uses. She inched her shoulders a bit higher, wondering if she'd be able to sleep in her position that night. A cold breeze fluttered fitfully through the shuttered window. She couldn't keep it flung wide open, her Dad and everyone security conscious, but she'd found a way to cheat on the closed window a bit.

Lariel's guards had not yet arrived but had sent word that they would be in Calcort in the morning, so they were very close. Close enough that they might even press on through the night to make the city. The quarantine, in its third day, kept the vineyard quarter secured off, as Sevryn had predicted, making guarding her much easier. And efficient. Nutmeg sighed. If Grace and Sevryn had really wanted her safe, why hadn't they stayed? But she knew better than that. It had just been nice having Grace close again.

Nutmeg turned her chin, looking across the room, to the corner where she had a safe buried under the floorboards. She had almost told Rivergrace about the burden and gift Warlord Bistel had laid upon her. Almost. Wiser not to, she supposed, but she trusted her sister. Grace should know.

Nutmeg got up, not gracefully or with the bounce of energy for which she'd been known, but well enough, and went to the corner. She moved the small vanity dresser that covered the floorboards where her father had cleverly carpentered a cubby hole, without asking why, or even remembering later that he had, although she knew Tolby never missed anything. He probably assumed that she had some keepsakes from Jeredon she wished to keep safe and private. He would never in a million years have guessed the safe spot held a journal written by a Vaelinar warlord and entrusted to her upon his death.

She pressed the three boards which opened and then slid away to reveal her hiding spot. Wrapped in oilcloth and then silk, she took the journal out and laid it upon her knees as she sat down, her back to the vanity dresser. Her baby kicked wildly, either in excitement for her change in position or because the journal, with an aura even her Dweller eyes could recognize, revealed itself.

Nutmeg stroked her fingertips over the worn leather. "Do you see it, baby?" she whispered. "The way you saw the door? I swear I felt you grow quiet when I looked at it. I'd not a chance of seeing it on my own, I know that. I felt you grow still and knowing and warm with the seeing of it, through me. It had to be you, Tree's blood, I never saw that way afore." She wiped a wispy, tickling lock of hair from her forehead. She did not know what Rivergrace saw when she looked at things with those beautiful eyes which marked her indelibly as a Vaelinar, eyes of aquamarine, stormy blue, and the deepest blue of a bottomless lake. Did she see the aura that Nutmeg had seen? The door of ashen gray, the look of dead and tempered wood, with its lock of sooty black? The green-gold of the living vineyard around it, or the silvery bloom around Grace herself, and the shadow that Sevryn cast wherever he walked. She'd feared to ask her sister. What if no one alive saw what she saw, and she only imagined it, or the strain of having a child had driven her slightly crazy? It did not help that the visions she had came and went, fleetingly. "Look on this now, if you can. This is not from your father, but it is part of your bloodline, and we have to keep it safe." Meg sighed. Bad enough that she carried the child of a Vaelinar power line, but if she did see—she was invested with abilities she ought not to have. Kernan witchery was not greatly appreciated among the people. Vaelinar power even less so. She would have to be even more cautious than before. Meg rubbed a tiny yet growing furrow between her brows.

She had another burden she'd vowed to keep safe, one that was as hidden as her child was obvious. She'd thought, briefly, to share it with Rivergrace but then changed her mind, and Nutmeg still did not know if she shied away from sharing because she did not want to be thought of as stealing from a dead man's body or if she so coveted the thing, she could not bear to share it with anyone. Her hands shook a little as she clasped the journal tightly.

The leather smelled of a masculine scent, and woodsmoke, and horse sweat. Bistel must have carried it wherever he went, tucked inside his shirt and leathers and mail. It carried a wealth of years upon it, worn leather but polished from the touch of hands upon it, Bistel's hands, opening it time and time again, to read and write within. Nutmeg opened it carefully.

She'd done so once, when she had first gotten it. Written by a Vaelinar for Vaelinar, she expected to make no sense of it, and had not, except for dates here and there, time spans that impressed upon her the sheer enormity of Bistel's lifespan, hundreds of years longer than she could ever hope to live. She wondered if, should she learn to read the words, she might discover that all those years actually made him wiser as well as older. If life were just at all, it would have. But life, as she had learned all too well, had little sense of justice. The pages were a creamy white and she touched them tentatively, afraid of their possible fragility, but they met her fingertips with a resilient surface. Not an ordinary paper, then, perhaps a parchment of some sort. She leaned close, peering. Whatever it was, the pages glowed. Then she leaned back. The baby shifted a little inside of her, and she could almost imagine a tiny hand reaching out.

"They don't glow, normally, do they?" Meg whispered. No one answered her in any way, and she turned the blank page.

Boldly printed, the words leaped out at her. A TREATMENT ON THE CREATION OF VAELINAR WAYS.

Underneath, in smaller yet no less compelling letters, was written: And the Downfall of Bloodlines Tied to Unsuccessful Creations.

Meg sat back as if shoved, closing the book abruptly. She knew that Bistel and his people worked a Magic upon Kerith that those native to her world could not. They could sway and even change the laws of earth, air, fire, and water,

twist them, braid them, to make new creations that were
nothing like illusions or sleight of hand. They were major
changes branded upon Kerith, changes that often went
against the very Laws of Nature, and for lack of a better
word, they were called Ways. Ways like the Ferryman of the
Nylara who could traverse that broad and raging river no
matter what the weather, or season, or flood level. Ways like
the Shining Sisters. Ways that had stayed, and a few that had
been destroyed, like the great Jewel of Tomarq. Ways that,
for all their wonder, were each and every one singular and
could no longer be made by most of the Vaelinars who
walked Kernan lands. The talent and strength it took must
have been prodigious and for this, the rest of them could
only give thanks, or they might have seen the Vaelinars
mold their world into a totally unfamiliar landscape. Those
days were gone.

Her hands shook. Unless, perhaps, one could read and
understand this book. What she held, what Bistel had given
her guardianship over, was nothing less than a kingmaker.
The Vaelinar who possessed this book and could use it,
would wield untold power, for it seemed to Nutmeg that
Bistel had taken the unfathomable and made it understand-
able. The ild Fallyn would kill for it. Meg's head jerked upright. Perhaps they already had. If she had thought they
might come after Jeredon's heir, it meant nothing next to
the tome she held. Her life would be tenuous indeed if they
had an inkling of what she held. Her death sentence would
become not only desirable but a necessity if they knew of
this treasure. She had not told anyone, but she had no idea
whose eyes might have viewed Bistel's final moments. She
pressed the book to her burgeoning stomach. Bistel had
known the charge he'd laid upon her, and what she would
do to uphold it. "Never," she whispered fiercely. "They
won't have it. By all the Gods of Kerith and beyond. *Never.*"

It wasn't till candlemarks later, her cubbyhole closed and
dresser back in place and her curly head pillowed in near
perfect comfort, on the verge of drifting away to sleep, that
her eyes flew open in realization. She'd read it.

Read every foreign symbol as easily as the tally books she helped keep for their orchards and vineyards, and patterns for fancy ball gowns, and those silly rags of gossip passed around on the streets for only one penny. How she managed it, she could not guess. There wasn't a babe born who could talk, read, and write straight out of the womb. So what ability did Jeredon's child have that could enable her to interpret the unknown? Nutmeg's eyelids fluttered. There were days, she thought, as she settled back down to sleepiness, that were almost too much to take in.

Chapter
Sixteen

THE TROOPS STATIONED AT THE BATTLEFIELD where the Rivers Ashenbrook and stony Ravela crossed had grown bored. They were not bred to wait endlessly, but to shore their courage up at a moment's notice and wade into a fray. No major attacks on the horizon, or even minor skirmishes, and the soldiers retreated into dreary activities: mending armor, repairing weapons, drinking and gambling. They found a fruit which could be stewed and fermented into a potent brandy, supplemented by their daily ration of beer. They quarreled and brawled among their various Vaelinar factions, although grievances were kept to a minimum and grudges were mediated speedily by commanders who had no wish for lifelong feuds to flare up at such close quarters. Life was not good, but it was bearable. Their thoughts and attentions turned inward; few if any, noticed the curious ones who scrounged about the broken-rock hillsides, looking for artifacts and oddities. The battlefield had already been well scavenged. All that remained were odds and ends: a torn leather boot here, a tarnishing belt buckle there, a broken arrowhead over yonder. Items of real interest had been found weeks and weeks ago, and only the extremely bored even bothered to search the area. With little interest in yet another futile mission, rather like waiting for the enemy, soldiers ignored the last of the scavengers.

No one noticed the ragged Vaelinar who searched the steep slope leading from the now collapsed tunnel on the mountain where the Raymy had burst forth with their ungodly horde. No one paid any attention as he stooped over each and every bone that lay bleaching in the sun or moldering in the shaded nooks and crannies of the rockfall. His clothes of nondescript color, neither gray nor tan but close to the dirt and rock he combed through, drew no attention. He wore a hooded mantle and carried a large sack tied to his belt, to convey whatever treasures he found. He must have found little. The sack never seemed to fill nor his efforts to wane. He had not been there long, but how long no one could say. Nor could anyone say what he looked like, because none of them had been interested enough to approach him to take his measure.

That undoubtedly had saved them their lives, boring as they might have been. Quendius carried a very long and sharp sword at his back, one that he knew how to swing quite well. His light soot-colored skin stayed shadowed by his hooded mantle, and his dark eyes, set deep within his face, showed little light or forbearance for any of the soldiers stationed on the plains below him. He squatted by bones and turned them over in his hands, one by one, examining them minutely, looking for something—or someone.

On the tenth day of his scavenging, the rogue weaponmaker stood, stretching his back, and gazing down on the encampment. No one noticed him then as they had not really noticed him earlier. He scratched at a Kernan "see me not" fetish sewn to the neck of his tunic. It smelled . . . no, it *stank,* but he could not deny that it worked. Not a great magic like Vaelinars wove, but good enough for his purposes. He made a mental note to find the hedge witches who'd gathered and cured the fetish and recruit them, willing or not, in his future efforts. As for now . . . Quendius turned his head to gaze about what remained of the killing ground.

Narskap had died here. His eccentric, deadly, and faithful hound of a man had turned on him, and died here. Death was too easy, too simple to lose Narskap in. His body had not been collected for burning, as the soldiers' corpses had been, nor had he been left to the carrion feeders because no sign could be found of his bones, however scattered about the rockfall they might have been.

No. Narskap had died and yet risen to walk away from the battlefield. That was the only answer the days of his searching could provide. No one would have claimed his body because he had been first to the site, only to find it gone. In the aftermath of battle, Quendius thought perhaps he'd misremembered the spot. But again, no. Perhaps he thought himself freed from Quendius now. He would be wrong if he did. Quendius dusted his hands off in finality. Narskap had but one weak link in the chain of his existence, be it living, dead, or Undead, and that would be his daughter. She was the flame that drew his moth-like existence, like it or not, and that was where Quendius would find him.

If not, holding the girl might provide him with a few distractions. He wrapped his dirt-colored mantle about him more closely and climbed the rockfall toward the setting sun, where his camp and horse waited. Yes. He wanted that girl. He knew where she would be, hidden under the cloak of the Warrior Queen at Larandaril.

He knew exactly where to go to retrieve her.

Chapter
Seventeen

SPRING TICKLED ALONG the southern reaches of the First Home, but on the mountainous seascape where Fortress ild Fallyn held its foothold, the wind and clouds kept the sun and warmth at bay akin to late winter. The seascape along this part of the rugged coast reared up particularly wildly and the fortress built upon its cliffs was created at great sacrifice and with powerful magic. Such a sacrifice that it was said, quietly, the ild Fallyn bloodline had never again been so Talented. Words never spoken near its fortress walls or among the sheltered population imprisoned within.

With the lessening chill as daylight stole into the fortress, Ceyla woke reluctantly, her meager blankets cocooning the scant heat about her body. She hesitated to stretch her limbs out as her body demanded she do, knowing she would lose whatever heat she held. From the deep breathing around her, she could tell that few in the longhouse had awakened yet. Birdsong stayed silent, so the faint winging of dawn hadn't warmed the stone walls or dense woods about them yet. Still, she rolled a little in her cot.

Someone leaned over her shoulder, breath in her ear, saying, "Quiet."

She frozc. The hand on her shoulder squeezed slightly. "They took Marisanna last night."

No! She hadn't awakened enough yet to learn that what was wrong with her morning was not the cold, not the hunger, but the fact that her cot was empty save for herself. Ceyla put her own hand out. "No," she whimpered.

"She hasn't come back." The hand squeezed again, and then the informer moved away from her cot, padding silently into the darkness.

Not Marisanna. No. Ceyla curled up tightly, eyes squeezing out tears, chest convulsed to stay silent.

Her bunkmate, far older and a little wiser, suddenly gone, and she hadn't even noticed the emptiness next to her. Marisanna had warned Ceyla that this might happen. "I've had three children, all boys," she'd noted. "Not a one of them shows a hint of Talent. I'm no good to them, and I know too much now, so I will disappear one day. When it happens, you mustn't ask about me. You must forget me."

"How can you ask this of me?"

Marisanna had looked at her, with eyes of smoke gray and faint jade green, with vivid sparks of emerald in their depths. Vaelinar eyes. "I don't want your death on my conscience."

"How would you know? You'd be gone!"

"Maybe. Maybe not."

"If they take you—"

"If they take me, the easiest way to dispose of me is to push me off the sea cliffs." Marisanna had paused for a long time. "The fall probably won't kill me as they think it will."

"Probably? How? What do you mean?"

"My children don't carry the spark, but I hold it deep within me. I can levitate as they do, the ild Fallyn. Not often or as well, but I can. If they throw me off a cliff into the sea, I'll find my freedom. I'll either fly or die." She had given a dry chuckle. "One way or another. Do you understand?"

"You can't be sure."

"No. But you can't mourn over uncertainty, can you?"

"Why are you telling me this?"

"Because we share blankets? Because you remind me of the daughter I'd hoped to have one day? Because we are both subjects here? Or . . ." Marisanna had tilted her head slightly. "Because I know you have a Talent, too, although you've hidden it very, very well. Keep my secret as I keep yours." Marisanna had tucked a wayward strand of hair behind Ceyla's ear then. "Hope for me as I hope for you."

Ceyla stayed in the hollow of her cot for long moments, sorting her memories from her dreams. She put one hand over to the other hollow, long cold. Gone without a leave-taking. Ceyla must have slept the sleep of the exhausted. And she had had dreams, vivid ones that now crowded back into her head behind her eyes, shoving as if they could burst out into being. She put the heel of her hand to her right eye, then her left as if she could stay the hurtful bulge that she felt though it did not seem to actually exist. Secrets, pushing, demanding, to be loosed. Dreams of secrets and now Marisanna taken. She took a deep breath and got out of bed, into a day that promised only a bone-chilling future as she dressed.

Ceyla shivered into her shawl, its thin wrapping pulled up around her head and ears as well as her neck and shoulders — as if that could seriously keep her from freezing — and made her cautious way across the subjects' grounds. Few had risen yet to do their chores and exercises, the dank morning keeping those in their cots who dared. Other subjects were already buried deep in the tasks of keeping the stronghold running. It was hard work, brutal work in the winter, and no one could afford to be looking about in idleness. She could creep along, most likely unseen, if she took great care. And she had to. A sharp splinter in her heart drove her to seek solace despite the weather. She could no more ignore its pain than she could the icy spring descending upon the stronghold.

Mist off the angry sea tide kept the cold low-lying and enveloping the land. It clawed at the shore like an angry, spitting cat, its breath sea salt and biting, wind whipping at her like a lashing feline tail. Shivering, she ran hunched over, trying not to think of better days. She found a spot at the stronghold wall where she could look over, across the boundary expanse to the cliffs, which arched in a curve to the sharp rocks below. She saw nothing on those rocks. Not like in past days when broken bodies could be discovered there, bones shattered and lungs filled with sea water. Escapees, they were told. And some might have been. Others were no doubt sacrifices to the ild Fallyn blueprints.

Because she could not see Marisanna did not mean that she did not lie down there somewhere, arms and legs akimbo, rags soaked in sea water and blood. But Ceyla grasped at the secret she'd been granted as if it could help, staring into the wind until salt spray dried her skin and stung her eyes, and could not aid her.

"They threw her over last night."

Ceyla jumped and would have screamed, but the fear so constricted her throat she couldn't get the sound up and out as she spun back against the wall, facing the young man who'd accosted her. "Nahaal."

He lifted and dropped a shoulder, peering past her to the rocks, the wind whipping back his hair from a face that, if he mourned, showed no sign of it. She supposed that if he looked closely at her, he might see the same blankness. The ild Fallyn did that to one. Weakness could never be shown.

"I have not seen her body wash up."

She couldn't bear his words. They poked into her hearing like sharp sticks, and she turned away from him.

He made a scornful noise. "She wanted to be thrown over." He pushed Ceyla away from the wall and with a grunt of effort, went over it, floating and landing halfway down, boots skidding over the spray and moss-slick rocks. He regained his footing while she stared. Marisanna always said her sons had no Talent, yet here was Nahaal . . . had she even known? Did anyone here know? She hugged her arms around here, trying to shut out the wind and shut in her questions. The ild Fallyn must know, for he wore decent clothing and he hadn't been sent out to do hard labor. Yet.

Nahaal bent and picked among the sharp stones for a moment and stood, with a rag wind-whipped in his hand. He made another leap and came down next to Ceyla. He put the rag in her hand. "So much for my mother's hopes. Don't linger here. I might have to tell them you were here, and secrets never sit well with our masters. I have lessons." He strode off, covering the ground in huge, leaping, strides.

Ceyla looked at what she held, remembering Marisanna's brightly colored shawl, a scrap of it sodden and smelling of salt and blotched with what might have been water-diluted blood. She squeezed her fingers tightly about it. The ild Fallyn knew about Nahaal and tossed his mother over anyway. Nothing could save any of them. She wanted to call after him and remind him of that, but she pressed her lips together tightly.

She leaned over for one last look and saw—or hoped she saw—a bright-colored flash moving stealthily at the cliff's bottom, near the sands. Did something or someone move down there? Despite the shredded cloth she held? Ceyla held her breath as if it could help her see better. Marisanna had held hope for freedom. She tucked the possibility away inside her. Soft words in the night, a comforting touch on her shoulder, a knowing look in friendly eyes. That could not be lost. Not if she held tightly onto them. Ceyla opened her fingers and let the sea wind take the scrap from her hand, deciding that would not be how she would remember her friend.

Memories would not comfort her, would not soothe her mind with balm, and so she turned away, her gaze sweeping over the stronghold grounds—or at least that small portion that she was familiar with as a subject and worker. She drew her shawl up to cover the back of her neck. It would never be warm here the way it had been in the countryside she remembered from her early youth, with sand dunes and grasses that swept over them, a beach so hot it could burn the soles of your bare feet in the summer. She remembered those days to keep her warmer at night, burning the reserves of her own fuel to keep going. Her body had always been slender and spare, boyish with little plumpness to keep her buffered. Now she was scarcely more than stick thin. While other subjects thrived under the ild Fallyn yoke, she did not. She had no Talent the Vaelinar could discern, but they would not throw her away, not just yet. Not until she had been bred back and her children could be tested, as one tests a litter of hounds to see their mettle. Marisanna's fate awaited her.

Ceyla shuddered. She checked her thoughts and corrected herself. Ild Fallyn hounds got more regard than the subjects did. They looked at her eyes, the royal Vaelinar did, at her eyes of brown and caramel and gold and said to each other, there should be Talent here. Vaelinar magic. But where? And she would not answer them, not yet, not if she could keep her soul from them. The ild Fallyn sought to bring back their blood, blood thinned by Kernan partners over the centuries, but not with kindness and a welcoming warmth. No. They were trying to breed the Kernan out, and enrich the Vaelinar bloodlines, a mission that would take decades, if not centuries, but then the Vaelinars had the lifespan to make such plans. But the only breeders who lived were the ones with promise.

She counted herself lucky that she had had a childhood outside the gates of the ild Fallyn fortress. Many here had not. But that same luck rubbed and chaffed her, for Ceyla had memories to haunt her that the others did not, memories that gave her discontent and unhappiness as much as they soothed her. She knew what she missed beyond those armored gates. The others did not or chose not to. Looking at them and living with them drove home one further point: she would never be allowed to go back. When the ild Fallyns were done with her, she would be discarded as well. Even breeding successfully would be no guarantee.

She held no wish to be like Tench, most Vaelinar-like of any of them, and with more than a passing resemblance to the Warrior Queen's late brother Jeredon, or so those who had seen both, could testify. After the abortive war at the River Ashenbrook, Tench had been gathered up from the barracks of the subjects and disappeared within the fortress halls, never to be seen again. Was he the father, as some dared to whisper, of Lady Tressandre's unborn child rather than the Anderieon heir she claimed? Perhaps. Likely. No one could know for sure, at least not from Tench's witness. He had vanished.

Nor would she become like Nahaal, cold at his mother's death, the only spark in him a seeming pride in what she now knew meant he had a gleam of Talent. He'd always been brash and confident. Ceyla wondered how Marisanna could have overlooked him. He would be trouble to her now, now that Marisanna was gone and Ceyla had seen his ability. He would be after her, demanding payment for the reveal.

Her day would come. She'd been raped and often, she had no hope of avoiding that, but conception had been withheld and now that she'd matured, even the choice of her body would be taken from her. She had to prove herself. She kept her meager Talent as hidden and under wraps as she could, and it was perhaps because of that very Talent that she could anticipate the means with which her captors would test her to reveal herself. If they decided she could not be bred, and she could not be successfully categorized, she would be locked into drudgery until the stress of her toils, age, and, perhaps, Tressandre's legendary temper killed her.

Ceyla ducked her head and made her way to a kind of freedom. There was a corner where the worlds met, the actual grounds of the ild Fallyn fortress abutted the forbidden quarters of the subjects. Here, a few things grew like trees and flowers. One such blossomed now and later in the year, she would comb through it carefully, harvesting what little fruit it might bear in the thin and bitter summer. More importantly, the corner stood neglected. No gardener worked here, and the patch drew no attention or visitor except for

herself. She sought it out when she could, just to touch
something that grew unfettered, unstained, and untainted
by the hand of her captors. The stone wall buckled in an odd
way about it, giving a niche where there ought not to be
one, as if the mason had planned an alcove for a statue or
perhaps a fountain, and then been forced to abandon it. She
could just fit into it, the scrawny tree hiding her further in
its shadows, and be safe for a while.

Her brow throbbed. She clenched her fist and pressed it
to her forehead, willing away the beginning ache. It would
not be enough. It was never enough! Caught where she
should not be, with the pain about to descend upon her in
drowning waves, she shrank into her forbidden corner of
the courtyard where eyes and ears could spy upon the ild
Fallyn themselves if one was stupid enough to try it. She
had never been here before when the avalanche came down
upon her. That usually happened at night, uneasy sleep becoming torturous dreams, so torturous that she even welcomed the occasional rape by a guard of the subjects, for
that pain was less and she could endure it. The brutal ad-
vances were sanctioned unless the subject had been marked
for breeding and then they would cease. When that time
came, Ceyla knew that her days were numbered. Marisanna
had consoled her before. Now she would face it alone.

A trumpet blared through her worries, and a man bellowed in answer.

"Open the gates!"

Her temple throbbed at the sound of the gatekeeper's
voice, and then at the great gears for the gates grinding into
motion, their vibration moving through the very ground.
With creaks and groans, the massive wooden portal split
and swung up, and black-and-silver-garbed riders came
trotting in, the manes of their tashya horses flying, as they
herded in a stumbling group of prisoners. Or perhaps these
were volunteers hoping to pass ild Fallyn Talent screenings.
Or maybe, they were slaves brought from the East and
transported to the western coast. She couldn't tell from
their mud-coated garments and faces. They staggered

against one another, a few holding out hands to those who seemed most exhausted, their expressions numbed despite their efforts for their companions. She remembered those first days as if they were yesterday. It was the days in between which had become a blur to her.

As the horsemen began to dismount, a visible stir went through the troops. They opened a pathway through the center of their gathering, stable lads coming out and yanking the horses aside as well, as a regal-looking woman came out of the fortress main doors, tapping a riding crop against the side of her leg. Hair the color of wild honey tumbled from the high tiara that crowned her forehead, but she did not need the jewelry to define her. Anyone there—or anywhere—would have known who she was. Her blouse of black and silver shimmered like silk in the weak sunlight, while her trousers seemed to be made of soft ebony leather. Her dark boots shone. Tressandre ild Fallyn approached the ragged line of recruits and strode by them, slowly, gauging the worth of each by some calculation only she understood. At the end of the row, she turned on heel. She traced her steps back down the row, faster now, stopping every once in a while to assess one of the recruits more closely.

Ceyla found her hand on her throat, stealing up to her mouth, in case she cried aloud. She shivered as she watched the inspection, yet she could not turn her eyes away. Dreams and visions did not have to tell her what might well happen. She'd seen it before and unless she died in the coming night or escaped, she'd see it again.

Tressandre's voice carried clearly through the air. "Dwellers," she stated. "How many times have I told you Dweller breeds are useless to us? They are like Bolgers. Animals. I won't have them in our programs! Who thought he knew better than my edict and brought them in?"

One of the riders fell to his knees. His young face creased in dismay. Ceyla did not recognize him, but she seldom got a look at the ild Fallyn elite in the compound except for deliveries like this. The heavy doors, which led to the fortress and grounds proper, were unbarred only rarely. She curled her fingers upon her skin, willing him not to speak, for there was nothing he could say which would please or stay Tressandre in what she would do next.

"Forgive me, most excellent one. These three all show Talent in goodly amount, and I did not wish to overlook them if they might hold any value to you." He pointed to a girl, one Ceyla had thought a child as she'd been when brought in, but who now obviously was not, although young. "Show her the fire," he demanded.

The Dweller stood on one foot and then the other, trembling. The two Kernan- and Vaelinar-blooded on either side of her shuffled as far away as they could.

"Show her!" he shouted at her. "If you wish to live."

Ceyla shuttered her eyes a moment. When she looked again from her hiding place, the Dweller girl had her thin arms stretched in front of her, and flame danced in each palm. The yellow-orange aura reflected upon her face, but she did not seem to mind the heat although Ceyla could see that the flames were hot as tiny waves in the image rippled upward.

The riding crop tapped twice at Tressandre's side. "And the other one. What does it do?" she said, her tone bored.

"It . . . he . . ." the ild Fallyn rider said, "Projects."

"Projects."

"He gives off illusions. Fleeting yes, but with training they can become stronger."

Tressandre tilted her head. "What sort of illusions?"

The rider got to his feet and paced down the row to the young man. "Show her," he said impatiently, as if the Dweller breed should have known what would be asked of him.

The young man shuddered. He had been one of the ones who stumbled most coming into the yard. "Water," he husked, his voice barely audible to Ceyla. "I need water."

Tressandre pointed the crop at him. "Why should I waste water on you?"

"Because," he answered slowly, and his entire body began to waver. Ragged cloth rippled. Skin stretched and expanded. Height shot upward. "Because I can buy and sell you."

A tall and sturdy Kernan trader, richly clothed, pointed haughtily back at Tressandre. His words brought a collective gasp from those about him and Tressandre jerked her chin in the air.

Ceyla felt her mouth fall open. Her astonishment lasted but a few seconds, for that was how long the illusion sustained itself, fleeting seconds. The prosperous trader wavered and began to fall apart, layer by layer. As the Dweller began to appear again, he fell forward to one knee, shaking, once more ragged.

"Interesting," she drawled. She looked the subject over again. "But not interesting enough. Maybe if he could have held the image for more than a breath or three. Dweller blood is vastly inferior, even to Kernan lines. These are curs, all of them. I work to restore our bloodlines. Can none of you understand the import of that? Powers that had been ours and will be ours once again? Nothing is achieved without sacrifice and yet you—" She stabbed her crop at the offending rider. "Ignore my mandate. Ignore our greatest purposes. Ignore the heritage of ild Fallyn!" She tucked her crop under her arm, turning on her heel, and heading back to the doors that had produced her. "Test the others. Pray they prove worthy of our teaching. As for these three, kill them."

Ceyla threw her arms over her head and ducked her chin down, curling into herself, so that she could not see, but she heard the screams despite all her hopes that she would not. She had lived through that first culling as she still lived this day, but nothing remained certain. She sank into herself knowing the end of her time might come this moment, this aching and blinding moment as she pressed herself into shadow and the crack in the stone wall, and pushed her fingers into her mouth to stifle her moans and perhaps a lucent outcry.

She could feel the overwhelming cloud begin to drop on her. No, no, no, this could not be happening to her. She

doubled over, digging her heels into the broken stone and
dirt, pushing herself into a painful knot as if that pain could
stave off the other. Not now, not here, not in the daylight,
not with riders within hearing distance. Her mind could not
fill with the crushing visions of others that did not belong to
her, that made little sense to her, that scrambled her own
being until she hardly knew who or when she was. She
could not serve the tide of otherness. But it filled her. Her
pitiful attempts to save herself were swept away by a tsunami. Insanity came rushing in, pushing her sense of self
aside until she could only cower and dimly await its cessa-
tion.

She knew she was crazy. One couldn't dream the way she
did and not be crazy. The minute her affliction became
known, she would be killed. Defective. Blood no one in
their right mind would want carried on. She would be well
and truly worthless. Useless. Insane.

The torrent rushed in and she sank under its weight,
sank and drowned.

When the rush receded, her hearing returned first, a faint
roar obscuring the clarity as though she actually floated underwater. She could feel her awareness bobbing upward
into the afternoon, sun a bit warmer than it had been in the
early morning. She drifted like an insignificant scrap of flot-
sam rising to the surface of the tide, bobbing aimlessly here
and there upon the foam of the sea. Ceyla uncurled the tiniest bit. She ached in her bones and her nerves felt like fiery
wires throughout her body, her skin tight and tender. Voices
drummed upon her hearing with the fervor of a high tide
beating upon the rocks. Rather than struggle with it, she let
the buoyancy of her consciousness carry her upward until
she was fully aware, her head throbbing with the remnants
of the attack, and her eyes squinted against the flood of
sunlight. Rolled into a ball and tucked away into the stone
wall's niche, Ceyla lay still, her stomach fighting the attack

as it always did—she was invariably sick as a dog or raven-
ously hungry or, worse, both. This time she was hungry and
warred with herself to move, to find, to eat, to replenish
whatever stores the insanity always sucked out of her as
though she might be some succulent fruit. She turned her
face into her hands, her fingers still in her mouth and spat
them out before she started gnawing on them like some
mewling babe. Sounds kept beating upon her ears and
slowly she separated them into words that made sense.

From above her, from little used parapets, voices drifted
downward.

"... remains difficult to gather without attracting undue
attention."

"But you have made the efforts I prescribed to you and
taken the precautions." Tressandre's voice, tones like liquid
gold but words bitten off sharply. Ceyla held her breath desperately upon recognizing her dread mistress' voice.

"Of course."

"Good. Because trust me, our queen Lariel is fixed upon
the Raymy. It would take a munificent mistake on your part
to draw her attention. See that it doesn't happen."

"We do our best."

"See that you continue to do so. Make no mistake. I am
readying for that opening of the gate to our homelands and
when it does, I want our forces prepared to act. We will take
our heritage that was stripped from us and we will restore
our legacy as it was meant to be, and we will come to the
aid of our long lost Trevilara, queen and country. She will
want to be generous in her rewards, to all of us. That is my
pledge to you. All that was taken from us here, we will have
within our grasp again. We are already in position and anything can, and will, happen on a battlefield. No one will
stand in our way when it is time for us to make our move."

The other made a sound of appreciation, a low murmur
that Ceyla could not hear distinctly, but she knew in her gut
what it meant. The other was groveling in his gratitude,
much like one of the subjects trying for extra bread crusts,
and it made her sick to hear it.

"Don't thank me now. Hold your gratitude until we've accomplished what we intend."

"Nevertheless, you have my life, Lady Tressandre. You have but to ask for it."

"If I do, it will not be for my sake but for the sake of the heir I carry. You know that, don't you?"

"We would all die for you and the baby. The monstrosity." There came a noise as the speaker spat upon the courtyard flagstones. "The monstrosity that Lariel intends to name her heir, Dweller and Gods know what else, because I cannot believe that Jeredon would have touched the beastly female, that *thing* shames and dooms us all."

"I hold hope that Lariel will see the truth and the justice of our position. If not, well, there are others to judge her. What is important for us today and tomorrow, is to purify our blood and Talents after decades of bowing to lesser ones so that we might be accepted," and here the word dripped with sarcasm, "rather than rule as we were intended. If the gate cannot be opened to return us, to restore us to our rightful place, then we must carve it here. Out of stone and flesh, if we must."

"From your lips to the ears of the Gods!"

"Not them," Tressandre hushed the speaker. "For They sleep. From my lips to the ears and hearts of Vaelinar such as yourself who know and understand of what I speak. The day grows late. I can't keep you longer, for the roads are still uncertain these days."

"I'll carry what you've told me."

"Do that," Tressandre said. "And we cannot fail."

There was a long pause, followed by the clatter of a horse's hooves and then the thudding of the great gates which kept the fortress sheltered. "Fool." Tressandre made a noise through her teeth that was both dismissive and scornful before her footfalls could be heard on the courtyard paving moving away.

Silence but for the drumming of her own blood in her ears fell upon Ceyla. She stretched her body open slowly,

with aches and pins and needles attacking her every movement. She'd heard too much. The next time her insanity fell
upon her, those words could come tumbling out of her
mouth, giving her and any who heard them a death sentence for spying. Tressandre plotted treason. All suspected
it. Few had proof. And whatever else might happen, Ceyla
could not give that proof, for no one would believe her but
the guilty party herself, and she would be just as dead. Not
to mention the disaster that her fit itself might prove. She
had no memory of the visions that had danced within her
twisted mind, but she knew they would resurface, unbidden.
Crazy Ceyla, the other subjects called her, and they had a
right to. No, she could not stay. It would bring death upon
her and many others if she did. Better to flee and die alone,
trying to escape.

    She carried her meager belongings always with her, in a
bundle tied under her skirt. It hampered her walking sometimes, giving her an odd gait that merely added to the hu-
miliation already heaped upon her shoulders. She had
nothing to go back for. Marisanna, gone. No meal would give
her the sustenance she needed nor would it yield enough to
stock her for a journey. Best to go now. She'd already been
missing for the afternoon while under the spell of her
warped mind. Ceyla heaved a sigh and stepped back. She
already knew how she would get out. Like a wisp of a ghost,
she could see it in her mind, playing from a dream of the
past or even from this very day. These phantoms of actions
danced behind her eyes until she could see little else. She
had to leave. Now. And in the way she saw without seeing.
She knotted her shawl tightly about her head and neck, tying it like a thin and worn scarf. She would crawl on her
belly under the high rock walls of the fortress, from the kennel runs where one enterprising hound tunneled away under the wall and the kennel boy too lazy to take mortar to
the stone work to repair it, merely piled up loose rock to
cover the holes. She knew she would make it that far. Unfortunately, her insanity chose not to tell her if it would be

safe on the other side or how far she would get. She would be blinded as to her future. Rather like the hound.

But like the hound, a compulsion had been laid on her to get away, to dig away at the fence that held her, and to escape. She could not turn back. She would run. In a day. Maybe a handful of days, but run she would.

Chapter Eighteen

LAMPS LIT THE GREAT CONFERENCE ROOM on the third floor of the manor. Their light spilled out of the windows into the domain of Larandaril, blessed valley of the sacred river, which bled off to the west and into the sea, carrying prosperity and commerce wherever it flowed. Lariel gazed out the windows, as quiet murmurs rose and fell at her back. She watched for late arrivals, knowing that Bistane might be close but not yet there, and Sevryn was traveling trails of his own, after having sent her dire news.

Despite the men who sat at her table, she felt alone. Terribly, unendingly, alone. She had called for a conference, yet the man whose advice meant most to her would never talk to her again. She clenched her hands, felt a pang of pain for an absent digit in her left, and unclenched quickly, to rub her scar. She no longer looked down at her hand and felt a faint surprise at the maiming; it had finally become a part of her. Perhaps the day would come when the loss of her brother would grow as dim.

She turned about in the lamplight. Indoors, the faceted

glow spread into every corner and reflected warmly off the heavily polished table that dominated the area. Dinner had been served and cleared. Tapestries were drawn against the windows that normally looked out upon the vistas of the kingdom, beautiful and lush, a land blessed with bounty, a jewel in the grasp of the Vaelinar. Inland from the hard-scrabble coasts of the peninsula continent referred to by the natives as the First Home, Larandaril cupped a life that, while not easy, gave up its bounty far more willingly than the rugged coastlines. She'd remade the pact her grand-father had with those Gods and demigods of the region, and held to it, and so the land cleaved to them and their welfare. There were those, of their own race, and of the native races of Kerith, who resented that pact, but Lariel knew the price beyond even that of her flesh and doubted that anyone else would have given it over. The land held them, but they also held the land. Reflected in the lamps' glow also were the figures of the handful gathered about it, standing and sit-ting, their finely boned faces and curving tipped ears lend-ing them an arrogance they wore as easily as the fine clothes and armor upon their bodies. As she turned to face them, and their voices quieted even more, her fondness for them braced her. Perhaps she was not quite as alone as she felt. All the men in the room knew that while Lariel Anderieon might ask them for their lives, her rival Tressandre ild Fallyn was more likely to take their lives and brutally, at that. Lara could never drag out of them what they would not willingly give. Their opinion mattered, it would be listened to, before the Warrior Queen put her thoughts into action. For a mo-ment, she saw the great bulk of Osten Drebukar at the table which made her blink and as she did, the much younger though no less doughty figure of his nephew Farlen occu-pied his place. Another loss she could not quite accept but must, there being no choice. The men turned to her as if knowing the moment had come.

She stirred now as if feeling the weight of their thoughts, but it was not she who spoke.

Farlen's hand chopped the air as did his words. "The

Ferryman's hold on our enemy is weakening. He is a dam which will break. When he does, we'll be wiped out unless we're ready. Sevryn's messages attest to that."

"And what was your first warning? The dairyman who had two dozen Raymy drop into his pastures from out of the sky? Or mayhap it was the lace makers' guild up the coast that suddenly found a handful of odd lace makers armed to the teeth within their circles? Indeed, I am told their guests were *all* teeth. Or did you not pay attention until they attacked at Calcort?" Tranta bit his caustic words off crisply. Only two of station occupied the vast room, the other two, scribes, sat with their pens busily scratching. Tranta ran fingers through his sea-blue hair. "I daresay it's not the Ferryman we need to fear but Daravan."

They spoke bitterly of the savior who had stepped into a war, a war they had been losing, and swept up their enemy in a tidal wave of river water, and carried them into a breach of time and place which only he and his brother, the Ferryman who tamed the most untamable rivers, could make. Daravan had warned them that he would lose his hold and they had better be prepared for the return. That had been two seasons ago, and the Vaclinars and their allies had no idea when the portal would shatter, when the Ferryman and his Way would collapse, the enemy spilling once more onto the lands they hoped to desecrate and conquer.

"We are like an archer with his bow long raised and string pulled tautly back, and praying only to be able to finally loose the arrow. We need an end to this."

Lariel ran her fingertips across the mail she wore still, as she had been doing every day since deciding a war was coming which must be fought, frowned, and said, "Do either of you know if it will rain the week after next?"

Farlen knotted his lips and then his brow, pondering, before giving up and saying, "Highness, it is spring, and the rainy season, but I can't foretell the patterns of the clouds more than common sense and a day or two will give you. I could send out and see if we can find a Kernan witch who reads the weather, but there's no answer I could give you."

Lariel looked to Tranta who shrugged, saying, "You ask if either of us is a diviner, and the answer is: no. Not with regard to the weather or to the collapse of the Ferryman. Such power in a Way has never been heard of or seen before, and none of us can duplicate a magic like that. Kerith seems to be shrugging off our weavings on this world. When will Daravan's hold shatter?" Tranta shrugged. "We only know that it will."

Farlen, looking every bit as forbidding as his uncle had looked in his heyday, merely growled a retort back in his teeth and slumped down in his immense chair. He flexed a large hand. "Has it occurred to you that these Raymy are hardly our concern? They were savaging these lands long before we arrived, and will likely do so after we return to our lawful home."

Something flashed across Lara's face so quickly that it was scarcely traceable, but Tranta saw it. His eyebrow rose ever so slightly at her as she put one hand, knuckled, onto the table. Underneath her chain mail, her dress of a soft but luxuriant green rustled, a sound faintly reminiscent of a rising storm wind through forest treetops. "No. What occurred to me," she answered slowly, "is that it took the race of the Mageborn to subdue them before, and there are no Mageborn who exist now. What powers they might have held and used were not recorded precisely enough for us to know what they were. The peoples who depended on them have no one now. No one except us, the invaders of Kerith, the intruders, the exiled. Should we care? Did we take their lands from them? Enslave some of them for decades? Yes, we taught them more than they might have known through the normal course of learning, but we took more than we gave. And, Farlen, it is our lands and our people who are threatened."

Tranta decided to wave a hand in conciliation. "I was fond of that dairyman," Tranta added. "Estate money is barely enough to replenish the herd and keep the farm going. If the son is able to step into his father's boots."

"They will manage," Lariel told him firmly. "As we all

will. I know the camps in the valley of the Ashenbrook are logistically difficult to keep, but we must. The valley is where the Ferryman made his stand and the Nylara is the river to which he was anchored for centuries. I have to maintain a lookout there as well. Common sense—and hope—tell us this is likely where the Raymy will flood our land when his hold is relinquished. The Ashenbrook first, but possibly the Nylara. When he can no longer hold the thousands he swept up, when the dam breaks, it should be here or here." She tapped her hand on the table. "We have to hope it is, because we cannot protect every small farm, village, and holding if it is not. The East remains in Galdarkan hands, and Gods know that Diort has his own burdens there to carry. We might call on him again or we might not." Her words faltered as her own indecision in that matter echoed.

"It may predict where the Ferryman feels he can make his last stand when his strength to hold the army of Raymy fails ... but it tells us nothing of what Daravan will make of the situation. The brothers may have disappeared as one, but it is Daravan who manipulated us for centuries, to keep us from learning of our true origins and our path home. His strategy nearly divided us even as we moved against the Raymy. And that, my queen," Tranta Istlanthir said as he turned to face her squarely, "that was what nearly lost us the first battle and may well undo us for the final."

Scribes wrote furiously.

"I can't wage a strike against an enemy which hasn't yet appeared. And I think all of you forget that Quendius had no small hand in this." Lariel raised a hand, rubbed her eyes, remembering the tiny fret lines she saw every day now in the mirror. Her blonde hair had always been shot with platinum, as light and gold and silvery as early morning light, so if the platinum strands had become more abundant, it was plain only to her. She fought to keep the strain of her emotions showing through her face and hands. "The weaponmaster gathered those troops and brought them down on us."

"He killed my brother and destroyed the Shield of Tomarq. That, we also know."

Lariel read the expression on his face.

Tranta lifted a shoulder and dropped it. "I am close to admitting defeat in restoring the Shield of Tomarq."

Lariel gave a slight tilt of her head. The fiery Jewel which rode the cliffs above the only natural harbor on the coast, and a considerable harbor it was, had been destroyed by Quendius and although she knew that the Istlanthir felt its loss deeply as part of their foundation, she had never held much hope for its restoration. It was a Way, the making of which gave the Istlanthir the foundation for their House, but those who had made it had passed, the secrets of their great working dying with them. That the Jewel had stood at all, taking the fire of the sun into its heart, and burning to cinders whoever trespassed on the waters below, had been nothing less than miraculous. Should one expect miracles to last forever? She said gently, "The Jewel was shattered. How could you hope to fuse it back together?"

"Because it always was, and is, more than a gemstone. I had hoped that the Way which ran through it might be instrumental . . ." His words trailed off, unwilling to surrender to a certain truth that he could not remake the shield. Yet Tranta had taken it upon himself to do just that, knowing that the great red stone, which moved in its cliff top cradle to eye the sea, had been one of the most significant and conspicuous of the elven Ways upon the lands. It knew those who trespasscd against its watch over the shores and bays. It called down the fire of the sun and moon and stars to burn away those who did so, and it had been unfailing in its trust in the centuries it had stood. Tranta had spent a lifetime climbing the sheer stone peaks above the harbor to reach it and make what minor repairs of the cradle were required from time to time. The stone itself had been immutable. He had first seen the spidery flaw in it to his great dismay, and it had been his brother who had died defending it when Quendius fired a Demon arrow into its depths, shattering gem and flesh.

Farlen cleared his throat. "Even if Drebukar could find another such gem in our mines, the size of a horse that one was, we could not say if it would replace the old one. And it was your parents who worked the magic within it. You know that, Tranta."

Tranta inclined his head for a moment, his throat pulsing as he swallowed. Then he looked up. "We have many fronts to protect and sitting on our asses in one place, the Ashenbrook, does not address our problems."

Farlen turned his big broad face toward Lariel. "On part of that, Istlanthir is correct," he said grudgingly. "But we dare not strike camps. We need to be in place, for when that wave breaks upon our shores, it will be nothing less than a tsunami. We know this. We've talked of little else for weeks."

"If it comes as a wave. What if it comes as fitful rains instead, drops here and drops there, until we're flooded? What if we are faced with hundreds of simple farmers who open their barns, walk to their pastures, visit their wells, only to find a company of the enemy ready to spring upon their throats? Pockets of them holed up in our countryside? A battalion ranging the streets of any of our cities?"

"What if, what if," Lariel answered bitterly. "What would you have me do?"

"Be flexible," both men answered in unison and then stared at each other a moment before looking back to her.

"I have Bistane traversing the northern portions. He guides his father's—" she paused to correct herself tersely, "*his* cavalries at will. That's all the flexibility we can afford and Bistane is only one warlord."

"The ild Fallyn have cavalries, too."

She raised her eyebrow at Farlen.

He muttered sulkily, "Well, they do."

"I'll never give an ild Fallyn command. They will go to war and ride at my request, and only then. That's the only way they can be contained because they only act when it suits them."

"You can't let old grudges keep you from a victory."

Lariel leaned over her forearm, staring down Farlen. "The old grudge you speak of freshened less than a breath before the Raymy attack, and if she had had her way,

Tressandre ild Fallyn would be sitting here today in my place. I blame her or Alton for Jeredon's death, though I can't prove it. Yet I would trust Tressandre before Quendius and it seems she's already tried to kill my heir."

"Harsh."

"But necessary."

Tranta pushed himself from the window and came to the table next to Lariel, sharing her space without touching her, his lamp-thrown shadow falling across her momentarily before he leaned over the map. "You have another choice."

"What?"

"Let Abayan Diort in, and give him territory to protect."

She gave a dry laugh. "And he is the reason I gathered my armies in the first place. Without an inkling that the Raymy were returning, I set myself against a dictator forcing clans of his people to unite under his banner, wanted or not. The only good he's done was to mobilize us, in defense against him."

"He is one of those wheels Daravan set to spinning, and he showed other colors when he found out the truth and honor that were needed. He has proven himself."

"Not to me," Farlen grumbled. His voice, not nearly as deep and basso profundo as his predecessor, still rattled comfortingly about the war room. The corner of Lariel's mouth twitched in fond remembrance. "I will, however, grudgingly admit to Tranta's point."

"He has to me." Tranta reached inside the cuff of his sleeve, withdrawing a small scroll of paper tied with a cord. "And Bistane agrees with me."

"I am ambushed."

He smiled softly at Lariel. "No, my lady Warrior Queen. You are merely being persuaded." He reached out, took her hand and turned it over, dropping the scroll into her open palm. If his touch upon her lingered more than necessary, both she and Farlen seemed to ignore it.

Tranta moved away then and tapped his chest. "Would I blame a companion who was not here to defend himself? Never."

Lariel opened the scroll and read it, a faint furrow between her eyes remaining as she did so. She let the paper snap back into place as she released it. "I'll think on this, gentlemen. Perhaps you forget that these lands are not mine to give away, none of them but Larandaril. At least you aren't pushing to have him court me." Both murmured, and she shushed them, slicing a finger through the air. "But before I do, I will ask my Hand what he thinks of this proposal." She stood. "When he returns. Any other news we should stew over?"

"Perhaps," he offered tentatively, "the Jewel can yet be of service. It still has certain protective qualities."

"I'll leave that to you. Then we are adjourned here for the moment. We speak of little new, but we all knew that. I . . ." her voice caught slightly. "I am not one to plot a war without the help of good friends and good advice. Stay the night and get a fresh start in the morning. Bistane has been delayed, but he should be here then, and I'll let him know what we've discussed. Sevryn carries more details that we should know." Her words sounded more hopeful than the tone of her voice.

Footfalls sounded in the hallway. Boots with studded heels, from the noise of them, resounding upon wooden planks where carpet had once lain and had been pulled up ever since an attack on this room had come with little warning and Osten Drebukar had been assassinated, his great bulk thrown across the doorway to protect the queen and others within. The scribes stopped scratching ink over paper and looked to the doorway in consternation.

Tranta raised an eyebrow. Lariel's chin went up in answer as she shrugged. She was not surprised at the late guest, for the border of Larandaril, though now open, still had wards that identified who passed it. She knew who crossed her boundaries, although she also knew the act might have been transitory and purposeless. She braced herself as talk stilled and the interloper paused in the doorway to lean upon the threshold.

Alton ild Fallyn, faint amusement in his smoky green

eyes and the lamplight giving his hair more gold than it normally held, he being a subdued shadow of his brilliantly green-eyed and wild-honey-haired sister, looked disinclined to enter without suitable recognition. If he resented being an echo of Tressandre, he had never shown it, wrapping himself in his own brand of arrogance. Indeed, his devotion to his sister often made others uncomfortable. He traced a slight bow to Lariel from the doorway. Trail dust lay upon his black-and-silver clothes and field mail, giving them a sooty and indistinctive look. "A council of war and I or my sister not invited?"

"A briefing is hardly a council, and for that I would not have wished to pull you from the lines. We are only dogs worrying at an old bone without meat. Though here you are, and it's fortunate. I will have fewer notes to send out. And yet, because you are here and not at your post, I have cause to worry. You have news? Shall I ring for supper?"

"Supper, I have eaten, but I do carry news. May I sit and share?"

"Always, my lord Alton, are you welcome at Larandaril."

A glint flashed in his eyes as he entered the room fully. "And so much more pleasant it is to visit Larandaril these days, with its borders open."

"As they should be during times of war to our friends and allies. Luckily, I can always close them if necessary."

"Still, it is nice not to have the threat of imminent death lingering against the back of one's neck like a sharp, cold chill."

"Oh, the threat is still there, Alton ild Fallyn. Just not as swift and without explanation as it might have once been. The borders of Larandaril have been lowered but not elim-inated." And Lariel smiled slowly as she spoke. "Our ene-mies are still recognized. Your business must be important, to have brought you from the lines without my knowledge or leave."

Tranta muttered something no one else in the room caught although Lara leveled her sharp gaze on him for a moment, and he fell silent. The lines of his body, however, took on a defensive stance, for there was no love between the House of Istlanthir and the Hold of ild Fallyn. The corner of Alton's mouth quirked as he strode to a place at the far end of the table and sprawled into a chair, a crust of dirt falling off the toe of his boot as he ignored the import of Lariel's statement. "News, then, as the hour grows late, and I presume we're all wearied. M'lady Lariel, Warrior Queen of the Vaelinar and princess of Larandaril, greetings from my sister Tressandre ild Fallyn, heir of the Fortress of ild Fallyn."

"And greetings returned," replied Lara, her tone deliberate and heavy as if the formal words offended her somewhat. Farlen twitched as if thinking to move himself between them, yet failing to do so.

Alton's teeth showed faintly through his smile. "I bring you news of joy. Tressandre ild Fallyn is with child, carrying your brother Jeredon's progeny."

A long silence fell upon his words, broken finally by Lariel taking a slow, deep breath.

Farlen did move then, saying, "It is probable she is pregnant. How is it possible it is Jeredon's? The man is dead."

Both of the other men stared at him, and Drebukar's ears reddened a touch. "Don't," Tranta told him, "make me explain sex to you."

Lariel's fingers sliced through the air. "My brother has been dead these many months, and it hurts me to think Tressandre withheld this from us."

"She delayed to make certain that she would be able to carry it, not wishing to raise anyone's hopes for a pureblooded heir. The rigors of the battlefield and training for further warfare do mark a woman's body more than a man's, though I own she has, and always will, hold her own among any. She does, however, now celebrate the pregnancy and offers the realization that a pure Vaelinar would be a far better heir than the Dweller crossbred Nutmeg Farbranch is carrying."

"How noble of her. Has anyone confirmed it yet?"

"Two healers and a priest who swears he can read the soul blossoming within."

"I seldom believe a Kernan priest," Farlen muttered. "If a priest was to be of any use, he would tell us what sex the child is, boy or girl."

"We've no reading on that yet," Alton agreed with Farlen, "although a hale babe would be a blessing under any gender, would it not?" His mild green gaze alighted on Lariel and lingered.

"Of course it would." Lariel lifted her chin almost imperceptibly. "Tell Tressandre that we welcome her news, and look forward to the day when we can see my brother's child born and healthy. I can hardly wait to recognize the stamp of his features on the child."

"And so I will." Alton got lazily to his feet, returning to the threshold and then pausing as if he'd almost forgotten something. "Shall I tell her you are preparing a Writ of Succession?"

"There is already a Writ in place, for the issue of Jeredon Eladar and Nutmeg Farbranch."

Alton canted an eyebrow. "My sister told me you would speak thusly, but I disagreed with her. Never, I said, would Lariel Anderieon replace a pureblood Vaelinar with a halfbreed."

"Then you are both wrong. It is not the fullness of the blood that will decide me on my heir."

Tranta and Farlen grew very still. The look between Lara and Alton held, and strengthened.

"You doubt, then, that she carries a child?"

"Oh, I am most certain she does. I think higher of Tressandre than that. What doubting I would have, if any, would be the paternity of it. If I had such a reservation. And, if I did, I would hold onto it until after the birth when things might be ... clearer."

"Sometimes when we hesitate until we can see clearer, we end up blinded entirely by our delay."

"That is possible. But hardly probable." Lariel's hand

twitched by her side. "The ild Fallyn must have forgotten that I have Talents as well as they."

"We would never be that hasty as to forget. Tressandre has bid me, then, to leave you with this information. In lieu of support from the family of her child's father, she may be forced to look elsewhere. Perhaps among those who seek to return and reestablish our lost roots. She is not threatening action but only telling you that it must be among her considerations." Alton gave a half-salute and retreated from the room, his boots telling of his movement down the hallway, quick and decisive but not quick enough to be call a full-fledged run.

Farlen let out a growl when the steps grew dim.

"She means to go to the Restorationists. How do you intend to deal with them?"

"Is that what they call themselves now? How can they hope to return to a . . . a rift which cannot be opened by their command and which holds only the unknown before them? We were exiled. Do they think to return and find welcome arms? They are idiots."

Farlen and Tranta nodded. She considered both of them a moment before answering slowly, distinctly, spelling out her judgment. "We've a war to finish, first. Then we shall deal with our countrymen who wish to attempt to return. The portal which the Ferryman left in his wake is both unstable and very weak, and I doubt their gateway is usable. If it were, we would know for a certainty that is where the Ferryman will return. For all the dreams of those who'd go back, I don't believe the way home is there. There has been no traffic through it, be it as slight as a gnat or formidable as the Ferryman and his tide of Raymy." Not in the weeks since those in battle had seen a glimpse of their home world, lost Trevilara, through the Way the Ferryman had opened. Home. Thought lost forever, and banished from their memory, and yet seen once more in the direst of circumstances. But it had been glimpsed, undeniably, and Daravan, the Ferryman, and the army of Raymy had gone there, indisputably, before the portal all but shut. That moment, to those who had seen, stayed emblazoned in their memory. It had happened once. Surely it could happen again, and there were bound to be those who wished to try going back even though Kerith had been the world for Vaelinars for centuries.

"There are those who wish to return now."

"Leaving our allies on their own to fight the reptiles?"

"Even so."

"They think they can force the gate."

Farlen shifted his weight. "Their actions tell us they do. I haven't the reports to give us details yet, however. Other than that they will be manipulated, if not headed by, the ild Fallyn."

Lariel sat down. "Madmen will always want more than they should expect." She traced a design on the tabletop. "I have other, more immediate problems. It can't be true," she remarked quietly.

"Of course not." Tranta moved a step closer to her. "Tressandre doesn't know the meaning of truth. Why didn't you reject her out of hand?" He gestured. "The sheer politics of it."

"I can't blatantly call her a liar to her face. There are too many who already mutter under their breath that I might favor Nutmeg and we can't even be certain who called for her death, not yet. I can't, without definitive proof, reject Tressandre's claim. You must know that, both of you." She rubbed an eyebrow thoughtfully before continuing.

"She is too late. My brother Jeredon did not marry Nutmeg Farbranch, but he knew she was with child, and he acknowledged this to me before witnesses and before we parted." She stopped, the sound of her lies drumming in her ears. Nothing on the expressions before her denied her words. Then she plunged ahead with what she did know. "He also said he would contrive a dalliance with Tressandre to distract her and her brother from Nutmeg, to protect her from any possible ill reaction from Vaelinars, since she is a Dweller." Farlen canted an eyebrow, but Lariel charged on. "As Lariel Anderieon, I will consider Tressandre's claim and the child will be welcomed into our line, but it won't displace Jeredon's legitimately recognized heir. If it . . . if it appears to be Jeredon's, I have to consider a joint rule. If she wishes to be so foolish as to take her child with her when they secede, then I will have no choice but to remove the child as an heir of House Anderieon. What she does beyond the Ways of Kerith, I can't condone or support if she's foolish enough to try to go back. As a Restorationist, she must make that judgment on her own whether 'tis better to take her baby into an unknown or remain here and raise it within our House, braiding an alliance between our two lines. I pray that she will see fit to conduct herself as benefits all Vaelinars." She paused, out of breath.

"Will you acknowledge it as Jeredon's?"

"How can I? We know it can't possibly be, but I will not start another war by openly denying it. By putting the child into our line, I can possibly keep Tressandre from both corrupting and manipulating yet another innocent life. Yet I can, and will, secretly make a determination that will hold all the proof we need of the paternity. The Anderieons mark their own, have no doubt of it, gentlemen."

Her last words fell into their silence. Finally, Tranta stirred. "Sometimes I forget you were tutored occasionally by Gilgarran as well as your grandfather."

"Let me bring Sevryn back to the fold and we can discuss it," Lariel answered wryly. "If we can find him first. I am told he has escaped the quarantine at Calcort, which means he is likely on his way here."

Both men smiled at that. Born on the streets, Sevryn could disappear into the villages or cities at will, and not be seen or heard of for seasons at a time. His elusiveness had always been on the queen's behalf and often her behest as well, but now he was much more accountable. His lady Rivergrace had tamed him. He never went far or long now, without her knowing of it. All Lariel had to do was reach out and tap into that source, and she would find her retainer. But the loyalties of Rivergrace still bothered Lariel. Not raised Vaelinar or perhaps not even full-blooded Vaelinar, her abilities and her mindset remained paradoxical, and in these times, when Lara had to be dead certain of those she depended upon, she could not. Where did her passions lie, where did she intend to journey, and how did the touch of the Gods affect her, if at all? No, she could not use Grace to keep her pledged man in hand, and Sevryn had made it clear that he would honor until death his pledge to Lariel. She had no evidence to make herself wary of him. Still, he had a mind and means of his own. He was up to something, of that Lariel could be certain.

She had to know what it was.

Chapter Nineteen

THERE WAS NOT A DAY when Sevryn did not think of revenge. He did not seek the thought out, not anymore, but it invariably found him. When it did, he would weave a web in his mind of the how and the way and the when, although never the why because the why of it had sunk into his very bones and never allowed him to forget. The threads of his thoughts trapped him as much as it caught his prey. Sevryn could say, now, that Rivergrace had freed him from most of those thoughts. She gave him the freedom to breathe, as it were, as long as she was close and safe, and when they reached Larandaril, a great stone left his chest and he breathed more easily.

He had a duty to report to his queen, as Queen's Hand, but he wanted to settle Rivergrace in first . . .

He lifted her down from her mount and whirled her, until her breathless laughter filled his ears and soul, and then he set her down on her feet, and backed away just enough to give her room to fill her lungs. She reached up and tweaked his ear as she tucked his hair behind it. He fixed his gaze upon her face as if he could drink her in. He touched her nose. "You've gained a freckle or two."

"Trips on the road will do that."

"You could take a covered carriage."

"Me? In a carriage? Never." She smiled wider. "How could I feel the rain in the air or trail my fingers across the river waters?"

He did not add that their travels had given him thought, the barest of hints, the thinnest of threads, of another plot beginning to be spun, but it didn't involve Nutmeg or Jeredon's unborn child. What, exactly, Sevryn could not yet be certain, only that as Gilgarran's apprentice, he'd been taught that any conspiracy should be at least threefold to be successful. The attack at Calcort had only been the first layer. He knew he would have to discuss matters with Lariel and leave yet again. That knowledge made him hold Rivergrace even tighter.

She had caught her breath, and the humor danced still in her eyes until he said, "She'll send me out again."

"Now?"

"She has to. I can hear things no one else can."

"I know." She touched his chin. "Would you tell me if you had?"

"I keep my queen's secrets," he said, a slight warning in his voice.

"I've always wondered if there'd been any sighting of my father."

"He fell. We both know that."

"And we both know he carried Cerat within him."

Souldrinker. He cupped her face. "Grace, if we were going to talk about this, it was best done under open skies coming here, where other ears couldn't hear."

"I know, I know." She turned her face away from him. Her auburn hair caught the muzzled sunlight in the manor stairwell and burned gold among the strands. Subdued, she said, "I think Narskap would have crawled away, if he could have."

"There are more important questions to be asked first. But I will always try to find you an answer."

She reached back then, to take his hand and squeeze it. "Thank you." She hesitated. "There's a gathering here."

"Ah. We'll take the back stairs up, then." He turned out the horses, then came back and laced his fingers through hers. "Quiet as mice, all right?"

Grace blushed faintly. He knew her abhorrence of politics and arguments, not that the down-to-earth Dwellers she sprang from didn't appreciate a good talk, but they were a frank people and the machinations of the Vaelinar drew their scorn. "You should join them."

"I should, but I won't." He lifted her in his arms and carried her up the stairs to her rooms.

There, laughing, she tugged off his riding leathers and he freed her from her clothes, and she welcomed him home as passionately and tenderly as he had dreamed she would. After, she pillowed her head on his chest, listening, he knew, to the beat of his heart.

"She'll be calling for you."

"If she can find me."

Rivergrace let out a snort, then covered her face in chagrin, and laughed harder. She managed, "How could she not?"

Sevryn raised an eyebrow. "She might not look here."

"Never here."

"She might not know I'm back yet."

"The stable boys don't know?"

"Of course they do, but they don't always tell everything they know." He flicked his hand toward his nearby pile of clothing, and a silver coin flashed between his fingers. "The lads have always appreciated me." He tucked the coin behind her ear.

She smothered another laugh on his chest, her breath warm and moist and fresh. He buried his other hand in her hair. "Stay, then."

"As long as I can."

She slid her arms about him and burrowed even closer.

The thunder of steps down the hallway from the floor above caught them standing at the doors to Rivergrace's small flat of rooms, his hands holding hers, readying to sneak down the back stairs for breakfast in the morning.

Lariel leaned over the railing, her hair tumbling unbrushed down about her shoulders, and faint bruises of unrest and unhappiness staining her eyes. "Sevryn! Tree's blood, no one told me you were back! I saw Aymaran grazing in the pastures."

He smiled wryly at the presence of his beloved stallion betraying them. He bowed slightly. He was her man, and this was her war, and she did not waste time.

"Forgive me. I have need of you, Sevryn."

Sevryn, his hand dropping away from its caress, met the gaze of his Warrior Queen and friend as she looked down from the railing above.

"It's always nice to be wanted."

"I don't doubt that. Have you been here long?"

"Not long enough." He let his gaze slide over Rivergrace's face. "We got in last night."

Lariel paused. "Have the replacement guards arrived at Calcort?"

"Not when we'd left."

"And the Raymy?"

"They dropped like bloated frogs, here and there, from the sky according to reports, and nothing like the army we expect. At this rate, and from the size of the force that disappeared, I'd say the sky could rain the enemy for a century or two before they're all accounted for." He frowned. "It's the disease that threatens us."

"One or two at a time, we can easily handle that but why do I doubt we'd be that lucky?" She tilted her head. "War is nothing I'd leave to chance. Nor plague. What other news?"

"Abayan Diort returns from his lands in the east to Ashenbrook, purportedly to lend assistance on the field."

Lara bared her teeth and absently tapped a fingernail on them. It was a gesture that, he realized in a moment of shock, Jeredon used to do, which was why it was utterly

foreign and startling to see her do it. She dropped her hand.
"The Galdarkan leader presumes too much. He hasn't been
invited this time."

"Perhaps he doesn't think he needs an invitation?"

"We'll see about that. In the meantime, there's this need
I have of you." She turned on heel on the landing above,
ready to walk away.

"I presume now?" Sevryn remarked.

Lara smiled wryly over her shoulder. "As always."

"My time is yours." He touched a kiss to his fingertips, let
them graze Rivergrace's forehead before turning away and
following Lara up the stairwell. The upper floors of the
manor were, as always these days, quiet. Many of those who
had been housed in this home of the Anderieon family were
now off encamped at the Ashenbrook.

Lara took a deep breath on the steps ahead of him and
rolled one shoulder slightly, as if shrugging off tension. "My
apologies."

Sevryn kept his tone as light and formal as hers. "None
needed."

Lara shook her head, her own silvery and blonde hair
cascading about her. The light chain mail, her leisure wear
for days now, caught at the metallic glints of her hair, hardening it. Her soft leather boots made little noise now climbing the stairs while his hard riding boots made considerably
more. Despite her lead, he'd caught up with her by the next
flight and they climbed to the final floor in silence.

She seemed still in a mood to apologize, pausing at the
door to her official apartment. "Usually I would ask this of
Jeredon—" A sadness passed through her eyes.

"I understand. How can I help you?"

She stood in the doorway, weight balanced at a slight tilt,
her hesitance evident in every fiber of her posture, expression, and speech. After a long pause, she said, "You are my
Hand."

"And have served you well, I hope." They both knew he
served more in his capacity as her Voice because his most
major Talent lay in his own voice, in his ability to persuade,

cajole, and command through his words. He seldom had to raise a weapon in her service although he was more than capable of doing so, and had. Publicly as well as privately.

"You have. What I ask now is your silence and trust."

His eyebrow ticked slightly as if it wished to rise on its own and he fought it. "Lara?"

"I have, for most of my life, kept my Talents quiet and undefined. I was taught to do so by my grandfather."

"Doubtless old Anderieon had a good reason."

"There is no doubt of it. Jeredon, as close to me as any could get, was really the only one who had any idea of what I can do." She added softly, in an under voice, not to him but to herself, "I miss my brother."

Sevryn made the slightest movement forward. "I'll do what I can to replace him."

She nodded and threw the door open wide to allow him in. He followed her to the far end of her apartment where a windowed turret held a spectacular view of the valley of Larandaril, across its pastures to its forests and hills, with the River Andredia ribboning through it. He saw a great carved chair sitting, turned to the window. Its arms were scarred where nails . . . or perhaps knives . . . had scored it over the years.

"I need you to stand watch." Lara sat down on the throne-like chair, but perched on the edge of it, still unsettled. "Had you heard—on the road, sometimes news travels fast, but I know you travel roads that few do. Tressandre claims to be carrying Jeredon's child. I'm attacked on those two fronts, as well as by those who want to force a return to Trevilara. I'm in the dark, and I can't let that continue."

"And you have hopes of changing that . . . how?"

She bent her face away from him, seemingly intent on unbuckling her weapons belt and removing it. She tossed it to the floor with a clank and a thump, far away from her reach. When she did look back to him, a stern expression ruled her face. "Sevryn, we haven't taken any formal oaths to each other; we've been locked in trust since the day we met, when you chose to save me and my brother, when you were nothing more than another half-breed living on the streets. I don't want to negate that trust, but now I must ask for your oath. What you witness here you will never reveal in any way to another living soul, under any condition. And if I cannot return safely, you will destroy the body that waits here."

Sevryn blinked. After a long moment in which his heart beat one, two, and then three times, he said, "Lariel?"

"Swear."

"With no further explanation?"

"With trust comes faith, they tell me." She sat unmoving. Unforgiving of his question.

Sevryn found his head dipping in an almost imperceptible nod. He cleared his throat. "I so swear, Queen Lariel."

"I take your oath as offered." She reached in her bodice and withdrew a small, sealed envelope. "If you are forced to take harsh measures, this letter will pardon you. Without explanation, but pardon nonetheless. Keep it. Burn it before leaving these apartments once I have finished and returned. Is that clear?"

"Clear as muddy water, Your Highness." He took the smallish envelope, stamped and sealed, and stowed it in a vest pocket.

The corner of her mouth quirked. "That's all the explanation you'll get from me before the task. Otherwise, what curiosity would keep you here?"

"Like Jeredon, not curiosity but love and duty."

"Ah." A sweet yet sad smile fleeted across her face. "Well said. All right, then." Lara sat back in her chair and made herself as comfortable as she could in the seemingly impossibly stark frame. "Oh, and by anyone, I meant your love, as well."

"Lara!" Sevryn let himself sound even more affronted and wounded than he was. "An oath is an oath."

"Yes, well. I know that Rivergrace is the sun to your shadow, the soul that completes your own, and you've not only lived but died together. Still . . . you can't share this with her."

"I will not."

"All right. Sorry to be placing a secret between the two of you."

"If she doesn't know about it, she won't know it's there, will she?" Sevryn tried to smile at Lariel, successfully because she returned it. He concentrated on holding it even after she looked back to her window and knew that she had placed a burden upon him which he did not wish but which he could not refuse. This was what it was meant to have a place by those who governed, if they did it wisely, and even if they did not. There would be moments of power and privy and a good many might benefit the many but be ignoble acts in and of themselves. He'd gone down that road before although Lara and Jeredon had never insisted upon secrecy before. This made the act she contemplated now all the more serious. He shifted his weight.

The sound of his boot leather upon her wooden floorboards brought Lara back from her contemplation. She tilted her head, not toward him, but as though she might find a better view out her window if she looked slightly toward the left . . .

"What I am about to do," she said softly, "Vaelinars cannot do. It's a Talent that few had ever held and those who have, were executed for, at the earliest known age of its manifestation. I travel with other souls."

"Foresight?" He knew of the rarity of the ability, but had never heard of a death sentence for having it.

Lara gave a quick shake of her head. "No. I'm speaking of possession. Possession that transcends both time and distance." She dipped her hand into a pocket and brought it out filled with material of the softest yet strongest spinnings. "Bind my wrists to the arms of the chair to make sure that I cannot loose my hands. Under no circumstance do you want my hands loose." She paused. "Other souls are not always kind or gentle or willing to travel with mine. And if I cannot come back, you can't take the chance of another soul coming into this body. There is too much power at stake. Do you understand?"

"Not entirely but enough." He cleared his throat a bit. "Has it ever happened before?"

"Several times with me." She ran a finger over the gouges in the wood. "But I've always been able to take control back. Still, I asked this of Jeredon, and I have to ask it of you."

"I agree. I'll do whatever needs to be done."

"Good." She went quiet as he bound her wrists, tested them when he asked her to, and stayed quiet again as he redid the knots on one of the scarves. When Sevryn stepped back, they both inhaled and exhaled sharply as if clearing away the cobwebs from what they did.

He took his position at her right. "How long?"

"Never more than a few candlemarks. I see what I need to see or if it's total folly fairly quickly." She bit her lower lip. "Coming back . . ."

"Is there anything I can do to ease the journey?"

"Call my name. You know that we take it, our label, into ourselves, given or invented, we weave it into our beings whether we love it or loathe it, and we will always answer to it if we are able." She put her booted feet upon the tiny wooden stool as if just noticing it, and rested the back of her head against the throne, and her attention on the window.

"All right. How will I know when you've. . . . gone?"

"You'll know," she answered faintly and went silent.

Sevryn wondered about that. He went to the bureau nearby, where another chair rested, and candles sat in handmade holders, clumsy holders. He picked one up, wondering why it had even been fired and painted, and saw her initials in the underside. The second bore Jeredon's. They had made these when they were children, probably little more than beginning to walk and play and craft at things. He set hers down and lit it, so he could mark the time.

He stood at her shoulder for the first mark and then finally returned to the chair and sat, watching the window itself as if he could see in its reflections what she might be seeing. At the passing of the second mark, the candle flame flickered and nearly guttered out as she violently kicked the stool from under her feet and her body went slack.

She was gone.

He could see her breathing. Her chest rose and fell in the tiniest of breaths, in a rhythm long and drawn out so that he feared he might miss a breath altogether and think she'd stopped. Small bubbles upon her slack lip. Her eyelids fluttered as if her closed eyes watched some violent dream yet refused to open. Gently, he slid the stool back into place so that her feet might not dangle in the air. He sat on the edge of his chair and prayed that he would not have to carry out her orders.

It had been said, over the decades, or actually whispered, that Lara could see through the eyes of the vantane, those great war hawks that the Vaelinar had brought with them to the world of Kerith. He knew it was likely she did, for she often had oversight that only those airborne could have held. But this. This confession of riding souls, of possession . . . could she mean it? He knew that Gilgarran had held suspicions about her Talents for the last few centuries, but he'd never put more than that to pen and paper, nor had he ever voiced them to Sevryn. Sevryn was a half-breed and not one raised in the shadows of any of the Holdings or Fortresses. He'd been abandoned on the village streets by his mother, and he knew almost as little about the Kernan as he did the Vaelinar. What he knew, he'd gleaned himself and hoarded, treasures of stories, scraps of family interaction, little bits of kindnesses punctuated by huge hunks of cruelty. Once among the Vaelinars themselves, he'd grown into his skin as it were, first under the tutelage of Gilgarran and then with the help of Lara and Jeredon. But Vaelinars rarely talked about their Talents, their true breadth and depth, because that made them vulnerable to others. That they had Talent showed in their multicolored eyes, although he was a throwback in that his eyes were a plain gray of Kernan heritage, and more than that the Vaelinar did not put on display. One either had Talent or one did not.

He had never heard of, not even whispered of or speculated about, an ability like that one Lara just described to him. Foresight was observed either in the body of the seer or from the outside, a detached observer, often with many entanglements so one single true path was near impossible to discern. The future was comprised of too many threads for its weave and final pattern to be perceived more than a day or two in advance. Sevryn found that comforting. Nothing could be set in stone as they all had a hand in making tomorrow, and all could change their contribution. But this. Lara spoke of total possession, of seeing the future and its outcome through another's body and soul . . . the thought of it rankled through him, setting the hairs on the back of his neck on end. What of that person? Where did its essence go when possessed? Had one ever been thrown back here, into Lara's body until she came to reclaim it? Her words hinted that it had. Her bonds told him that it was possible. Her actions spoke that it could well happen again, and if she were not able to regain herself, he had his orders. He chafed his arms uncomfortably.

He could see why she'd sworn him to an oath. Even that might not persuade her of his discretion. He could not lie to himself. His life would be forfeit if the Warrior Queen thought him a liability and at the very least, Rivergrace could be held hostage to his intentions. He did not have the upper hand in this bargain, and none of the wiles Gilgarran had taught him about becoming a Vaelinar that came readily to mind could give him the advantage. He would have to be very circumspect about Lariel now. She was his friend and benefactor, but she was also what Sinok Anderieon had made her, a truly formidable Warrior Queen.

The candle sputtered when it hit its second mark. Sevryn's gaze darted to it. He watched it closely for a moment or two and then realized the candle had been dipped with marks embedded in it, so that it might be read more easily. These candles had been made specifically for those waiting in vigil. Watching. Studying.

He crossed his booted ankles and began to take his weapons out, one by one, to sharpen and oil and examine for defects in blade or balance, a ritual he normally did in the evening before going to bed, much like a woman might

bathe and take an accounting of her body's health and
beauty, line by line, freckle by freckle, asset by asset before
rising from her tub to garb herself for the day's, or night's,
affairs. Although, truth be told, he'd only known one woman
who was that vain about her body: Tressandre ild Fallyn.
And she, also telling the truth, would then spend even more
time on her weaponry than he did. He had not enjoyed his
brief servitude as her lover.

Sevryn put his head down, after checking on Lara's
evenly breathing form for a long moment, and immersed
himself in his work. The day would be long and, he feared,
the night longer. He relaxed for a moment, and that's when
he lost himself.

Chapter Twenty

H E FELT HIS HEART GO DOWN HIS THROAT, and the thoughts in his mind scatter like a flock of birds an archer had shot an arrow through. Nothing remained of him but that which he caught by a will of iron, and felt himself imprisoned. Within what, he had no notion. A scene unfolded before him of a Larandaril he both knew and did not know. He was both there and not there.

He watched as they carried the Warrior King on a litter into the Dead Circle. A moment of panic hit him and yet it played across his eyes as a memory, so real it must once have happened. Sinok Anderieon sat up as they lowered the bower, swinging his legs over and crossing his arms, his brow lowered defiantly. He wore his mail but no helm; instead he used a bejeweled leather strap to hold back his silvery-white mane of hair from his forehead. He stared across the Circle. In the beautiful, enchanted valley of Larandaril, this alone was its singular blight. Perhaps it encompassed all the blight that might ever have entered but magic kept it out, one could not know; but nothing lived, crawled, or flew across its expanse. It was as if it had been blasted into the ground and lay, quietly lethal and sterile, for the rest of its existence.

One could step into the Circle. One could step out again, but whether the experience would be survived depended upon the reason for visiting the spot in the first place. Today, survival would have a high cost and perhaps not visit the trespasser at all.

The bearers of his litter, armsmen, not slaves, fell back several paces and into guarded stances. He looked once over his shoulder, the irony that a Warrior King might need protection not lost on Sinok Anderieon. He put his hand to his back sheath and withdrew the gleaming blade as if to signal that he was not as aged and helpless as observers might hope. The brisk late spring day brought spots of color to his otherwise graying complexion, perhaps the only obvious sign of ill health about him other than the way he had entered the arena.

He would not have been carried in if he had had any other choice. To expose a weakness among those gathered here, his peers, his own Vaelinars, was deadly. He looked about him, taking stock in the way a fighter did. Sevryn took stock even as the old king did, recognizing figures of past power. Gilgarran. Daravan. Bistel. The Istlanthir and Drebukars were here, and the ild Fallyns. Others who he could not discount but no one he feared more than the Hold he had recognized first: ild Fallyn. Lifting his chin, the old king met a gaze across the Circle, and Lariel, his granddaughter, did her best not to shy away from the Warrior King's intensity. She toed the line, waiting for the order to enter the Circle.

He strode across the Dead Circle as if breasting a river in full flood, deliberate, slow, and chest forward. He might be taking a risk but it was unlikely. He had been there before and strode as if he remembered it well; it was when he was on the young side of his prime, and it was where he won the confirmation of his title of Warrior King. He had gained it in battle and proved it in this arena. It was whispered in Sevryn's time that the trials Anderieon had faced were what had poisoned the Dead Circle. But only whispered.

Now it was another's time.

The call and chatter of nesting birds, which had quieted when the various personages came to ring the circle and then risen back to an unafraid raucous volume, silenced again. It was as though nothing dared to breathe while Sinok Andericon was in motion. He came to a halt at the far side of the circle where the candidates stood, sat, and squatted in waiting. He held his hand out.

"Lariel."

Grandfather. Father.

The realization of Sinok's place in her lineage jolted him. And that is when Sevryn knew what imprisoned him.

Not what, but who . . . he lay like a speck within Lara's mind. Her memory. The young Vaelinar with hair of many shades of gold both light and dark, with a touch of silvery platinum smiled faintly before answering his summons.

Lariel held an unquestionable poise before her grandfather and his enemies, unaware Sevryn rested inside her thoughts. She was, as always, uniquely herself. Her posture echoed the manner that was reminiscent of Sinok and that was as well, because she was his granddaughter and daughter, a thought that battled itself inside her. Sevryn tried to wrap his own mind about the incest and betrayal of Lariel's mother and could not. The young man she stood with looked after the two of them as she moved to answer Sinok. He was a grandson, but he bore little resemblance to the Warrior King except that his face was as finely carved and handsome as theirs. He wore a scattering of years more than Lariel but Jeredon Eladar did not show dismay that his sister was called forth before he was. In the set of his shoulders, it could be read that he did not expect to be. He was not the preferred heir of the old man. Sevryn rejoiced to see his old friend again but mourned what he knew of him through Lariel's thoughts.

Sinok clasped Lara by her wrists. He looked her up and down. "You are well equipped."

"Jeredon and Osten made a few suggestions."

"Wise of you to heed them." Both ignored the irony that

the two advisers were among the other candidates. Jeredon equipped himself like the ranger and hunter he preferred to be, and Osten leaned upon a great poleax, one of his more favored weapons, seeming unconcerned though his keen gaze was focused upon them. The son of the House of Drebukar was an opposite to Jeredon. He was nearly as broad as he was tall, muscular and heavy browed, and solemn of face. He wore his great sword strapped to his back and a throwing ax on his left hip. He, no doubt, had more weaponry placed within easy reach upon his person, but the mail and hard leathers that armored his body made it difficult to see them.

Jeredon had a baldric filled with throwing daggers, each of them as sharp as any razor, blades whisper-thin and handles balanced for the long throw. He had other knives for short throws and hand-to-hand, if needed, but had not equipped himself with them that morning. His hair looked as chestnut as the field foxes they had scattered before them in the grasses and brush when they rode in with the dawn, his hair braided and tied back tightly. The only weapon of any extravagance upon him was the longbow and a multitude of arrows filling his quiver. Jeredon returned a nod when he felt his grandfather's gaze upon him, and before he turned away from the Warrior King's harsh assessment, he threw a wink to his younger sister.

She felt it as she might a warming coal placed upon her heart: welcome and, in the chill of this morning, necessary.

Sinok took her by the wrists again and drew her close as if embracing her. Instead, he whispered into her ear, "You are my heir and choice. Remember that. This is only formality." Before he broke away, he slipped a dagger up each of her sleeves. The metal felt cold and deadly against her skin.

He kissed her forehead roughly even as he pushed her away.

Lara watched him return to his position across the Dead Circle and seat himself on the edge of the litter as if he sat a throne, which the Warrior King did not own but made out of any chair he possessed. As plain as any statement, he told her across the distance, that attitude owned the title, attitude and the ability to back it up. She toed the half-helm at her feet. When she put it on, she would tell herself that she had begun and would not stop till she had achieved that which her grandfather and Warrior King wished of her . . . or she was incapacitated.

She did not have the attitude. She knew that. She could call it up, more so than Jeredon who had never had the killing spirit that Sinok Anderieon wished engendered in his get, but never enough to truly please her grandfather. She did, however, have the ability, including the Vaelinar Talent that he had bid her keep hidden her whole life. There were many among the Vaelinars who whispered that she did not hold the power and Talents that ran in their bodies, but she did. It manifested itself early and often, and Sinok had taught her how to lash it down and tame it and use it only when she called it out. During those early years she had been a difficult and frightening and . . . occasionally . . . fatal child to nurture. Those servants who had dealt with her had been taken away and she never saw them again although she was almost certain Sinok had had them put to death. He did not wish his granddaughter's nature exposed.

Nor would he wish her to expose herself today. Not fully. Even as he expected her to prevail, he expected her to be circumspect in all things, for the day would come when she would need all she held within and without herself to triumph.

Instead, she had shown a brief and fleeting Talent in public to possess animal minds, particularly those of the war hawks, giving her some slight advantage over the battlefield. That Sinok had encouraged in her, weak though it had been at first, cultivating it until it, though not greatly valued among the Vaelinars, at least kept the rumors down that she was not worthy to be a candidate as his heir.

She stepped back, and Jeredon moved forward at her back.

"What did he gift you?"

"Two daggers. Throwers, I think."

"Only two? Likely to have poisoned blades. Take care if you must handle them."

She gave the slightest of nods. She had not yet donned her helm, so her hair hung unbridled over her shoulders and cascaded down her back. "And you," she murmured. "Remember the ild Fallyn can fly."

"Levitate," he corrected in his best big brotherly tone, before adding, "No doubt the reason I am here. I am used to bringing down the winged." He shifted his weight and the arrows in his back quiver gave the faintest of rattles.

At their right, the ild Fallyn candidates sat as quietly as great cats, their eyes of jade and smoky green watching them without blinking. Tressandre had hidden most of her beauty under the ebony-and-silver colors of her arms and armor, and her brother Alton stayed off her left hand, an echo of the same. Unlike Lara and Jeredon, the two were as ruthless and capable as their parent might hope. If any candidate here could take the position from her, it would be one of the ild Fallyn. By any means.

Osten coughed to clear his throat. The Drebukar was here because he deserved to be, but she knew that he had no great desire to reign over the sacred valley of Larandaril and the unruly families of the Vaelinars. Not that the Warrior King or Queen did so. No one House ruled, but the Council was undeniably influenced heavily by the Warrior King. The Drebukars were the stout shields that protected leaders, the savvy advice in the ear that gave leaders a battlefield advantage, but they did not carry the leaping insight, the drive, the vision that leaders often carried. To their credit, they knew and understood that.

Perhaps it had been different in the beginning, in their own lands, but as invaders here on Kerith and in the provinces known as the First Home, on the western coast of this sprawling continent, they could only guess at the true intent of the roles and titles they assumed. The Istlanthir were not here because they had their hold and their kingdom: the wide blue sea. They were staunch allies, but they also held an allegiance, a yearning, for the wilderness that lashed its tides upon their coastline. They cared not to rule land, but to conquer the unconquerable sea.

She looked to her father's right hand, where Bistel Van-tane stood, his silvered hair bare to the early morning sun, his heavy mail shining, his sword point down as if it could be a staff. He had a staff, a great piece of aryn wood slung across his shoulders, for the warlord was both a reaper of men and grain. His fields to the north rippled with winter wheat and ripened in the summer with the sweetest of or-chards, both fruit and nut, and the aryn trees, which grew best at his behest, made a living wall against the chaotic debris to the east, where the Mageborn had ruined the lands.

Bistel's son Bistane stood at his elbow, striding back and forth unhappily, for he had not been allowed to throw in his name as a candidate. Jeredon's peer, he had the right, but Bistel had stayed his hand. Perhaps he did not wish to cross the wishes of Sinok or perhaps he thought that the candi-dates might not leave a survivor standing, in which case, Bistane would be a necessary substitute. Or, perhaps even, since Bistel was already warlord in his own right, he thought it unnecessary for his son to participate in this trial.

From this distance, a look at the strong-nosed warlord could not give her a definitive answer to that question. He stood as still and silent as Bistane moved restlessly. Bistane looked at her across the distance, his face skewed in an ex-pression she could only read as dismay and anger. She could not signal him back that she would rather he not be in the circle, as she did not wish to face him.

There were other Forts and Houses with candidates. Bannoc whom she'd faced down before, pacing warily, as if knowing that he was doomed to fall again but fated to be within the circle anyway. Quarrin of the faraway Hold of Bytrax, a Hold which stood no more since a tsunami had swept away the ocean shore of their lands, but as a family they still remained. Quarrin had become their one hope to be given new lands and restore their name. He had the faintly silvery skin and metallic hair of his lineage and wore

a veil across his face in the manner of many Vaelinars who
had gone to the Eastern lands which had not been marred
by the Mageborn Wars. His sword held a great, curving
sweep and even though he wore his battle gear, she could
hear the faint sound of the bells upon his pant legs as he
moved slightly.

Those bells.

They would be the death of him, she thought, signaling
his movement almost before he would think to act.

Findorel, face etched deeply with lines, was near to Anderieon in age but obviously saw no reason why he was not
fit to take up the challenge to become Warrior King. She did
not fear him as much as the others, if only because his hands
shook now and then, and she knew a weakness ran through
his Fort's lineage, the quaking illness, and that he was already afflicted with it. If he should gain the title today, it
would likely be stripped away from him for infirmity. Still,
he intended to try. Lariel would take advantage of his stubbornness as well as his experience.

Lithe Samboca whirled away before she could meet his
eye, but he had always been a loner, not shy but almost as if
the company of another was unbearable. She had always
thought him strongly empathic, born and bred to be a
healer, but he was fascinated with the cutting edge of ob-
jects with a far darker purpose and so he was here, seeking
the title of Warrior King. If he won it, she pondered, he
would lock himself away in a tower without human contact
unless it was to battle and kill. A shiver of cold went down
her spine.

There were the charcoal-skinned twins of the far south-
east, two women with faces like sharp iron whom she had
defeated in skirmishes before, together and separately. She
did not overly worry about them unless she found herself
greatly outnumbered. Then and only then could the Iron
Wolf sisters hope to harry her to ground.

A quarter of the circle away stood a puzzling figure, one
who had petitioned to be allowed the challenge, but who, as
the very last of her line, gambled much. She could wait and

marry, and hope to perpetuate her bloodline the safe way—
or she could charge in headlong, and hope to gain a kingdom by winning this morning. Tiiva Pantoreth stood,
dressed in hand-me-down leathers and mail, her spine
straight, her chin up, her copper skin as dazzling as an early
sunrise, her thick, coiled hair bound into a snood of fine
mail, perhaps the only object about her that hinted of a
former glory. Her weapons at hand were serviceable, and
from the way she had stretched out and exercised a while
ago, she was good with them. She would need to be. She
glanced at Lara as if sensing her appraisal, and they locked
gazes for a long moment. Tiiva's mouth pursed slightly as if
she might say something, but she did not.

To her left, in the shadow, stood a figure all in black,
difficult to see, difficult to watch even with her full attention, masked as well, and for all his sinuous grace, she could
not have said if he were male or female although she
thought male. Nor could she name his House. She and Jeredon had eyed him when they rode in. He had already been
here, crouched at the edge of the Dead Circle, and her
brother had not responded to her muttered "Kobrir" when
spotting him.

Surely not. Not one of the assassin brotherhood. They
were not even Vaelinar. She had waited for the man to be
hustled off, but it had not happened. His presence was not
only tolerated but evidently had been invited.

She said very quietly to Jeredon, "Watch the Kobrir."

His eyebrow arched and he moved slightly, surveying
their area. After a long pause, he noted, "I no longer see one."

She shot a glance back at the shadows. The Kobrir had
not moved. In fact, as if feeling her eyes on him, his head
turned and his gaze caught hers. He dipped his head in the
barest of perceptible nods, before turning his attention back
to the circle.

Jeredon didn't see him. Nor, she thought as she scanned
the others, did anyone else. Surely she was wrong in that.
Could her grandfather see him? She could not tell across
the distance.

Tiiva Pantoreth tossed her head slightly, her glorious hair cascading over her shoulders as she took off her chain mail snood and then put it back on. A heat rolled through the morning mist, a heat smelling of musk and flowers and the faint aroma of a woman. It grew in lushness as it swept the grounds, grew in intensity and thickness until Lara felt cloaked in it, bathed in its warmth and alluring sensuality. She shifted her weight uneasily, distracted, wondering what had come over her. And then she realized it came from Pantoreth.

She radiated . . . no, smoldered in the new day sun. Lara could feel the heat tumbling off her, a sensual warmth that shivered over her own skin and warmed the pit of her stomach. Her heartbeat quickened. That would be one of Tiiva's Talents, sensuality, seduction, a call so forceful and primal that Lara found herself wanting to answer. No one else so much as stirred and Lara realized she'd felt the other gathering the power to herself before using it. She could feel it being drawn from the essence of all around her and took half a step forward toward Tiiva with eyes narrowed and mouth drawn. "Do not," she said softly, her voice pitched for Tiiva alone, "finish what you are thinking of doing."

Tiiva blinked. A long, slow, deliberate shuttering of her eyes. The corner of her mouth quirked upward slightly as she tilted her head and looked away, and the heat of the morning bled away as she let the power slip through her fingers.

There were half a dozen others. She had looked them over, noting their strengths, their probable Talents from their Houses, and not seen anyone she had not already bested in training tournaments. They would enter the Circle. Those who were pushed or dragged out were disqualified. The last one standing captured the title.

Or perhaps not even standing. Just . . . living. Lariel wet lips suddenly gone dry and put her hands up to sweep her mane of hair into a knot and placed the half-helm on her head. As if her movement had been a signal to him, Sinok Anderieon straightened his right arm toward the sky.

"At the fall of this banner, the battle begins."

He dropped the bit of silken cloth. It caught a draft, or perhaps a bit of ild Fallyn levitation, for it did not immediately drop. It wafted downward, gliding back and forth on a gentle updraft, moving on its own timeline, while she counted her heartbeats to steady them. She saw where the scarf would land, on his booted foot, right at the demarcation of the circle. That had significance, she thought fleetingly, but could not finish her observation as Jeredon let out a long, measured breath behind her. She knew where he was at all times, a sense between them that twins often had, though they were only siblings. She had hunted often enough with him and he with her that each knew instinctively where to place themselves to be most effective and yet stay out of each other's way. The same with what skirmishes they had faced. Of all people on Kerith, he was her most valued. He always had been and she could not foresee a day when he would not be.

She watched the banner drift slowly to its inevitable position, aware that others about the Circle stirred into movement, readying to strike, and she knew that the ild Fallyn could stay gravity with their powers. And that they would be in place first accordingly. It struck her what her grandfather planned. This was a battle, no doubt about it—but no battle was ever won strictly on the strength of arms alone. It took strategy and cunning . . . and in this case, would no doubt take holding the possession of that banner. It had not been stipulated. Crafty old man that Sinok was, it would never have been mentioned overtly. But he had said at the dinner last night for all to expect the unexpected, to be prepared for the unannounced, and to capture the essence of what would be demanded of them in the future.

This would be the most intensive maneuver to capture the flag that she could ever imagine. To win, she must get herself to the circle's center so that she could capture it when she willed to do so, and to defend it if anyone else had intuited Sinok's intention.

"Now," she whispered to Jeredon and sprang into the air,

readying to turn with weapons drawn, before the world returned to normal.

Osten moved along with them, a movement she sensed
rather than saw, his bulk stirring the very air and trembling
the earth slightly with its impact. He brought with him the
steadiness of stone and the quickness of liquid silver.

Even with her preemptive move, she barely missed
Tressandre's strike. Curved steel swung at her elbow, shearing off her bracer, sending a thrum up her arm, a message
of warning. Lara landed, kicking out and swinging her leg
about as she did, to bring it up, around and then behind to
brace her. Her boot caught Tressandre in the jaw, snapping
her head back and she retreated, shaking her head, an angry
red blossoming across her throat.

Across the circle, Fin had already slashed and put one of
the Iron Wolves out of the circle. She could see a movement
toward the downed woman, healers in motion. It mattered
little. One less, the better. Tiiva stepped across the circle
deliberately and into sparring position opposite the veteran, dropping her shoulder slightly as she brought her katana up. She faced Fin, kicking back with one leg, dropping
her cloak on the ground as she did so, serving notice that
she would take no prisoners.

Lara jerked her attention back to their duel. She parried
Tressandre away again, more worried about Alton. Alton
had been tempered by the ild Fallyn like a smithy does forg-
ing a sword, all to succeed not only his own hierarchy but
that of Sinok and Bistel as well. The ild Fallyn would have
it all and even then, Lara realized, would not be sated. Jeredon grunted as he leaped into the air, avoiding Alton ild
Fallyn's rolling tackle, meant to sweep his legs from under
him, and with that, the main event fell into position.

It would be the two of them against the two ild Fallyn.

For long moments, that was exactly how it played out.
And then Lara felt the others still standing moving into
play behind them. Osten muttered a guttural oath and
shifted his bulk, she could feel the ground practically
shake under his booted feet as he did so and she knew that

the survivors had decided to join ranks, at least for the moment.

Her ears rang with the noise of clashing weapons, grunts of strain, the slap of armor being hit and hit hard, the gasps of effort and pain, and a muttered aside here and there. She knew Jeredon guarded her back as she guarded his. Tressandre leaped away for a breather, but a flicker in her gaze gave away her real reason and Lara took a bob to her right, and parried a slicing blow, thigh-high, from Quarrin, his bells shivering as they met. His blade slid downward, and he used his balance to throw a kick at her. She saw it coming. With a twist, she kept it from slamming into her temple, taking it on the point of her shoulder instead, but it still rocked her. She went with it, letting its momentum take her down to one knee, and it was there that her power thrilled through her, and she knew what the next few moments could hold for her. A leap, a turn, a killing thrust . . . it brought the taste of bitter, metallic blood to her throat to see it, to hold it in her thoughts, the inevitable which had not, but would, happen.

Lara went down, rolled, and kicked back up, making it to her feet and steadying herself. She took a deep breath. Sequence one, broken. No time to celebrate. She had two on her before she could take a deep breath, but Jeredon took out the second with a wicked slash low to the ankle and Findorel fell with a sharp cry, not cut but feeling the blow through his shattered bone. She grabbed his wrist and dragged him out of the circle, getting a breather for herself for no one attacks a rescue operation. They did not dare, nor did they mind observing the nicety, for it put her face-to-face with three who did not want to let her back into the depths of the circle. Alton ild Fallyn, Quarrin, and Tiiva.

She reacted to the sound of the bells, betraying the southerner's gathering of muscles, and she put the butt of her sword hilt into his head, behind his ear. He dropped. She put a hip into Tiiva and spun past her, only to see as she did that Tiiva went after Alton instead of her own exposed flank.

The lunge failed as Alton went to one knee, letting her

speed carry her past him, and when he rolled off, his gaze
was on Lara, not the Pantoreth fighter.

There would be no further pretense here this morning.

It would not be a matter of one of them pushing the
other out of the Circle. No.

This was for the death.

Alton leaped, both hands filled with his silvery blades, and
he took flight with that astonishing lightness that graced the
heirs of ild Fallyn. Sequence two, begun. Lara slipped her
dagger from her left sleeve and readied to throw it.

She had not foreseen what happened next.

With a curse and a defiant shout, Osten stepped in front
of her. Alton came down, his sword cleaving Osten's face in
two and her friend went down in a wash of crimson. She felt
the warmth splatter her own face. Jeredon gave out a maddened cry, pushing Alton away from Osten. He took a slash
from Tressandre on his backhand even as he bent over Osten
to protect him, reminding Lara of the mother bird who feigns
injury and covers her chicks' bodies with her wings as she
does. She drove in to drive Tressandre off and ducked as
Tress spun away and then came back, her mouth twisted in a
sneer, but Lara had stepped back, grabbing the lithe Bannoc
who had fallen and staggered back into the fray, and used
him as a shield. He deflected the shot, but not without injury,
and Lara swung him by his wrist off his feet and out of the
circle where he fell into the arms of a waiting healer.

She staggered back into an embrace, hot mouth against
the side of her neck, and felt a blade edge along her throat,
just under the protective strap of her helm. "Did you see
this, I wonder," Samboca hissed into her ear. He kicked her
ankles apart and tightened his grip. She looked into Jeredon's wide eyes, knowing her front was exposed to any who
might want to put a sword into her ribs, exposed except for
him. He stood over Osten's moaning figure, his eyes locked
into hers. And then he dropped his gaze to her right hand,
where she still held her throwing dagger, the last-minute
gift of Sinok.

Undoubtedly poisoned. All she needed was a graze. But held as she was, any slight tensing of her muscles would telegraph her intention, her planned movement, her action, and her throat would be cut. Even now, she wondered why Samboca hesitated. Then she knew why he had asked the question he had. He'd felt as she had. He would feel as she would. He held a shadow of her forbidden Talent.

Corrupted empathic senses. He'd read her.

"Will you bleed as much as Osten?" Samboca purred. The heat of his words flowed down her neck, but she stilled any response to that, unwilling to feed the bridge of feelings they shared.

Instead, she watched Tiiva Pantoreth bear down on the two of them, her sword loose in her hand, her face expressionless, the copper of her skin glowing with the exertion of the sparring, her eyes focused on Lariel's face.

Samboca locked his arms tighter. "Sweet to kill," he murmured. "Sweeter yet to be killed without dying." He would enjoy being entwined with her as she died more than he would enjoy slitting her throat. He stood steady and gave the last survivor of House Pantoreth her target.

Tiiva took a steadying breath and drove her blade deep. Samboca gasped before Lara did. He rocked back on one heel, arms loosened with the feel of the steel driving deep, hotly, fatally . . . into his torso.

He gurgled a protest at Tiiva, loosed one arm and feebly tried to stab back at her as she said, "It seems I missed Anderieon." She twisted and slammed her blade downward before tugging it out of Samboca's body.

Lara threw off the arm spasming about her neck and shoved Samboca away. He crumpled, blood foaming from his mouth in a wrenching gurgle, and curled upon himself as if the death agony was almost more than he could bear. He looked up at Lara. She heard his last whisper.

"What . . . did . . . you see?"

What she had seen, she would never reveal, and as he lay dying, he could never reveal that she *could* see. The House of Pantoreth had not only saved her life, but preserved her future. Why?

Tiiva gave her a nod as she stepped back and cleaned her blade in the sterile dirt of the dead circle. Lara moved to the side, heard the faint sound of bells and whirled, letting her dagger fly. It sank hilt-deep into Quarrin's neck, the veils of his headgear torn and fluttering, then turning crimson as his eyes rolled back in his head.

Now only a handful remained.

She turned and ran.

She could hear the gasps of surprise from observers ringing the circle. She dove at her grandfather's boots and took the banner from the ground, from just inside the circle where he had nudged it and when she rolled to her feet, she held it aloft with a cry of triumph before stuffing it into her chain mail.

Surprise, then dismay crossed Alton ild Fallyn's face as he and his sister realized that besting in arms was only part of the prize, and they had yet to take either Lara or Jeredon down or obtain the flag.

She took three quick, yet deep breaths, charging tired muscles to answer her yet again.

Tressandre smiled slowly, her lush mouth curving into a grim line. Her hips swayed as she settled into her stance, and she quirked an eyebrow, waiting for Lariel.

It crossed Lara's mind then and only then that she had been waiting for Alton to take the initiative, getting into position for the final attack, when it was Tressandre she ought to be fearing.

Tressandre who held the ambition.

Tressandre who would stop at nothing.

She should have known.

Now she would never forget. Lara took the battle to Tressandre, and prayed that Jeredon could handle Alton.

And she watched for Tiiva at her back.

Tressandre moved like quicksilver, black-and-silver shadows of grace and deadly precision. A smear of blood graced one high cheekbone. A bracer hung raggedly from her left wrist, perhaps broken by a shot from Osten's axe earlier. But she stood unshaken and raised her left hand to beckon.

Come and get me.

Lara smiled. *Oh, I will.*

But not in a way that Tressandre could expect.

Her katana in her right hand, she pulled the second dagger with her left and threw it even as she moved in with a confident lunge. Tress knocked the dagger out of the air instinctively with her own drawn sword, but that opened up her flank for attack . . . and Lara answered with a slash across the ribs that drew a gasp from Tressandre even as Lara spun away, and fell back on guard for a response. It came immediately, Tressandre's smoldering calm utterly broken.

The blows came fast and furious. Lara parried, answered, and circled, her ears filled with the scream and ring of metal against metal and Tressandre's short grunts of exertion as she pounded at Lara's skills. They fought with swords and kick blows, turns and lunges, until both fell back for a long moment, gulping down air and energy, steadying themselves for another bout. From the corner of her eye, and the look of shock on Tressandre's face, she sensed a wild movement.

It was then Alton leaped.

His sweeping sword aimed at Lariel's neck. She looked up, with no place to go, caught between the point of Tressandre's blade and his fall. Her brother lunged to shield her, his body twisting through the air. Alton's blade drove on.

He impaled Jeredon through the shoulder, even as Jeredon stabbed his own sword upward, thrusting it through Alton's thigh. Face-to-face, they tumbled to the ground and lay still.

"Coward," spat Jeredon.

Pain creased Alton's handsome, sulky face as he responded, "Loser. Always in your sister's shadow."

"By my own will. I am not a dog begging to be allowed at my sister's heels."

They strove against each other a moment, setting their blades even deeper.

Lara heard the barest of movements and swung about, catching Tressandre's weapon on the tip of hers and tossing it off, thrusting it from her grip, disarming her. Grimacing, Tressandre put her hand to the inside of her baldric, filling her palm with the many-edged silver of a throwing star. Lara stepped back and then made a running leap of her own, both heels, into Tressandre's chest. She flew back, out of the circle, and onto her ass even as Lara fell flat and fought for air.

She looked up. A shadow against the sky caught her gaze.

The Kobrir looked down at her and shook his head. He pointed to her flank. She flung herself to her right and got to one elbow, to see Tiiva Pantoreth begin a move.

Whatever it might have been, Lara did not allow her to finish. Her senses flared. She scrambled to her feet and, grabbing Tiiva by her slender wrist, whipped her out of the circle before she even knew she'd been caught.

Then there were just the three of them, Alton and Jeredon muttering low curses into each other's pale faces while their blood slowly stained the dirt, still grappling and making it impossible for either one to get to his feet.

Lariel gathered herself, weak in the legs though she felt, arms aquiver with the weight of her weapon, and she pulled the banner from the neck of her chain mail. She put the tip of her sword through it and held it aloft.

"I stand alone!" she cried.

And so she did.

After Alton and Jeredon had been carried from the field, and after Sinok had sat down triumphantly on his litter, and after Tressandre had promised her an uneasy future with her title, and after Tiiva Pantoreth had been made seneschal of the manor of Larandaril for her effort against Samboca, Lara finally left the Dead Circle. Osten had been carried off, his face staunched and forever a ruin of what it had been, and the bodies of those with failed hopes taken to be attended for the rites of death.

No one stayed to talk with her. No one but a shadowy man who seemed not to be noticed.

Lara looked at the darkness-swathed Kobrir. "I owe you thanks."

"You need to learn to think like an assassin. There are no friends, only foes. And more importantly, when you drop a foe, make sure he stays down."

The corners of her eyes crinkled a bit as she eyed him more closely. She saw storm-gray eyes watching her through his mask, but they were not the eyes of a Vaelinar. "Who *are* you?"

"That is not the question you should be asking. The question you should be asking is—who will I be?"

In a flash she did not see, his hand shot out, and a thin blade traced her bare throat, eliciting the smallest of blood trickles before he turned and disappeared.

In her mind then, Lara did not know the assassin.

But Sevryn did.

Chapter Twenty-One

SEVRYN ALMOST FREED HIMSELF. Her surprise and shock as her own blood dribbled over her fingers nearly drove a wedge between their minds so that he could separate himself, but it was not enough. Her ties to him were tempered and layered like steel in a well-forged blade. Nothing less would surprise him. He knew Lara's will almost as well as he knew his own. Perhaps better than he knew Rivergrace, for he had been at the Warrior Queen's side far longer. She clung tenaciously to him now without even knowing how she had bound him to her consciousness. He was her anchor. He was to bring her back . . . except that she had dragged him along.

Sevryn wrested a niche for himself, a Way within the Way that she fabricated as she searched for the future. He found a place next to her temple, so that he could see through her eyes, hear through her ear, and possibly even speak through her mouth if he had to. He made himself as small and inconspicuous as possible, as though she carried a gnat with her, and fought to stay as he had made himself. He knew nothing of her Talent except what he was experiencing and from what little Lariel had told him, he doubted she knew a great deal of it herself. If she had suspected in any way that he or Jeredon or whomever else she might have used as an anchor would be open to her memories, or soul, she might never have allowed it. She could not have afforded the chance. He rode inside a pocket of her mind now that gave him a window he wished he did not have.

There were many things about the Warrior Queen he did not want to know. There were far more things about himself that he did not wish her to learn. He hunkered down, finding a place of calm, putting himself into a position of ease and yet readiness, a position that was only figurative within Lara's mind but which he felt that his own physical body would take. He sat with both legs in front of him, knees bent and feet flat, his sword across the tops of his knees, his palms upon the blade. He had often meditated like this, and his mind and body fell into the routine, guarded, centered, and yet at a kind of peace. He didn't think she could find him here, even if Lara searched, and he sheltered himself from the storm of her thoughts and memories skittering around him like storm clouds lashed ahead of a strong wind.

Like dreamtime, it seemed to stretch forever and yet, when Lara stirred, coming to a sudden and sharp consciousness, it seemed as if no time at all had passed. Yet he knew better, for the blade had grown warm under his hands. He came alert. A whirlwind of her thoughts wrapped around him—sight, sound, and smell—until he realized what she searched for: that first moment of battle when the enemy engages and the body reacts with the recognition of that encounter, readying to fight back or run, as that enemy is recognized. The Raymy. Lara searched for the Raymy. Unwilling to wait indefinitely for the devastating wave that would mark the return of the reptilian soldiers, she was going to meet them on a future day, possessing a body which might or might not withstand the attack.

He sensed Daravan, but the man twisted out of her reach time and time again, and he would not give away the secret of their returning. Sevryn held his breath as he felt Lara

sifting through souls as one might sift the wheat from the
chaff, lives running through her fingers like grain. He tried
to turn away from the invasion and could not, although he
managed to buffer himself from the wrongness of her actions. She was desperate. He could feel the panicky edge of
her own thoughts and emotions even as she searched
harder and faster. Then she had the unwilling, unsuspecting
host she searched for, and dragged Sevryn in with her.

The vision of forest and meadow burst before Sevryn in
vibrant greens and the myriad colors of wildflowers. He felt
the bow in his hands, an arrow idly held before being set to
the string, his heart beating in time with that of the archer.
He recognized the man even as Lara did: Chastain, a disci-
ple of her brother Jeredon, a good man, young, eager, and
in this moment, frightened as he stepped in to flank Lara
herself and the air rang with the noise of swords being
drawn, horses being reined around tightly into formation,
shields being brought up, orders shouted across the din of
men, and Raymy moving into contention. Hundreds upon
hundreds of Raymy. They stank of saltwater and a dry,
musty under odor. Lizards did not carry an animal stink to
the Vaelinar nose, although perhaps they did to the war
dogs that barked loudly and bounded across the fields.

The vision showed Sevryn that they had not stepped into
this possessed body at the beginning of the fight, however.
A regrouping perhaps, a defensive formation, because he
could now see across the grasses where many dead lay and
a thought ran across Chastain's mind that his quiver must
be less than half full now and that he would have to draw
his sword and close on the enemy soon. When the queen
did.

Now Sevryn had to hang tightly onto himself, for he was
drawn not only into Chastain but into Lara herself, warrior
Lara, Lara looking across the field and assessing what she
needed to do to stand against the Raymy. Assessing where
she was and how to best hold the ground and where best to
retreat strategically if necessary, waiting for Bistane. Yes,
she waited for Bistane and his troops, on the way, so close

and yet so far. Ironic that the ild Fallyn were here and he was not, but that was war, was it not? Enemies always close.

Far off, the horns sounded. Lara's heartbeat jumped. Here came Bistane, as hoped for, as promised, as *needed*. A flurry began among the Raymy as they knew they were being flanked, and half their forces began to swing around, to face attack on another front, and set themselves into position. She could not allow them that luxury. Lara stretched her neck, and bellowed, "Archers!"

Off to her right, she could hear Sevryn echoing in his Voice, using that Talent of his, to repeat the order, making sure that it would not only be heard, but followed: "Archers! To the fore! Set and fire!"

Caught in her mindset and that of Chastain, he could see only a peripheral movement in the corner of his eye, which the possessed Lara noted had to be Sevryn and mostly likely Rivergrace. She did not turn her attention to them, worrying instead about the Raymy and their placement to face Bistane, wondering how she might warn him, then deciding the warlord, young as he was, had inherited all his father's finer instincts.

Yet, Sevryn and Lara as observers, could not ascertain the where of the battlefield, only a hint as to the when, that it was early enough in the spring that maiden's nod still bloomed among the grasses, and that the wind carried a sharp edge of chill to it. As one mind, they noted no sign of Abayan Diort or his Galdarkan forces in the battle. Whether that was for good or ill would be decided on the outcome. He had either abandoned them or failed in his vow to support the war. Or perhaps he was behind them, holding a strategic point, and they had outflanked his position. Lara could not tell from her possession of her future self, as if something blocked all but the most rudimentary knowledge. Perhaps it was Fate protecting itself.

Perhaps the Warrior Queen simply did not know.

The Raymy decided that they would leave a token resistance to Bistane on their flank, and that their real goal would be to take down the Vaelinars they faced, and they turned almost en masse to Lara and her battalion. Archers fired. Arrows blackened the sky momentarily before falling in a wooden rain that took its toll, but not enough.

Never enough.

He heard a cry. Rivergrace's soft, yet strong voice rang out in denial. "Never!" A golden river of flame sprang up, walling them away from the Raymy. He could feel the power sucked from him/them to fuel it, feel an answering weakness which they/possessed Lara could ill afford and yet . . . and yet . . . the flames stopped the Raymy. He could feel the searing heat across the meadow, smell the cloth and leather gear of the fighters smolder, and flesh of the dead begin to crisp. He gagged. Lara choked. All one and the same.

A strangled cry behind them. A virulent curse. One of the ild Fallyn. Behind them? No, thought Sevryn. Lara would never be stupid enough to leave both ild Fallyn behind her. Would she? Even in the heat of battle?

Possessed Lara reined her horse sharply, sword out, turning as Sevryn called out, "LARA!"

Turning in her saddle, turning in the meadow, even as the tide of the battle surged around her. Now Lara sensed the danger and began to pull back, out of her future self, the scene dimming, sound bleeding away, color fading. A rider all in Kobrir black, face all that was recognizable, drawing a sword to charge at her.

Future Sevryn coming at her, blade in hand, swinging. Gray-and-black–shadowed garb surrounding him.

Silvery blade catching the rays of the sun.

A heavy impact and slice of pain. Sharp, tearing pain. Lara pitching forward in her saddle, losing her seat.

Losing her life.

Chapter Twenty-Two

HE FOUND HIMSELF. He surged out of Lara's memories and possession whole, if shaken, his body dripping with sweat, his sword in his hands as he'd imagined it, on his feet in the attack defense position. Defense, not offense. It couldn't have been him. He did not have the angle but another had. His forearms ached all the way to his shoulders. He'd taken a blow to his weapon, deflecting it. But not enough. Not enough to save her entirely from harm. And then, he was back, here and now. Lara sat in her wooden throne, nails dug into the arms, leaving new and ugly grooves in the wood. A slack expression rode her face, and underneath her blue-veined eyelids her eyes moved restlessly as those caught in a nightmare or fever-delirium did. He wanted to rouse her, but he couldn't. If she had seen as he thought she did, if she remembered as he remembered, she would believe that he had tried to kill her. The blows had been that close, shearing through the air and blades skimming off one another. She would think the worst of him.

But he had not. He knew it as well as he knew his love

for Rivergrace. He knew it as well as he had ever known anything in his soul.

But he could not disprove it.

If he stayed at Larandaril, he was a dead man. The same for Grace. When Lara came to, she would not, could not, allow him to live, knowing what he knew and having tried to do what she thought she saw and felt. She couldn't afford to take the time to wonder, to puzzle things out, and had no one she could trust from whom to seek advice. She would have to act and act decisively. A cold shiver touched the back of his neck as he relived a moment of cold steel slicing deep.

He touched two fingers to her temple and loosed his Voice. "Sleep."

She took a shuddering breath and her body sagged down onto the throne. Sevryn considered her for long moments. Dare he try more? Dare he twist and corrupt his ability even as she had, to save his life? He might be able to re-braid her observations.

He wouldn't do it for himself. He knew how to survive. How to dodge and dissemble. He might do it for Rivergrace, but . . .

What if Lara also forgot the information she'd staked everything to gain? What if she forgot about the Raymy? Bistane? All she'd hoped to learn. She'd hoped to turn the tide of war in her favor, and she might have. He would be but a single fatality in that effort if he failed to keep himself alive. If he twisted her mind now, there might be hundreds, even thousands more if the return of the Raymy army was not met in force. This was war.

Sevryn sighed. He traced his fingers across her forehead, moving a tangle of hair from her eyes for when she would awaken. His Voice still rested deep within his throat as he spoke to her. "Think well of me. Even when you do not wish to do so, think well of me. Know that I lived as a brother to you and Jeredon. Remember that even when confronted with what you think you know. That's all I ask." He had so much more he wanted to say, but he cleared his throat instead, stifling his impulse. He'd made his decision and now he must live with it.

He did not dare to stay at Larandaril to see if he had persuaded her.

Sevryn turned away from Lara to abandon the only true home he had known for most of the decades of his life. Life as a Vaelinar half-breed had been dangerous, but life as a full-blooded Vaelinar was far more treacherous. Lara and Larandaril had been a haven, though surrounded by a sinister moat of Vaelinar schemes. She and Jeredon had thrived on it while Sevryn settled for survival.

He went directly to Rivergrace's apartments. She sprawled on the divan by the window, her gaze fixed on the scene beyond. She came to her feet gracefully but said nothing as he raised his palm. "Pack. Take as little as you can but everything you need."

"How long a trip?"

He paused a moment. "We're likely not coming back."

"Lara?"

"I've lost her trust."

Her eyes widened, those lovely eyes with hues of blue and aquamarine and a dancing gray-blue, but she didn't ask anything further. Wordlessly, she turned and began to gather things. Extra pair of boots. A waterproof hooded cloak. A few vials and pots of creams and medicines. Two pairs of riding pants, one pair of suede chaps. A skirt. Two shirts, and one overtunic. She paused at the last item: a cloak he did not remember seeing before but surely he had, there were few secrets between the two of them. This rippled as a kind of nothingness, rather than a dark material, and he blinked as he tried to fix his eyes upon it; but before he could say anything to question the garment, she had it placed out of sight in her saddlebags. A few more things packed in. Her slim hands paused over the leather flaps of the bags. She took the second pair of boots out, hesitating.

"Take them," he said. "We may not have time to find a cobbler or wait for his crafting."

Rivergrace nodded. She tucked them back in and re-

arranged a few items. Her packs were full but not overly so.
She could carry them herself if she had to, and their burden
would be negligible to her mount. He had taught her a few
things, it seemed.

"Yours?"

"Never unpacked." He went to the door.

Rivergrace took a step to follow before turning around
and scanning the room. She scooped up a last item, a ribbon-
tied packet of letters from her desk. He recognized Nutmeg's
bold and sassy scrawl and smiled. Nimbly adding them to her
bags, she slipped out the doorway ahead of him. They took
the backstairs, which were now steeped in shadow, and no
one saw them leaving after he gathered his things.

He left his beloved Aymaran grazing in the pasture. Rivergrace watched him curiously as he selected two good, honest horses: Glow for her and Pavan for himself and she
helped him saddle them. If she had had any doubt that he
did not think they were returning, that proved it. Whatever
he thought they might face, there were certain parts of his
heart he would not subject to the trials ahead. She wondered if he had battled with himself whether or not to bring
her as well, but squelched the question.

She swung up, two sets of packs now on each horse, the
second set full of grain and hardtack biscuits which the
tashya, the hot-blooded horses of the Vaelinar, particularly
thrived upon in hard times. Glow flicked her black-tipped
ears forward and back as Grace settled in the saddle, pushing her boots deeper into the stirrups. Glow slid one fore
hoof forward to paw at the ground in dainty impatience as
her gold-dappled hide rippled. Sevryn mounted and pivoted his horse about, not a word or whistle or last apple
thrown to Aymaran in farewell. She thought she saw a tear
sparkle in his eye momentarily, but then his back faced her
and she urged Glow after them.

No return.

Glow eagerly caught up with Pavan and his rider and
they loped abreast at an easy pace. It was then Rivergrace
asked him, "What are you thinking?"

"I am thinking what I will do about the ild Fallyn."

She had no response to that, realizing that he was leaving the Queen but would not leave her vulnerable, not if there was any way he could help it. She had no advice to give him. The only way the ild Fallyn could not make trouble was if they were dead, and he would not be the first to consider the enterprise, knowing that all other similar enterprises had failed.

Dusk began to filter quietly, like lavender smoke, through the greening woods at the top of the ridge. He reined to a halt and Pavan turned his head to nip impishly at Glow's neck. The mare danced away a step. He shifted in his saddle to consider Rivergrace with his gray eyes: deep, contemplative eyes that always seemed to see right into her, with a trust that was complete and loving. She felt a warming tingle up the back of her neck.

"Which way?"

"We need to move quickly and unseen, but with the Ferryman gone, I can't use his Way to cover ground."

She could feel the night begin to gather in the condensation about her, ephemeral yet inexorable, as the balance in air and ground changed with evening's coolness. If she wished, if she would allow it, sparkling dewdrops would cloak her, drawn to her. Rivergrace would not, although the dampness didn't bother her, it was the chill. Early spring dew still remembered winter's ice. "Mageborn tunnels."

"The question there would be, are either of us Kernan enough to read the sigils."

"And the closest one collapsed."

"That, too, being a problem."

She knew that the labyrinth of tunnels could be their death; they'd wandered them before out of desperation, but they had also served a purpose. A faint sheen of uneasiness rose on her forehead, a queasiness, and she dried it away with the back of her hand. "I don't want to go underground."

His gaze rested on her. "If we simply ride, we will be overtaken. She'll send out hawks. We can't outrun messengers on wing."

Whatever had happened between Sevryn and Lariel? She opened her mouth to ask, when something brushed past her cheek like a tendril of unruly hair demanding attention. She put her hand up to sweep it away and found nothing, not even a wisp of spidersilk. Grace turned her face to follow the sensation of what seemed to be there but was not. Nothing. Yet something. She pushed it out of her mind, returning to Sevryn and their dilemma.

"Bregan could read the sigils."

"Do you think any trader could?" he responded.

"Doubtful. You have more experience with traders than I do. Mistress Robin Greathouse is Dweller and although she has . . . quirks . . . nothing like Bregan's ability with the tunnels."

Something pulled on the edge of her cloak. Rivergrace glanced down at her boot to see if it was caught on the hem. Nothing.

"What is it?"

She met his gaze. Uneasily, she answered, "I don't know."

"We can't stay up here on the ridgeline." He laid his reins against the side of Pavan's arched neck, and the horse responded with a step forward. "We may have no choice but to try a tunnel."

Dew settled on her in a weightless cloudburst, enveloping her in tiny, sparkling droplets. She smoothed her hand through them, little stings of water with the bite of winter still within, yet bursting with . . .

She looked up. "Sevryn!"

He halted Pavan and looked back over his shoulder. "Is something wrong?"

"I can use the rivers."

"The Ferryman is gone."

She held her hand up and dew streamed through her fingers like moonlight, coalescing into a stream of moisture. "I can use the rivers."

"All right, then. The Andredia? We'll have to circle around to where it flows out of Larandaril, and do so very circumspectly, but we can make it by midevening."

Normally she would be hesitant, a little doubtful of her abilities as she still came into understanding of them, but even the barest thought of the sacred river flooded through her mind, pulling at her, a tide not to be ignored or crossed. She nodded. "Even the Andredia."

He turned their horses about yet again, as the lavender mist of dusk deepened into purple, and long shadows lengthened into night.

Those same shadows proved to be midnight highways for many in the restless night.

Chapter
Twenty-Three

Tressandre

"HOW LONG HAS THE SUBJECT been missing?" Wrapped in shimmering black-and-silver cloth, the speaker might have been a storm cloud, but the ild Fallyns always preferred those colors. It was not the clothing the guardsmen watched warily, it was the expression on Tressandre ild Fallyn's face and in her infamous, fierce jade eyes. Being fitted for an outfit of some sort, she stood on a cushioned stool so that the aged seamstress could have better access to her elegant figure. Dressed in little more than the skin she'd been born with, Tressandre did not seem to care about the intrusion as Heroma measured and cut, pinned and basted. Bare skin peeked intriguingly through sashes of cloth as the guardsmen straightened from their bow and the veteran answered.

"Since the noon meal, as closely as we can figure."

"As closely as you can figure."

The tall, redheaded guard shifted his weight. Younger, he let his gaze feast on her. He might be punished for his stare—or he might be rewarded. She was the power in the fortress although her older brother Alton had ridden in late during the night and now slept. They would not have gone to him anyway, not when Tressandre was in the keep. She was the undeniable mistress. Boldness fueled his words. "Those posted on duty thought she'd gone for a tumble. It's common enough."

The jade eyes glinted. "Indeed. Perhaps we're feeding them too much if they can afford to miss a meal to rut." Tressandre lifted her arm at a murmured request. "How did she get out?"

"That has not been determined yet. Over the wall seems likeliest."

"For a chit of little Talent, she seems to have stirred up quite a hornet's nest." At another soft request from the seamstress, she lifted her cascading mane of dark blonde hair, her aroma of cinnamon and night rose scenting the air. "Nonetheless, her act can't be tolerated. I want the hounds and trackers after her, and no one is to return until they find her or her remains. She is not important to our project, but she has a mouth and she has memory, and those I will have safely contained or silenced. She matters to no one but the three of us, and the three of us want her accounted for. Am I clear?"

"Crystal."

"Good. I have business elsewhere, but if I hear that you need my help, I will not hesitate to give it."

The guardsmen paled a bit. "That will not be necessary, Lady ild Fallyn."

"I am certain it will not. Now take care of matters." Tressandre sliced a dismissal through the air and the two backed out of the drawing room with great speed. She watched them go, a frown lining her brow. She did not need trouble among the subjects. The name of the one gone missing did not carry any recognition, so it was not one of those they'd found useful. She brushed her dark blonde hair from her shoulders and twisted it into a knot at the back of her neck, her arms rippling with both muscle and grace as she did so. She looked down at the woman attempting to pin trousers in place. "Did you place the name, Heroma?"

"No, milady, but then I seldom have dealings with the outer hold."

"Just as well." Tressandre looked at herself critically in the two standing mirrors opposite them. The bent and wiry woman working on her did not seem to notice or take care of her reflection, creased and white-haired, hands a bit gnarled from years of tailoring as her fingers hurried up and down the cloth, pinning here, releasing there. "Stomach. I need more stomach."

The seamstress, on her knees on a padded stool, craned her neck to look upward. "Milady Tressandre, I cannot make it both ways. I cannot create a stomach where you have none, nor can I pretend to hide said stomach as though you did not wish it revealed simultaneously."

"Of course you can, Heroma. You can work miracles with a bolt of cloth."

The seamstress stabbed pins into the cushion at her wrist. "It's a riding costume, milady. Not that you should be riding at all this early in your term to protect the child, but I positively cannot tailor it and give you a belly where you haven't any yet!"

"I'll use a pillow if necessary. Small and firm. I am pregnant and will show it."

"And the riding?"

Tressandre rolled her eyes, the smoky bits going light and dark silver against the rich, jade-green background of her pupils. "I suppose you would have me use a carriage."

"It would not hurt. Your blessed mother had two miscarriages before Alton and another before you."

Tressandre turned a bit, angling her jaw and looking at herself in the closest mirror as if barely listening. She tugged at the ill-fitting blouse and trousers with a frown. "And were we not worth waiting for?"

"The two of you fill and carry the legacy of ild Fallyn to greatest expectation, but that is hardly the point in this discussion. You carry the Anderieon heir. Babies compromise the best intentions."

"Baby this and baby that. The child isn't important, it's the political legacy that is important. Don't worry unnecessarily. You see that I have a proper maternity trousseau, and

I will have a child, Heroma, if I have to pluck it from a pair of unwary arms."

The corner of the seamstress' mouth gathered and she grew silent. She pulled and pinned for a few moments, said quietly, "I will have a pillow and strapping made" and got to her feet. She took the hand Tressandre extended as she did so. "We'll have these made at once, and I've patterns for the others. Gowns, skirts, blousing and so on. I'll have to make adjustments." Her mouth thinned. "I cannot tell yet how you will increase in the bust, but there's time enough for that. I'll have a costume for you tomorrow and we'll go from there."

"Well and good." Tressandre kicked the garments off and Heroma caught them, tucked them under her arm, and left with a nod of her head. Tressandre waited until the seamstress left, her soft-soled boots walking slowly yet firmly down the hallway, and then leaned for a bell rope, yanking it. She did not have to wait long.

Alton, eyes still a bit crusted from sleep and face slack from being pressed against a mattress, appeared at the door. He lifted an eyebrow at the pieces of fabric lying about the room as his sister stepped down off her cushion. "How is old Heroma? Bossy, as usual?"

"I want her dead. As soon as you can arrange it."

"What?"

Tressandre wound a stray bit of her hair about her finger. "I believe you heard."

"Heard but did not believe."

"Dead. By tomorrow evening. Make it quick, I won't have Heroma suffer. A broken neck, perhaps, suffered during a fall down the stairs. See to it."

"Lady sister, she's been with us for untold years. She might as well be our grandmother." He rubbed the corner of one eye and flicked a bit of crystal from his finger.

"All the more reason she should not suffer." Tressandre lifted her chin, daring Alton to get off another word, but he closed his mouth on it. She smiled briefly. "When our enemies investigate the word of my pregnancy, and they *will* investigate, she is our weakest link. She is old and frail though she admits it not, and they'll break her like a twig. I want her spared that."

"A certain death stacked against an uncertain torture?"

"Do you not agree with me?"

He traded looks with her before dropping his gaze. "I always agree with you, sooner or later." He smothered a yawn on the back of his hand. "Tonight, then."

Tressandre looked at him over her shoulder. "No. Tomorrow night. She has some work to finish for me, first."

"Ah, good. Then I can finish my sleep. The ride from Ashenbrook to Larandaril and then home is a hard one without the Ferryman to give quick passage." He scrubbed at his eyes again, looking for a moment like the tousled boy, handsome and carefree, that she remembered from her own early days when she used to watch him whenever she could. "If that is all right with you?"

She turned away from him with a languid move. "As long as you finish it in my bed." She put her hand behind her, stretching it out to him, and he reached forward to take it.

Ceyla

At first she was uncertain she heard the hounds. Their voices rose and fell with the thin whistling of the wind through the evergreens as night began to fall and the branches moved restlessly. Needles and limbs whipped at her as Ceyla moved through them, running when she could and stumbling more often as both the lack of light and the roughness of ground tripped her up. She had half a day on her pursuers, but they were used to the hunt. If she went to water, the still icy and swift flowing river would kill her before her hunters did. If she did not, her scent would linger for the hounds to pick up. She'd hoped being in the dog pens, her odor might be muddled, but the noise growing on the wind told her that her ruse had not worked. She might not live the night, despite her earlier belief that she would. One never set out to fail, she told herself, ducking her head further, her palms raw as she propelled herself forward, holding her hands out to shield herself. Going back was not an option, for there would be no mercy. They would flay the skin off her body and the armor from her mind, use her up and leave her lying exposed to die a lingering death. This, she knew. This, she had seen far more than she'd seen her success.

But she had seen her success. More than once. Enough to give her the courage to try. Never trying or giving up ensured her failure, and so she had screwed up her courage to do whatever she could.

Her breath whistled through her throat like the wind in the trees, cold and chill and scraping her inside out. She stumbled into tree trunks more than once, left shoulder aching and both elbows smarting. Her feet had stung, but now they were numb. Ceyla thought she could feel the soles of her shoes part, flapping about her ankles but she couldn't be sure. It would be better to be running on raw pain rather than stumps that she could not feel or maneuver upon at all. She lurched and skidded across dirt and needle glossed pathways unseen where only animals traveled and heard the hounds grow inexorably closer.

The river sounded in her ears. There would be no soft banks to ease down, the river in these mountains cut deep through sharp and towering cliffs. She had to take one of the suspension bridges if she wished to cross and if the ild Fallyn hunted truly, they already had guards there alerted. She had planned to travel underneath the bridge, skittering along its belly like some ceiling spider after arriving unnoticed. Now . . . what chance? The river itself, dark and deep and fierce, rushed through the gully. And, too, the river, if she survived it, would carry her back, back toward the fortress and its escarpment footing near the sea. Backward in her flight and hopes. Always back.

Unless she just let the river take her down and drown her and everything would cease. Her hopes, her fears, her . . . dreams.

Ceyla plowed to a halt and shook herself. Blood roared hotly through her head. Her ears tingled, her throat tightened. And her feet managed an answering throb of life. If this were only for herself, she could falter. She could consider defeat.

But it had never been just about herself, and her dreams would never let it be. So. She gathered herself with a long, scorching breath that seared its way into her throat and lungs and sighed out softly again. No turning back. She would find a way.

As she staggered back into motion, her wish to feel her feet flared into jagged, tearing pain and she gasped, tears running unbidden down her face. What folly that had been! Raggedly, she stayed in motion, lurching this way and that, stabbing flashes of agony driving her across the ground. Then, along with the howling, came the smell.

Ceyla scrubbed the back of her hand across her nose, wiping away tears and snot and the noxious odor. She blinked. There was no possible way she could smell the hounds at this distance, not even with her preternatural skill. Nor had any hound she ever winded stunk like this . . . never.

Then her face broke into a smile, a wide, gaping, gasping for breath smile, but one nonetheless. Some stinkdog had made its den nearby, leagues and leagues away from its normal habitat, but slimed the ground and bed with its scent and the mucus that it shed to coat and protect its skin. There wasn't a hunting dog who could wind her own scent through the detritus of a stinkdog!

Ceyla clawed her way through the bush and when she was certain, how could she not be, of the den's location, fell to her hands and knees and crept forward.

The animal could be vicious. It was, under any circumstances, unpleasant. But she would approach unthreatening, not weak if different, and unchallenging. Ceyla calmed her

breathing and moved, slowly, bit by bit, her eyes watering as
the odor grew more and more vile. She could hear the rustle
of the harsh grasses and needles and a grunt. She could feel
the body heat rolling off the roused beast and hesitated a
moment, savoring the warmth. The howling behind her
grew louder, and she could now hear the individual barks
and bays of the pack tracking her. She hadn't much time.

Her palm slipped on a glob of mucus. Repelled, she
snatched her hand back and the stinkdog growled deeply in
warning. She wanted to shake her hand clean, but this was
what she'd come for! Teeth clenched, she wiped her hand
over her scarf and hair. Then she crawled forward into more
of the disgusting stuff, until she found a patch she could
lower herself into and roll. Gods. She shuddered as she did
so and her throat clenched, holding back her desire to
vomit. The stinkdog opened its eyes. They caught the glow
of the barely revealed moon in the sky as it looked toward
her. Ceyla froze.

It opened and closed its jaws as if yawning or chewing. It
moved about on its bed to face her. She could hear it snuf-
fle.

Did her eyes reflect a stare back into its own? She held
her face steady, crouched on the ground, lower than the
head of the beast, tensing to get to her feet and run if it
decided to charge.

The stinkdog chomped and slurped its jaws again, then
put its muzzle down and closed its eyes to mere slits. Not a
welcome, exactly, but not hostility either.

Ceyla finished coating herself, in quick, sure movements.
The mucus stuck to her from head to toe until even her
nose eventually gave up and refused to function, overcome
by the stench. She would, she thought, smell it in her dreams
until the day she died.

Which, hopefully, would now be a long way off.

She did not get to her feet and leave the den until the
glowing, slit eyes closed and she could hear the creature's
deep breathing. Then she moved off, careful not to slough
off any of the coating as she went, and when she had gotten

downslope, she turned in guilt. The hounds would scent her this far, if no farther. She could not leave the animal on its own.

Tired, weaving on her feet, the bridge within sprinting distance, she closed her eyes. Ceyla let herself sink, sink, and sink until she found the edge of sleep in her exhaustion. And on that edge, she found the rhythm of the stinkdog in its sleep and she sent it a picture of peril, of dogs baying in killing excitement as they charged toward it.

Then she opened her eyes and ran.

Behind her, she could hear the animal get to its feet with a muffled bellow as it prepared its defense instinctively. She could do no more than give it warning and let it choose its fight.

The rest, short as it had been, gave her a last jolt of stamina. She sprinted toward the suspension bridge, torches placed upon its length to illuminate it in the darkness, its base well buried into the side of the mountain, its scalloped sides an artistic rendering of cable and steel. Only the ild Fallyn Talent could have built such a structure, for they had the inherent ability to levitate, making the building of such possible. She had crossed it once, many, many years ago, young and small and fighting her captors, but she had made note with her sharp eyes and memory of this eventual road to freedom.

Unfortunately, the very slime and scum that disguised her scent would impede her ability to climb. Couldn't be helped. Her hands were already raw. Ceyla ducked in under the foot of the bridge and pulled loose some well-woven rope and stout but pliable leather she had been secreting for seasons. When she had prepared herself, she reached up. The underside of the bridge was as she remembered . . . she having thrown herself off the wagon bed and tumbled down the hill to nearly fall off the cliff's edge into the river, so that she could lie underneath the structure and spy on its construction. Then, the span between hand and footholds were beyond a child's reach. Then, the structure had seemed insurmountable, yet another obstacle she could not hope to defeat.

Now she had hopes.

Far behind her, the howling of the hounds broke up. Faltered. Faded and then regathered strongly, then stuttered again. Fighting? Scattering? Confused? She could only surmise.

Once under the bridge, they had little hope of tracking her.

Ceyla tightened her harness and took hold of the rough metal and wood that was the underside of the soaring structure. Night had fallen deeply and, under the shadowed bridge, she could see little even as her eyes adapted. She lay back on a strut and shut out the sounds around her: the foaming river below, the baying hounds in the distance, the creak and sway of the bridge itself as it moved in the wind. She concentrated instead on the structure, on the rough surface with its many angles and joints, places that might be climbed and swung from, caught and crossed by . . . if only she could see. If only she knew what she faced. Or had faced.

Ceyla brushed her hand across her pack and liberated her herb pouch. She could not see the small bags tied within, but each had been wrapped and knotted differently so that she could identify them by touch alone, if she had to. A slim bag came open reluctantly as she undid it, and the faint, musky smell of the cured leaves within stained the air. She drew a pinch, only the merest of a pinch to her lips. Dare she? She did. The crumbling herb left a smoky and bitter taste behind as she retied the bag and secured it back in her pack. A sip of water did little to dispel it. More water would dilute it and wash it out of her system quicker, so she had to endure the bitterness. Better if she had taken a flint and set it alight so that she could inhale the smoke, but that might draw attention when she could not afford it. So, instead, Ceyla wrapped her arms tightly about her strut and waited for her mind to catch the bit of dreamspark she'd ingested. It grew in her. She could feel it uncoiling and reaching, stretching throughout her body, hot and sharp, and then it hit her mind.

She could let it carry her off into dreams unwanted, but Ceyla had no intention of closing her eyes to unhampered power. She curled the herb like smoke through her vision, twisting it, until she stood, sun dappling her body, murmuring voices behind her, the restless stamp of horses, the smell of fall leaves crushed underfoot, and she made her way down the embankment carefully.

"Take care, m'lady."

The words, male-voiced, so far away behind her as barely to be heard at all, filled with concern and—what? Authority. She must take care. She had been given no choice, but neither did she have time. Only the briefest of moments to look back under the bridge, to look back at the way she had traversed in the dead of night, and see what she had accomplished. Only a breath or two in which to examine the feat and to know, to remember, what it was she had done. Ceyla slid to the bottommost anchor of the span, wrapping an arm about a bit of shrub that stubbornly split the rocky foundation and grew, as spindly as an old garden rope—and as strong.

She narrowed her eyes and put her free hand up for shade. She could see the underneath of the span now. Where handholds and footholds might be gotten. How long the swing out must be in the dead center of the underbelly, right over the frothing, raging river down below. It made her breathless to look at it, to think that she had crossed it at night, how perilous it had been, and how she could only have made it because of this moment, looking back.

She examined it for every breath she could manage, aware of the male figure coming up behind her and putting an arm about her waist as if to steady her . . . or reclaim her. The ild Fallyn who'd built this had used magic to do it. Ordinary craftsmen could not have accomplished it. But once built, one did not need levitation to scale its underside. This she knew. She stood here, did she not? Stood and looked back? But in a hundred other visions, she did not finish her journey. The hunters and dogs found her, pulling her from her perch. Or the river claimed her falling body. Or the harness she'd wrought so cleverly had tangled and she died, dangling there, hanged. But in this moment, in this vision, she examined the bridge and sent her thoughts backward, ever backward, so that a slave running for her freedom might catch them.

All it took was one vision seen rightfully.

In the heat of the day, in the cold of the night, Ceyla shivered and sweated. The dreamspark boiled from her body, from her pores, her skin stinking of its odor and then, in another breath, all had faded.

Ceyla dragged her hand across her forehead, and then scrubbed her hand dry on the seat of her pants. She could hear again, from far away, the sound of the hounds. They were on the trail once more. Her whole body shook as she clenched her eyes shut for a moment, could feel the sweat even from her eyelids; moisture poured from her body as the dreamspark violently burned its way out. And then it was gone, leaving her shaking like a newborn thing, about to mewl in distress, helpless and weak, the price of the seeing she'd done. In this moment, it might serve her, or she might yet fail. In another moment, somewhere else, she would gather the strength to go on. Or she could muster it now. In this self.

Ceyla tried to swallow, but she nearly choked on the dryness in her throat, left behind by the quick ravage of the dreamspark through her system. She could hear a hound bell, not so far now, a pack leader telling his mates that here, here, here, he'd found a scent despite the slime, despite the stink of the beast, here was the trail.

Ceyla fastened her harness and pushed off, swinging through the night. She'd done it, once. She'd come back to look at what she'd done, so that she might remember it when she looked forward. A tangled vision but true. Only once.

That would have to be enough to carry her through.

Chapter
Twenty-Four

EVEN IN THE DARK OF NIGHT, Bistane saw shadows. A warlord, son of a warlord, he could not discount nerves but neither could he afford to court them. Yet, he felt the quickening of movement, sensed more by the stirring of air and leaf and gravel around him than by sight, and even this had begun to change. He could see things others couldn't, not the threads of the physical, but what he feared was not physical. He reined his horse in as they drew near Lariel's stables. This was not his home, but Bistane had been here often enough that he knew it well and it mattered little that he did not walk on his own ground. The feeling of oddness, of a presence where there should be none, stalked him whether he was astride, as he rode now, or walked in the light of day where shadows ought to be expected. In those times when the eerie sense followed him, he thought he saw his father, Bistel Vantane, pacing with a warlord's marked confidence next to him and then marching away, off on some ghostly business that Bistane could neither detect nor decipher.

It was only habit and imagination, he told himself. His

father's death was but recent and his presence such a strong one that it was difficult to perceive a world without him. For what reason would he be haunted than by sheer familiarity of his father's authority and advice in his life? No other that he could think of. He had been a good son, a strong and temperate son, and there had been little strife between them once he had grown "into his boots" as the elder Vantane liked to put it. Bistane had little regret with reference to his father. Their only contention had been when Vantane sired another son and brought him to the hold, but even then, there was no doubting that the warlord held enough love for them both. And, Bistane had been grown by then. Matured. He held no shame that he had a Dweller-blooded half brother although his father thought it best to keep the relationship quiet. Verdayne had been raised somewhat like a frolicking puppy until he grew sturdy legs and a love of the land that all Vantanes held. The aryn trees seemed to listen to him. He filled a hole that neither Bistel nor Bistane had known existed until Verdayne occupied it proudly. Bistel liked to say that Verdayne held the best of the Dwellers within himself, but Bistane knew only that his younger brother held a consistent joy he did not, and he shared it.

Bistane dismounted in the lee side of the Larandaril stables and stretched his legs, taking stock of the lateness of the night and the quiet of the yard and wondered if Verdayne saw ghosts, too. He should ask him sometime. And then, disquiet hit the chill and damp air, a feeling of being held back as strong as if a firm hand had fallen upon his forearm to pull him aside. Bistane put his hand on his horse's muzzle to keep him quiet and shouldered him back into a corner until he knew what had fallen on him, what shivered his senses in the air about him. He took caution even in the heart of his queen's kingdom, for he'd passed Alton ild Fallyn on the road a few days ago, in the black-and-silver livery of his bloodline and wrapped in a temper darker than the shadows of midevening that shrouded them both, lashing into his horse. He had used his sword to clear his path of stray branches as though he were cutting down bandits, hooves drumming as

he disappeared. Bistane had felt his lip curl back over his
teeth as he sucked a breath inward. Well enough that he had
pulled aside, out of caution. There was no love at all between
the ild Fallyns and the Vantanes, and under these circumstances, yes, Alton might well have attacked him, claiming
that he had been lying in wait to do the same. Blood spilled
here and now would do no one any good, although doubtless
the ild Fallyn could twist it to their advantage, regardless if
Alton lived or died. Another of the few grievances he and his
father had had between them. Bistel had counseled him:
"You cannot feud with the ild Fallyn, even if they are as
treacherous as the centuries are long, and they are, make no
mistake of that. But there is no good end to fueling such hatred between our Houses, and no end at all until one side or
the other is obliterated from the face of Kerith. So stay your
hand, my son, and let time, and others, work the vengeance
you seek."

He inhaled lightly. Still ghost-ridden, Bistane stayed
himself a moment or so longer, thoughtfully, before taking
the backdoor through the kitchen after turning his horse
into pasture under the still sleepy-eyed guardianship of the
stable boy who had spared him a grateful salute for the coin
tipped into his hand.

The warmth of Lariel's manor rose to meet Bistane. It
enveloped him, smelling of yeast for risen dough about to
be put into the ovens and of flowers which dotted the various counters and tables and of the scented oils which
burned softly in the wall sconces and ceiling lanterns. He
found comfort in Lariel's home as he did within his own
walls. Once little more than a hunting lodge, it had been
built upon over the centuries until it sprawled, a gracious
and secure manor house, and the touch of its female ruler
could be felt throughout every beam, brick, and weaving.
As a lad, he could remember the fierce Warrior King, who'd
held court in these buildings, his voice like steel cutting
through ethereal distance and solid wall to find and beat
down whoever he could when displeased. The old Anderieon, as Bistel had often referred to him, was a lean and

shaggy war dog who could and would just as soon sever
your tendons with his fangs as give you a lick in welcome.
He remembered being afraid to his bones of the towering
man with the fine, high cheekbones that cut the panes of his
face into a terrible severity. The old Anderieon. Bistane
shivered a bit in memorial before entering the manor.

Farlen met him. He bowed deeply. "Warlord. The Queen
is in consultation."

"Not recovering from Lord Alton's spat of ill-humor?"

"You knew he was here?"

"I passed him on the road. It seemed wise to not let him
be aware of me."

The corner of Farlen's mouth quirked. "I suspect it is he
who needs recovery, if any is needed. No, she is having
words with Lord Dardanon."

"Oh, Sevryn's back, is he? I should like to hear what he
has to say, as well."

A cloud passed over Farlen's features. "She's not to be
disturbed. They just went behind closed doors. I cannot tell
you if it will be long or short." He put a hand on Bistane's
shoulder. "Alton came to put in Tressandre's claim that she
carries a child from Jeredon."

"What?!"

"Yes, well, it would indeed be miraculous. Whoever's son
it is, he'll find her teats like ice when he tries to suckle. But
there will be enough discussion on that in the morning. Let
me see you fed, and your room made up, and you can rest
from your journey. A bit of sleep might do you good."

"If sleep could." He did not rest well at home. He
doubted he would rest well here, particularly with that news
to chew on. The only bed that gave him much sleep at all
was hard ground, and little enough of that. One did not ride,
these days, or make camp, without caution. You slept, if at
all, with one eye open. He managed a smile. "A hot meal
sounds appealing."

He ate in his chambers, unwilling to speak with anyone until he'd heard whatever Lara would tell him. She kept her own counsel and he disliked not being privy to many of her ideas. She hadn't seen fit to send him news by bird, but then she knew he was already on the road and would hear soon enough. They warred arm in arm, but she did not hold the same trust in him that she had in his father. Why would she? He had not proven himself, not in her eyes and not in his.

Suddenly tired beyond measure, he wrapped himself in a blanket and sank into whatever sleep he could find.

He woke deep into the night. No sound, muffled or otherwise, echoed through the old wood and stone of the great manor house. He brought his own hot water up from pots always kept simmering on the kitchen hearth to make himself fit for the queen, whenever she decided to send for him.

He sang to himself as he stripped down to wash what he could of the road dirt off him, enjoying the hot water even if not a full bath.

Bistane dashed his razor into the last of the bathwater, cleaning it, as his voice trailed off. He couldn't sing for her anymore. She'd lost her joyousness when she'd lost Jeredon. When she did listen to him at all, it was to hear the echoes of his father's voice within his words, the refrain of his father's advice and wisdom. It was as though he, as himself, did not exist at all except as a reflection of Bistel Vantane. He peered at himself in the small mirror, propped against the wall, and saw little to shore up his estimate of himself. He knew who he was before his father's untimely death. Now . . . he had doubts, he supposed. Not that he was untried in life or in battle. He had not been at his father's side when he was cut down. He had failed in that regard.

Bistane looked down, realized his fist was clenched. He opened his hand slowly. He must have had it clenched for long moments, for his fingers had gone both stiff and pale, cramping when he tried to open them. In that regard, he was definitely his father's son. He could have a stubborn will when set to it.

He picked up a towel to dry his face. Time to show that

will, then. He was tired of waiting for Lariel to acknowledge his presence, to summon him; whether she had deigned to give him a night's peace or had forgotten about him altogether, he had no idea. Whichever it was, he wasn't going to suffer it a moment longer.

Bistane straightened his shirt, pivoted on heel, and went to find the woman, deep into the night or not.

He passed two servant girls on the stairs. They ducked their heads and said nothing although he could hear faint giggles in his wake. Did they know he was headed toward the queen's apartment? Or did they simply giggle because that's what young lasses did? He used to understand such things, he thought. Or maybe that was because, once, he used to assume the attention was directed on him. Further doubt marked him when he heard one of the girls' last words as they turned the corner, "Lord Tranta makes me blush, too . . ."

He turned down the spacious wing where Lariel lived, had lived, with her brother. The traitorous seneschal Tiiva had had rooms here, too, he remembered although he had never been inclined to visit them. Tiiva, in her voluminous gowns of silk and satin, with a dagger sheath hidden in her sleeves. Disappeared and hoped dead, deceitful, alluring Tiiva.

You can never tell an enemy by the foulness of their features or words. Yes, my father, I remember your saying that well. Bistane neared the doors marked discreetly in the far corner with Lara's crest and slowed, brushing the palm of his hand over his hair. Did he still have that wild lick of hair that always showed up when he'd been sleeping? He thought he'd combed it down when he'd washed, but—

Bistane bit off a curse under his breath. It did not matter. Nothing mattered but that Lara turn her eyes on him and finally see him and not the late, great Bistel. He was as deeply loyal to her service, but he was his own man. She had to see that of him, sooner or later. Did she not?

Bistane stopped in his tracks. The door hung slightly ajar, latch out of place. Hastily entered or exited, he could not tell. But amiss. He drew his dagger hissing quietly from its sheath, put a booted foot in the door to ease it open, and slipped in.

The rooms were draped for nighttime, the heavy curtains still down on the windows of the far wall. But she had neither dined nor slept in the first two rooms, and he turned the corner beyond them, to enter a room he had seen a few times in his capacity as his father's aide when she conferred with Bistel. An odd room, spare, with a table and a heavy wooden chair that sat, throne-like, in front of a window that took in the horizon of the forested hills of Larandaril. He could see as he moved into it that the drapes had not been brought down here, and silvery moonlight bathed the room.

A muffled sound drew him closer. When he came to the chair, he saw Lariel, tied to the arms, slumped as if asleep and fighting a dread nightmare, her body twitching and her face etched deeply in strain and tension, her mouth half-open as if she tried to scream. "Lara!"

Kneeling, he cut her bonds. Was this how Sevryn had left her, or had someone else been in this room? He cradled her face between his hands. "Lara. You're all right. I'm here. Wake. You're all right!"

Her eyes flicked open for a moment as if she fought sleep with every ounce of her being. He cradled her tighter, her smooth skin chill under his palms. Her chest heaved as she sucked down air like a drowning person, and her arms came up to claw at him. He grasped one strong wrist and then the other to keep her from harming either himself or her.

And then her eyes flew open and stayed that way, pupils distended, the whites of her eyes showing as well, like a frightened animal.

Suddenly she screamed, "Assassin!"

Chapter
Twenty-Five

L ARA BOLTED UPRIGHT INTO HIS ARMS, shuddering, taking another breath to cry aloud again, and he put his palm over her mouth. "You're all right," he whispered in her ear as he pulled her close. "Calm. Quiet. Center yourself. No one is here but us."

After long moments, her trembling quieted and her breathing returned to normal, so he took his palm from her lips. She did not move away from his comforting embrace immediately. When she did, she put her chin up and the woman he knew as Lara became the Warrior Queen.

"Treachery," she said.

"So I gathered. I found you tied here. Unharmed yet beset."

She pushed her hair from her face, tossing it back as she stood. She took a step. Tottered as she did so. Bistane moved close again, lending his support, half-walking and half-carrying her to her writing desk in the main rooms.

She sat down and watched as he lit two lamps. "Get Farlen. And Sevryn."

"I will, but . . ." he paused. "I was told Sevryn was here with you, consulting."

"He was." She frowned. "Just find him for me."

The seneschal he found easily, sleeping in his rooms a floor below. Of Sevryn Dardanon there was no sign, nor of Rivergrace either. Bistane returned uneasily to Lara. If Sevryn were the assassin of which she spoke, nothing could have stopped him from his goal. Yet she lived still. Unless Lara was not his target.

Dawn was threatening at her windows as he entered her rooms. She stood up at his news, straightening herself as if putting on yet another layer of armor. "Mount a guard. I will find them." Her hand clenched and unclenched. "He is in my service and she may think she follows in the steps of a River Goddess, but this is my kingdom, and *I will find them!*"

Sevryn raced the horses as far as they could at night. At dawn, they paused to rest the horses and take a bit of food. Sevryn climbed a tree to be certain of his scouting and came down with nothing to report but a troubled look on his face.

Grace put her hand over his. "Yet you saw nothing."

"No and that worries me more than seeing horsemen on our trail. Because she will come after us, I am certain."

"What did you do? Or is it me? Have I done something?"

He bent and brushed his lips over her hand covering his. "Never you, though I don't doubt she bristles a bit at your lack of experience with Vaelinar scheming."

"Bristle? It's more than that. Ever since I found Fire, she's feared me."

"Fire is a power that isn't easily controlled, even within the bricks of a hearth. She may be wary of you, but Lara's not the kind of person who will kill someone who makes her uneasy." He shifted his weight and shook his head. "No, it's me and what I've done is not what I've done yet. It's what she may fear that I will do."

"Must you speak in riddles?"

The corner of his mouth quirked. "It seems I must. I gave her an oath, Grace, and beyond that, there are things you're better off not knowing, if we can't win free of Larandaril. Just know that she thinks I may try to kill her."

She tilted her head. "Will you?"

"No. Not unless she threatens you and there's no other recourse."

"But she trails us now."

He put his finger on her chin. "Because she thinks she has reason to."

"How could she think such a thing?"

"That, you're better off not knowing and I gave my word. And she is wrong. Very wrong." He turned his face away.

"We can't waste time here if she means to take us prisoner."

"No, but I can't spend the horses too dearly yet either. We'll go again in a few moments. Glow and Pavan need to crop a bit. If she means to imprison us, we're not likely to find replacement mounts or other aid easily."

"We'll be on the run."

"Probably."

"Where are we headed?"

"Ild Fallyn Stronghold."

"What?" Her face paled.

"It's not what you think." He captured her hand, as she jerked away from him. "Never that. I'll never join them not even if Lara and all the lords were on our heels."

"Then why?"

"If Lara believes, as I think she might, that I've turned against her, then she stands alone except for Bistane and Tranta. I won't leave her vulnerable." His lips thinned. "I intend to take a bit of diplomacy into my own hands."

She gripped his hand tightly then. "Sevryn."

"Don't judge me."

"I'm not, how can I? Yet you speak of murder."

"Not exactly. Alton will get a challenge. He'll take it. That should cripple Tressandre long enough for Lariel to get her support consolidated. That's all she will need."

"How can you even think of that?"

Sevryn studied her. She wore her distress openly, as she did most of her emotions and feelings in her expression, not masked as the high elven practiced. Not deceitful. "The question should be: how can you not? If ever a bug deserved to be squashed, it's Alton." He touched her chin. "It's a blessing that you don't, but you have to understand, the ild Fallyns have had Lara's death planned for centuries. Now that I'm no longer under Lara's constraints, I can work to ensure their plans will never succeed. She won't appreciate it, but I can't walk away free until I've done this."

"And then?"

"And then, you and I will discover the Eastern lands, beyond the wastes of the Mageborn, and far away to the Eastern sea."

Darkness clouded her eyes. "Nutmeg . . ."

"We could stop and take her with us. And Lily and Tolby and all your brothers." Sevryn grinned at her then. "I wouldn't mind uprooting the Farbranch family."

"That might take a bit of digging."

"I'd make time for it."

"All the while ducking Lariel?"

"Anything to make you happy."

She laughed then, thin and light, but still a laugh. He turned her about and brought her into his embrace, and they were both quiet for long moments, watching the horses graze, as the dawn came up bright and proper.

Pavan threw his head up, a gleam in his eye. He arched his neck as if to whicker, but Sevryn got to the horse first, hand on his nose, bringing it to his chest to muffle him. The horse stomped a hoof. Around them, the clearing became startlingly, suddenly, quiet. Birds that had woken before dawn broke stopped their singing and noise-making. Rodents schussing through the grasses to find shoots and seeds to nibble lay low, inaudible, as though a massive predator now stalked the area. One must. The only sound that had not changed except perhaps that it had grown louder was the flow of the River Andredia. Its waters could be heard

even more clearly moving over the sand and stone of its
bed, swiftly but not flooding. Sweetwater, undeniable in the
way it washed through her senses. Yet, the clarity and purity
of the river did not wash away her apprehension that something close by was terribly wrong. Rivergrace looked to
Sevryn, and as she did, she drew her short sword.

Unlike him, she dropped to her knees and began a slow,
inexorable crawl to the river. Behind her came a long pause
and then she heard Sevryn follow her. He reached out and
gripped her boot. "Grace. There is no way to make the
horses crawl."

She curled up to look back at him and then realized what
he meant. Her face warmed. "Then we might as well run for
it."

"Done!" He handed her to her feet and literally tossed
her aboard Glow, throwing the reins into her hands before
turning and doing a running mount onto his horse.

As they kicked their horses into a run, birds burst out of
cover to take wing behind them, adding to the sudden
change from tension to fear. Grace leaned low over the
neck of her mare, urging her faster. A whoop sounded behind them, leaving no doubt they had been seen.

But they had plenty of horse under them, crediting
Sevryn's caution, while the pursuers had to be riding mounts
nearly played out, having ridden at top speed to catch up
with them. Glow put her ears back at Grace's words, and
stretched out her nimble legs to eat the ground beneath
them even faster, dodging the shrubs and low brush, her
hooves cutting the distance away. The River Andredia rib-
boned before them, dark blue and white, frothing on the
rocky coves as it made its way out of the valley Larandaril.
What she thought she could accomplish there, she was not
certain, but she knew it was their only chance.

Pavan drew even with Glow, their heads bobbing together, as they raced across the field toward the Andredia.
His nostrils flared wide and he snorted, stretching his body
out, his hot-blooded nature bringing out the desire to race
and win, his senses driving him to run flat out. Clods of

spring-tender grass clumps flew through the air. Glow answered his challenge by putting her ears down even further and angling away from him to give herself racing room.

Grace wrapped her hand about the right rein and began to tug on it, slowly, steadily, turning her mare in her path else they would not stop at the river but ford it at speed, and she didn't want that. They had to be in the water. She did not breathe until Glow plunged into it, plowing a spray of ice-cold water about all of them, tossing her head and snorting as she beat Pavan by a mere step. Sevryn twisted in the saddle. He said nothing, but his brow went up in question. She put her hand up for silence. His mouth twitched. She looked to him, and her own brow quirked. He lifted a shoulder in a shrug and looked down at his hands, each filled with a throwing dagger.

Rivergrace lifted her own hands. The waters of the Andredia reached up in misty waves to fill her fingers before running through them. Glow tossed her head uneasily as water sprayed about her. The same unease filled her rider. Grace felt the Andredia sink through her skin, into her veins, into her very soul . . . cold and icy, fresh melted from the mountains, carried out of the font hidden within them, and down the hillsides throughout the valley. She could feel more than that in it, however. There was rainwater, fallen from the skies and drifting from far, far away, distilled from the air and seas themselves. They had no calling for the Andredia, but they had an answering for her. The Andredia did not want to give in to her will, would not let her braid it as she wished, did not want to bend to her asking, but she persisted. She was more than the heir to the Silverwing waters, more than the heir to its mad Goddess. She felt the ire of the Andredia's soul and reminded it that she had helped to cleanse it, not that long ago. It owed her, though water seldom felt that it owed any living thing on the face of the earth. It simply *was*.

"What are you doing?"

Rivergrace did not glance up, merely letting a "Shush" go, her face bent to the river around them. Glow danced in the flow, splashing it vigorously, her chestnut dappled hide shivering. It was chilling her. It had already seeped icy fingers into Grace.

"Surrender now, and there will be no arms pulled against you."

Her attention snapped up, as did Sevryn's. Lariel sat her golden and silver-white steed, her shoulders thrown back, her mail gleaming in the early morning sun, and her eyes bruised with fatigue or perhaps it was sorrow.

"We deserve our freedom."

"You gave an oath to me, Sevryn Dardanon."

"I have given you more than one oath, my Warrior Queen, and upheld every one of them."

Rivergrace's fingers moved on their own volition, weaving, braiding, bending the recalcitrant river to her will. If not for the rainwater in it, it would not have listened to her at all, not with the queen of Larandaril so close. It finally conceded to carry one away, but only one. Rivergrace stayed cold. She told the river what she wished and it agreed to follow her desire.

She dropped her hands to her reins, fingers bone chilled, numbed with her effort, trembling in her saddle. Glow took a side step toward the river's bank.

"How can I know that?" Lara asked sadly.

"At least one of those oaths will not be entirely fulfilled until one or the other of us is dead, for it is the vow of a lifetime, and cannot be upheld until our lives run out."

Her gaze locked on Sevryn. "Do you tempt me?"

"No. I remind you that I have given you my word, and I see no evidence that anything I have done is treasonous." Sevryn kept his daggers in his hands, but they rested easy on his thighs, and he made no move although Pavan, like his stable mate, danced a little nervously in the rushing tide of the Andredia.

Bistane kneed his horse in front of Lariel, partially blocking her, though whether it was to protect her or intercede for Sevryn, could not be discerned. "Come with us, you two, before the river freezes both of you. We need to sit and talk. I have word from the north and our queen has her own confidences to share."

"I'll come." Rivergrace lifted her hand and made a summoning gesture. The Andredia answered with a roar, as she kicked her mare out of its waters, and onto the earth clear of its agitation.

"No!" Lara kicked her mount forward, knocking Bistane's to one side in her fury. "How dare you seize the Andredia! I am its force, its power, its benefactor by pact, and it will do my will! It answers to no one but me."

Rivergrace swayed in her saddle as Lara raised her fist, and an unseen but not unfelt power surged through the air. It smashed into her with a thunderous boom as though lightning had sundered the air. With great effort, she clung to her seat in her saddle and took a deep breath before turning to the other and smiling, sadly, answering, "Not entirely." She made a final movement with her hand, before beckoning to Sevryn, calling out, "Aderro! Good fortune."

"No! Don't do this, Grace! Don't do this. Trust me!" He dug his heel deep into Pavan's flanks, but the horse stayed froze in fear at the panic in his rider's voice. Sevryn cursed and jerked hard at the bridle and bit. The tashya stayed frozen in place, withers quivering, otherwise unmoving. He lifted a leg to throw himself off, to go after Rivergrace, to stop her sacrifice. He did not make it.

The air roared as a wall of water rose upstream. The waters of the Andredia reared in a flood tide, white spray and towering. The flash flood hit Sevryn and his mount full tide, sweeping them away as the horse screamed in terror. Sevryn bent forward to lace his arms about the creature's neck in a frantic gesture to stay mounted. White foam rose like fog, obscuring them as they disappeared in the fury.

Bistane jumped from his horse and ran to Rivergrace's side, grabbing the headstall with one hand and her arm with the other, both bracing her and protecting her from Lariel who threw her head back with a keening cry of anger.

Chapter Twenty-Six

RIVERGRACE THREW HERSELF off her horse, landing on both feet but with knees that threatened to give out from under her, even as she dared not show any weakness. Sevryn's anger swept away downriver, out of hearing, and she swallowed tightly. He would hate her for what she had done. Her heartbeat drummed in her throat and black stars danced at the edge of her vision. She shoved her feelings into the pit of her stomach to summon a smile at Lariel. "Trap me if you can."

Lariel stood in her stirrups, reins knotted tightly around one fist as she raised her other hand, baring her teeth in a fierce growl as she swung her horse around to face Rivergrace. Her eyes flashed multiple hues of blue punctuated with flashes of gold and silver. "You were a guest on my land and in my kingdom."

"Guest or well-regarded prisoner, I was never certain. But I have never acted as less than an ally."

"You are my hostage for Sevryn Dardanon."

"Never," she answered. She couldn't allow Lara to make her into a chain to bind him. She threw her head back, gathering her abilities within her, assessing what she could do to face Lariel and live. The woman who snubbed her horse into submission did not look at all like the young woman she'd made friends with, once upon a time. This then, was the person that men met upon the battlefield, and fell back from in awed retreat. "Whatever you think he has done, you don't understand, nor do you understand the range of what I can do." The air shivered about her with a rising heat from Lariel, but she ignored it. Water shimmered about her, drops too tiny to be seen or even to feel, but she felt them. They called to her and she called to her element. With a confidence she did not know she could feel, she lifted her arms and surrendered to the water. Rather than gather it to herself, she gave in to it. She could feel herself thin and grow unsubstantial, her life pulses change into an airiness that scared yet thrilled her, weariness leaving her body and bones as she became nothing more than a damp mist on the air, her empty clothes dropping to the ground. Glow whickered nervously and stepped away from her.

She ran . . . no, floated . . . away from cries and shouts on the air after her, noise that buffeted her misty being harmlessly, if annoyingly. She had not known she could do this, but she had thought she might be able to, from the way the dew condensed on her and tickled her skin and whispered to her that she could follow it wherever it went . . . and now, she did. She let the wind take her, high up into the hills of Larandaril, with the pounding of hoofbeats being left farther and farther behind her, just as she had left her cloak of flesh behind. They would not catch her, not just yet, not in this form, although she could not hold it long or she would lose herself entirely and disappear into the fogs on the hills forever. She drifted on the wind, driven, a spray splashing upon the high ridges that ringed Larandaril, and she nearly lost herself in the fog.

Her watery self did not consider this a bad thing: it was the way of water. Evaporation, condensation, precipitation and all over again, a cycle of nature. She was outside that cycle, outside the nature of water even as she wore its form. She had to remember that. Remember or be lost forever.

The air still held a bite from winter, but the chill felt good upon her face as she turned it toward the sky laced with clouds. She could feel the moisture beading in the sky, not heavy enough for rain but gathering. To the east, to Abayan Diort's dry lands, this rain would come. It would please him, this spring storm, and his farmers, and the lakes and streams of his hard-pressed land. The knowledge brought a smile to her face. If only it could always be so. But there would be storms and droughts and little else she could do anything about except to sense and know beforehand. The knowledge prickled along her skin and through her body before sinking deep into her bones. She could, if she wished, release the rain that gathered now in premature, misty sprinkles here, but they did not need it and she hesitated to interfere with the natural way of things. She had not been taught to be a Goddess, but she did not have to be to know there was a responsibility in the ways of nature. And, after all, if she was a Goddess, it was only as a minor River Goddess, in place of the one who had gone ... did Goddesses go insane? Perhaps her predecessor had gone demonic. It wasn't something she liked to dwell upon. She had been branded with the fire from the same Demon. Did she carry the same fate as well? The backlash which ostracized her warned her that it was a clear possibility. Lara's harsh words gnawed at her, because finding out the truth might endanger all those she loved, and she had to know the truth, if she hoped to be able to hide or quell her secrets.

She could hear the call of dark water more clearly now that she was far from Vaelinar shouts and pursuit. It touched her, faint, yet persistent, as one might hear a drip from a leaking roof hidden deep within the eaves. She did not think it had tainted her or was even sure that it had the ability to do so. Here was a power and a pervasive one. Rivergrace hesitated, momentarily thinking of turning back to whatever punishment Lariel might yet impose. Perhaps she deserved it.

Her mother Lily would tell her emphatically, no; she was not nor could she become Narskap. The weaving of her life had been different and, though a thread here and there might be the same, the pattern emerging was so different as to be night and day. For one, she was mortal. Her flesh, her heart, her soul, her loves and hates all mortal. And there it was, the truth that should blind all of them. She couldn't be a Goddess or a hound to evil because she *was* mortal. What she held within her was only the ability to read the waters of the rivers and of the clouds and to know its mind. Added to that the ability to call Fire, and control it briefly, aim it before loosing it, setting it within a parameter that it could not cross until it burned to bitter ashes. To harness Fire cost her reserves of strength that calling Water never did. Water came to her as naturally as breath, and she could feel it in any living object. Any water-Talented Vaelinar could do the same.

Only no one in their living memory had touched a Goddess of Kerith. She had not only touched the Being but had been cradled by Her for decades of her early life, held in a protective cocoon of not-being yet preserved, until the Goddess released her in her all-too mortal form.

Rivergrace thought of flesh. If it were not for Sevryn, and Nutmeg, and all her Farbranches—Lily and Tolby and her three brothers—she would not know who she was. They anchored her, but she held a core inside herself that made that possible. She would not accept Lara's condemnation for being different. Like a twig or a slender sapling, she had bowed as much as she could. Now it was time to seek the sun and grow as she was meant to grow, strong as well as supple. She was the daughter of Dwellers who believed in strong roots and had given them to her. She would betray herself as well as them if she stayed in the shadows of Vaelinar distrust. She would be who she was meant to be.

She smiled within her misty self as she crossed a brooklet of river water, and sent a prayer to all those she loved so much through it, knowing that it would be carried into the valley and then into the sacred Andredia before heading to the vast sea. She passed along dewed grasses into the foot-hills and the darkness of a cave where water called her yet again, to answer a voice she did not know.

The chase lost far behind her, she paused, a wisp upon a rocky outcrop just behind the border of Lara's lands. The mountains here, sharp hills really, with catacombs which had caught her once before, called out to her now.

Stone, sharp and cold, with a voice that begged to be heard.

She paused and listened for a long time. No. Not rock. Not granite and jasper and agate and plain old dirt. Another kind of water trapped deep within its confines, like a dark jewel in its shadows. It was water that called to her, water deep and secret. It called to be discovered. She hovered on the hill, undecided, until a rising breeze threatened to dissipate her altogether sending her fleeing into the mouth of the stone hill. With a chilling efficiency, it sucked her in, her senses sent whirling about her until she screamed, knowing and fearing that the cavern mouth was undoing her entirely.

Suddenly, she sat stark naked on the cold stone floor, physical and whole, shaking in every limb, stony pebbles bruising her flesh. Grace anchored her quivering hands over her mouth and jaw, holding her lips still and steadying herself until her breathing quieted and her hard-drumming heart slowed. Finally, she moved her hands up her face to rub her eyes. Had she lost any of herself to the mist, to the rocks? She couldn't tell. Physically, she had all the flesh she'd been born with. Spiritually, she could not take an inventory. Were there memories torn from her? Whole lives missing?

Grace pulled a lock of her hair, a gesture Nutmeg used to do whenever she fussed, saying, "Stop that!"

Her words fell on deaf stone. She got to her feet carefully, her eyes adjusting to the dark. She hated it and, worse, she stood barefoot. She had the tender-soled feet of the shod class of society, and walking here would be excruciating eventually, notwithstanding her nakedness. Despite the fact she had been deposited so far inland of the tunnel, she thought she knew her direction and that the mouth of the cave lay at her back. She could turn about. It wouldn't solve her nudity, but she would find the sun and fresh air even though the voice of the dark water now tugged at her, as if realizing she had arrived to accede to its demand. It tugged determinedly at her as it held a leash to her heart, pulling harshly. Sharp pains lanced through her chest as she took a wobbly step backward. Water could not rule her if she did not let it. She raised a hand instinctively, filling it with fire, and cut the invisible cord with a slash of her fingers. The dark water recoiled as it was wont to do in the face of its opposite.

Rivergrace drew herself up, straight and tall. There had been a time when closed-in spaces and darkness gnawed at her, captured her, and held her still and tight in fright so sharp that she could not escape. No more. Perhaps she had grown from those days when she was no higher than her mother's knee and they both were enslaved in the mines, or perhaps it was because she had faced darkness and more in caves often enough that it no longer held a threat. Rivergrace did not count the dark side of the earth as a friend either, but it no longer ruled her. There were many things these days that had no power to control her. She would ferret out what cowered in the depths, determine what comprised it, and what she might do about it. She smiled faintly as she walked into the deeps, her fingers trailing lightly upon the right side walls, keeping track of her path as her senses sought that which called her. The walls were sculpted yet rough and grainy from the centuries that had passed since their first carving under the hills. Great, scaled worms had traveled them, according to the Bolger tales, followed centuries later by the Mageborn who'd woven their own magic on the earth to make themselves pathways for war and intrigue. She could not know of either, being young even by Kerith standards. She did know that the stone and the water were far older than any worm or magician. Far, far older, as old as the birth of the world itself, for how could it be otherwise?

She supposed her sister might have a Dweller's tale of the birth of these serpentine trails.

She had wanted to stay with Meg, Gods knew that she did, but events wouldn't allow it. She knew that the pregnancy was difficult and that, although Nutmeg grumbled about hers, it was probably far more difficult than she'd allowed. Dweller babes were stubborn and oft did what they willed, and as for Vaelinar children . . . well, they were fey. What else could they be?

Rivergrace stumbled heavily over an unseen obstacle, going to one knee, landing on her hands in the gravel. She smothered a curse she had learned in Bistane's great army. It sounded harsh the moment it escaped her, and echoed like a stone thrown against quarry slates before its noise passed. There are some words that should never be said, particularly in the dark, and she regretted it the second it passed her lips. She held her breath as if it might bring some retort back to her, but heard nothing.

She got up, dusting her palms. She never thought she'd be wishing for a gown, although she dressed plainly, compared to the gowns that elegant Tiiva and Lariel wore about the manor and grounds, but she often resented even the plain dress she had adopted. Better to have the homespun pants she and Nutmeg used to run about in, the better to scale ladders and carts and apple trees. She narrowed her eyes and took a look at what had tripped her. A half-buried ivory dome caught the light. Either a water-polished stone or a skull sunk deep in the tunnel's floor, and she shied away from it, leaving its mystery unsolved. It gleamed at her, a fallen star in the tunnel, catching her eye. Then she saw, clumped not far beyond it, unusual ripples in the dusty floor.

Bending, she ran her fingers through the dust and touched cloth. She lifted the garments and shook them out, turning her head to avoid the clouds unsuccessfully, sneezing loudly as she tried to see what it was she held. Kernan country garb, a woman. Grace buried a fist in the fabric. Still good, not rotting, although the skull had seemed polished

by age. Dubious fortune she could not overlook, she pulled
the clothing on, shuddering as the grit slid over her bare
skin, finding the blouse a bit too big, and the divided skirt
could have used a belt. There were herbs in the pockets. A
Kernan wisewoman, then, out herbing on the fertile ridges
just above Larandaril. Boots would have been perfect.
Grace dragged her toes along the cave floor, shuddering
when she kicked aside more bones, and then found the rugged shoes the woman had died in. She turned the bone fragments out, shaking them down to rattle among the stones
and pebbles before they finally quieted.

She had to sit to put the shoes on. Sturdy leather creaked
as she tried her feet in them, found them adequate, if too
wide. She had Vaelinar bones, after all, and when she stood,
her skirt would be several hands too short. Sliding her left
hand into her pocket, her fingers touched upon iron and
traced its curvature and length. A wicked blade, a pruning
knife, sharp and hooked. A long pocket on the right hip
held a short sword. An errant sting in her fingers told her
that it had retained its sharpness over the years. Rivergrace
breathed deeply. Dressed and armed, by the ill-fortune of
another. Had the wisewoman, Kernan witch born, also
heeded the call of the water? Had she drunk from it, caught
thirsty in this dry and dusty tunnel? Grace pushed her hair
back from her brow. She would remember not to.

She moved on, every now and then catching the smell of
the water, and then finally hearing it, faintly, pooled and yet
dripping within the depths ahead of her. If the water did not
sing her out as it had sung her in, she might be lost and
wandering for quite a long time, her fate not much different
than that of the skeleton she'd stumbled over. As she walked,
the echo of her steps changed, and she became aware the
ceiling grew higher and higher still until she could look up
and see splinters of sky and cloud. That eased her a bit. She
could feel her dread of closed-in places lift a little, even as
dirt and pebbles skidded down from the roof opening to
shower her. Grace eyed the roof carefully. She might not be

able to climb out, but that did not mean something could not fall in. Moving cautiously, she started forward again.

The tunnel began to curve to her left, and the sound of water became clearer with every step until split rock overhead let in waning rays to cast a wavering light upon a pool in front of her, where the entry widened into a small cavern and she could feel the dampness in the air. She knelt upon the slick stones that formed a lip at her end, and stretched her fingers out to the pool. As soon as she broke its cool, wet surface, sparks of light green seemed to emanate and mist off the water and a voice intoned, "Welcome." It came from everywhere and nowhere.

Drops trailed from her fingertips as she sat back, craning her neck to look about her, shadows draping close and revealing little. The stone beneath her knees vibrated still, as if it had been struck to produce the sound, and she wondered if she had truly heard it or simply felt its resonance throughout her body. She watched as the last droplets of pool water fell from her hand, each sending up a glowing splash and a ripple as it hit. If she were a wee creature, with soaring antennae from her brows and wings buzzing on her back, would she feel the striking of the drop on the water just as she, human, had felt the shock of speech against the very rocks? Rivergrace frowned. She dashed the last of the dampness from her hand and scrubbed it dry against her skirts vigorously before she became lost in thoughts she seldom thought or had time to dwell upon. The philosophical lassitude which had enveloped her immediately faded. Bespelled. She had nearly fallen headfirst into its net. The corner of her mouth twitched wryly. Nutmeg would never have succumbed to such a trap. Ever practical, ever in motion, the Dweller in her sister did not lend itself to windy platitudes. Do and be done with it! Then tell a colorful tale describing the deed. That would be the Dweller way.

She looked down at the cavern's lake. It pooled power. It reeked of power and because it did, she knew she had to be circumspect. She could not charge at it like some child with a bully stick and hope to beat it into submission. Like water itself, it would be fluid and slippery and damn near uncatchable.

She tilted her head. "You called, I have answered."

"Many are called. So few answer."

The sound this time came faintly, scarcely audible and far short of the power available, leaving her unable to decide if the remark queried or complained of her. The contact felt like nothing she had ever experienced before. This was not the River Goddess she'd sheltered once only to lose to the insanity of Cerat the Souldrinker. Another God? She didn't think so. The only power she knew of, inside these tunnels, was that of the Mageborn, and they had not been alive to touch the peoples of Kerith in a thousand years or more. So what had called to her, and how, and did they call to her or just to anyone? Had there been magic in the long gone rockeaters which had carved these tunnels? That, in the few tales that Rufus had told her from early Bolger days, had never even been hinted at. It was the venom and spittle of the rockeater serpents, and the rough scales of their hides as they bored, that ate through this stone, not magic. Not power. She could not call herself a true judge of magic, however, for even among the Vaelinars she was untrained and knew little. From what she did know, Vaelinars did not work magic. The effects were the same, but they saw the world with eyes of varied and remarkable colors, a seeing of the threads and strands which comprised the many elements of the world and which could be plucked, strung and unstrung, knotted and severed, rewoven and cast aside, like an instrumentalist with their instrument. It was not magic. It was the seeing and touching of what they saw which gave them their myriad powers. Not that they meddled more than by the merest of touches. Most had not the capability to do what they might dream of with what they perceived. Only once in a while was a great reworking accomplished, a Way, which might establish the fortune of a Vaelinar bloodline for generations to come. Mostly, Vaelinar magic consisted of a small pluck here or a faint strum there. A larger effect would come from a strike or a hammer upon the elements. And then, there were those unspoken disasters, those attempts to alter reality, which exploded upon the world and for which an entire bloodline could be sentenced to death. Vaelinar justice. Reach for power, but suffer the consequences if you fail.

A small chill ran across the back of Rivergrace's neck. There were whispers that such a happening had sentenced her own family to termination and that her father had fled to an even harsher taskmaster who had promised him hiding and given him enslavement. Did she believe that Fyrvae now named Narskap had come from such a background? She did not know. She hardly knew herself, let alone a father and mother she had lost when very young. It could be true. It equally could not be true, and used to mislead her. If the Vaelinars were experts in the weaving of the elements of the world, they were even more masterful at weaving the emotions and thoughts of those who lived upon it. Her Dweller upbringing had hardly prepared her for the insinuations of the Vaelinars. Her first lessons had been hard given and harder to receive, but she was learning. It did not mean that she had no friends among her own people, but that her people held a different code for the world and how it was meant to work. If you asked Tolby Farbranch how the world should work, he would tell you of seasons, seasons of planting and nurturing and harvest and storage for the seasons of want. He would tell you of teamwork and family and trust and love and courage. He would tell you of unwanted rain and the fury of wind untold and the gentle touch of a spring sun. If you asked the Vaelinar, they would tell you of Houses and Strongholds and Fortresses, of warlords and Warrior Queens and cunning craftsmen, of heralded Ways and fouled pools of failure where no man could hope to live, of a heritage torn away by a mysterious enchantment, and of a heritage returned by an even more mysterious Ferryman. They might tell you of their superiority and the yoke that this world placed upon them, and of their eternal longing to return to that which birthed them. They might tell you of the burden of living centuries in a

lifetime, anchored to a land of commoners, dreaming of uncommon abilities. Every once in a while, you could find a
rare one who would speak to you of family, friends, honor,
and love. Such a man she loved.

Rivergrace waited a few more heartbeats before standing.

As if suddenly remembering her, the lake woke. "Look,"
the power whispered. "And see."

She dropped her gaze to the still waters of the deep pool,
its surface barely lit by the light which trickled down from
above, a thin and wavering orange illumination that smudged
more than it delineated. If she saw more than herself, it was
only as a shadow in the deep dark pool. Rivergrace saw a
ripple across the pool, and felt her whole body tense as
something she could not describe or hear filled her senses.
A mist rose from the edges of the water, ringing the area,
giving it a border as if it were a dark and foreboding mirror.
The air grew deadly cold. She could feel the frost without
seeing it, yet her skin burned with the icy touch.

Without her willingness, her gaze was drawn to the dark
water. Rivergrace knew that she would see what was going
to be shown to her without her approval. She feared for her
soul as the power stripped away the very permission she
had fought throughout her adult life to gain for every action. She saw Sevryn and images that made little or no sense
to her in their savagery. It caught her breath in her throat
and she gritted her teeth against her reaction, not wanting
to give the images more power than they already had. She
watched and did not understand, and feared. Would she remember later or would the visions disappear into her very
soul, forgotten but infusing their power into everything she
thought and did? She bent her head to watch more closely,
willing herself never to forget. Understanding would come
later.

Visions faded. She knelt down, hand out, chasing them.
"More."

"More?" The power shivered about her.

"I have to *know*."

"And if knowing unmakes you, unravels you again?"

"Then it's my willing, not yours. Not theirs. Mine."

"You asked," said the voice of the dark water. "I grant."

Silver glinted off the water pool mirror. It seemed to splash off the ceiling and walls of the small cavern, dancing sparks that spit and shimmered over the dirt and stone. They did not fade but held wherever they touched, small stars drawn down and pinned to the earth, giving off an aura of being untouchable for all their closeness. She became the silver among the inky darkness, and her thoughts raced away.

She felt the coursing halt and she tried to pull back, feeling herself fall into another flesh, captured, possessed, and she fought, rearing up in fear. Dark magic coiled about her strongly. *Wait. Watch. Know.* Rivergrace laced her fingers close and prayed it would be anchor enough and let her mind stay where it had been sent, and she became another.

Chapter
Twenty-Seven

A STRANGE SKIN HELD HER. The smell of the sea enveloped her, as did this other, this one who thought of herself as Roanne. Rivergrace let herself slide deeper into the other's thoughts and hoped not to be perceived. She stood upon weathered planks. The dock shifted uneasily upon the harbor's tide, the ship tied to its side rolling with it, dockworkers cursing as their footing unbalanced on the plank ramps and their loads grew unsteady. The edifice had not been made to be permanent or hold adamant against the tug of the ocean. It had been built hastily, and illegally, and would be torn down the moment the ship shoved off, its boards dried and fed into fireplaces scattered throughout the small port. No sign of their leaving would remain other than a wake upon the waves which would, as in the way of all ocean's faring, last but a moment or two. No trace of their mooring, no track of their leaving, no sign of their traitorous plans would remain behind save for people who knew that a trading ship had put up its sails and nothing more than that.

A morning wind rose up, stiff and cold and brisk, a few drops of rain slanting upon it. Roanne drew her cloak close about her in a futile effort to stave off the cold uneasiness that tugged at her. All passengers were already aboard, and her parents had yet to come to the docks. She had come from her dorms, with what items and books she had carried with her into her apprenticeship, and they were coming from the family's country home with their things. She had seen little enough of them over the past few seasons, except to make this plan, and now she fretted.

Captain Galbert's first, Nethen, shouted down. "Make ready to cast off! The Tide Caller waits for no man!" His voice softened a bit as he added to her, "Lady Marant. We can hold no longer. All our informants, all our omens, say that now is the time, if we are to follow the Tide Caller."

The Tide Caller. Black phantom. A God or Demon? No one knew. Only that he had appeared, tearing a hole in their ensorcelled world, and the philosophers of magic held that he would disappear through that same hole . . . and beyond him, perhaps, freedom. He rode a tide that Queen Trevilara could not control, could not block, could not send a plague against. His was a singular magic, which the old tyrant did not hold and should be unable to counter. Or so they prayed. So thin a grasp to believe upon, just as she held now. Something flickered down a long alleyway. "I see a carriage. Please." She shaded her eyes to look across the morning fog and haze where, amid the smoke of the plague bonfires, she could indeed see the carriage, the two-in-hand approaching. The crest on the doors had been draped over, but she knew the horses, knew them well. One of them she had helped birth and then wean before the horse master took over to train it to harness as it grew. Roanne held her breath. The carriage halted a cautious length away, horses restive, and her father leaped from inside. He did not wait to help another occupant out, and her heart quailed inside of her.

"Mother?"

"She's not coming." Her father drew close enough that their voices would carry only between the two of them, the din of the dockworkers readying to shove off and the thin wail of the sea wind cloaking their words.

Roanne's hand went up in entreaty. "Go back! Convince her. Tell her this is our only chance. Tell her she has to come with us! I can beg the captain to wait a little longer. Please. We can't leave her behind."

"I'm not coming either."

Cold pierced her chest. "No."

"She came down with a fever last night. We can't take a chance, Roanne, on infecting you or the other passengers. A ship is close quarters." He turned his face away for a moment. "It's better this way."

The coldness in her chest spread outward, infected all of her limbs. "It doesn't have to be the plague. We've been resistant. Let me go to her. It could be any one of a handful of spring fevers. The alphistol bloomed early, she always gets wheezes and hives from them. It could be something minor. Father, I can help!"

"No." He cut the air between them with his hand, his gloved hand, and she realized he wouldn't touch her. Not truly. "This isn't a chance we're willing to take, and Captain Galbert would be the first to agree. You have to go for us, Roanne. Follow the Tide Caller. Do the House of Marant proud, as you have always done. When it comes to it, I—I admit I haven't the courage. You sail to a rift in the very fabric of the world itself. Who can hope to survive that? I can't. I know you do, and I pray you will, but I can't go with you or even follow after. Your mother is sick, but her reason becomes my excuse. Forgive me."

"Father."

He shook his head. She saw the track of tears down his cheek.

"You're not a coward!"

"Oh, I am. Just never in the ways I thought I would be." Someone high up on deck yelled something incomprehensible down at them, but Roanne knew it must be an exhortation to hurry. Her father beckoned to the driver who set the handbrake and climbed down, pulling a shroud-covered chest from under the seat. The driver carried it to the plague bonfire, showed it to the priestess standing there who inspected it, ordered the shroud off and burned, and gave permission for a loader to take it aboard. Roanne watched her even as her voice threatened to freeze in her throat.

"Father, please . . ."

He looked into her eyes, the only way he would come close to her. "Our heritage and history rests in there. It's the best we can give you, Roanne. Daughter. The chest is air- and watertight, within another chest that is also airtight and watertight. The handles on either end are sturdy. It will act as a float, and can hold you up, if need be."

If the ship came to grief. But she was already held fast in grief's grip, her eyes tight upon her father's face. The House Marant, one of the queen's oldest and most loyal families, had fallen to this, their death and despair as the queen became inexorably a thing too awful to bear. If her mother did not have the plague, if her father did not sicken as well, could they withstand much longer that thing of darkness that ruled their country? They faced death, and worse, by staying. Her fleeing would endanger them, and she'd no doubt her father knew that well.

"Have you . . . other plans?"

"We do, but I won't speak of them here." His steady gaze flinched. He touched a gloved finger to her cheek. "Gods willing, there will come a day when we . . . when we meet again."

"Lady Marant!" First Mate Nethan called hoarsely. "We are weighing anchor! We cannot wait longer."

Her eyes brimmed. She knew she couldn't dissuade him, and she didn't have the courage inside her to stay and face with him what she knew they would face. "Please. Don't hate me for leaving, Father."

"Never. And you must not pity us for staying. You go for all of us. Carry our love and pride, always!" He choked. "Now . . . go," he said, his voice coarsening, and she heard the tears checked within it.

Roanne leaned to kiss him, and he flinched backward, fastening a scarf over his face quickly. He grabbed her hand and put it to his chest in the only salute of farewell he dared allow. "Live well and long and in love and honor," he told

her. Then he took her hand, steering her to the bonfire
where the cleansing priestess awaited.

Smoke and cinders puffed in her face, stinging her eyes,
and when she had blinked them away, her father's hand had
left hers, and the carriage itself was pulling away in haste,
before either of them could change their minds.

The priestess looked her over. She could feel the woman
peeling away the layers of her skin, searching, digging, for
signs of plague. The dowager had never liked her and had
scorned all her clumsy attempts at learning in her apprenticeship, but they knew each other well. She had other teachers
she valued and revered, but fate had made it this one who
would see her take her good-byes. The woman's thin lips
peeled back from her teeth in distaste as she bit off her
words. "Burn the cloak," the woman said. "Then board."

As reviled as her former teacher was, Roanne knew that
the priestess had been born to be a healer and now all that
was left to her was the scourging, the purging against the
plague that ravaged all of their people. Her natural Talents
had been honed, sharpened, to do one thing: identify and
then burn away the disease. She could not heal. She could
only destroy the source, help stand against the contagion.
And when this ship pulled away from the dock, the priestess would be the one woman left in the small village who
knew exactly who had boarded and what their intent had
been. They would not let her live with that knowledge. She
felt an unbidden surge of sympathy for the woman. They
had knocked heads because Roanne had refused to sharpen
her skills for cleansing only—repudiating the course the
priestess had been forced to take. Yes, the scourging might
prevent the plague but to relinquish the hope of healing
it . . . that had been a possibility Roanne could not sacrifice.
Did the two women hate each other because of their
choices? Once. But not today. She saw an expression pass
over the dowager's face and knew that she would not be
betrayed even as the consequences frightened the priestess.

Roanne began to shrug out of her cloak, her sleeve covering her face and said quietly, "Leave. Cut your tongue out

and run as fast as you can. It's the only way you'll be safe."
She dropped a handful of coins into the hand held out for
the offending garment before draping the cloak in place.

The priestess' eyes widened as the color drained from
her face. She answered with the barest nod of her head.

The tongue would grow back, in time, for she was a
healer yet, of sorts. But it was the only way those who would
kill her would tire of trailing her and let her slip away, thinking their job was done anyway. Tongue gone and fled, she
would not, could not, betray them.

Roanne kicked off her outer gown for good measure, dropping it as well onto the bonfire. She had dressed in layers, new
clothes, untouched, under the old, for just such a measure.
Smoke puffed up, rank and thick, obscuring the priestess from
her view and trailing upward to a canopy strung over it, protection from the dreary skies. What must burn would burn. As
she ran for the boardwalk, it began to rain in earnest, hard,
sleeting drops that stung her skin like fiery ice. It did not taste
at all like the salty tears already wetting her face. Two sailors
handed her on board, helping her up the last few steps, throwing the ramp off behind her, the ship groaning as it prepared
to shove off. She shook them off and clambered her way to the
upper deck. The coldness stiffening her began to thaw a little.
First Mate Nethen held her elbow to steady her as she stood
at the railing and watched the ship being towed out upon the
tide. All ties loosed. All ropes cut or thrown aside. All hatches
for boarding and loading battened shut. All land and family
and kingdom and alliance abandoned.

Roanne knotted her hands upon the railing. She tried to
find a word or two of hope to throw into the wind and rain
and felt them leave her throat but could not hear them over
the creak of wood and rope and the cries of the sailors.

Through a thin veil of smoke, she saw the priestess move
away from the fire and lift one hand in a sign of benediction.

So be it.

Rivergrace sat with her hand to her mouth, jolted back to
the reality of cold stone and broken sunlight filtering
through the escarpment. Tears dried on her cheek. She
blinked upward, even as a small rivulet of sand and grit
began to trickle down from above. She swallowed, feeling
the movement of her tongue between her teeth. Had this
other girl truly suggested that it would be better to have a
tongue cut out than be forced to speak?

She dropped her hand and touched the lip of the pool.
Dark water licked at her fingers like a hungry pup and she
drew her hand back hastily. No water for thirst here. It
would consume her long before she could take a drink. The
feeling of it, almost like slime, dripped off her hand in thick
plops. She wanted to wipe it off on her clothes but feared
spreading the contamination. Thoughts tumbled through
her head. The plague had come from Trevilara with the Raymy,
a weapon of war. The Tide Caller could be none other than
Daravan or his phantom brother Ferryman. The rift, on one
side at least, was opening wide enough and often enough that
people sailed to it, hoping for escape. She closed her eyes
tightly. She knew of no refugees being taken in, but the First
Home had a vast coastline. She had much to think about,
and pushed back on her heels to stand.

"I am done here."

"Ahhhh." The water sighed against her thoughts. "But I
am not."

She stood, an agonizing effort against a gravity that
would flatten her to the ground that would keep her fixed
in place against her will. Bones trembled, sinews tightened
and then crackled with the effort, but stand she did, drops
of sweat running over her face like raindrops or tears, and
her mouth went even drier. She placed the palms of her
hands carefully against the rock wall, feeling its texture cut
into her skin: rough, gritty, solid, unthinking. She turned her
face away from the pool even as it cajoled her.

"I am water, but I bridge. I know what I am from what
has touched me, from what will touch me, what will cross

me. But because I am water, I can be shaped by a vessel. You are such a vessel."

"Anyone who tries the shaping of such as you are plays with darkness. You infiltrate."

"A vessel cannot hold water without becoming damp, that is true. Still. Listen. I have more to show you."

"No." Grace pressed herself tighter against the wall, grounding herself in the solid feel of the stone, the minerals trapped inside it, the quiet depths of its existence. With a clarity she wished she didn't have, she knew she had begun to understand most of what the pool had shown her, the blurred images, the shadowy specters, the barest silhouettes of truth cast across the waters. Her knowledge would lead her to a course that would change her forever. She longed for Sevryn. But this course would make that impossible. She'd put a gap between them. Pain pierced her. He was already angry with her for making a decision to protect him; she'd heard the outrage in his voice. But this was different, far different, and there would be no going back from the path she intended to take, a Way of sorts, as another Vaelinar might view it, into a future she could only hope she could manipulate.

She had choices. A myriad of them. But, as it often was with choices, she had no method of telling which would be the best, in the end. All she could do was weigh them now and make the best judgment she could, and she had done that.

Rivergrace pushed herself away from the tunnel wall, headed back the way she had come in, knowing it now whether in thready light or pitch-black darkness.

"AN OPEN ACT OF TREASON," Lara said stubbornly, her jaw set as the words left her mouth.

"You can't treat it as such."

"And why not?" She swung on Bistane.

"Because we are at war and because, within our own ranks, we have enemies."

"I count him as one of them."

With a faint sigh, Bistane sat on the corner of her desk. "You don't know that. Despite your anger, despite what you think he might have done, I see no evidence of any wrongdoing, Lara, and if you have secrets you fear his revealing, there's no word on the wind of any such betrayal." The other two men in the office kept their silence.

Her mouth twisted bitterly. "You doubt me? Who do you think tied me to my chair?"

He considered her face. "Under the right circumstances, almost any lover might have," he answered lightly.

"He's not my lover!" Her blue eyes reflected icily at him.

"I found you in no harm except for nightmares."

Lara looked away from him, but not before giving him an expression of contempt.

"He is your Hand, Lara. He's done more for you than perhaps anyone save Jeredon, and your brother is gone. You've kept him close and he's kept your commands, odious as they have been from time to time. You've asked much from him and, as far as I know, he's delivered it."

"He fled."

"It would appear from your actions now that he had reason to."

"Don't try to lecture me further, Bistane. You haven't your father's experience or authority to do so." She looked back to him, her brows drawn tightly in disdain.

It hurt him to meet her expression, but he did, saying quietly, "I have the experience even if you won't credit me for it. But you misunderstand me. This is not a lecture, this is a discussion, and I won't be left out of your council. I deserve it; I have earned it." His voice tightened. "Since you dismiss me, I'll leave you with the information I came to tell you, and it's not good news."

Lara put her hand up, taking in a breath with a sound as if it must have cut like a knife into her lungs. "Forgive me, Bis. It's not just Sevryn. I would hold Rivergrace as a surety against his actions, but I don't know if I can trust her as I want to. She has abilities; you saw them at the Andredia. My river, but she commanded it. What else could she wrest away from me?"

The other two men in the room, had remained quiet, but Tranta stirred now. "M'lady, Rivergrace has never done you malicious harm."

"No. No, but she hasn't been raised as we were, trained as we were, and she has ties to this world that none of us has, ties to Kerith Gods which seemed to both aid and war with her Vaelinar Talents. I don't fear her, but I do hold her with great . . ." Lara paused, as if picking out a word after deliberation, "concern."

"She's aided you with those same abilities."

After another long moment, she continued, "At Ashen-brook, true, but upon that battlefield, with others in hand—Daravan and the Ferryman—I can't swear as to whose power it might have been or who initiated it, and what we saw then we are unlikely to ever see again, a braiding of Talents. She might be able, but does she have the heart to do it?"

"We all fear the unknown, Lara."

She shook her head slowly. "I've seen her turn a river into fire, Bistane, and if she did not use that power tonight, but held it in reserve in case she needed to, then she is even more dangerous. To all of us and to herself. I love her, but I can't trust her."

"You don't trust because you have doubt. You haven't condemned her because of that same doubt. We all know her. She's good and loving, but with a core of stone, like that which lies in the riverbeds, solid and polished and all the more beautiful for the wear of the water. Dweller-raised, she has her . . . eccentricities, but I wouldn't even fault those."

"But is she one of us? Truly?"

"If you count on blood alone to be one of us, what have you to say for the likes of Quendius?"

She took in a slight hiss through her teeth. "It wasn't our blood that made him thus."

"Perhaps. Or lack of it doesn't make her what she is."

"In another time, perhaps, I might be able to give her the time she needs. I haven't got that liberty now, Bistane."

"You would punish her for being unpolished?"

"I can't afford to have a tool whose temper cannot be judged, whose use is unknown and uncertain and whose attraction is a distraction among those I do know well." Lara moved back, put her hand to the nape of her neck, and rubbed gently. "Nor a prisoner."

"What are you going to do?"

"I don't know. The only sure remedy is one I can't face right now."

Bistane put his hand on her shoulder. "Then don't."

"One life against many? You know what I have to choose."

"What I know, Lara," Tranta murmured, "is that Bistane is right in that we have many enemies and few enough friends. We don't have the experience among us that we used to: Osten is gone, Bistel is gone, Gilgarran and Daravan, gone, Jeredon and my brother."

Bistane smiled and gripped her shoulder gently, feeling the heat of her body through fabric, the smell of her subtle perfume in the strands of her hair. "If being a pawn were treasonous, there would be many of us condemned. We don't always know who uses it." He leaned forward and took a subtle inhalation, breathing her in. She turned slightly, so that their cheeks almost brushed.

"Which should I take comfort in? Your advice ... or your presence?"

Clearing his throat, Bistane moved away from her. "Whichever you need most from me." The prick of her contempt had faded away until all that he felt now was being moved by her, as he always did, his body hardening to her closeness and his own feelings for her. She knew that of him, surely, not quite but almost lovers. He ached for her to allow him to close that gap between them, but he would not let it happen because she felt weak and helpless. He would wait. As he had for a long time, and could a while longer. Either of them might succumb to a momentary weakness, but neither of them would respect that, and if any relationship lay in their future, respect had to be partnered with the passion. She deserved and he demanded nothing less.

Farlen shifted his massive shoulders, an oft-seen habit of Osten Drebukar. He stated, "I have men searching downstream on the Andredia, to see if Sevryn survived the flash flood and where he might have washed ashore."

"Oh, he's gone. Where, I don't know, but I've no doubt Grace had the river carry him free, far beyond where I could have reached out for him." Lara made a tiny sound that might have been a sigh before turning about, twisting her fingers together. "What's done is done. Tranta has a long way to get back to the shore, and Farlen has a day of plotting logistics ahead of him yet. You've ridden a long way, and in the night, to find me. Give us your news. I'll have mulled wine brought up and the first of the breakfast bread."

"That would be appreciated. Who stands watch on your door?"

"Tranta, if you do not mind."

He did, slightly, and there was a small hitch in his stride as he filled the threshold and said, "Of course not."

Laughing Tranta, lord of the sea and his only true rival, if he really had any, for Lara's attention. But he would not gain Lariel's regard by disliking Tranta. And who could dislike the man anyway? He couldn't, if it were not for her.

"Nothing you could messenger?"

"Not reliably." He slid his coat off his fighting leathers. "It is a rather long story." He waited until Lara seated herself as a maid came in with a tray quickly brought in and left, while Tranta took up a stoic stance at the door of the apartment facing into the hall, a goblet of wine in one hand and a pull of butter-soaked bread in the other, the back of his gleaming head of sea-blue hair to them. Bistane knew he would listen, but his words were not meant for Lariel alone. He took his chair to relate his visit. He spoke as if it were only a tale to be told, much as he had shared his experience with his brother, and when he finished, the room sat in quiet for a moment until Lara took a deep breath.

She stirred, smoothing the napkin over her lap distractedly. "What of the books?"

"We unwrapped the book Azel had marked as most advanced and found it in deplorable condition, as he warned we would. My brother secured it even more thoroughly than our good scholar had. It should last until Verdayne reaches Calcort although it may be in nothing but crumbles and ash if it does not. He carries a second, one barely touched, or at least that was its condition when Verdayne secured it. It's virulent, whatever it is. If it is caused by pests, they are so tiny they can't be sighted easily."

"What if we are carrying the curse to Calcort? I don't

want to see the contamination spread. All those libraries, all those books."

"Azel says his ordinary books and scrolls have not been infected. So far."

Lara tilted her head to one side, a fall of silver-and-blonde hair cascading down her shoulder as she did. "The *Books of All Truth* are a Way. Is it coming undone?"

Tranta shifted uneasily in the threshold, and Bistane scratched the side of his jaw as her words fell ominously between them. Farlen made a deep noise of distress like a groan stifled in his vast Drebukar frame. Bistane gathered himself and leaned forward. "Pray it isn't so, lady queen."

Chapter
Twenty-Nine

CEYLA LAY IN THE FALLEN TRUNK of the great tree, an aryn tree no less, and shivered despite the fact she no longer had feeling in her hands or feet, the decomposing matter inside as damp as it was outside, rain drizzling inside to find her no matter how deep she tried to burrow. She was now into her second day of running. The foul weather had given her two strokes of luck ... the first being that the hounds had lost her scent (and the water washed her clean of the awful slime) and the second being that one of the hunters had gotten near her without knowing it before his horse slipped on the wet needles and leaves on the forest bed, throwing him and running off. She'd been the one to catch the horse and it stood now, half-dozing, as she tried to catch a small stretch of sleep. The rider had died of his injuries. Ceyla had rolled his body under a thicket of silver finger and led the horse away until she could find a tall enough stump or fallen tree to mount from, and ridden away as far as she could. They wouldn't find the body for days, until the corpse stench could draw the hounds, and by then she should be south and east toward her destination.

Should be. Would be. Could be. For a dizzying moment, the threads of many futures dazzled her thought and sight, and then one *twanged* true and her vision cleared again to the here and now.

Ceyla put the heel of her hand to her brow. Never had she been so struck and staggered by the futures ranging before her, all vaguely different and vaguely familiar at the same time, with a driving goal to reach that she could not forget or let go. That one thread, that tight and thrumming singleton that drove her and seemingly bound her fate, now told her to sleep. Sleep a while and then ride, ride to the one she must meet. The feeling in her limbs would return with a burning vengeance and she would stay alive and whole until she met the man of her destiny upon the road.

And then she knew little of what might happen beyond that.

She pressed the heel of her palm tightly against her temple as if it could wipe away the painful throbbing of her mind. It worked for the briefest of moments and then her thoughts broke through in a lightning-strike surge so strong that it flung her back against the rough trunk of the tree with a smack that sent a different sort of pain through her skull.

She needed sleep! Her body begged her for it and her mind perversely held it just out of her reach, spinning thought after thought instead. None and all could be true, and Ceyla no longer cared. She'd started on one path and would remain dogged to it no matter what frayed and scattered pathways seemed determined to sprout before her inner vision. She could not choose them all!

Chapter
Thirty

The Andredia surged around Sevryn and the horse, frothing snow white like an incoming wave onto a beach, but it carried them. Pavan struggled to keep his head up, nostrils flared huge in terror, hooves striking as he attempted to paddle to no avail, but it was all unnecessary. Through the icy sting of its spray and chill white fog of its rush, Sevryn could feel the intent of the river embodied in the way it rose under them, pushing them forward. Nearly knocked from the saddle as Pavan flailed, Sevryn kicked his feet free and held on to the horse's mane, letting his body ride the river wave. The moment he was immersed in the river, the shock of it hit him. He rode cradled in the essence of a wild, untamed thing that resented and defied his nature even as it answered the will that Grace had laid upon it. They sped downriver, surging at a pace that took his breath away, and he had no doubt that when the Andredia felt it had delivered them, they would come ashore hard enough to break bones. To that end, he tried to talk to the water's essence, using his Voice to reach the sentience buried deep in its elemental being, to find the thread of its existence that Gilgarran had taught him all things in cre-

ation were woven of, each different and yet the same. The
hope that his Talent could even reach the thing Rivergrace
had made out of her desperation thinned as the water crested
mindlessly, sweeping him and Pavan downstream. His sense
of time swept away with the river. He could have been caught
in the flood for moments or for days, timed only by the fact
he felt thirst and hunger, and he heard Pavan's equine stomach rumble loudly.

The river quivered underneath them, like a ferry lurching away from shore. He called to it, reaching down into his
Voice, coaxing it to beach them, assuring it that it was time
their journey come to an end. He could feel it absorbing his
words, sucking them down into the white-frothy maelstrom
of its inner being, digesting them, as it were. Whether it
thought or reasoned well enough that he could control it, he
had no idea. When he looked at it, he could not see the
threads Grace had woven together, the woof and warp of
what she'd created to spirit him away.

He put his hand on Pavan's neck. The horse's skin quickened under his touch, and he swung his head about to nervously chew on Sevryn's sleeve. He answered by rubbing
the horse's nose a bit, then scratching him under his chin to
soothe him. As he did so, the river began to give way, freeing both of them. Their feet and hooves sank suddenly into
watery foam and then their conveyance fell apart.

They washed ashore violently, both of them going over
and rolling in the tide of water, the horse squealing in fear.
Sevryn kicked free of the animal, afraid of the damage Pavan's flailing hooves could do, and as soon as he landed, he
tackled the animal's neck, keeping him down, as the water
drained away from their bodies with a powerful suction that
threatened to drag them back into the river again. The Andredia curled back with nothing left but foam before Sevryn
got off Pavan's neck and urged the gelding to his feet. The
horse got up and stood, head hanging, legs braced, breathing as heavily as if he'd run across the meadows to get here.
Sevryn knuckled him between the ears.

"I know how you feel."

"Now you talk horses," a heavy voice grumbled at him.

Sevryn swung his head about so quickly that water sprayed from him, as he squinted his eyes to look up the banks of the river. A bowed figure in browned leathers grunted back at him, his heavy scent drifting down to Sevryn on the wind. More animal than man, his leathery face grizzled and tusks at the corners of his mouth yellow with age, the Bolger straightened up with another grunt, as if his bones might ache, which they certainly might, for the male was old enough to be the grandfather of his entire tribe.

"And what are you doing here?" Sevryn asked in astonishment.

"Told to go fishing. Not told what fish."

"You were told to be here?" Who could have known they'd meet? How could anyone know the river would carry him thus far and no farther?

Rufus shrugged. The Bolger lumbered across the grassy bank to meet him, taking up the reins of the tashya who seemed beaten by the ordeal. He bent to run his thickly scarred hands over the horse's legs. Years as a foundry worker had remade his hands into clumsy looking, heavy instruments but that would be untrue. They held as much gentleness as any man's, and were as capable of wielding almost any weapon. Bolgers were beasts with human intelligence, and a shrewd, savvy outlook on life. He and Rufus had history forged in the slavery of Quendius, and years before that, the Bolger had known Rivergrace as a small child while she was held captive in the mines Quendius ran. Rufus still called her "Little Flower" for the pretties the child had shared with him. He had, in the decades Sevryn knew him, transcended what the man thought of Bolgers. Rufus patted the horse when he was finished examining him. "Legs good. Cut. I fix. But good."

"Who told you to go fishing?"

"Tribe shaman. Dreamed it. Said future would float down this river." Rufus grinned around his yellowed tusks. "Here."

Rufus shrugged and waved his arm to indicate the banks.

"Half a day walk. Here, there, looking, waiting." He stopped and eyed Sevryn with his round, dark eye in a brow that now bristled with silver-and-gray hairs. "Ugly fish."

"Yeah, yeah." Sevryn grinned. "You look pretty good to me. Anything to eat back at your camp?"

"Some." Through the heavy tusks at the corner of his jaws, Rufus made a chirping noise at Pavan; the horse perked up a little and followed after him as he led the way back up into the forests far below Larandaril.

"Tell me about this shaman."

Rufus strolled along in his bow-legged gait for long moments, his brow lowered, thinking. "Shaman is shaman." He squinted sideways at Sevryn. "Gods awakening. Trouble soon."

"He foresaw it?"

Rufus gave a gesture that was more shrug than nod. A practical man, the Bolger had never struck Sevryn as particularly superstitious, yet here he camped at his shaman's directive.

"Where's Rivergrace? Did you fish her out, too?"

Rufus stopped dead in his tracks. He half-swung about on Sevryn, his lip curled. "You lost Little Flower?"

Sevryn gathered himself. "She sent me downriver. I was hoping she'd followed."

The Bolger looked flatly at him for long moments before saying, "Not see," and turning away. Sevryn let his breath out very slowly.

Rufus built up a campfire, fed him, rubbed Pavan down with great handfuls of dried grass until the horse's coat shone. Then he made poultices for three cuts he'd found on the horse's slender legs, before setting the animal out to graze the rest of the day away. With the same kind of quiet care, he saw to Sevryn as well, content to wait on the story that brought the two of them together on the riverbanks of the lower Andredia. Rufus pitched his mule close to the horse, and the two mounts ate in companionship, their tails busy against whatever flying pests might bother them as they grazed. Rufus readied a meal for the two of them.

Drier, and a lot less hungry, and listening to his horse crop away eagerly at the grasses behind them, Sevryn filled the Bolger in on the happenings as he knew them. Rufus absorbed his words in near silence, a habit of his that Sevryn knew did not reflect on his comprehension. The Bolger had always been a male of few words.

"Little one with big mouth very big with baby, then."

"Very."

Rufus nodded. "I should go."

"She could use you, but I need you with me, first."

"What?"

"I intend to find Bregan Oxfort."

Rufus nodded. "Payback."

"Of a sort. I need to know why he betrayed us, and didn't expect that I wouldn't come after him when he did. I imagine he's gone back to his holdings near Hawthorne."

Rufus scratched his nearly bald pate. "Aye." His jaw worked as if he chewed on something. "Fancy boot." The Bolger named him for the intricate metalwork and geared brace of Vaelinar make on his weakened leg. Yet Rufus seemed a little disgruntled.

"What is it?"

"Not find Little Flower?"

Sevryn looked at his boots, drying in the heat of the banked campfire. "I want to," he answered directly. "Everything in me tells me to go back and get her, but she set me free on purpose. This is something I have to do."

"Bregan."

"Yes, and the ild Fallyns. Bregan owes me, and I'll take it out of his hide, and he'll take me through the ild Fallyn gates if it kills him."

"Ahhh," Rufus rumbled. "Plan."

"Yes. I have a plan." Not, at the moment, a well-formulated one, but definitely in the preparation stages. "You with me?"

Rufus gave a lopsided grin. "Against trader? Fallyn? Gods

know yes." He folded his arms across his barrel chest, protected only by a boiled leather vest, an old one that had seen almost as many years as the Bolger. "Show me Kobrir."

Sevryn hesitated a moment, before reaching inside his shirt to his inner holster and bringing out the dagger. With another hitch, he found the cuffs and dropped them to the ground beside the dagger. Rufus sidled over to look at them, to examine them minutely with his coal-dark eyes. He stabbed a finger at the weapon.

Sevryn picked it up and turned the dagger over in his hands. "Gilgarran's," he told the Bolger squatting next to him. "Different than the one he used when he trained me, although not by much." He slipped a dagger out of his boot. "He added a channel, here, like this. This is mine, but I patterned it on his. Good balance, good for . . ." he paused. "Wet work."

Rufus made a rumble at the back of his throat. He stabbed a big-knuckled finger at the first dagger. "Not old master forge."

"Not Quendius?" Sevryn returned his weapon to its sheath as he turned Gilgarran's over in his hand again. "I didn't think so, but I wasn't sure. Who, then, is the question. Possibly the ones who made the daggers the Kobrir use. They, too, are similar. The metal is high quality, good ores, good tempering, good pounding." And he fetched out a dagger he'd taken off an assassin's body. The workmanship could be seen to be strong in resemblance, although the quality of the blade for the Kobrir was superior and the stylized K buried deep in the butt end of the haft. There was either a flaw or a mark on the lettering for each dagger. Sevryn peered at it and could not read it. He lifted his chin. "We need a jeweler. He'll have a lens that could read this." He scratched his nail over it lightly. "Both daggers with a flaw on the owner's initial? Unlikely. I'm betting it's a maker's mark. Or a forge stamp."

"Likely." Rufus agreed. He shifted his weight on his haunches. He glared down at the cuffs. "Little Flower."

"I'll kill anyone who tries to put her in them."

Rufus put his big hand down, balancing on his knuckles. "Many questions."

"And I intend to get answers, starting with Bregan." He continued to check himself over, a deft touch here and there, reassuring himself of his armory, a ritual he did almost unconsciously. "Three days to get to Hawthorne, if we ruin good horses. Longer still, to ild Fallyn Stronghold."

"Mule not keep up."

"This isn't your journey, Rufus. You don't have to keep up with me. You've fulfilled your shaman's wishes, and I owe you for it."

The Bolger squinted at him. "Little Flower safe. Little Flower's man keep safe."

Sevryn understood the being's affinity for Rivergrace. She had befriended him when both suffered imprisonment under Quendius. She had shown him a child's simple love and hope, and he'd never forgotten it. "I could use your help," he admitted. "You're a good man to have at my back."

Rufus grunted. "Why run horse?"

"Not enough time."

Rufus shifted a little, as if to ease aching knees in his squat, and said nothing. They both knew that Sevryn wanted to know why the trader had set him up, if his story that a God had instructed him to do so was truth, and if it was . . . how a God might have spoken to Bregan . . . and what the assassins of the cult Kobrir wanted by manipulating those events. What did a king of assassins truly want from Sevryn? He doubted it would be as simple as distracting him from the return of the Raymy and the queen's service. With the Kobrir, as with the ild Fallyn, there would be gears within wheels within circles. He had no choice but to go where the obvious led him, for now.

"I guide."

Sevryn raised an eyebrow. "I know where I am going."

Rufus flared his nostrils in a restrained snort. "Fast." He dragged a thick finger through the stable dirt, leaving a wriggling path. "Worm's way."

"Pathways of the Mageborn." He'd been taken that way

before. He had no doubt Rufus knew them. What he *did* doubt was that the tunneling of the ancient magicians would carry him from this backwater smuggler's cove to Hawthorne.

The Bolger shook his head. "Worm's way." He jabbed a thumb at the rugged cliffs of the coastline in the distance. "Many worms. Many wriggles."

He had never run across one of the great worms who had eaten through stone like a hot dagger through butter, and he hoped he never would. The beasts were so long gone from the memory of men that there were not even stories of them, or bones in the rock, or old paintings upon cavern walls. It was as though they had existed in a time beyond mind. But the Bolgers knew them. They might carry the folklore. The men of Kerith, the Kernans, the Dwellers, the Galdarkans, and the Vaelinars, all of them discounted the Bolgers in their humanity. Perhaps it was an even graver mistake than many were coming to believe. "How do you know of these serpents?"

Rufus met his gaze for a long time, unblinking, as if weighing him down to his soul. Then he wiped his tusked mouth with the back of his hand, preparing to talk with difficulty the languages of true men that his tusks warped and distorted, for his own language was virtually unknown by any outside his race. Sevryn felt a pang as he recognized the gesture. Rufus adjusted his position, hiked up his apron, and then jerked a thumb in the vague direction of south. "We not from here. Like you."

Sevryn nodded.

"Home that way. Wise old women tell."

He realized he was going to hear a tale that only the shamans of the clans told. He put his hand on Rufus' arm. "You don't have to tell me."

"Hear me. Learn," Rufus answered firmly, as if Sevryn might be an impatient and squirming child. Sevryn hid his smile and settled back, his mind smoothing out the Bolger's painstaking and halting words.

"Our home is south. Another land from long ago. It is wild, new. Hard to live for farmers, easier for hunters. We hunted the big worms, and they hunted us. Our father's fathers knew them well. (Rufus indicated a long stretch of time that Sevryn knew meant longer than two generations and nodded his understanding.) It was our home. Marshes, hills, forests, valley, lakes. We knew only this because it was the way things were, as the sun rises on one side of the land and sets on the other. But times change. A great sickness ran through the pigs and large rats that the worms ate and the snakes found themselves without easy food. The lives of our father's fathers became even more difficult. Still, it was our home. Perhaps things would change again. We waited.

"Their prey died off. We lost the animals we hunted, and we became the worms' only food. They began to sicken, too, and poisoned our lands and our rivers. The worms turned on each other. Their battles destroyed much. We could not stay. We took our lives, our tools, and we left. Moved north across deep water. Many died, many lived. Strange country, strange peoples, strange Gods. It is not our home. It is only where we must live. We are not liked. (Rufus shrugged.) But we know the sign of the worm when we see it, yet it is good these are old signs, older even than our father's fathers. We know the worm is gone, but we know our old enemy well. We know how to use its trails and dens. Often we hide in the shadow of the old enemy from the new ones. Then the Mages came. They laid their magic on the worm trails. It sinks into the rocks. It grows and spreads, even to where the Mages did not see, could not even guess what lay along the paths of the great worms. We felt it. We know. We watched as the Mages turned on each other like the serpents did. Magic spilled out like poison. We would have laughed, but we were afraid their war would ruin our new land. It almost did. But the peoples here fought back, and the Mages died, and there is still much good land here. Some of it is bad. Most is good. Like its peoples. We stay as long as we can. Some of us returned to our home, but they never sent word if they could live or not. So we endure." (Rufus shrugged again and

turned both of his great, leathery hands palm up, signifying
the end of his tale.)

Sevryn nodded his head several times. "You have great
courage, and now I realize your wisdom is even greater."

Rufus tilted his head slightly, brow wrinkling deeply,
and then he grinned. He beat his chest. "About time." He
stood, his joints popping faintly as he did so. "Get fancy
boot. We go."

The horse disliked the method of travel, but the mule
seemed used to it, or perhaps he just had the level head that
most mules had. His calm eventually soothed Pavan over
the course of their journey, and they emerged from the
stony, dank confines of the worm trails just above Hawthorne and not far from the cliffs that had once held the
great Jewel of Tomarq. Sevryn realized as they walked their
mounts out and the sun shone fitfully through wispy spring
clouds that the Bolgers could have, if their clans united,
overrun most of the fortifications along the coast through
those same trails and wondered why the Bolger wars had
been lost by Rufus' people. It had been the Vaelinars who'd
stopped them and the thought trailed fitfully through
Sevryn's mind, along with a myriad of others, that the Bolgers might have pulled back when they faced magic once
again and, fearing its horribly destructive ends, had given
themselves up to defeat. But it was only a flickering thought
and one he did not voice aloud as they mounted up to gain
Hawthorne's bridges and city streets.

They caught Bregan in one of the outermost disreputa-
ble bars at what Rufus called "the stinking end" of the city.

Chapter
Thirty-One

RUFUS GRUNTED. His heavy head swung about, and he moved into a trot, hauling Sevryn after him, his broad nose wrinkling as he caught wind of their prey. "We find," he told Sevryn as if an explanation was needed, and protesting in every muscle and bone, he followed the Bolger.

Coursing through the evening dark of the port brought its own challenge in broken and wavering streets, ramshackle buildings, and surly townsfolk who thought little of a Bolger and a Vaelinar shouldering their way through their population. Rufus answered angry growls in kind with his own. Finally they came upon a building that seemed to be more inn than drinking hole, and Rufus shoved Sevryn inside first, following on his heels. The Kernan innkeeper swung about, wiping his beefy hands on his stained shirt and lowering his eyebrows at the sight of Rufus. His mouth twisted on the words he might have been going to utter and he told Sevryn, "Long as th' beast's with you." He jabbed a thumb toward the common room. "Fire and chow in there."

And so was a slumped trader prince, head in hands, looking moodily at the hearth. Sevryn crossed the floor in four

strides, clenched a fist, and swung before Bregan even knew
he was in the room.

Bregan held a small cut of prime red meat to his swollen
face, watching Sevryn ruefully with the other eye. They sat
in a small corner of the bar, little more than a hut in this sea
harbor city. Whatever privacy could be extended to them
had begun when he hauled Bregan's limp form into the corner. It would have to do. Awake now, the trader looked as
rough as Sevryn felt, clothes torn and hanging, bruises and
gashes on every bit of exposed skin, and swelling now going
purple despite the cuts of meat to take the heat from them.
Most of the damage had been inflicted long before Sevryn
found him. Bregan spat to the side, a pink blob of froth, and
poked his tongue at his teeth.

"Don't fuss at them if they're loose."

Bregan rolled his eye. "I *know* that." He adjusted his
makeshift compress. "I just don't know if you loosened
them or . . . or . . . ." He left off talking and just shrugged.

"Does it matter? You deserve to not have a tooth left in
your head. You set me up and, worse, left the heir to the
Anderieons open to assassination."

Rufus grunted his agreement with Sevryn, the Bolger
hunched over in the corner behind them, his back against
the wall.

"I assure you that was by mere coincidence."

"Coincidence?"

"The Kobrir, I knew about. I thought I knew about them,
that is—I wasn't sure. I wasn't told everything. As for the ild
Fallyn or whoever tried a strike at the Dweller lass," he
dropped the meat from his eye and peered at Sevryn. "It
was bound to happen sooner or later, but I had no inkling
of when or where." He curled his arms up over his head.
"I'm a dead man. I know that. Kill me now and end it. I
could do nothing other than what I did because the Gods
sent me to betray you."

"Gods? What do you know of Gods?"

Bregan uncurled a bit. "Ironic, I know. I made a fortune on listening shrines, did I not? Listening to Gods everyone thought had gone deaf centuries ago. But now I'm struck with a truth I cannot forget or dodge. The Gods of Kernan are awakening. I'm not certain I want to be alive when They become fully aware again."

"Keep talking in circles, and I'll be able to solve that one for you."

Bregan dropped a hand down to the back of Sevryn's wrist. "You think you're threatening me, but all I hear are promises to take me out of my misery, and I'm thankful for it."

Sevryn shook off his hand. "You've gone mad."

"Do you think so? I agree."

"Even a madman needs friends." Sevryn sat back, baffled by Bregan's behavior.

The other shuttered his one open eye momentarily before looking back to Sevryn. "You think you need to tell me that? Garner Farbranch, nearly your brother, is my friend. Indeed, he is probably the only friend I have ever had who does not think of cozying up to the traders' guild. Do you think I wished to betray that? What profit would come to me from hearing the Gods, eh? They bring nothing but trouble. Yet I did. I had but to walk close to one of those cursed shrines, which I designed and pandered by the hundreds to mobs hungry for the words of the Gods when and if They ever began to talk to us again—and I *heard*. It reached out and grabbed me, held me transfixed, so that I could not move until I had heard every hallowed word. The only shrine ever to do so, I might add. If a curse would make me deaf, then blight me. I would accept it willingly!" He dropped the cut of meat to the table, leaning forward in earnest, his face lopsided with his injury, his eyes both blazing. "I heard Them, I tell you, and They told me to bring you to the knives of the Kobrir."

"Just me?"

"As if you are not enough? Should the Gods have

thrown in all who remain of Lariel's court as well? Yes, just you. Why, I cannot say because I have no inkling."

"Well, then," Sevryn commented mildly, keeping a hold on his concern and his temper. "The Kobrir must have heard Them as well. They were waiting, were they not?"

Rufus leaned on the knuckles of one hand.

Bregan's battered mouth opened and shut without sound, gaping like a fish out of water and floundering on a riverbank, before he got out. "Must have. Must have done. How else could they have been here? Why did I not think of that?"

Sevryn found a cold, fresh cut of meat, put the point of his dagger into it and tossed it at Bregan. "Because you did not think."

He caught the hunk neatly and applied it. "There is that. If I have been used, at least it was not for your death. You sit there very much alive."

"That scarcely excuses you."

"No, and I will be in your debt for the rest of my life, however long it shall be." His free hand moved uneasily upon the tabletop. "One does not serve the Gods easily and with impunity."

Sevryn noted that Bregan worked with the spoken word as a craftsman did a tool, even as he himself did with his Talent of Voice, but he couldn't discern any malice or deception as he listened, only true remorse and puzzlement. He had not told Bregan of the message itself, only that one had been delivered. He would not divulge that to anyone else except for . . . his thoughts caught and stumbled. He had been about to tell himself Jeredon, but his friend was beyond all confidences now. He felt a small pang not only for himself but for Trader Bregan who had just come to understand the true worth of a good friend.

He did not doubt that Bregan thought he knew what he'd heard, but he doubted the origin. He lifted his wine mug to hide the expression on his face as he mulled over what Bregan had told him. A cryptic message did not sit well with him. He was still of a mind not to let the Kobrir get away with it, but night had fallen well and truly and he doubted he had little chance tracking shadows in the dark. So, for the moment, his only source of information was the man who had betrayed him and who, from what had been said, was as surprised at the ambush as Sevryn.

The Gods, it appeared, had not spilled any of their secrets.

Bregan had been told to bring him, and he had. Sevryn's need to accompany a caravan for some protection and disguise had merely fallen in well with the trader's needs. As he sat across the table, expressions of confusion and guilt filtered across Bregan's face, to be shut aside quickly and replaced with a trader's carefully neutral and studied look.

Sevryn put his mug down. The wine of this hole in the ground was strangely passable, unexpected in this rustic place. Perhaps there were men of money who had laid a cellar down here, coming in from time to time. He had never been a fisherman himself, but there were men of estates who enjoyed an empty coast and good fishing waters from time to time. To think of it, he had never been a man of any estate. His only worldly goods were those the queen held for him, and his actions had now forfeited that. The Queen's Hands seldom retired. They usually died with their boots on.

As he had nearly done.

"Tell me where you heard this voice."

Bregan flinched slightly, his good eye widening at Sevryn. "Where? At a shrine, as I told you."

"But where?"

"Ah. On Temple Row. The lanes there are rife with them," Bregan added ruefully.

No surprise there. "Would you know this one particular shrine again if you came across it?"

"Yes."

"How?"

"It rather made an impact on me," Bregan told him dryly. "And the owners tend to decorate them, make them their own, put family signs on them and so forth, stock the incense bowls with their own herbs. Unless it has been taken from Temple Row, I can find it."

"Good."

Bregan drew his legs under him with effort. "Are we leaving tonight?"

"Morning will be good enough. I've sent for a healer who should be here sometime before then."

"I thank you for that, then."

"Will you thank me if I can prove to you it was not the Gods who spoke?"

Bregan's face went white under the crimson-and-purple mottling, making his bruises stand out starkly. "What do you mean?"

"I mean that any hedge wizard, with the right trappings could make you see and hear things as he wished you to. The only question I have is . . . why."

Bregan slumped back in his chair, defeated. "Why, indeed? Why would I think that, after centuries of silence, the Gods would deign to speak to me? I have never been a paragon of anything except trading."

"Except that whoever did speak to you knew that you could speak to me, and I would listen."

"If the Kobrir wanted you or me to be dead, we would be." Bregan dropped his meaty compress to the table. Rufus took it up to spear on a cooking fork and thrust it into the small hearth's fire, adding it to the other steak, which he already had roasting.

Sevryn watched as the trader wrung his hands together. He cleared his throat, and Bregan fixed his gaze on him once more. "And after we find out who convinced you to betray me, I need to hire your caravan out."

"Oh."

"And you with it, of course."

Bregan licked his lips as if they'd suddenly gone dry. "And I would do this for what amount of money?"

"I don't intend to give you any."

"I see. Well, under the circumstances, I suppose that is fair enough." Bregan hitched a short breath before leaning over the table intently, his voice low, his words sharp. "I will give you that debt as paid if you do something for me."

"And that would be what?"

"Teach me magic."

"What? You have gone mad."

"Not yet, not quite fully. You're Vaelinar. You know the workings of power. Teach me."

"I can't teach you what isn't born in you."

Bregan reached out with both his hands to grab Sevryn by the wrists. "This is a genuine bargain, Sevryn Dardanon. I will give you a caravan and guide it into the very mouth of hell for you, but you must teach me about magic on the way. Do we have a deal?"

Sevryn stared into the other's eyes. He saw desperation rooted deeply in their gleam. "I will try. I can't make any promises."

"Noted. Our deal is struck, then." Bregan let loose of him and leaned back, exhaling in a long, shaky sigh.

Temple Row was even more crowded than he remembered. It had always drawn the desperate looking for luck and the rich paying to keep it, but the throngs of everyday folk he saw as he threaded the street amazed him. A smell of incense mingled with the siren smell of the sea. It fused with the noise of the street, with the chanting of the priests and their acolytes from the various temple and chapel facades, the hawking of the street vendors, the prayers and arguments of the throng. Sevryn wove his way through, his senses plucking at the threads of the street even though the sensations rose in an overwhelming tide. *Concentrate*, Gilgarran would have rebuked him. He opened his mind and then closed it, bit by bit, searching for that one thread, that one jarring note that he remembered, that singular thread which would lead him where he wanted to be. A baker shoved him aside with a massive shoulder, his burly form still smelling of the rising dough and the wood ovens. A textiles worker, a bundle of fabric samples hanging from his belt, worked his way against the tide, anxiety etched deeply into his brow. Sevryn nearly knocked a very pregnant mother of three off her feet, righted her, and dusted her off even as he dodged the man.

Bregan had little more luck with the masses, and finally both fell in behind Rufus who cleared a tolerable path with his Bolger presence and irritated growl. But all these people . . . congregating here, in the middle of their workday as if they were searching for something, something tangible, something vital they seemed to feel was missing from their lives and that, Gods promised, it would be provided here. He had never found it to be so. When he ran on the streets, chanting a God's name had never protected him from flying fists and feet, or any pestilence of nature. He had only had himself to rely upon. He could understand it more if the current held a sense of hope, of optimism, but all he could feel here was one of desperation. Desperate, harried people in search of comfort and a turning of the tide which carried them. He found that cold and frightening. Sevryn shrugged deeper into his coat.

Bregan tugged on his sleeve. "There is a shrine," he shouted near Sevryn's ear. "Women swear by it. It grants love and children. You should stop by it while you are here and drop a coin and a bit of scent stick."

"Are you sure they swear by it? Mayhap they swear *at* it," Sevryn remarked as he dodged a herd of children tumbling by like puppies in a pack.

"Do you not wish to make her happy?"

"She is happy." And Sevryn sincerely doubted anything from this crowded street of pilgrims in despair would improve Rivergrace's lot. Rufus snarled ahead of them, whether in response to Bregan's query or at a tall, weed-thin butcher who blocked their way, he could not tell.

Perhaps it was the coppery tang of blood from the man's boots or apron that set it off, but Sevryn caught that for which he searched. He stopped in his tracks, Bregan bumping into him. The trader winced as he caught his elbow. "Are we near?"

"The Shrine of the Lovers? Nay, it's a good alley or two behind us . . ."

Sevryn leaned close to Bregan's jaw. "Fool. *Are we close?*"

Another quiver ran through the trader. He swallowed once or twice as if unable to speak, and then ground out, "In the shadows ahead. To your right hand."

Sevryn stared. He had not seen the boil of darkness before but now that Bregan directed him, he saw it clearly some paces ahead, the townsfolk and those who came to worship skirting it uneasily. He let his mind spill over it. What had been there no longer was, but its cloud lingered with a greasy, repellent feel, meant to turn people away. Another day and the sheer wash of humanity through this street and its side feeders would not even know this place existed, if they could even detect it now, beyond the feelings it projected.

Sevryn gave a whistle as he steered Bregan toward the cloud. Rufus came up short in his position as point and fell in at Sevryn's flank instead. The Bolger wrinkled his nose as they drew near.

"Stinks."

"Oh, and that's the turtle calling the tortoise slow," Bregan said lightly, nervously, as Sevryn propelled him into place. He stopped as if he had hit a wall.

Sevryn caught the same sense of it that Rufus had, it stank, not in an aromatic way, but in a skin-prickling, nerve-tugging way. With misgivings, he nudged at Bregan. "Is this the shrine?"

"I . . . I . . ."

"Is it?" He edged them closer and then he could actually scent its odor, a bare but distinctive one. Sevryn felt a surety in his bones; he knew the smell now, faint though it was, the drug a potent hallucinogenic which left its victims in a highly suggestible state. It was exceedingly rare and expensive, and few would know of it. He would not except for Gilgarran's expansive teaching, and he doubted anyone outside of the Kobrir might use it since Gilgarran's death except . . . except who? A thought dangled just outside his capture of it, taunting him. He shook it off when Bregan shrugged out of his hold.

But it was not to flee. The trader went to one knee, his golden brace folding fluidly with his movement, and he put a hand on the small, ceramic shrine that sat with its back to a thin chapel stall's wall. The haze Sevryn had seen and felt roiled around them as Bregan did so, a disturbance in its veil.

"A street vendor pushed a stick of incense in my hand," Bregan murmured, his head bent in memory. "He was full of—like they all are—hope for the shrines. He begged me to honor the street with my prayers. The market had begun to drop off a bit for the shrines, and I knew it could use a boost. Why not show some piety? I thought it might be fitting to light it and set it somewhere. These . . ." and he gestured vaguely at the one shrine and then out at all the others littering the street, "these came out of my enterprise. So why not? I don't believe in them, I never did, but they needed to." He dropped his hand back onto his leg. "There is always money to be had by selling what people need."

"Or by convincing them they need it."

"You try to give me guilt, but I won't take it. The Gods used to speak to us. We were not often left to wonder what we should do or where we should go with our lives when we stood at a crossroads. We did not feel adrift. Now, we do. You might be thankful for that. If the Gods had spoken to us and told us to destroy you, we would have risen up, every one of us, with whatever we could wield to do so. But they remained silent, and are silent still, so you live amongst us for centuries with impunity."

"Do you threaten that state?"

"Not I." Bregan looked up at him. "But you, with half a Vaelinar heart and half a Kernan heart, have heard the whispers. You know that even after all the time has passed, the elven are still strangers at our doorsteps. Sometimes welcome and sometimes not."

Sevryn did not answer that. He looked at the wall. How would the Kobrir have known which shrine Bregan would choose to do his homage at? Could it have been as simple as having made this one undesirable to all others as it was now, and a busy trader, oblivious to the distaste and in a hurry?

"Rufus, think you can get behind that wall?"

The Bolger scratched his pate. He moved away from them, crowds shifting to avoid him as he did so, despite the fact that a sparse number of Bolgers moved among the acolytes and temples, doing odd jobs of manual labor. One stopped to watch the clan chieftain curiously, and then dropped his gaze quickly and moved back to his sweeping when a young Kernan snapped a few words at him. In moments, Rufus disappeared and then, he could hear a knocking along the wall that stopped only when Sevryn knocked back when he reached a position.

"That was clear enough," Bregan said dryly. "Think they sat back there and waited for me, or anyone, to pay homage?"

"I think it's likely they did. Can you smell what you burned here?"

The other leaned forward slightly and took several deep inhalations, before shaking his head. "There is something, but I can't quite make it out. Can you?"

"Yes, but it's faint. When it was freshly burned, you would have not noticed it much more, it's an inconspicuous little herb but one that can give quite a kick. We call it dreamspark."

"A well-laid trap, for anyone."

"No. Just for you, Bregan, I think."

"Why so?"

"There are not many people who could lure me as you did. They needed a person of some reputation, and power, position, and of value to the queen. This person had to catch my ear and have a good chance of succeeding in having me follow their lead."

"So I was the lucky fellow."

Sevryn made a diffident gesture. "They would have had better luck getting to you than to my lady Rivergrace or one of the Farbranches."

Bregan's lip curled. "And they bent my will easily."

"Not they, the dreamspark. As for that, you have certain habits that make it easy to lead you down this particular lane. You drink a bit, and you're more susceptible when drunk than you like to think you are."

"I drink a bit."

"Yes, sorry, was that not common knowledge?"

Rufus rumbled from behind the thin patchwork wall, "Fancy boot empty many jugs."

Bregan straightened. "If you want to count the numbers of gutters I've seen to those you've crawled in, I'd be more than willing."

"I was standing in those gutters and it was not my choice," Sevryn corrected him and skinned his lips back from his teeth in a slight smile. "At least we both made it out."

"Did we?" Bregan stared down at the small shrine, his face etched in disgust. "Truth is only as good as the men who profess it while lies prosper off any tongue." He kicked the ceramic sculpture in disgust. "I pandered to this deception." His voice rose. "All false. Lies! They needed a fool, and they found one!"

In the streets people began to slow and murmur, gazes fixed on them. Sevryn could feel a wave of uneasy attention as they jostled into position to watch. Bregan seemed oblivious to the attention he attracted. He kicked the shrine again, rebounding it off the wall, and it broke into three pieces, ash from incense scattering as it did. Rufus made a noise from behind as the object shattered. Muffled as it was, the growing crowd heard it.

"What was that?"

"I heard something . . . did you?"

"The Gods speak!"

Sevryn turned abruptly to spot whoever uttered that last, but the crowd had grown so dense and fluid that he could not catch sight of any one face. Bregan's voice rose harshly as he attacked another shrine, smashing it, sending pieces skittering over the alley's cove. A rising wail followed the shards.

"My shrine! My shrine! My prayers for my wife, my sister! What are you doing? That was my shrine. What are you doing?"

"Drunken fool . . ."

Bregan whirled at that, pointing a finger at the curtain of townsfolk. "It doesn't take too much wine to know that this is a piece of pottery, nothing more! Are you idiots? What do you believe? If I told you this . . . this worthless piece of clay could raise the dead, would you believe me?" He toed a piece at his foot and then stomped his boot heel onto it, grinding it down into poorly fired clay dust. "It's dirt! Nothing more!" His voice rose with that of the inconsolable wailer who fell onto his side, weeping.

Sevryn whistled sharply for Rufus as distraught people pushed closer, surrounding them, pressing them toward the walls. His fine-tuned senses lightninged over his body in protest at the closeness, and he swung about, taking stock of the situation. Agitation rose through the observers like a tide, crashing through them and carrying others off into shouts of protest against Bregan's action as well as those who cried in sympathy with the prostrate man now lying in the alley. His gut clenched at the emotional waves rising like a flood tide about them. He gathered his Voice and spoke, but his own words remained unheard, drying in his throat, falling from his mouth like useless, nonexistent sounds. Sevryn stepped back in surprise. Never had his Voice failed him. Never.

He reached for Bregan's elbow. "That's enough."

Bregan threw him off. He plowed toward other niches, other shrines, bellowing as he shoved his way through. "Fools, all of you are fools! The Gods are deaf and mute to idiots." Incense sticks flew, smoking and still alight, as he kicked and booted the clay monuments to scattered shards. That quickly, the situation went from dangerous to explosive, as if Bregan had lit a fuse.

The crowd surged. Blows and kicks went flying. Sevryn grabbed for Bregan, getting only the sleeve of his coat and yanking him out of the reach of the people. Rufus appeared at his flank, out of breath and scuffed, as if he had fought his way through the outer ring of townsfolk to get to him, and perhaps he had. The noise of fisticuffs and breaking pottery filled the air, hoarse cries of "Blasphemy!" and worse roared against his ears, and Bregan fought his hold even as others fought to tear him free and bear him away. Pain stung along his ribs and someone stomped his boot toes hard and he cursed as he spun Bregan around into the arms of the waiting Rufus before using his body to simply block and bully their way out of the fray. Body already sore and bruised, he felt like a battered piece of meat as he hauled and bluffed his way out, knuckles stinging and his nerves strung tightly as he kept his hands from the hilts of his knives. No bloodshed. Grunts and curses echoed his shoves and body blocks, and when they emerged from the fray, it felt like he'd unstoppered a very stubborn jug.

Suddenly, they were free.

And just as quickly, a shout of annoyance and discovery sent the crowd at their throats.

He pulled his hand knives then, sparing as he could be, watching agitators spring back in dismay as they felt the sting and saw the blood. Improvised weapons came to hand as he pushed Bregan and Rufus down the street ahead of him. One man pulled off his rugged boots and flung them about by the laces. Awning poles were stripped loose and plied about head and ears, missing Sevryn as he ducked lithely away but landing blows on many another head. Rufus stripped free a pair for himself. The Bolger applied it where he thought it would do the most good and, leaving a trail of bloody noses, thrashed ears, and sliced arms behind them, they made it off Temple Row and into the relatively clear passage of the main thoroughfare of Hawthorne. They looked back over their shoulders to see the mob chasing after them.

"Run," muttered Sevryn, jerking at Bregan's collar. He jabbed a thumb in Rufus' direction. "Get the mule, horses. Meet me outside the town gates."

Rufus dropped his battered and splintering awning pole and ran in the opposite direction, leather apron flapping about his bandied legs. Bregan reeled in Sevryn's wake as they ran, with the howling mob at their heels. With little or no hope of the City Guard intervening, Sevryn guided his charge through the winding streets as he remembered them, and by the time they made their way to a city gate at one of the seven bridges linking Hawthorne to the mainland, Bregan wheezed like a pipe player and Sevryn's nose ran pink from a blow he'd taken and the heavy breathing he was doing. He wiped his upper lip dry on the back of his hand.

Rufus had the horses and mule. One chance in seven he'd find the right gate, but Sevryn knew that the Bolger had an eerie sense of direction, and he'd charted his course based on Sevryn's initial path of escape.

He threw Bregan on his horse. "Get home. Can you ride?"

"Always." The trader struggled upright. He'd taken a blow to the forehead that left a small gash in his brow, and purpling to the side of his neck.

"I've business elsewhere." Sevryn mounted in a flying leap. "Try to stay out of trouble, then."

"Without argument." Bregan turned his horse about and put a heel in its flanks, sending it into a gallop through the gate and thundering onto the bridge.

Sevryn pointed to the southernmost gates and bridges. "That way."

The lane circumnavigating the city boundaries was narrow, but they could still ride two abreast, and so they did, kicking the city gate shut behind them, startling both guards who had been staring, mouths open, at them since they'd burst on the scene. Evidently they'd been trained to keep invaders out, not in.

Sevryn lifted his reins, to urge a swift, running walk from his horse. Gilgarran would have had his hide for precipitating a riot. Could have been prevented, should have been foreseeable. Had he grown soft, in some ways, in the service of the queen? Thinking of the departed man brought up another thought, frothing to the top of his mind. Gilgarran would have used dreamspark, and had upon occasion. But so had Daravan. The machinations here, bringing Bregan to

Temple Row and then exposing him to the drug and waiting to plant whispers in his hallucinating mind, yes, that was a labyrinth of planning not coincidence. Bregan had been the prey, and he'd fallen into the trap. Who besides Gilgarran might deal in such mental devices? Perhaps Daravan, who was more than a match for his old mentor in elaborate deceptions. But Daravan was caught up in the Ferryman's journey, was he not? Unless, like the handfuls of Raymy spilled here and there, the man had been deposited back on Kerith and no one the wiser. That thought grabbed him for a long moment.

If Daravan had come back, and thought to threaten Rivergrace with a web of machinations, he would find a way to kill the wily bastard, come hell or high water.

A dry whirling sound came from behind them, atop the gate. Sevryn jerked about to see what it was. He caught the barest glimpse of an object sailing at his head before an explosion of pain, a darkness etched with sparks, was followed by musty nothingness.

Chapter
Thirty-Two

RIVERGRACE EMERGED from the graying darkness of the cave, her eyes narrowed against the sun. From its slant, she'd been inside the cave far longer than she would have guessed. She drew in a long, slow breath, enjoying the clean air free of the smell of cold rock and lichen and dust. As she stepped farther out, something moved furtively in a line of shrubs, something unseen but heavier than just a scurry upon the ground. She turned to it, listening. All noise hushed. Not even the buzz of an insect wing. The lack of noise told her more than the sound before had. She was not the only one who paused, held their breath, and listened for an enemy. It was not her imagination unnerved by what she had seen and learned from the dark water. Lariel might have tracked her down. This ridge ran along the border of her kingdom, and Lara had a bonding with it that was laced tightly with her Vaelinar powers as well as the powers of Kerith itself. She knew who trespassed on her borders, and although Grace was near certain she stood beyond them now, she couldn't be absolutely sure, and even if she did—she stood so close to them, that the land itself might betray

her. How she might have to react to that betrayal shook her
for a moment.

She would change; it was inevitable, and this must be the
beginning of it. Rivergrace pressed a hand to her eyes, shuttering them for a moment, hoping for clarity when she reopened them. It might work. Chances were it would not.
Yet, when she looked upon the scene again and swept her
gaze about, she could see a multitude of threads in all the
colors of the landscape, each one waiting to be plucked or
braided or snapped—and thus altered forever. Did she dare
take the responsibility? A failure to accept those consequences had destroyed the House of her father, or what had
once been her father.

She took in a long, slow, soft breath as if she could taste
any mischief on the wind, as an animal would scent trouble.
A hush stayed over the area. The feeling that pressure built,
swelling and expanding, until it exploded and inundated the
surroundings, cloaked her. A storm gathered, but not a
storm of electricity and rain. That she could handle, even
draw upon, replenish herself as she replenished its essence.
She was water and, in some little respect, fire, but she was
nothing of what she sensed approaching. Grace took in another soft breath, deep and quiet, a gentle hiss between her
teeth and through her nostrils.

She balanced her weight and brushed her cloak from her
side, wrapped it about her left arm to shield it and slowly
withdrew her short sword. With a certainty and fluidity she
was not sure she really felt, she moved into a defensive position, keeping part of the broken rock of the cave entrance
at her back. The steel glittered dully in her hold, a muted
silver like a river in the high mountains just beginning to
thaw from its winter ice.

She let her senses rove, wondering if Lariel had dared to
send the guard after her. Perhaps something that ran feral
through the ridgeline wilderness stalked her. She turned to
her right and took three silent steps to where she had abandoned her mist form and where the cave had first welcomed her. Grass lay bent and bruised, its aroma wafting

up. Something with heavy footsteps had trod here after her own foggy passage. She frowned.

A twig snapped. Her head shot up and she searched the nearby trees, hugged by scraggly shrub, but saw nothing. Smelled nothing. Heard not another sound more. Anger bled out through her nerves, and fear rushed in to replace it. She'd resisted the dark water, but this, in the light of day, chilled her blood. Danger stalking through sunlight made it that much more potent. She backed up a step into the undergrowth and nearly stumbled on a clump of fallen leaves and twigs. A scuff of her boot toe brought to light the desiccated corpses hidden there.

She stared in shock at the sudden death. Three young hens, once fat and rich of plumage, lay next to each other, shrunken down as if drained of every drop of moisture their carcasses had once held. She had no inkling of how long ago they might have been killed or even how they had been killed or what kind of predator would hide the evidence. What would do such a thing ... kill, blood, and yet leave the meat? One carcass would be enough for ritual, as reprehensible as she found the thought. But three? Uneasily, she shoveled debris back over the bodies and stepped away. The nerves along the back of her neck tingled in warning. Holding her breath, Grace refocused on listening. Something furtive moved again. More than the noise of the movement, she caught a sense of size. Something big vacated one area and flowed into another, and that something was big, or at least bigger than she was. Yet nothing of shadow or substance met her sight. She frowned and scanned the area about her slowly, carefully. Something on the run toward her shattered the calm.

The brush and trees around her began to thrash their branches and roar with wind like an incoming ocean tide. It almost smothered the noise of pounding hooves.

Rivergrace backed into a defensible position, tightened her grip on her sword, and waited.

Raiders, and riding hard. They swept along the ridge, daring the border of Larandaril as if they knew the magical toll it could take out of their hides and were uncaring of the consequence, their whips in hand and knives in their teeth as they bent over the short, stubby manes of their ponies.

Grace broke her position to run sideways in the opposite direction, grabbing the long, green limbs of a sapling and letting it spring back as the raiders rode past, the ones in front curbing their horses hard and wheeling around even as the tree snapped through the air, knocking one of them from his saddle into a hard fall, head- and neck-first into the ground. Without seeing if he stirred, she ran back to her original chosen place to dig her heels in, and knew her eyes had gone more gray than blue, the storm-ridden color of an icy lake. Ponies turned and leaped against boot heels jabbing their flanks as bits cut their protesting mouths. Four remaining raiders came at her. Not so many, she told herself. Sevryn could have taken them down with thrown daggers before he'd even draw his sword. Men, if only just, with the hard-eyed intensity of Kernan and Vaelinar tainted with Kernan blood, their faces weathered by sun and weather and scarred by fighting.

She reached for the Fire inside of her, the anger, that she had unleashed for Sevryn and Hosmer on the streets of Calcort but found herself empty. Worse, she found herself tender and aching inside as if her torrent of magic had left her torn and burned herself, worse than merely being emptied. She shoved back a flinch and curled her mouth into a downward grimace. She gave them not a word, not the satisfaction of perhaps hearing the fear in her voice, as they came at her.

The moves Sevryn and Lariel had drilled into her took over. She barely felt herself stand until the last moment, then step aside, calmly slashing at the exposed mid-thigh of the closest rider and watching the blood spurt free as she did, splattering her and soaking him, as she ducked under the swing of his sword. His hoarse voice filled the air with curses. A whip lashed out, catching her shoulder, ripping through fabric and stinging her skin, but she did not feel it until she had moved back into place and then took a lunging jump at the third rider who had fallen behind. The trees and shrubs limited her accessibility, and she used that as a natural barrier to shield her flanks as she took a deep breath and gathered her nerve and cut the pony down—ah, tree's blood, she hated to do that as the animal let out a scream and went sliding to its knees to plunge floundering upon the ground, rider half-pinned under it. She came around sharply and took a second slice at the animal, to put it down humanely, her heart pounding in her chest as she did. It was but an animal, a beast made to service the savages that rode it, and she could not let it suffer. Grace did not mind that her boot heel came down in a vicious stomp on the pinned rider's throat as he grunted and tried to pull himself free.

And then there were two. The downed rider, his face laid open to the bone from the lash of the green-skinned sapling, and his fellow, still mounted and wheeling about to her blind side, whip and knife in his free hand, reins knotted about the other. They spread apart until she could not watch one without losing track of the other, and knew they had her as long as they flanked her. She had but one option.

Grace moved into the shrubbery as if hoping it could shield her entirely, and with a sharp cry, fell, her leg betraying her and crumpling as she tripped, dropping her sword. The raider on foot let out a triumphant grunt and bounded after her. She rolled in agony and came up with her dirks buried in her fists and felt his hot breath as it stunk in her face and she gutted him, right to left and then left to right as he fell on her. She shoved his body aside as a horse whinnied sharply. A fist hit her temple, crushing sight from her eyes and air from her lungs, as pain flashed black, then red and orange. She struggled in vain to get to her knees and could feel herself topple for real, world going dark, even as she had a sense of whatever it was that had run the ridges and stayed murderously quiet in the shadow while she fought, as it sprang free and deadly. She lost her battle to stay conscious.

Chapter Thirty-Three

A T LAST HE HAD SOMETHING of what he'd come for. He sat, drawing shadows in around him, his hands crossed on his horse's withers in front of him, big hands, scarred by untold decades of work on weaponry and the use of them. Quendius watched as the girl collapsed, having already given the signal for capture rather than kill. He lifted one hand to scratch a rough nail along the line of his jaw, waiting but not as patiently as he would have liked. He frowned, his Vaelinarran eyes scouring the ridgeline, but he did not see as his fellows did, even though he had the multi-colored eyes. No. They betrayed him, just as everything else in his life had, at one time or another. He felt as a blind man might feel, bitter and disoriented, blockaded from his potential, denied his birthright. Angry. But at least he was away from the banks of the Ashenbrook, where everything had gone to death and ash. It had been reborn with the advent of the rains, brought at last to these drought-stricken lands by the woman who lay struck down before him. She might have more use than he'd originally planned. He had no more use for greenery than he had for ash, but he understood the value of both to others. He waited.

A second wing of his raiders swept over the ridge, even as a being tall and spare, dressed in little more than rags, came out of the shelter of trees and brush, and with a sweep of his arms and swords moved into a fighting stance over the sprawled body of the fallen girl. A noise of satisfaction fell from Quendius. The lone fighter gave a rising growl, a sound barely more than human, but he had little to fear as the raiders fought to keep their mounts from bolting. The riders yanked at their headstalls and drummed their heels against their mounts' sides to drive them at their quarry without effect. Its very scent seemed to fill the ponies' nostrils to send them plunging and bucking away, their riders cursing and spurring them into sullen obedience when they finally gained some control, far enough away that the ponies shuddered to a halt. Two of his best whirled their mounts and whipped them back around, driving them at the defender by brute force. Two more raiders fell, lifeless, from their saddles as they got within sword reach of the lone defender. Quendius rose in his stirrups, his chest bare even in the raw spring air, an open vest of white, curled wool his only upper garment except for his weapons harness. "Enough." He cut the air with both his hand and voice.

His horse did not fight his command to advance close to the ragged, wiry being who defended the fallen girl. It sashayed sideways until Quendius pulled it to a halt. He leveled his gaze on the lone swordsman and his face creased into a wide, humorless smile. "I should have known months ago and made my search easier. You would be where the girl is. I finally intuited that much. If you lived at all, if you held any semblance of life, you would be where your daughter is. Surrender. You're the quarry, not her." Quendius put his hand out as if to accept a proffered blade.

The swordsman looked at the weaponsmith, color drained from his lean face as hope fled, to leave his eyes hollow in his skull, his teeth bared in a feral snarl. He shifted his blade in his hands, fingers in claw curls about the hilt, presenting only his flank to vulnerability.

Quendius studied him. "My hound," he said finally. "Did you think we could be unbonded by such a thing as betrayal? I'm here for you. I know that you knew I would follow you if at all possible, and I have. Though," and he paused. "You've done all you could to make it impossible. But not enough." He withdrew his outheld hand.

The swordsman bent long enough to gather a fallen short sword from the bent grasses under his feet and secured that in offense as well, his stare unblinking.

"I can always make her my target, Narskap, but it would be a waste. As long as she's alive, I have your balls in a vise. We both know that. Perhaps you seek to protect her from what you see when you close your eyes. What might a dead man see when he looks upon sleep?" Quendius shrugged. "So, given that, move away from her and give me your weapon. You are my hound, and you will always be my hound. Even death hasn't taken that leash from you, and I venture to say that nothing ever will." Quendius swept his piercing gaze over the other. "Or is it undeath? You are both and neither. Maker and unmaker. Once you tricked Gods and Demons into the weapons you forged, sucked them into the mineral marrow of your creations. Do you now trick them to overlook your meager soul? I thought you had lived and crawled away from me on Ashenbrook's battlefield, but now that I finally have you in front of me, I see that you didn't live. It's no wonder the ponies wouldn't get near you. They can smell the rank otherness of your form." Quendius leaned over in his saddle, dark eyes blazing at Narskap. "Do you think? Can you speak? Or do you find existence an instinct only, too long ingrained in your flesh to let it go?"

"I think." Words rattled out of the spare man's throat, like pebbles cascading along a dried-up creek bed. A very long pause followed. "I live."

Quendius let his gaze drop to his forearm, where a sword had struck a passing blow. The flesh parted, but blood only welled up in sparse drops, like a desert reluctant to give up its water. Even as he looked at it, the gap closed and flesh began to seal to flesh. That sight drew his close attention, a greedy interest.

Quendius swung off his horse. "You cannot live."

"I live!"

Quendius shook his head slowly.

"No. No, you don't." He moved to Narskap, took the sword from his hand without protest, and laid his palm on the other's chest after twitching aside clothing that was little more than rags. "I feel no heartbeat there. Can you? Does your heart rattle in your rib cage like a frightened, imprisoned bird? No. Does your pulse drum in your neck until you think your head might explode from the force of it? No. Do you pant with eagerness, hound, to be on the hunt? Or in tiredness from the exertion of the trail? No again. You have no breath other than what it takes to speak, I watched your throat. I watch you now. What are you, my hound? What have you made of yourself?"

"Leave us be," Narskap said. His breath, if what it was could be called breath, held a dry, musty odor like a root cellar that had been closed up overlong. Not unpleasant but not alive.

"I can't," Quendius answered simply. "Especially not now. Not without answers to the questions I have. Do you feel pain?" He took the surrendered sword and drew a long gash down Narskap's chest.

Narskap hissed as his skin opened, and he jerked his head back, lips curled.

"Some pain, it would seem." Quendius touched the tip of the blade to the wound as a single, crimson drop welled up. The blood smoked as it ran onto the sword. "Damn these eyes. If it weren't for these, perhaps I could see. What are you, Narskap?"

Narskap said heavily, "Your hound."

Quendius smiled grimly. "Perhaps I earned that. But it's not the answer I seek this time. Never mind. We have time. You more than I, it seems."

With his free hand, he signaled his remaining raiders. "Mount up. Catch the free ponies. Take the bodies. I want little left behind. This is still within Larandaril's reach, and I want no clues. Be careful with the girl. I don't want her marred." He turned his attention back on Narskap. "Don't think to return her to Larandaril to be free. I've taken much time and pain to place someone deep within the Warrior Queen's little kingdom. She will be shocked if and when she discovers the traitor, for this alliance is probably one of the best I've ever forged. But if I must sacrifice my hard work to keep Rivergrace hostage, I will, make no mistake. Her only chance is with you, Narskap, father that you want to be, however awkwardly. Obey me, Narskap, as you were bent to obey me from the very first, and if you don't, she won't be the last to suffer. Do you understand me?"

A very long moment paused, and then Narskap's chest rose and fell as though he had to remember how to speak. The long gash closed despite the upheaval of his body. "I do."

"Good. In return, I promise you a very eager pupil. I am your apprentice as well as your master. I want you to unveil this new Talent of yours in every aspect. I have a feeling that I've finally found what I was born to do." Quendius twitched a hand, and two raiders leaned from their mounts to grasp Narskap by the arms and toss him aboard a riderless pony. He waited until all of his men had left and raked his eyes one last time over Rivergrace's sprawled form lashed to another, lagging into line just ahead of him. Quendius mounted and drew even.

"He thinks he will protect you," he murmured to her still form. "But not even in total obedience will he keep me from what I intend." The corner of his mouth pulled in what, for him, was a smile.

Rivergrace woke slowly. Her limp body rocked back and forth to the gait of the horse she straddled, her head and neck flopping painfully every now and then, and it was the pain, a lightning surge through her muscles and somewhere at the back of her eyes, that woke her completely. She became aware of an arm across her rib cage, holding her close to a body that was not warm but chilled. Captive. Her skin shivered as she thought of becoming mist again and dissolving away from her captor's hold, but it held her as tightly as he did, unwilling to let her go, and she didn't have the strength to force it. She was caught, well and truly. Her eyelids fluttered as she tried to look down and see who—or what—held her. A breath tickled her ear. "Gather your strength."

The words were no warmer than the figure that held her. Rivergrace contained the shiver that swept through her. The arm about her rib cage was clothed in little more than rags, the skin tight and drawn, sinews and bones delineated clearly under it. A man more skeleton than mortal. She tilted her head slightly.

"Father?"

"Once. And yet, it seems, always."

"You're not well." She traced a fingertip along the back of his wrist, not daring to say more.

"I am dead, Grace, or to be more precise, Undead."

He said it so quietly that she nearly believed it. "I looked for your body at Ashenbrook."

"I was already gone. You wouldn't have found me."

"And now?"

"I abide. But what I am shouldn't worry you."

"You tell me you're Undead and I shouldn't worry?"

"I exist. I remember; I learn. I breathe just enough to form words when I wish to use them. My heart beats just enough to move blood through my body. But I don't need to breathe to continue existing, nor does my heart need to keep beating. Occasionally it stops altogether. I can even heal although that is most sluggish and requires . . . outside intervention."

She did not want to ask what he meant by that. "How did this happen?"

"First, you die. And what comes after, you needn't know. It's not a burden I would give you."

"There must be something I can do!"

"Nothing."

"You don't know that."

A soft sound that might have been a chuckle if there had been enough breath behind it. "I'm fairly certain." A long pause followed. "I thank you for your worry."

"You're my father."

"I haven't been your father for most of our lives. I'm not so Undead that I can't feel the pain of saying that."

Rivergrace straightened in her father's hold, her body aching. "We have to get away."

"No. Not yet. We're here to learn."

"Learn what?"

"Look to your fore. Tell me what your Vaelinar eyes see."

She straightened in his hold. In front of them rode a tall, arrogant man sitting confidently in his saddle, flanked by two men on either side. The flanking riders were ragtag warriors, but the man who led them was of a category altogether different: Quendius, the weaponmaster. The man who lived for wars and their consequences, a man who would rather rule ashes than not rule at all. She sucked in a tight breath before spitting out his name.

"Yes, you know him, but tell me . . . what do you *see?*"

The back of her head pounded dully at her, the sunlight shone a little too brightly, and her ribs and one knee let out a lightning jab of pain every now and then as the horse swayed under them, and she did not want to look at Quendius. Narskap snuggled his arm about her a little more tightly in reassurance.

"I don't want to look at him."

"Try it anyway. You are Vaelinar, yes, but you have a Kerith River Goddess bound into your very being and . . . something else. You should be able to see what I can only sense, and most others are blind to. Study him, Rivergrace." His words were low, pitched for her ears alone, but there was steel tempered in them, steel that made her flinch as he uttered them.

"Anything you can see in him, any weakness, may be our key to surviving his intentions."

"Escaping is our survival."

"Not all things are escapable." His embrace left her ribs as he lifted his hand to under her chin, forcing her to focus on Quendius. "*Look.*"

She swallowed tightly. Viewed mostly from the rear, a little to the side, Quendius sat tall in his saddle, broad-shouldered, silver-gray bared arms freed by the sleeveless vest he wore. Those same arms were corded with muscle, strength learned from decades of working at the forge and in the field with the weapons he tempered. The legs were equally as strong, no weakness in the calves as the leather pants curved tightly to them. Grace closed her eyes a moment, and then reopened them. She was not at all sure what Narskap asked of her. Healers could look at a person and sometimes pick out the thread that did not belong in their complex weaving, that thread being the illness or injury that plagued them. But she wasn't a healer in Vaelinar terms. She could heal and did, by virtue of touch, absorbing that into herself that she found wrong when she touched someone. It was not a skill she practiced often, and her vision had little to do with it. Narskap removed his hand from her throat and chin, sun moving to dapple her chilled skin where he had touched her. Quendius had none of the lines of refined strength that attracted her in Sevryn. Instead, his was a crude and demanding strength, one that she found intimidating to look at. And, yet, it seemed that portrait was one that Quendius fought to project: hardened strength, not one of refinement or power coiled in waiting. Head on, strong-as-a-bull qualities.

"Lily was a weaver. Tell me how that man is woven."

"I can't do that!"

"I think you can. Try for me."

Rivergrace made a small sound of exasperation before narrowing her eyes at Quendius. He wasn't a man she wished to be on the same continent with, let alone within riding distance. If he were a weaving on Lily's loom, he'd be threads of arrogance, crossed by others of violence, the warp and weft of his existence. There would be other threads to fill in the pattern: anger, hate, a sly intelligence, a joy at the pain of others, all these things she knew about him. There was much she didn't know about him and never would want to: those areas were huge, gaping holes in the weave. But as she worked in her mind and then looked at him, she saw.

Saw the bared threads of the man's existence. She sucked in a long, slow breath, her hands dropping to her father's arm and gripping tightly to steady herself.

"What is it?"

"I can't describe it." She took a breath that quavered as it filled her lungs. "He's coated with this oily darkness. It slithers around him as though it were alive. There are huge gaps in his weave, and among all the darkness, all the wrong and knotted patterns, there are silver-and-gold threads that don't seem to belong. I can't . . . I can't see anything else." Nor could she bear to, she thought, no matter what her father asked of her. The sight of Quendius stuck in her throat with a sick, stinking coating that threatened to suffocate her as if merely by looking she drank it in. She shuddered.

Narskap put one scarred hand over her eyes. "Do not follow his web."

She closed her eyes behind the coolness of his palm. "The silver threads are Vaelinar. I've seen them before."

"His heritage. But why gold? There is nothing of light about the man at all."

"I don't know." She put her hands up to bring his down.

"You didn't see the magic in him? His Talent?"

"No."

"He has the eyes! He has to have a Talent in his blood."

"Sevryn doesn't have the eyes, yet he does have the magic. It could be the reverse with Quendius."

"No. I smell it on him from time to time. Magic has a stink to it."

She took his hand from her eyes to look at the man riding several horse lengths ahead of them. "If he does, then it comes from the abyss." Her head throbbed, but she picked at the essence of magics about them, and when she touched again upon the oily, dark strings emanating from Quendius, her heart took a leap that felt as though it landed at the back of her throat. She examined the web carefully, even as doing so repulsed her.

Then she spoke ever so softly. "Narskap. He sees, but he does not see as we do, and he hasn't discovered it yet. We see the threads of life that weave our world about us. He sees only the thread of death. If he learns to tug on those threads, to weave them as he wills or to snap them entirely, he will learn to destroy at will. Can't you see it on him?"

Narskap didn't answer for a very long time, until he had breathed again, and his breaths were so far apart she could barely discern them, and would not if she hadn't been leaning against him. The Undead breathe, but very rarely. "Are you certain?"

"Yes, as you should be. I have died once, and you stand on the threshold between. If anyone can be certain, it should be us."

"He's had centuries to learn himself and although he creates tools of destruction, he's never shown an inkling that he needs no tools. He seeks chaos and thrives in it."

"He may be blind to his abilities, but he won't always be. He has been content to use you, but what happens when that no longer satisfies him? We need to leave him dead behind us." She said it barely audibly, the words disgusting her as she uttered them, but she knew they were true.

"Not yet. I don't know what we might unleash if we do. I'm not saying that you're not right. I'm saying only that the universes have their laws and I don't know yet what kind of backlash we invite when we deal with Quendius."

"Backlash?"

"What if meeting death is all it takes for him to learn what he is capable of? We could unleash the very Talents we fear. You've reminded me that I ought to be able to see more than you of his potentials. I've been studying him from the living side. Now, I need to walk among the ashes." Narskap raised his hand again, to place his cool palm on her forehead. "Now rest a bit."

His touch felt oddly soothing as she closed her eyes and relaxed in her father's hold. She remembered days from so long ago she barely knew how to walk, exploring the vast underground river in the mining cavern where they lived, the three of them, her mother and father like silver flames in the semidarkness. Her singing. His strong arms rocking her to sleep. Protecting her. His strong voice talking with her mother, planning on how to free them. The horse moving in a swaying walk that lulled her back to sleep, despite her worry.

"Mik is nearly dead."

Rivergrace stirred at the gravelly voice. Narskap put a heel to his mount's flank, swinging him about to watch.

The raider speaking reined his horse up and lifted his short sword, prepared to hasten the event, knowing his commander would demand the man abandoned immediately.

Quendius put his hand up. "Leave him. I have a need for him yet."

The blade halted in midair, a silvery splinter that caught the sun and looked as if it could part the sky itself. Quendius smiled at it as if in memory of his forges and his men, and of their workings in fine weapons. He wheeled his horse around to block the horse next to him, threading his way through the pack to clasp his hand upon Narskap's bony shoulder. "It is your turn." He ignored Rivergrace as though she did not, for the moment, exist. He had been ignoring her for days.

Her Undead father moved his head about slowly, bones creaking under paper-thin skin. "For what?" A peculiar tension brought his shoulders back.

"Initiate him." He tightened his hand on Narskap's shoulder. "It's time for you to teach me, and show me how to make Mik into what you've become."

They all of them smelled of campfire smoke and sweat and horse lather, odors that overwhelmed Grace, all except for Narskap who smelled of horse, a little, and . . . what? A dried herb and perhaps a faint, musty smell, like something which had been put in a trunk long ago and just brought back to light. He no longer smelled of the living. Grace felt him shift behind her. "And you believe this is something I know how to do."

"I have the proof before me."

"You assume it was voluntary. And, even if it were something I knew how to do, why would I wish to curse another being with *this?*"

"Your wishes hardly matter to me as long as Rivergrace's welfare concerns you. I thought we had an agreement, you and I." Quendius tilted his head as if listening to the lifeblood rattling in the throat of the dying man. "We have little time. This isn't a choice you get to make, I've made it for you."

Narskap's attention went to Mik and flicked back to Quendius. "If you would be a God, be a compassionate one and let him go. If not, do it yourself." He raked a hand over his face, welts tore through his cheek and then sealed, all without pain or blood. Quendius watched the gesture hungrily. "I would wish this on no man."

"And I," Quendius said, leaning out of his saddle and into Narskap's face, "would do it to any. Give me an army, Narskap, an army that does not feel pain or stop fighting to bleed. If you don't, your precious daughter and her family will suffer as long as they have a thumbnail's worth of skin upon their bodies and a drop of blood to lose. I will enjoy finding ways to keep them alive while I invent their torture." Then and only then did he drop his hot gaze on Rivergrace, and she found her heart quaking as he did. She thought of the short sword sheathed on her father's hip and the palm of her hand itched.

She could feel him straighten and raise his chin. "You don't want to threaten me."

"Oh, but I do, dear hound. I have spent many a decade threatening you, and it simply binds you closer to my heels and my wishes. Now do this for me, or Mik will spend the last candlemark of his life in more agony than a dying man deserves to be, followed shortly by your girl."

Narskap shifted away from him, from his hold on his shoulder and putting his sword out of Rivergrace's reach as though he had read her desperate thought to take it from his hand and drive it home, and swung down from his mount. The horse dropped his head to the ground and began to lip dispiritedly at bruised grass sprouts. They traded a long look. She shook her head ever so faintly. Narskap's only response was to lift a bony shoulder and drop it, nearly imperceptibly, as if to negate her concern. He looked to Quendius. "As you wish."

Quendius smiled thinly in triumph.

The raider chief and another of his men cut the lashes that had bound the mortally wounded brigand to his saddle and lifted Mik to the ground. Narskap's shadow fell over him, a casting hardly more substantial than he was, thin and wavering. Mik's eyelids batted wildly as he groaned and then subsided into the choking rattling noise he had been making. Rivergrace saw Narskap's eyes widen and a glint lit them, a gleam from deep within him that shut her, and all else around him, out. She put her hand over her mouth as she realized how lost he was. The metallic smell of fresh blood flooded her senses and she realized it would drive away the other's control. She dug her hands into the saddle to steady herself as she watched his face and lost all that she knew of the man who had been her father and the being who had been her nemesis as he became something *else* altogether.

Narskap went to one knee beside the injured man's sodden flank. He forgot Quendius. He forgot Rivergrace. All he could remember was fresh blood.

The taste of it lay on his tongue though he never brought

his fingers to his mouth as he touched the man, the warmth
of it warmed him like a banked fire, and the sticky, silken
sensation of it washed over him as though he'd bathed himself in the man's essence. He could feel a life stirring in him
that he had not felt in weeks, not since he had died, or
nearly died, on the fields of Ashenbrook. It awakened and
stretched rasping claws through him from the inside out
and he knew that this thing, this obscenity that kept him
pretending to live was hungry. It had him and it hungered
for more.

And as it did, he finally knew what it was that had kept
him alive, and Narskap mourned the knowledge as Cerat,
Demon Souldrinker and ancient nemesis, reached through
him and hooked a claw in Mik.

It slurped at the dying man. It ripped hanks of flesh from
him, though no one could see it but Narskap, as the victim
groaned and let out a shriek and drummed his heels on the
ground with the last of his strength. Even as Cerat de-
voured, the Demon offered a deal to its meal. A life for a
life, more or less, and Narskap could feel a burning at his
fingers as the power to consummate filled his hand. A touch,
a tacit agreement, and the tattered man would become what
Narskap was. "You don't want this," Narskap whispered
hoarsely, in a voice low enough for only the two of them to
hear. Mik's eyelids flung wide open and he stared into
Narskap, raised his hands and grabbed Narskap by the collar, forcing him down into Mik's face and for the briefest of
moments, Narskap saw Cerat's white-hot gleam burning
back at him. Mik opened his mouth, working for words, and
never found them.

He batted Mik's hands away and let the Souldrinker
take what it could. The man went still immediately, and the
warmth left him as if it had never been, Cerat sucking what
he could from the dead corpse but not finding the anchor it
needed to stay and reanimate him, because Narskap
blocked him from that last, satisfying morsel.

Narskap rocked back on his heels. Bloody sweat dotted
his brow before he wiped it away on the back of his arm. He

looked up to find Quendius watching him closely. "I almost had him."

"I know." The corner of Quendius' mouth drew back wryly. "Better luck next time." He straightened. "Bury what you can, shallow, we've got ground to cover."

Narskap struggled to his feet and none of the raiders put out a hand to help him. Blood drenched his fingers, and he looked at himself, but the urge to lick them clean had fled. He dumped part of his waterskin over them and wiped himself as best he could, the warmth gone, the stickiness gone, the aching promise gone.

Quendius held his horse's reins out to him. "No matter," he said. His glance ranged over his remaining men, those hale and those wounded. "You'll have more practice. You're almost certain to have it right before I decide to kill River-grace."

Chapter
Thirty-Four

CEYLA FELL AS MUCH as she dismounted from the fork of the tree that held her tired, punished body, dropping to the underground with a crackle and a snap of breaking twigs. At least, she prayed they were twigs. She stayed in a crouch while she took an inventory of her body—aches, bruises, and all—before moving cautiously to her feet. The sweeping branches of the tree enveloped her, almost as though she had wings, and kept her hidden in the early evening shadows. Deep in sleep during the day, she heard, or thought she had heard, horsemen moving through at a distance and listened intently now, wondering if she could still hear them. Or even if she had heard them at all. Only the muted sounds of twilight reached her, that time when wildlife of the day began to seek shelter and the nocturnal citizens began to rustle awake. Like those caught in the dusk, she needed to find water and she drifted out of her leafy wings to search for it.

She'd been untroubled by visions the last two days, sleeping the sleep of the exhausted when she'd found shelter, which Ceyla welcomed, but at the same time she felt cast adrift. Other than the singular destiny burning inside her, she was now more or less on her own. It was times like these that left her wondering if she knew what she thought she knew or if she were simply insane. She squeezed a fist closed. No use thinking that way, or any other way, because she had little control over what happened to her mind. It guided her, it obstructed her, but she did not know life without it. What others thought, how they thought, she could only suppose because she was different and would always be different. Her nails bit into her palm.

It came to her that she heard no sounds of the horse. Nothing. She'd left him lightly hobbled so that he could graze, but no cropping or any other sign that he existed met her listening. Horses were not noisy creatures, but they had patterns of sound Ceyla could expect to hear.

A breeze ruffled through the edge of the forest, bringing with it the furtive sounds of those awakening into the night. The touch of wind felt good on her face although she knew she might be chilled and damp before dawn rose again. She took cautious steps toward the noise, thinking she might be tracking those headed for water even though she could not yet hear the water itself. The horse would surely have sought out water; she'd just be following. Ceyla kept moving, stretching her sore muscles, feeling the scabs on her various scratches tug on her legs as she did. Her stomach knotted in a hunger cramp. She needed food, more than roots and berries if she could find it, but even a quantity of those would fill her growling need. She pushed forward faster, eager to find water and perhaps a fish in its depths.

Ceyla heard a distinctive noise. She moved in its direction, listening intently as she did, unable to identify just what it was she heard. Hooves? Or something else? She stilled again, frozen in her footsteps. A leaf, dangling from an overhead branch, tickled her forehead. She batted it away irritably. Then the smell came to her. Tentative, weak, coppery. Could it be . . . ? She inhaled again, gently, mouth half-open, tasting as much as she smelled. Yes. Blood on the air. Ceyla turned her head, undecided which direction to go.

She needed water. Predators hunted those who moved to water instinctively, day after day. Inevitably. Predators went where the prey went.

Or the blood sign could mean that an attack had occurred nearby, for an altogether different reason. Her hobbled horse ... anything. She stayed frozen in indecision. She needed water. Without the horse, she needed boots or shoes. She would not get far on bare feet. She needed help. Or a plan. Or ...

She heard a groan. A low, from the gut groan that raised the hairs on the back of her neck. Ceyla turned on one heel, preparing to run. But she did not. Whatever it was that groaned needed help. She knew that. It might or might not have anything to do with the blood scent, but chances were it did. She didn't have to be a seer to make that connection. It could even be her horse, mortally wounded, and needing a merciful ending, if nothing else. She owed it that much. She pushed a foot forward, and then had to follow it. One halting, pushing footstep at a time, she moved closer to the noise and the smell. Before she broke through the shelter of the brush and saplings, she could see it: her horse's carcass, exsanguinated and ripped to pieces, in a bruised patch of grass and dirt. She bit the inside of her cheek sharply to keep from crying out or being sick. It had been torn down and then shredded apart, although the blood loss was far less than she would have imagined. Limbs had been ripped off and then gnawed upon. The entrails bulged out of the stomach's cavern, piling onto the forest floor. The face of the animal was ripped to tatters as if that and the tender area under the throat were where it had been attacked first.

Ceyla turned her face away. Had she crippled it so much with the hobble that it couldn't have fought back, couldn't have run? She didn't think so. She didn't *know*. All she knew was that it was dead. Perhaps one day a vision would show her how and why, but she couldn't depend on that. Her visions did not exist to make her life easier.

She shoved a fist into her mouth to keep herself quiet,

and began to skirt the death scene. There was still the matter of water. Still the matter of the groan.

Ceyla eased through the undergrowth as quietly as she could, hunching over to hide herself within it, gnawing on her fingers anxiously as she moved. She had nothing, nothing except her wits and she wasn't even sure about them at this point. A noise like . . . like a shower of gravel and dirt cascading upon ground halted her in her tracks again.

She had no idea what would make a sound like that. Or why. She knew the where of it by this time, in a break just beyond the canopy of trees and brush, out in the open. Exactly where she did not want to be. She put her hand out to the trunk of the nearest sizable tree. The feel of rough bark biting into her palm calmed her a bit. This, she knew. This pain was familiar.

As quickly and quietly as she could, she scaled the tree. Up and up until the branches could barely hold her weight before lying down on one to see what she could see. She inched as far out on it as she dared before coming to a halt, slowing down her breathing, hoping her pulse would follow, concentrating on being nothing more than a leaf upon the waving bough. Moments slowed. Her panic ebbed. She blinked a few times to clear her vision and looked down. At first Ceyla did not see what could possibly have made the noises she'd heard, particularly the shifting of rock and pebble, and then she saw, half-shadowed, what looked to be a shallow grave. It made no sense to her until she heard the low groan again, rising in both agony and decibels, as the grave rippled and then heaved upward. A shower of dirt and gravel fell off the hump to either side, raining upon the ground.

Something that was not dead had been buried down below. It had not stayed there. It had erupted, desperately. It looked as if it had returned, more than once, hollowing a den from its grave.

Her first instinct shook her. He needed help, surely. She should go see how badly injured he was, find out what had happened, see what she could do. But the shock of seeing him—it—rise from the ground froze her in her perch. Blood and gore covered his ragged clothing, but it was fresh, glistening under the dirt and grime, not the rusty brown color of old blood. The wet shine of it caught the glare of the sun like a crimson mirror. Ceyla flinched, her gaze darting away from what she watched. Whatever it was or wherever it came from, she felt certain it was a principal player in the death scene she'd just skirted and that whatever foresight had kept her from rushing to help, she thanked prayerfully. Its odor rose with it, a miasma of fetid odors that forced her hand to her nose and mouth to keep from spitting it back out and giving herself away. She didn't know if it could climb, but she certainly knew that it could kill.

As for who or what had buried it, there seemed to be a good possibility that it had buried itself for the sun filtering through the surroundings bothered it. It groaned and mumbled, hunched over and shambled forward in whatever shadows it could find. Ceyla watched it stumble out of her sight and when it had completely disappeared, she found her fist remaining in her mouth to keep silence. She wanted to stay in the tree a very long time to keep safe, but as the sun would eventually fall in the sky and the shadows lengthen, she would become more and more unsafe. Better to run now, while she could stay with the sun shining full upon her.

Ceyla sprinted.

A scream like that of a mountain bobcat split the air behind her, a shout and a growl swallowing it up and Ceyla sobbed, certain that whatever it was, was on her. She stumbled and went down, somersaulting through the bushes and shrubbery, stopping only when coming up hard against a sapling that bent as it bore her weight.

Only then did she realize that nothing chased her, that the battle sounded behind her, that the thing had found a different target. Ceyla rolled upward to one knee, branches stabbing at her and her body aching, but knelt, alert, like an animal sensing whatever it could.

She could hear the furious battle muted only by distance

and the forest itself, limbs twitching in the wind and animals scurrying away from the furor. Hoofbeats drummed her way and Ceyla leaped to her feet into the pathway of a tashya horse, head up and eyes wild, reins flapping about its neck and chest. It slowed at the sight of her, and she grabbed for the leathers, thinking the horse would pull her arm out of her shoulder as it dragged her along before abruptly stopping. It let out a low, sobbing snort, and rolled its near eye at her, the whites blazing. Ceyla put her hand on its muzzle and murmured comforting sounds to it, even as she listened to the noise of a far-off fight. The noise stopped after a handful of breaths. She pulled the horse's head down to her chest and held it very still, not wanting it to whicker or whinny, alerting the survivor of the battle.

No more sound reached her, though she strained to hear. The tashya's ears flickered forward and back, and it stomped a foot at being held in such a confined way. Ceyla kneed it in the chest and bit out a discouraging sound. The horse stilled.

The smell of smoke reached her. That comforted her more than the silence. Whoever survived was burning the body, and she doubted the half-alive, shambling thing she'd seen could think to do such a thing. She cheered the victor and his actions. Burning it was the only smart thing to do. Leaving the body could only spread the contagion and for all she knew, it could come alive yet again.

Ceyla's hand closed on the horse's reins. A distant whicker hung on the air, and her horse trembled in its need to answer it. She pinched its nostrils tight with her free hand until she was certain the horse relaxed. Then, and only then, she swung the horse around, put her foot in the stirrup, grabbed the saddle, and mounted.

Whoever the victor was, he had a horse or pony at hand, and would not need this one. She did. Ceyla sat for a moment, casting through her scattered thoughts, before finding the one, the singular need, that drove her. She turned the horse, put a heel to its flank, and continued on her journey. Tree branches grabbed at her sleeves and whipped at her face as she took the tashya winding through the groves, lit by an unquenchable desire to reach her destination, a thirst that would kill her if she could not slake it.

She rode for two days. Not running but without stop. Both she and the horse were drenched with sweat and tottering with exhaustion when she reached the outskirts of a vast encampment, one heralded by the scent of its campfires and the aroma of its horse lines. Its people were golden-skinned, and they put their hands up eagerly to lift her off her mount, which promptly dropped to the ground with a shuddering sigh of relief. She staggered away from the fallen horse. They stared at her for a long moment.

"A Vaelinar is come to us!" they shouted, and they brought her to their king.

Chapter
Thirty-Five

VERDAYNE STAYED ON ONE KNEE, catching his breath and studying the remains of the creature he'd just dispatched. He could not count it human now, but it had been once. He would burn its remains the way he and his father burned aryns corrupted with black thread — using fire and salt — for there was no way he wanted to see this thing rise yet again. Even as he watched it, he thought he saw a quivering in the fingers of one detached hand, lying among chunks of flesh hacked apart which had bled only when his sword had finally pierced the thing's guts. As if it had no blood in its body save that which it had drunk from an earlier kill.

He got up, sword in hand. His tashya had run after dumping him unceremoniously when the thing had attacked, but his cart ponies had stayed, quivering in their harness and rolling eyes that showed far too much white in their fright. He rubbed both muzzles with his free hand and murmured words of praise to them. Not relinquishing his sword, he gathered his bag of salt, his flint, and tossed them near the remains, slowing only to pitch dry kindling across the battleground as well.

The salt he scattered first, and then lit a fire over it, a pyre of sorts, for a being who did not deserve an honorable burial but got one of sorts anyway. Through the flickering flames, he studied what was left of the body. A soldier, though a poor enough one. Mercenary. And, around here, that meant a man who rode under Quendius.

Verdayne spat to one side. That knowledge meant that he would have to look for black thread as he made his way to Calcort, for he knew that Quendius had murdered Magdan while they were bringing in saplings to replace the great aryns corrupted by the blight that had seemingly come out of nowhere, with devastating effectiveness. He could not prove Quendius had spread the blight as well, any more than Magdan could, but the old man had muttered epithets about it often enough. He looked to the north, a tug deep in his heart to follow after, to see if he could catch the weaponmaster's trail. Quendius moved in shadow and his domain in the badlands had never been found, at least not by anyone who lived to tell the tale. He was as close now as anyone had been to a warm lead in decades—and he couldn't take it.

He rubbed the back of his hand across his forehead. Revenge wasn't his charge. The black thread among the aryns was. His family had laid that burden on him, and he'd accepted it. It was the same blight on the books he carried for Tolby's examination. From tree to page to ... where? His father would have cut, salted, and burned whole groves to prevent the contagion from raging across the land. Could he be so bold as to do the same? Destroy the great library lest one unaffected book held the seeds to corrupt another? He didn't think he had it in him to lay waste without more proof. Certainly Bistane had not thought destruction an answer. With any hope, Tolby Farbranch could tell him what they must—what he must—do when he showed Dayne what his tinctures could do. Page by page they could save a book. He did not know if that would help at all in the larger scheme of things.

When the fire had burned, an evening mist drew its cooling arm into the forest, and he dared to shovel dirt over the ashes, thinking furiously as he worked.

If he had his tashya, he'd cut his ponies loose and send them to Pepper Straightplow, a Dweller farmer who lived within two days' ride of this grove, but he'd not found a sign of the hot-blooded Vaelinar steed, so cart travel was all that was left to him. He whistled them up and fed both a ration of grain and spoke to them, low but commanding, telling them what he expected of them. They would take him to Calcort at the fastest pace they could manage until their tendons bowed and their wind broke, if he asked it of them. He was not quite that demanding.

Not quite.

Chapter Thirty-Six

SAND CRACKLED OVER HIS EYELIDS as Sevryn opened his eyes. It husked its way through his throat as he inhaled to take a breath and speak. It rattled at the bottom of his rib cage as he sat up. A Kobrir leaned over him. He felt the presence of others watching him in the shadows ringing him.

"Might you be the king of assassins?" He got the words out and then had to spit off to the side to clear his aching throat.

The Kobrir tilted his head to let out a barking laugh, a laugh similar to one Sevryn had once heard from a man who'd survived a knife to the throat. He had never heard a Kobrir laugh, but he thought perhaps this one carried similar scars.

"Do you think," and the being wrapped all in dark clothing, with even his face veiled in black, leaned close. "Do you think we would bring you all this way and save you the work of your quest?"

From the harshness and growl of his words, Sevryn thought his assessment of a badly scarred windpipe correct.

He wiped the back of his hand across his eyes. "I did not ask to be abducted."

"Perhaps you would rather we'd killed you."

"If you could have."

Another barking laugh. "You're not as invincible as you might think."

"True. Your drugs brought me down." Sevryn stood cautiously, stretching his limbs as he did, gauging his balance and strength. Besides the feeling that he was half made of grit, he seemed to have no detrimental side effects. Water would cure his ills . . . he hoped. The drugs used might have an ill effect entirely the other way. He would be cautious drinking at first.

As if reading his thoughts, the Kobrir offered him a waterskin. Sevryn bowed and took it, wet his mouth, spat out the water, and then took two cautious sips before handing it back. The Kobrir's face, what could be seen behind the masking and veil, gave away a raised eyebrow. "Not thirsty?"

"All in good time."

"Careful. That is good. Always take care among your enemies, and be even more careful among your friends." He tossed the waterskin at Sevryn's boots. "We gave you a journey, but circumstances have changed, and we find ourselves now in a race against time. We cannot wait for you to find your way."

"Not to mention that I have side trips planned." Where was Grace now? Did Lara hold her? Did she think he hated her for sending him on without her? There was a distance between them he dared not let grow, or they might never find their way back to each other.

"True. To your best interests, perhaps, but not ours." The Kobrir beckoned over one shoulder. "When you are ready, your trial begins. Perhaps you are worthy of the quest we gave you, and perhaps not. We would have ascertained this more slowly, but as I said—"

"You're in a hurry."

"Indeed."

Sevryn bent slightly to pick up the waterskin. He took a

full drink this time, and waited as it coursed through him, rinsing away the gritty aftereffects of whatever drug they'd given him. An inhalant. He would have to learn and remember it as it could come in handy. He drank another mouthful, before fastening the skin to his belt. He was far from hydrated, but he could function. He and the Kobrir watching him traded nods.

The speaker pointed at the shadows and said: "Begin." He faded back into the gray edges of the shadows where he could be both seen and unseen, his silhouette blurring. Sevryn looked up. He stood in a rock formation that was more cave than not, its ceiling wide open to the sky and elements, a jagged bowl. He marked the speaker's position by a rock formation before turning to the opponent who seemed to appear out of nowhere.

This Kobrir was incredibly slender and wiry. Corded muscles showed under his wrappings, but none of it bulky. Sevryn noted that this man would be fast and could probably outleap him, if it came to it. He passed the back of his wrist over his eyes again, clearing the last of the clouds from them. Then he patted himself down. They'd left him with his weapons. He smiled at that. The Kobrir answered his smile with a wide one of his own.

"You will use one of our weapons."

"This is an *ithrel*," the wiry Kobrir told him. "It is used thusly." He opened the wicked looking blade and handle with a hard flick of his wrist, sliced through the air at its greatest extension, and then closed it down to its shortest length, filling his hand with it to make a cut by Sevryn's head. So close, it left a tang behind of metal shavings and oil, the scent of its recent sharpening filling Sevryn's nostrils. He pulled his chin in with a blink. The Kobrir looked at him intently. "Understand?"

Others in the shadows stirred at his back wordlessly.

"Best me, and you may pass." The Kobrir tossed the weapon at him, taking a step backward to fall into a stance, filling his empty hands with another ithrel in the time between one breath and another as Sevryn caught it up.

The warmth behind fell back hastily, freeing him to move as he must. He flicked the ithrel open. It took a strong wrist flick to make the weapon answer, and by the time he had it positioned, the Kobrir had stepped in and shaved the air by his face with the whispering blade. Sevryn pivoted out of range before the other could test him again. The danger here would be to assume he knew anything of the weapon, its balance and even its range. He swung back, found it parried, and the force of the blow vibrated heavily down, almost numbing his fingers. An unexpected aspect of the fight. He swapped it from hand to hand and back again, settling it tighter, settling the grip deep into his palm. He thought he saw a ghost of a smile flash across the other's half-masked face.

Yes, the ithrel held undoubted advantages to one used to handling it.

Within seconds, he realized the advantages and disadvantages of the weapon. If he took the time to think about it, he would find himself dropped in his tracks. No. This is where his innate abilities and his decades of training told him, telegraphed instinctively through his muscles, his nerves, his frame, what he need to know to handle the ithrel. To think about it, to reason, to do anything but react would take far too long to be able to defend himself. Turning the ithrel in his hands, he took his measure not of the weapon but of the being facing him, one of the elusive Kobrir who might—or might not—be human.

Slight, wrapped in dark cloth that took advantage of the dappled shadows of the forest as easily as it did the harsher shadows of alleyways and foreboding buildings, the Kobrir moved with an uncanny suppleness. He bent where you could not expect a man to bend, leaned at an angle you dared not think a human could defy the pull of the earth, and leaped effortlessly. But his eyes were still eyes, not like the wet bulbs of a Raymy or the red-slit pupils of a Raver. This enemy was both common and uncommon.

Sevryn could take his measure quickly and almost without thought, as he had been trained by Gilgarran to do. After a flurry of exchanges, initiated and parried, he knew that the man had a definite tell: his glance would dart to the left just before he drove in with a series of attacks. It would not be enough to defeat him, but it was enough for Sevryn to realize his own strategy.

It was for this, after all, that Gilgarran had trained him. Not necessarily the weapon, but for the meeting and measuring of an enemy. Trained to determine how best to dispatch him, whether by blade or guile, by attack or espionage, but always to be formidable ... and effective. From the day he had been scavenging in an alley, in a slightly less than reputable side of town, and Gilgarran had literally dropped on him from out of the sky or, more precisely, from a leap off a second-floor balcony, Sevryn had been an apprentice in matters he often did not understand. To this day, with Gilgarran long dead at the hands of the weaponmaker Quendius, Sevryn did not have a complete overview of Gilgarran's agenda and network. He had been but a single strand in a complicated web, and even by following as many strands as he could discover, the final weaving could not be seen or its purpose discerned. Gilgarran had been one of the few Vaelinar who had originally supported Lariel in her ascendency to Warrior Queen, but that had only been one tiny gossamer pattern of Gilgarran's desires. To fathom more would take a lifetime he did not feel like pursuing. He had his own pattern to weave and complete. And this, what Gilgarran had trained him for, was part of it.

Someone let out a small gasp behind him as the very fabric of the moment parted across him, slashed by the ithrel moving swiftly over him. He parried it, twisted the blade back on his own, metal whining as surfaces ground over each other before separating. The bones in his hands and arms vibrated, his teeth clicked together, his elbows flexed to answer the move. And here, he thought as his body fought, was the difference between what Gilgarran had trained him for, and what he had become. He was no longer only an assassin. What he plotted as he stood here was not to kill but to answer the blows being delivered, to divert them, to turn death aside, to present such a challenge that the other would fall back, would retreat, would give up and run or surrender rather than meet the inevitability of the death he carried. He was more than an assassin. He was the judgment between life and death. Or so he had trained himself to become.

He would kill if necessary, if death was all the opponent could offer. But he stepped into the fray not to deliver death but protection to those targeted, to shield the life/lives at his back, to withstand the expertise of those determined to dishonor life.

A thin smile tugged at his mouth. The Kobrir's gaze darted to his left. Sevryn moved with more than the speed of the cutting ithrel, flicked his wrist to open the weapon, and cut deep, blood spurting out as he did so, spattering him with coppery scented warmth as the Kobrir's grip disintegrated with the blow. The slender being staggered back, wound his hand in a sleeve of cloth, ripping it free from his other arm, and fell back into fighting stance, his wound staunched down to dull thuds of blood spattering to the ground at their feet. Blood loss would end their battle now, if one of them did not down the other first. The Kobrir swapped hands and Sevryn's smile tightened but did not lessen.

He, too, knew how to fight with either hand. He shifted his own ithrel. The pupils of the Kobrir's dark eyes widened a bit, and then narrowed. He should know, Sevryn thought, that his opponent would do no less. He, Sevryn, had known. If the Kobrir could misjudge him in this, what other mistakes would the famed assassin make?

Tender-hearted Rivergrace, in an unspoken plea for compassion, would have had him withdraw from the challenge. She carried his soul, after all. But he could not. He—they—had come too far to quit. The shield did not buckle simply because it had been struck. That was its purpose.

The Kobrir pressed. If his movements had been swift before, now they were blinding, seeking a quick and decisive end. His own heartbeat drummed the strokes left he could deliver before he would be too weakened to fight. He drove in at Sevryn with a surety in each delivery, sending Sevryn

back on his heels. His forearm stung and his sleeve separated into shreds on his arm.

Blood for blood, then, although his flowed far less speedily and from far shallower a wound. He would not stand in
this cavern till they both dropped. He gave off his own tell,
one he had deliberately primed the Kobrir to recognize. He
dropped his chin, signaling his intent to lunge on his right
foot to deliver an attack.

The Kobrir answered as he thought he would, and their
ithrels locked in a parry on their left sides, meeting each
other, crisscrossing in front of them, bringing them face-to-
face.

The difference was that Sevryn had filled his right hand
with his dirk and held it to the side of the assassin's neck,
bringing blood quickly to the point as he did.

The Kobrir's eyes widened as he froze in place.

"I was taught," Sevryn said, "never to fight one-handed
if I still had two hands." He pushed the dirk's point a little
deeper. Blood sprang freely.

"I give," the Kobrir answered. "You have bested me."
The ithrel fell from his hold and he went to one knee, free
to feel his pain, to grasp his wounded hand.

Shadows moved in to lift his weakened form and carry
him from the rock-bounded arena. Sevryn slipped the waterskin from his belt. It had done what he had hoped it
might: at least one knife-scoring showed along its leathern
side as it had blocked his open flank. Smiling wryly, he un-
corked it and finished the water.

As he lowered the skin, an old Kobrir approached him.
Still in dark wrappings, his age was apparent from the stoop
of his back and shoulders and hesitancy of his walk. Sevryn
watched him. This fellow may not have the agility required of
an assassin, but he doubted that he was any less dangerous.

His suspicions were confirmed when the old Kobrir
struck, a blade slicing across the back of Sevryn's wrist before he could pull out of reach. Not a killing blow by any
means unless the blade had been poisoned.

He could feel the surge of kedant through his blood before

he dropped back on his heels, out of range. The heat of it, the power of it, sang through his veins, offering him wonders he did not dare to accept. Sevryn gave a shake of his head.

"I am immune to kedant."

The old Kobrir cackled. "'Bout time, boy, 'bout time. Few Vaelinars recognize its potency. I could not take your word for it, however." He sat cross-legged, after replacing his knife in a wrist sheath.

"I take it your lethal ways are more subtle."

"Age has forced me to find death down other paths? Yes." His statement hissed into silence as he watched Sevryn's face, still tracking, no doubt, the heat of the kedant in his body.

"You're the one who drugged me."

"Might have been. I made the dust."

"What was it?"

"Another lesson, another time. A common but colorful field weed soaked in a special liquid, dried and ground."

Sevryn finished his water, the glittering eyes of the old Kobrir fast upon him. He sat down then, but not as the other had. He kept one knee up, for leverage in getting to his feet quickly. From the murmuring of shadows behind him, he sensed that most of the watchers had dispersed. A long dry lecture, no doubt, awaited him.

He tossed Sevryn a bandaging rag for the slice from the ithrel. "One learns to survive. If you survive, you can heal. You may not be whole, but you will be healed, and you have endured."

"As you have." Sevryn tied the bandage off with the aid of his teeth and the one available hand. The fabric held the scent of herbs he was familiar with, healing fragrances.

He could not underestimate this seemingly affable elder in front of him, a man with more blades secreted about his body and, no doubt, more venoms and powders. "This is another lesson."

"It is." The old Kobrir laughed, a rich deep chuckle with a bubbling at the end of it which he interrupted by coughing harshly. A wise old Kobrir who had, perhaps, been exposed to a few too many of his poisons.

"The way of the blade is not unlike the way of our lives. We are forged: beaten, sharpened, tempered, and then used, only to be beaten and sharpened again and used again until our metal grows brittle and dull. But even an old knife has its uses as a garrote stick perhaps or, at the very least, a weeder in the herb garden." The old Kobrir chuckled at himself. "Not that I would denigrate the power of herbs. Our best healants and poisons come from the garden, as innocent as those stems, leaves, and buds may look. But then you are well aware of that, as well as that venom for which you've built a healthy tolerance."

"Hallucinogens?"

"Without a doubt." The Kobrir pursed his thin lips.

"Which one of you drugged the Trader Bregan and why?" More importantly, for whom, but he knew he would not get that secret yet.

"I cannot break the confidence of a contract."

"That, in itself, tells me he was a target. It seems your brotherhood added intents of its own to it."

"Perhaps. I could not say."

Or would not. Sevryn found himself not trusting the elder being in front of him.

"There are many weapons in our arsenal."

"And I know many of them, and you are likely to teach me others, but what I want to know is this: why am I a student of yours? What do you expect of me?"

"I want you to pick the weapon mostly likely to kill me."

Without a word, Sevryn struck, his hand flat and taut as a blade, punching into the Kobrir's neck. The assassin had time only for surprise to widen his pupils before he crumpled onto his side, quite dead. A pouch rolled from the palm of his off-hand as he did. A deadly dust, Sevryn could imagine, ready to blow into his face.

Before he had recoiled, Sevryn said, "I know you are watching. I presume this is what you wanted."

A dry cough sounded from behind him, as well as the near noiseless sweep of two sets of footfalls leaving behind him. "He was a teacher. Although we prefer giving our teachers time so that they may impart their knowledge, I cannot argue that a teacher is truly finished when the student can best him. You caught him most unaware."

Sevryn got to his feet and turned to face the last observer. "Again, I would say to you: why?"

The Kobrir facing him put a slender hand up to drop the veil from his face and to unwrap the black cloth about his head. When he finished, he looked at Sevryn with a slight tilt to his expression. "As you can see, we are not from here, even as you Vaelinar are not."

He stared at a face the likes of which he had never seen before. Wide, flat nose, high cheekbones so sharp they could cut the air, a mouth which revealed more teeth than it should as the assassin smiled at him, a squared jaw to accommodate those teeth ... yes, teeth of a carnivore, no doubt of it. He wondered that, in all the close encounters he'd had with Kobrir, none of them had ever bitten him. It would have been formidable. It might have revealed that which was being revealed to him now. Sevryn studied the curve of his opponent's neck, long and elegant and, unless Sevryn were very wrong about what he saw, too many vertebrae. The Kobrir would have a far easier time of it turning his head to scan his flanks or even partially behind him. A handy condition for a fighter.

Sevryn took a step back. The Kobrir had never left their dead behind. Never. In any attack, there were always those whose single purpose was to retrieve the bodies, and they had done so with extreme success. Sevryn had never had more than a moment or two to look at them before being drawn away.

"You reveal yourself now. Am I allowed to ask where you belong, if not here?"

"We believe we are come from what you Vaelinar refer to as the lost Trevilara. We cannot be certain. Our lives and our histories are not as long or as well documented as yours. For a long time, we hoped we could ask you—that is, one of you—where our ancestors were birthed. It doesn't matter in many ways because we are almost certain we would not be welcomed back. We were sent here to be killers. We have succeeded, and yet failed. Vaelinars still live."

"You were to kill all of us."

The lips peeled back from those too many teeth again. "I think we were meant to. Certainly, at key moments in your history here, to impede growth. But as good as we are at killing, you and yours are better at surviving."

"Why stop at me?"

"Because, Sevryn, we have a small knot of magic amongst ourselves, courtesy of our birthright from Trevilara, and that fistful of power has told us to do what we've never done before: break a contract. Break a contract, spare the intended target, and reveal ourselves and pray that our feeble oracular vision is correct, and we have done as we should."

"Sparing me. Sparing Rivergrace."

The Kobrir inclined his head. Smoothly. Gracefully. Eloquently. What blood did he have in him besides human? Feline? Reptile? Sevryn tried to place it and couldn't. "We see a world coming in which we could have a place, or we could be driven out forever. We dwindle. We would like to embrace that which has been denied to us."

"You sent me on a search."

"One that was suggested to us by that kernel of foresight. A path which we had never hoped could exist, but which possibility has now been suggested to us."

Sevryn shook his head slowly. "I'm not your savior."

"Of course not. You're but a . . . how best to describe it . . . a finger in what we hope will become a fist."

"And it starts with finding the king of assassins."

Another graceful nod. "So it was given to us."

"Then lead me to him."

The Kobrir shook his head slowly side to side. "I cannot."

Sevryn could feel anger start a slow burn in him. "I cannot be delayed."

The Kobrir wrapped his head again, quickly, deftly, and replaced his veil. "Another lesson."

"And I complete it by killing you?"

"If that is how you must show your mastery."

Sevryn balanced himself. "One last question before the lesson."

"All right."

"Do you work for the ild Fallyn now?"

The Kobrir canted his gaze again. "I thought you understood, Sevryn Dardanon. For the first time in our history upon Kerith, we work for ourselves." Silver flashed in his hands and Sevryn found himself under attack.

He fought as his opponent did, with sword in one hand and dagger in the off-hand, the dagger being both shield and weapon. They clashed high and low, forcing each other back a step and forward a step, their movements so quick his eyes could not follow what his instincts told him to do, but he met every blow just as every move of his was answered. He sensed only the dull thuds when his blades parried successfully and did not feel a sharp scoring when he did not, for he kept up. How, he could not have told, because he did not think. He reacted. Years of training gave his muscles and reflexes a mind, a pattern, of their own.

The Kobrir stopped by flexing both blades in his hands outward, palms forward, and taking two rapid steps back, out of Sevryn's reach, as the fact a halt had been called reached his mind. He relaxed his blade and took a step back himself, not trusting himself to be totally out of reach of his opponent. He had not been breathing deeply. He took one now as he balanced himself.

Only then did he realize he'd been struck. The inside of his left wrist sleeve hung open, smeared with blood, though nothing dripped. His opponent, however, seemed to be untouched.

"How was it you found the skill to oppose me?"

"Training."

The Kobrir nodded. "Successful training. You did not have to think. That would have slowed you down enough for me to inflict far more damage. But it is necessary to think when you face another. To determine how to react. To determine when to fall back. When to press. What do you watch?"

Sevryn considered the question seriously. He could not tell what he watched in an opponent. Often, the eyes or hands, tell-givers of another's body. But not always. Not in this instance. He shook his head. "I couldn't tell you."

"Then let me tell you. I watch the shoulders. It is the center of our balance. To shift our weight, to attack, retreat, strike, parry, we must move our shoulders. Our feet follow. Our hands, elbows, our gaze follows. Even those you call Ravers and those we all call the Raymy, carry the balance of their structure in the shoulders. The Ravers are insectoid, so that occasionally changes, but they seem to prefer to fight upright, and if they do, that's where they carry their balance. The only change I make for an opponent is if I fight a woman. Women carry their balance in their pelvis. It is the center of their gravity, even a female who is prepubescent. Knowing that, I can make the adjustment. They are often trained by men, so they try to imitate the shoulder carry. A rare woman fighter does not. And if she is left-handed, she can be extremely dangerous for even the best trained man to face."

"She would have an advantage."

"Yes. But only if she knew it." The Kobrir's lips tightened in a half-smile. "Your opponent often thinks they have the advantage: height, speed, arm length, weapon. Those are advantages that are transient. As soon as you have noted what they have, that advantage is gone. You know how to counter it, fend it off, get under or around it. The assassin you do not want to face is one that has partnered with the animal. I have only met one or two in my readings who did so, but they were invincible. A four- or six-legged partner with speed or bulk or cunning gives a near unalterable benefit."

"What about the Bolger?"

"Strong, but slow. They can only offset their slowness by fighting at pole length or by throwing. I knew a Bolger with a net once who was extremely hard to bring down." The Kobrir took two long and slow breaths. "I am going to come at you again, half-speed. I want you to counter what my shoulders tell you I'm going to do. Move at any pace you find natural, I will meet it if necessary."

Sevryn had time enough to breathe deep before the Kobrir lunged at him. He saw his shoulder dip to the left ever so slightly, signaling a move to the left side, his right. An attack then, over or under his offensive hand. That was the last moment he had to think coherently. He noted the slowing of speed and found himself knowing the other's move just before he made it, although he couldn't say if he had spotted it through the balance shift of the other's shoulders or his own deeply ingrained training. He felt an easiness and began to press the other, quickening his attacks. The Kobrir answered in kind. Sparks flew now and then as the blades rang off each other. He could feel the burn in the muscles down the back of his neck and shoulder, and where he'd been hit earlier began a dull aching throb. Yet Sevryn did not slow. He felt a kind of fierce joy in the spar. The Kobrir finally halted it by leaping back before bringing his hands up.

It was only then, as sweat trickled down his rib cage, that he felt the sting of having been scored by the other's blade. Sevryn winced as he put a finger to it. Only the tiniest of surface slashes, not deep but long.

"You've done well. Tomorrow we practice again."

"The day's not over."

The Kobrir inclined his head. "And you are in a hurry."

"With a purpose, yes." Worthy lessons, but they were keeping him from Rivergrace.

"The rest of the day, you will practice breathing. Your muscles are tired, your legs are nearly dead, and all because you cannot breathe deeply enough while you fight. Another will be along to teach you those lessons." The Kobrir saluted him with both blades, stepped back, and disappeared into the shadows ringing the cave.

It did not help that his lungs ached, reinforcing the truth. Sevryn retreated to his bedroll, sat and began to sharpen, and then oil his blades. They had taken nicks, and he worked long to remove the imperfections. When he looked up, another Kobrir had come in and silently sat down in front of him, watching. As soon as awareness hit Sevryn, the Kobrir's hand shot out, throwing him down and he suddenly lost all ability to breathe. Dark spots began to dance before his eyes in another moment as his heels drummed the dirt and he fought to break free.

"Do not fight," the Kobrir whispered. "I will release you. Breathe deeply. Then I will take hold of you again. When you can resist my hold without falling unconscious, the lesson is finished."

It seemed to last hours. Gulp air down and be assailed, and try not to run out of breath before being released. Again. And again. Until finally Sevryn likened it to swimming underwater and found a relaxation in lying in the other's inexorable hold, his lungs slowly realizing that no more air was forthcoming, and his mind beginning to shout at him that he had to breathe. Those moments came farther and farther apart until . . .

The paralyzing hold on him let go and the assassin vanished, as had his brothers, leaving Sevryn alone on his now twisted and knotted bedroll. He could smell his sweat, sharp and pungent, as he filled his grateful lungs. With dinner, the silent woman who served him also brought a jar of water and two bathing cloths. He observed her as she bent to set the tray down, noting the wiry lines of her body, her hips, the fighting scars along one wrist as her sleeve slid up, and the fact she wore her weapon on her right hip for a left-handed draw. This one was undoubtedly like the Kobrir woman his dueling partner had warned him about, formidable in her own right. He wondered if he was supposed to test her and himself, but he was too tired and sore to make the attempt. Perhaps tomorrow night.

When Sevryn lay down to sleep, he fell soon but not so deeply that he did not count the sentries who came throughout the night to check on him and then left. Four, in all.

Chapter
Thirty-Seven

T HE STREET WAS ON FIRE or he would have seen
her.

Verdayne pulled his ponies to a halt, their heads high
and their nostrils flared with the sight of flame and smoke
dancing in front of them. They were all weary though he
hadn't driven them into the ground as he feared he would
have, but last night had showed the lanterns and torches of
Calcort glowing not too far away in the evening and he'd
pitched camp to let them all sleep soundly. The ponies had
gone to their knees and then hung their heads before giving
in to rest, but he'd heard them up before dawn, greedily
cropping at the spring grass, filling their round little bellies.
He'd waited till the sun had come up soundly, warming the
ground and chasing off the little mists of cold, early spring
before harnessing them to complete their journey, his own
hunger slaked by a crumbling biscuit. His tashya had carried the good saddlebags with sweet jerky and bags of
toasted nuts.

Verdayne stood up in the cart bed, taking in the sight in
amazement. The street was on fire because a Vaelinar had

set it so, gold and blue and reddish flames fencing off a considerable part of the quarter's district. Town guards had told
him of the quarantine when he'd entered, but he'd had no
idea of the scope. Even knowing that could not have prepared him for the sight, and then the Raymy came pelting
down the street, weapons gripped, roaming in their odd gait
of some on two feet and others on fours, moving rapidly. He
watched the flames as they did, perplexed on how to cross,
because the fire burned between him and the vineyard
quarter, which was where he most desperately needed to be,
at Tolby Farbranch's holdings. The near wheel pony flung up
her head and snorted. Her tension ran down the harness
lines to his hands. They would not stand here quietly for
long, their fear of the searing heat taking hold.

Nor, it seemed, would the Raymy. Hot and blazing
though it was, there were spots where the wall did not burn
as brightly nor as high, and if it had been meant to contain
them, and Verdayne looked down the side street where fire
ran along its gutters as far as he could see—if it had been
meant to contain them, it had not been meant to burn indefinitely. Could not, fueled by nothing except magic, and
that waned almost with every heartbeat. Movement ticked
at the end of the street. Calcort guards. He could see them,
on foot, weapons drawn, and coming after the Raymy on
the run.

They would not make it in time. He could see the Raymy
bunching, trotting at the far perimeter of the firewall, ready
to jump its boundary. The beasts had decided to take their
chances with the flames.

Verdayne drew his sword. Wrapped the reins about his
right hand still telegraphing the extreme nervousness and
tension through the harness, leaned forward on the balls of
his feet, and shouted at his ponies. They bolted in panic.

The fire parted as they swept through. It crackled and
spat and licked at him, but they moved so quickly it hardly
touched the cart. A dust cloud roared up about them, and
then they thrust through to the other side. Verdayne felt
intense heat one second and nothing the next as he pulled

on the reins and shoved a foot onto the brake so the cart
skewed about and slid sideways through the far barrier of
the flames, coming to a halt on the other side of it, so close
he could hear the sparks snap and crackle as they bit at him.

The Raymy came leaping after. He sliced at the first one,
downing it, and caught the second with his back swing. A
third he slammed in the gut as it hurdled over him in an
all-out dive for freedom. The last four landed just short of
the cart, caught between it and the fire. A clawed hand
swept at him, catching his leathers and pulling him from the
cart bed. He rolled, hoping to land on his feet, his leather
ripping free as he twisted. Dirt caught him, on hip and elbow, not as successful a maneuver as he'd hoped. He kicked
out, catching the nearest reptile by the ankles, sweeping his
legs from under him, even as he got to his own feet. A short
sword slammed edge down into the dirt, the sound of its
movement slicing past his temple. Verdayne dodged, and
then pivoted to his right almost as quickly, hoping to con-
found any sword strokes, his left arm up to catch any blades
on his bracer.

He used the cart bed to protect his back, but it also hampered his movement as the Raymy closed in on him. Another handful breached the firewall, and Verdayne felt the
stench of their bodies clog his nostrils along with the choking smoke of the flames. They respected his sweeping cuts,
but made trills and guttural hisses to one another, and he
knew they would close in on him. He would lose by sheer
numbers.

The cart shuddered as his ponies stamped and whinnied
in terror. He spun about, his sword falling across the harness,
slicing them free, and he slapped the one caramel-spotted
butt close to him in encouragement. A Raymy bounded in
vain after them, tripping over the harness that flapped behind them and entangled his feet. A guardsman sprinted past
Verdayne to cut the creature down in two slices and a deep-
throated jab. A sea of mottled gray-green skins surrounded
him and that was the last he saw clearly although he could
hear the grunts and cries of one guardsman to another

sounding from within the fray. Survival kept him too busy to account for the others. His arms grew numb, one from wielding his blade, the other from blocking whatever blows he could catch on his bracer, but at the same time, he noted that the opposition fell back quicker than he had expected, panting and growling and hissing from their wattled throats as they did.

A guardsman caught one by the forearm as it staggered back from Verdayne, and spun it around, throwing him back into the flames.

"Plague," he said. "Keep out of the gore." Then he was off, fending two of the beasts away from Verdayne.

He found himself all alone, with one in front backed up against a cart wheel which grabbed at his sword hilt when he swung it, and caught it, wood splintering but not giving.

From his right flank came a muffled curse and a long knife whipping past him and into the Raymy's throat. It blinked its large wet eyes, gurgled from deep in its wattle, and toppled.

"Well, a'right then," his rescuer said. "Going to stand in the middle of a plague-ridden street or move out of the way?"

Verdayne turned. His jaw fell as an enormously pregnant girl stood at his elbow, bent slightly to stab her long knife into the street dirt, cleaning it off as best she could. Her curls bounced about her shoulders as she looked up to meet his stare. Her prettiness stopped his words cold in his throat.

"What? Are you telling me you didn't see me when you put the cart in my path, nearly running me down?" Her eyes sparkled. "How could you miss me?"

Verdayne managed to close his mouth. "I was a bit busy at the time."

"Busy thinking?"

"Something like that."

"Hoping to be deep as a well and ending up a puddle."

He felt his face warm. "I was thinking something had to be done."

She gave a breathy snort. "Well, you did it. You drove through a wall of fire."

He closed the distance between them. "Which is failing. I saw it—they saw it." He took her elbow. "You need to get off the street before any more Raymy come through."

"Or fire-eating ponies pulling carts." She looked past him, and a look of pure joy replaced the mischievous glint in her golden-brown eyes. "Hosmer!"

"Meg! What are you doing hereabouts?" A stout Dweller wearing a captain's rank in the City Guard swept her up in an awkward embrace. They forgot Verdayne for a moment, so he took a step back, eyeing his ponyless cart. He found a rag to clean his weapons.

The lass laughed. "What do I look like I'm doing? Taking up half the street! I slipped my guard to take a walk. My legs still work, aye? This gentleman here says the fire is burning out."

"It is, but I think that's our last nest of Raymy run to ground and quite successfully, too. We'll dispose of the bodies, make a sweep of the quarantine area, and I may be home for dinner. And if I make it home, you and I will have a talk about slipping your guards!"

She beamed in spite of his scolding tone. "First time in days. I won't tell Mother and ruin the surprise." She turned away, ignoring Verdayne.

Captain Hosmer gave Verdayne a wry look. He saluted them both before trotting off to join the troops who were busy dragging the bodies down the street to a central pyre.

He put a hand out to stop the Dweller lass in her tracks. "Don't go just yet." He realized who she was but not quite how to approach his task, feeling all upended. He needed an introduction, but her brother had gone off.

She looked back over her shoulder and one eyebrow went up ever so slightly. "No?"

Verdayne gave a slight bow. "My thanks for the timely rescue."

"And welcome t'you."

He did not step away. Her other eyebrow arched to join the first in faint surprise as she swung about to face him.

"Would you know where the Farbranch vineyard is?"

"I might. And who would be asking?"

"Verdayne of House Vantane."

"Oh." Her face paled quite suddenly. "Bistel's . . ."

"Son. One of them."

"I know Bistane."

"He's been around a lot longer." Verdayne readied to catch her if she swayed or got any paler. "Miss Nutmeg."

"So you're one of those. Born to the manor and high-minded about my imagined place in the world. You can just turn heel and head back to th' Hold because I'm not about to be renouncing my claim, not that it's mine anyway, it's Queen Lariel's, and I haven't seen the man yet who can tell that woman what to do—well, Lord Bistel came close, but he's gone now—and she's the one who decided that this babe has got to be important to Larandaril and everyone else, not me. The baby is important to me, that's not what I meant. It's the succession that's a problem. As for thinking I've disgraced Dwellers everywhere, you can just tuck that notion back under your hat if you have one, along with your ears, and if you can't manage to do that, Hosmer will be helpin' you." She ran a little short of breath and stopped, pale features giving way to apple-shaded cheeks of indignation.

Verdayne rocked back on his heels. "Of course you are. Don't. Aren't." And Bistane had thought she might need saving from her predicament. She sounded as though she quite had the bull by the horns. Still, there was the matter of working with her father. He rubbed the palm of one hand on the thigh of his trousers. "But you're not why I've come to Calcort. I've been sent to find Tolby Farbranch."

"And why would that be?"

"We need his help. The library of Ferstanthe is failing. The books carry a blight on them, like the black thread, and we hope he has a cure. His spray has been of some help, and I've come to encourage more. More than the books, the living aryns are falling prey to it, and that would be my concern, Mistress Farbranch."

Her eyes searched his face, and her jawline softened. "I

beg you forgive me for my tirade, then. This . . . babe . . . has been a bit worrisome."

"You have every pardon you need from me." He paused. "You were with Lord Bistel on the field, were you not? Did he die a good death?"

Her mouth curved slightly. "A brave one. He didn't seem to be in pain, though he had no doubt he was dying. He was . . . Taken . . . as curious a sight as I've ever seen."

Verdayne's mouth felt almost too dry for words. He'd seen Taken deaths before. Most were incredibly difficult and heart-rending to watch, as if the Gods of death in two worlds fought over the scraps of flesh and soul. "Taken?"

"Peacefully. Back to his home, he said."

"Peaceful."

"Aye. A moment here and then, in a long moment, gone." He let out a breath.

"Well, then." She looked back down the street, saying, "I imagine your cart ponies have already made it there. We have a sweet water well in the courtyard. Push your cart aside, and I'll leave a note for Hosmer to have it towed after." She shoved a dimpled hand into her dress, finding a scrap of paper and a stub of chalk to write with as he took out the bundles he dared not leave behind. With the cart so marked, he shouldered it to the side.

Nutmeg took a deep breath before leading the way.

It wasn't a far piece as walks go, but he had no need to have the cider house and vineyards marked, for the house and outbuildings were the last homes on the street, with stony hills of vineyards stretching far beyond until impenetrable cliffs halted even their rows of burgeoning grape vines. Two tall Vaelinar stood in the street, booted feet spread and arms crossed their chests, in daunting poses that made him think of his younger days when his father had a guard or two for him . . . and he'd done the same as Nutmeg, slipping by them whenever he could. He couldn't imagine that Nutmeg would have her ears boxed for it, but when Tolby Farbranch stepped out with them, he knew that words would be had.

She slowed slightly. He could guess her apprehension. He touched her elbow lightly. "I know of your sister River-grace, but I imagine you have brothers, too?"

"Three," she said, before looking at him. "Garner, the oldest, Hosmer you met, and the youngest is Keldan. Keldan has a way with horses and other four-legged beasts, as well as Dad's talent for the fields."

"You know about brothers, then. Imagine me, with one centuries older than my years, and taller, and likely to live centuries after, telling every tale he can remember of every foolish thing I've ever done or am likely to do."

"What a . . . a legacy," she managed.

The lively color of her cheeks had evened out. He hadn't meant to rile her any more than she had meant to shock him. Who knows what she thought he'd intended. He had an in-kling when a brace of guards straightened up, anticipating her approach to the steading. Beyond them, a graying but still in his prime Dweller was looking over Verdayne's fled cart ponies.

She eyed the waiting Vaelinar guards. "Sweet apples," she muttered. "They look vexed."

"Could you blame them? They answer to Queen Lariel for you. Not to mention they are humiliated they lost . . ." he beckoned his hand over her ample body, "you."

She giggled at that. "It wasn't easy, mind you."

"Of course not. But still. Don't think they won't hear the end of it for weeks."

Nutmeg put her hand over her mouth. She ducked her chin in an attempt to look humble as she neared her father.

"Dad, this is Verdayne of House Vantane, come to seek your help," she blurted as they drew close and Tolby looked him over, the corner of his mouth twitching.

"Went down to escort him, did you?"

"A-course not, how could I know he'd be coming? I thought to take a walk."

"Through the vineyards, you told us," muttered the right-hand guard, his pointed ears pinned back to his head.

"But the vineyards are that way." Nutmeg gazed off in

their general direction. "And I just came from down the street. You must have misheard me."

The left-hand guard pulled her booted feet together, the heels making a sharp click. "Mistress Farbranch, you risk more than you know."

Tolby's hand cut through the air. "She's my daughter. I will deal with her." His gaze fixed on Verdayne. "I think we might have more important problems than a walk gone awry."

"We do, sir. Best discussed inside, and if you have a pair of clean gloves, that will help." Dayne hefted his bundle in his hand.

Tolby's eyebrow arched sharply, and Verdayne realized exactly who Nutmeg had inherited that expression from.

Chapter Thirty-Eight

"THERE ARE SECRETS IN BOOKS of the Vaelinar that, apparently, someone wished never to be set free."

"I wouldn't say that," Verdayne responded to Tolby.

"I do, and the evidence is before us, for those who have eyes t' see. This book," and he stabbed a strong finger downward at a shriveling, blackened text, "was contaminated directly. This book," and he waved his hand over a second across the table from him, "bears a portion of the contagion because it contacted the first directly on the shelves, while this one—" and Tolby strode to the end of his table to lean over a third book, "shows nothing of the contamination at all. No contact, either directly or indirectly."

"So how does that prove your point?"

"They were infected deliberately."

"I can see that." Verdayne pushed a hank of hair off his forehead. "But not the other."

Tolby gave him a wink from an eye creased by sun and weather. "Read the titles, son."

He frowned and leaned on elbows to join Tolby. "*THE FIRST HOUSES. MARKING THE ELVEN WAYS.*"

"Aye. Some of your earliest histories, I imagine."

Verdayne pushed his hair back again with an impatient shove as he felt his face warm, and he took great care not to glance at the lass sitting quietly at the table's far end. "I don't know how I missed it."

"Because you were looking at the mold, not the subject. All the books are valuable to you and Ferstanthe, it never occurred to you to wonder why, eh?"

He deflected with a question of his own. "So that means we pull all the books off the shelves and keep them from contact with the infected tomes?"

"Not quite. The very air carries mold and spores, some good, some ill. All the books in a closed area like your great library at Ferstanthe stand to be infected if given enough time. Particularly books kept in a back, enclosed area, as these appear to have been. This last book here seems to be clean, but it can hold a dust within it that will eventually turn black and then spread. These are your great books of mystery, are they not? By that, I mean, it's said that certain of your volumes are more important than others. Books in the sacred section hold writings that cannot lie and must be saved to the end of days, when they will have great import."

Verdayne shifted from one foot to another. "So I have understood," he responded slowly. Tolby Farbranch asked questions of him he wasn't sure he should answer. He did not want Azel or his brother after his hide for mishandling this.

"They pose the greatest danger to themselves and to the rest of the library. Removing them and subjecting them to the curative of the sun won't be enough, as I'm sure Azel has already discovered, which is why he put them into Bistane's hands and then yours. No ordinary measure will scour this mold from your library." Tolby ran his hand over his chin. They were weathered hands, tanned and callused, scarred here and there from hard work and misadventure. "You're thinking of the spray I use in the orchards against the black thread. It's been working for your groves, aye?"

"For the newly infected, yes. Where black thread has

eaten in past the bark, ofttimes all we can do is bring the tree down and burn it. It hits the aryns hard."

The two traded stares. The aryns, while not native to Kerith and its lands, were a hardy tree that once established could withstand pestilence, drought, flood, and even fire. That a mold might bring them down seemed unthinkable, yet it happened.

Tolby made a sucking noise through his teeth. "Well, then. We've our work cut out for us. I cannot add moisture willy-nilly to these pages, so I'll have to reformulate my tincture." He moved back to the first book. "We'll have to use this for test and trial, yet it may damage what is left. Do I have your permission?"

Did he have the right to order the book destroyed? And yet, it was already crumbling into a black sponge, and it had been sent for a purpose. "Of course, Master Farbranch."

Tolby cleared his throat. "If we're to be friends and partners in this enterprise, you'd best get around to calling me Tolby."

"Tolby, then. I hate to see it lost, but this is a war, isn't it?"

"Agreed. The first thing you must do is send word to Ferstanthe that they have a traitor or an infiltrator among them."

He fought to keep his face neutral. "You are certain."

"Without having been there to witness, as certain as I can be. This didn't happen by accident. We know that, as I said earlier, by the fact these are some of your more sacred writings, and that they are kept isolated to protect them, yet they're contaminated."

"Is there enough evidence here to tell who might have done it?"

Tolby shook his head. "Only that it was done."

"It couldn't be a mistake."

Tolby gave Verdayne a hard stare. "Could you have gotten to these books by mishap? Or anyone?"

"No, but—" He paused. "Azel holds these in trust. His students are hand-picked and taught well."

"He recently begin to allow students from all of Kerith. Not Vaelinar alone?"

"Yes." Verdayne thought a moment, and then shook his head. "You don't know what you're saying."

"I know exactly what I am saying."

"To be a student in Ferstanthe is to be given a great opportunity. Especially for those not Vaelinar. To risk that opportunity, the learning, the trust . . ." He shook his head again.

"I'm not saying it's one of the new students. There are those Vaelinar who believe that they should be held apart from the rest of us on Kerith, that they and they alone are unique and gifted. This could be an act of jealousy or anger. It could have been done to throw suspicion on the library's new open policy. It could have been done to destroy the Way of Ferstanthe." He paused before adding softly, "Don't think Azel won't be considering this himself. He is a most wise man, from what I've heard of him. This is nothing you need put in a letter. He will understand without your putting it into a lot of words, and there is no one you can accuse anyway."

Those words settled him and his jaw relaxed. "I'll send birds out as soon as we take a break."

"Good. I'll have Keldan show you the way. He's seeing to getting your harness mended and your ponies settled down."

"I drove them hard. I hate to leave my charges to someone else." A good horseman took care of his mounts himself or delegated the task to those he trusted.

"This," Tolby pointed out, "cannot afford to wait while you rub down and feed a tired pony. Besides, Keldan is having a look at the bloodlines and conformation."

Nutmeg spoke for the first time since she'd come in and sat down. "Sometimes I think he is half a horse himself."

Verdayne chuckled at that before bending over the books again, this time turning pages with hands now carefully covered with linen handkerchiefs that were far less cumbersome than leather working gloves. Working together with Tolby, they slipped protective pieces of bark between each page to separate them.

Nutmeg sat at the other end of the table, uncharacteristi-
cally silent, watching her father and this new man studying
the task together. An odd sense of seeing into her future as
a mother crept over her as she watched Verdayne who undoubtedly held Dweller blood in him but also a strong indication of the high elven. His dark curled hair could not hide
ears that were tipped in a graceful curve mounting to a
point. He towered above Tolby and would be taller even
than Garner who was the tallest of all her brothers, and yet,
compared to her Vaelinar guards from Larandaril, he stood
nearly a head shorter.

She watched him run his fingers through his hair again
as he bent over the books. That bit of hair could use a good
trimming. She might suggest a barber who could tame it, if
he wished. She watched him shift his weight and draw his
brows together in thought, his shoulders straightening.
Dweller blood lent him a strength to his frame, offsetting
Vaelinar slenderness. And he had mannerisms . . . so like
the Vaelinar and at the same time so like her own Dweller
folk. He moved and worked like her own, but he chose his
words as carefully as any Vaelinar used to meanings within
meanings and schemes within schemes. Was she looking at
a person and seeing what her child would be like when
grown? She had not paid much attention to the mixed
bloods that populated Calcort, not wondering before. Did
she watch the future in front of her?

He shot her a glance as if feeling her watch him. Heat
stained her cheeks for a moment as she looked away quickly
to her father as he tested the moisture content of the pages
in front of him but not before she noticed what handsome
eyes he had. Thick, full lashes framed dark blue on top of
lighter blue, giving him a gaze of deep indigo, and not likely
one would notice the color stacked upon color, but she had
noticed almost right away. As a weaver and tailor's daughter, Nutmeg appreciated the interplay and beauty of color.
She wondered what Talents Verdayne carried as his legacy.
Her hand moved unconsciously to lay over the curve of her
stomach. What eyes, indeed, would her child have?

If he was going to be the Warrior Queen's heir, it would be best if he looked as Vaelinar as possible, to put aside some of the challenges he would inevitably have to face. But still ... to hold a Talent in secret without the telltale giveaway eye colors as Sevryn did ... that might be an advantage.

Sweet apples, Nutmeg thought, and resolved to stop staring at Verdayne. She was beginning to think like a Vaelinar schemer, a regular Tressandre ild Fallyn! Although she would like another look into those lovely eyes ... she smacked her knee lightly. Enough, and done!

They had work to do.

Chapter Thirty-Nine

CEYLA SAT ON HER HEELS, hands dangling at her knees, as the great Galdarkan considered her. Abayan Diort, skin of golden hue with eyes as sharp as a bird of prey upon her face, took her measure. She could hardly bear to look upon him, as a hundred futures wheeled through her thoughts, each of them bearing him within it like a golden torch blazing furiously. It dizzied her so that she could hardly think and even as she tried, nausea rose from her gut as it clenched. She knew which future she ought to concentrate on, but she could not decide for him. Would not. She had reached him last night and blurted out the divination that had driven her to escape from the fortress and reach him at all odds before collapsing. When they woke her this morning, his handmaidens told her she'd slept two days, yet she still did not feel rested.

Or perhaps fear gripped her.

"You look better this day," Abayan said. His voice held a deep tone to it, and she could tell if it deepened even more, in command or anger, it would rumble like that of a great beast. She shivered. She had awakened that beast. "Do you remember what you said to me?"

How could she forget? "I said that you must move your army and take Larandaril."

"Yet we are still encamped."

She did not answer, uncertain if it was a question he leveled at her.

"Your name?"

"Ceyla."

"Of what House or Hold or Fortress?"

"I came from the ild Fallyns, but they didn't send me. They hunted me when I fled the Fortress." She could tell him she'd been a slave, but she did not think that would win her any sympathy or trust.

"And you managed to elude them. Weaponless. On foot." He looked down at her feet, which were now bare. "Barefooted most of the way until you stole another's shoes."

She lifted and dropped a shoulder diffidently. The condition of her feet was no secret nor was the ill-fitting pair of shoes taken from her. "He was dead. He no longer needed them."

"How did he die?"

Ceyla looked away from the Galdarkan's face. "I don't remember. I might have killed him. He might have been felled by accident as I took as rough a trail as I could to try to keep the trackers off me." She could feel his steady gaze remain upon her.

"How did you come by the idea that I must move upon Larandaril?"

"It came to me. I can't explain it." She studied her knees, hidden by the lightweight soft cloth of the women's trousers she'd been given. Her blouse had embroidery on it of winged birds, decorating the v-neckline and hem that fell over her slim hips. Everyday clothes and yet the finest she'd ever worn. Her own clothes, stained, torn, muddied, slimed, had been burned. Now she looked like any of the Galdarkans until one considered her pale complexion and eyes and

hair color and stature. Alien in almost every way she could
consider. Her mouth twisted wryly at the thought. She realized that Abayan Diort waited for more of an answer. Her
gaze flickered up. "I see things. Feel them. They come true.
I cannot depend on its happening, but it kept me free of the
trackers. I had no choice, you see. I had to find you. I had to
tell you what I'd seen. If I hadn't come to you, sooner or
later, it would have burst out of me and then *they* would
have known, and we would both have been betrayed. I had
no choice!"

"You fear those who raised you?"

Ceyla bit the corner of her lip. The pain, quick and sharp
and then gone, left her with a coppery taste on her tongue.
Now that he'd asked for it, she had to give away her truth.
"I was brought to the fortress when I was very young. Enslaved. Those of us without obvious Talent despite our
blood are taught a little and worked hard. We are bred if we
have some possibilities. Those who do not . . . disappear."

Abayan frowned. Strong features stamped his face,
square jaw, square face, deep-set eyes that missed little detail. A well-muscled neck sloping into powerful shoulders
and chest. He looked like a conqueror. "Is this a habit
among your people?"

"I don't know. All I know are the ild Fallyn, and I fear
them. If you make me leave, they will find me. Take me
back. And eventually kill me."

"Your words tell me it will not be a quick death."

"I don't think it will be. They will want to know whatever
I can tell them, even if I will not."

He inclined his head gravely. "I grant you sanctuary here,
as long as you wish it, Ceyla. You're a guest of myself and
my host until you wish to leave of your own free will." He
leaned forward then, his eyes narrowing. "But I, too, need
to know whatever you can tell me."

She raised one hand, palm up. "I see you in the fields
adorned with maiden's nod in full flower, followed by your
army. A great battle awaits you, an important one. Your

true destiny awaits you there, if you have the courage to claim it."

"Against Queen Lariel?"

She could not speak for a moment. It felt as through her tongue had cleaved to the roof of her mouth. In desperation, she looked around her and found a gourd of water. Ceyla grabbed it and took a long swallow. Warm but sweet water: the Galdarkans had found a good source nearby. She lowered the gourd but kept her hand wrapped tightly about it. "I can't tell you. I don't see everything."

"Just enough to cause me a considerable amount of trouble," Abayan said dryly. "Tell me this, if you can. Do you see the Warrior Queen at all?"

Her head whirled violently, and she closed her eyes or she would be sick and spew. From between her clenched teeth, she answered. "Yes. She is geared for battle. But I do not see her facing you. Yet."

"Yet."

She wrenched her eyes open. "I see possibilities. As you make each decision and move into the future I have beheld, it changes. Clarifies. That I can tell you."

He leaned back in his chair at that. The leather frame creaked slightly under his weight, though he was not a heavy man, his form leanly muscled. He looked up, away from her, considering the sky or perhaps its drifting clouds. The sunlight gilded his skin even more golden. "If I do not march?"

Ceyla swallowed tightly. "Death. All along these lands. Darkness. A great plague falls on us all. We fight ourselves. We fight strangers. You have to march. You must!"

He looked upon her again. "I can't bring war upon Larandaril."

"I'm not asking you to."

The corner of his mouth pulled up wryly. "And yet you do."

"You must march to where I direct you. I know that in my very bones, and yet I can't tell you why. That is your fate, yet to be written."

"And revealed to you."

She stood up carefully from her squat and then kneeled before him. "It may be. It may not. All I can tell you is that I threw away what life I had to reach you, and to tell you this much. It was a wretched life, but it was *mine*. This is yours. I'm only a visitor within it."

He stood then as well. "A Vaelinar comes to your door," he said softly, as if to himself. He laughed without humor. Stretching his arms out, he looked at his hands, at the backs of them and then his palms when he turned them over, his brows knotted in thought as he did. Then he spread his hands wide.

Abayan beckoned at her. "Go. Take your ease while you can. We decamp and march in the morning. We are an army that moves mostly on foot. It will take us a while to reach this destiny you've promised me."

Chapter Forty

GRACE PUT HER HAND to the back of her neck and tried to rub away the knots, her horse jarring as it trotted. If Sevryn were there, he'd lean over and pull on her reins, bringing them both to a halt, and his hands would find the tight places instinctively to soothe her. Her heart ached to know where he was and how he fared, if Lariel had caught him anyway, or if he'd made it away safely. Dust from the trail rose around her. "I can't do this."

"You can and you must." Narskap studied her.

Rivergrace reined her horse to a halt and pretended to adjust a stirrup. He fell back, with a mercenary behind them watching them both, his expression bored. Quendius did not seem to notice or care as he rode on.

"You deal in death."

"We all deal in death, my daughter. We're born to die."

"You know what I mean. Kill him now. End this."

"If I kill him now, I will simply push him across a threshold that he will master, and once he's done that, none of us will be able to deal with him." Narskap's whispery voice rasped across her nerves.

"He treats with Cerat."

Narskap laid his dry hand on the back of her wrist. "No. I deal with Cerat. He can't touch Cerat without me."

She looked into his eyes. *Souldrinker. Soulstealer.* She knew Cerat's voice well, and could not hear it in her father, and yet she knew that Cerat sat deep within Narskap. Perhaps caged. Perhaps in charge. "Let me go. If you love me like the father you once were, let me go."

"I can't. I have some lessons to teach, and then a place to bring you. From there . . ." His expression cleared to a careful neutral. He said nothing more and turned away from her but not before she saw a single tear track down his cheek.

A tear tinged with blood.

She put her boot back in her stirrup to urge her horse after him and knew she would have to kill them both. If they could be killed. The thought plunged inside her, knowing that she wished her father dead. But the being he'd become under decades of service for Quendius had done more than lead him into being Undead. He'd changed long before that. Lost his name. Juggled sanity. She knew that she could study him for years without finding a trace of the young man who had married her mother against the wishes of both their Houses, and loved her, and fathered a child with her. That man had disappeared long ago even as she had toddled after him, and she could no more resurrect him than she could clearly remember him from those times.

Now he labored to recast and forge her in the same mold he had followed. She couldn't allow it, even if it meant saving her life. What kind of life would that be? Not hers. Never hers. Surviving at any cost meant nothing.

Grace wiped the back of her hand across her forehead, though it did little good to clear her head. They'd been riding for days and the forests and valleys of the First Home faded behind her. They headed north and east to what some called the badlands, where magics of the Mageborn Wars twisted and warped the geography, and even groves of the aryns could not hold back the chaos. Quendius had staked a claim there. She knew once she saw it, she would never

leave his custody until she died or he did. Sevryn wouldn't
be able to trace her there. Twisted magics would likely block
any touch between the two of them. His seat of power had
never been known, although Quendius had held the forge
and mines where her family had slaved for him. That had
only been one of his holdings. Seeing the place he called
home would be deadly for her.

A small freshet of water cut through the ground ahead
of them, scarcely enough for the horses' hooves to splash as
they waded through it. She slid to the ground anyway, and
went to one knee in it, washing her face and hands upstream a little of the muddied crossing.

As she plunged her hands into the water, her soul cried
out for Sevryn. The River Goddess who had entwined with
her gave her the power to touch through water . . . if he was
touching it also. Small comfort that could be, for those times
could be few and far between, unless he searched for her as
well. And he would be, unless Lara had caught him. She
prayed he would be.

No answer came to her. She stayed in the water another
heartbeat, then two, reaching for him, knowing that the
odds he touched water at the same time were like being
struck by lightning on a clear day unless he searched ac-
tively. She needed to know that he lived somewhere, safe
and sound, clear of Lara's anger and vengeance. She wanted
him to know what had befallen her. She sent her heart and
soul shivering through the water, searching for him and
found nothing but the cool wetness. Rivergrace sighed. It
might be the last she could speak and share with him.

"Get up."

Anger flared as she doused her face with water again
and got to her feet. Quendius had circled around and come
back to the brooklet's bank, staring down at her. She
thought of setting the river on fire, but the cost to her would
be too high. It wouldn't bring him down, but it would drain
her of the strength she so badly needed now. Nor could she
melt into the river as she wanted to do, as the rivulet called
her to do, giving way into mere droplets of water and mist

to float away. That would also take too great a toll of her mind and body. She wasn't strong enough.

Not now. Not yet.

"I'm tired," she simply said. She picked up her horse's reins, turned the stirrup to put her foot into it and mounted.

"At least you live," Quendius answered her as she rode past him.

Sevryn

They brought him out of the caverns early in the morning. Already the sunlight glanced off the rock in white-hot spears, and Sevryn could feel the furnace this place would be in the summer at the height of the sun's power. He didn't wonder the Kobrir could find a refuge in this place, for no one would live here unless out of necessity. Although there would be hidden valleys and fonts of water here, it was still a blasted land with little to recommend it. He narrowed his eyes against the glare and put one hand up to shade his face so that he could follow the trail they led him down. Pebbles and sand rolled from his boots as he walked. Scrub grass stubbornly grew from cracks in the rock and shale, stabbing green shafts upward that yellowed and browned as they reached the full sun, and tried to wrap about his ankles. He didn't find the area familiar though he'd traveled a lot of territory under Gilgarran's tutelage and during his service to Lariel.

He couldn't be sure what they had planned for him since taking him out of the arena. Perhaps to a wider forum, perhaps to another purpose altogether. The Kobrir bracketing him had not spoken since getting him on his feet and on the move.

Insects hummed, and he could hear birds on the wing, their fast shadows darting across the white rocks. The smell

of greenery reached him, and so he was not surprised when
the rocks split open, their wall tumbling down, and a valley
of not inconsiderable size met his eyesight.

A river tumbled through it, swift enough now from melt-
ing snows and spring rains, but one which might sink into
little more than mud flats when summer heat reached its
fullness. Water! He could search for Rivergrace as soon as
they gave him a bit of freedom. He felt an ache at the back
of his throat that came not from thirst but from loss. Sevryn
turned his head and saw terraces, cultivated and growing,
and canals for irrigation watering bordering each area.

They had been here a long time, the Kobrir. Sevryn
looked about, searching for evidence that might show how
long, and from where they came.

The sheer rock sides of the valley could well shield it
from direct snowfall, although not icy temperatures, but
chances were a community could live here through nearly
any season and stay self-sufficient. The wind and airflow
over the cliffs would protect them to some degree, making
it a valley that could hold life well year-round. It was no
wonder their home base had never been discovered.

The captor following him touched his shoulder and
pointed when he had his attention. "Down there."

A pathway snaked through the terraces to a garden near
the bottom, staked and growing with herbs. Some he recognized, some he did not. He wondered if they would try to
poison him again. As he reached the garden, they pointed
him toward a well, sunk deep into the ground, a stone ring
cupping it. An empty wooden bucket with a long, thick rope
tied to its bail lay on its side next to the well.

"Draw a bucket and seek the master." The Kobrir
pointed toward a bent figure, in dark colors so old and
faded they appeared a warm brown rather than the sharp
black of the assassin cult.

He thought he'd killed the old master, but apparently
there was more than one in that ranking. The bucket fell a
good distance before it hit water, and he hauled it up, water
splashing to and fro as he did. He still had a pretty full

bucket in his hands as he pulled it from the well and the cold wetness hitting him as he hefted it with both hands felt good. He thought of Grace as it did. Did Lara hold her? Had she gotten free on her own? She lived, he felt that in the very marrow of his bones, but did she live well?

He would go to the river, free-running water, when they let him, and see if the water carried her voice, her thoughts within it.

"Bring that here, boy."

The hunched figure in faded brown had turned and glared at him, face wrinkled behind the Kobrir veiling mask.

Sevryn answered by obeying. Crossing the ground between them, he held the bucket out. Water spilled out over his hands and for a moment, a brief but shattering moment, he heard an echo of Rivergrace in his mind. It could be no other but her thrilling through the drops, warm where the water chilled, elusive as it ran through his fingers. He could feel a love that filled him and then a touch of fear that shivered down the back of his neck. *Narskap has me.*

Had he heard that? Or did he imagine the words flowing through the touch of her element? He tried to catch her voice, her sense, her words, and keep her with him but could not hold on, any more than he could keep spilled water from running through his fingers and all he had left filled him with uneasy knowledge. He trusted Narskap no more than Quendius or than he currently trusted Lariel.

His thoughts and her touch evaporated. He found himself returning the glare of the bowed-over Kobrir gardener. The man snatched the bucket from his hands. The old man bent to water tiny seedlings he had buried up to their neck in the dirt, a sandy loam that nestled them gently. Sevryn took the bucket back and refilled it a second time, although the water no longer held an echo of Rivergrace in its shimmer.

"Recognize this plant?" the gardener asked as he finished watering.

"I believe the Kernans call it pinch-wart."

"Excellent. Yes, that is it. The tales of old women say to

chew a leaf and then apply it to tag-warts and moles you wish to remove. Never treat more than three blemishes at a time, they warn." The gardener straightened laboriously. "They are right. The leaf does not work unless the person needing it is the one chewing it—something about the saliva—and it is highly toxic. More than three leaves can kill you." He smiled, a half-toothless grin. "We do not use it for warts."

He did not imagine they did. The gardener grabbed up a walking stick and moved through the plots. Sevryn trailed him warily, staying out of range of the stick should the Kobrir decide to turn and swing it.

"Stay close to me," the old gardener muttered. "I'm an old man, I have no strength to yell."

"I think you have all the strength you need," Sevryn told him. "I killed your associate. It would not be unreasonable to think you would hold me to answer for it."

"That was my son, and he fell to his own foolishness for his treatment of you. I taught him better." The old gardener sniffed before turning back to his herb beds. He pointed them out, one by one, seeing if Sevryn could identify them and their properties. He kept up, naming more than half of them and their usages, both common and uncommon, to the Kobrir's satisfaction. It unnerved him a bit to know that a good many of the flowers beloved in the gardens of Kerith had lethal properties. One of them, the drought-loving neriarad, was bitterly toxic in every part of its existence: leaf, stem, flower, and seed. It grew lavishly in the wild, and he scrubbed his hands together as he passed the towering shrub, making a mental note to warn Rivergrace and Nutmeg of it.

He spent the day working with the gardener, weeding, watering, transplanting, harvesting. The Kobrir laughed at him for not being able to always smell the difference from one herb to the next, noting his vulnerability in that sense while Sevryn noted that the gardener had a touch of blindness for color. He did not always see that an herb's leaf carried a hue over color on its frilled edge or striping its stem.

Not all the garden's crop was used for poison or hallucinogens. More than half carried medicinal properties, useful ones that he committed to memory as he handled them. When the day's sun had begun to pass into a mellow streak on the horizon, the gardener dismissed him abruptly.

"Leave me. I'm done with you." He waved Sevryn off and stood with his walking stick in both hands across his chest as though he might attack after all.

Sevryn climbed up the valley's stone staircase where the smell of cooking fires hit him when he reached the crest, a welcome aroma. When he reached the sandy floor, a veiled woman pointed him to a vacant spot by her campfire.

When his dinner, a stew of some kind, arrived in its bowl, she knelt by him with a plate. Various compartments held ground-up spices and her eyes smiled at him.

"Choose three," she said. "To savor your meal."

Sevryn examined the platter. He recognized the frilled edge of at least one herb, chopped up nearly unrecognizably but for that one particular. A most unpleasant topping. This, he realized, was not dinner but a test of what he had learned from the ancient herbalist and gardener.

The woman tilted her head at his reluctance. "It is a simple thing."

Beyond him, at other cooking fires, Kobrir gathered and chose their seasonings with abandon, looking now and then and laughing as he paused, hand outstretched over the platter.

He had no doubt if he were to exchange one spice platter for another, he would find considerable differences. He pondered challenging another for his spices, but knew it would not likely be accepted.

They were waiting to see if he poisoned himself.

The smoke of the fires overwhelmed his senses. Even if he were to hold the spice to his nose, he couldn't be certain of what he smelled. He had to rely on his other senses. A Vaelinar first and a hungry man second.

Gilgarran used to rail at him to look and truly see. As if he had an eye in his hand, Sevryn let himself examine each compartment with his Vaelinar self.

A sickly yellow hue hung over more than half the plate, with a single vibrant green over a crushed leaf in the middle. He reached for that, a pinch and held it before his nose to be certain.

Yes. This had both a mint flavor and a heat to it. Not toxic although if used in great quantities, the food would be too spicy to eat comfortably. He crushed it further in his fingers as he sprinkled it over his stew. The servant woman gave no indication at all of her opinion of his choice, not even a tightening of the fine wrinkles at the corner of her dark brown eyes.

He knew common salt when he saw it, or thought he did, but when he reached to it, his Vaelinar sight flashed a brilliant red for a moment. He pulled his hand back. He might want his dish salted but did not dare to try that crystal.

"Two more spices are needed, master, before your trial is done."

He looked up at her and nodded in understanding. Quickly then, using his knowledge of that morning, he picked a small dried fruit that helped with digestion and lastly, a dull gray-brown seed that could also impart, he hoped, a bit of salt to the stew. Both looked and felt green as he handled them.

The Kobrir server smiled. "Perhaps another seasoning?"

He looked at the platter. He thought he recognized dried silvery green stems from a wild onion shoot, but decided against it. "I am done, thank you."

She bowed her head before straightening and bearing the dish off. When she knelt again, it was beside the gardener who sat in the shadows, and she pointed out to him which herbs Sevryn had chosen. The gardener considered the serving dish before lifting his head and leveling his gaze on Sevryn.

The stare was meant to unnerve him. The man thought to shake his confidence in his choosing. He waved away the platter and the woman, and she retreated into an alcove in the rocks, which might or might not lead elsewhere.

Sevryn swirled his bowl about to integrate his seasonings

and lifted it to his mouth. The gravy had a pungent, rich flavor to it, with an undertone of that minty herb. The meat was chewy but tender, and he counted three different root vegetables in it. He enjoyed the stew down to its last drop, and a Kobrir dining nearby passed him a hunk of bread to mop up the bowl. They had stopped watching him.

It was not until hours later when he dropped off to sleep after oiling and caring for the weapons they allowed him and his shackles had been refastened with the weapons put out of reach that he knew he had passed the trial, for his stomach settled untroubled. As he closed his eyes, thinking of Narskap and Rivergrace, he realized that he would have to take care with everything he ate. He would be a fool to think the trial need be passed just once.

He would search their ranks until he found the damned king as they required of him, and then he would find Rivergrace.

Chapter Forty-One

VERDAYNE HAD NO TROUBLE matching his steps to Nutmeg's, but he felt unsure about the entire exercise. He had, however, felt even more uncertain about her going off alone. Although she wouldn't be alone; at least one of Lariel's guards trailed behind them. "Are you certain you should be out here walking? Maybe Keldan could give me the tour."

Nutmeg shot him a look that said she thought he was daft, but she smiled as well. "I cannot think of a single woman with child I've ever heard about whose legs fell off because she took a walk."

Now he could only hope the guard could not hear them. "I did not mean—"

She took her straw hat off and shook her head about like a recalcitrant mountain pony before jamming it back on. "Not that I expect you would have experience with another woman, but you worked a farm. There must be some idea in that pretty head of yours how to treat a brood mare."

He wasn't sure which insulted him more: his implied lack of knowledge of animal husbandry or the fact she called him pretty. Verdayne felt the tips of his ears grow hot. He wanted to correct her and say that she was the pretty one, but that struck him as even more inappropriate. He cursed himself for deciding to accompany her. It couldn't possibly end up well. "I merely wish to be considerate."

"Aye, a-course you do." She trailed her fingers through the thick growth of grape leaves as they passed. "And Dad thought I should take you through our grapes where you can see what he has had to spray and the results."

He decided from the way she tackled the sloping vine-yard that she was not only Dweller but part goat. He found himself catching his breath from time to time when she slowed to show him a particular vine and the new grapes hanging downward from it, with the frosted sheen already developing over its globes that would impart a great deal of the wine's personality to it even though they were scarcely bigger than peas now. He didn't know if she stopped just to educate him or catch her breath herself, but he certainly appreciated it. By the time they reached the far quarter against the infamous cliffs of Calcort, the tips of his ears burned again from the sun's touch, and he wished he had brought his hat.

She took him among the rows. "'Twasn't black thread, but it was a mold that hit these five rows. We took a chance on spraying, rather than cutting them back and burning the cuttings. You can see the leaves have stains on them, but the mold is gone and the grapes forming seem to be all right."

"Will you harvest and press them then?"

"Perhaps. Dad would rather be safe than sorry, and I would agree with him. We might work this part of the vine-yard separate. We have three varieties of grape here a-purpose, and it wouldn't hurt to treat this acreage as a fourth. Suppose the grapes held an unseen poison that we in our greediness turned into wine?" She shook her head. "We do well enough here, we can afford to lose a bit of the crop for sale. It's a risk all farmers and growers take, aye? Wind and sun and hail, not enough rain and too much rain . . . all risks." Meg paused. "Dad thinks that his spray, concentrated and more potent, will kill that black thread of yours. He's not certain, mind you, but it's the place he wants to start."

Verdayne turned a leaf over in his hands. He could feel the health and vigor in it. "I agree," he said. "It's a good place to start."

She nodded. "He's making the concentrate now." She turned away. "Take care, there are some nasty wasps gathering nectar and pollen hereabouts—"

She hadn't finished the sentence when he heard a shrill buzz and felt sharp jabs along his forearm as he let the grape leaves fall back into place. She looked back abruptly at his stifled curse. "I should have spoken sooner."

"No mind. I've worked groves, I'm used to stings . . ." His voice trailed off. Hot agony lanced through his arm, sending jabs of pain that didn't stop till they rammed the base of his skull. She grabbed his shoulder.

"Back to the house. As quickly as you can make it."

His vision blurred slightly as he turned to look down at her, and then it cleared. Then it blurred again. "At least," he managed, "it's mostly downhill from here."

"Indeed it is. The guard and I can roll you if need be." She glanced around but saw no sign of their escort. "Or not."

"I can make it," Verdayne grumbled and then his head swam again.

Nutmeg gave a little snort. "Lean on me. As you remarked, it is downhill."

She sat him in the kitchen, after hailing the house and finding it empty. Her forehead furrowed, and then she tossed her hat on the counter and rolled up her sleeves, then his.

Nutmeg looked in dismay at his arm. "I've got to draw the stinger out or it'll keep swelling." Her glance moved to his face. "Can you swallow? Is your throat closing?"

"No," he answered wryly. "I think I can rule out death by sting."

"For the moment, anyway." She poked her finger at his wound, rewarded by his hiss and flinch. "It can build. Let me run over to the herbalist. She'll have something."

"Nothing in your overstocked Dweller cabinets that will do?"

"Sorry, no. None of us ever got stung like that." She could feel his intent gaze on her as she wrung out the cloth and soaked it in cold water again, before wringing it and applying it to his forearm.

"You shouldn't have to fuss over me."

"Any Dweller knows that red markings on an insect is the world's way of telling us to be careful. Even birds think twice before they snap up a crimson stinger."

"But first," Verdayne said through gritted teeth as the heat and pain of the stinger worsened, "one has to see them to avoid them. We don't have them up north, or I'd have known to look for them."

"Ah, so that's your excuse! Ignorance!" Nutmeg shot to her feet. "I'm off to the herbalist. Stay off your feet . . ."

"I know, so the poison doesn't circulate." He put his other hand up to wipe away the beads of sweat dotting his forehead. "I'll wait. But, please, don't run."

"Not long!" Nutmeg threw the door open and dashed out of the kitchen. Her guards startled, spears and swords coming up. "And there you are. Just me," she yelled over her shoulder at them before pelting across the street and down a few house estates. She halted long before she got there, the baby kicking hard in complaint as she paused to hike up the straps of her belly sling and catch her breath.

The herbalist was working in her front garden, her head down, her curly hair bouncing about her shoulders in unruly waves. As much gray as auburn, Nutmeg didn't think of her as a true redhead until the Kernan woman lifted her face to look at her, and the fair, fair skin decorated with a bounty of freckles faced her. She must have, Meg realized, been a flaming beauty of a redhead once in her past. Now, time and weather had tracked her face and taken the color from her hair, leaving her merely handsome.

"Mrs. Simples," Nutmeg started and then halted, knowing this not to be her name but unable to think of it no matter how she grasped for it. The neighborhood children called her Mrs. Simples, but she had grown far beyond that, she'd thought.

"Nutmeg! Whatever are you doing racing around? You'll stretch your skin and sprain your back. That's quite a burden you're carrying." The herbalist straightened with a basket hanging on her wrist. "Or do you need me?"

"Oh, not that, at least not yet. Our guest has been attacked by crimson stingers. Have you a paste or ointment for that?"

"Drawn the stinger out yet?"

"No, his wound swelled over almost immediately."

"Hmmm. That guest of yours would be the Vaelinar breed of Lord Bistel?"

"Yes'm."

"It's the high elven in him. All right, then, you'll need a hot poultice to draw the stinger out, and then a mint drink to cool the poison fever. Get him to drink chilled water as well, if you can, when you give him these. He should stay quiet the rest of the day and let that stout Dweller heart beat the poison out of his body." Shucking her gloves, the herbalist led the way into her home, its very walls saturated with the fragrance of the herbs and flowers dried within them since the day it had been built. Nutmeg looked at the low-hanging beams which served as drying racks indoors, although she knew the woman's backyard flourished with similar racks. Still, in a spring where rain and mist sprang up unexpectedly, the safest place for drying seemed to be inside. The various scents woke memories in her, but not pleasant ones. The healing tents on the battlefield smelled like this, when not overwhelmed by the smell of blood and gore. Nutmeg paused on the threshold.

"Come in, child, come in. I need to show you how to mix this." The herbalist's hands fairly flew over the shelves, picking covered jars down and ladling a spoonful of this and a pinch of that into a small, common clay bowl. Nutmeg

neared the rickety wooden table slowly, trying to identify
some of the powders but only having success with one, a
common enough kitchen powder used in some batters as a
dough riser. When she was finished with her mixture, the
herbalist tied a cloth over it and pushed it aside. "Hot water,
hot as you can stand to the touch. Mix it well, and then paint
it over the wound, as much of it on the stinger site as you
can. Lay the cloth over it and let it dry. Takes a short while,
not as long as clay but about the same. Peel it off, it should
draw the stinger with it. Along with a patch or two of skin,
no doubt." She smiled, showing that she had lost some
lovely white teeth in that wide smile of hers. "Then clean
the wound with plain water and put some of this ointment
on it." She set down a different pot in front of Nutmeg.

"Oh, that smells wonderful." The aroma tickled her nose
delightfully.

"Keep it. Use it on those stretch marks of yours. I've
been meaning to send some down, but those guards of
yours are a bit off-putting."

Nutmeg chuckled. "They're supposed to be."

"Aye, well I know." The herbalist pushed both clay pots
across the table at her. "Settle with me later when your victim is resting comfortably."

"I will." Nutmeg put the pots into her apron pockets.
Both felt heavier than they had in her hands. She had begun
to turn away when the herbalist caught her elbow.

"How do you feel?"

Nutmeg looked into concerned hazel eyes. "I feel very
pregnant," she answered softly.

"Of course! You seem to be carrying it well, for a
Vaelinar child." The herbalist tapped her chin. "They carry
longer than Dwellers, some as long as a year and a third."

A chill rippled down Nutmeg's spine. Did that mean that
Tressandre might possibly actually be carrying a child by
Jeredon? The herbalist misread Meg's reaction. She put her
hand out. "Oh, you won't be that long, child, no worries!
But you're closer than you think, yet not as close as you

hope. I know you're tired of this burden in some ways." Her hand went to the sling strap and hiked it yet a little tighter. "Nice harness, this. Does it help?"

"Yes. I've even begun wearing it to bed."

"Good. Good." The herbalist stepped back. "Best get back to your patient. That high elven blood of his is not as tolerant to the stinger as ours are."

"Oh!" Nutmeg had almost forgotten Verdayne for a moment, although she didn't know how she could. Perhaps it had been something about the herbalist's manner. She turned toward home and went to Verdayne as quickly as she could manage, her thoughts still wrapped about the fact that the herbalist seemed to have an idea when this heavy stomach of hers might finally yield.

Dayne's eyes misted as she put the plaster on, his forearm nearly twice its normal size and a patchy red in color. She smoothed the cloth over the clay-like mixture and saw the pain fade from his face, a fine wrinkle at a time, until he sat quiet, pale, but without the deep lines etched into his face.

He looked up at her. "What now?"

"We wait for that to dry and then pull it off you."

"It'll bring the stingers."

"It should."

"Good. For a moment when you first opened the jar, I thought you'd come back just to bake bread."

Nutmeg laughed. "It did smell like it, didn't it? The rest of the ingredients aren't nearly as common, though."

They sat in silence for long moments, waiting for the clay upon his arm to dry. He looked up to find her watching.

"What is it?"

Nutmeg almost did not respond before answering, "She said you had a strong Dweller heart in you."

"Ahhhh. As compared to you, who have no heart." Verdayne shot to his feet. "I'm sorry—I didn't mean that. Not at all." He swayed.

"Of course you did, in a way. We're nothing if not direct. Now off your feet." She sat very still for a heartbeat or two in his silence. She swallowed. "It's a'right. I might deserve it, a bit. I don't wear black for him. You cannot hear me cry, so it's no wonder you doubt my feelings."

"I could never doubt your love for that child or your family." He stood rigidly, waiting until she took a deep sigh of a breath before he sat back down abruptly.

"Dweller tact," he repeated.

"It's why we have such thick heads. Or maybe because we have such thick heads, it's necessary that we have no tact. It's a matter of getting the attention."

The corner of Verdayne's mouth quirked. "There must be kinder ways of bludgeoning someone."

"Ah, but time is always of the essence." Nutmeg put her hand out and tested the poultice. Drying but not dry. "Perhaps you've forgotten that we're nowhere near as long-lived as the Vaelinar."

"I could never forget that. I've seen my mother and brothers and sisters pass. Nieces and nephew. Great-grand nieces and nephews draw near their prime." Verdayne's brows knotted a bit. "My mother not so quickly as the others. It's an old wives' tale, I suppose, but the lovers of Vaelinars do seem to inherit a certain longevity."

"Really."

He nodded. "My mother lived to be almost a hundred. Long enough to see me from my childhood into my youth. Not that I expect to ever approach my father's age, his years far longer than even most Vaelinars, but I'm just shy of a hundred and fifty years now and, barring accidents or war, should make two hundred or so."

Nutmeg breathed out, as if suddenly aware she'd been holding her breath. "So my child will live a span."

"Did you think he wouldn't?"

"I didn't know. I've thought upon it, but it's not the sort of question you can ask just anyone. It borders on rude."

"I suppose not. Asking, that is. There are more Vaelinars than you think who have a Dweller hidden away in their cupboards, though."

A thought flickered through Nutmeg. "It must have been hard on you, watching your family pass."

"Bistel kept me closer to him. I never quite understood why, but I've been thinking on it a lot since he died, and I think it was to protect me from my mortality. That and the fact that he had loved my mother, and wanted to give her the respect he felt she deserved. He would not marry her, but he intended to honor her in other ways. He tried to give her land when she married, but she'd have none of it."

"Oh?"

Verdayne shook his head. "No. She asked for a mill. She said with Bistel bringing winter wheat to the north that there would be a great need for a good mill, and she was right. She and her eventual husband and sons expanded it three times over, and now it's a grand old mill, still grinding away, and the family is a prosperous one."

Nutmeg eyed him. Finally, she gave a slight shrug. "I can't see you as a miller."

"No?" He gave a soft laugh. "Me neither. Though my father gathered a few of my kind at the manor to help raise me, no one was a tradesman. I grew closest to the gardener . . . though that title was not enough to describe all that he did for Lord Bistel . . . but he taught me much about the groves and fields. And he a Vaelinar."

"He's gone?"

"Yes. Murdered a few seasons ago." Dayne picked at the edge of his poultice.

"Murdered?"

"I saw the body."

"So it wasn't all honey growing up as Bistel's son? Privileges and honor, a secure place in his graces."

"What? Why would you think that? Or think of it at all?"

"He kept you close. Gave you friends and family that were like you. Made sure your own family didn't grow bitter against you. He didn't push you off to find out for yourself what the world thinks of half-blood."

"I know what Kerith thinks of us."

"Ah," said Nutmeg. "You've not had the delight of women cross the street to spit on you, then. From all races. Or had assassins set upon you. Or had a House decide that you were nothing more than a smudge of dirt that needed to be wiped off the face of Kerith."

He frowned sharply. "I would not have let any of them happen to you! Assassins, we had. Bistane and I handled most of them, though my father took out a few. It's part of being a successor. Perhaps you hadn't thought of that when you decided to carry Jeredon's baby."

"If anything." Nutmeg reached out and ripped the poultice off Verdayne's arm. He let out a smothered noise as it tore arm hair and four fat stingers and a bit of blood and skin from him. "Sometimes we fall in love without thinking at all, and that's the real tragedy. That and losing the — the wonder of it and the desire to ever do it again." She pushed the ointment at him. "That," she added, "should take the bitterness away."

He took it off the table and got to his feet, crossing the room in a few strides before he turned at the doorway. "I'm not bitter because my father took me to his estates and raised me, but for every day you've been scorned and spit upon, think of my experience in decades. Things were worse until I finally grew taller than Bistel's war sword, but it was all to be expected. I tussled with Bistane as your brothers probably tested one another, and suffered the hatred of others because all Vaelinars are hated. I decided a long time ago not to see the world through the veil of those memories. My father gave me love and discipline, and my brother who lives today loves me no less than the brothers that time took away from me ages ago. Your babe will be born with his own sight, but you're the one who will give him vision." Verdayne took a long breath as if he might say more. Instead, he pivoted and left.

Nutmeg sat back in her chair, as spent as if she'd run across the wide vineyard.

Chapter Forty-Two

Ild Fallyn

IT WAS NOT THAT HER BROTHER was useless. On the contrary, Alton served a number of very important uses. It was that he did not always show the insight, the ingenuity that she expected of him. Tressandre stood reminded that she needed to retain the option of doing things herself when he brought back word that the escaped woman had eluded them all and disappeared into the wilderness. Half his retinue had died or suffered crippling injury. She could not fault the effort he'd put into his attempt to capture and return her. Why had the wretch bolted? Where might she have gone? Those were questions to which she wanted answers. She searched through her fortress looking for them.

That was how she found the miserable youth now huddled in front of her on the flooring. He clutched a pillow to his chest, doubled over as if hatching it, his tears soaking into the silken cover and his begrimed fingers sinking deeply into it in his white-knuckled hold. The pillow wouldn't save him, of course. It wouldn't even come close to protecting him. At least, for the moment, it seemed to have stopped his wails.

Tressandre stopped pacing to look at him more closely. He might have been the equivalent of ten Vaelinar years old. Perhaps even closer to thirteen. He'd been at the fortress for a decade and had not, according to the yard supervisor, shown Talent of any sort. He was due to be culled then, sent to the fields or forests for work, or simply dispatched for his knowledge. Males on the edge of puberty either bloomed with their Talent or had none. She didn't have to be patient with them as she did the females, who matured later and slower. He did not know that he neared the end of his usefulness to the ild Fallyn, or perhaps he sensed it vaguely, but it didn't account for his extreme distress.

No. He feared her in the immediate moment, and rightly so. Tressandre gave a small, secret smile. Very rightly so. She made certain to have earned the fear and respect they gave her.

She leaned forward slightly to tap her whip on his shoulder. He flinched and inhaled a sharp, gasping breath, but held his tears back as she'd told him.

"Now, then. You know a bit of this Ceyla."

He nodded and took a gulping, snotty inhalation, pressing the cushion closer. Tressandre stared at the top of his head. That pillow would be thrown out and burned. Possibly the whole divan. And, certainly, the carpet. The tip of the whip bounced in the air impatiently. "Tell me."

"I have ... I have ... Talent," he gulped. "Not much. Not yet. But I can hear ..."

"Hear?"

"Things. Things people say to themselves."

"All the time?"

He shook his head. "Sometimes. It bursts in my head. It hurts. My ears buzz like I was stuck in a hornet hive. There's words in the buzz. Voices." He twisted his neck so he could look up at her. "I heard you think you would burn everything just because—because I touched it."

"And because you're filthy." Unapologetically, Tressandre dropped onto a tuffet upholstered in a matching silk coverlet nearby.

He nodded miserably and put his face back in his pillow.

She ground her teeth. "I haven't all day. Tell me what you promised to tell me and we shall see what your fate might be."

"Cey—Ceyla talked in her sleep sometimes. Like a fevered dream. No one else could understand her."

"But you could."

"Because I heard her in my head, too. She could get loud." He relinquished the pillow with one hand and thumped the side of his skull. It did not sound like the thumping of a ripe melon she'd anticipated. "She knew something. Saw it. She had to leave and carry the message. It clawed at her mind. She had to go!"

"She saw something?"

"She did. No one else knew, but I guessed at it. Before a thing would happen, she would see it. Not everything of course, but important things."

Tressandre flexed her whip in her hands. A seer . . . a Vaelinar with Foresight . . . and her brother had missed it? She would doubt the probability of such a Talent because of its rarity, but evidence suggested that Ceyla might indeed have had it, enough of it, and could have used it in her escape. It would have given her a great advantage, even if the Talent was a new, raw, untrained ability. Yes, a great advantage. If true, she wanted the girl. Tressandre would have to exert whatever means she had to get that girl back.

She got to her feet. The boy heard her stand and drew himself inward even more, rolling into a ball about his pillow center. He was all elbows and big feet and scrawny arms as she looked down at him.

"What are you going to do to me?"

"That depends," Tressandre whispered as she leaned down to his ear. "What did you hear from her thoughts that drove her to run away?"

"A battle. A great battle coming, and she had to gather the Galdarkan Abayan Diort and bring him to it." He looked up, his nose swollen red and leaking, his eyes smeared pink with tears and fear, and his lower lip tucked between his teeth.

"Where?"

"I don't know. It's all I heard that I could make out. I promise, mistress, I promise that is all I know!"

"It can't be all. What is a battle without a battlefield? It's not enough to know soon, I need to know *where*." Her knuckles went white. She could feel her icy skin stretch across the bones of her fingers.

"I can't—I can't tell you what I don't know. I can't. I can't." He curled back into a ball, huddling, awaiting a blow of anger.

Tressandre looked down. Her mouth curled. "No matter."

"Is that . . . is that enough?"

"To save you? It might be. You will have to pray it will be." Tressandre stood and crossed the room in three great strides, throwing open the closed doors. Her retainer standing outside startled, jumping to his feet.

"Get me Alton. Immediately! And the birdmaster. I have messages to send. I want the light cavalry ready to mount up." Tressandre could not contain her smile. Lariel had not been so vulnerable in decades. Nor did she intend to let Diort gather the prize which she had hunted, plotted, and waited so many years to gather for herself and her family. She would find him, and then she would settle with the Anderieon House.

Behind her, the lad sobbed again, this time in relief.

Chapter
Forty-Three

NUTMEG BROUGHT THE JOURNAL out when the entire house fell into quiet except for the soft creaks and moans of the wood, which always spoke as hot and cold, light and dark, affected it. Nutmeg cradled it between her palms. She should give it to Verdayne. That had been part of Bistel's command to her, but only part of it, because he'd told her to give it to her sons first, and hold it until they felt ready to give it to his sons.

Her sons.

She would have this child and someday another, if Bistel were as good a prophet as he'd been a warlord. That thought curved her mouth in a pensive smile as she rested her arms upon her swollen belly. That meant she might love again someday. Marry. And go through this all over again, perhaps not so alone next time.

She lifted her chin, looking off into the darkness. Not that she could feel herself entirely alone this time. Her family enveloped her. She was selfish, she realized. She might not have Jeredon, but she had family. It was not the same, but she certainly wasn't bereft. As for passing it on, she didn't feel quite ready yet. She wished that Bistel had been a bit clearer in his wishes.

Nutmeg leaned over and lit a candle. Its glow brightened the room perhaps more than it ought and the leather cover of her book gleamed richly in its illumination. Why had Bistel not left the book in the archives? It might, indeed, be the very book meant to be destroyed by whoever had infiltrated the library. On that count, it might endanger her now. Not enough to be hunted for the possible heir she carried, but to add this to the pot, Nutmeg knew she might be hunted relentlessly until she gave up the secret she held. The warlord had laid a terrible burden and charge upon her. Why? She was no great hero or warrior. Had he seen more in her than she saw in herself? Without the child she carried, she couldn't even read it. Perhaps he had never meant to give it to someone who could. If so, he didn't know her. No hero, maybe, but as stubborn as any Dweller could be. Nutmeg would have worked at it, like a knot in an old, frayed rope, until she puzzled it loose and open to her. Maybe he had seen that in her and counted on it.

Maybe this, maybe that. She couldn't ever know—Bistel was far beyond her reach!

Nutmeg opened the book and ran the tip of her finger down its crackling page. Within her, she could feel the baby stir slightly, grown so that now he (he?) could not have much room and as if to prove it, she could feel a pain in her rib cage as a hand or foot stretched out. Whoever it was, they could no more resist the book than she could.

She didn't know a time when the Ways didn't exist, just as she had never known a history when the Vaelinars had not been there to manipulate it. She'd crossed at the behest of the Ferryman who had tamed an untamable river, and proved he could cross not only water but time. The shores of the First Home lands had been protected by the Shield of Tomarq. And a half dozen other Ways shuttled the fortunes of the Vaelinars, and eventually the other peoples of Kerith, back and forth.

Yet, like anything built by a mortal people, the Ways did

not seem limitless. She'd heard whispers at Larandaril that Ways were failing. Unraveling. The elemental strands of Kerith falling back into their proper place, no matter how the Vaelinars had twisted them to be, her world resisting its invaders down to its very core. Like the terrible aftermath of the Mageborn Wars, magic unleashed by a failing Way could be devastating. A book like this—and Nutmeg stroked her finger upon the page again—could stabilize and restore the Ways to their former glory, or make it possible to create new, wondrous Ways, something not attempted in centuries. The toll for failure had been too high, the methods not understood and thought lost forever. But not to everyone.

Not lost to Bistel Vantane. His mighty aryns were thought to have been the first Way created on Kerith, a tree blossoming out of a staff, a tree which could even stand against the corrupted magics and chaos left behind by the Mageborn Wars, groves growing and even thriving in the blighted lands where pools of miasma twisted Kerith forever. Had he thought to create again? Something? What? Or had he hoped to keep Ways from ever being created again? The power involved, the power bestowed upon the makers . . . Vaelinars who invoked Ways would be nothing less than gods.

Nutmeg closed the book on her finger. Even if no one lived who could truly use the book she held, there would always be those who would think they could. Perhaps she held a key which could unlock any door, even a door that should never be opened. The light in the room shimmered as she looked across it, its glow falling among the shadows to be shivered away by what she could not see, like a golden thread disappearing in a weave of dark threads, there but not always seen, not unless the weaver wished it to be seen.

As if it were a Way that could be designed, patterned, and crafted by her.

Nutmeg stifled the small, startled noise she made at that thought, dropping Bistel's book into her lap. Had she thought that or had it come from within, from the independent mind forming within her? A thought that never should have been formed to begin with.

We are not ones to play Gods, she told herself. She laid both hands palm down on her stomach. *Never think otherwise. Sweet apples! We do not change our world to be what we want it to be.*

And yet ... do we not plant groves? Plow fields? Seed for harvests?

We do change worlds. Every day.

That is different.

How is it different?

That thought froze her, motionless, for a very long time without an answer while the candle guttered low beside her, till she eventually stirred abruptly to pinch the wick out and let the room fall into total darkness.

Tree's blood ... what did she carry inside her?

Chapter
Forty-Four

CLOUDS SENT DARTING SHADOWS over the green hills and forest of Larandaril. The River Andredia flowed strong and swift, white curls upon its rapids as winter runoff swelled its banks. Yet, uneasiness weighed down upon her charge, her domain, and that tugged upon her heart. She finally decided to speak aloud some of her thoughts.

"We almost had him at Hawthorne."

"The confusion would have been perfect cover; unfortunately, the riot was too massive for our men to converge on Sevryn, and he was pulled away from us."

"It's been days and no further sighting."

"Not yet."

Lariel turned in her chair, seeking the window and its framed view of her beautiful river valley, lush with springtime and maiden's nod and not finding the sight as soothing as usual. She was seething, she thought to her faint surprise, and that was not something she did. Her grandfather had done much of it; and, although she couldn't be absolutely certain, she was fairly certain Tressandre and Alton ild

Fallyn seethed. They all had the same hardheaded temper-
aments about being obeyed absolutely and never crossed,
as if humans could reliably be depended upon to do such
things. She had thought herself a little more bendable.

Apparently not. Would her inflexibility cost her as dearly
as it had Sinok? She couldn't allow it to, but she carried a
knowledge buried deep inside her. A moment would come
when fate needed her. She'd seen it. She had to live to fulfill
that moment, and that meant her life could not end at
Sevryn's hand. It could not! Doubt riddled her now. She
carried within her that endpoint which she had shared with
no one, not even Jeredon, but it loomed inevitably ahead of
her. She accepted that. Now, however, she feared she would
not carry out her part as seen, and that would be unaccept-
able. Kerith and all its peoples faced the unthinkable if she
did not carry her burden forth to that future.

Lara ran her fingers through her hair, pushing it back
from her temples and jawline, thrusting the heavy curls
back upon her shoulders. No more would she allow Sevryn
to be a traitor against her. She could not. She had too much
at stake. House Vantane could have taken the title from her
if they wished, but Bistel had had power of his own and had
never wished for the kingdom of Larandaril. He possessed
his own lands to nourish, his own peoples to protect. Bistane and the other son—she could not quite recall his name
at the moment—she did not think either of Bistel's heirs
would do anything other than follow in their father's footsteps. No. She knew a web of conspiracies tightened to take
her throne from her, and some of her enemies had not yet
been revealed, but she feared Tressandre through experience and now Sevryn. What he knew about her Talents
would make her cast out from the Vaelinars, that which her
grandfather had known, nurtured, and guarded until death.
She closed her eyes momentarily. The old Warrior King had
even killed those servants around her as she grew up who
might have suspected her Talents. She remembered a day
when she had pled for Jeredon's life as well. He had finally
relented and let her brother live. His actions had led to

much speculation that she had little or no Talent, but Sinok Anderieon dealt with that as he did most of life: he tore through it. Now she seemed called upon to do the same.

If she had Sevryn in hand, perhaps she could take his measure. Perhaps she could avoid the inevitable, now that her temper seemed cooled and logic could prevail. He'd been loyal to her and Jeredon all these many years, had he not? What made her think he would turn against her now? Gilgarran had trained him. That in itself made him an unknown quantity. Who knew what Gilgarran's end game, so untimely cut short, had been?

Behind her closed lids, she saw again what she'd seen through Chastain's eyes on an unknown battlefield, quite near in the future: Sevryn, clothed in the dark weavings of the Kobrir assassins, advancing on her, silvery blades in hand, close enough to kill her—

Lara wrenched her eyes open. Her memory staggered to a halt, even as her heartbeat jolted in fear. She knew what she saw. *What she felt.* Even as she fought within herself, she knew what she had seen.

Lara looked at Drebukar and stifled a faint sigh, managing it as a slightly longer than necessary pause. "We've sent the last of the troops out successfully?"

"On their way. Our presence here is strategic only, three squads apportioned over the valley to keep some semblance of security. These last we've sent out should bolster our presence considerably. We are ready at Ashenbrook."

"We need to be. Reports of Raymy drops are coming in all along the coast, indicating Daravan's hold is weakening. I think we can expect to see the mass of that army dropped at the river within the next handful of weeks."

"Our troops are prepared."

She smiled ruefully. "Overprepared, I should imagine. It's been long seasons since the last engagement and we can only keep their edge for so long before it becomes tiresome. Not to mention expensive."

"They'll be ready," he repeated firmly.

"I think we should join them shortly."

He inclined his head, a gesture so like his father that when he lifted his face back into full view, Lara found herself shocked that the scar cleaving his skull in two was missing. To hide her momentary lapse, she turned away from him, who was not Osten though her heart and mind thought he should be.

"What word on Rivergrace, if any?"

"She's not returned to Calcort. No involvement where Sevryn slipped our hold, but I can't confirm that. They may still be separated, but I can't imagine he'd stay away from her long. If we could find her, we would no doubt find him sooner or later. Master Trader Bregan has gone to ground. It's said he's dismissed all his servants—those who hadn't already quit—and doesn't come out of his manor. It's said he's gone out of his mind."

"Bregan," Lara repeated. "His caravans are still running?"

"His is a well-oiled empire. It would take more than a few weeks in seclusion to undermine it."

"Let us hope so. Half our supply contracts are with his House. Keep an eye on him, if you can. I'd like to know what's unhinged him if it's something other than his propensity for strong drink. Put eyes on elder Bregan, too. I know the two of them hit heads often enough. If we can't find out directly, the father might be more talkative. Nothing obvious, though. I need subtlety."

"I'll see to it. We have good contacts in Hawthorne."

"We should. I spend enough money there." Lara eased back in her chair. "Thank you for the briefing."

"Anything else?"

"Not for a while. I'll call."

Farlen bowed sharply and left her. Lara stood up, changed her clothes, and then donned her chainmail. Then she took a sword and shield off the wall, shoved her table and chairs aside, and began to drill as her grandfather had drummed into her very being oh so long ago. She did not intend to stop until she could no longer hold her weapons at all. She aimed at shadows with and without substance.

Rivergrace knelt upon the ground, fussing over her shoes. Horses stamped tiredly behind her and blew hot breaths. Her father's shadow fell over her and she wondered for a moment that he could even throw a shadow. Its silhouette looked more whole than he did and she put a finger out to touch it, thinking of the legacy he insisted on passing on to her. She did not want to tangle and untangle the very threads of mortality. Worse, it tired her, leeched the strength out of her very bones, and she might never have the strength she needed to escape. She approached that point at which she no longer knew herself, and feared that when she did finally reunite with Sevryn, he would despise her. He dealt with death, but cleanly. None of this enslaving of souls or feeding of Demons. He would hate her as she'd begun to hate herself. A long breath sighed out of her.

"What is it, Grace?" His voice. As dry as he was. As quiet. As flat and unnatural toned. Perpetually tired, perpetually existing despite it. Would he have her end up as he did?

Her fingers twitched and she answered softly, "I can't do it."

"Can't or won't?"

She looked to Narskap. "Both. It is death and I don't want to deal with it."

"It's worse than that, it's Undeath and unnatural, but this is what we need to sow, for the moment. You must trust me, Grace. Trust me as if I have always been the father you loved once."

His breath heated her ears as he spoke, bending close to her, seeming as if he did not speak at all, but she heard him. She concentrated on braiding the brittle laces of her old shoes carefully. The shoulder of the ancient apron she wore shrugged off her shoulder, and Grace tugged it back into place irritably, brushing off dried flakes as she did.

"Where on earth did you find those clothes?"

"On a dead woman in a cavern. I had need of them and she no longer did."

"I'll get you something more suitable as soon as we reach the ranch. I doubt if he burned Tiiva's clothes."

Rivergrace twisted about to look up at Narskap. "Tiiva was there?"

"After Lariel turned her out of Larandaril. She held an uneasy alliance with Quendius, but he soon found her guilty of disloyalty. Did you think she had run to Abayan Diort?"

"We weren't certain where she had sought refuge, what alliances she might have made before she turned up in bits when Quendius used her to breach the border."

Narskap nodded. "He took her soul with one of the arrows corrupted by Cerat. It was not a mortal wound though deadly. She lived long enough to ride to Larandaril, and there he killed her to cross the border, which still knew her essence and opened for her. Lariel had exiled her but not removed her signature to access the border. Even in death she managed to betray you."

"He killed her?"

Narskap moved away and nodded. "Or perhaps he had me kill her. Some moments are hazy in my memory."

Her mouth tasted coppery. Rivergrace brushed the back of her hand across dry lips. Tiiva of House Pantoreth, the last of that bloodline, with her brilliant hair and skin, and elaborate gowns, running Lara's household as if it were a mighty empire. Perhaps, for her, it had been, though ultimately unsatisfying. Rivergrace had never felt accepted by the woman, never Vaelinar enough. She did not think she could stand wearing whatever wardrobe the beautiful but arrogant woman had left behind. She stood, slipping her hand in one of the many herbalist pockets of the apron. Ground-up bits of leaf and stem met her touch. Narskap had turned away, so she lifted her fingers to sniff them and almost sneezed in surprise.

Deadly hawk's cap, unless she was mistaken. She brushed her fingers off carefully and made note to wash them as soon as she could, lest she poison herself. She watched the back of Narskap's head. It wouldn't work on him, but it would probably take down Quendius if she could dose his food. It might be her only chance.

Narskap turned back and crooked a finger.

"Rest is done."

Rivergrace straightened her apron and approached, wiping her thoughts from her mind. She would have to consider her actions and what Narskap had said earlier. Was Death only a threshold that Quendius might enter and return even more formidable than he already was? Was Cerat his latest alliance? How far dared she go along the pathway Narskap had drawn before she had gone too far to ever go back?

Before she would lose all she loved and who loved her? Her thoughts reached out to Sevryn but could not find him.

Chapter Forty-Five

THIS WAS HIS THIRD DAY in the gardens. Sevryn had tired of it the first day, but the late afternoon on the second day he'd been taken from the dirt to the sand of the arena, and no doubt this day would be no different.

"And this is hawk's cap." The herbalist's crooked fingers caressed the plant gently. Shadows striped him as if he might be a beast crouched to pounce from the garden depths. He ached from bruises taken in his beatings but not from the exercise. The Kobrir were not tasking him any harder than he'd trained himself in the days when Cerat had raged inside of him and he'd feared to let Rivergrace know him. The garden held a kind of peace to it that tried to lull him, and he could not allow that. He cleared his throat and gathered his thoughts.

"I know of it," Sevryn told him. He squatted by the bent man. "Not deadly until dried. The sun seems to anchor a potency within it, for whatever reason, otherwise it actually has a medicinal use as a purge."

"Unless great quantities are eaten, yes. But once dried, it becomes a hundred times deadlier." His teacher smiled. "What would you do with it dried?"

"I could use it like kedant, make a dip out of it to treat my blades, but it doesn't work as well in the bloodstream. It needs to be eaten. It's far too bitter to put in a drink. You could treat a pickled dish with it and it might not be too discernible that way."

The Kobrir nodded. "Excellent. We make a dry capsule of it. There are those who will consume it regardless of taste."

"For what reason?"

"It will abort the unwanted. A child or even a tumor. It takes but a pinch for that, and if the host body is strong enough, it can withstand the effects."

This usage came as news to him. "It physically aborts a tumor?"

"No, no." The elder dropped his jaw in a soundless laugh. "How could you even ask such a stupid question? But no. It stops the growth and, if dosed a few more times, makes it shrink upon itself until there is nothing left of it."

"If the host is strong enough to survive the hawk's cap."

Another nod. "If would be the question, would it not? But if death is a certainty, perhaps an almost death would seem to be a respite? The dose is given over weeks, perhaps even months, to give the host time to work at keeping its strength. Sometimes we must kill to live, eh?" The herbalist got to his feet with bones that creaked and knees that popped audibly as he straightened.

"You seem the master here."

The herbalist folded his hands together. His dark eyes gleamed from their depths within his wrinkled face. "Many are masters here."

"You've set a task on me to find your king. But I've work of my own that needs to be done, and I can't afford the delays."

"Can you afford to live?"

"It's not my life that worries me. I have other concerns."

"Other journeys."

Sevryn did not turn away from the unblinking gaze. "Yes. Important journeys."

"You must find our king for us. This is a matter that will envelop all of us, whether one wears the black or not. It is a matter of many lives and many deaths."

"He would be the most powerful of all of us. I take it he's gone rogue?"

The herbalist looked away, breaking the tension between them. "I cannot say."

"Or won't."

"No. I cannot tell you what I don't know. All I can tell you is that what seems important to us only is of real importance to you, as well."

He didn't feel reassured. "Tell me where your king was last seen. How your contracts are made. Give me my weapons and let me go, and I'll hunt him down for you."

"Not yet." The herbalist flexed, and his back gave an obliging crick-crack. He pointed downslope to where underbrush thickened and shadows grew darker, playing upon the ground. "It's grown warm. Perhaps you would enjoy a swim? There is a tarn there, in the valley's corner." The herbalist shot him a look. "It is said to be bottomless."

His shirt clung to his ribs with sweat. Sevryn considered a swim in what would undoubtedly be a snow-fed, cold-water lake as he had not been able to bathe in days. The possibility of touching Rivergrace within the water's pool beckoned to him. The ache of her loss grew with every passing moment. Days of fight sweat and farming dust felt caked over him. He could use the cleanse.

"A swim is just what I need." The old man watched him as he shed his shirt and boots, hiked down to the tarn's sloping bank, and stood for a moment, watching its waters before putting his hands over his head and diving in.

Not that he trusted a single invitation from the Kobrir.

Icy waters parted as he plunged in. The shock felt good, kicking the weariness out of his system, bringing him wide awake and alert. It was, as he'd decided, a snow-fed pool, clean water as his examination of the growth and animal life about its edges indicated. The danger here, if any, came from its sheer iciness and what it might hold within. He ducked under once or twice but found its depths too dark to see clearly. One lap and he readied himself to climb out, knowing the coldness would affect him shortly.

Something grabbed him from behind, taking hold of his ankle and not letting go.

He dove downward instead of trying to make the bank, reaching for the long knife tucked into his pants' waistband at the small of his back. The sudden reversal of his body weight loosened the hold, and he was able to twist free. Muddied waters hid all but a shadow of his attacker as he curled to meet him. He angled to his left in what he hoped would be a feint, and his attacker kicked forward.

Wrapped in dark cloth, the Kobrir could hardly be seen in the deep blue waters and the mud churned up from the bank. Remembering that the old man had warned him the lake was bottomless, he stayed near the edge of it, for he would gain the only propellant he could get from kicking out from there. His limbs began to numb. He wouldn't last long, but the other had the same disadvantage. He pushed out away from it and at the trailing bubbles he could see, drifting upward to the surface like pearls. He rammed into his opponent and they locked, hand to hand.

The assassin had a grip of iron. Seviyn did not try to wiggle out, exertion that would only tire him; instead he played into it. On the streets long ago, he'd learned that strength alone did not win a wrestling match, particularly if that strength could be leveraged against the wielder. He fought back now in the same way, giving when his opponent expected a push, pushing back with his legs, entwining them, holding his opponent fully below water with him. Now they both held their breath, feeling their pulse in their ears, the leaden response of their arms to what they asked of them.

The cold would kill them nearly as soon as the lack of air. He could feel it penetrating, dulling his effort. It made his whole body heavy, almost too heavy to move, and his mind tried to slow with it. Heavy and dull. His mouth thinned. He could hold his opponent dear and near, hoping that the other would fall into unconsciousness before he did, but that would be a close call. The other felt icy in his embrace.

Sevryn arched his back suddenly, breaking free of the other's hold by sheer, now unexpected force. He kicked free, hit the lake's bank with both feet and drove himself upward, knife in hand, stabbing as he went.

He hit. Solidly. The blade wrenched against his hold. He could see a cloud as dark as ink spurt out even as he twisted upon himself, reversing his upward climb. No air for him yet. Not until he had his opponent and weapons in hand.

Not with his arms but his legs; he reached out to grasp the other. They clashed again, twisting and churning in the water. The Kobrir hit him, hard and solidly, in the rib cage, exploding what little air he had left in a spew. Sevryn bit his lips, hard, as he clamped his legs and thighs. Then with all the quickly draining strength left in him, he pulled toward the shore and climbed the lake's banks hand over hand. Rock edges sliced at him, moss denied him purchase, and mud sloughed up everywhere as he fought for a hold.

Dark water churned furiously about him. Deeper than he'd thought, weighed down by the other's body fighting him every handhold of the way, he climbed the stony bank like he would a wall. His lungs ached. He tasted blood through the teeth that sealed his lips from gulping for air. Rocks pulled loose as he clawed at them and then grasped for the next, desperation giving him new strength. Get out now or die.

He pulled himself upward and into the air, its acrid dryness hitting him full-force and he thought to just collapse there, half-in and half-out of the water, but he still held his attacker imprisoned in his legs. Sevryn reached down to grab the Kobrir by whatever he could best get hold of—turned out to be an upper arm—and hauled him out as well. His legs unlocked stiffly, and he rolled over and then got up, staggering out of weapon's reach before going to his knees on the hot soil and feeling the sun blaze down upon his shoulders.

The Kobrir still bled. He writhed and curled into himself, too spent to even pull his feet from the lake. On the hill above, the herbalist gave a sharp whistle. Kobrir sprang up from everywhere, grabbed their kin, and bore him away.

The old one tottered down the hill. Sevryn looked up at him warily, his hands on his knees, as he filled his lungs and felt the pin and needle feelings coming back into his limbs.

"You did well. But then you suspected."

"Why wouldn't I? No Kobrir gives a gift without expecting a price."

The herbalist held up his index finger, crooked by age and wear. "No being gives a gift without expectations. You would do well to remember, no matter who you deal with."

Sevryn felt the corner of his mouth stretch and moving faster than he thought he could, he pivoted and threw his weapon at a shadow behind him. The knife hit deep, and the Kobrir collapsed with a surprised sigh. Sevryn moved to him and took the dagger out.

He looked back over his shoulder. "Even advice has its price, eh?" The water settled into its deep blue and calm seeming and Sevryn realized he had not felt or heard a single echo of Rivergrace within its depths. He hadn't searched for it and, truth be told, it would have distracted him. Yet he yearned to have heard the echo of her essence in the cold, clear water, her silken touch on his very being. He craved it. He lived to receive and return it in kind. He prayed that what the Kobrir planned for him did not change him into a being from whom she would turn away. He cleaned his knife on his wet pants and went to retrieve his shirt with a quick look at the fallen bodies behind him. Never turn your back on the Kobrir.

Chapter
Forty-Six

COULD ROADS BE HAUNTED? Even with five hundred soldiers and cavalrymen at your heels, stomping and marching and bellyaching? Bistane stood in his stirrups for a moment, easing his thigh muscles and knees, and fought the impulse to look over his shoulder even as uneasiness danced along the back of his neck and tingled up his spine. He'd ridden this trail before, with his father and the rest of their troops, down to where the Rivers Ashenbrook and Revela crossed to meet the enemy. Inevitably memories would plague him, but he felt more than that, a familiar touch, a remnant of a well-known tone upon the air. He thought he'd left his father's shade at home, but it seemed not.

Lengthening shadows told him the day was nearly done, and he put up a hand in signal that a suitable place for camping should be found along the river. He watched as his captains deployed scouts on his order.

He wouldn't pitch a tent tonight, but decided to sleep outside in the mild spring night while he could, for the farther south he went, the more capricious the weather could be until the stolid days of summer set in. Bistane toyed with the idea of camping amongst his troops or opting for solitude. He did not want to be crowded, preferring some measure of solitude, and rode up to Lamdur to tell that captain of his decision.

Lamdur looked at him dourly. The campaign had burnished his copper skin and lightened his brown hair with streaks of gold and silver to frame his sharply etched face. He'd seen much under Bistel and now Bistane. "Not wanting to sleep among the great unwashed? I don't blame you. I'll have a wineskin cooled and set aside for your dinner. I would appreciate it, however, if you let me know where you will be making camp, my lord."

"Done. I'll probably be on the river ahead of everyone."

"Before the scouts go through?" Lamdur rubbed the bridge of his nose where it had been broken at least once. It was the only coarse bone in his face. "I would advise against that."

"And I wouldn't take the advice."

Lamdur nodded curtly. "Yes, sir." He wheeled his horse away, headed to the rear to the supply wagons, no doubt to make good on his pledge of having a cooled wineskin ready.

Bistane was more than ready for it when he shackled his horse and put the rubbing cloths he'd used on the animal over the saddle for the night. Daylight dappled the riverbank. When he looked at it closely, he could see the tiny streams of light and the minute beads of water making the bigger picture. He could not, like Rivergrace, summon the water, nor could he set fire to running along it as she had done at Ashenbrook. He could, if he wished, set the air to humming with the music he had always felt in his veins. Raise a breeze to stir the heat off the land or drive the pollen gently over the fields to fertilize the crops. Churn a twister away from its ill-fated journey, though that took almost his last heartbeat of strength to accomplish. He could make his weapons sing, sending them unerringly to their target as the metal thrummed to a beat only he could hear. His father had talked of the same phenomenon. Dayne didn't hold a similar affinity to weapons although he had been taught to use them exceedingly well. That pleased Bistane although he knew it probably should not, but he liked being his father's son. Verdayne had other abilities, including one or two that he had shared only with their father, secrets kept from him. Bistane attributed it to being in control, a trait he shared.

Or he had until Bistel had begun to haunt him. Bistane sat in the small clearing by the river, ahead of the noise and stink of the army following him, and hoisted the promised and delivered wineskin. He took a long draft and then rubbed eyes grown weary. Sunlight shivered and dappled its way through the canopy, and sparkled off the river, and he dabbed at his eyes again. He watched the area carefully, his eyesight not as it should be, both less and more than he expected, with a glimmering of Talent about it. He closed his eyes tightly for a moment, but when he reopened them, he could not shut away the sight he saw.

"When you were a lad, you used to beg for time with me."

"That was when you lived and breathed." Bistane saluted the vision in front of him, Bistel clad in battle leathers as he wore much of his life, even when at the fields and groves he loved. He looked as he had always looked through the prime of his life, without even his death wound to mark him. "Now it is just plain unsettling."

Did he see a ghost indeed—or did he see into a plane of existence where ghosts might come and go? Did he believe anything he saw? Why would such a thing befall him? He stared at his wineskin a moment but knew he couldn't blame the vintage.

"Why?" Bistel eased himself onto a fallen log, bending his knees carefully to sit, and leaned forward with his elbows on those same knees.

"Why do I see you? I have no idea. Perhaps you have unfinished business. It bothers me that a man as long-lived and achieved as you are—were—can suffer from such a thing, and it bodes ill for my own rest in peace whenever it might occur."

A breeze that did not exist for Bistane appeared to lightly ruffle his father's snow-white hair. "I am surprised and that pleases me. You rarely showed such depths when I was around."

"When you were around," Bistane pointed out, "we were generally at war with someone. When we weren't, you were off gardening."

His father's mouth twisted to one side. "I never puttered around. I did not garden."

Bistane took a draught from his wineskin. "No, you didn't. I apologize. You were as good a farmer and orchard man as any ever born on this world. Verdayne follows closely after you in that, far more closely than I although I have my Talents."

His ghost nodded. "I am blessed with two very strong sons."

"Might I ask why you don't haunt the other one?"

"What makes you think I don't?"

That startled Bistane for a very long moment during which he capped and uncapped his wineskin several times, thoroughly uncertain if another drink would help the situation. He finally lowered it and pondered the brilliantly blue stare of his father's eyes. "I think Verdayne would say something."

"Your brother keeps his silence on a good many things. I believe he's decided that, since his time is much more finite than yours, that learning is a priority for him, and he cannot listen when he is speaking."

"Now that is unfair."

"But likely true."

"Its veracity doesn't make it any easier to accept." Bistane opened his wineskin after all and took a third long draught from it, feeling it warm his gullet and belly as he did. When he closed the skin up this time, he wrapped its lace about it, and threw it to one side. Bistel raised a white eyebrow.

"I never argued better when I was drunk."

"Most can't. Have you a meal on you?"

Bistane paused in mid-movement as he reached for his saddlebags. "What? Do you eat? Are you hungry?"

"Of course not. I meant for yourself. An army is best kept only a little hungry."

He stretched to draw the leather bag into his lap. "Fresh bread, a hunk of cheese, and some jerky. However, I told the cooks to slaughter three of the herd for the men tonight, before you scold me for poor rations."

"They deserve a full belly before tomorrow's march."

Bistane spread his napkin out over his leg to balance his dinner upon it. "And that brings us, no doubt, to why you're here tonight."

"Am I here? Or are you seeing where I am?"

"I don't know. Are you in a mood to tell me?"

The corner of Bistel's mouth quirked. "I'm afraid I have no answer for this, other than you seem to have a hold on me."

"Then, dear father, I release you. Both of us need our peace."

Moments ticked by and neither moved.

"It doesn't seem to have worked," Bistane remarked.

"No."

"Moving on, then. You were saying something about tomorrow's march."

"You have only a few days to bring the army to where it will be sorely needed."

"Is this why I'm seeing you?"

Bistel raked his fingers through his snow-white hair. "Again, I can't answer that. But I do know a few things about warfare and mounting armies and strategies, and I know where your army will be most needed."

He lifted his bread and cheese to his lips. "Then I am listening."

And so he did while the ghost told him what was on his mind.

Nutmeg couldn't sleep. She hadn't heard from Grace since she'd left, and the short words she'd had from her replacement guards told her only that Sevryn and Rivergrace were not currently in Lariel's favor. Why? What events had turned and which way? She would gladly have tortured any of the guards if they'd have said more than that little, but Vaelinars were famed for their tight-lipped ways, brought up amidst plots where a single word might give a kingdom away. The only thing she had gleaned from them in the past few days had been surprise at Verdayne Vantane's arrival. They had neither expected him nor quite knew what to do about him. They gave him the deference of a lord—he was Bistel's acknowledged son, after all—but they didn't care to do it. Nutmeg had never been immersed in court intrigue, but she knew when a bow had been slighted by both its depth and length. Verdayne got their minimal respect. She didn't know if he knew it, but his words with her suggested that he did. Was that why Bistel had sent him? Oh, Bistane had issued the orders, but she'd little doubt that the old war-lord himself had told Bistel that, when the time came, he should send Verdayne to the Farbranch holdings in Calcort. But why? Had he sensed even then she carried a child, a child who would face all the disadvantages his own son faced?

What did Verdayne see in her?

Nutmeg leaned as close to the edge of the bureau as she could get, notwithstanding the current size of her belly, and peered at the mirror fastened to the wall in front of her. She could get closer if she shoved the dresser aside, but the noise of that might awaken the house and she had no intention of any of her family (brothers) crowding into her room to see what the commotion was. Besides, it wasn't her belly she was looking at.

It was her eyes. Filled with merriment, usually, Dweller good humor at the rest of the world. She knew it. Jeredon had told her often enough, but she didn't need the telling of it to know she had good eyes. Bright. Set off by thick lashes and a dusting of freckles below, across her nose. She was a comely lass, for all the dark circles now and the faint lines of worry at the corners of her eyes.

Nutmeg squinted hard and pushed against the bureau, jutting her chin out and staring at herself. The babe didn't like the hard edge of wood pushing into his domain and pushed back with a stubborn hand or foot. She rubbed her stomach ruefully and gave way just a touch.

"I have to see," she told her irritable child. She rubbed her hand across her brow. She leaned close again.

Her eyes. Staring back. Frowning at her from the mirror's surface. Nutmeg started to let her breath out in a slow, measured, exhale of relief.

And then the shadow came up.

Oh, no, Nutmeg said silently, her mouth moving but the words stifled. *No.* Another color shadowed her eyes, over her caramel-brown eyes, a ring of golden, with bright sparks of green.

Vaelinar eyes.

She shut her eyelids tightly. *No.*

Chapter
Forty-Seven

NUTMEG LIT TWO MORE CANDLES and peered into the flaring light. She couldn't be seeing what she was seeing, but the extra illumination only sent more shadows darting about her rather than clarity. Her nose practically pressed to the glass, going cross-eyed, she finally closed her mouth in dismay. Perhaps in the morning light.

And if the daytime showed no difference? Hurriedly, Meg swept up her hair and looked at one ear and then the other. They remained the same, round-edged, delicate shells of Dweller ears they'd always been. Not like Garner whose ears seemed a bit jugged, or Keldan who had ears with very little lobe to them, still normal but not as pretty as hers — and hers were still hers.

The candle flames wavered, as the bureau translated her trembling and shook itself, making the illumination dance. Nutmeg backed away from her dresser before bending over and blowing all the candles out, leaving her in the dark and still shaking.

She curled up on her mattress. Once her body had begun to change, she knew she would inevitably no longer be the

same. In a way, she had welcomed the rest from chasing
about the countryside, involved in the intrigue that Vaelinars lived and breathed, only to find that it had followed
her home. It was not the home she had thought she would
have at this point in her life, but her parents' home. She had
envisioned one of her own, perhaps even a home that was
a tinker's wagon like the Dweller Robin Greathouse's, a
woman Master Trader with a bit of her own magic. The days
she had come to their old home on the banks of the Silverwing had been filled with new goods, do-hickeys and sometimes toys that delighted all of them, news from faraway
and, occasionally, a magical prophecy or so from Mistress
Greathouse. Lily wove some beautiful fabrics which could
be traded for a great deal, and sometimes she tailored outfits from her best yardage, outfits that fetched a pretty price
from the trader and would be sold for even more elsewhere,
after being tucked away in the wagon Robin called home. A
home that indeed traveled about but still provided security
and sanity, the only intrigue being the laws and taxes placed
on those who traded. Or perhaps even a home like the
herbalist down the street had, a small fence in front to keep
her favorite flowers and herbs from being trampled by pass-
ersby, a whitewashed house with an arch over the front
door, and fragrant from the drying flora hanging from the
rafters. With, of course, at least one pair of childish feet racing to and fro.

Nutmeg pressed fingertips to her temple. No, she hadn't
foreseen a bit of this, and that was her own shortcoming, not
thinking ahead. A Dweller, an orchardist, a rancher thought
ahead season to season, crop to crop, and she had that ingrained in her—she who could plan for a decade ahead in
seeds and grafting and harvesting—and she hadn't thought
more than a handful of days ahead in her own life. When
she finally closed her eyes and slept, it was only because she
was so tired that she had no choice, her thoughts having
raced her into the ground.

The heat of the sun streaming through her curtains
warmed her cheek, waking her. She uncurled stiffly and

made her way to the mirror, blinking the sleep from her eyes. Hunger rumbled deep in her stomach and Nutmeg curved one hand over herself. She was always hungry! She could hear sounds throughout the house that meant her parents were up, Tolby's low voice registering as his deep tones vibrated through the wood. Leaning close, she stared at her face in her mirror again.

When had she gotten dark circles under her eyes? The tiny cut of a wrinkle at each corner? She brushed at her face as if she could whisk away the flaws even as she leaned closer to look for what she feared most. She knew the laugh lines at the corner of her mother's eyes. And there were mornings when Lily awoke, and dark circles marked her worries from the night that carried into the daylight. Nutmeg knew her mother's face well and celebrated every facet of it, a gem honed by life and laughter. Yet her eyes, though sometimes crinkled in cheer and sometimes dewed by sorrow or thoughtfulness, had always been her mother's without the deep etchings.

Nutmeg blinked several times and then leaned close, opening her lids wide. In the next moment, she held her breath. The candlelight had not lied to her. She saw herself looking back with Vaelinar eyes.

Nutmeg took a step back. Her hands shook, fluttering on the air like butterflies that she could not catch and still. Her heartbeat, once so familiar, now thumped heavily in her chest. She forced her hands down and took a deep breath. She backed up slowly across her room, not so many steps to take although her knees felt as if they could not bear her weight or even work properly, and one of the floor planks creaked as she stepped over it. The noise filled her ears and mind, driving everything else out for a blink of a moment. When her thoughts roared back in, the first one was of her book. Bistel's book. She had questions. It had answers.

Nutmeg spun on her heel and lunged at the hiding place, fumbling until she got the book free and open. Vaelinars remade things. They twisted and tangled the very threads of creation on Kerith until they created a Way. That Way might stabilize, in spite of being out of the order, or it might snap back into place, creating a—well, Bistel hadn't explained it quite so that she could understand it, but the reaction was invariably lethal. Ways that remained were workings that paralleled nature most closely, so that the threads that had been rewoven did not or could not revert to their natural state. Vaelinar eyes could see the possibilities, could differentiate the fibers of the world that might be tweaked.

She had to narrow her eyes to read the writing as the pages danced in and out of focus. The baby jumped in her stomach, a hard kick to the ribs, pushing out what little breath she had left, and Nutmeg bent over, gasping. She breathed deeply until her ears stopped sounding like the Silverwing River in full flood tide and her heartbeat slowed so that it no longer drummed in her chest and throat. She lifted her chin and then straightened carefully, putting her shoulders back. *You gave me Vaelinar eyes.*

So that you can see. A small voice from within said. The voice of common sense, or an echo of her parents' voices, or . . .

She curved the book over her stomach, as if it were a shield.

You can't give me that which I don't already have. I have eyes, so you changed them.

I could give you another eye, if you wanted it.

She felt a tingle in her forehead, between her knotted eyebrows. She clapped a hand to the spot. *No!*

The tingle stopped.

She could feel her child squirm inside her, as if uncomfortable, cramped inside her. Then, the barest of whispers in her mind.

I can do this.

Her mirror groaned. Nutmeg whirled to see it . . . its silvered reflective surface . . . turn to wood. Apple wood, smoothed and varnished and beautiful, but wood. Indisputably wood. She retraced her journey across the room to test it with her fingertips.

Now you can't see your eyes and be unhappy.

She could feel the grain of the wood. Where it had been planed and then gently buffed for a finish. She could almost smell the scent of apples imbued in it. Wood, where there had been glass and silver paint. Not one thing evolved to another part of its natural state but one thing taken away and another element replacing it altogether.

Not possible.

Nutmeg took a step back. She couldn't let what her mirror had become be seen. Questions would be asked that she feared she couldn't evade properly, not for long. "Change it back." Her voice shook. She cleared her throat. She stretched out her hand and flattened her palm upon the surface. "Back to glass. A mirror, as it was."

She did not get a voice in return, but a feeling of great weariness swept her. Her hands began to tremble again, this time not from shock but from fatigue. She tightened her jaw. "It must go back. It must. I have no safe way to explain what happened." She clutched Bistel's journal in her left hand so tightly her knuckles went white.

The wood grain under her touch began to grow chilled, so icy she snatched her hand back. She could see the surface roiling, a silvery brew that boiled within the frame, a storm of change that had none of the control from before. A cold sweat broke out on her forehead, and slid down her temples, the bridge of her nose, the side of her face as though she stood in a wintery rain. The wood did not want to give way to the glass. The metamorphosis fought itself, wavering from one element to another, bubbling in and out as it warped, filling her small bedroom with the stink of molten metal and glass as well as the aroma of fresh sawed wood. The frame bowed out as though it might fly into a hundred pieces, shoving Nutmeg back a few steps in fear. Then, suddenly, it sank into itself, metal frame with glass and its silvery paint backing it, not quite the same as before but close enough, for this mirror looked fresh and new, not the fading and slightly spotted mirror that had reigned above her dresser for as long as she could remember.

Her stomach cramped, hard, and Nutmeg let out a cry of

pain. Her right leg gave out from under her as though it had suddenly gone boneless and she began to fall. Her cry rose in fear as she thought, "I'm going down." She threw the leather journal as far under her bed as she could, as her body, traitor, gave way and another hard, long cramp ruled her, squeezing the breath from her and she thought she could feel her child's body arch in pain and then go horribly still inside her.

She hit the floor as the door was flung open, her vision filling with the sight of Verdayne's tall form on the threshold. "Nutmeg!"

Chapter
Forty-Eight

"**N**O, YOU'RE NOT IN LABOR. For the fourth time." Lily coaxed a white rag gently over Nutmeg's pale face.

"Although that day is not so far off," the herbalist murmured, pouring clear water into her cup of mashed leaves and stirring it up to benefit her patient.

"How can you tell?"

"I think anyone could tell from the size of your stomach, my dear. If not soon, you'll burst of that child." She smiled, not ungently, sliding one hand under Nutmeg's head and guiding the cup to her lips.

"'S not funny," Meg got out before the tea overwhelmed her words. She gulped down the brew, shuddering with every other swallow, finished, and gasped out, "Tree's blood, that's awful!"

"It's meant for th' babe. It's very weak inside of you, a shock to both of you. Whatever were you doing?"

"Besides fainting?"

Lily reached over and pinched her ear, hard.

"Ow!"

"Wretched child. I know it's hard to get comfortable, but you need to settle now and then, for both your sakes."

"I'm not going to stay a-bed from now till I pop."

"And no one said you had to. After today." The herbalist stood briskly, dusting her hands. "I've left enough leaf that she can have another cup this eve, and that should do them. If you need me for other matters"—and the two women traded a glance that Nutmeg knew they thought she wouldn't catch but she did—"I'll be about most of the day. I've some shopping to do now that the quarantine's been lifted."

Lily bent to the dresser across the room and frowned a bit at the mirror, before picking up a generous fold of yard goods and passing it to the herbalist, along with a few sparkling coins. "Thank you, for everything."

The herbalist took both offerings, beaming. "And thank you, Mistress Farbranch! I'll be seeing you soon, no doubt."

She pushed gently past Verdayne who stood in the doorway as if his feet had taken root there, neither in nor out, but steady. They exchanged a nod, but then his attention riveted back on Nutmeg. She tilted her head away so as not to look at him.

"Nutmeg . . . has that mirror always been like that?" Lily turned back to the object, running her fingertips over the carved frame, apple wood, quite charming.

Meg's thoughts skittered. The plain metal frame had quite vanished. "Mother. Of course it has. Don't you remember?"

Lily tilted her head. "I suppose I do. This has been quite a year to fill my head, hasn't it?" She pulled the light sheet up over Nutmeg. "Now rest. I'll leave you to thank Verdayne for his timely rescue, and then I want you to nap. I have some matters at the shop to attend to, but I'll be home in early afternoon to fix lunch and get supper going. Stay off your feet," she finished firmly.

Verdayne waited until her footsteps had quite faded and Nutmeg decided finally to look at him. "Are you better?"

"A-course I am."

"You gave us a fright."

Her lips twitched as she nearly answered, "Not before I had a fright," but did not. Instead, she tightened her mouth. This was not a man she wanted to be sharing things with. Even if he did look oddly handsome standing at the door to her bedroom. He was as different from Jeredon as he could be, and yet oddly the same. Her ears warmed and she tugged at her right one.

"You fell." Verdayne scanned the floorboards between them. "Not a rough place to stumble on." He looked at her face again as if he could read it. "I thought I heard—" He shook his head.

"Heard what?"

"You'll think me soft in the head like a rotten apple."

"Already do. What did you think you heard?"

"I heard metal . . . well, metal makes a sound when it's being tempered, placed in a saltwater bath, more than the sizzle, it . . . whines. And I heard wood creaking, like a tree does just before it cracks open and loses a limb or two in dry heat."

"Was that all?"

His jaw worked, and then he shook his head. "Not all." He shifted weight. "Thought I heard a baby cry. Not loud. Muffled, as if from a distance."

She hadn't heard that. She'd been too busy with the roar of a river in her ears, and her eyesight darkening. She moved a little in her bed, trying to sit higher. One elbow stung like the devil had bitten it. She supposed she'd have a bruise the size of her head on it, soon. He stood, waiting for her response. "That proves it, then."

"Proves what?"

"Rotten apples have a great imagination."

Verdayne laughed, a rich deep sound that shivered over her skin and sank where it tingled along her bones and made her smile back. "Still, then, you are better?"

"I'm a'right. Just as shiny as a new leaf."

"You don't mind being . . . different."

Her skin, which had been warming steadily, suddenly went chill. "What do you mean?"

"Different."

"Explain yourself."

He took a deep breath. "If you're not used to seeing, it's difficult."

"Do try."

"Threads of being . . ." he beckoned about the room, the empty air, nothing, and everything. "They have a way of shining when they've recently been manipulated. I can see it. Some of Vaelinar blood can see it. Most can't, although they can see the results quite well. Just not the aura of the making, which I can plainly see. As you said it, a shiny new leaf." He looked at her squarely. "You glow, Nutmeg, and not with your health, your maternity, not like that, although you do, no doubt about it, but this aura— Even from across the room, I can see that your eyes have changed. A touch about the ears. Your hands." He fell quiet.

Nutmeg spread her hands upon her quilt. Sturdy Dweller hands, calluses from working at the loom, sewing, harvest, picking. A small white scar across one knuckle from—what was that from? One of the small battles she and Rivergrace had been in. Perhaps from a Raver cut. She inhaled deeply. Her fingers did seem more slender. A bit longer. More like her mother's hands now than her father's though she had never thought so before. She knotted her hands up.

"Your head is full of empty air."

"Perhaps, but I can see. Can you, Nutmeg?"

She did not want to look at his face again, but she had the sense that Verdayne would stand in her doorway until the Gods and Tolby decided to move him. So she met his gaze again, solidly. The corner of his mouth quirked. "Your eyes are quite lovely. They were before, no question there, but now . . ."

Her mouth twisted. "I don't want to change."

"Then don't."

"I didn't! He . . . he did it. And he can't, not anymore."

"He?"

She curved one hand over her stomach.

"He."

"I think it's a he, but whatever. As stubborn as I am. As capricious as Jeredon could be." She took a deep breath, feeling suddenly as if she stopped breathing for too long a moment. "He wanted me to see as he does. Will. Should."

He leaned a shoulder against the doorjamb. "I've not heard of such a thing before, but then, I haven't been around long."

"Longer than I have." The answer might be in Bistel's journal, but she would have to crawl on her knees to retrieve it and certainly had no idea of doing that until she was entirely alone and undisturbed.

"That may become different as well."

His words troubled her, down many different paths. To be around her child longer, that would be good. To see her parents and brothers diminish, and perhaps even their children as well, would be heartbreaking. She saw the expression on his face, concern and understanding, and knew what he had already faced. "I never thought I would feel sorry for the length of a Vaelinar life."

His lips curved slightly. "I know."

"You can't say anything."

"I will not. But mothers are observant and Lily may already have noticed more than your mirror." He craned his neck to look at it. "What happened there?"

"I was distressed about my eyes. He changed it to wood so that I would not have a reflection."

Verdayne's eyebrow lifted. "One element to another?"

How quickly he'd picked up on that. She wished now she hadn't said anything. "Yes."

"Unheard of. The energy and Talent involved—no wonder you fainted. He must have drawn on every reserve his tiny body had to do it, and yours as well."

Now fear crept deeply into her. "I could have lost him?"

"I'm not a healer or midwife, but it might have gone badly. Don't ask too much of him, even as a small child. He has to grow into a power like that."

"You promise you will not say anything."

Verdayne watched her face for a very long time, his now wearing a carefully schooled Vaelinar neutral expression.

"You can't. It's going to be hard enough for him ..."

"Do you know why Jeredon was not made Warrior King after Sinok?"

"No. Vaelinar politics, I assume, not that I pay more attention than I have to."

"You'd do well to study their history now, it will serve you and the child. Jeredon was not considered very Talented, and what Talent he did have was not extremely strong. It appears to have skipped a generation. Perhaps even two, considering his mother and father."

"Sinok was strong."

"Extremely. And so is Lariel although her Talents have never been entirely revealed. My father had faith in her but never told me why."

"His faith was enough for you?"

He nodded. "Always. Bistel was an extremely good judge of people. It's one of the things that make him, made him, the leader he was. A good judge of people and of soil."

The baby turned sluggishly inside of her, as if stretching, and she moved onto one hip to help him adjust. He watched carefully before asking, "Does it hurt?"

"Hurt?"

"When he moves."

"Sometimes. He likes to put his foot into my rib cage. His elbow sometimes makes it difficult to lie down just right, and he always, always, gets more active just when I'm ready to sleep."

"Huh."

"You're a farmer."

"True, but it's difficult to ask one of my horses why she's stamping her feet and switching her tail in irritation. I can tell she's bothered but not why." He laughed again, very softly. "Not that I'm comparing you."

"Oh, well, why not? Tree's blood, I'm as big as any mountain pony." Nutmeg pfoofed stray hairs from her face in irritation.

"I should leave you to rest."

And she should tell him about his father's journal, but

how could she? He had told her to hold onto it, and pass it
on to her sons when she was ready. Sons . . . oh, rotten apples, could she be carrying twins?

Something of her thought must have shown on her face.
"What's wrong?"

"Nothing. I just thought of getting bigger."

He backed a step out. "You definitely need to nap. Lily
will be boxing my ears if you're still awake when she returns." He bowed. "Call if you need me. I will be . . . listening." He closed the door softly behind him.

Nutmeg pushed back on her pillows. Bother. He would
undoubtedly hear her if she got up and tried to retrieve the
journal. Some business would best be left until the depths
of the night. Again.

She sighed. The baby turned again inside of her, a bit
more lively, and she knew he was feeling stronger.

You can see, she thought she heard.

Nutmeg turned her cheek to her pillow. Yes, she could
see. But did she want to? Was she strong enough to?

There would be no knowing until she was on the other side,
would there? Her glance fell on the strangely beguiling carriage Lord Tranta had sent them, a carriage that looked more
like a ship sailing on restless seas than a baby's cart. She hoped
that he'd gotten the thank you letter she'd finally posted. He
seemed a lonely man, that one, although she'd seen the way he
looked at Lariel sometimes. It was a look she used to crave
from Jeredon, although she didn't know if she'd ever received
one. Men tended to look when ladies could not see.

She settled her shoulder into the mattress and told herself she did not regret a single moment with Jeredon, as
over and done with as it all seemed now.

And she found herself strangely sorry that Verdayne had
left her doorway.

He'd said she glowed. And had lovely eyes.

Chapter Forty-Nine

SEA WINDS ROARED off the coast and up the cliff, with a sound more ferocious than a tempest through a forest, and they sounded in his dreams, calling him to ride tides from the known to the unknown.

Tranta woke, one arm thrown over his chest, with the wind still tugging at his dreams, and the morning sun dragging them away from him. He rolled to his side and rested on his elbow, watching the waves below the cliff crest and fall, foam and ebb. Birds kited above the waves, diving vigorously now and then to pull a fish from the waters. He watched them use the wind, however strong, however contrary, to their advantage, wings outspread as they soared in place, eyes cast on the glittering ocean, seeing what even he could not from the cliff. He took the challenge, though, eyeing the waves as closely as the birds did, in hopes of seeing life darting below the surface.

He looked for more than prey—or perhaps it would be more accurate to say that he had a different prey on his mind, and it wasn't the Raymy either. Tranta shaded his eyes. He did not expect to see what had plagued his dreams

for the last week: a floundering ship on the horizon, ragged
sails attempting a tacking maneuver to close on the shore,
against the tide, against the wind, against all common sense,
in desperation. Why not try to ride the storm out in calmer
seas? Why not wait for the tide to turn? He had the sense
that whoever crewed that ship had run out of time, and the
urgency of their need drove deep into him, even in his sleep.
Even looking for it in his dreams, Tranta hadn't been able to
see the ship easily: its wooden construction had all been
painted a sea-gray and its sails were dyed the same, as if
someone had deliberately wanted to make it difficult to de-
lineate upon the ocean. He had spotted it because a lightning bolt had illuminated it on a storm-dark day—in his
dream—and he wondered idly if he would have the same
luck in real life.

Because it *was* coming. He would bet every last shattered bit of his precious Jewel of Tomarq that the ship sailed
toward its doom. He felt it down to his very bones that what
he had dreamed sailed mercilessly toward him. Last night
had been the eighth night of that dream. The only variation
was if he got to it in time to save the passengers. Sometimes
he did; more often he did not and could only watch, horri-
fied, as they went down on their storm-tossed ship.

But not today. Today the sky was impressively cloudless
and calm. Only the wind spoke of weather brewing and yet
to come. Only the wind.

Tranta rolled to his back. The chill in the sea mist told
him it was just after dawn, the sun behind him reinforced
that, the wind nudged at him to awaken, but he felt like a
bit more sleep. He'd been at his forge until late, and his
muscles still ached and eyes still burned from the brightness
of the fire he'd banked. He'd sent a bird off to Lariel two
days ago when he knew he'd drawn close to the end of the
task he'd set himself. It couldn't hurt, surely, to rest a bit now
he'd finished his task. His eyelids closed slowly and he
slipped back into a dream where he searched for a sea-gray
ship that fought to make shore before it sank.

When he woke again, the sun was branding his cheek

and forehead. He rolled with a muffled curse and got to one
knee, searching for the waterskin and for an ointment. He'd
been on the cliff for days and knew better. When he finished, he stood and went to get some food: smoked fish,
bread and cheese, and a quinberry, still a little tart for being
early in its harvest, but welcomingly juicy. He ate as he
stood, overlooking his signposts and what he had salvaged
from his Jewel of Tomarq.

She faced in now in a hundred different poses, faceted
and sparkling red-orange in the sun, shining so brightly that
he narrowed his eyes. A hundred signposts, each adorned
with a miniature of the cradle which had held the original
Jewel, a cradle that rocked up and down, and side to side,
propelled by the wind, sun, and the Jewel's own will, so that
its eye could view the horizon in front of it. He put his hand
out and flicked the nearest one into greater motion. It immediately swung alertly toward him, and then relaxed into
a gentle rocking movement.

"You know me," he murmured. "Even as I know you. I
wonder if the Drebukar had any inkling at all what they
found when they mined you out of the earth. Or perhaps it
was my own Istlanthir who imbued you with the guardian
spirit that still shines out of you, regardless of your circumstances. Whatever you are, you are more than a Way, for you
are sentient." He stroked the side of the faceted gem close
to him. A hundred signposts he'd had fashioned and three
staffs. One for Lariel. One for Bistel. The third, he had not
chosen a Vaelinar to carry. Perhaps even Abayan Diort
though that Galdarkan carried his own magic. Who might
best be protected by the guardian of Tomarq?

Lara should arrive at the cliff late that day or perhaps
early on the morrow. She'd be pleased when she saw what
he'd fashioned: how could she not? And he did want to
please her, his heart did, although . . .

And Tranta turned his eyes to the sea. Lara had never
mentioned a marriage, an alliance between them, although
they'd been close all their lives and he thought he knew well
why. His truest heart lay out there somewhere, beyond the

waves, calling to him on the trade winds. Was it the ocean himself or merely the desire to travel on it, to discover, to master the tides? Whatever it was, it did not matter to Tranta which might hold him on land—it wouldn't hold him for long. Not throughout all the seasons. He would return, as all men of the sea returned to shore, but he would always go back out again, if he could.

Was that why he dreamed of a sea-gray ship going to its doom? That if he followed his heart, the rest of his fate would fail?

"Perhaps," he said softly to himself, "I should take the third staff with me. You would be upset if I left you entirely, would you not?" and he turned his face back to the many facets of his Jewel, his eyes dazzled. "We have a visitor coming," he told her and walked among the posts, ensuring that each and every one of the cradles that held a piece of her worked properly and that it held her safely.

He still had shards too small to use and could not bear to throw them away, nor would he sell them to a jeweler to adorn bracelets and tiaras and cuffs. The Jewel of Tomarq deserved a dignity beyond that. She had watched their coast for centuries before her downfall. He would not let her remains be turned to mere baubles. As he moved among her red-gold brilliance, a tiny thought at the back of his mind occurred to him: that he had never felt as one with the Jewel before nor regarded her so highly and with an intelligence of her own, as much a woman as the Warrior Queen. Should he think it odd? Yet how could he think otherwise, given the evidence. The thought evaporated from his mind before he could focus upon it and drifted away, like foam on the outgoing tide.

"We have a queen to show what we can do," he told her as he moved among her many flames. "I want her to be as impressed as I am."

The Jewel of Tomarq did not answer him. Tranta smiled wryly as he gathered his tool belt and went to work.

He worked on the cradles till the sun had peaked in the sky and began to slide away toward the ocean. Then he stood and stretched, easing cramped muscles in his neck and shoulders, and reaching for a waterskin. Before him, on the makeshift workbench he'd put together, lay a girdle of sorts, a chain mail belt and he had installed on its top tier and lowest tier, eye drops of the ruby jewel, not certain what purpose the armament might serve other than to bedazzle the eye. He tapped it thoughtfully with one nail as he put his waterskin down. "A pretty thing for any lady, but will you save her life?"

"And is that what you mean it to do?"

Tranta's head snapped about and he saw Lariel sitting on the other side of the chasm, her hands folded in her lap, her horse and guards secured at the bottom of the slope, out of earshot.

"Lara! How long have you been sitting there?"

"Not that long. A welcome rest after a hard ride. Will you lower the bridge for me? I see what you've made." She stood, dusting herself off. Her blonde and silvery hair caught the gleam of the lowering sun and sent it shooting like sparks through her strands.

He lowered the bridge as requested and held it steady while she joined him. She wore riding leathers and light chain, adequate protection on the road although not likely to offer much if an attack had been pressed, but then she'd come with speed and that meant watching weight. He took her hand as she stepped off the wood-and-rope bridge.

"So what have you done with our broken shield? It looks like you have scaled it down, but surely you can't mean for us to have a fence along the coastline?" Lariel strode into the center of his works, her brilliant blue eyes not missing a detail of his efforts.

"If I am correct, four of these posts, positioned properly, can handle the guardianship of Hawthorne's harbor. The Jewel can't strike as far as she did, nor as hot, but she certainly has retained all her capabilities to react to danger."

"You've replicated the cradle."

"To some extent, yes."

"Do we need to assign a watchman then, for each post, to aim the Jewel?"

He could see the calculation in her eyes, of manning each signpost on shifts around the clock, and the cost of doing that. Tranta shifted his weight. "The posts don't need to be manned."

Lara stopped in her tracks, half-turning. "What?"

"Just as the Jewel of Tomarq operated independently when in one singular piece, so does each of these signposts operate. She has retained her ability to scrutinize the surroundings and react accordingly."

Lara murmured something which sounded to him as if she said, "Gods in heavens" before catching herself and finishing her walk through his latest creations.

"Her beam is not as far-reaching as it was, but it is still very effective, and if there is need, the other signposts will join as sentinels."

Lara blinked. "Meaning . . ."

"If the beam is not sufficient to render her target helpless, the other signposts close by will also strike. If one fiery beam does not take our enemy down, rest assured that two or three most certainly can. In a way, the Jewel is far more efficient now. Energy is not being wasted on broad sweeps."

"But." Lara paused, and then started again. "How does it know? How does it know whom to strike? If I dress as a smuggler to approach the shore, will it cut me down? Will it take out a landing boat of ild Fallyn if they invade up the coast?"

"How did it always know before? It is a Way, Lara, and it's always known our enemies, from the day it was created. I can't be clearer than that."

"There have always been traitors."

"And there always will be; it seems ingrained in our nature. Will the Jewel strike against a traitor? Probably not until such a one is embroiled deep in the traitorous act, because it is not more godlike than you or I. If you're asking me if it will strike someone down merely because there is darkness in one's heart, I can't tell you that." He spread his hands, palms up.

Lara gave a soft laugh. "Of course you can't. Although our lives would certainly be easier if you could."

"Now you speak of Sevryn."

"Yes. And Rivergrace, I suppose." Lara pulled up a three-legged stool and sat upon it. "Or anyone else . . . can you imagine marching someone in front of these to see if our Shield would react to them?"

"The Jewel was never meant to act as a jury of peers. It is meant as a guardian in hard times, when armed incursions have already declared their intentions and need to be acted against. I don't think it was given the extreme sentience to judge much further than that."

She nodded and shifted her chain mail shirt about herself, easing it a bit. She saw the jewelry lying out on his worktable. "And what is this?"

He folded his legs and sat on the ground opposite her. The cliff here was beach as much as it was rock, with scruffy tufts of grass too stubborn to not grow here, and sand that shone with tiny bits of rock and shell. He pulled the girdle into a more recognizable shape. "I'm not sure what it is," he admitted. "I have fragments I can't find a use for, yet, and I won't let them be turned into vanity pieces. Now this," and he stirred it with a fingertip, "this could be a valuable piece of armor if it works as I think it will."

"Have you tested it?"

"I just finished it as you sat there."

"What do we need to do?"

He pursed his lips in thought. "I suppose we need a volunteer to wear it and a volunteer to attempt an attack."

"Do you think it might react to ward off an attacker?"

"It should. I don't know if it would merely be a deterrent or if it could cripple the attacker, however. I'd hate to boil one of your guardsmen inside his armor."

"That serious a response?"

"Possibly." He calculated mentally. "Yes, quite possibly."

An expression he could not read passed across Lariel's face. She looked down for a moment, perhaps to finish her thought or hide it, he couldn't be certain. "You wear it and I'll come at you."

He shook his head. "No, nor will you wear it while I attack. First, if we have any confidence in the Jewel at all, she'll know the difference. Second, if we're wrong, and she can't determine the difference between a feigned attack and a real one, someone could get seriously hurt."

"Then the item is useless if you can't test it and predict its use."

"The Jewel of Tomarq has never been useless."

Lara closed her mouth, her lips in a soft line, as she examined his face. She sat back a little. "You would take it on face value."

"We wouldn't have to. I imagine if we search one of the prisons in Hawthorne, we could find a thief who'd be quite interested in taking the piece off you, whether you were alive or not, if he thought he could get away with it. Would you set a man up like that?"

"Why not, if he'd savage me?" Lara leaned out and shouted down the slope to her guardsmen, "Find me a thief from the jails across the bay. A good one, a desperate and hungry one."

Two of her men answered with a salute, mounted and rode off.

"You're serious?"

"I want to know what it does if I'm going to wear it."

Tranta looked at her. "I didn't say I'd made it for you."

"If not me, who then?"

He couldn't say because he hadn't anyone in mind, but he opened his mouth to gainsay her and then could not. Perhaps he'd had her in mind all along. Perhaps the Jewel had.

She nodded briskly. "See? And I have a need for it, I think. There is a battle coming."

"Here?"

"Ashenbrook and Ravela, most likely, although if Daravan loses his grip on his tide of Raymy, it could be anywhere. They've been dropping in handfuls, here and there. Worse, Calcort reports their invaders carried plague. I not only have to stop them in their tracks, I have to burn them where they stand." Lara smiled ruefully. "I could use the

Shield back in her old glory. I need a guardian against wars and traitors."

"I tried."

"Tranta! Never think you've failed. Look at these posts—sentinels made from the debris of the Shield's destruction. No one else would have even attempted it, let alone succeeded." Lara leaned close to him. "You've done a marvelous job."

"You're pleased, then?"

"As soon as we can test one or two of the pieces, we'll huddle over a map and decide where best to strategically place them. You've made the posts substantial, I imagine they can be sunk into any foundation on almost any part of the coastline and be fairly permanent."

"For centuries, I had thought. If the wood rots, the cradle can be attached to a new post. The Jewel will not diminish, as stone does not. Nor do I think anyone would be fool enough to pry them away."

Lara touched the girdle. "Give or take a link or two, I think it will fit."

The corner of Tranta's mouth quirked a little. "It should," he admitted. He had danced with the Warrior Queen often enough that he had a good idea of the span of her waist.

"Excellent. It's late enough for a dinner. Cross the chasm and eat with us?"

Tranta stood and gave her a hand up. "With pleasure."

They had finished a modest supper and a wineskin among the four of them and retreated into a game of pieces heading far into the night when the two guardsmen returned. Lara stood with interest as they rode into the fire's light, leading a tired Kernan pony by rope halter with a ragged man perched on its back. His smell preceded him.

He threw one leg over the horse's withers and crooked it there, leaning forward with an easy smile. "So this is the lady who sent for a true man."

"And found him in a jail," rumbled Guardsman Niforan at Tranta's elbow. He set down the wineskin he'd been holding to serve Lariel.

She put her hand on his forearm. "At ease. I did send for him."

Niforan stood back, but Tranta could feel the tension radiating from him. He stood, went to his workbench and crossed back over the bridge, where he handed the girdle to Lara with a bow. The Kernan thief's gaze fixed upon the glittering jewelry. She strung it between her fingers and walked toward the thief. "I need some help fastening this."

He slid off the horse, eager to oblige, his hands fastening the girdle about her waist deftly, his fingertips soothing down each link and facet of the jeweled armor. Lara stepped back out of reach quickly, her nostrils flaring slightly at what Tranta thought was probably his odor.

She considered the Kernan who was tall for his kind, although not for a Vaelinar, their eyes met on a level. "You've a name, I suppose?"

"Hariston." He gave an incline of his chin. "Harry, they call me."

"Appropriate." Tranta paused. "Your hair does seem to have a life of its own." He eyed what seemed to be small creatures moving through long, greasy hanks of mud-brown hair, probably not too much different from the way it might look when the man hadn't been imprisoned.

Harry eyed him. "You with hair that is not born of this or any other world."

Tranta smiled with one side of his mouth as he tucked his sea-blue locks behind one ear. "I would not have it any other way."

Lara looked between the two of them. "My lover," her eyes lingered on Tranta, "and I have a bet."

Harry rubbed his hands together enthusiastically. "I hold a certain relish for gambling. Where do I figure in this little wager of yours?"

"Why, you are the central figure."

"Tell me." Harry stood, appearing at ease though Tranta

marked his posture well: weight shifted slightly forward, ready to move, arms and shoulders loose. More than a thief, this one, he thought. Perhaps dangerously more.

"Lara—"

"What?"

"I don't think this is wise."

Her gaze flashed at him briefly. "Nonsense. You just hate to lose a wager."

"Ask him if he's ready to lose his life."

Tranta caught Harry's attention with that. "A life or death proposition?"

Lara made a diffident movement with her hand. "Life if you win, back to jail if you lose. And likely your death there, right? Although you seem to be faring well."

"Haven't had the trial yet, Lady Vaelinar. That will make the difference." His attention came back to her as she moved, and her girdle flashed fiery brilliant in the campfire's light.

"Get my girdle and you're free to go."

He looked at her, one eye squinted. "That's it? That's all?"

"You have to go through Tranta and then me to do it. That should be enough," she said tranquilly.

Harry turned round to survey the group. "What about this lot?" He indicated Niforan and the other three guards.

"They will not interfere."

"And I have your word on that?"

"You do."

Harry spat to one side, just missing Niforan's boots. They stared at one another coldly. Hariston wiped the back of his hand across his mouth. "Vaelinar word don't amount to much."

"Then we might have a problem agreeing to our wager. I offer freedom and gold, and you don't trust my offer." Lara started to turn her back.

"Don't be hasty. What if I wanted to keep that?" Eyes fastened on the bejeweled girdle again as if it had lit a lust inside him that could not be put out by either fear or common sense.

"It's not part of the wager."

Harry's fingers twitched against his thighs. "But I want it."

Tranta put up his hand. "A moment." He crossed the bridge, wooden planks thumping under his boots, rope creaking and straining in his haste, and made his way to his bench. There he cupped a handful of the slivers and tear-drop shards, wrapped them in a sweat rag, and bore them back to the campfire. When he opened the rag to show the Kernan, a multitude of the gems shimmered in his palm. "This plus the gold."

Harry licked his lips. He gave a nod. "Done. But I will do whatever I have to for it."

Lara smiled slowly. "You took a knife off me when you helped fasten the belt on. Is that weapon enough for you?"

A wicked smile crossed the Kernan's face. "I could do with another."

At Lariel's nod, Niforan tossed him a long sword and then retreated. Lara gave him another wave. "Retreat to the base of the slope."

"Milady—"

"Take the others and go."

He started to speak again, but she sliced her hand through the air, silencing him. Smothering his protest, he took his horse and beckoned for the others to follow. Lara called after him, "If this man makes it down the slope, he's to be allowed to go free."

The Vaelinar stopped in his tracks, back stiffening. He muttered, "Aye," before starting downward again, into the night.

Harry waited until they were long gone, even the muffled hoofbeats of the horses, before grinning. "Lord and Lady Vaelinar." He tossed his head, his lank and skinny strands falling back.

"Do you know us?"

"No, and I don't want to." He began a slow pace to his left, drawing Tranta's wary attention. "You are lords and ladies. I doubt you've ever lived in a street, a ditch, a cave, in your life." His hands tightened about his weapons. "You think this is a game. Never is, for the likes of me. Haven't had the trial yet, but they want me for thievery. And murder. Don't like jail. Like court even less." When he had paced as far to his left as he apparently wished, Harry began to pace to the right. Tranta marked that he was learning the ground he stood on, its hardness and softness, stones and roots, not easily seen by firelight. Harry kept smiling. "So who is it you usually have do your killing for you? A swordsman like the guardsmen? Perhaps a sellsword like the Kobrir?"

"I usually don't have much need for killing," Lara responded.

Tranta dropped his ragful of gems at his feet to keep his hands free, feeling uneasier by the breath. "Lara, I begin to think Niforan had the right of it—"

The Kernan gusted a laugh. He stopped in his pacing. "Now, are the two of you thinking of backing out of your bet? That's not the way it's done. Although I wouldn't put it past a Vaelinar. Lower than Bolgers in my sight."

Lara did not draw her dagger, but unwrapped a chain bracelet from about her wrist, and began to swing it. The movement caught Tranta's gaze, just for a moment.

The wrong moment.

Hariston lunged but not at sword's point, not at chest or arm or head, no, he went low, bowling Tranta's legs out from under him even as he reached out and sliced Lara's leg, cutting through riding leathers like a hot knife through butter. He rolled and vaulted to his feet, coming up with a boot at Tranta's throat as Lara crumpled in spite of herself, with a tiny noise of dismay. Tranta felt her hot blood splatter his face even as he fought to breathe under the Kernan's heel. *Underestimated*, Tranta thought. The thief lifted his boot enough to kick him in the jaw, and he saw stars, his ears roaring with the blow. He rolled to his side, ears ringing, eyes losing sight, fighting it, fighting to get up and protect Lara, sucking down wind not only to breathe but to yell for help. Far, far underestimated the hunger in this thief.

And the quickness. Harry tossed the long sword aside, sweeping his hand toward the girdle to rip it off Lara even as she curled in reflexive pain, her hands going to her leg, trying to stop the spurt of blood. The second dagger began its silvery arc toward the curve of her throat.

Someone screamed.

Tranta thought it was Lara as he rolled up and staggered to his feet.

The scream stopped abruptly as it hit its highest register. Gurgled into a deep moan of the most intense pain and then that stopped as well. Tranta rubbed at his eyes, readying to tackle the Kernan as the thief wobbled back onto his boot heels, both arms outstretched.

Or what was left of his arms.

Burning coals, stinking of seared flesh dropped and sizzled in the scrub grass at their feet. Nothing remained of his arms below the elbow. Harry's head turned, jerkily, a quarter of a turn, and his jaw dropped as if he might say one last thing, but he did not. He pitched face forward and hit the ground, quite dead.

Tranta did not feel much more steady on his feet, but he lurched to Lara and knelt down. "Hold this," she said, and grabbed for his fingers, put his index tip into the hole on her leg, as her eyes rolled back in her head and she passed out.

He felt the blood flow slow to a trickle as he held the hole, and drank down as much air as he could get into his lungs before he bellowed for her guardsmen.

Then he looked down on her, and the jeweled girdle, and thought that he needed to make her a choker as well, that their fiery brilliance was not all that different from the fresh blood glistening on his hand in the firelight.

And that the Jewel of Tomarq shielded Lariel quite well.

Chapter
Fifty

DESERT HEAT CRACKLED along his back, warning of an even more dangerous baking once the summer months set in. Sevryn had been there long enough that they gossiped in front of him: no word of Rivergrace, but Lariel, it was said, had been spotted riding from Hawthorne, shining in the sun as if the Jewel of Tomarq itself rode on her shoulder, and he'd no idea what to make of that except that *he had no more time*. Sevryn had beaten every fighter he knew in camp, most of them more than once. The most dangerous one he'd met had been a woman, as the old Kobrir had warned him, and a left-handed woman at that. She'd come within a palm's width of hamstringing him and although he'd prevailed, he was not happy that he had maimed her doing it. She did not accept his apologies after but scowled as if he insulted her for being the lesser skilled and weaker. Part of him feared that he might meet with her again, in the dark under dire circumstances, and the outcome would be even more harsh.

But if she stood between him and his freedom, she would go down. He'd wasted enough time. He'd let the Kobrir ed-

ucate and hone him, but he had no more time. The ild Fallyn
waited for no one. As for Rivergrace, nothing from any who
had seen her, and no recent sign from the waters she might
have touched. He paused, on his knees, hands in the dirt
grubbing weeds, realizing he'd said that last aloud.

"You have said that before," the old Kobrir remarked, settling back on his haunches. The lowering sun slanted shadows
across his unreadable eyes.

"Because it is all the more true. Is this bringing me closer
to finding your king for you? You set me on that road—let
me go follow it."

"It may not be a road to your liking."

"It never was, but you used a threat to urge me upon it.
I take that threat seriously." Sevryn glared into the mild
eyes watching him behind a Kobrir mask. Fading eyes, yes,
but a stare returned steadily into his. The old man was as
unyielding as the dry land about him, this sere land they
called home.

He had it placed in the map of his memories finally, not
far south and east of Larandaril, over the small break of
stony hills that had capped the Mageborn Wars badlands
from the more verdant First Home lands, this spine-
breaking land. There was a river close by, a major river that
would disappear into the mountains themselves and then
open up to tumble down toward the sacred Andredia which
flowed into and out of the Warrior Queen's holdings. A wall
of chaos bordered this patch of land, making it inhospitable
to enter and warning off any trade caravan because of the
uncertain magics. It seemed, now, to Sevryn that the magics
were not so pooled here, except for that wall, and once
passed, the Kobrir had not only a gate few would breach,
but a welcome curtain drawn over their existence. It was
possible they had a few aryns planted along that curtain.
Yes, water was dear here, but it would rain enough that it
could be stored, and they had the deep lake in the valley
which could be used, no doubt fed by underground water
sources. If it rained at all, the aryns could hold. The sun was
a little too hot here, but the Kobrir weathered it well

enough. And they were a little too isolated here, but again, they were a cult of killers. Better for them, or they'd have been rooted out and put to the sword long ago.

The herbalist stirred. "You may think you're ready. Perhaps you are, Sevryn Dardanon. You rarely were defeated by us, even before this training. Queen Lariel misses her Hand."

"I did more talking for her than fighting."

"Even so." He stood. "Come with me one more time."

Hope surged through Sevryn as he got to his feet eagerly, more than ready to follow the old one again into the terraced garden of his herbs for both healing and killing. He trotted down familiar paths, noting the herbs about ready to be picked, the flowers of some just beginning to bud, knowing them with a familiarity he had not had before.

They continued past the lake, into a ground he had not yet seen. A thorny growth covered a small patch; the herbalist stopped at the edge of it. Very tiny blue flowers peeked out of velvety leaves, protected by a fine layer of thistle-like undergrowth, and the stems wound up, about and around with long, wicked thorns to finish the guardianship.

"This is the king's bed."

Sevryn shifted his weight. Thoughts sifted through him. A final trial? Was this the "king of assassins" they had urged him to find? Would he be required to survive whatever test the plant held for him? His mouth dried. Whatever skills he had in fighting would not help him now. He thought of all he'd learned the past days from this Kobrir and wondered if there was anything that could serve as an antidote to the king's bed.

The Kobrir seemed to be waiting for his response.

"Why name it that?"

A twitch of a smile behind the veil. "Because it puts every king down to rest. That rest has all the appearances of death, but it is not, not for many, many weeks when the body finally wears down because it cannot wake."

"A coma."

"Rather like that, yes. I am told that the subject is fully

awake and aware while in its grip but unable to respond."
The man cut his hand through the air. "I would not like to
go like that."

"Nor I. Which part of it do you use?"

"The buds only. Squeezed for the juices. Put upon the tip
of a dagger. Jabbed into the muscle tissue. Hit the heart or
lungs and there is no recovery. Muscle tissue and the subject
succumbs to the rest. Oddly enough, the body will heal itself
of all but the turpitude if tended diligently. Once the antidote is given, the subject recovers, often healthier than before."

Sevryn frowned, not sure if he quite understood. "If
other blows have been struck, they still heal?"

"Yes."

Sevryn took that in. A strike near the heart or lungs
would be invaluable. "And you show me this why?"

"We are giving you a vial. Prepare your weapons when
you know you're closing in. When you meet our king, you
must strike. You must bring him to the rest. That will deliver
him to us, and from there, he is ours."

"He doesn't want to be king of the assassins?"

"I am certain he does."

"But you don't want him to be."

"Perhaps. Such things are not easy to know, are they?
Perhaps we are in need of his counsel, and that has not been
forthcoming. Perhaps we fear he attempts too much and
must be slowed before we are all lost. Perhaps we are jeal-
ous. Perhaps we are tired. Perhaps we are about to be led by
another with more potential. Who knows."

"If you do not, I certainly can't begin to." Sevryn gave
him a slight bow. "The antidote?"

"A maiden. All kings respond to maidens who bow before him, do they not? But that is for us to give."

"I understand." He didn't, quite, know what that last bit
meant but it wasn't his problem, as they said. "Tomorrow,
then."

"Yes. First light."

"And to where do you send me?"

"To the battleground, one of yours, not ours," the old Kobrir said. He made a motion.

Out of the thorny shadows stepped the woman fighter he'd cut so badly. She did not wear a veil over her face, and the neck of her shirt also lay open, to allow the air to reach the wound and finish the remarkable healing that had already taken place. Both surprised him, the woman and the healing. She held clothing over her arm. "I am to dress you."

The herbalist gave a stiff bow and backed away. "I leave you for the moment. When I return, I carry the vials of the king's rest."

She did not move closer until the older master had gone. Sevryn turned to her with curiosity. "Why you?"

"Why not me?"

He wondered if she held a dagger under the clothing, one last challenge to meet, but she laid each piece across the ground and folding her legs, went to her knees, and waited for him to disrobe. Sevryn did so, also wondering why these clothes were any different than the ones he'd been given earlier, but as she held out each piece, he could see their weaving was finer, tougher, and darker but in shadows of gray, not like the blacks they wore. The bottom half was no problem, but she watched him critically as he began to pull on the shirt, which wrapped about and cross-tied. "No," she corrected and put her hand out.

She changed the fold and sat back again.

"What is your name?"

The Kobrir's gaze flecked up to his face and back down to his chest. "Why?"

"I've met dozens of you in the ring, but not one has given me a name." Sevryn was not convinced that he had met more than a few handful, over and over, with different battle tactic specialties, but he had no intention of letting the Kobrir know he thought their population as thin as he did.

"Perhaps it is not our wish to do so. We may meet again, on the street, in the shadows, or on contract. Is it easier to kill someone whose name you know? I do not believe so."

"It's all a business to you anyway. Traders call one another by name."

The side of her mouth he had not cut twitched slightly. "So if we trade blows, we should know each other? Very well. I am Bretta."

"Thank you. And you all seem to know my name, but I am Sevryn."

"Indeed we know you. You are the man who will find our king."

"And what do you think about that?"

Something flashed deep in her eyes. "He must be found. He made us. He led us here. He put us to work. He told us there would be an end to our road, but we've never reached it. He has lied to us. There must be an accounting."

"So this will not be a happy reunion."

Bretta got to her feet smoothly. "Let us hope it will be a just one." She held up the hood and veil. "You are almost dressed. You'll come back to the fire, eat and sleep, and a guide will be given to you."

And almost completely informed, although he knew there were some vital answers lying in wait for him, like an assassin in ambush. Uncertain as the future was, he welcomed it. Any step on that road would carry him back to his heart.

Rivergrace

"Now braid the strands tightly," Narskap told her.

"I know, I know," she said, and shuddered as she could feel Cerat gnawing at her, at the leads she was giving him, even that tiniest portion of the Souldrinking God, readying to go into the man whose heart and soul strings she held, the soldier that Quendius had near killed for them, to make into one of his Undead. It was not the first time today she was doing her weaving for Narskap, nor would it be the last; with each one, she felt more loathsome. She could not return from this. Could never explain it or expect an understanding of it from Sevryn or Nutmeg, let alone hope for redemption. No one but Narskap could even come close to understanding, and he simply did not care, having lost that ability.

"This is vile."

"He will most certainly die if you stop. At least he'll have some sort of existence under Cerat's reign."

"How can that be good enough?"

"Almost everyone dying will tell you that any semblance of life is good enough. Otherwise it's a dark edge we slip over." His hands cupped hers. "This way and that."

"I know."

"Then do it."

"It fights me."

"You fight it."

Rivergrace tossed her head a bit to get a stray bit of hair from the corner of her eye. "I hate this."

"I know. But it will be vitally important later."

"Why?"

Narskap became very still. He rarely breathed except to talk and she'd gotten used to the eerie stillness behind her unless he was talking, but now he let out a brief sigh. "Trust me only in that it will."

Trust in this man, this being, was not easily come by, and he knew that well, so she did not respond. She fumbled the pattern once, and his rough hands moved quickly over hers, smoothing it out.

"How clearly can you see these threads?" he asked her.

"The gold is life. Very distinct. It's more than gold, really, but it has a fullness to it—I can't quite explain. If I were weaving, it would be like the difference between a thread and a yarn."

"But I know what you are saying. And the black thread is death."

"It's not black."

"Is it not?" Narskap's expression, like granite, rarely changed, but she thought she saw a crack.

"No." Rivergrace shook her head slightly. "Black is a color. This is an absence of color and warmth. It is a denial of all the gold thread holds. It is like the opposite of existence."

"But you can see it? This absence?"

"I've been doing this with you for days. Of course I can see it, or I couldn't be working with it, but I can't describe it, except that it's anathema. It's loathsome." She wanted to worry her fingers together at the thought but could not, not as long as she held this man's threads. This dying man was bargaining with all he was worth to keep on living, somehow.

"You are fire and ice. And this is nothingness."

"Yes. I think you can describe it like that." She paused as the man before them staggered to one knee. She frowned, twitched her wrists, and then tied the braid off.

"Are you done?"

"He either stands and exists or falls and dies. I can tell which I think would be better for him—for any of them— but you don't wish to hear it. You know it yourself." She broke away from the bare embrace Narskap held her in, and finally chafed her arms as if cold or so she could shrug off the indescribable feeling that crept up her fingers. She did not look back as the man gave a grunt and clambered up to his feet. He swayed as unsteadily as a newborn foal.

Narskap shouted, "Get him to blood, or we'll lose him yet." He followed after Rivergrace's footsteps as she walked away, not wanting to see the thing eating.

She sat down as far from the camp as Quendius had made clear she could go, mopping her forehead with the back of her sleeve. She felt sweaty and dusty, but that was dirt she could wash away. The stain of what she had just done, and had been doing, sank below her skin. To her very bones. She could hear a cheer behind them. They had made another Undead. Most of the troop they rode with now consisted of Undead, the ones who'd survived Quendius' and their meddling. She wanted to shrink at the sight of them, but she feared to show them any emotion, any weakness, any frailty.

She'd been taken hostage so that Narskap would do the bidding of Quendius, but now that he'd drawn her in, made her his apprentice, his partner, she doubted that she'd ever be freed. She was as much a prisoner to her father as to the other. She was as valuable now to Quendius and his plans as Narskap was, and the Gods knew that the hound was never free of his leash.

Rivergrace looked at the ground below her feet. Even if she escaped, where would she go? Who would have her now, tainted with the stink of the Undead? How could she ever face Sevryn or Nutmeg and let them see what she had done, what she could do, what she had become? She had bent a little each day to stay alive a little longer until she had come to this. Had it been worth it? She didn't know. She couldn't know until Narskap did what he had promised, what he had held for her, to end Quendius. Even then, she wondered if it would be worth it. The death of Quendius would not roll back the days to when she was innocent of manipulating life and death.

She put the base of her hands to her temples and held her head. The spring season called her, the dew forming on the early evening grasses and leaves, the promise of a shower upon the land only a day or two away. She could dissolve into a mist again and this time not come back. Scatter herself to the land so that it might live and her stain be gone . . .

"There is a purpose," Narskap said. "For which you must live. Even if you don't understand it now, you will." As if he could read her thoughts. Perhaps he could.

"Empty words."

"No. A promise. What I do, I had planned to do alone, but I can't. It will take the two of us to bring Quendius down."

"And yet you keep making him stronger."

"Perhaps."

She turned to look at her father. At the stranger,

Narskap. She had learned long ago that she could not really reconcile the two men, but Narskap survived because he was the stronger. And within that strength, he held tightly to the remains of himself as husband and father, sheltered closely, so that virtually no one but herself could see the difference. But she did. For a moment, she felt a surge of hope.

He lifted a finger. "Not even in our thoughts."

He stood and left her alone then, wondering how she could trust him. Then she scrubbed her face with her hands.

No hope. Quendius would sniff it out and quash it. That is what the hound of the weaponmaster meant.

Show no hope.

But deep inside, Rivergrace cupped it close, like a golden thread of life.

Chapter
Fifty-One

LARIEL STARED across the room. "What word of Sevryn Dardanon and Rivergrace Farbranch?"

Farlen thumped his substantial body down on the edge of Lariel's desk. "None. Nothing has been seen of either." He watched as she eased herself onto her chair, tilting her face away from him, not wishing him to see what the mirror showed her every morning: dark circles under her eyes and new fine lines creasing the corners of them. "Our inquiries have been discreet but fruitless." He wiped absently at a gravy stain on his shirtsleeve.

"Nothing."

"It doesn't mean they aren't out there, although with Rivergrace . . ." He shrugged. "She commands her element of water too well. She could be the sacred River Andredia for all we know."

"I doubt that. And, if she were, I would know it."

"She turned to mist and disappeared."

Lariel stared at him. "She used the cover of mist to hide her escape. Nothing more. Don't attribute qualities to her she doesn't possess. She wasn't raised as one of us nor trained as one."

"Agreed," although the sharp line between Farlen's heavy brows did the opposite. "As for Sevryn, we know he can be as elusive as he wishes to be."

"He must be found." She rapped her nails in irritation and then laid her hands flat for a fleeting moment. The scar at the base of her missing finger had begun to lose the coloration of newness. She considered it.

Farlen scratched his scalp for a moment, vigorously, before asking, "What did Tranta have for you?"

"Good news, after all this. The Jewel's Way remains. Although broken in pieces, it still holds guardianship. He's made lampposts of the fragments, and we'll use them at the harbors and coastal cities."

He sounded dubious. "They work? Will they still flare out and burn invaders?"

She touched the gold-and-ruby pectoral at her throat. "They work exceedingly well." She smiled faintly at Farlen. "Your two Houses did a mighty working with that Shield."

"Not likely to ever be duplicated. It's good the Way wasn't shattered as well although I will say from what I know of it, all we did was find the gem. It's the Istlanthir who worked it." His eyes scanned her waist. "He made the girdle as well? Like the collar?"

"Yes. The posts that Tranta has fashioned work differently. They have the same cradle the great Jewel had, so they retain an independent movement, side to side, up and down . . . it's quite remarkable to see them at work. The Jewels maneuver the cradle. At first I thought it might be a random movement, like the wind, but no. There is a sentience there, Farlen. The Istlanthir often talked about it as though it were alive, but I never quite believed it until I saw it. Tranta has managed to preserve it, through sheer determination. We tested it." Lara's voice faltered then, and she cleared her throat lightly. "His adaptations work devastatingly well." She shook her head in slight disbelief. "Will it save us? Not from a massive invasion, but then the original Jewel couldn't have either, until it was massed at Hawthorne, and although it's a natural harbor with easy shores to approach, we would be foolish to think that's the only point to invade. We've a long coast." She inhaled tightly. "As for invasions, have we any more reports of Raymy movement?"

"Two more drops." He hesitated in that deliberate, Drebukar way of his, so like Osten it made her heart sorrow for a moment at the death of her old friend. "Like the contagion in Calcort, they seem plague-ridden. It gives them no quarter, they fight as ferociously as ever, but now we've carcasses we must treat carefully, as well as wounded."

"Anyone contaminated yet?"

"A handful." He looked at her steadily. "No one survived."

"No one?"

"They were already wounded from the fighting, so perhaps . . ." he shrugged, his leather shoulder pads creaking. "I would hate to hazard a guess at how destructive the illness can be."

"Plague." Lariel's hands went into rapid motion again, reaching for a pen and the small message sheets for the birds. "We need to apprise all the healers we can reach, Hawthorne, Calcort, as far north as we dare send. Have the traders send word to their east-going caravans as well. Although I doubt the Raymy will hit there, it could still be carried."

"Abayan Diort?"

"By all means, if you can reach him, give him word as well. I had hoped the quarantine at Calcort was an aberration, but we cannot believe that now. Bistane is how close to Ashenbrook? I have to make plans to pull out and meet him there."

Before Farlen could answer, the windows of the manor darkened and began to shake. The wooden frames creaked and spoke to one another, and the plaster holding the glass panes within them began to crack and powder and the glass

itself rattled. Thunder began rolling through the valley of
Larandaril, vibrating the very stones of her home as it
KER-acked repeatedly. Clouds rushed in overhead, dark
and crowding, boiling together and shredding apart noisily.
It grew in tenor and strength, rolling into booms and shouts
of fury. The stones echoed it, shuddering, and great crackling noises rent the manor. The walls did not split but
sounded in low, deep tones. The flooring boomed below as
if it were a giant drum being struck over and over. Lariel
pitched to her feet and ran to the nearest window. Black
skies where only a blue and clouded sky had reigned just
moments before. She threw the window open, the wind
tearing the frame from her hand and throwing it back with
a crash. Farlen moved as if he could protect her, from what
neither of them could guess.

She smelled the sea come storming in. Salt and brine
filled her senses and stung her eyes like spray off coastal
rocks.

The clouds opened and poured, in buckets. The air
turned the color of iron from the rain and the forests, barns,
and pastures could not be seen through it. It rattled over the
manor like a hailstorm except there were no icy bits bouncing about, just fat, heavy raindrops. She put her hand out
and the fierceness of the rain stung her skin to a bright pink
immediately. Then, as abruptly as it had come in, the rain
shut off, water funneling everywhere, across the ground and
the stone courtyard, the manor house in a wet sheen, her
face damp with it. The last of the rolling thunder bled away,
taking the water with it, and the noise, but not the black of
the sky.

She licked her lips. Tasted her fingertips.

Salt. Her senses had not failed her.

"What does it mean?"

Lariel shook her head, Farlen looming at her back. "I
don't know."

Farlen cleared his throat. "You asked of Lord Bistane,"
he offered, trying to return to a norm. "We only know he's
en route."

Lariel stayed at the window, watching the dark clouds peel away from the capricious spring sky in shreds, going, going, gone. "Good," she answered quietly. "Everyone is gone that I dare send. We need to follow."

"We can move whenever you order."

She closed the window shutter and latched it firmly, pressing her fingers tightly against the wood so that Farlen could not see the tremor she felt in them. Lara's mouth felt too dry to speak easily. She moved inexorably but blindly toward that moment of betrayal she had foreseen. Had she seen truly? Did she prepare to march toward her own death? She took a deep breath. She still had time. She had the Jewels about her throat and waist. She could prevail.

"Good." She added, "See if the water below is salted."

Farlen quirked an eyebrow at her as he got to his feet and went to do as she asked. Fairly certain he would return with a positive response, she pondered what it meant. Sea spouts sometimes came in with sudden storms. Fish had been dropped a league or two in from the shore, as if snatched up in an unearthly net. It wasn't unheard of. But not as far inland as Larandaril.

Except they hadn't had a storm, not really, just that momentary buffeting which had come from out of nowhere. A storm that had, literally, just dropped out of the sky. Lara looked back to the window. "What are you bringing us, Daravan?" she murmured. "And most importantly, when?" It must be soon, she answered herself. Very, if unpredictably, soon.

Chapter
Fifty-Two

VERDAYNE DIDN'T STIR as Nutmeg entered the great barn and cider mill where he and Tolby had laid out the work they had planned to do, but Tolby dropped a shoulder to look about at her. "Put a scarf over your face," he instructed. "I'll not have you breathing in fumes or mold whilst I'm working."

Lily had draped a wrap over her shoulders when she'd left the farmhouse, undoubtedly guessing where she headed, and so Nutmeg wrapped it lightly over her nose and mouth despite the heat which had gathered in the barn during the day. She saw that Tolby had had glass covers made, great spherical lids, to place over each book. Both men peered back down at them as she joined them.

"This one," Tolby said, and tapped the lid. It rang faintly. "Far too gone for us to save, but it responds to the spray nonetheless."

Nutmeg leaned close. "What do you mean?" Her father hadn't been talking to her, but she had no intention of being left out of the conversation, since walking and talking was about all the exercise left to her now. And thinking. The two

Vaelinar guards, dark-haired Hiela with faintly copper-toned skin that reminded Nutmeg of the shifty Tiiva and silver-haired Unar with sooty-skin that reminded her of the weaponmaster Quendius, took up places just outside the barn and proceeded to play an obscure Vaelinar game that had something to do with the palms of their hands and the backs of them, and manipulating a hide-bound ball no bigger than their thumbs back and forth. She supposed it had something to do with keeping them dexterous although she'd never seen Sevryn play it, and he had the quickest hands of any she'd ever seen, even Jeredon. It kept the guards occupied, which meant they probably weren't listening very much, if at all. "The book has stopped falling apart?"

"Indeed. But we can't regenerate it."

"Makes sense." She frowned at Verdayne. "Can't make something out of nothing."

"Well . . . not in this case, at any rate."

She looked at it, knowing she could read it if she brought her power up, but not wanting to, in case either of them would notice. "Was it something important?"

"*Books of All Truth* are all considered important."

"I know that but, Important. Even amongst the likes of those."

Verdayne looked at her. "We cannot lie when we write them, or the library won't accept them. It is a compact, a vow, made to the library. It was done so that we might have the truth at hand when we needed it, regardless of how it reflected on the writer of that journal or the other participants in that history."

She gave an impatient huff. "That, I know. Everyone knows." She shifted weight. Her ankles had swollen and she felt clumsy, but her mind worked. Or it was supposed to! "They can only write the truth as they know it. That doesn't always mean absolute truth."

"And that's the thorn of it, isn't it? When the time comes, it's hoped that scholars can overlay the many books and find a righteous perspective. But what's within here is as close to truth as can be hoped." Dayne smiled tentatively at her.

She didn't know what made her cross at him, sometimes. Sometimes all she wanted was a kind word from him. Nutmeg crossed her arms over her stomach and decided to stay silent.

Tolby, ignoring them, raised the second lid and carefully, with a sprayer like the ones he used on his precious orchards and vineyards, misted a bit of fluid onto the waiting book. He lowered the lid quickly.

"So . . . what are the scholars waiting for?"

"Waiting for what?" Verdayne had looked down to see what Tolby was doing, and his attention snapped back up.

"You keep saying, when the time comes. What time will that be?"

"I'm no scholar. I suppose it's when they think things are dire and cannot get any worse."

Nutmeg moved to stand by her father. "That's no fun."

"Fun?"

"Fun. There must be all sorts of information you could use now. Helpful facts. Explanations."

The corner of Verdayne's mouth quirked. It made the line of his strong jaw even more definitive. She watched it. "Scholars are of the opinion that when the *Books of All Truth* are so consulted, their mission will be fulfilled and they will fall to ash."

"Rotten apples! They disappear?"

"So it is thought. Any look at them would have to be quick and thorough before they're lost forever."

She folded her arms. "Ridiculous. They're disappearing now."

"Because they're diseased."

"Or," and she lifted an index finger, "because other Ways are failing, too."

Verdayne closed on the two of them and lowered his voice, despite the fact that the two guards at the door were chatting (or perhaps chanting, Nutmeg couldn't quite be sure) and involved in their game. "We only know of a few. It could be aberrations."

"Perhaps," Nutmeg told him, "but I've been about Larandaril and there's rumors."

Tolby put his hand on hers. "There are always rumors, Meg. That doesna mean you can go about repeating them."

"These are true rumors." She pointed at Verdayne.

He shook his head. "Never. I don't know what you've heard, so I can't verify that. I know what I've seen myself, and those are not rumors. The aryns are failing. Not all, and not many—yet. But this same mold which corrupts the books is very similar to what eats away at the borders of our groves. Yet it might not be the failing of a Way. The debris from the wars of the Mageborn is dangerous and not studied because of it. We could be facing something none of us has yet identified."

She shoved her unruly bangs from her face. "Word pinching."

"Word . . . what?"

"Like a baker shoving and pulling at dough about to make a pie crust out of it, you're pinching at words." She paused as the baby put out a hand or foot and shoved it quite hard into her rib cage, making her catch her breath a bit.

"I do not pinch at words."

"Then why, for the sake of all that grows green, can't you say magic going bad is bad magic?"

His mouth thinned before her answered. "Because it's not that simple."

"Nothing is except for you, perhaps!"

"Nutmeg! Lord Verdayne is our guest here and you've no cause for that."

She stepped back, her face warming at Tolby's reprimand. She looked down. Swollen ankles, tight sandals, dirty barn floor. "My regrets, *Lord Verdayne*."

"Accepted, although I admit you have a point. Of sorts."

"Of sorts?" Her voice rose.

"There is bad magic and there is magic which has failed. If—or when—it fails, it simply dissipates. It doesn't turn into a morass of chaos and toxin."

"Like that?" Nutmeg pointed at the near-destroyed book.

His jaw worked. "Ah."

Tolby took her hand and pointed it at the bell in the center. "On the other hand, sometimes mold is merely mold." He looked down at his handiwork and smiled.

The newly misted book looked near pristine at the page where it lay open, with only a slight rust stain where black mold had been festering but moments before and even that disappearing. Verdayne leaned in. "Very effective, Master Tolby!"

"With little damage to the ink or binding."

"So it seems! We'll have to treat it page by page."

"I think that's wisest. And dry between each application. We don't want to warp it, nor do we want to give the mold a chance t'come back." Tolby scratched the back of his head. "I've enough on hand to do the job here, but we'll have to tincture far more for Ferstanthe."

"Will there be any trouble transporting it? How virulent is it?"

"Stoppered kegs should be good enough. I might have a bit of trouble rounding up all the herbs I need—once I start buying, the price will shoot up. Demand and all bein' what it is."

"We can afford it," Verdayne told him firmly. "Perhaps you should make the solution at the library itself. I can send to Azel to gather the quantities."

Tolby shook his head. "I won't be leaving my stead here at this time of year, but I could send Keldan. The lad has a good head." He looked past Verdayne to Nutmeg. "I'd send you, lass, but I think the journey would be difficult on you, and your mother would never forgive me for putting distance between her and that baby. She'd have my head."

"On a stick," agreed Nutmeg. She leaned over the first bell-shaped lid. "Was this treated already?"

"With an earlier potion. We thought to strengthen it a bit."

She nodded. "Good. Because the mold is coming back here, ever so slightly, on the edge."

Tolby bent over. He swore. "There's the fly in our success."

"No, no, that could be expected with the weaker application. Reapply, let it dry, and we'll check it in the morning." Verdayne lifted the cover.

Nutmeg took it from his hands. "Men," she said. "Treating the book and not the dish." She showed him the inside lip of the glass bell. "Spray everything. It contaminated itself again."

Tolby peered down his nose. "She's right. There's mold on the glass. Not much, but it doesna take much."

"We'll have to put scalding water over the lids after you spray the books. Then dry them." She set the lid aside. "Would not hurt to scour the table as well. Any decent cook could have told you both that."

Dayne gave her a slight bow. "Your sharp eyes saved us a bit of work on that. We might have been set back days."

"Aye," her father said and hugged her about the shoulders. "Now I suggest you get inside and put your feet up for a while, or Lily will have my head on a stick anyway."

"Going, going," Nutmeg said reluctantly. "But only to save you."

She left the barn, dropping the scarf from her face gratefully, the cooler air pleasant on her face. Her two guards abruptly left their game and fell into place, one at her flank and the other at her heels. They left her, reluctantly, when she closed her bedroom door.

Nutmeg bent over as far as she could comfortably to stare at the shadows under her bedstead. Then, carefully, she lowered herself to her knees and scuttled under as far as she could until she found Bistel's journal and fetched it out. Getting up took a moment or two, and left her huffing a bit for breath, the worn leather book firmly in her hands. When she sat in her corner chair, she opened it, sunlight coming through her window in slats, patterned by the half-opened shutter.

She could read it now, without strain or worry, and opened it to a page at random. Bistel's careful penmanship filled her vision. "My aryns," it read, "both define and deny all that I have written heretofore about Ways. Firstly, it involved an item that was living. An item that was not native to Kerith. And, for all that I was the one who planted it and willed it to grow, I had not made preparations to create a Way nor did I generate incredible amounts of power and Talent to induce it to do so. That a greenstick staff would grow—that in itself was somewhat remarkable, although the staff had developed tiny buds suggesting that it wished to grow—that it would grow if only given a chance—and I could feel the intense need and longing within the staff to do so. I planted it with a tremendous surge of hope within myself that it would succeed at its goal, fulfilling both our longing, myself and the staff's.

"That it grew, and its seeds grew, and its saplings flourished, and that they became a barrier against the corrupted energies left by the Mageborn Wars, astonished no one more than I. And yet, the phenomenon pleased no one more than I. The aryn tree grows to be a majestic, logging-worthy tree, with immense benefits while it grows and flourishes. It resists insects and fire. It increases the watershed capability of any plain on which it is introduced. Its bark can be eaten by forest animals in times of famine, and the tree survives. Its canopy does not starve the forest so that other saplings can flourish. Its boughs are fragrant, I'm told its needles make an excellent herbal tea with healing properties, if steeped properly, and when it drops a limb and goes to the lumber mill, the wood is hard, well-grained, and faintly aromatic.

"All of that takes a back seat to what has become its primary purpose, which is to absorb and filter the chaotic evils of magic dregs left behind by decades of war long before we came to tread these lands. The aryns do not do this overnight; it has taken decades, even a few centuries, to cleanse the soils and borders they guard. Their presence is valuable and desired. Thus it bothers me that they now seem to be under attack, from a pernicious mold, which is not accidentally introduced nor exists naturally. I believe this same mold is a variant of the one introduced to the library of Ferstanthe.

While I cannot with any certainty point out the perpetrator, I have narrowed it down to a few possibilities: a Master and his apprentice. It is a crime of more than opportunity, it is aimed at the very hearts of the Vaelinar."

Nutmeg closed the book on her finger. So Bistel had known of the library's problems even before Azel d'Ferstanthe had. She wondered how he'd given notice to the big, burly librarian before the battle that was to take his life. She knew he had, he must have, but even so he did not trust the library enough to leave this book there.

Perhaps the mold had even been spread to destroy this book, if he'd left it behind. She frowned.

Yet another reason not to reveal its existence, even with Verdayne here and being so . . . appealing. Strong, perceptive, and appealing.

Nutmeg sighed. The baby moved sluggishly inside her, as if stretching a bit and finding little room to do so. Her skin ached. She stood and put the book back in its hiding place, manipulating the wood boards carefully so they would not creak and then found her skin cream. A light rub and perhaps a nap before she started dinner. That sounded like something she could handle, in place of Vaelinar mysteries and destinies. She put her head down, wondering what Rivergrace would make of Verdayne.

Chapter
Fifty-Three

RIVERGRACE DISMOUNTED at the edge of a tiny freshet and drank first, despite the horse's impatiently yanking at its reins, for he would muddy the waters if she let him drink first. Only a moment or two after she gulped down what she could, he nudged her aside with his thick, heavy head, chomping at his bit, and took her place.

She stepped back after tying the reins loosely to the saddle, giving the beast enough room to drop his head for grazing as well, and walked back to a knoll and sat wearily. Her legs ached, her clothes felt as if they could walk away without her in them, and her thoughts were not her own. Not really, not anymore. She could feel the tiny fibrous tethers of the others tied to herself, her making of them. They drank at the brook's edge as well, slurping through mouths that sounded as if they must be numb, but she could feel the real thirst that drove them—blood.

Grace closed her eyes. Quendius would let them beat the meadow for whatever they could scare up and devour. Mice, hares, even the disgusting stinkdog made prey for the Undead. They would cut off limber tree switches and walk through the growth, scaring up whatever they could and then pounce on it, devouring squealing bodies alive. She opened her eyes, knowing herself not to be safe if she did not keep watch, not even with her father about. Did their desire for blood influence him? It had to. She held no confirmation of it, but she knew it had to, if she as a living being felt the palpable hunger. She wouldn't watch it and wished she could not hear the hunt.

Quendius walked past her without a glance. He moved to each of the Undead in his charge now, nearly twenty, for he had picked up a patrol or two and no one escaped his sword now. Each man stopped as he approached them. Then he did something Grace had never seen him do, and she felt it to the very core of her being.

He put his palm on the chest of each of his men. When he moved away, he carried a bit of their thread with him, a thread torn from Grace and from Narskap, for she saw him stagger and go to one knee, his face even more pale than his Undead state normally colored it. She felt a twisting ache inside of her but kept herself steady and her face neutral. She could not let him know he affected her somehow. Quendius raised his face to the sky and grunted faintly each time, as if he felt the impact of what he was doing. When he had finished, he swung about and eyed Narskap.

"You've done good work for me." He pressed the heel of his hand to his own chest. "Cerat holds them for me, as you promised. It stands for me to gather more and have an army no one can face. The Demon smells a war brewing. All I must do is let them fight themselves, and reap the dead." He looked briefly at Rivergrace before turning and walking upriver to find clean water of his own.

Narskap searched wildly until he met her gaze and they stared at one another. Dread gathered in her bones and sent a chill arching through her as she realized whatever Quendius had done had shocked Narskap. Fear shivered deep inside of her at the look on his face as he ducked away from her quickly. It did not stop when a flock of silverwings streaked the sky overhead and circled about her before winging off.

She knew the birds well. They were wont to follow her whenever she traveled their territory, often thought to be favored by the Goddess of the Silverwing River. She'd always considered them lucky.

Grace turned about. She had not, she realized, been paying much attention to their travels, thinking they had continued to move north and east toward the badlands, which hid the fortress Quendius called home. But silverwings did not range so far north or east.

No. Quendius had slowly circled them. They were headed south and were far closer than she realized, not far from the Silverwing River and the sacred Andredia.

She forgot to breathe for a moment. Would it bring her back toward Sevryn, or would she be lost forever?

Quendius lifted his hand and turned, tugging on all of them invisibly. "We have a war to scavenge. Every being that falls will become a brother of ours! We ride and we ride hard."

The Undead let out a grunting cheer.

Chapter Fifty-Four

Sevryn

SEVRYN SLEPT as he'd trained himself to do, dropped into a light doze that would refresh him but not cloud his awareness of what happened around him. When the Kobrir sleeping around him had dropped into that trough that the dead of night often brings, he rose and made his way to the latrines as quietly as he could but not so quietly that it seemed he wanted to avoid detection. To be too quiet would betray that it was silence and sneaking that he sought, bringing attention he did not wish. To be too loud would be just as problematic.

Once in the relative solitude of the jakes, he undressed quickly, stripping down and repositioning each of his weapons in a different, more expedient location, including the ithrel. Bretta's sharp eyes had caught the placement of each and every one as he'd dressed before, and he'd no doubt that she had noted the positioning carefully and reported it. He'd taught himself years ago to position his weapons where they would likely not be spotted, and thus when he reached to draw one, he would not be noticed. Surprise was as much an element of his success as ability. His training now gave him even more of an edge and he wouldn't relinquish that because Bretta had watched him arm and dress. Why? Because they told him he had graduated and he knew full well they had not given him a final exam.

When he returned to his sleeping spot, at least two nearby Kobrir stirred and turned, noting his activity even if they did not react openly to it, and he curled into his blanket, his wariness ever sharper. The morning would bring the answers he sought—and more questions, he was certain, he'd overlooked asking.

He woke just before what he knew to be dawn. He could feel the bare warmth of the sun just touching the bones of this desert, and its glow ate across the sands and up into the rock. The rustle of moving bodies, combined with the sharp tang of fires, stirred in the morning breeze. The pungent aroma of spices being tossed directly onto the firewood as well as into the cooking pots sizzled into the air as he stretched and moved toward the cooks. He searched, as he always did, within himself for signs of Rivergrace. He ached for the barest touch of her, at the thought of stroking the curve of her throat, of untangling her hair from her temple, of feeling her lips swell beneath his. What would she think of him now, what the Kobrir had made of him, finishing the job that Gilgarran had begun and Quendius had, unwittingly, contributed to, as well? Would she accept him as she always had? Would she understand that what he had done and would do, would be for her? She would not, he thought, as gentle as her soul was, but she might listen to him long enough to explain . . . once he found her. And he would find her as soon as he won his freedom here and took care of the obstacles that threatened her.

They parted for him as he strode near. They stared without staring, their gazes darting away as soon as they had been noticed, tugging their veils into place in case they had revealed something unseemly. As he walked through, he noted at least eight fighters missing.

Eight, then. Or more. If he had been one of them, he would not have tipped his hand as to how many able-bodied fighters he had. He didn't expect they had either. They had always had his fear, but now they had earned his respect. He still did not know what they were as a people ... they had a sinuous quality to their movement as if they might have joints he did not, and bent in ways he could not ... and they had not dropped the veil of secrecy from their lives despite his living in the midst of them. Not much of it, at any rate. He knew a little more than he had and, as far as he could tell, he knew as much of them as anyone alive on Kerith today.

And that, too, made him cautious about stepping away from them. There would be those who would argue he was not worthy, he would never be worthy. There would be a few who merely regarded him as a contract to be collected upon, and he knew that Lariel had most likely put a price on his head. It would have been done discreetly, but he had little doubt. It was probably what he would have done in her position, barring taking care of the problem himself. She could not: she had to keep her hands relatively clean and direct a defensive war against an enemy who would not give her advance warning. But he would have trusted her, despite the seeming betrayal, because they had years between them of loyal service and friendship. *He would have trusted her until proven otherwise.*

The last of the Kobrir parted before him and he saw that they had led him to a massive cavern arena he'd never seen. It had little ceiling left, the elements having broken through ages ago, and sun and shade striped the area brightly, the sharp rock walls sending spear-like projections against that backdrop. He halted, heard the murmur of voices drop to nothing behind him, and did not turn. One voice instructed him: Find your guide. He sidestepped into a shadow and loosed his Voice, telling the rock and sand and shale to accept him, and melded into their presence.

Still as stone. Dark as shade. He balanced on the soft soles of his shoes, his senses so alive that he could nearly feel every grain of sand and rock beneath him. He inhaled as quietly as he knew how, sussing the air long and slow and deep inside his lungs. When he moved, he did so as a splinter of darkness, another step, then two, sidelong to pause again, his eyes growing in his ability to see in the dark, knowing that as he adjusted, so did his opponents. They would not see him, however, not as long as the shadows held him close as a brother.

In that closeness, he found his first opponent and took him out, quietly, silently, with no more sound than an outward gust of breath from the fallen Kobrir. In other circumstances, Sevryn would have left him dead. This time he left him unconscious and curled on his side. He moved away from the fallen quickly before being revealed.

Stone fingers pointed his way to another assassin. Sevryn used one hand and the crook of his elbow this time disliking the noise of the first conquest. When the man fell limp in his hold, he left him propped against the cavern wall where he'd found him and none the wiser that he did not just simply remain lying in wait for Sevryn to pass.

Three, four and five were nearly as easy. Five almost broke his cover, thrashing one leg out as he fell into unconsciousness, but Sevryn flicked his shadowy coverage about them and the movement was swallowed up hungrily. He saw then his objective, a hunched-over being at the far end of the cavern's progress, his head in a burlap bag and his voice mumbling in a low-pitched monologue which might or might not contain sanity. His guide.

Sevryn watched the wretched being for a moment, wondering if the ordeal would be worth it. As he sidled through another spear-like patch of darkness, he suddenly realized that he had left himself wide open and flung his head back, looking up—even as Bretta plunged down at him.

He had only a flash of her face, her dive tearing her veil free as she leaped upon him, and then they were hand-to-hand and she fighting as though her life depended upon it. She curled her hand upon his neck, clawing deep and brought him down into the dirt with her. Her scar turned livid as he used her weight to anchor his twisting somersault back to his feet, and she scrambled up.

He balanced himself and watched her find her center, her lips curled back as though she were some great, feral beast he faced. His pact with stone and shadow faded away as the two of them stood exposed by the striped rays of sun slanting down on them, and he heard the murmurs of surprised Kobrir as he seemingly appeared out of nowhere. His attention locked on Bretta, her center of balance, and aware of her speed, rage-fueled this time. She slipped a little to her right. He mimicked her movement. Dust rose in the tiniest of clouds from their feet. He listened, not to their breathing or their steps, but to minor sounds in the background. Sounds of stealth, if he could catch any, for certainly there were still Kobrir he had to pass once he got through Bretta. They would not rush him yet, giving Bretta her chance to best him.

She palmed a dagger, a small one with a jagged edge, unfamiliar to him, but Sevryn knew it would slice wickedly and painfully. He disarmed her and took the time—and taking a blow just off a kidney—to toss it far across the arena where she could not easily retrieve it. As he took three deep, grunting breaths to shrug off the pain of her hit, he reflected that she'd probably meant the dagger as a loss, getting in a blow that could have doubled him over in pain. She'd missed her target but just barely, and pain radiated throughout the small of his back, agony that faded even as he shoved it aside to focus on her.

Bretta curled her fingers slightly and beckoned, a nearly imperceptible motion. She wanted him on the offensive. Sevryn danced a step back, refusing to step into her opening. Her lip curled in unspoken contempt. She lunged at him, both hands spread, and he parried her attack at her wrists, slipping one hand up and the other down—which was just what she wanted, as she grabbed his forearm with a grip of iron and his left hip with another claw-like hold.

But she didn't find the weapons she thought to find there. She blinked twice, the only surprise she showed, as he spun out of her hold and dropped back a step to bring up his ithrel, the weapon she thought she'd imprisoned along his flank. Her mouth closed tightly as he nodded to one side in sardonic apology and his calf felt bared now, with the weapon pulled away from his skin and out of his wrappings. The pupils of her eyes flared in surprise even as he struck, and she ducked away out of sheer instinct, the ithrel shaving the top of her right shoulder, parting the fabric of her shirt with the faintest of whispers and leaving a long, crimson line after it. He'd claimed first blood.

No time to note it, let alone celebrate, for she dropped to one knee and loosed throwing stars at him. One buried itself in his shin guard, and the other sliced past his ear with its signature air-splitting noise. He flicked the buried one back at her. Bretta batted it away with a backhand even as her glove parted, sliced open, and blood welled out.

Second blood. None of them so deep as to cause either of them any pain or even slow down their attack, for nothing even close to a bleeder had been hit, but he had to wonder. Wonder when she'd become so clumsy or was she, like a mother bird with a broken wing, decoying him into an action that would prove fatal to him?

She'd dropped down from above. Was she positioning him for another? Sevryn took four running steps to his left and vaulted onto a low boulder that hugged the arena's rock wall, scattering a knot of observers who darted off for safer climes as he swapped holds on his ithrel and looked up just long enough to target. He cocked his hand and threw, the ithrel tumbling end over end before *thudding* deeply into a long, dark shadow that perched out of place along the broken stone rim. The Kobrir dropped with a soft moan, to curl upon the sands.

Bretta let out a cry, a half-shriek torn from low in her throat, and rushed him.

He jumped as she did and they clashed in midair, hands and feet blurring as she attacked and he defended, landed and rolled under her kicks, to come up free and breathing hard. She lunged at him again, her fingers laced, her hands

in one fist. He scrambled under her assault and came up
with both hands to break her hold and got a kick in the
lower stomach for his effort and a second to his right knee.
His leg gave way, and Sevryn rolled as he went down. Red
pain lanced through his knee, but he wasn't hurt as badly as
she'd intended. He proved it by getting up on that leg and
bouncing to his feet. Her face creased in a frown, her scar
deepening into an ugly purple-red.

He took the fight to her, then, determined to close it before she forced him to hurt her as badly as he had the first
time they'd met with blows. She fought him as daringly as
she had in the past, and he reacted as his body had been
trained and retrained, with no time to think between blows
and parries, forcing her to be the first to step back and take
a deep breath. His knee sent lightning pains into his thigh
as he put his weight fully on it, but he did not react to it. He
could not let her know he had a weakness. Blood ran its way
down her hand to drip sullenly into the dirt, and she
shrugged her head to one side, easing a neck muscle.

He didn't follow the movement with his gaze as she'd
wanted him to. He'd seen her do it before, and this time
with her foot lashed out in a vicious arc aimed at his temple,
he ducked under it, her leg now thrown over his shoulder,
and dumped her onto her back. He twisted her over onto
her face and jumped with both knees to her kidneys, to a
choked squeal of pain. Vicious, low and necessary, for Bretta
had made it plan she would not stop at halting him in his
tracks. She intended to kill him. To defeat her, he'd half-
killed her.

Bretta let out a tiny whine as he crossed her arms behind
her back and used the blood-soaked rag of her sleeve to
bind her hands together. She kicked viciously at him as he
stood up, grazing the knee she'd damaged, but he danced
back to look down at her as she rolled to her back, glaring
up at him.

He turned on heel and resumed his walk to the waiting
guide who knelt even more hunched upon himself, muttering or incanting below his breath. Not Kobrir, maybe not

even human at all, a wretched being curled up and ranting in a broken, barely audible voice. Sevryn thought it a bad joke.

Tired of games, bruised and hurting, Sevryn made short work of the two Kobrir who jumped him just short of his goal. He heard bones crack and sinews tear as he thrust them aside and knew a moment of fleeting regret as he passed over their writhing forms in the dirt.

One stride away from his guide, he turned. Kobrir filled the far end of the roughly circular arena where he'd started his journey. Did they ready themselves to rush him one last time?

He lifted both hands. "Are we done now?"

The herbalist materialized from out of the rock shadows and tossed him a small, closed pouch. It landed with a thump at his feet. "We are done. You are just beginning."

Sevryn slid the toe of his foot under it, kicking it into midair where he caught it and tucked it inside the fold of his shirt after feeling its contents. Two hard vials lay within: the king's rest, as promised. And the cuffs they'd given him originally, taken back and now restored, as well as the marked dagger.

He turned back to the guide. The man, if it was a man, stank, sweating out booze and bad food and little sleep. A stream of low and muttered nonsense issued from the filthy bag over its head, its edges damp with spittle.

He bent and pulled the hood off.

Bregan Oxfort babbled up at him, blinking blindly into the light.

Chapter
Fifty-Five

NUTMEG SAT AT HER LOOM, working at creating a fabric she intended to use for the baby's winter season, to sew a sleeping bag against the drafty cold. She worked steadily, hands and feet moving in concert, the old wooden loom somewhat noisy as she moved it in a steady rhythm, her thoughts drifting far away. The mild thump and creak of the wood and the noise of fiber upon fiber as she passed the shuttles back and forth and corrected her tensions from time to time occupied her. It did not compare with the two great looms at her mother's shop, with treadles and tension bars and the ability to create not only more intricate patterns but also finer cloth, but she'd grown up with a loom much like this one and it granted a certain serenity with its working. She listened to the muted clatter and tried to ignore the thoughts beating on the inside of her skull. Where was Rivergrace? Why did her Vaelinar guards seem intent on knowing if she had heard from her sister? What was happening at Ashenbrook? She had caught them talking about wanting to join their fellows there but they quickly stopped speaking if she drew near, thinking she had not heard them. If asked, they closed their lips mutely. Her Vaelinar guards saying little made Nutmeg more than suspicious at their tight-lipped demeanor.

She sat up, arching her back and shoulders to ease the tension. A hard thump somewhere deep in the house made the timbers vibrate and a muffled shout followed. She stood abruptly. Shadows swept over the windows, darkening the room, and she could hear thunder rolling from far away, gaining on Calcort even though she couldn't see lightning striking. The walls shuddered. Bric-a-brac on shelves about the room danced in place uneasily. She put her hand out to steady herself, but it wasn't a quake. The shaking came with the low rumble, a vibration that seemed to sink all the way into the bedrock below Calcort's foundations. The whole city trembled at it. A wind came up with a sound like the rushing of a river at full flood tide, and the air filled with a salty musk. She could hear the sharp, piercing shrieks of birds as they flew past the farmhouse, fleeing. Then, all went silent except for that rumbling which grew ever steadily louder and nearer. The sun fled, a dark curtain dropping over the house.

Nutmeg lifted her chin in wonder and a bit of fear. She patted her thigh, where she kept a scabbard strapped, a thin but deadly blade inside it. She even slept with it now, when she could sleep. Her gaze darted to the short sword leaning against the wall nearby. Better the sword.

She could hear the rain start, heavy thudding drops that gave way to a cascade of water. She stepped to the window, and all she could see through the breaks in the shutters made it look as if she stood under a waterfall. The roof groaned with the weight being deluged upon it. Hard thumps fell onto the roof, and the house continued to shudder under the assault.

She stepped back abruptly as the door to the room banged open, Dayne filling it.

"We're under attack."

"Who?"

"Raymy. They're dropping from the sky like hailstones."

She went to the nearest cloak peg and grabbed her sword and harness strap from it. No more going about the waist, she thought ruefully, and simply slung it from her shoulder. "Where are we going?"

"Wherever we can," he answered grimly.

Garner met up with Verdayne in the hall.

"When did you get home?"

"Late last night." He looked rumpled and tired, but he wore rings on his fingers and a heavy gold chain about his neck. Gambling evidently agreed with him. He looked at Nutmeg and back to Bistel's half-Dweller son. "Can you use those?" His gaze fixed on the sword and dagger in Verdayne's hands.

"Quite well, actually."

"Then you stay with her."

"I have no intentions of going elsewhere. You?"

"With my father and brothers, at the yard. There's attackers among the Raymy. We'll be fine as long as they don't use fire." Garner made a face. "Even this rain can't hold, and the timbers here are old and dry."

"If they do use fire?"

"Get down in the root cellar and have Nutmeg show you the tunnel. It heads into the fields."

She felt the blood drain from her face. "Garner, I can't get through the tunnel in this condition."

He looked upon her, seeing what he'd missed in the season he'd been roving. "Tree's blood. Then get out the back through the vineyards, and to the caves beyond. Just get there, however you can. I'll hold them off."

"We'll manage," Verdayne said firmly, putting his hand on Nutmeg's wrist. "I understand you're a betting man. Odds?"

"Odds are it's Nutmeg they're after, driving the Raymy before them as a decoy."

"I'll take that bet." He pulled Nutmeg toward him firmly. "They'll have to get through me."

"They?" Nutmeg looked from one to another.

Her brother took her hand a moment and squeezed it. "I understand they're wearing the black and silver."

No disguise for the murderers this time. She bit her lip and then took a brave breath. "I understand."

Garner gave a sharp nod, darting away toward the front of the house at Tolby's bellow.

Nutmeg hated that her heart pounded. She wanted to go back to her room and retrieve those things she couldn't be without: the shawl that Rivergrace had woven to be a baby blanket, the small ring Jeredon had given her without ties, Bistel's journal. The journal she'd tucked in its secret spot in the adobe foot of the bedroom wall where it would most likely survive any fire, the mud bricks as thick as two feet, but flame would destroy her other memories to ash left out in the open as they were. Still, only things. She told herself that as she could hear Vaelinar high cries and taunts over the clash of weapons.

She pulled herself together. "This way."

"The cellar?"

"I thought we discussed that? I'd never get this great belly through th' kitchen door and down the ladder. No, the backdoor to the yards is this way." She shuddered as something screamed. "We may have to fight our way through, but once we hit the maze of the vineyards, we're free."

"Or trapped. They can burn through those vines if they know we're in them."

She threw him a look, knowing her face must have paled for she felt the warmth leave her cheeks. Then she shook her head vigorously. "Let them. They're green enough, it'll be hard to spark them and that should slow 'em down. The grapes will regrow, but they'll not catch us." She did not say that rebuilding the vineyards would take years, but Verdayne undoubtedly knew that and that if Tolby Farbranch had a choice between sacrificing the vines or his daughter, he'd pick the vines. She pushed her way outside into a nearly black wash of rain and cloud that pummeled her so that she ducked her head and hunched over in an effort not to be beaten to death. She could almost hear Verdayne follow her out, but only because the door made a muffled bump at his heels. The thunder had slowed to a vibrating

growl, low and hard to hear but pressuring her ears all the
same. She could smell the fish-and-salt odor of the ocean; it
dwarfed her other senses, and she could taste the salt with
every breath as it filled her nostrils and coated her lips. The
brine made her almost instantly thirsty, and they'd left with
nothing but weapons.

She scurried across the herb garden and through the
flower beds, knowing the pelting rain would hide their foot-
prints in mere moments as mud and water splashed about
her ankles. Behind her, Verdayne let out a muffled curse
and then a grunt as if he hefted something off his blades.
She threw a look back over her shoulder and saw two dark
figures behind her, one tumbling to the ground. She ran
faster.

Something splashed at her heels. "Verdayne?"

"Behind you. Keep going."

That was the nut of it, though, wasn't it? The baby
crowded her lungs and her stomach. She waddled, rotten
apples, like an old biddy. She could hardly eat or breathe
deep some days, and now, gasping for air already and hardly
running faster than a crazed turtle, she didn't know how far
she could go. But there wasn't a question in Nutmeg's mind
that she stop. Tressandre ild Fallyn's men would rip this
child from her body, killing it and her in the process. She
had not a doubt that those were the orders. She crouched
over, for the vines were only now reaching toward the sky
with their creepers and would grow much higher. Now she
had to bend and shuffle as fast as she could. Mud pulled at
her steps, weighing her feet down, as the pouring rain made
it difficult to even see her way—but she opened her newly
made Vaelinar sight, and the green threads of the growing
fields caught her eye and tugged her way to them. And, to
her astonishment, the rain tasted of salt, as though the skies
wept heavily upon Calcort. Pray it did not last long, or the
salt would kill the vines without any other help.

Nothing else jumped at them as they entered the vineyard. She stopped for a moment to catch her breath and
scan their path. The terraced fields need not be a one-way

trap. She could take him to the stone door where she'd taken Rivergrace and Sevryn and hope that one of the two of them could get it open. Once inside, the tunnels would take them through the stony hills to the river on the other side or, if they stayed to the tunnels, farther beyond. And, more importantly, it would be a locked stone door between them and pursuers.

She caught the sense of the door, hidden up the hill and over a terrace or two, like a beacon shining at her. Nutmeg had never seen it in that light before, but then ... she brushed her hand over her face, trying to dry it a bit. She hadn't had eyes like this before either.

Verdayne hovered at her shoulder. "My lady?"

"I'm fine. Just a bit winded. Stay close." She took off toward the tunnel door, not running, but settling for a jog, and put her hands to her sling, tightening it a bit, so her stomach wouldn't jostle about, stretching her skin painfully and making things even more uncomfortable. Halfway up the steep terrace, she felt Verdayne's hand against her lower back, pushing ever so slightly, helping her make the grade.

They reached the top as the darkness of the clouds began to part, the wind tearing them away in long, black wisps, and she went to her knees.

"Nutmeg!"

"Hush and get down! You'll be seen." She yanked at his knee; he fell beside her in a rough kneel. Her skin stung from the hard rain, more so now that it had begun to let up and she could feel something beyond burning numbness. She wondered if her face would have bruises, tiny purple dots all over it as if she'd been in a hailstorm, when this was all over.

"What did you kill back there?"

"Raymy. It sort of fell off the roof behind us and came up fighting."

Nutmeg wiped her eyes dry. "I've heard of toads being carried in the rain and then dropped far and away from their pond, but not lizard Demons." She inhaled deeply. "At least the rain up here has lost its salt or the grapes would be done for, anyway." She tapped a bunch hanging near her face, little green globes not yet swelled with juice and flavor. She pointed out the direction she intended to take and began to creep that way, not standing until they went over the stony ridge. Mud-caked, she stomped her boots once or twice and watched the sludge slowly run off her clothes.

"I'm going to need a bath."

Verdayne laughed softly. "At the very least. What other plans do you have?"

"There's a door that way, cut into the stone. There are limestone caves and caverns that run under these hills, although most have been deliberately shut off. This one hasn't."

He raised an eyebrow. "Something left of the Mage-born?"

"Probably. Or just smugglers looking for a back way into Calcort. More likely smugglers. Th' city has a history of them as any river or port city has, eh?"

He straightened to his full height behind her, eyeing the horizon they'd just left. "Seems too quiet."

"Because of the storm. They'll be dazed for a bit, uncertain." She followed his line of sight. "Do you think they held the house?"

"Not for lack of trying. Tolby knows how to handle himself and your brother Garner has used the pointy end of a sword more than once, I think. And Hosmer, certainly."

"Against Vaelinars."

"Better Vaelinars than Kobrir."

She blew a breath out at that. He was right, of course, too right. "Do you think they knew that the Raymy would drop like that? How could the ild Fallyn have guessed that?"

"It's possible. I haven't seen it, but it's said there's been Raymy sightings all up and down the coast. Clouds come in, and Raymy drop from the sky. They might have already been here, planning their move, and saw the storm coming in." Verdayne paused and then put his hand to her cheek, gently. "Enough talk. Voices carry on a wet day."

She nodded then, and strangely missed the warm
strength of his fingers upon her face as he took his hand
away. With a kick to her ribs from the inside, she began to
make her way to the corner of the vineyards where stone
met the soil.

When they finally arrived, she was too out of breath to
do more than point at it, bend over, and attempt to catch up.

Verdayne brushed past her, his back to her, as he examined the door closely. "Smugglers might have used these
caves, but that carving should tell you it wasn't made by
them."

Nutmeg didn't answer. Hanging her head down, she
caught sight of the lower trail . . . and raised her head slowly,
as five Vaelinars slipped in silently to surround them. She
let loose a pungent curse word and Verdayne froze.

"There's no running," Tressandre ild Fallyn said, slipping
a hood from her hair, freeing silken tresses, and smiling, her
eyes not warming but staying alert and focused on her prey
as she stepped forward from her escort.

When Verdayne turned, he did so in one smooth movement that left him with his arms out, a bladed barrier between them and Nutmeg. The sun shone after the storm, the
wind dropped to the barest of warming breezes, and the
Vaelinars stank of blood.

"You can't have him," Nutmeg told her.

The Lady of ild Fallyn's gaze slid over her. "Him? Are
you sure? You can't be certain."

Nutmeg shut her mouth tightly, feeling her lips thin.

Tressandre's eyes of jade and smoke narrowed to bore
into her. "Perhaps you are. A mother knows these things,
after all." She caressed her own, barely visible bump. "That
would complicate things, however. As for having him, well,
I doubt you are in a spot to negotiate."

"We'll both die before I let you take him."

Verdayne echoed a firm, "Stay clear."

"Who knew the Dwellers could be so fierce?" Tressandre
paced slowly, watching them, before adding, "Perhaps you
have a trace of Bolger blood in you? Yes. I think that must

be it. Stubborn, coarse, somewhat less than human ... I sense it in both of you. Which makes our dear unborn prince even more of a dubious mix than we'd thought. What a shame our Jeredon hadn't been more forward thinking before scattering his seed so hastily."

Nutmeg could feel her face flame and she spat back, "At least it's his seed I carry. Who knows what fathered yours."

One of the Vaelinars surged forward, but Tressandre caught him on her forearm. "Patience, patience," she told him. "You can tear her apart later. As for your aspersions, sturdy little breeder, no one is here to listen to them. You'll never see your ambitions for Larandaril come to fruition, unlike this vineyard." Tressandre looked about her momentarily, and then her gaze came to rest on the stone door behind them. "How interesting," she murmured. "What have you hidden here? It looks most convenient for us to make our way out of the city unhindered."

She turned to look at the last Vaelinar, hooded, who stood with sword ready in his white-knuckled hand. "Dear brother. Is there any need to backtrack our trail?"

"None at all," Alton answered, sweeping his own hood back. "Our dear cousin has his orders and will be following them handily, I trust. We can make our way to the battlefield directly. Or home."

"Hmmmm." Tressandre swept her consideration over Nutmeg, from her muddy boots to her rain-frizzed hair. "She might make it that far. If not, my plans are flexible."

Mageborn tunnels or not, her heart sank at the notion of walking all the way to Ashenbrook, let alone the coast. It would take weeks. She swayed a bit, brushing up against Verdayne. The touch of him, tall, proud, his muscles tensed and protective gave her a bit of hope. She wasn't alone in this. She put her chin up. Defiance bubbled inside her throat, but she swallowed it back. Better to let Tressandre think her cowed and unable to fight back, because she intended to, and intended that it be successful. "I cannot walk far," she murmured, but put her hand on Verdayne's back to reassure him.

Tressandre lifted and dropped a shoulder diffidently. "I might be able to persuade you, if I feel like it." She turned her attention to the stone door. "Who can open this?"

Nutmeg pivoted. "I can," she said firmly, and put her hand to the engravings. The door swung open to the noise of gravel being tumbled, and hinges complaining, and dark, damp air rushed out to greet them. She thought she could also smell the fresh water-and-flower scent of Rivergrace who had passed here only a few weeks ago.

"Disarm them both." Verdayne's body stiffened and she smiled at him. "Unless," she added, "you wish to be left behind on the trail."

"Try to keep them," Alton told him, "and she gets a knife to the kidney."

"Try to disarm me and you get one to the gullet before you can touch her."

"Boys," said Tressandre softly. "Stop trying to impress me. Time matters more to me than bravado." She reached out to jerk Nutmeg's sheath from her shoulder and tossed it scornfully behind her in one moment, and in the second, she had disarmed Verdayne before he could blink. She tossed his weapons after, brushing past them all to step into the tunnels. Crimson flushed Alton's high cheekbones as he shoved his knife back into his belt. He kicked the weapons aside before stepping after his sister.

Verdayne put his hand on Nutmeg's elbow, his words pitched only for her ears to catch. "Don't worry. I won't let them hurt our baby."

Chapter
Fifty-Six

A CHILL IN THE SEA AIR misted over Tranta as he bundled up his signal posts for transport. He tied them tightly, not wanting a rough ride to damage the inset Jewels he had painstakingly mounted. Each of these posts held, if not the full sentience of the toppled Way, a strong echo of it, and he handled each accordingly. He looked off the cliff, out over the ocean, where a shelf of dark cloud had begun to move in swiftly as squalls could, dipping so low that he could barely tell where the ocean met the storm. Waves churned, whitecaps sailed forth from them, and kites hung on the air, calling mournfully. He stood on the highest cliff, the Jewel of Tomarq's base, reluctant to give up her post, yet knew he must. Reluctant to return to the land, when here he could almost believe himself a kite, wings spread, hovering just off the currents of the sea. A yearning ran through him. Perhaps when the battles were over, he could convince Lara to let him sail out from the coast, to see what lay beyond it, what far islands awaited. He could use the riddle of the Raymy to convince her, for surely they came from elsewhere on Kerith, and their native lands ought to be discovered. With or without her patronage, he could go where he pleased, once the sentinel wall went up. There would be little or no maintenance, and any fool could tell if there was an invasion or not . . .

He straightened. A glimmer of movement caught his eye on the far horizon. A ship? So far out on the waves that it could scarcely be seen? It rode up and down on the troughs violently, dipping so high and so low that its timbers must be creaking loudly in protest and her sails lashed down, to keep the storm from driving her round and about in circles or snapping a mast. If it still had a mast. He narrowed his eyes, hoping to see it better. It remained an elusive speck to his vision, but Tranta remained certain it was a ship. He wondered if it would stay on its heading toward Hawthorne and what his new sentinels would make of it as friend or foe. If it could make a landing, it wouldn't be until full dusk unless it anchored in calmer waters and waited until the light of the morrow. If he were captain, he'd wait . . . but then, he wasn't. Not a captain of this or any other ship. Yet.

He bent to lash together another bundle, the last. The Sentinels he'd selected for the cliff he'd place over the next day or two, after shipping the others out. He'd already packed the spare fragments into a chest and sent it to the House for safekeeping, anticipating that he might be smithing more Jewel-adorned chain armor if Lara's pieces worked well, demand coming from those fashionably adorned who also went to war. A mere handful of stones lined his pocket, giving him comfort that he probably only imagined. He had already decided that he would pick and choose his clients and the ild Fallyn would not be among them. There would be protests and possibly even threats of boycotting and such, but he planned to shrug them off by explaining the scarcity of fragments that could be set. No one knew how much of his Jewel remained intact and usable but him, and he planned on keeping that information to himself. Tomarq was more than a precious gem, and her shards were meant for more than baubles to adorn the vain.

He could see her sentinel ability being replicated in a number of crucial ways.

Boots thudded to the ground behind him. Tranta turned in bewilderment, having pulled up his bridge in the early morning, and saw a man in black and silver striding toward him. His short sword glistened wetly in the afternoon light. He wore a tight smile on his young face that spread as Tranta met his expression. The levitator flexed up and down on his toes mockingly.

"Surprised? Easy to feel invulnerable when you have a drawbridge way up here."

Obviously, he wasn't invulnerable if he had a trespasser on his workshop grounds. "What do you want?"

"Your work." And the ild Fallyn gave a short bow at his waist, with a flourish of his sword, already dry in the crisp sea wind.

"Then it won't worry you if I say, over my dead body."

"You would merely follow in the footsteps of your guard, down the slope."

No surprise, there. Tranta thought fleetingly of the cliff's edge at his back. He'd been sent over it once before, a great fall, one that had crippled him for a time. He doubted he would survive a second fall. Ancestors of his had not, but the Shield of Tomarq had been a demanding mistress in her time, and Tranta had often taken the climb up the nearly sheer cliff to appease both himself and her. She respected that, he thought, and possibly guarded him in her own way. She had rested nearly unassailable, a queen in her own right, and appreciated those who knew the dangers of tending to her. He knew well the heights she ruled. He wondered what the son of the Fortress ild Fallyn had in mind for him.

"No words for them? No vows of vengeance for their murder?"

"They knew their service," he answered flatly. He would not let the killer toy with him, familiar with the bent of those who wore the black and silver. He'd never met one without a mean and sadistic streak, however civilized they pretended to be. He flicked a hand in the air. *Get on with it.*

The swordsman walked a few steps to his right, short gliding steps. He stood on the throat of the cliff approach, narrowing his path, but Tranta didn't expect him to worry about it. He, his quarry, stood dead ahead where the cliff widened, and the great gem had rested in her golden cradle which still rode the cliff's edge because he hadn't dismantled it yet. It still moved, silently, restlessly, side to side in its gyroscopic arc, as though the Shield were yet enthroned within it. All that gold, glinting hard as the sun lowered in the skies toward the storm front, which had not yet shielded its last, glittering rays. The cradle had to be sending spears of light into the ild Fallyn's face. Tranta sidestepped himself, so that he would not shadow the other's vision.

"You carry a bit of the ild Fallyn look to your face, but not much. If I had to guess—and it seems I do—you're a result of their breeding back program, for purity in their bloodlines. You might be, by some stretch of the imagination, a second cousin or so."

The man's jaw tightened and his mouth twisted. "My name is Nahaal, and they call me cousin."

"Ah. I am Tranta Istlanthir, and my House calls me son."

The tip of the other's sword jerked upward in his hand.

Touchy. He would remember that. "I have sworn the ild Fallyn as my enemy."

Nahaal said, "Conveniently, I will be your death." Nahaal's ears twitched. He wore his hair tucked behind them, points proudly exposed, as if declaring the strength of his blood. He had never been told, Tranta warranted, that their twitch served as a tell to his intent.

Tranta shook his head slowly. He waved a hand about him, indicating the remains of the Shield of Tomarq and answered, "No. She'll be my death."

"A smashed gem."

"A queen of gems and a Way. She may be scattered, but she still reigns up here."

"She is broken. Even Ways die."

"Not her. Believe me or not, at your peril." He moved in the opposite direction, watching as the sun bedazzled

Nahaal's face. The other squinted his eyes and mimicked Tranta's stance, but not as successfully as he liked.

Tranta would not have the sun in his opponent's face as long as he liked and needed to take advantage of what time he had. Nahaal moved impatiently, but Tranta, having watched the warlord Bistel and his son Bistane for much of his life, decided that the ild Fallyn attempted to draw him out. He did not respond except to pace another cautious step to his side. Once he drew, he knew the other would press him. Even as he moved, he realized that Nahaal did not intend for him to live. It would be enough to disable him and take the Sentinels, but those hadn't been the orders given. Alton ild Fallyn hated him as much as he hated in return, and he wasn't meant to survive this encounter.

Tranta took a carefully measured step backward. A glint in the other's eyes deepened.

"It's not the death trap you imagine," he informed his opponent. "I've lived through one fall off this cliff which increases the odds I'll survive a second."

Nahaal jumped. He leaped high, as if thinking that Tranta would leap to meet him but did not have the advantage of levitation, and that his blow would be superiorly overhead, slicing downward.

But Tranta hit the ground and rolled, this time in the opposite direction of where he had been sidling sideways, as the sword blade whiffed through the air harmlessly. He drew his curved sword and long sword as he got back up, crossed them, and waited. The sea never smelled more powerful in the wind and spray coming off the water to his back. It renewed his yearning to sail on its waters, singing of the joy of following the tide to his innermost self. That voice should distract him, but instead it buoyed him, letting him believe that a day would come when he could yield to it. A day beyond this one. A lifetime that ticked another season or two longer when death stared him in the eye.

Tranta knew that whatever happened here, whatever the outcome, it would be discovered shortly. He'd already ordered freight wagons to come and pick up their loads of the

Sentinels. The guards who now lay dead at the foot of the slope would be discovered. The looted work yard would then be revealed upon further inspection. Whether his body would be found there within it or not still lay in his hands and his workings. He still had a grip on his destiny.

Nahaal closed on him. Blades rang. His hands moved of their own volition. Parry, block, attack, retreat, set, and block again. Nahaal's breath came in a near bellow, fueled by his fury, unable to get past Tranta's defense.

He sprang back for a needed breather; Tranta did not press him, feeling an aching burn in his biceps and wrists.

"The ild Fallyn lie," Tranta said conversationally, trying to keep his own breathing smooth as if he had been little more than tried. "I am not the target they told you I would be. While it's true my contemporaries—Bistane and Sevryn—are far more Talented, I have a certain ability."

Nahaal's nose ran. He wiped it on the back of his wrist and made a scoffing sound. "We enjoy toying with our prey." He centered himself with bravado.

Tranta opened his mouth to reply, "I am Shielded," but Nahaal threw from his left hand and the dagger sank deeply into his right flank with a vicious smack, knocking him back a step. His breath left him in a surprised whoosh. He crossed his chest with his long sword as Nahaal closed and he sank his own left-handed sword deep into the other's boot, nailing him in place momentarily as he staggered back another step.

He pushed his hand into his pocket flap. Tomarq's splintered and shattered bits filled his hand, beyond warm to the touch as the last of the clear, lancing sunrays came over the cliff.

He threw his handful of rare gems into Nahaal's face as the swordsman closed for the kill. They burst into flame at sunlight's touch, driving Nahaal onto his heels with a sharp cry of both fear and pain as he pushed his arms up in defense. The hair fringing his face burst into flame that sputtered out.

Tranta's hands twitched to take the blade from his side,

but he knew better. He closed on the other, injured flank turned away so that Nahaal could not twist or turn the dagger deeper. He brought his long sword up, but Nahaal, face blistered and eyes streaming in agony, parried him. The swords sang as they ran off each other.

Nahaal pulled Tranta's weapon from his foot, and came at him again, both hands full, his face contorted, his vest smoking in fits and spurts where molten glass still rested in its folds.

Tranta ducked from the inevitable sword blow, but Nahaal did not swing. He slid to one knee, hooking his free foot out and catching Tranta behind the ankle, sending him backward.

And nothing lay behind him.

Tranta felt himself pitch off the cliff's edge, and Nahaal's eyes narrowed in triumph.

He fell but not before he reached for and grabbed the ild Fallyn's ankle and took Nahaal down with him, the edge of the cliff crumbling about them. The sea wind whistled up as he tried to twist in the air so that he could see the ocean looming underneath. A gull sounded a forlorn cry as they tumbled past. He wondered if the levitator could regain his senses well enough to protect them from the harsh landing awaiting them.

Chapter
Fifty-Seven

BREGAN CLEANED OUT the wooden bowl with two fingers and sucked the last of the gravy off them, smacking his lips when he finally dropped the bowl. The broken canyon walls cast long, warped shadows across the two of them. The Kobrir had pulled back, so far back Sevryn could not see a one of them, although he sensed them. Bregan examined his nail as if he might gnaw on that before licking his finger off one last time. He looked up at Sevryn hopefully, and Sevryn shook his head. "Tight rations around here. That's the last of it."

The Kernan trader wiped his hands on already filthy pants. "Better than nothing."

"You look like you've eaten a lot of nothing."

Bregan rubbed the back of his neck thoughtfully. "When did we part?"

"It's been a few weeks. Not that I would call it a parting. That's twice now you've left me to Kobrir hands."

"It's been forever to me." Bregan got to his feet, shakily. He reeked of body sweat and fear and stale, greasy food. Deep lines creased his Kernan face, eyes nearly hidden in their folds, a man who had once been young and who now looked aged. He patted down his leg brace, which spiraled brightly about his limb, untouched by age or dirt.

"They've held you that long? Here?"

"Held me? No, they came and got me a night or so ago." Bregan's hair stood straight up as he combed two fingers through it. "I think I lost my mind. I don't know why they brought me to you. I don't know what day it is. I hardly know when my feet are on the ground and my head in the air. Not anymore. Not anymore." He shook his head slowly.

Sevryn studied him, not a clue rising in his thoughts as to why the Kobrir had brought the trader as a guide. He would not waste more time. "Did they tell you why they brought you?"

Bregan rubbed his chin, his fingers making rasping noises on the long stubble that was fighting to become a beard, his eyes going unfocused as he thought of something in the far past . . . if he thought at all. His head jerked to one side. "They put a bag over my head. I couldn't see shit. Everywhere is dark. Everywhere." He jerked again, and turned to stare into the shadows. The cave's mouth yawned to one side of them. Sevryn thought it to be the entrance to the caverns he'd first awakened in, but could not be certain of that. This region appeared riddled with caves that buckled out of the hard earth, their roofs and sides broken, cracked out like an egg, with other, deeper caverns still in the stone behind them.

"I hate the dark." Bregan quivered. His jaw dropped. A bit of drool started to string out of the corner of his mouth.

Sevryn slapped his shoulder, hard, worried the Kernan trader would fall back into the near mindless babbling he'd first been greeted with. "Focus!" he snapped.

"On the dark?" Bregan's face twisted. "Imbris!" he shouted, his voice breaking in the middle of the word like that of a youth aching for manhood. "Imbris!"

And the cave mouth lit up.

"There. There," mumbled Bregan brokenly. "You can't see that. No one else can. But I do. N'kessak!"

And the cave went ebony again.

Bregan groaned and sank back to the ground, his braced leg sticking out awkwardly in front of him. He covered his face with his hands. A sob escaped his begrimed fingers.

"Do it again."

Bregan rocked back and forth. Sevryn leaned over and snatched his hands from his face. "Do it again. Say imbris."

Bregan's mouth moved impotently three or four times before he got the word out. Quavering, barely audible, wretchedly spoken.

The cavern bloomed with illumination.

Sevryn turned around to eye it better. Not torchlight, not wavering, either on—or off. He'd seen this before with the touch plates on the tunnels of the Mageborn, but no one had known the language to speak. Now Bregan had . . . what had Bregan done? Guessed it? Learned it? Read it from the touch plates? Figured out how to manipulate relics of the old sorcerers?

He reached back down and turned Bregan's face forcibly to the cave's brightly lit maw. "Look at it. Look."

"I—I—" Bregan leaned over and retched, loudly, but nothing spilled from his mouth. He swallowed, hard. "Light."

"Yes. It's lighted. You did that."

"You . . . see it?"

"Yes." He jerked Bregan to his feet and walked him to the cavern. Six strides, no more, and each one as difficult as if pulling a house behind him. "Make it go dark."

Bregan licked his lips. "N . . . n'kessak."

The light went dark. It didn't fade away, like dawn giving up to dusk, or a candle guttering out. It was all or nothing. A brilliant match struck and then put out.

Sevryn put his hand on Bregan's shoulder and squeezed roughly. "You're not crazy, man. You've got a bit of magic in you." What kind of magic, he hesitated to guess, although one thought pushed itself stubbornly forward in his mind. He did not utter it, thinking that Bregan tottered on the brink as it was. He stared at the inky pool. "Imbris," he said

quietly and firmly, but the cavern did not answer him.
Magic, indeed, but not one that would answer his Vaelinar
blood.

"Imbris," echoed Bregan and the pool blazed up, its
white light so bright that they both turned their gaze away
momentarily.

Sevryn returned to pick up the meager pack that consti-
tuted Bregan's belongings, and his own much larger and
heavier pack. Waterskins were lashed onto it tightly, and
deep inside the interior pocket, a velvet pouch held two
vials, as promised. He shouldered the pack.

Steering Bregan inside the cavern, he heard a voice call
out behind them. He turned as a hand fell on his arm, a
hand he knew well, browned and spotted from the sun, with
dirt from the herb gardens ground into the cuticles and under the nails.

"Find the king of assassins."

"I have been charged," he answered. "And accept my
duty."

"Are you certain of that?"

He studied the Kobrir face, hidden by veil, familiar hard
expression glinting in the dark brown eyes. "I'm certain of
knowing my word. The rest of the quest is beyond me until
I know who the king is."

The herbalist shook his head slowly. "This man only
shows you the way. You should, by now, know whom it is
you are seeking. That difficulty may break you."

Sevryn could only stare for a long moment, as certain
thoughts began to fall into place in his mind. A being who
could enchant metal that would enslave Vaelinar. A being
who had warped the essence of the Kobrir before bringing
them to Kerith and using them as he willed even as he
ruled them. A being who had been twisting threads and
weaving them to his favor for centuries. A being of subtlety
who might as well be made of the shadows. A cold chill
went through him. He had to have seen it before, and
looked away, denying the truth. Now he knew why Gilgarran had picked him up out of the mud and trained him the

way he had so many decades ago. Now he knew why the Kobrir had been so intent on honing his edges. And why he must kill. None of them would have a destiny if he did not.

Daravan. A man few would deign to face, and the Kobrir had known that, as well. The man Sevryn had found to be his father, although he did not seem to have a single paternal instinct within him. Not even for the race he had created/corrupted. He knew his primary target and then beyond him, would be the person who had created him and sent him. He had wanted to kill the ild Fallyn and Quendius, but he knew now that they would have to wait. Not long, but wait they must.

His mouth had dried, but he managed to say, "I know," to the herbalist as he pulled his wrist from his hold. The other stared into his eyes a long moment before nodding his head and stepping back. Sevryn felt as if he were an arrow, loosed into the air, soaring inevitably toward its destination. His thoughts dizzied for a second, weightless.

Bregan stumbled over a rock and Sevryn grabbed to keep the trader on his feet, and the cave went dead silent around them as if they, and only they, existed. Into that noiseless realm, Sevryn said, "Take me to Daravan."

"How, by all the Gods, do you expect me to do that?" Bregan shook under his hold.

"Because the Kobrir told me you would. Tell those voices of yours to guide you."

"Do you think I don't plead with them? Every moment I breathe? To go and leave me be?"

"And now you are asking them directions. If you're of no use to me, tell me why I shouldn't just leave you here for the Gods to play with as they will?"

Bregan flung a hand up. "You can't leave me!"

"As you've left me to die twice? What makes you think I won't? That I shouldn't?" He shook Bregan by the collar. "Or that I won't leave you to the assassins and let them persuade you however they will?" He knotted his fingers ever more tightly in the stinking shirt.

Bregan shut his eyes tightly. "Mercy," he mumbled. "Not

that you show it within you, but your lady Rivergrace sees it, she must. Mercy."

Sevryn gave him a final, violent shake, spinning Bregan away from him. The trader threw his arms about his head and curled down to his knees. His mouth closed on a sob, muffling the noise into mewling.

Sevryn watched for a moment as he decided whether to leave him or push him forward, jolted a bit by Bregan's reference to Rivergrace, and knowing that the other was right. She was indeed his soul, if he still had one. He put his head back, looking at the rugged stone roof above him. A thought struck him, and he stuck a hand inside his garment and drew forth the pouch given to him, working its drawstring until it opened. He took out the dagger he felt almost certainly belonged to Daravan. He took the trader's slack left hand in his and wrapped his fingers about the object. "Bregan, I need you to take me through these tunnels. For her sake, not mine. For the people behind us, the Kobrir. For the armies waiting for the return of the Raymy. I was made to strike, but you have to find me the target, the man who bore this weapon."

The mewling faded. When Bregan looked up, his face was streaked where tears had cleansed him. He scrubbed his hands over his head, ruffling his scalp. He took a deep breath and nearly choked on it. Laboriously, straightening his brace out and then under him, he got to his feet. He looked to Sevryn and said hoarsely, "This way." He shoved his hand forward, dagger slicing the air, and followed after it.

They traveled, Bregan alternating like the madman on the brink that he was, from sane to babbling to weeping to sullenly silent. He fought with Sevryn for water, like a small child pawing at him, and Sevryn finally gave him one of the water containers when they'd drunk it nearly dry. Bregan rationed himself then, touching it on his belt frequently and telling himself that he must have patience, that he must not squander the water.

The plates set into the tunnels they followed did not respond to Bregan until he slapped his palm on them and either read or intuited the symbols embedded there. Once or twice, peevish at Sevryn's presence, he snapped out n'kessak, plunging the tunnel into impenetrable darkness. It did not last long as Sevryn hauled him onward, heedless of rock outcroppings to slam an elbow into, unsteady footing to stumble over, or the occasional overhang to bang a head upon. Then he slapped the walls and begged for light until they illumined. They rested only when Sevryn felt as if he must, letting Bregan slide down into a heap and muttering the word for darkness until it was answered, and his hoarse voice lost in the echoing blackness.

Time swallowed itself. Sevryn felt fairly certain they'd been in the tunnels four days because the water hides had been drunk dry and his lips gone cracked when a grayish light filtered down in front of them, a natural light, an opening to the tunnel's end. The Mageborn tunnels swallowed time and distance, making navigation difficult, but he'd traveled them before and had some inkling.

Sevryn moved his hands over his Kobrir garb, checking his weapons, checking how accessible they were and how easily his hands could flex to pull them, feeling stiff and unyielding at first, as though his body had begun to turn to stone like the path they traveled. Bregan leaned against the cave wall, gulping down air as though it were water and could save him.

He did not, could not, quiet when Sevryn motioned to him. Sevryn moved in beside him and slipped his hand over the trader's mouth and nose, silencing him as he would a bellows. Bregan squirmed and clawed at his hands, but Sevryn said in his ear, "Water. I can almost hear it, but you must be quiet." The other stilled.

Sevryn listened another moment before nodding. "Down here." He stepped into shadows leading away from the graying dawn of an exit, and the sound of lapping water gained strength. It did not smell, at least not to their nostrils, which gave some hope it would be drinkable, sweet water. The gray dawning of a promised exit faded until, like a slip of the moon in the night sky, all they could see was its edge as he knelt down by the water.

Bregan watched him. "Is it good?"

Sevryn examined the edge of the small pool. There were animal tracks, most of them small and secretive, leading in and away. He saw no skeletons nearby. "I think so." He dipped a hand in and tasted it. "A bit odd, but drinkable."

Bregan fell to his knees and then his stomach.

"Wait." Sevryn put his arm out. He fished in his backpack for a packet he hoped he had stored deeply inside. "Yes." He found what he needed, pinched a bit between his thumb and index finger, and dipped it in the water.

The gray-green plant stayed the same color, darkened by the moisture.

"All right." He released Bregan who ducked his head into the water with a sobbing sound.

While the trader drank and drank until Sevryn feared he might founder himself, he got his skins out and set to filling them, and tugged the third one free from the other's belt and filled that one. He thought they were at journey's end, and both the Ashenbrook and the Ravela would have clean water, but he was never one to assume that he could reach it safely. Where Daravan appeared, there would almost certainly be Raymy, and possibly Raymy with plague. That could affect the rivers if a battle were being waged on their shores. Bodies fell into water. Water would be poisoned with their gore and blood and decay . . . and quite likely, disease.

Bregan got to his feet, stomach bloating, and let out a belch that actually brought sand dribbling down the nearest wall. He scrubbed at his face. "Did I get you there?"

"Don't know yet. Will you be all right if I leave you here?"

In the twilight of the cave, Bregan's eyes narrowed. "Why?"

"I'm not sure what I'll meet out there. You're relatively safe in here."

The trader's mouth worked, and then he shrugged. "Any jerky left?"

Sevryn unhooked a pouch from his belt and tossed it over. "Little enough."

"Anything. That water is rattling around my insides like a drunk trying to get attention with a tin cup in an iron cell." Fumbling a bit, he set to opening the pouch.

Sevryn went in search of the dawning light.

He stood in the tunnel opening for a moment, letting his eyes take in the natural light. Morning, he thought, and stepped toward the outside.

He did not stand in the valley where the Ashenbrook and Ravela Rivers bounded a past battleground. He watched as Lariel and Jeredon rode in quietly; she seemed to notice him but said nothing.

It took another moment for him to recognize where, a barren circle spread before him, and a pallet with a febrile king being set down at the far end, and combatants gathering. Spring, when the grass grew a sweet yellow-green and flowers bloomed abundantly except here.

"My Gods."

He stood at the time and place where Lariel Anderieon had earned her title of Warrior Queen.

And he did not understand why or how. Bregan had led him back in time.

Sevryn went to cover, calling for a sapling to own his shadow within its own slender seeming, and melded into it. Lara paced once or twice before him, and flashed a glance over him, slowing, and he knew she saw him despite his hiding.

No one else took notice. That would be as he remembered from her memory, if she did not lie to herself. People did, often. And even if they did not, the years often bent and faded what was true and what was not.

Bregan had, indeed, brought him to Daravan. But not a
Daravan he could kill, not here and now, without changing
the history of the last few centuries, and he dare not tamper
with a Way such as that.

He watched again what he'd learned from Lara's memory, but his attention stayed on Daravan at the other side of
the Dead Circle, the Vaelinar who stood in the shadow of
Sinok Anderieon and wondered what he intended there.

Sevryn spoke to the tree's shadow hiding him and moved
quietly about the Circle, from shadow to shadow, unnoticed as
the savage combat held the attention of all. It gave him a pang
to see both Jeredon and Osten at work, both friends, both
dead, and yet here . . . as young and in their prime as ever he
had seen them, and not in Lariel's thoughts this time. They
sparred and covered her, and each other, grunting and shouting and even laughing with their efforts. He could, if he wished,
reach out to touch them. Warn them. Protect them. Bitter-
sweet to see them and know he could do nothing. Could not
stop their untimely deaths in his lifetime. Could not save them
from plots and conspiracies, and not from love and war.

At last his turning took him within a handful of paces of
Daravan. Daravan whose Vaelinar gaze stayed raptly on Lariel
and her every movement as if he might devour her. Was it
admiration or ambition burning in his eyes? Gilgarran,
Sevryn's mentor, looked younger than he had when training
Sevryn, but then . . . he had been, then. Several hundred years
younger. His attention seemed split between Lara and Daravan, his wiry form tense. In his cupped hand at his thigh, he
palmed a small but lethal blade. Who for? Daravan? Sinok? It
would not be used—at least, in Lara's memory it had not. But
Sevryn moved through a different perspective now.

If Gilgarran sensed him in the shadows, it might even be
used on him.

Sevryn stilled his breathing and even his thoughts, except to reach out and watch the threads of existence stretching about him, weaving and reweaving in tangled patterns
about Lara as she fought to stay alive and earn her title.

His breath hissed between his teeth at the treacheries

and unexpected alliances, and the skill of the combatants until Lara, tired but still alive, lay for a moment on her back. He had worked his way, unthinking, to the edge of the Dead Circle where she'd fallen. Their eyes met. He knew Tiiva lurked on her flank and made a motion to warn her, unheeding of changing history because when he'd viewed this scene through Lara's eyes, he had indeed signaled her in warning. So how could he not now?

And then the challenges played out as they had been meant to and he did not know if he had unwittingly changed history or not, because Lara remembered the Kobrir assassin. Daravan walked away without a sound, but Gilgarran went to old Sinok and accompanied him, and soon no one stood at the Dead Circle but the two of them.

Lara looked at him as a shadow-swathed Kobrir. "I owe you thanks."

She could not depend on him, for he would not be there again, not for decades upon decades. He looked at her young and hopeful face. "You need to learn to think like an assassin. There are no friends, only foes. And more importantly, when you drop a foe, make sure they stay down."

She considered him longer, thinking. He could not let her think.

"Who *are* you?"

"That is not the question you should be asking. The question you should be asking is—who will I be?"

"Are you here to kill me?"

He dropped into his Voice. "No, my lady, not in this or any other time. Nor shall you remember these words until you have the greatest need."

In a flash he did not let her see, his hand shot out, and his thin blade traced her bare throat, eliciting the smallest of blood trickles before he turned and disappeared.

Inside the tunnel, he bent over, hands on his knees, more shaken than he wanted to admit. When he stood, Sevryn strode to the pool where Bregan sat, back to the wall, eyes closed in sleep. He grabbed him by the collar and dragged him back into the depth of the tunnel with the trader awakening and twisting in his hold, voice cracking in fear.

When Sevryn had gotten so far back into the rock-strewn path that the edge of light bleeding in could no longer be seen, as if it had never existed, he stopped, throwing Bregan to one side as the other yelled for illumination and mercy.

Bregan threw dirt and rocks at him until, weak, he could throw no more, and the ineffective barrage sank to the cave's flooring as he did.

"You're as bat-shitty crazy as I am." Bregan bowed both hands over his head as if afraid Sevryn would seize him again or beat his brains out against the cavern wall.

Sevryn leaned over. "You will," he said slowly, "take us back into the tunnel until you feel a difference in the path, a shifting, a change, and then bring us back to the time and place you are supposed to deliver me."

"Wha—what are you talking about?"

"Get up. Get up and do it."

Bregan waved about them. "We're in solid rock. Do you think I know where we are?"

They were face-to-face. Sevryn bared his teeth. "You fool of a Mageborn. If anyone knows where we are, you do."

"Mageborn." Bregan's teeth clicked shut. He reared back, scooting along the dirt floor. He wiped his eyes clean of dust and disbelief. "The Mageborn are dead. They destroyed themselves before you lot were thrown cursed into our lands. I know that. You know it."

"Did you think just any Kernan could do a bit of magic? Could read the tunnel signs? Could summon bright light out of ancient, forgotten sigils? Anyone?"

"I . . ." Bregan swallowed. "I thought I'd gone crazy. The Gods speaking to me." He whispered, "They called me Mageborn in my delusions, in my rage, in my stupor. I knew I had lost my senses. I can't be one of them reborn. I don't have the guts."

"Oh, there's little doubt of that. History proved that

most of the Mageborn were, as you put it, bat-shit crazy. As for the Gods talking to you, there will never be a better time to listen. Now get up and get me where I need to be."

"I'm afraid to hear what They want to say to me."

"Right now, I'm the one you need to fear." He put his hand under Bregan's elbow. He could feel the man draw away from him.

"I want no trade with Gods," Bregan muttered.

That made two of them.

Chapter Fifty-Eight

BISTANE HALTED HIS HORSE as his two scouts came pounding up, their tashyas wet with foam and nostrils flared as they fought for air. Greenery slashed by hooves sprayed the area about them as they plunged to a halt. Leathers creaked and metal jangled as the horses danced in place and snorted vigorously, tossing their heads. He unhooked his water flask and threw it to his riders, waiting until they had washed their mouths out and then drunk deeply. "What is it?"

"Ild Fallyn troops. Riding on a parallel track to ours, half a day ahead."

His lips thinned. Ill news indeed, but then word of that line rarely brought any other kind of news. He scanned the landscape about him, the forests thickening as they moved uphill, ridges awaiting them, to slow them down and perhaps provide gateways to ambush. He knew this wilderness but slightly, and he did not like what he saw. Too much unknown, too much rough territory. "How many?"

"We crossed a handful, but it appeared they have split off from a considerably larger-sized force."

He did not, as his father would not have, demean their skills by asking if they were certain. They would not have pelted back to report unless they were. He crossed his wrists on the saddle in front of him, taking stock. Some answers would be more important than others. "Were you seen?"

"Not by any who lived."

Nor did he ask again if they were sure. "Were you able to question any of them before their unfortunate demise?"

"One. Calcort has been overrun by Raymy, a huge fall of the lizards. They came in like a tide. He claims that the Dweller who carries Jeredon's heir is in ild Fallyn hands, captured in the fray, and Tressandre has ordered her imprisoned. I cannot confirm the veracity of his words as his companion died too suddenly to corroborate the story."

"Nutmeg Farbranch was taken from Calcort."

" Yes, and . . . your brother, Verdayne."

Bistane's jaw stiffened. If only he had not sent Verdayne with the books, but he could not be in both places and there had been no better man for the job. The job before him might not matter at all if the library fell to destruction. He swallowed his regret. "Being held for ransom?"

"The scout said nothing of the sort." The scout hesitated. "We have no proof and what the ild Fallyn scum knew, he heard from camp gossip as Tressandre and Alton were to join them shortly. He believed it true and was quite proud of it. He recognized our colors. He told me—" the speaker paused before swallowing tightly. "He told me to tell you that your father's bastard was being attended to and that he would be taught how to serve the Vaelinars properly."

He frowned but answered lightly, "If they do indeed have Dayne, he will be surprising them. My brother is no less stubborn than any of us and no less skilled with a weapon. He will let them think what they want, and turn their inattention on them as soon as he can. He will be very tough to kill." And if they did, ild Fallyn would pay. His father might have tempered his actions toward that lineage in the past, but he no longer felt a need to honor old counsel. And as for ghosts, why had Bistel said nothing about

Dayne's capture? Did the spirit world move around in the dark much as any world did? What good was a haunt without answers? His frown knotted tighter.

"Should we send out a detail to see if we can find them?"

Bistane thought a very, very long moment. If he were to send anybody, he'd have to send his very best, and he had a grave need for his very best at the moment. He could neither afford the loss of ten riders to send out or the exposure of his troop movement if any of the other ild Fallyn discovered them. He would have to trust that Dayne could hold his own. "No. Whatever the ild Fallyn are up to out here, I fear we'll know soon enough, and I don't want to tip my hand before. We cannot move to capture the hostages without more information and time, and our current engagement holds my complete attention for the moment."

"As you wish, Warlord."

"Not what I wish, but what must be." He nodded slowly. "Get fresh horses. Get replacements if you feel you need it. See that the other scouts know where you marked their position and likely progress. I don't want any more encounters. We're too close to where we have to be."

"But that is well."

"That is very well." He meant to be close. He had to be close. Lives depended upon it.

"If we should encounter other ild Fallyn, however, I want that confirmation that they've taken the girl and my brother hostage. As well as to what they're up to."

"Aye, my lord."

Clouds swooped overhead with the speed and intensity of birds on the wing, a blight on what had been an otherwise ordinary and pleasant late spring afternoon. Bistane looked up as the skies darkened ominously with a keening of wind and then lightened again, the storm breaking up even as it streaked by. Ebony banners marked the passage as if a God struck his colors defiantly. The wind screeched past, snatching at him vigorously and then letting go like a wisp of smoke. No storm moved like that, in heartbeats instead of candlemarks. No natural storm.

"Do you smell that?"

"Like the spray off the sea, sir, almost." The scout whirled his horse about as if he could keep pace with the lightning-fast clouds.

"Yes. Almost exactly like that." Bistane tracked its movement roughly, and the tension that stiffened his body translated to his horse, which made a two-step shy off the trail anxiously. Bistane reined the horse back and made note of the storm clouds streaking past. "It's gone now, but it will come to a landing somewhere. Like a water spout or wind devil, and Gods help those in the vicinity."

"What do you think it brings?"

"More than rain and wind." He hooked his water flask back onto his saddle. "Time is wasting."

The head scout and his follower threw him what passed for a salute, wheeled their tired horses and made off to do as he'd ordered. He craned his neck to catch the last of the storm tide as it rolled past them, leaving the air in its wake with a dank and salty stink. He could not fathom how feathery clouds could rain down a dire enemy from the very sky itself, but he feared that this storm was capable of just that. From what sea to their sky? On what wings did the Raymy travel? And yet, it was not worry about the Raymy that spurred him. He kept staring as if he might see beyond even a Vaelinar's vision, perhaps into the future, perhaps back to the land which had birthed the storm and cast it whirling. The vision he wished did not come to him. He lifted his helm and brushed his hair off his forehead, and settled the helm back again. Always far more questions than answers came to him.

He didn't like not going after Verdayne or that sassy bit of a woman, Nutmeg. He loved his brother and held a certain fondness for the outspoken Dweller who many saw as no more than Rivergrace's shadow but which he had learned was far from the reality. As for the other, it was not that Dayne would appreciate a rescue from him; he would not if his faculties and all his limbs were still intact, but his brotherly instincts called for him to ride to a rescue. Bistane had been given a task, and he could not stray from it, or outcomes would be dire. Even if he brought his army in time, the prospects were not good. He told himself Dayne would understand. And, if his brother didn't survive, he would have to live with his decision.

Bistane put his heel to his own mount and rode to the head of the column. Cavalry, archers, and infantry all saluted as he passed them by, buoyed by good meals before he asked this forced march of them. They would grumble in another day or two, but he hoped they would reach their destination by then. He would stay ahead of them now until they reached the battlefields. He'd slipped into the front of the formation when he became aware that he did not ride alone—his father's ghostly white mount and transparent figure rode next to him, the sight of the apparition stinging his eyes. Why see him now? What good did it do? The other wavered in his view as if both there and not. An unnamed feeling surged through Bistane. Was the ghost here—or was Bistane somehow viewing where the ghost reigned? What advantage did that give him if the ghost could not even warn him that the ild Fallyns were also driving an army this way?

He wiped his brow as if that might clear both his thoughts and his sight.

"I don't seek this," he said quietly, "seeing you, and if you must speak to me, at least tell me about Verdayne."

Bistel turned his chiseled face toward him, snow-white hair uncovered by his usual war helm. The blue-upon-piercing-blue eyes weighed him. He knew that visage, that expression, that careful measurement so well. Bistane waited for his father to speak, but if Bistel had an opinion about his not riding in pursuit of Verdayne and Nutmeg, he did not express it. Nor did he say anything about anything. Bistane put a gloved hand to the back of his neck where prickles raced up and down, and smoothed his skin. Gods but he hated being haunted.

Chapter
Fifty-Nine

NAILS RAKED THE SIDE OF HER HOOD, tearing at the fabric like daggers. Sunlight splintered in through flaws in the rough weave, but she did not have to see to know who clawed at her. Nutmeg held herself as still as she could in the saddle, unflinching, although every instinct reacted. To show fear would only make the moment last longer. She would not give Tressandre the joy she sought in tormenting her.

"You will miss me, little beast." Tressandre gave a shallow, hissing laugh.

"As a stinkdog misses its slime?"

Tressandre slapped her, sharp and hard despite the baffling of the cloth hood covering her face. She recoiled with the blow, ears ringing. Nutmeg tasted blood at the corner of her mouth and curled her fingers tighter into her saddle leathers to keep her balance.

"I should have made you walk every step," ild Fallyn hissed at her ear. "But your waddling makes me late to a triumph for which I've long fought. Don't despair. You'll still have company on this little journey, and they will see to it that your dungeon room is waiting for you. As dungeons go, it's not much, but then you're used to grubbing in dirt. It should be quite homey."

The voice withdrew, and a horse jingled his bit. Tressandre said coldly, "If anything befalls this lump, make sure you cut the baby alive from her belly. I want that child!"

Horses nickered as hooves drummed and dust rose that penetrated even the rough cloth about her. When she could breathe evenly again, her mount jerked into movement. Though she had ridden quite a bit in her life, and it was better than walking, the discomfort made her bite her swollen lip. Every jar sent lightning up her spine and through her hips. Her horse stumbled a step and slowed.

A hand took her by the elbow after fumbling a bit, and Nutmeg recognized Dayne's hold. The hood over her head rustled as he bent close enough to touch it and whisper, "We have fewer than half the guards we had before. And Tressandre and Alton are gone."

"You heard what she said?"

"Yes." His hand tightened on her. "And the blow. Are you hurt?"

"It only smarts a little. I should have kept my lips tight."

"You? Refrain?"

She freed one hand from the saddle flap to put it over his. "My own fault, and I know it. My mouth is faster than my reason."

"Rest as you much as you can." He held her hand and squeezed it. "You'll have need of your strength before this sun sets. Our weakness is our advantage." Another squeeze as if pressing the meaning of his words into her before he let go as one of the guards grunted at them, and she could feel a horse being ridden in between them, separating them.

He planned something. He'd tried to tell her. These four left to escort them had not seen him fight, had no idea who they faced. And she could do for at least one, push come to shove. As for weakness, her biggest one was her condition. Cut lip or not, Nutmeg began to smile.

Her expression faded as the day wore on, and the pace

of the horses quickened. She grew thirsty although not hungry, but they made no stop at the peak of the day. Her horse had begun an annoying wheeze emphasized whenever Nutmeg bounced in the saddle, which happened more frequently than she liked. She wished for one of the Eastern horses that Keldan had told her about, horses with a running walk gait that made the rider feel almost as if they sat a rocking chair instead of a mount. She'd doubted his tale then, but he'd sworn its veracity. Even a tashya did not have that smooth a movement. The insides of her calves and thighs began to sting and the small of her back kept cramping.

A bird's sharp whistle pierced her growing discomfort, bouncing off the landscape that she could not see, but as near as she could tell, it came from behind. She jerked in her saddle. She knew that whistle and knew it well. It had called her home from the groves and orchards almost every day of her life when small. Her hands itched to rip the hood from her head so that she could look about. Nutmeg grabbed at her horse's mane and found a rein to yank on sharply, bringing the beast to a stiff-legged halt.

"I need water to drink and after bouncin' me all over the face of Kerith, I need to pee." She put her shoulders back and stiffened defiantly. Before the sound of her voice faded, the bird whistled again, long and loud and keen. Close music to her ears.

Her hood came off roughly and she sat, fresh air flooding her nostrils and sunlight stinging her eyes. She blinked as Dayne had his hood removed and she waited for a hand down from her saddle and the glory of a spring day invaded her senses. Nutmeg took a deep, grateful breath. She saw the four still with them, hardened men, the leader a man with a scarred and leathern face that boded no good. He had dead eyes, she thought, and shivered. Dayne reached her first, his warm and steady hands on her waist, his expression solemn but a warmth deep in his eyes, and she slid off slowly into his care. In his ear, she said, "That's no bird cry. That's Tolby Farbranch and he's on our heels." She pretended to turn clumsily in his hands and went to one knee.

His hands stiffened. "Then now is the time," he whispered as he bent over in concern, his body sheltering hers protectively. His voice raised. "Are you all right?"

She gave a tiny snort. "If I was a'right, would I still be on the ground? My butt hurts and my stomach—" she paused and doubled over a bit, stifling a groan. She rolled an eye up at Dayne.

"How can I help?"

She moaned again, barely audible as she muffled her mouth against her arm.

Would they think labor had begun? Dayne took an odd step away from her, centering himself.

"What's wrong? Get her the water she wanted and find her a bush. I don't want any trouble from you lot."

The four milled about, two with eyes on them and two others with eyes to the country about them. She feared if they overplayed her indisposed moment, the troops might do just what Tressandre had ordered: cut the baby from her body and leave her for dead. She reached up to Dayne, hands going cold with the thought. His were warm and strong, but he firmly withdrew his sword hand and squeezed hers together with the other. He began to haul her upward, but he mouthed, "Fall."

She didn't think she could fall. At least not gracefully. If she went down now, she'd be like a newly picked apple falling out of its bushel and bouncing off the wagon to roll all over the ground, bruised and mashed. She winced at the thought even as she pulled her hands free from his and went tumbling on her backside, figuring sore as it was, it was better suited to land upon than any other part of her anatomy. Discomfort shot up her spine and she let out a yelp far louder than she'd intended. Dayne shouted, reaching down for her, and Tressandre's men whirled their mounts about. She rolled to one knee and let out a gasp.

Her skirts bunched under her and she felt crushed grass and dirt grind into her knee. The leather sheath strapped to her thigh warmed her fingers as she slid her hand over it and tugged on the hilt protruding from its depths. The slim, lethal shape filled her grasp. Nutmeg smiled and then twisted her lips into a grimace as boots thundered toward her. The grizzled veteran hit the ground first and advanced on them. His second in command stared coldly at them, while the two on point at the front stayed back. One of them unslung a bow but did not fit an arrow to the string.

The one afoot shouldered Dayne aside, muttering, "What in the cold hells is going on?" and putting out a booted foot to shove her aside as he passed. Nutmeg let out a tiny growl, folding her arms to protect herself. He shoved his toe into her again. "I say we save the trouble and take the runt's baby."

"And what would you do to feed it while we rode?"

"Let it squall for its mother's milk. Water is good enough for it. It'd live till we hit the fort." He scowled down at Nutmeg. "They're keeping us from ild Fallyn victory. We've been waiting decades upon decades to see Queen Lariel's head spitted on our lady's sword. Now that day is here, but we have to escort this turd."

The trooper in second charge returned, "Doesn't matter where we are. We still share in Tressandre's glory."

"You're a stupid shit if you think hearing the others talk about seeing the last battle will make up for not being in it! I say we slice her open now. With only the frigging brat to mind, we can make twice the time. Maybe even get to the field in time. This lump of turds here isn't worth saving."

"They left orders—"

"They're always leavin' orders. We follow them, as we can." The trooper glared down at Nutmeg, his eyes narrowed, and his hand started toward the sword hilt on his left hip. "I think I'm going to like doing this." His sword made a noise as he pulled it clear and bent over. "Look in my eyes, mongrel."

A ray of sun glinted off the steel edge into her eyes. Nutmeg rolled to her side, both hands on her dagger, and jammed it deep into the side of his throat before she tore it free. Hot blood splattered her face as her target made a deep, gargling noise and went for her, hands clawed. Dayne kneed him aside, grabbed the sword and sprang at the second guard, catching him in mid-dismount, the sword burying itself to the hilt with the man's momentum.

That left two as the archer grabbed an arrow and nocked it, drawing his arm back. Nutmeg rolled under her horse's legs, one arm curled over her head if it should kick, the animal whickering in distress at the smell of blood a-wash over her and pooling on the ground as ild Fallyn's man kicked his way into death.

Verdayne, bowed by the weight of his victim, went to the ground fighting. Nutmeg saw the archer aim at him as he tussled, and sucked in her breath to cry an alarm, but couldn't catch her breath as a spasm grabbed her torso.

It didn't take that long to fire an arrow. It couldn't. But she'd no way to stop time in its tracks as it seemed to have done. As she caught her breath, she saw the archer reel back in his saddle, falling as his horse danced away in alarm and then bolted as it dumped its rider altogether. The man rolled onto his back with a moan, clawing at the bolt buried deep in his flank. The horse stamping its hooves about her made a sideway hop, one hoof clipping her elbow as it did, and then tossed its head and tail up, galloping away. Pain lashed through her, and she grabbed at her arm.

Verdayne staggered to his feet as his wounded assailant latched onto his ankle and hauled him back. He slapped down with his bloody sword, and a scream cut the air.

The last remaining trooper curbed his horse in place, twisting in his saddle, looking for the unseen bowman who'd cut down his companion. As he reined his mount about and put a heel to it, fleeing, an arrow whizzed through the air, burying itself in his back. Dayne jumped up and caught him, dragging him out of his saddle and slitting his throat before he hit the ground.

Nutmeg finally got a smothered protest out. Dayne came to her, went to one knee, and picked her up in his arms. His warmth and strength surrounded her, and she buried her face against his shoulder. "No help for it," he said, holding her close. "We cannot afford to leave anyone alive." He ripped his sleeve off and cleaned her face.

Hoofbeats trotted up. "I've been wondering when you'd make your move."

Verdayne grinned up at Tolby Farbranch sitting atop his sturdy Kernan mountain pony with a second on a lead. "I'm good," he said, "but I could not take on both Tressandre and Alton by myself. Waiting seemed more prudent than fighting."

"Right to be levelheaded about it," Tolby agreed. He kicked his feet out of the stirrups and hit the ground lightly. "Meg, tell me you're all right."

"If I could breathe," and Nutmeg fought for more air. "I would." Her arm hurt like the time her old cart pony had stepped on her, but nothing could override the spasms. Dayne and Tolby grasped her arms and helped her to her feet but the next spasm brought her crouching down again.

"Rotten apples," she managed. "I don't want to be spoiling your rescue, but I think—" and she sucked down another gasp of air. "I think I'm having a baby."

"ARE YOU SURE, Meg?"

"Well, no," she answered her father. "But it seems likely."

Tolby looked rough, as if he had been riding hard after them all those days, heedless of dirt thrown in his face and branches whipping across his body, and he mopped his brow on the back of his sleeve. "Then you've got to get back on a horse, because we need to get to fresh water. Can you do it?"

"Water?" repeated Dayne. "Seems like we need a homestead with a midwife."

"Don't insult my dad. He birthed all of us."

"Your mother did most of that work, child," Tolby said gently. "I only helped a little, but I know what to do." He changed his grip to steady her, and she cried out sharply. He pulled back his hand, filled with fresh blood. "I thought you said you were all right." He tugged on the ragged slash in her sleeve. "This is a good cut here. I'll bind it now, but we've got to clean it good and stitch it soon as we stop." True to his words, he ripped off the bottom hem of his tucked-in shirt, the only clean part of his garment, and strapped her upper arm firmly. "Hurt?"

"Aye, but so does everything else." Nutmeg gave a shaky laugh. They got her mounted with only a small squeak or two of discomfort, and then she looked down at her father. "What's Dayne riding? This pony won't carry all of us."

"This, I can handle," he said wryly, and clasped a hand on Tolby's shoulder before letting out a piercing whistle.

Tolby got on his horse and gathered the reins. "Will you be following me?"

"Wait a moment." Dayne walked among the bodies, gathering weapons and wiping them on the trampled grass and dirt. Before he'd finished and straightened, one of the fled horses came trotting back, ears pitched forward in curiosity.

Dayne spoke to it in a soothing voice as he put a firm hand on the bridle, gave a jump to get his foot in the stirrup, and swung the horse about.

Tolby nodded. "Good lad."

"Was that Vaelinar magic?"

Dayne laughed at Nutmeg. "No, no. Just a lot of work mucking out the stalls and taking care of those beasts. Any horse worth his oats and in hearing distance knows that means a feed bucket. They know a stable lad when they hear one!"

Nutmeg sniffed. "Long as they take a bite out of you and not me when they're not getting what you promised."

Dayne let out an unexpected roar of a laugh. Tolby took point, saying his caravaner days gave him a fair idea where the water might flow. He tracked them deeper into the line of foothills and greenery, winding their mounts back and forth, letting the trees envelop them. Meg felt their coolness fall upon her gently, the wind murmuring softly through leafy branches, and she closed her eyes and tried to send soothing thoughts to her restless child. He did not answer her, but she could feel the rapid beating of his heart fluttering inside of her. She sent mothering thoughts, thoughts of warmth and protection and love. Whether they reached her anxious child, she did not know. She thought of all the times her mother and her father, and even her brothers, held her, giving comfort and hope, and sent those memories inward. She sent the feeling of finding Rivergrace, thin and with fresh scars from shackles and cuffs on her small limbs, of pulling her from the raging Silverwing River to safety and warming her with her own small body, and declaring that she'd found a sister. Of how she and Grace had embraced so tightly at this last leave-taking, of her sorrow and joy. Her fingers laced tightly to the swell of the saddle in front of her, to the fringes that had been stitched upon it for just such a hold. When the spasm came again after long moments of rest, it gripped her so tightly that she clenched and ground her teeth so that she would not scream and scare her father and Dayne.

It was then the warmth and love she'd been sending within returned. It rose up and wrapped about her, cocooning her, taking the pain if not the pressure away as if her son answered the only way he knew how. Long moments passed that she held to that answer, not hearing either her father's or Dayne's voices as they spoke, or the clop of the horses' hooves on the ground, or the birdsong from the canopy above them as they passed through.

Sometime later, she became aware they'd halted.

Nutmeg opened her eyes. Tolby, on the ground, reached up and wrapped his hand about her boot toes. "Stay sitting a mite, while we build a bit of a cot for you, all right? And a fire. I'll have water boiling in no time."

"Dad," she said.

"Aye, Meg?"

"I love you. And Mother and everyone."

"Well enough, and we all know that. You've never been one not to show it." He squeezed her foot. "Things will be all right." He took his knife from his belt and began to systematically strip bushes of their long, fragrant limbs as Dayne hobbled their two horses in a small pasture next to a brook that bubbled cheerfully past them. Nutmeg watched it curling past. No Silverwing or even close to an Andredia, but the lush trees lining its bank spoke that it was a loyal and steady provider to the area.

Dayne dropped a considerable bundle of firewood in

front of him. He had evidently been picking it up along the
way and balancing it on the saddle in front of him as he
rode, for both he and his mount were flecked with bits of
bark and dried leaf. Nutmeg curbed her smile of amusement. The moment fled quickly enough as a hard, pressing
spasm gripped her and shook her tightly. Dayne rushed to
her. He took her hand in his.

"Bad?"

She nodded. He pressed her hand tightly between his.
"Let me get that fire built, and then I'll get you down."

Another nod was all she could manage.

The moments knotted together, pain and release, pain and
fear, pain and being helped down off her horse. Walking
helped ease her stiffness, and Tolby sat her down on a weathered old tree stump he'd cleared free of leaves and brush. The
leafy cot stretched next to it and she looked at it longingly.
Flames leaped up and smoke tickled her nose as she perched
there on the stump instead. He'd brought water from the
creek in his rain slicker to fill the collapsible bucket he always
packed in his saddlebags. She'd been on trips when it had
boiled stews and soups, and occasionally even klah so potent
you could stand a stick straight up in the drink, but never just
plain water. When steam began wafting up, her father squatted next to her. "First, the arm," he said.

"Dad—"

"I know what I'm doing," he said firmly, as he began un-
wrapping the wound. "I want this cleaned and stitched up
before I have to worry about any other problems."

"But—"

He held up a finger. Nutmeg sealed her lips together
tightly knowing that her stubbornness came from this man
and she was not likely to best him in a contest of wills.
Dayne clucked his tongue as he watched over Tolby's shoulder.

"Close," he commented. "But mainly a deep flesh wound."

"Aye," Tolby agreed. "Good luck on that one. Bring me
some of that boiled water."

Dayne searched the gear packed on his horse until he

found a tin cup, as well as a fairly clean and folded blanket. He fired the cup before filling it with water and bringing it over. Tolby nodded in approval as he opened one of his own kits, a kit often used for fishing with a curved hook and fine, strong thread but today would be used to close her cut. He waited until the water cooled to bearable and then set about cleaning her cut.

It hurt. It hurt enough that it sliced clean across her other hurts, the pain of the labor, so that she scarcely noticed the major event. He stitched her cleanly and quickly, talking to her as he did. "This will leave a touch of a scar, but that will be fine, even with such a fair skin as you have. It's a marking of life, a trophy of winning through the hardness of it, Meg, my child."

"I don't mind."

"And well you shouldn't. Few of us get through our years without an award or two. It adds to the beauty, not takes away."

"Dad! As if I'd worry about such a thing."

"Good." He nodded. "That's my girl." He took another stitch. "Almost done here, and I think you're about done, too."

Her mouth opened. "I—" and then a mighty spasm took her, and as her father knotted off the last stitch, she surged to her feet.

"Squat," he told her. "Like you were milking one of the goats but without a stool. It'll help."

She did, and it did. He gathered up her skirts as he ordered Dayne to bring the boiling pot over to him.

"I'm washing up," he said to Dayne. "You, too, in case you have to help catch."

Dayne's face flushed for a moment. "She's not a cow," he responded softly, as he rolled his remaining sleeve to over his elbow and washed.

"Never, but catching a baby is not all that much different."

And then Nutmeg heard words, but little made sense as her body seized her and did what it must to bring her child into the world. Moments passed. Long, awful, dread moments that left her gasping in between with relief, only to be seized up again, over and over. She felt it at last as the child passed and rocked back onto the branchy cot, on her elbow and her father cried out, "Well done, Meg. A beautiful baby girl."

"Girl? It . . . It can't be."

Dayne mopped her forehead. "A wee, perfect little girl. She looks like you, in a very pinkish and somewhat . . . well, I can see you in her squeezed-up little face."

Tolby took care of the rest, then wrapped up the baby in his slicker and held her up so that Nutmeg could see her tiny, perfect hands with fingers already trying to grip, and little feet with exquisite little toes, and a wispy brush of dark hair upon her head. She reached for the child in wonder. "So it's you I'm meeting, finally," she told her baby.

Baby eyes did not reveal her Vaelinar bloodlines, nor did her heart-shaped face with pudgy cheeks except for the tiny, tip-ended rosebud ears, but that no longer mattered. One look and she had Nutmeg's soul. She held her close as the child wailed its first cries and then softened, chortling for her. She held her baby close.

But a girl. How could it be? Nutmeg ran her fingers over the downy soft bit of hair. A beautiful, wonderful girl.

And then another, hard spasm took her.

"Hold on," said Dayne. "She's crowning again. There's another."

Tolby took her girl from her, and put her gently on the leafy cot, tucking her in before turning to Nutmeg. "Are you sure?"

"A-course he's sure!" Meg snapped, her body rigid. "This is not bobbing for apples and fun." A growling groan escaped her, shutting away whatever else she might have said. She threw her arms up to Tolby and Dayne to grip her wrists and she held on for dear life. She lost all sense of time, all but blacking out and then she felt the pressure push the baby through, a relief through the pain.

She could hear the offended squall. Dayne gripped her firmly.

"A boy," Tolby announced, "and as like to Jeredon as could be, with a touch of you."

A boy. The boy.

Nutmeg gave a tired, wobbling smile before passing out.

She woke groggily with the late afternoon sun still slanting across her and knew she hadn't been out long, woodsmoke stinging her nostrils. One of the babies gave a fitful cry.

Dayne and her father had been talking. They stopped and turned to her. "Better?"

"Always. They must be hungry. Give them here."

"Are you up to it?"

"I had better be, hadn't I, with two of them?" She held out her arms in welcome. "The boy is Evarton, and my girl is Merri."

"You sound certain," Dayne commented as he snuggled little Merri into the crook of her arm.

She felt no doubt. "I am. For Jeredon Eladar, and Merri for . . . us. Because that is a Dweller-sounding name."

Dayne turned away as she began to suckle a child on each breast, the business of doing it harder and definitely more painful than she'd imagined, but she knew it would soon be routine. If she could handle two babies. She was ample enough, she supposed, but wet nurses had been around almost as long as mothers, and she might have to find one. Evarton fastened his eyes on her as he pulled, but Merri squinched hers shut tight as if concentrating all that she was on this drinking business. She put her chin to the top of his head. "All babies' eyes are muddied a bit and change color, and I can imagine yours will be like his, green with streaks of amber." Evarton made a noise of contentment. Merri fisted one tiny hand and waved it about.

Tolby cleared his throat. "We have been talking."

"Imagine that." Meg looked at him.

"I have a question for you, first."

"And it would be. . . ."

"Did anyone ever suspect you were carrying two?"

Meg thought a moment before shaking her head sharply. "Never. Not even Mother."

The two men nodded sagely. "Then we have a suggestion. Find a wet nurse and leave Evarton behind for a bit, in safety."

She frowned. "And why would I leave my son behind?"

"Tressandre. She would probably feel far less threatened if you produce your daughter, so like us and so unlike the Vaelinar."

The words fell like rocks upon a tight drum skin. Nutmeg waited a moment to take them in. They made no sense at first, and she swirled them around in her head until they did. Her eyes opened a bit wider.

"And if Tressandre doesn't feel charitable? What if she decides that being Dweller is far more despicable and Merri becomes the target of all her venom? That sentiment would back her if she assassinated a mongrel? Use her for bait? How could you say such a thing?" She took a deep breath. Both babies stopped suckling a moment and Merri's little face bunched up unhappily. "And how long would I leave Evarton 'in safety'?"

"A year, perhaps two, at the most. While Tressandre has her child and Lariel proves her claim insubstantial."

"You want me to give away one of my babies for years? How would he even know me when I took him back? How would I repair the hole in my heart for doing such a thing? How could you ask it of me?"

"It might be best," Dayne answered softly.

"Never will I sell myself short again because of Vaelinar politics. These are my children and I will raise them close and well. Don't ever tell me to give either of them up again."

Tolby's face creased in sadness. "Are you certain, Meg?"

"Never more. Only the years will tell if I'm right, but I won't be trading one for the other. We will keep them safe." She tightened her embrace about them. Merri began to drink again, but Evarton, who had never stopped, seemed full and laid his cheek against her bosom and watched her. She looked up to see Dayne watching her.

He gave a brief, crooked smile before turning back to the fire. He'd done some hunting evidently because she could smell meat roasting on a spit as he busied himself tending it. He said something she didn't catch. "What was that?"

"I said I would be one of their guardians. If you'll have me."

Her face warmed. "How could I not?"

He twisted around. "There are a hundred ways and more you could turn me away, Nutmeg Farbranch. I pray you use none of them."

She saw the intensity of his expression and in his eyes as he braced himself. He expected her to refuse him, but how could she? Disappointment chilled her, deep inside, that he asked for the babies and not for her as well. Not that she thought he wanted her in that way, or even that she was ready after losing Jeredon, but disappointment wended its way throughout, despite all that. Someday she would want again. Look for love again. And she had begun to think when she did, that Dayne would be the one she searched for. She could think of no one else she'd rather have in her heart.

Words jostled against her tongue and lips, refused to issue, not until she had thought long what to say and swallowed twice against a dry mouth to say them. "Verdayne Vantane, I would be honored for you to be a guardian for my children."

"Good." He nodded. "Because that is the way it will be, regardless of your permission."

She sputtered slightly, and Tolby chuckled.

He tapped his belt knife on the spit. "Supper is ready, and I suggest we make plans before we sleep. The spring sun should wake us early, and we need to be on our way. There's a war brewing out there, and I intend to have our babies in a safe haven before it hits. May the plots and conspiracies of our kin pass us by."

"Amen to that!" Tolby answered.

Meg hugged her children close. From his lips to the ears of the Gods, wherever They might be sleeping.

Chapter
Sixty-One

Lariel

LARA EMERGED into the late morning from the man-
or's kitchen door and enjoyed the sunlight as it came
down to bathe her. The gold about her throat warmed against
her bare skin and seemed to tighten about her waist. She
smoothed the Jeweled armor down over her chain, her fingertips catching a buzzing tingle as she did so. She pulled her
gloves across her fingers, waiting as Chastain led her gelding
Yarthan out of the yard, and made an inspection of his harness before placing himself at his headstall, holding him for
her to mount.

She stepped forward. "The battalion is readied?"

"Waiting on the road."

"And the company to remain behind?"

"Patrolling, my lady, as you commanded."

Lariel stood by her horse's stirrup in hesitation, a nag-
ging thought at the back of her mind that she could not
banish even as she could not quite bring it up clearly so that
she might understand why she hesitated, why she worried.
She slapped her gloves across the palms of her hands.

"My lady?"

"I have forgotten something. And it vexes me not to know what it might be."

He opened his mouth and then shut it, having evidently been taught sometime in his young past that it was not wise to interrupt thoughts at such a time. The corner of his mouth skewed tightly.

She rubbed at the spot between her finely arched eyebrows, and then shook her head. Lariel sighed. "Still no word from Calcort?"

"Not yet this day, but the bird handler did not seem worried. The winds and uncertain weather, he thought, would have delayed any flight."

Her guards would have, she knew, not waited for a certain time of day to send off a bird if Nutmeg had gone into labor. The word would have been sent off immediately. She had to assume that no message meant all was well. Would be well. If Jeredon had any way to work his will upon this world, he would be watching Nutmeg and his unborn child. She believed that. As for things undone or forgotten, she couldn't linger.

"On to Ashenbrook, then." She pulled her gloves on emphatically and then swung up. Her gelding lifted his head high and let out a challenging whicker as she settled into the saddle and shoved her boots in securely, taking up the reins.

They had barely ridden out of the manor's yards when the wind came whistling in. It turned the helm on her head chill even with the leather lining and she put a hand up to make sure it stayed snug on her head. Yarthan wheeled and trumpeted a protest into the storm front, nostrils flared, and pawed a front hoof on the road. Roaring in fiercely, the wind lifted his mane from his arched neck and buffeted Lara so that she grabbed for a hold.

Chastain's horse wheeled in panicked circles until he got hold of her and curbed her to a standstill. The trees about them whipped in a frenzy and beyond, where the River Andredia flowed, she could hear a torrent, as if the storm filled the river and sent it cascading harshly down the banks. The air smelled of the sea and of spent lightning.

"I don't like this," her armsman muttered. He clapped a hand to his sword hilt.

"Would you strike down a lightning bolt? We have no power against this." She swung her horse about. "We've objectives we can handle. Join the battalion while we can. Make the border of Larandaril. Ashenbrook can no longer wait!" She shook her reins and Yarthan sprang forward, head down, as if he thought he could outrace the storm. The clouds behind clashed against one another and the boom of thunder began to shake and rattle down the valley and across the groves. She could hear tree branches crack and fall. She bent low over her horse's neck and chirped to urge him into a pounding run.

They reached her battalion at the edge of the border, in a wide, far-reaching meadow bounded by forest on either side, her men in armor and leather hunkered down for a siege, the cavalry dealing with white-eyed horses who reared and spooked against the incoming storm. Clouds blackened the sky, and she reeled Yarthan about, eyeing this far reach of Larandaril, a border she'd crossed to go to war at Ashenbrook several times over the past year, and what she saw struck her heart as solidly as if someone had reached out and punched her.

Maiden's nod, pink-throated blossoms thrashing in the wind, the wildflower growing in abundance over the green grasses, everywhere she looked. Near her manor, they grew in handfuls here and there—but in this place, in this time, they looked like a pink flood upon the green. Her eyes widened at the sight. At what she'd seen in prophecy. What she'd viewed, through Chastain's eyes when she'd possessed him. When Sevryn had found the corrupted side of her soul. When the nodding pink blossoms filled the fields and her vision. When she'd come to meet a death she could not possibly meet, not and have the world of Kerith survive what was yet to come.

Everywhere. She knew that meadow. The flowers. Chastain by her side. *She knew.* The time of her death loomed over her. No matter what she had done, it had found her.

Lara's hands tightened into fists. Yarthan, on the bit, whickered a protest as her hold bruised his mouth and rose into a half-rear in the air. "Seventh Battalion!"

Her captain, a hard-bitten man who had spent most of his years riding under Bistel and had come to Lariel only upon his death, put his hand up. "Ready on your command." He had blue-violet eyes, and hair that gleamed the color of bronze, and a network of crinkles about his eyes, and one corner of his mouth rode higher than another, thanks to an old scar. He had once been a contemporary of Bistel, and was made of that same steel, to the core. Before she could answer his unasked question, the skies opened up and rain came down in crushing blows, a torrential rain that stank of brine and seaweed. It flooded the ground, frothing into whitecaps about the horses' dancing hooves and Lara pulled her sword, swearing. She looked up into a boiling sky and still more rain plummeted earthward in a curtain so dense she could barely see through it. And then the Raymy tumbled after, stinking of the ocean and wet leather and plague.

"Forward, attention!" shouted Gandathar, clearing his steel of his leather and putting himself between her and the first rolling bodies to drop upon the ground in salted, stinking pools of water. Her troops sprang to attention, dispatching the first few groups with relative ease, as the Raymy warriors seemed disoriented, getting to their feet with dazed grunts, but the skies kept raining, as far as she could see, lizard warriors.

Daravan's tide flooded back, rolling over Larandaril. Not Ashenbrook where it had been taken up. Not where she had the bulk of her troops quartered, as did Bistane and, even reluctantly, the ild Fallyn, and the rest of their allies.

Not where the defenses had been built up carefully in wait. Not where the offensive troops had been quartered for seasons, drilling and anxious, waiting and eager. Not where any of the military minds at her disposal had planned for the Raymy to be. Daravan had weakened beyond any of their expectations.

"Gandathar. Clear a handful of men. Send them back to the birdmaster, have him send word the troops must come here, at all haste."

Her captain nodded sharply and spun about, pointing five times. The cavalrymen raced past her, horses' hooves thundering and swerving past the struggling masses of lizard warriors. The last man put his horse into a leap over a knot of Raymy and one of them rose up, bounding as they could do on froglike legs, sword impaling the jumper deep into its gut, bringing down the horse crying in agony and the rider in silence as he tried to roll free. Both horse and soldier disappeared in a sea of gray-green flesh as savage cries filled the air.

Only four left to make it back to the manor and send word for reinforcements. Lara turned away, unable to help, knowing it useless to watch, her own position slowly being ringed in as masses of Raymy got to their feet and the rain kept pouring. She wiped the stinging from her eyes and filled both hands with her steel, guiding Yarthan with her knees as he'd been trained. The golden pectoral and girdle flashed as she leaned, twisted and struck, regained her balance and leaned another way to parry a blow, and growl a return warning as lizards reared their warty heads to hiss at her. Yarthan backed slowly into a fortified circle of fighters, all of them facing outward, as Raymy began to press into a formation around them.

"Hold!" ordered Gandathar. "Don't let them break us."

A tall order for a small group of men. From the center of the battalion, archers loosed a flight of arrows that cleared the path around them, Raymy falling with gurgling cries and their more cautious fellows pulling back.

Gandathar made it to her knee. "What shall we do?"

"As you ordered," Lara answered grimly. "Hold." She looked out over the meadow and remembered that, in her vision, the sun had been shining when Sevryn had struck her down. Had she augured the day wrongly? Or did she yet have time?

She dared not trust to a fate she'd foreseen. Her time was here and now.

She heard a gurgling scream to the rear of their position and turned her head to see one Raymy fall on a wounded horse, tearing it to ribbons like a hunger-crazed hound.

She spoke a soothing word to Yarthan to steady the horse and stood her ground as a wing of fighters, their warty skin glistening in the rain, hopped forward in advance.

When night fell, the rain stopped, if rain it had been. It felt and smelled like an ocean had descended upon them, drowning them under brined waves that caked the skin and stung the eyes and nostrils and almost hid the stench of the diseased enemy. And when night fell, it fell blackly, under storm clouds still hiding the sky, a thousand stars muted. They banked no fires for themselves or the wounded. They dismounted and let their tired horses stand quietly, and set sentries on the outer ring of defense, but the Raymy had fallen back as well, yellowed eyes glittering in the dusk until they could no longer be seen. No sign had been reported of Daravan. They must have taken him apart. Lara sank to her haunches and checked her blades by running bare fingers over them, found a whetstone, and began working the notches out.

"Will they try a nighttime attack?"

"I can't say. Their eyes are different than ours. If I had to venture a guess, and I doubt any of us want to stake our lives on a guess, I'd say they cannot see well in the dark. I don't remember that from Ashenbrook. It could be the disease. I know that it's affected their stamina. If it hadn't, we'd all be dead. As it is, we've fought hard but taken far fewer casualties than I would have expected." She paused. "We have to hold. It will be days before anyone can reach us. They are all marshaling at Ashenbrook. It's where we met them last. It's where they were swept up from. It's where they should have returned!"

"But they did not, and now it's up to us."

"Can we hold?"

"We've no choice. We have some tactical advantage in

that they are plagued by illness and their own weakness. Since they're Raymy, I'll take any advantage I can get."

"They seem disorderly and disoriented. We can outthink them. We should be able to outlast them."

Gandathar inclined his head. "That, my lady queen, is my deduction." He handed her a hunk of jerky. "I set sentries but only half the number I would normally have put out. Better to have rested men at dawn."

"I want us moving before dawn."

"Where to?"

"To the far side of the meadow, into the grove's edge. I want what men can get up into the trees — archers, spearmen — to do so."

"Attack from above." His lower lip tightened. "Might help."

"Axmen are to drop branches down. We need to build a barricade."

"Of course." Gandathar stood. "We should start now."

"It would be wise, but in shifts. We all need to be ready at dawn and that means some sleep."

"We will have sleep enough when we're dead."

She made a noise at that. He patted her on the shoulder as he moved away and quietly, so quietly she barely heard his voice, began to cull his axmen from those gathered. Lara chewed at a corner of the dried meat and discovered that she hungered and finished the bit eagerly. The stringy meat left threads in her teeth that she picked at carefully, before finding a waterskin and drinking sparingly of it. The Andredia flowed not far away, but she could not measure the risk it would take to reach it. Not with the Raymy overwhelming the countryside. Low, murmured conversations surrounded her, quiet voices, not wanting to lure the enemy out, but still needing the connection of talking, punctuated by the sound of soft snores as the exhausted slept. Now and then, Lara could hear the high-pitched whistling hiss of a Raymy accosted by a fellow reptile as they battled among themselves. They ate their dead. They might be feasting now.

She could hope, but knew it would be in vain, that they

might destroy themselves overnight. They would not. And if another storm blew in, there could be greater numbers yet to drop. Where was Daravan when they needed him again? She remembered the fields of battle at Ashenbrook and Ravela and knew the opposition had come pouring out of a mountainside and into the stony valley, seemingly without end. She feared there were more to come. Could they hold out? Would anyone be able to reach them in time? She had no answers.

And she felt alone.

Chapter
Sixty-Two

"ANY NEWS IN THE NIGHT?" Lariel woke to a day not yet dawned, still curtained by heavy night, and one that had not yielded much sleep. Her captain stood over her, barely distinguishable in his blues, his quiet touch alerting her.

"None worth noting," Gandathar said, passing down a pannikin of porridge that smelled both sweet and savory, though thin enough to drink.

"Their numbers held, then."

"Unfortunately."

She sipped the porridge down. It tasted surprisingly good, and she could only wish there were more of it but knew there wouldn't be. "At least they have not increased."

"Right at that, my lady. I had a few fires struck. I've had the lads boiling water and making sure they keep as clean as possible. The corruption is as far downwind as we could manage it." He paused. "Even the skraw are cautious scavenging the bodies."

Carrion even the scavengers avoided? That could only

reinforce her caution. The Raymy died, becoming plague dead that only cold earth and scalding fire might welcome.

"Fence up?"

"Not only up, but sharpened. It should hold a substantial charge, and then the boys will only have to watch those coming over the top or flanking us."

"You let me sleep too long."

"You gave your orders. We knew what to do, and your mind needs to be clear."

She cleaned the pannikin out with a swirl of her finger and licked that clean. "Excellent. Now we move into position."

"Nearly all the men are already withdrawn to position."

Lara blinked in surprise. That meant he had left her open, exposed to the enemy if the Raymy could have seen better in the dark.

"It's all right, my lady. I left the archers behind, and ten of our best swordsmen." He put out his hand to help her to her feet. She stood without touching him, though her mail weighed her down, her body used to its burden.

Chastain stood beyond her captain, his bow in his hand, arrow ready, and attention across the meadow warily. Lariel watched him for a moment. Would he know when she entered his mind? Would she have to make sure that he did not survive this engagement even if he deserved to? *And where was Sevryn?* She turned away.

They backed up to their new position, facing toward the enemy, moving together in a concerted effort, and she was almost disappointed when they made it without incident. Gandathar let out a muted sigh. She listened to the sound of the horse line behind them. The cooling canopy of the grove, intermittent though it was because the trees here had been thinned by logging, would still protect them when the sun came out. If it came out.

They attacked at dawn. Silently, out of the grasses, rearing up and at the barricade before the Raymy were even sighted from the treetops, their mottled skins perfect camouflage in the flattened grasses. Lara watched as Gandathar set the archers into place. She went to the horse line and tacked Yarthan up, his ears flicking forward and back alertly, his nostrils snuffling at the blood already being spilled in the morning. He ducked his head so she could pull his headstall up and over and fasten it securely. His withers danced as if her hands tickled him when she put the blanket and saddle on, but the blanket did more than pad the saddle's weight, it protected his flanks and much of his stomach from injury, the fabric and fibers of such a weave that even arrowheads couldn't pierce it easily. Lara tightened the girth firmly. "You'll be better protected than I will," she told the gelding. "Mostly." Her gold Sentinel jewelry from Tranta glinted in tiny, sun-catching flashes about her.

She could hear Gandathar barking short commands and her men answering above the grunts and hisses of the Raymy as they clashed. A look back over her shoulder revealed that the Raymy were coming over the barricade—not easily and not quickly, but inexorably. Cued by her actions at the horse line, a dozen of her armsmen were mounting up as well so that when she swung up into her saddle and Yarthan came about, she had a detail at her heels. She used her pole arms, snugging the heel of her poleax deep in its pocket in the corner of her saddle harness, and shook the reins at Yarthan as she cried "For Larandaril!" and charged out of the forest, angled at the Raymy flank. Battle cries followed her.

The first hit jolted her teeth in their sockets and felt as if it knocked her elbow into her shoulder. Her target fell hissing and growling, but it did not get up. She freed her weapon and reset it quickly as the Raymy began to swing about, realizing the enemy angled at them. After that, she could only concentrate on keeping alive, keeping her horse on its feet and her in its saddle as the Raymy fought to cross their meridian.

Gandathar handed her the reins to a fresh mount and threw her aboard with a sharpened sword and a small shield at some time when the sun had sunk past its high mark in the sky. She relinquished the poleax only when he did so, letting it drop to the ground. Her hand and arm felt numb. Her *mind* felt numb.

"Casualties?"

"They're taking the worst of it by far, my lady." Her captain did not look her in the eyes. He watched as she washed perfunctorily and then lifted a waterskin, gulping its contents down a throat both hoarse and dry that water seemed to help little. "You could take a breather."

"Are you?"

"Only long enough to see you remounted."

"Can you afford even that?" She started to turn about in a circle and he caught her stirrup, staying the horse in its tracks.

"What we can't afford, Lariel, is losing you."

"We need to take the offensive instead of defensive. If we keep falling back, they will have us cornered in another day or two." Her left hand ached, the joint missing a finger gnawed at her. She rubbed her gauntlet without thinking. "We have to stop them, even if only for a day or two." The sky darkened overhead, rumbling ominously as she spoke and they both looked upward. The clouds, whenever they drew close and dark, rained more enemy down.

"What do you suggest?"

"Clear the field. Put the fear of Dhuriel in them." Dhuriel, their God of Fire, meant more than mere sparks and a warm hearth. She talked conflagration on a massive scale. She waited.

Gandathar looked, his gaze examining the field closely, littered with piles of bodies here and there. Some of them the Raymy worried at, feeding. Others had not yet been molested. One eyebrow lifted.

"Do you see a pattern?" she asked of him.

"I do, and I commend you. Clever. You need a torch, not a sword."

"I need both, and I need a skin of that excellent oil that burns with very little persuasion."

He went and fetched both, handing them to her. "It's good to know that stinkdogs have some worth in the world." He wore a second skin over his shoulder.

"I'll take the left flank."

"Then I the right. Use your shield, my lady! They're getting the hang of spears and, I daresay, a few archers among them."

"The same for you." He lit her torch before soaking and lighting one himself, Lara waiting until he was ready.

Then they left the relative safety of the grove and went to set fire to pyres of the dead that she and her armsmen had been compiling through the day. She leaned from her saddle, squirting the noxious smelling liquid over the tumbled forms of the Raymy dead and what looked like one Vaelinar under them. She murmured, "Nevinaya aliora," in farewell to her own as she waved the torch over the bodies and the oil flumed upward in a violent explosion of flame as her horse leaped aside from the heat and roar. Nevinaya aliora, *Remember the soul*, indeed.

Lara wheeled her horse away from the pyre and raced for the second, others across the field going up in the same blaze of glory, smoke guttering up with a stink that brought tears to her eyes. The next three piles held only Raymy bodies and she said nothing over them, not even breathing if she could help it as she layered the accelerant over the stack. That last stack brought her within range of the fighters, and their croaking and hissing threatened her. A well-thrown spear arched over her shield and shoulder as she ducked her head to wheel her horse about. It clattered to the ground impotently and her horse did a little bucking leap over it as they ran off.

She shook the reins and leaned low over his neck, signaling a jump. They cleared the barrier as her men yelled a welcome.

They quieted as she raised her hand. "Smoke covers the field. It gives us eight major points of concealment to advance. Muster and find your leader and do so. It's time we showed them what Vaelinar steel can do!"

And so they did.

But when her horse finally staggered to a weary halt, head down and sobbing for breath, and she sat with legs so numb she did not know if she could sit her mount any longer, she knew that the only thing saving her at that moment was the rapidly falling dusk. The pyres now guttered low, with a fog of smoke overlying the meadow, maiden's nod long trampled into nothingness and the smell of burning flesh overrunning her senses. She should seek a healer but knew the only one they had would be overwhelmed, and he was more of an archer than a healer anyway ... she'd sent all her resources to Ashenbrook.

"Queen Lariel."

She lifted her gaze.

Chastain stood at the withers of her horse, his hand out to help her down. She studied him, torn by her emotions. If he had died during the day, then her vision of her death might not yet await her. She would have lost a good armsman but perhaps a destiny as well. Guilt flooded her at the thought, and she looked away, smoothing her expression and hoping he had not read it.

She took his hand and swung down. She would have to kill him if he remembered in his future that she had possessed his mind. Why not now? What could she change if she did?

His hand pressed upon hers firmly, assuring that she stayed on her feet, tired as she was.

Why not indeed? Sinok would have done it. Her grandfather had done a good many things that appalled her and yet saved the kingdoms for both the natives of Kerith and the Vaelinar.

"My lady?" He watched her face quizzically.

Lara shook her head briskly. "Nothing, Chastain. Nothing at all. A momentary ghost."

"There are many tonight," he returned grimly.

"How many fallen?"

"Near half."

That news, despite his hold on her, did stagger her. "That many?"

"I fear so."

"Captain Gandathar?"

"Injured although still able to sit a horse, hold a sword, and bark orders."

She firmly but gently removed Chastain's hold on her arm. "I'll see him, then, when I've gotten my own hurts cleaned. Is there anyone who can tend my horse?"

Chastain whistled sharply and a young Vaelinar limped over, his ankle firmly splinted. "Take my lady's mount for her?"

"Gladly." He took the reins before ducking his face, but she could not see a glimmer of resentment for being called up while injured, and she thanked him.

Then she went to get the bad news, and the worse news, of the day.

Gandathar sat on the ground, his back to a tree, his left arm resting across his knee. He watched as she settled herself, no less gingerly than it looked like he shifted to make room for her.

"Chastain told me it was bad."

"It is. More than half fallen. We have most of our dead behind the lines so that we do not have to listen to the Raymy savage them, but that's little consolation."

"Can we hold another day?"

He did not answer.

She leaned forward. "I'm not asking if it will be enough. Only if we can hold one more day."

The rough nature of his face hid his feelings. "I can't promise you that, Lara. We're doing our best, all of us, but we are outnumbered."

She nodded and cupped her hand over his knee for a moment. "Understandably." She leaned her head back against the tree bark. She looked up at her leafy support, a Larandaril evergreen, nourished by one of the tiny brooks that fed into the sacred Andredia. Raymy blocked the Andredia from her. She resented them for that almost as much as for the deaths of her men and women.

An agonized nicker broke the muted silence of the camp. The sound of it sent shivers over her skin. "The horses?"

"We can't do much for the wounded. We haven't enough skilled vets here, but we are doing what we can. The few are working on the men."

She pressed her eyelids shut a moment. When Lara opened them, she said, "Send the horses out at dawn. The wounded we absolutely cannot save and yet can be driven in a herd."

Gandathar tilted his head questioningly.

"The Raymy are voracious scavengers. We've destroyed their dead, contaminated them. They hunger at least as badly as we do. Send them meat on the hoof."

"My lady."

"I know." She struggled to her feet. "It will give us an advantage which we seem desperately to need, to pull back yet again. The forest grows thicker here. Some of us can disappear into it to survive. Someone must survive, to tell the others what has happened."

He gave a grudging nod. "So ordered."

She left him gnawing at her words as if he could chew them and spit them out, but they both knew that their choices consisted of difficult and none.

She went to the horse lines and gave what comfort she could, knowing it would not be enough for either them or her. In the morning she would have to muster whatever courage she held, knowing that her vision had failed her and that not just her, but all of them, were fated to die in this trampled valley.

Chapter
Sixty-Three

A BAYAN DIORT RODE down a narrow canyon, a harrowing neck of an entrance that spoke of ambush to a military man, one he would prefer not to have taken but to which Ceyla had guided him resolutely The little slip of a Vaelinarran woman refused to bow before his authority and experience. They had argued but briefly, his stubbornness equaled only by her own. If it had not been part of her prophetic seeing, he would have disdained her directions and taken his army the way he wished. Anywhere but this choking stone canyon The noise of their movement brought crumbles of rock and pebbles trickling down, even avalanches of sand which coalesced into a smoky fog rising from horse hooves and footfalls to tickle the back of the throat and dry the eyes. He turned in his saddle to look at Ceyla riding at his flank. She didn't notice his glance, all her attention seemingly focused on keeping on top of her mount, with a mixed expression on her face that revealed fear and effort, her hands knotted into both the reins and mane. His mount's hooves clicked on the stones and sent them skittering away. Ceyla's eyelids bolted open and her face pinked as she saw Abayan watching her.

"Are we close?"

"I don't know where we are, just where we're going. The sight—" she started to gesture its vagueness, but ended up desperately grabbing for balance. "I think you'll know it when you get there."

"I should expect a battle. If so, we will know long before we reach it."

"You should expect your destiny."

"Perhaps I should ask if I will live to fulfill it."

Ceyla grinned before putting a hand up to hide her face self-consciously. She wore traditional Galdarkan garb and her filmy sleeve slid back, revealing her delicate arm. "One hopes. Finding a destiny is a journey. Fulfilling it should be another journey as well." She anchored herself firmly yet again.

"Even as young a prophet as you should know that some journeys are very short."

Her answer tumbled out without thought. "Not yours."

"Well, then. I'll take that as good news." He shrugged back around in his saddle until all she could see were his broad shoulders, golden skin rippling with his muscle. "Very good news."

Ahead of him, the man on point raised his hand, giving an all clear. That should have lightened his spirit, but Abayan did not try to fight the feeling inside him that something waited, just ahead, something close and something dangerous. A being could crouch among the broken foot of the hillsides and not be seen until too late. Not an army. Not a handful of men. A single man, deadly and—

Abayan brought his horse to a sudden halt. He shaded his eyes. A furtive movement between him and the point man far ahead. He stayed rock-still in his saddle, watching that splinter of movement to see what might happen. Had he seen it? Had he imagined it? He narrowed his eyes as his gut tightened in anticipation. His intensity communicated along the reins to his mount who threw his head up alertly.

The army at his back stood at attention as well, noise muffled by the crooked canyon, but still undeniable: stomps, the creak of leathers as soldiers rose in their stirrups or sat back to relax in their saddles or freed bows from their harnesses and brought them to ready. Horses whickered softly and chomped at their bits. He heard all of that.

What he did not hear was noise from in front of him. Silence rested where there ought to have been bird chatter, an occasional song, the tap of claw on rock as rodents or lizards skittered. Their coming would have sent wildlife fleeing, but they hadn't passed yet. Hadn't drawn close enough. No, the silence here was commanded by a presence just ahead, and that was what he watched.

A shape emerged from what had seemed only to be a slight crack in the granite and shale wall ahead. A Kobrir, black clothing so covered in dirt that he appeared to be gray, unfolded, hands at shoulder height and seemingly empty.

Before Diort could utter a word, Ceyla warned. "Steady." Did she mean it for him and not the assassin? Had she lied but moments ago? His mouth dried. Was this to be his fate? Had the ild Fallyn sent him a false prophet to lead him astray? He cursed himself as a fool, a most unworthy Galdarkan. His hand twitched as he let it fall on his sword's hilt. If he had his will, he'd have pulled Rakka, the earth-shattering war hammer which had once been his, the instrument which he had used to build his new empire, the weapon which had helped stem the tide of Raymy at Ashenbrook River and had died in the doing of it. If a war hammer could die. The weapon remained, but it had emptied of the powers imbued in it, and now stayed holstered near his stirrup as a massive hammer which could do damage but nothing like the legends he and it had put into modern memory. He wondered if it was his turn to be emptied and remembered only by past deeds.

The Kobrir spoke. "Lord Diort. I am unarmed."

Abayan frowned and heeled his horse a step or two closer. "I know that voice. Is that Sevryn Dardanon behind the assassin's cover? Or have the Kobrir become even more cunning, imitating one of the Queen's own?"

"Indeed. There's a long story here about why I wear an assassin's garb that I would willingly tell you, but I think we both have a place to be. Time is not in our favor. May I ride with you?"

A second being emerged groveling from the hillside, clutching at Sevryn's knees. "Don't leave me! Don't!" Then, as if realizing he was exposed in full, dazzling sunlight, the man shrank down, throwing his arm over his eyes. As ragged as if he'd just stumbled out of a ghetto, Master Trader Bregan cowered at Sevryn's feet, the only thing recognizable about him the Vaelinar brace that ran the length of his leg and articulated as well as any limb.

Abayan fastened his gaze on Bregan, not understanding what he saw, both revolted and fascinated by the esteemed trader's obvious downfall. "Time," agreed Diort, "is of the essence, but there's at least part of a tale here which has to be told."

"Indeed," murmured Ceyla behind him. "Guardian King Diort."

Her words pierced his attention. He twisted to consider her. He was a warlord. He had gathered hundreds to follow him. Reinforced dozens of city states behind him. Yet her naming of him struck something buried inside him that sounded like a deep chord, plucking at his very soul. He did not like that, but he could not deny it, either. Unsettled, he looked back to Sevryn and the beggar. "Trader Bregan," he acknowledged.

The man rolled his head from under his arm to peer up at him. Ceyla crowded her horse close, and Bregan's gaze flicked from Diort back to her and returned to Diort. "L-Lord Diort," he managed.

Sevryn nudged him. "Stand up, Bregan."

"Must I?"

"It would be best."

Bregan stood, pulling himself up hand over hand on Sevryn's stern figure. Sevryn appeared not to notice the handling he received until his companion straightened and then he reached over and dusted Bregan off, somewhat.

Ceyla did not stay at Diort's side. She kneed her horse forward until she was close enough to touch either of the men if she but leaned out of the saddle, her expression intent upon Bregan. When she finally reined to a stop nearly on top of the trader, she said, "Tell him."

None of the three men spoke, silenced by confusion. She reached down to Bregan, and said again, urgently, "Tell him!"

Bregan coughed into his hands.

"You mean him to speak of what?" asked Diort mildly of Ceyla.

She pivoted about and stared him in the eyes for a long moment before only nodding and turning back to the Kernan trader. Sevryn dropped his hand on Bregan's shoulder. He flinched.

"The news will out, one way or another. Might as well begin here," Sevryn said.

Bregan shuffled a filthy boot, scuffing up even more dust and grime. "I—" His voice broke.

They waited. Bregan gathered himself, as painful a mental process as Abayan Diort had ever witnessed. He could not afford to wait, but he had been compelled. For no discernible reason, his heart knotted in sympathy. He leaned forward slightly. "We're listening. I hold an entire army at my back, and yet we wait to hear what you have to say."

Sevryn dropped his hand on the other's shoulder and squeezed Bregan comfortingly. Bregan threw his chin up. "The Gods have spoken to me. I didn't ask for it, and I can't help it. They . . . they tell me I am Mageborn." He reeled away and thudded against the canyon wall as if spent.

Abayan's breath left him as painfully and suddenly as if someone had swung his war hammer into his chest. Diort swayed back. He fought for air.

Ceyla looked to him, triumph on her face. "This is what I dreamed."

Diort ignored her. "What do you mean?" he demanded of Bregan when he could breathe again.

"He means that he has magic," Sevryn answered. "That the tunnels of the Mageborn answer to him. That he believes he has heard the voices of your Gods. That he has been driven nearly mad by what cannot be happening but what seems to be happening."

"Magic."

"Old Kerith magic. The kind not seen in centuries upon centuries."

"With good reason. They destroyed themselves."

Sevryn smiled slightly upon Diort. "But they created the Galdarkan."

Diort did not smile back. "You would undo all that I have built if I accept this man for what he claims."

"Your kin were made to be guardians, to protect and guide the magic and madness of these men. You have risen to reweave that empire, but this time with Galdarkan common sense and leadership, bringing a sense of unity back to that which was shattered. Will you abandon it now?" Sevryn cocked his head.

"I can't deny that, but—" Abayan shifted uneasily.

Bregan lurched forward and put his hands on Diort's booted foot. "I didn't want this," he husked. "I wouldn't pretend it for a hundred Trade empires."

Clouds that had cleared for the morning threatened to darken the skies again, and a faraway thunder rumbled heavily. They all looked to it. The moment shredded away. Diort rubbed the back of his neck. Fate tugged at him.

"I haven't much time," Sevryn reminded.

"None of us have. Why are you here?"

"Bregan guided us, but I imagine we all go to the same meeting."

"Yes," Ceyla answered quickly. She swung down to press the reins at Sevryn. "Take my horse." She unloosed the second waterskin and held it to her chest as she clambered over the trail and sat in the shade of the standing men.

Again she would contradict his orders. Diort frowned down at her. "I won't leave you here."

"Oh," and she smiled brightly at Diort. "I don't expect

you will, but here is where I need to wait. I've done what I had to do. My prophecy is finished."

"You would not see the end of it?"

"It's enough to have seen the beginning. You're the one meant to see the ending."

He felt uncertainty again, a feeling that he had trained himself against, replacing it with confidence and experience, but she shook him yet again. He would not argue with her again, not with hundreds of troops behind him watching, even if they were unsure of what they watched. His little prophet going toe to toe with him would not need much translation to become army gossip. He would have to leave Ceyla behind. Diort tapped his chest. "You have a place with me even if you never utter another oracle in your lifetime. I've pledged that."

"Then you'll come back for me when it's time." She watched as Sevryn mounted.

Bregan stood hesitantly. The fading sun gleamed dully off his brace, the only thing about him which shed dust as if determined not to be dirty. Diort put his hand out, saying "You'll ride behind me. I'll get you a horse of your own as soon as I can." He kicked his foot out of his stirrup so that Bregan could use it to mount and swing up behind him.

When all had settled, Diort said, "We ride to war."

"We know," Bregan muttered at his shoulder. "I suppose you want to know what the Gods had to say."

"That might be helpful."

"Some of Them are very angry."

"Helpful *and* prudent. And the others?"

"Not all are fully awakened. When They are, there will be a judgment."

"But not today."

The man at his back leaned very close to his ear. "I can't always make sense of anything."

"When you can, speak to me."

Ceyla watched them ride out of hearing, and then the army passed her by as well. She was still watching as the point man rode back to Abayan, throwing himself off his mount and to the ground, flattening himself in abject apology for having missed the men among the rocks. Diort did what he did, what a decent, honorable leader must. He picked the man up and sent him back on his way, chastised but not broken.

He knew she watched him, because he felt the weight of her regard on the back of his neck. He would not turn back to view her, because she had said her good-byes and promised him there would be a return and what more could he ask of a prophet? But as he led his column into the valley where she had told him war awaited, he wondered if she had counseled him properly and if the role she had foretold would really be the role he rode to play. Trader Bregan tightened his arm about Diort's rib cage. He stank like a man who had been living in a gutter and perhaps he had. He seemed maddened. Diort considered what Ceyla had told him very carefully. What good would it do his world to have the Mageborn return, despite the fact he had been created to care for them, to defend the law and bring justice for them, and yet the need to care for Bregan had settled in his very bones. He wanted to deny the urge to nurture the man, a foreign emotion making itself at home in his body. But what would it mean to deny that for which he had been born? Ceyla had called him the Guardian King. She had come to him, telling him she would point him toward the true meaning of his life. He had chosen to believe her without knowing all of the consequences, events that overshadowed all the hard work of the past few decades drawing his broken people together. He had hoped she would show him the way to complete his working, not giving him an invalid to take care of. Oracles had never been known to be crystal clear, although she had seemed clearer than most. He should have turned a deaf ear to her. Death could find him and this feeble newborn Mage easily on a battlefield. That might resolve much of the uncertainty that settled over him now.

After all, it was better to have Death come to your door than a Vaelinar.

Chapter
Sixty-Four

L ARA WOKE with a certainty in mind: that she needed
to reach the pure blue waters of the Andredia. Her
four-fingered hand twinged ferociously, bringing her out of
her half dreams even if the sound of the encampment waking and getting to its feet, gathering arms, the stamping of
nervous horse hooves did not. She had made a pact with
flesh and soul, and now the Andredia wanted her, piercing
even her exhausted dreams. The air sang with high-pitched
hissing, warning that the Raymy advanced. She opened her
eyes, right hand tightly grasping her left as if she could
squeeze the pain out of it. More than pain racked her body.
She carried the memory of Sinok Anderieon rasping to her
as he passed his title to her. *You are the heir to Larandaril
and the pact we forged with the sacred River Andredia. You
will face, or your heir will face, the destiny I had thought
would be mine. There is a time of reckoning coming for our
presence here. The Gods of this world will awaken and when
They do, there will a conflagration beyond imagination. You
must live! You must live and keep the peace with the Andredia and Kerith so that our people live.*

She bent over her hand, cradling it, overcome by the pain of the memory and of the maiming. The pact had almost been damaged beyond remedy when Quendius poisoned the font of the river itself, and she had sacrificed not only her finger but a good part of her soul to the Andredia to restore it, binding her forever to it.

Sevryn and Rivergrace. Jeredon and Nutmeg. They had fought with her to get to the Andredia. To destroy the sword Cerat possessed. To give her the opportunity to reforge the sacred bond. One was now dead. Two disgraced by betrayal. The fourth bearing her heir. The depth of her sacrifice she wouldn't know until her own end. Had she given up love and children? Did she regret it? She couldn't because she had never thought all lost, not until this morning. Her foretold assassination neared. The Andredia called out for her now, its banks defiled with swarming, diseased Raymy and the corruption and death they left on her shores. She had to get to the river. Vision or not, living or doomed to die, a fulfillment awaited. More than Sinok filled her mind. Her brother Jeredon echoed in her thoughts as well, and Jeredon's as yet unknown child.

She got up, shoulder to a bent evergreen sapling that flexed and bowed under her weight as she levered herself up. She knotted her aching left hand in its needled branches, the greenery still spring soft, and the aroma of it sinking into her skin, a welcome change from the stink that seemed to cling everywhere else. Savoring the evergreen perfume, she stripped some needles from the branch, crushing them in her hand and combing her fingers through her hair so that the memory of the fragrance couldn't leave her.

She dressed stiffly but quickly, lastly smoothing the gold chain jewelry Tranta wrought for her over her mail. It had saved her more than once over the last few days, but she could see that the various inset Jewels gleamed less brightly than they had. She cleaned and polished each one gently before bringing the pectoral to her neck and fastening it in place, a ritual she repeated with the girdle before clasping it about her waist. Both chimed gently against the mail underneath as they settled. The Sentinels Tranta had transformed from the shattered death of the Jewel of Tomarq would line the shores and hearts of the provinces. Had old Sinok also seen them in his forewarning? There'd been no mention if he had.

Lara raised her head. Visions were not substitutes for actions. He had taught her that more than anything. Action. Firm, decisive, conclusive.

She could hear the horses she'd condemned being gathered together and herded out. Lame and halt, panting with fear and pain, the beasts let themselves be driven toward the meadow reeking of smoke and seared flesh. Lara went to join the stable hand who led them, her own face drawn with the anguish of these charges, her hands white and trembling upon their headstalls. Lara brushed the girl's hands aside. "I'll take them."

"But—"

"I will take them," she repeated firmly.

The stable hand nodded and let go reluctantly after running her fingers down the dish face and rubbing the soft muzzles of several of the horses before dropping back.

Lara stood still a moment and let her mind and thoughts go into the tashya surrounding her. Tired beasts all, sore and hurting, afraid and hungry. Valiant animals who exceeded their training, every one of them loyal and brave until this misery. She eased their minds. She took what pain she could from them, chased away what fear she touched, promised them green meadows beyond the horrors they would tread. Her own Yarthan stood among them, his head held high in valor, his off leg bowed with a tendon injury she did not know he'd taken. She went to him and scratched the underside of his jaw. He wasn't injured enough to send with the herd, yet she saw in his thoughts his stubbornness at being left behind. He'd broken loose from the horse lines to come with this bunch, unknowing of what awaited them. He would bear her when the time came. She left their dazed thoughts gently, withdrawing slowly.

They followed her quietly to their slaughter, finely

carved heads held up, ears pricked forward, eyes bright, necks arched, their bodies moving as willingly as they could despite their wounds and injuries, flesh numbed by her to their agony.

Not so Lara. Hot, wet drops stung her cheeks and sank into pools of dampness in the arch of her throat. The tashyas surrounded her, flashes of color and heat, muzzles lipping at her hair, her hands, her shoulders, faces rubbing at her back. It reminded her of her very early days when her grandfather used to take her out to the pastures, when the yearlings would circle her, nip and buck to show their cleverness, and the brood mares would press close to her to see if she had apples or other treats to eat. She had never wanted to leave.

Now she picked up her pace into a slow jog, the horses moving to keep up, some of them stumbling as their injuries impeded them although they no longer felt the pain. She drew her sword slowly as the ever-present hissing sound of the Raymy rose in a high-pitched whine. They saw the horses moving. Perhaps she could even be seen within the group that now muffled and protected her. She hoped the Raymy watched in curiosity, drawn to a standstill.

She chirped to Yarthan who obediently trotted up close to her, his lean body buffeting his way to her side. Wrapping her left hand in his mane to hold him next to her, she raised her blade and began to humanely bring down the horses closest to her.

Hot, coppery blood fountained. Huge, warm bodies buckled and thudded to the earth, the light going out of soft brown eyes as she targeted the jugular in their throats, moving from one to another as quickly as she could, leaping over them even as they fell, Yarthan nickering in fear, pulling himself free. Lara moved in a frenzy like some great predator jumping among them and striking before most even knew what befell them. They died as painlessly as she could manage and at the last, called for Yarthan again who rolled white-ringed eyes at her, both of them covered in blood, and he untrusting and panicked. She seized his mind.

He plunged to a halt, hooves planted to the meadow, fetlocks sticky with pooling blood, and she vaulted onto his bare back even as the Raymy cried out and stampeded toward her and the bounty of horsemeat she'd created.

Their reptilian, diseased stink overrode that of smoke and burned flesh, but the copper smell of newly spilled blood sickened her even more. Lara bent low over Yarthan's neck, coaxing him for what speed he could bring, lamed gait making him wobbly, but he tried for her, neck and head lowered, and ears pitched back to catch her sounds of encouragement. She cast a look over her shoulder. The Raymy swarmed at the slaughter point, horse bodies being torn apart with such vigor that it appeared they reared in the air, legs and hooves flailing, but she knew she had left no living tashyas behind her. She could see a knot of horsemen angling her way, Gandathar and Chastain in front, coming to join her. Because their mounts were sound and hers not, they began to catch up surely. She held her sword up and cried, "The Andredia!"

They reached her. Chastain riding up on her flank, as they entered the far edge of the thinning grove between her and the river. They slowed, as branches whipped at them and then, as Lariel saw the trees give way to brush and grass slopes that would dip to the river, she slowed her horse in triumph. Nearly there. Once at the Andredia, she could put her back to the sacred river and know that it would protect her.

The silence of the forest gave way to croaks and hisses of challenge as row after row of Raymy rose up to greet her, blocking the way.

She put her heel into Yarthan's flank, forcing him about, only to face her own men.

"We're trapped."

"Only until we get to the river," Gandathar told her. He signaled to one of the bowmen who shouldered his bow to unclip a horn from his belt. "Sound the rally to the queen."

"Sir. You bring them to their death."

"We vowed to do this."

Lara watched as the young man brought the horn to his lips. His first attempt failed; he lowered the instrument to wet his lips and cough. Then he inhaled deeply and brought the horn up.

It winded over the noise of the Raymy advancing through the marsh grasses and underbrush. It sounded over the nervous tramping of their mounts. It trumpeted over the beleaguered meadows and groves, carrying gloriously across that breadth of Larandaril and the Andredia and into the verdant hills that surrounded them. The mighty blast sounded for what seemed forever.

Her heartbeat slowed and steadied as the last moments of panic settled into resolution. "Well and then," she said to Gandathar. "Let's make this as expensive to them as we can."

Before her words faded, an echo came down off the ridge.

They turned in shock, and Gandathar tilted his head to listen. "That's no echo. That's a response! We have troops incoming! Reinforcements!"

Lara's throat tightened. They had done it. They had held until reinforcements could reach them. She thanked her dead, her living, in silent prayer.

And as they looked to the faraway ridge, movement filled their sight. Horsemen, several hundred, began pouring down into the valley. The wards of Larandaril, thrown open did not alert her as they should have, and Lara watched with sudden, icy apprehension.

She knew why the moment she spotted their colors—the black and silver of Fort ild Fallyn.

Chapter
Sixty-Five

SEVRYN DID NOT REACT as the young woman riding with Abayan Diort and who had named him Guardian handed off her reins to him, leaned close, and whispered. He knew nothing of her, but felt a flare of her Talent wash over him as her breath grazed his ear.

He had not reacted, uncertain of what she meant or wanted, giving only a near imperceptible nod that he'd heard when he put his foot into the stirrup. Her words shivered into his ear and stayed coiled there like a menacing serpent that he could neither disregard nor evict.

"When the time comes, leave him behind. Your own destiny quickens and beats as the heart does, while his is slow and steady. You cannot wait!"

And that, he thought to himself a day later, is why oracles gather such success (and failure) to their names with vague tellings that brooked interpretation in any direction and often could not be understood at all until the event had

passed. As he rode behind Diort and Bregan, he had no
more idea of her meaning now than he'd had when she'd
first spoken to him. Unlike the Galdarkan leader, he put no
faith in a Vaelinar prophet, but she left him debating his
options nonetheless. On this earliest of dawns, he itched
with uneasiness. He longed for Rivergrace even as the geas
laid upon him burned. He had a date with the king of assassins.

That's when he heard them: the horns on the wind. The
sounding reached all of them. Diort threw his hand up, halting the march, and asked of his nearest commander. "Is that
a rallying call?"

"It is, and an answer. But they are far apart."

Galdarkan signaled his herald. "Bring your horn out
when we are close, but no sooner. We march too far away to
make assurances. Order a double-march, but we cannot
move quicker. I won't separate my forces."

And that was when Sevryn understood the oracle's
warning. Diort would march his army as one, foot soldiers
with the cavalry, but he—he could not afford to stay behind.
Without a word, he whipped his horse out of line and sent
him pelting down the canyon and into Larandaril. Hard
ground gave way to lusher grasses and flowers blooming
only to be crushed under horse hooves as they pounded
their way into the Warrior Queen's kingdom. Shouts behind
him thinned and fell into silence as he sent his horse as fast
as he dared into the heart of Lariel's vision of her death.

The Galdarkan horse splashed into the edge of a brook,
spraying them both with water, and he felt Rivergrace in its
touch. In shock at the sudden awareness, he hauled on one
rein, turning his horse about sharply. Mud and water splattered them both as his horse danced about, tossing his head
up and down at the abrupt command from Sevryn. As the
droplets ran down his body, he could feel Grace's presence
caress him from head to toe. She lived! She was near. She
touched water as he did. He wanted to shout to bring her
nearer. Sevryn shifted his weight about, looking back into the
hills and high mountains that crowned this end of the valley;

stony precipices where the font from which the Andredia sprang lay hidden. He soaked in her essence like a starving man. She lived—she feared, she worried—but she lived. Everything else he could deal with, they could solve together, but he wasn't prepared to face death again just yet, and definitely not without her. She sensed him as his horse pawed the brook, sending up white feathers of water, as they connected again and he felt the thrill of recognition and then a jolt of— abhorrence? Fear. Guilt. She wore a cocoon of emotion about her, dark and tangled, and he felt her reject him. She shoved him away so abruptly that he nearly lost his stirrups and seat on his horse, as if physically shoved.

Sevryn threw his leg over the rump of his horse, landing in the brook up to his knees. He bent and washed his face in the frothing water and as he did, he felt her slip away from him, but he would not let her go. Not without sending his love and trust to her.

She lingered for a moment then, an almost palpable image, a longing and he knew he had not lost her, although she had thought to push him away. Narskap's Undead touch played over the last of Rivergrace before their connection broke, and that left Sevryn leading his horse out of the river and onto the farther bank, giving up a bit of precious time to wonder what had transpired. Did Narskap hold her? And if so, faithful hound that he was, where was Quendius?

His heart beat heavily. The thud of it in his chest reminded him of his other needs. He turned the horse about, swung up, and shook the reins, aiming the Galdarkan steed toward the sound of horns, not so faint and far away as they had been.

Lather clung to his mount and the horse breathed gustily as they finally headed to the Andredia and Sevryn could see the colors of House Vantane thundering down the hill toward him from the border on the horizon. He angled his horse to join them, his right hand thrust in the air with his palm open in surrender and the ranks opened to let him catch up with Bistane at the fore. Their horses kept pace with one another, the two of them riding in a brace.

"What in the name of dead Gods are you doing here?" he yelled to Bistane.

"Aptly put, as a ghost drove me here. We're riding on ild Fallyn heels. Lara is surrounded at Larandaril's heart." He considered Sevryn, his garb, his horse. "It appears you have a history. Are you still a traitor?"

"Never. There were circumstances—" Sevryn cut the air with his hand. "Tressandre brings her troops here?"

"And Raymy, coming back in tides. In for a fight?"

"I thought I was going to be in one alone."

Bistane threw him another sidelong glance, looking him over. "I should probably skewer you on sight."

"Then you won't know what I've been up to."

He waved a gloved hand up and down. "Seems rather obvious."

"Never have the Kobrir or Vaelinar been obvious."

Bistane laughed, a hearty sound easily heard over the pounding hooves of their horses. "Too true. Stay close. My men are spoiling for a fight, and I'd hate for one of them to mistake you for a target."

"What ghost?"

Bistane looked to him. "My father sent me here."

"Does he do well?"

"Who can say how a spirit does? I gather he doesn't wish Lariel to join their ancestors, however."

In answer, Sevryn kneed his horse closer and the two ran their horses as one.

So it was, that when they caught up to the battle, the ild Fallyn had Lara circled.

Cavalry and archers in black and silver grumbled as those in Vantane colors fought their way to their side, braiding their numbers together against the Raymy. Lara turned her pale face toward them and Sevryn felt that telltale heartbeat of his skip as he saw her covered in blood and thought he'd not come in time. Yet as she swung her shield arm up and her sword out, he could see weariness in her frame though her hands held steady. They'd both been there before, he thought, and her eyes sought his face, framed by Kobrir wrappings and she froze in motion.

War dogs leaped among the Raymy, belling and barking as they wove through the encircling ranks. Vantane armsmen cleaved their way behind him and set a perimeter. Sevryn kneed his tired mount close, closer, into position. The only one not yet drawn to the fray was his own heart and soul, but he feared to look away from Lariel to find her. Wherever Rivergrace was, he knew it was close. Perhaps as close as the waters of the Andredia itself.

A prophet and a ghost had driven two contingents here to meet. The ild Fallyn had come on their own, intending, no doubt, to cut off Lara on her way to the fields of Ashenbrook where all had thought the Raymy would fall. She was not meant to make it to rejoin the bulk of her troops. If all had gone as the ild Fallyn planned, there would be none who lived to tell the real tale.

He saw Alton trade a look with his sister. Tressandre bent over her mount, her face set in lines of fury, her hair of dark and wild honey billowing back from her face and half-helm, and her hand gesturing wildly.

A Raymy leaped up beside him. His horse shied out of swinging range, unseating Sevryn who managed to land with knees bent and body centered. The Raymy jabbed upward brutally, but he was not there, twisting away, with a kick to the back of the thing's knee, sending it down with a whistling screech and a sword jab to the back of its head. It stayed down. Sevryn turned to regain his horse, but the poor creature had bolted and not far, being cut down by Raymy at the edge of the fighting, on its haunches and thrashing. He did not watch longer.

He spoke to the shadows of the trees and saplings and stabbing branches of the shrub bushes, and even of the men and beasts that grappled in life-and-death struggles and used them to reach Lara's side. He moved unseen on foot, his Voice gaining allies to hide his movement in stealth. Her

horse stamped and blew foam on him as he drew near, and
he realized Lariel rode bareback without even so much as
a headstall to keep her balance or telegraph her wishes. He
remembered otherwise. He blinked. Things not so set in
stone as she and he had thought? How mutable could Fate
be? Clouds roared across the sun-dappled sky as an unknown storm wind drove them in furiously, an unnatural
storm that made Sevryn look up.

Lariel did the same. "Watch your backs," she called, unaware of his nearness, her voice louder and stronger than it
deserved to be, a leader's voice to her troops. "Close to the
Andredia if you can! Raymy will fall again!"

Chastain rallied, fighting to be at her side. So also did
troops wearing the black and silver. Sevryn wiped his hand
on his trousers, first one and then the other, to dry them, as
the pawns of Lariel's prophetic vision fell into place.

He worked his way closer toward her, determined to put
himself between her and Tressandre, when he saw his love
on the river.

Rivergrace strode out of the Andredia, river water running
off her form as if it were a cloak she wore. Rafts bumped to
shore behind her, things that might once have been men
shambling off rough wooden planks lashed together
crudely, and he could *see* thin lines of light and substance
connecting her to them. Behind her, Narskap scrambled
onto the riverbank as well, his ragged clothes hanging from
his skeleton-thin body and behind him—Sevryn felt his
own lips peel back in a feral grimace—strode Quendius. As
clouds lowered, the weaponmaster threw his head up and
laughed, a throat-rattling sound that brought anger boiling
up in Sevryn.

Sevryn moved instinctively toward the Andredia, out of
the shadows, out of position, drawn by Rivergrace even as
he forgot Lariel, propelled by hatred of Quendius. He could
see by all the hells of all the Gods the invisible shackles that

tied his love to his enemy, and to the Undead that gathered on the riverbanks. A cage of thread enveloped her, of black and gold, of smut and light, of substances he didn't understand but could see woven about her. The Undead mercenaries stood motionless, looking to their master for their orders.

The waters boiled against the small but potent army. Sevryn realized that Quendius had not come to wage war but to reap the harvest of dead. Dead that the river would carry to them as the battle carried to it.

Lara made a strangled sound deep in her throat. "Not my Andredia!" she cried and thrust her sword up. She would have charged Quendius as he would have had not the skies opened up yet again and the Raymy fell.

They came down, rolled to their feet, and moved into battle stance as they rose, with none of the dazed attitudes that had cloaked their earlier numbers. The sheer number of them cut the hills beyond from sight.

Lara shook herself. She stretched her body, threw back her head and bellowed "Archers! Archers! To the fore! Set and fire!" She wheeled her horse about. "Draw them in!" Lara ordered. "Set and shield." The thin forest at the river's edge gave her some cover, but not enough.

He could hear Alton ild Fallyn bellow, "To the Queen!"

Where was Bistane? Sevryn cast around wildly, but could not find him on horseback or on foot.

And then there was no more time as the inner circle and advancing Raymy clashed.

The sky rained death, blackened by arrows falling upon the Raymy, and bodies toppled. As before, not enough. Never enough to even slow them down. Sevryn gripped his weapons tightly. Raymy plowed into the Andredia, choking the river with their diseased flesh, and Quendius began a chant that would bind the river with its cargo to his will. He could feel the raw power rising. The weaponmaster had found a Talent . . . in death.

Sevryn felt her touch him before Rivergrace cried out, "Never!" She drew his power from him, causing him to lose

a step as he moved to meet a sword, and she stood in a void
between the forces, untouched by arrow or blade, her hands
moving. A golden river of flame fountained upward from
the ground, sucked from their power and hers, weakening
all of them even as it walled them in safety for the moment.
He gagged at the stench of burning and fought to keep on
his feet.

The Raymy fled the fire. They streamed across the broken ground in a fighting panic.

Behind him a strangled cry and a curse from Tressandre.
He remembered that pungent voice and the Foresight
grabbed him up, sent him pivoting on his heel. Ild Fallyn
behind them? Had the Raymy drawn their attention at that
crucial moment? Lariel would never allow the ild Fallyn
behind her, not after having Foreseen the disaster of this
time, could she?

Sevryn fell back a step, Alton in his range of eyesight,
and Tressandre at the corner of his vision. On foot, he raced
toward her, toward Alton who'd curved his sword close to
his body, kicking his horse at Lara. He called for the shadows and they answered him, cloaking his weaving run toward his queen and friend, abandoning Rivergrace, his
heart torn in two. He lunged at Lara. Chastain yelled in
warning, close and yet not close enough to aid.

It had all changed and yet remained the same. Sevryn
leaped in the air, turning, the back of his hand bringing his
weapon about when Lariel burst into orange flame, her jewelry flaring out at Alton ild Fallyn and his scream of terror
as the Sentinel set him alight. Sevryn let the sword go in a
throw that thudded deep into his throat, cutting that scream
short. As he came back to earth, his sleeve smoked in the
fury of her protective jewelry, golden links now charred and
dull. Lara turned to look at Sevryn in surprise. Turned as
her lamed horse stumbled, and she began to slip from his
back.

Tressandre ild Fallyn growled at them both and leaned
across her horse, steel in her hands. He swung across her to
parry Tressandre's blow. Too late. Just a bare heartbeat too late.

Their silvery blades clashed in the patchy gleam of the sun as it tried to break through storming clouds. They sang, howling against one another.

Tressandre's long dagger sank deep into Lara's flank, parting chain link and silk under tunic and flesh, driving home as Lariel gasped in pain. She pitched forward over her mount's shoulder, coming to earth, losing her seat.

Losing her command.

Losing her life.

Sevryn recovered, fingers loosening a throwing dagger from an ankle sheath, and Tressandre spat as it sank into the curve of her neck where it met her shoulder and armor could not protect her. She reined away from him as Lara fell at his feet, her life spurting out in crimson beats. Each fountain counted a failing heart.

He could hear Bistane yell sharply. Felt the press of mounted horsemen about him. Chastain lunged at Tressandre and cried out as she gutted him. His horse bolted at the chaos, carrying him out of reach, but it was Lara who commanded his attention.

"For ild Fallyn!" A chorus of voices chanted with Tressandre, and she disappeared in a cloud of guards that began to hack their way out. He did not see her again, but the Raymy toppled like trees being axed down for lumber.

He went to his knee.

He drew the painted dagger from his sleeve. The anointed blade. The one given to him for the king of assassins and he broke his vows, all of them, as he struck. He drove it into her exposed inner thigh where the chain mail coat could not protect her. Another spurt of blood spilled onto the ground, and then it stopped even as her face went pale and her eyes fluttered as she looked up at him. Her golden jewelry sizzled out, stones burnt to an ashy gray. Her body went still. A horse pounded close.

Bistane slid to the ground at a run. "Sevryn!"

He threw an arm across the other. "She's not dead. She's not dying. My blade is poisoned. It mimics death. Don't leave her side till she wakes. It may be days. It may be weeks. She will heal if you tend it. Don't take the blade out. Do you hear me? Do you understand? Don't take the blade out until she heals. The poison on the blade is the only thing keeping her alive as she heals."

Bistane looked at him with wild eyes. "I don't understand anything. Tressandre brought her down, but you gave the crowning blow . . ."

Lara made a small noise. Her lips worked. "No." She attempted to take Bistane's hand and failed. He reached down and took it up. Her eyelids fluttered again, butterflies slowly settling into place, and she grew still. Very still.

"She's not bleeding. She's not dead," he repeated firmly. "What have you done to her?"

"The Kobrir call it the king's rest. It will maintain her. I hope."

Bistane looked at him slowly. "You don't know."

"I know it's all the chance she has. That was a killing blow from Tressandre."

"There's an antidote?"

"Yes. The Kobrir have it."

Bistane let out a very long breath. "If they will relinquish it willingly. If not, I will persuade them." He smiled thinly before adding, "You got Alton."

"I know. Abayan Diort is on the way. Your numbers should be enough."

"You know that."

"I do."

Bistane looked distracted for a moment, looking at something beyond the two of them that Sevryn could not see, and then he nodded abruptly. "We can hold for Diort's forces."

Sevryn got to his feet. Bistane stayed kneeling by Lara, but he shouted orders about that his men broke into ranks to obey. The noise of the battle returned to hearing, as if they had been locked away and Sevryn searched frantically for sight of Rivergrace. And found her walking toward him.

Eyes of blue on blue and aquamarine and a touch of gray saddened as she looked at Lara. "It is all she feared."

He defended himself. "No. She's bound into a coma. She can awaken. I didn't kill her."

"The Kobrir dressed and armed you."

"But they don't command me."

Her mouth turned down at the corner as she heard his lie. He started toward her, but she put her hand up.

Grace turned halfway and saw Alton's cramped and half-burned form on the ground, his head nearly severed from his neck. She frowned. "Did I. . . ."

"No. No, that fire came from Lara. From Tranta's Sentinel, I believe."

Grace knelt beside her queen, her friend, her enemy and gently smoothed the platinum-streaked hair from Lariel's face. "Bits of the Jewel of Tomarq, I would guess, striking at an enemy." She tapped one ruby-faceted gem that had not burned out at the curve of Lara's throat. "Take care of her, Bistane."

"I will."

She then put her hand out to Sevryn. "Aderro." They entwined fingers as he pulled her back to her feet. He could feel the cage that enclosed her, as fine as spidersilk and as corrupt as Cerat, tethered souls caught and woven in a cold hell about her. His heartbeat leaped in his throat at the Demon touch. He recoiled, and she felt it.

"It's not your darkness that turns me away, but my own," she said softly.

"Grace . . ."

She shook her head quickly. "I follow my father," she said and then no more, lowering her gaze, her soft expression marred by guilt and shame. She pulled her hand from his and ran.

A bloody path led to the river and she returned to follow it, her wall of flames burning lower but still as hot. Narskap met her, taking her by the elbows, ignoring Sevryn in her wake.

"Remember this," he said. "Cerat is never diminished no matter how many times he is divided."

Rivergrace looked at him in suspicion. "What are you telling me?"

"What I must. He lives to corrupt. Innocence is the most perfect bait to catch him. He is most powerful whole." Narskap shook her lightly. "Will you remember?"

"You speak in riddles."

"You'll understand if you remember."

Sevryn closed with them, put his hand on Narskap's bony shoulder and spun him away.

"Leave her be," Sevryn growled. "Leave her be and back away!"

"I gave her life," Narskap said, brittle eyes burning into his. "I gave her death." With a move Sevryn did not see coming, with a Demon-given speed, he struck and Sevryn fell to the ground in a swell of black-and-red-driven pain. Rolling in half-blind agony, he watched in a blur as Narskap swept Rivergrace off her feet and carried her away.

"**B**RING HER TO ME." Quendius raised his chin in victory.

"No. You have what you need." Narskap stepped into the lapping waters of the Andredia and hauled the nearest raft onto the bank. He made the mistake of turning his back on Quendius as he did. "All the dead and dying you could wish for are here." He motioned to Rivergrace. "Step aboard."

"All I need but not all I want."

The weaponmaker caught Narskap by the throat. Rivergrace jolted forward a step and stopped as her father's eyes met hers, stern in their warning not to interfere. She smothered her anger in her throat and stayed. Waves of the Andredia danced close to her, the water agitated in white-and-crimson-dashed foam.

Quendius shook him like a hunting dog with prey gripped in its jaws. "Your service is no longer required. I know what it is you've done and how to do it. If I need assistance, she will grant it to me." He began to squeeze, his charcoal skin turning white about his heavy, scarred knuckles, hands closing inexorably about Narskap's neck. Rivergrace could feel the web of life threads that she had helped her father weave shake about her, a gossamer cage of lives held between life and death. They quivered and breathed, shook and billowed, and she knotted her hands to keep from losing them as they wore torn from their anchoring to Narskap. Narskap's breath escaped from his throat like steam from a whistling, fretting kettle as Quendius squeezed tighter and the sound turned to smothered grunts. He kicked futilely as Quendius hiked him in the air, but he looked at Rivergrace, unwaveringly, and she thought she saw a kind of resigned peace in his eyes.

"Before you leave, I'll take this, however." Quendius reached his other hand into Narskap's chest, pushing through skin and into the rib cage. Into muscle and bone, a great scarred hand that had forged weapons alongside Narskap for decades, its thick fingers sent rummaging past the heart until he found what it was he desired: the burning coal that was Cerat buried deep within Narskap's body.

Narskap wriggled and groaned as Quendius ripped the essence free. His gaze pulled from Rivergrace as Quendius tore him apart and held the chunk of liquefying Demon matter high. He held it triumphantly for a moment and then swallowed it whole, sparks and streams of fiery molten rock cascading between his fingers and then his lips as he did. He smacked his mouth in satisfaction and opened it to laugh. The Demon Cerat roared triumphantly from the depths of Quendius' throat and out his mouth.

For a moment it seemed as if his body would reject the substance. He quaked and bent over, retching. His body quaked as he pulled himself back into a stand and when he opened his mouth, Quendius howled a second time. A fiery shower issued as he did, sizzling and dancing to nothingness about his face and Grace held her breath, watching Narskap broken open and dying as he dangled from the fist that held him up. But that moment passed and Quendius stayed on his feet. He shook Narskap's limp body a last time before dropping it on the ground, ignoring the mouth that opened and made a last, pleading sound that never finished.

Narskap fell into a collapsed lump of rags, mummified

skin and bones, nothing even remotely like what had been a living man left to him. His ruins shuddered into quiet.

Quendius tapped his chest and a hundred or more threads shimmered as though they were strings on an instrument and he had plucked them. Rivergrace shook her head, her own ties to the army of Undead struck, and thrumming across her agonized self. She hugged herself close protectively, praying that Quendius could not see that she had the souls he claimed also anchored to her.

Overhead, the skies split. Her ears roared with the thunder and pressure of the storm lowering to rage over the battlefield. She looked up at a widening window into another world. Daravan had lost his hold on reality, and the worlds clashed together again. She could feel Kerith weaken as the lost Vaelinar world opened upon them. A Way that no one should ever have created gaped open.

Quendius smiled widely.

"You will come with me."

He turned and crossed the river, his Undead army at his heels, each man picking up a Vaelinar body and carrying it with him, multiplying his numbers with every step. He didn't look back as if assured she would follow. Rivergrace darted out, knowing she had to stop him even as she felt compelled to trail him. She sought flame in her body and found she'd gone cold, tired, burnt out. She had nothing left to seek there, and although water answered in its stead, she knew that water would not stop him, not unless she could mount a flood so high and furious it would drown all of them. She dropped her hands in defeat.

Her body trembled as she took an unwilling step after.

"You won't go with him."

She looked over her shoulder. "I have to."

"I'll hold you." He came from behind her, breathless, covered in blood and shadow. He would not let her leave him behind. Sevryn put his arm about her waist. His Kobrir cloth had slipped from his head. Blood trickled down from his scalp, and he leaned as much upon her for support as she upon him.

"Anchor me," she whispered to him.

"Always."

"I don't want to go with Quendius."

"Then you won't. Not like this." Sevryn's breath warmed the tip of her ear, his face closing to touch her cheek. She could feel her ties stretching tighter and tighter. The Andredia whipped up in agitation as black clouds swooped in like birds of prey bearing down on them. She could smell brine on the forest air. She thought, if she stood firm enough, she could stand with Sevryn forever.

Shadows appeared upon shadows. The very firmament of the grove and meadow seemed to ripple as if it were nothing but a painted page that the wind now tossed and turned and prepared to rip apart. The landscape seemed to stretch. The wind became visible as a rippling purple ribbon that both caressed and tore at the physical world. Rivergrace put her hand on Sevryn's shoulder. "Gods help us. Someone is securing that Way."

"Securing it."

"Creating it, and then weaving it permanently into Kerith. It wasn't created here, but it's being forced from the other side. Sevryn, we can't let that happen. It feels wrong."

"It could destroy Kerith. Or not. But I can feel its power, and its pull." He paused.

"That's what Quendius is waiting for, that open Gate."

"It has to be Daravan."

She'd seen it at Calcort when he'd barely sensed it, Daravan's manipulation of a Way, but now his skin prickled as if a thousand fire thorns had descended upon him. He couldn't doubt her. He flung his arm across her. "Stay with me."

"Sevryn, Quendius tows me after him. Sooner or later, I will follow. This cage of souls binds me. If I let them go, they will never have a chance to live or die as meant."

"They're mercenaries. Murderers."

"They're people. Not all are killers. Not all have a choice."

He heard it in her voice, that compassion for life. "Let them go. Let them be on Quendius."

"I can't. I helped weave their cage. You have to understand—I'm the monster, not them."

"Don't talk like that." But he knew what she meant, instinctively, because he thought of himself that way. A weapon forged and then honed by the Kobrir. He couldn't let himself be used, but knew inevitably that it would happen. "I'm holding you, not just because you asked, but because I love you. I've loved you since the moment I saw you; even when I died, I knew you and that I loved you. Let me hold you."

He moved restlessly and tightened his arms about her, feeling the tension in her body, feeling the energy sizzling through the gold-and-black threads that covered her like a gossamer web. He could feel her growing cold. He could feel himself in the chill.

An opening blinked and then grew wide. Where feathery evergreen should exist, a nothingness gaped out of which darkness escaped to wisp fleetingly across their view. The Way grew like a mouth, a maw of chaos that opened to swallow them down, or perhaps an Eye of Darkness peering into them, all of them. The wrongness of it sank into his very bones like a Kobrir venom.

A tall man stood in the center and strode across, and disappeared like the shadow he commanded. He shouted an order to be followed, a Voice that rang with Vaelinar magic to Sevryn's ear. It could only have come from Daravan, the man who'd given Sevryn that self-same Talent among others. A voice he'd never heard raised before, never heard in more than speaking tones, and now realized it had been uttering orders in whispers, subverting, pushing, shaping that which should never have been shaped, sculpting Fate as Daravan and Daravan alone wished it, and using the Kobrir to bring to death those who could hear and disobey.

Sevryn cursed in a low hiss.

Rivergrace turned her face toward his. "What is it?"

"The bastard is no hero who saved us all at Ashenbrook, who took his brother's brother and swept up the Raymy in a tide." Sevryn spat to the other side. "He retreated from forces who would have devastated his. He saved the Raymy, not us . . . and now he's brought them back to strike at the heart of Larandaril."

"But . . . Lara . . . the others . . . said he was losing control, that he'd held them back as long as he could."

"You just felt that Way being anchored here. Did he feel powerless to you?"

"No."

"Nothing Daravan does is by accident or from weakness. Not even his attack on Calcort."

She sucked down a breath. "He knew about Nutmeg and Lara's heir?"

"Somehow. He's not been in a void as we thought." He took a stride forward. He knew what he had been charged with by the Kobrir all those days ago. "I have to take him out."

She did not gainsay him, but she did warn him gently. "Hundreds of Raymy yet to come."

"All the more reason I make this stand now." He whirled about. "Get ready!" Sevryn cried, his warning augmented by his Voice, and the valley rang with it.

In answer, the bridge between worlds thundered.

Unthinkable. Masses yet to invade Larandaril, already driven down and besieged by a dread army. Even as they both thought it, they saw it. Line upon line of Raymy as they began to march through, a tide of gray-green reptilian flesh carrying steel. Rivergrace laid down a line of fire that channeled the march to turn away or it would consume them, her voice hoarse and her hands trembling with effort, but it was a weak line and she couldn't sustain it. He felt her pull strength from him, driving a chill deep into his bones. He fed her a little and then cut her off, needing his own core to fight Daravan when, if, he found him.

Behind them, Bistane shouted for his archers to fire, and the sky filled with spears of wood arching overhead, raining death anew on the first ranks of the Raymy trampling into the meadow. They fell in waves, but their fellows behind them surged over the dead and kept coming. Their grunts and hissing filled the air.

He had to close the Way; he could do that as soon as he found Daravan and separated him from his cloak of disguise to target a physical being. Sevryn paced, readying to face the unseeable, his breath hissing now and then in frustration. Nothing he had learned, on the streets as an abandoned boy, or from Gilgarran, or from Jeredon, or from the Kobrir, gave him the knowledge to unmask Daravan.

Rivergrace closed her eyes for a moment as if centering herself, then reached for and caught up his hand and pressed a thread into it, a thread he felt more than he could see with its luminescence from her heart. It stretched between them as thin as gossamer and resilient as spidersilk. It did not match the threads of her cage, but with silvers and blues shining throughout it. It touched him as intimately as she had ever touched him. He put a hand up, but his fingers slipped through it, leaving a shimmering note of her presence behind.

"If you lose me again," she said, "this is how to find me." She smiled, a sad and fleeting expression. "Please don't hate me more than you love me."

"I could never hate you."

She looked after Quendius and his Undead troop, disappeared through the eye of the Way. "I made them."

"Narskap made them. He used you as Quendius used him."

She shook her head. "No. I wove many of those threads." She took a deep breath. "I wanted to hold them as gently as possible, as close to life as possible, because I could feel the hunger in them to live. I don't know what lies ahead for them, but they pull me after as much as Quendius does."

"They are fodder for him, but souls to you. I can't hate you for that. Never."

Rivergrace raised her other hand in the air, her eyes half-closing, and a shimmer of dewdrops covered her skin wherever the air touched it. She reached up and touched his eyelids with dampened fingertips. "Look for shadow weave. Lily wove and sewed him a cloak of one. Look for it and summon it."

Call for it? He hadn't the time, Bistane's archers and Rivergrace's line of fire held the Raymy back, but only just. They would be overrun in moments and yet, now was all they had. He cupped her cheek as she stood on guard, the one hand raised to keep her flames up. Strain ran through her, but her soft skin felt warm to him and she looked at Sevryn long enough to smile again. "Now," she whispered.

So Sevryn called for the shadows. He touched his throat and shifted into his Voice, singing to the dusk not to hide him as he used them, but to part and reveal that which he needed to see. To betray that which the shadows meant to keep secret. To part and let the light inward, to illuminate what he needed to see. He could feel her touch on his eyelids still and, with a chill, the veil lifted from his vision and a clarity of crystal sharpness descended. Sevryn frowned at the brightness of the day as it flooded him, but now he saw a man-sized force of shadow moving at will and focused on it, like the hunter he was. He moved, not toward it, but to flank Daravan even as Grace dropped into her stance, her hands curling once again into the gesture for summoning flame, and as he set his position, she laid down a new wall of fire. She staggered back a step as heat roared up, between her and the Raymy, the armies of Kerith at her back. They let out a shout of joy and charged to take out the Raymy stumbling through the wall of flame with armor smoking and skins blistering.

They stood in the channel through which the army surged. Sevryn caught her up and carried her, running, out of their way.

Horns trumpeted on the smoky air. He could hear the shouts of Galdarkans as they thundered onto the field, breaking the walls of Raymy.

Assured, he stepped into darkness cast by a whip-lean sapling as he asked it to hide him. The scent of the evergreen sapling filled his nostrils. He withdrew his ithrel and his curved dagger as the vision Rivergrace had given him filled his senses once more, and he sang a last time, the shadows shredding at his summoning. Into his Voice, he put all he knew of Daravan, which seemed little, and all he wanted to know, which was vast.

Storm-dark clouds darted past him where there should be no cloud across his acute sight. He struck, left-handed, carving the clouds away and the noise of fabric ripping answered his blow, as well as a grunt and curse. The shadow weave parted, revealing the man wrapped within it. Daravan spun about, brought to a halt in front of him, looking down at him with eyes of storm gray and icy gray, frost-silvery hair braided back from his face. Daravan's sharp-paned face glared down upon him.

"Should I call you father?"

"I will never answer to that title." Daravan gestured. "You can't stop me."

"I have already given you pause." He watched as Daravan looked upon, and considered, the ithrel. One eyebrow arched.

"Step away while you can."

"Not just yet." Sevryn felt his ithrel and dagger hilts grow warm in his hold, familiar to his fingers and the palms of his hands. He did not have his second blade anointed with the king's rest readily available but stepped into his balance.

"You've no idea what's at stake here."

"I know," Sevryn said, even as he watched the other's stance and flex of tensed muscles, "that you have been engineering the demise of Vaelinar in this world since the day we were exiled to it. That you have deaths uncountable behind you and would have even more before you. That's all I need to know."

"No longer a hero, am I? But you don't ask yourself why."

"Knowing why won't stop me or justify you. Wasn't one world enough for her? It seems not."

Daravan pushed his cloak back from his shoulders. He

put a hand back, indicating the Way behind him, filled with jostling Raymy as they continued to advance, but the world behind them could be seen if one tried. "I serve my queen with all that I am."

"I don't care."

"We were at war! She only did that which she had to do to protect herself and her lands. And now I must help her undo the destiny she sent spiraling, and we will not die. Not there. Not when we cross to here. Give in and she will remember those who stood by her."

"Trevilara is no queen of mine. She is still at war from all that I've seen. Nothing gives her peace."

"I can."

Sevryn shook his head. "Not at the cost of Kerith."

"Kerith. A pot of mongrel flesh. It's the land that matters. The air. The seas. Kerith flesh. Bolgers aren't even human."

"They're more human than you."

Daravan's mouth twisted for a moment. Then he spat to one side. "I thought it might be you who finally came after me." Daravan shrugged back the hood on his cloak, the shadow weave billowing about him like black smoke. Vertical lines etched the starkness of his cheekbones and down into his face. Smaller crinkles flared the corners of his eyes as they narrowed on Sevryn. He made a gesture, and the Way fractured, sending lines of distortion through the ground to reach them. Sevryn staggered, placed in a world that no longer seemed firm. The shadows he had shredded flew up from the cracks, enveloping not only Daravan but him, and their touch made his teeth chatter with their cold. A blaze of white fire tightened about his chest, and he brushed it with the side of his hand.

Rivergrace. His darkening world lit up in silver and blue.

Daravan sliced a hand forward, and his flesh sizzled when he touched that shield she'd put upon him. The corner of Sevryn's mouth quirked.

"I was sent," Sevryn told him.

Daravan's eyes lit as he contemplated the meaning behind those words, that allies he might have anticipated had now stepped away from him. He looked at the ithrel once more. "Ahhh."

He might have said more, but he lunged, and Sevryn had readied for him. They clashed, the fractured world beneath their feet shifting and crumbling as they moved. Daravan slung his cloak forward, attempting to net him, but Sevryn slipped aside and tore it from his hands, coming up in Daravan's face as the shadow weave disintegrated about him. They clashed, Sevryn being surprised only that Daravan held weapons he hadn't even seen him pull. Steel rang.

Careless of him to have missed the weapons pulled. It was the only thought he had as they met, parried, swung, hit, shrugged off, turned and attacked, blocked, and the steel between them screed against their edges. His training centered him. His teachers' voices spoke firmly in his ear, telling him how to react. Daravan sank a vicious fist across his rib cage, a stinging blow that knocked the breath out of him, but his muscles answered with two fists and a backhanded slash of his own, driving Daravan away so that he could catch a breath. Daravan fell back out of range of the ithrel, a deep glimmer in his eyes.

Sevryn flexed his hands, resetting his hold on his blades. His knuckles stung, and he knew he'd hit hard.

"The assassins, the traitors, trained you well."

"Gilgarran gave me a good start. The Kobrir finished it." He chose to ignore the ache in his ribs. A fist was better than a knifepoint.

"I think he recognized me in you."

"At least he bothered to look at me as someone's son." Sevryn took a step to the side, then came back two steps in the opposite direction and closed on Daravan, silver flashing in his hands and coming away crimson.

Heat scored along his own shinbone. Kobrir cloth rippled open, and blood seeped out the length of his lower leg. He kicked aside and moved back into a defensive position. Shallow, it would close without attention, as long as Daravan did not have his blades doctored.

Sevryn caught his breath again and did not wish to waste it. He said nothing but waited for the sign Daravan would attack again. The barest of warnings. He dodged to the side, landing on his knee, and the knife that would have pierced his right lung jabbed past harmlessly. He whipped his feet out at Daravan's ankles, to bring the man down but catching him, not at his feet as planned but behind one knee, driving him off balance.

Daravan fell back with a grunt, caught by an evergreen sapling, which kept upright and hampered the backswing of his left arm.

Sevryn closed again. He thought he had the other at a disadvantage, but Daravan proved him wrong. Sevryn spun away, going to the ground and clawing out of range, coming up gasping and wary, hot blood trickling from an arm wound he hadn't even felt getting. Daravan gave him no quarter. He filled the air with throwing knives, Sevryn twisting and turning, spinning and coming away relatively unscathed, though his left sleeve now flapped loose. No hindrance to him and perhaps even a gain—Daravan would have to look through the tatters to find a solid target.

But the other arm, that worried him. Any significant bleeding slowed and weakened him—would bring him down as surely as a solid hit. He tore his left sleeve loose and knotted it tightly about his right bicep, moving always as he did, eyes on Daravan, denying him an easy target. Sweat trickled down Daravan's temples. That caught Sevryn by surprise, and he looked again. Then he realized . . . Daravan wore leathers under his clothes, armored underneath, protected from many of Sevryn's blows but given away by his own body heat. Sevryn smiled grimly to himself. He'd need to change tactics, no longer needing to wonder why his slicing attack hadn't given him the results he wished.

"Did you ever wonder where your mother went?" Daravan sounded winded a bit, but he bared his teeth in a savage grin.

"She went looking for you."

"No. No, she went looking for another Vaelinar who

would have her, searching for her own fading youth and beauty. She went chasing the street rumors that we Vaelinars give part of our long lives to those we bond with. She abandoned you to chase a new beginning for herself." Daravan stopped talking. Lunged at him.

Sevryn spun to his left and came back with a high, left-footed kick. The Kobrir Bretta had schooled him in that move. It took Daravan down.

He rolled to one knee and staggered up. The Way shifted under him, swelled and then closed, and then shuddered open again.

Sevryn watched the fabric of Kerith tremble at Daravan's weakness. They were all weak, and though he did not believe what Daravan told him, he could understand if that search for more life had drawn his mother away. He would do it if that's what it took to stay with Rivergrace. That need was a weakness he could understand.

"She needed a life," Sevryn told Daravan. "What was your excuse? Where were you, Father, when I grew?"

"Not tending a mowling mongrel." Daravan wiped the back of his hand across his face, smearing the blood Sevryn had drawn. "I saw you once, long enough to know you existed and that you had not a hint of Talent about you. Not in your eyes, not in your disgusting flesh. I love Trevilara and came to fulfill my duty to her. I spilled my seed in a weak moment or two. You came into being. But it was Lariel I wanted a child upon. Then my sacrifice would be worth it. We lose power you see—a child rips it from us whether we will it or not. Would I let a pretty piece of meat part her legs for me just so she could steal my magic? Not if I can help it. I should have killed you then, but you had nothing of me. Not until Gilgarran found you, and then it was too late."

"You wouldn't have fathered me even then."

"No. I still would have killed you. As I will put you down now."

They met again, blades clashing, arms and hands swinging, feet shifting. Met, spun away, turned back for another clash. Sevryn felt the blow that parted the skin on his right lower ribs but not the pain of it until warm, salty blood began to leak. He couldn't afford to bleed.

He sucked in a breath, and moved into a pattern the Kobrir had taught him well.

Daravan dodged low to his own left to avoid it, but he could not avoid the fisting blow aimed at his throat, Sevryn's ithrel between his knuckles.

One hit.

Daravan fell back. He clawed at the blade in his throat, dislodging it, face gone pale in three heartbeats, the front of his body dappled with fresh crimson, the hole in his throat pumping out more. He blinked as he looked at his hands and then put them back to his throat, trying to stop the flow.

"The queen must stand," he husked. "You cannot bring her down."

"She's a murderous bastard like you. Why not?"

"She is life. She is the only true Power."

"She is nothing to me, as I was nothing to you."

Daravan crumpled to his knees. He threw his head back to look up at Sevryn. "She's a great woman. I earned her love . . . I . . ." He did not finish, his breath and life whistling out of him, punctuated by a last gurgle. His body folded upon the ground.

Sevryn stood over it and regretted only that he had not left the man in a king's rest for the Kobrir to gather, as they had requested. A mercy on Daravan, he supposed, for he felt certain that what the Kobrir had planned was nothing less than a slow, harsh death in servitude much as they'd been condemned to by their creator's actions. This dead man could never have been his father. He had no memory of him except for feeling the echo of the ache his mother had felt before she, too, abandoned him. If he had any patriarch, it was Gilgarran. Gilgarran and the streets. He toed Daravan's dropped weapon far away from his open hand, the other still clutching at the gash in his neck futilely. Blood pooling into the grass and needles slowed into a sluggish crawl until the heart no longer beat. He turned away.

The open eye behind him opened and shut for the barest of breaths.

When it stared open again, the Raymy no longer marched through, the flood halted. He saw an ocean shore, marsh grasses tangled and brown, a red-brown scum floating in on the tide, but he had no time to watch. He could feel a pull on his heartstrings and then saw, in a cold fear, Rivergrace framed by the Way. Her hair blew loose in a wind that smelled strange and exotic.

Rivergrace stood in the halo of its aura before entering with a soft murmur. "Follow me."

Because he loved and trusted her, because he was an arrow that had to have an archer, he did without so much as a look backward.

Glossary

aderro: (Vaelinar corruption of the Dweller greeting, Derro). An endearment, meaning little one
alna: (Dweller) a fishing bird
alphistol: a garden flower
astiri: (Vaelinar) true path
avandara: (Vaelinar) verifier, truth-finder
Aymar: (Vaelinar) elemental God of the wind and air
Banh: (Vaelinar) elemental God of earth
Cerat: (Vaelinar) souldrinker
Calcort: a major trading city
Daran: (Vaelinar) the God of Dark, God of the Three
defer: (Kernan) a hot drink with spices and milk
Dhuriel: (Vaelinar) elemental God of fire
emeraldbark: (Dweller) a long-lived, tall, insect and fire resistant evergreen
forkhorn: (Kernan) a beast of burden, with wide, heavy horns
Hawthorne: capital of the free provinces
kedant: (Kernan) a potent poison from the kedant viper
klah: (Kernan) a strong, caffeine-laced drink from ground and stewed beans
Lina: (Vaelinar) elemental Goddess of water
Nar: (Vaelinar) the God of War, God of the Three

Neriarad: a flowering, drought-resistant shrub that is highly toxic in stem, seed, and flower

Nylara: (Kernan) a treacherous, vital river

Nevinaya aliora: (Vaelinar) You must remember the soul

quinberry: a tart yet sweet berry fruit

qynch oil: a pressed oil used as a base for many purposes, including cooking

Rakka: (Kernan) elemental Demon, he who follows in the wake of the earth mover, doing damage

Rockeater: a venomous, dry country serpent

skraw: (Kernan) a carrion eating bird

staghorns: elklike creatures

stinkdog: a beslimed, unpleasant porcine critter

Stonesend: a Dweller trading village

tashya: (Vaelinar) a hot-blooded breed of horse

teah: (Kernan) a hot drink brewed from leaves

ukalla: (Bolgish) a large hunting dog

Vae: (Vaelinar) Goddess of Light, God of the Three

Vantane: (Vaelinar) war falcon

velvethorn: a lithe deerlike creature

winterberry: a cherrylike fruit